Worldwide Praise for the Erotica of John Patrick and STARbooks!

"John Patrick is a modern master of the genre! ...This writing is what being brave is all about. It brings up the kinds of things that are usually kept so private that you think you're the only one who experiences them."
— *Gay Times, London*

"'Barely Legal' is a great potpourri... and the coverboy is gorgeous!"
— *Ian Young, Torso magazine*

"Collections of stories have become increasingly popular in the past couple of years: leading the way is the prolific and consistently entertaining John Patrick who, under the STARbooks imprint, has edited fifteen or more collections of erotica written another dozen books himself and published several handfuls more by other authors. ...Burly (500-plus pages) anthologies of erotic writing, the perfect bedside companions..."
— *Richard Labonte, Q Magazine*

"A huge collection of highly erotic, short and steamy one-handed tales. Perfect bedtime reading, though you probably won't get much sleep! Prepare to be shocked! Highly recommended!"
— *Vulcan magazine*

"Tantalizing tales of porn stars, hustlers, and other lost boys...John Patrick set the pace with 'Angel!'"
— *The Weekly News, Miami*

"...Some readers may find some of the scenes too explicit; others will enjoy the sudden, graphic sensations each page brings. Each of these romans á clef is written with sustained intensity. 'Angel' offers a strange, often poetic vision of sexual obsession. I recommend it to you."
— *Nouveau Midwest*

"'Angel' is mouthwatering and enticing..."
- *Rouge Magazine, London*

"'Superstars' is a fast read...if you'd like a nice round of fireworks before the Fourth, read this aloud at your next church picnic..."
- *Welcomat, Philadelphia*

"Yes, it's another of those bumper collections of steamy tales from STARbooks. The rate at which John Patrick turns out these compilations you'd be forgiven for thinking it's not exactly quality prose. Wrong. These stories are well-crafted, but not over-written, and have a profound effect in the pants department."
- *Vulcan magazine, London*

"For those who share Mr. Patrick's appreciation for cute young men, 'Legends' is a delightfully readable book...I am a fan of John Patrick's...His writing is clear and straight-forward and should be better known in the gay community."
- *Ian Young, Torso Magazine*

"...'Billy & David' is frank, intelligent, disarming. Few books approach the government's failure to respond to crisis in such a realistic, powerful manner."
- *RG Magazine, Montreal, Canada*

"...Touching and gallant in its concern for the sexually addicted, 'Angel' becomes a wonderfully seductive investigation of the mysterious disparity between lust and passion, obsession and desire."
-*Lambda Book Report*

"John Patrick has one of the best jobs a gay male writer could have. In his fiction, he tells tales of rampant sexuality. His non-fiction involves first person explorations of adult male video stars. Talk about choice assignments!"
-*Southern Exposure*

"The title for 'Boys of Spring' is taken from a poem by Dylan Thomas, so you can count on high caliber imagery throughout."
- *Walter Vatter, Editor, A Different Light Review*

STARbooks are Available at Fine Booksellers Everywhere

They're ready to graduate...

Juniors

A New Collection
of Erotic Tales
Edited By
JOHN PATRICK

STARbooks Press
Sarasota, FL

Books by John Patrick

Non-Fiction
A Charmed Life: Vince Cobretti
Lowe Down: Tim Lowe
The Best of the Superstars 1990
The Best of the Superstars 1991
The Best of the Superstars 1992
The Best of the Superstars 1993
The Best of the Superstars 1994
The Best of the Superstars 1995
The Best of the Superstars 1996
The Best of the Superstars 1997
What Went Wrong?
When Boys Are Bad
& Sex Goes Wrong
Legends: The World's Sexiest Men, Vols. 1 & 2
Legends (Third Edition)
Tarnished Angels (Ed.)

Fiction
Billy & David: A Deadly Minuet
The Bigger They Are...
The Younger They Are...
The Harder They Are...
Angel: The Complete Trilogy
Angel II: Stacy's Story
Angel: The Complete Quintet
A Natural Beauty (Editor)
The Kid (with Joe Leslie)
HUGE (Editor)
Strip: He Danced Alone
The Boys of Spring
Big Boys/Little Lies (Editor)
Boy Toy
Seduced (Editor)
Insatiable/Unforgettable (Editor)
Heartthrobs
Runaways/Kid Stuff (Editor)
Dangerous Boys/Rent Boys (Editor)
Barely Legal (Editor)
Country Boys/City Boys (Editor)
My Three Boys (Editor)
Mad About the Boys (Editor)
Lover Boys (Editor)
In the BOY ZONE (Editor)
Boys of the Night (Editor)
Secret Passions (Editor)
Beautiful Boys (Editor)
Juniors (Editor)

Entire Contents Copyrighted © 1997 by John Patrick, Sarasota, FL. All rights reserved.

Every effort has been made to credit copyrighted material. The author and the publisher regret any omissions and will correct them in future editions. Note: While the words "boy," "girl," "young man," "youngster," "gal," "kid," "student," "guy," "son," "youth," "fella," and other such terms are occasionally used in text, this work is generally about persons who are at least 18 years of age, unless otherwise noted.

First Edition Published in the U.S. in June, 1997
Library of Congress Card Catalogue No. 96-070309
ISBN No. 1-877978-89-2

Contents

Introduction:
READY TO GRADUATE
John Patrick...11
THE DRIVER:
A VIRGIN'S CONFESSION
John Patrick...29
HIS NEW BOSS
John Patrick...36
ONCE UPON AN ISLAND
Rudy Roberts...54
STRANGE BEDFELLOWS
Leo Cardini...70
A WILLING LEARNER
Peter Gilbert...85
A GOOD SPANKING
Peter Gilbert...93
GAME FOR ANYTHING
Peter Z. Pan...103
FADE TO BLACK
L. Amore...110
AFTER THE GAME
William Joseph...115
WHEREVER YOU WANT
TO PUT IT
Kevin Banton...123
WHEN BOB KISSED ME...
Greg Bowden...132
MAKING ENDS MEET
James Hosier...147
BRADY'S CROTCH
Jack Ricardo...155
BURT'S TRUNKS
Terry McLearn...163
NOVICES
Ken Anderson...172
NIGHT SCHOOL
Edmund Miller...182
CLASS ACTION
Chad Stuart...190
JUNIOR CUM LAUDE
Chad Stuart...231
AN ABUSE OF AUTHORITY
Dan Veen...256
A DAY AT THE BEACH
Jimmy D. ...271

OLD HABITS
Mark Anderson...275
IN ANGELO'S ROOM
William Cozad...284
HOTTER THAN HELL
Rick Hassett...290
JONAH'S ISLAND
Jarred Goodall...301
SPANISH SUMMER
David Laurents...313
STRANGERS
ON THE ROAD
David Laurents...320
FLEXIBILITY
Cory James Legassie...321
THE NEW PAGE
Edward Bangor...325
WILD IN THE WOODS
Rick Jackson, USMC...336
NAKED SKATEBOARD BOY
Frank Brooks...343
THE BIRTHDAY PRESENT
Ken Smith...360
THE SHOOTING CLUB
Peter Gilbert...370
A LONG HARDNESS
John Patrick...382
NEW YORK AVENUE
Daniel Robinson...391
HE HAD NO IDEA
Antler...392

Bonus Books

HUSTLING THE BONE
IN ATLANTIC CITY
Life is rough amid the glitter and
glamor of Atlantic City in this
new erotic novella by
Thom Nickels...393
And
IN THE PRESENCE
OF INNOCENCE
A Farmboy's Lusty Memoirs
by Thomas C. Humphrey...451

Editor's Note

Most of the stories appearing in this book take place prior to the years of The Plague; the editor and each of the authors represented herein advocate the practice of safe sex at all times.

And, because these stories trespass the boundaries of fiction and non-fiction, to respect the privacy of those involved, we've changed all of the names and other identifying details.

"...I was going out with one of my male schoolfriend's sisters, and in the summer I used to go camping a lot, mostly in the wilderness of the back garden. Anyway, one night her brother and I decided that we'd camp out together. We lay there chatting and listening to the radio, then he said to me, 'Are you gay?'

"For a second I wasn't sure what to say. All sorts of things flashed through my mind. What if I admit it, what will they say at school? I didn't want to lose a good friend. In the end I decided to admit it in a joking sense; that way if the worst came to the worst I could say that I was only kidding. 'Of course!' I said, waiting nervously for an answer.

"'Then fuck me,' he said."

– *Tony, interviewed for the survey published in the book "Proust, Cole Porter, Michelangelo, Marc Almond and me"*

INTRODUCTION: READY TO GRADUATE

John Patrick

The "graduations" we are discussing in this volume are from having no sex or having straight sex to having gay sex. This awakening can occur at any age, and the histories are always fascinating.

An Illinois man said he was in college before he went to a rest stop and knew from the writing on the wall that he had been missing out. "I had never gotten it on with another guy but dreamed about it constantly," he confessed in Boyd McDonald's *Raunch*. "Finally I couldn't stand it. The note on the wall said to meet 'Friday at 4 pm.' I decided it was now or never. I arrived at the rest stop shortly after four to find no one. I assumed I'd missed him but went on in the john to read the walls. The usual was there – 'If you want to suck, rub cock.' I read as much as I could as quickly as possible and then opened the door to head back to campus. There to my surprise was a car. Scared to death, I thought what the hell, I'm going to finally do it. I went out the door and rubbed my basket, not sure if I was doing what was expected or not. The man in the car just sat there. I got in my car thinking, "Great, what now?" To my surprise, he got out of his car. He got even with my car window, put his hand on his cock and squeezed like he knew what he was doing. I nodded and he went to the john. 'Great, what now?' I thought. 'Is everyone as dumb and awkward as I the first time?' So I chose to sit and wait and in a minute he stepped out, came over to my car, and got in. He was an older guy, perhaps in his late 30's, short and stocky, with a dark moustache. He asked me how I was and if I was from around there. I said fine to the first question and then lied to the second one.

"Before I knew it, he slid over and said, 'How about a kiss?' Before I could reply, his tongue was in my mouth and his hand was on my pants. I loved it. Boy, was I naive. I had never even considered kissing would be a part of this experience. He continued to mess around with my pants and asked what I

liked to do. I didn't know what the hell to say so I mumbled, 'I don't know.' He said, 'Do you like to suck?' 'Yes.' 'Do you like to fuck?' 'Yes.' 'You like to do anything?' 'Sure.' At least I was ready to give it a try. He fumbled with my zipper as we kissed some more and then asked if I could get it out. As he rubbed around my pants, I was so nervous I at first didn't even have a hard-on. But as I pulled it out, my nine inches sprang up. He grabbed on and asked if I wanted to go to a motel. I guess I passed his inspection. He said he'd pay for the room, but the catch was I was to go with him and leave my car. All this was too new and I felt too unsure, being without a way out. So I insisted that I follow him in my car. When I wouldn't give in, he suggested we go in the john and get it off. I stuffed my dick back in my pants and followed him inside. Once inside, he began to drop his pants and I followed.

"Before I could catch a look, he pulled me close and his tongue was not the only thing poking me this time. God, did it feel good.

"Before I could think, he was feeling my cock again and led my hand down to his. Still embracing tightly, I had to let my fingers be my eyes. Boy did they have fun. His cock was much smaller than mine, perhaps five or six inches, but thicker. I moved my hand down his hard cock and cradled his soft balls in my hand. He let out a sigh saying how good it felt.

"I could tell he was as hot as I was. He tried to once again insist that I go with him to a motel. I declined, however much I wanted to go. He asked, 'Do you like to take it up the ass?' As I responded yes, he said we *had* to go to bed. I was so willing to try anything I said yes in hopes he would try to fuck me right there even though I knew his thick cock would rip open my virgin hole. Enough was enough. He went down on me. Immediately my cock was buried in his throat and I found myself wondering if I'd come. The more he sucked the harder I fucked his mouth. I thought maybe it would be too much for him, but he didn't flinch a bit. In minutes I unloaded my cum. To my unhappiness, he took it all but spit it out in the john. I wanted him to swallow my first load. I figured my time had come to reciprocate and I knelt before his groin. This was really the first time I had to look the situation over. It looked as good as it had felt in my hand, although it was indeed short, at least

by my standards. It looked about three inches thick. It was nestled in a nice bunch of fur and had two wonderful balls hanging below.

"Although I know I was not as skilled as he was, I at least was enjoying myself. Then the disappointment: he grabbed my ears and plunged his meat in me repeatedly. Although I didn't mind the face fuck and sought to keep it up, the hold on my ears broke things up. I began to panic, stopped sucking, and said I had to go. We embraced, to my surprise, and kissed again. His rod was still hard and rubbing on me. I guess I wasn't a total disappointment; he asked when I'd see him again. I said next Friday. I guess he liked my cock as well as I liked his."

Arnie Kantrowitz, in his delightful memoir *Under the Rainbow*, remembers his sexual graduation. He says he was terrified of playing sports. Baseball was a disaster and "swimming wasn't much better. I nearly drowned because I was so entranced with the counselors' cocks bobbing blithely up and down as they tested the diving board.

"...I had my first erection when I was about twelve. I was riding my bicycle, bedecked with its colored handlebar streamers, bobbing plastic bird and Tab Hunter decal on the rear fender. Maybe the bicycle seat activated the hard-on, or maybe it was just time. I had no idea what it was about, not having had such delicate topics discussed with me in so many words. All I knew was that I liked it better when it was bigger, and I hoped it would be bigger the next time I went to see the family doctor, who was the only one left who still saw me naked. But it didn't take me long to figure out that a man is supposed to be ashamed if a bulge of desire can be seen in his pants. It's not civilized. And if the bulge should point at another man, it's not safe.

"I began my forays into adolescent sexual experimentation just before I was thirteen. Like most boys that age, I started playing around with my friends. It started with after-school visits. Just school chums horsing around and all that. I'll show you mine if you'll show me yours. 'Boys can see boys' (a motto of the public urinal). How about a little strip poker? Want to see my mother's diaphragm? How about my father's jockstrap? Let me see your dirty pictures (half a deck of straight porno playing

cards). Why don't we try this position out? I proffered half the invitations and accepted the other half. But I hadn't yet had my first orgasm, and watching a friend masturbate was an illumination of the first order. The 'white pee-pee' my mother had told me about hadn't prepared me for the beauty of a seemingly endless fountain of pearly semen spurting from the head of his cock. There was something sacred about it. It was only a matter of weeks until I could produce my own, and as soon as I learned what it felt like to come, I was hooked. I came whenever I could.

"One afternoon I had a friend over, and we had the house to ourselves. We started out doing homework together, and it wasn't long before we were touching and looking interested in each other. Of course, just making love was out of the question, since we were all-American Jewish boys, so we had to find an excuse. 'Want to wrestle?' he challenged. Now there was a new angle. 'Sure,' I murmured. 'What'll we wrestle for?' 'What do you mean, *for*?' I was willing to yield to his strength with a minimum of struggle. 'There has to be a prize for the winner.'

"I was beginning to catch on. The prize was each other. 'Suppose we do it like strip poker. The loser has to take something off after each round,' I suggested, wanting to increase the skin contact as much as possible. We wrestled for match after match, yielding and overcoming with ease, first one then the other, and with each match a shoe or a shirt or a pair of pants was quickly discarded until we were in our underwear, and soon out of it and trying out the delights of '69' without knowing they had a name, and having a frighteningly wonderful time, even if it was forbidden, lost in pleasure, until I heard the sound of the key turning in the lock. My mother was home!

"'Arnold?' she called. In the minute it took for her to cross the apartment from the front door to the door to my room, we hastily abandoned our passion and scrambled into our pants. We were just zipping up when she appeared in the doorway, a look of stark horror painted on her face. 'What are you two *doing?*' she sputtered. 'Hi, Mom. Oh, we were just wrestling,' I lied guiltily. She wasn't buying. 'I think you'd better go home now,' she told my friend. 'It's suppertime . . . and I don't think you should visit Arnold anymore.' He collected himself and

fled.

"Then came the inquisition. 'Arnold, what were you doing with him?' 'I told you, Mom, just wrestling.' 'Now remember, just tell me the truth, and you won't be punished. What do you mean, 'wrestling'?' 'You know, *wrestling,*' I insisted, my voice quivering with guilt. 'Did you *touch* each other?' She filled the word with obscenity. 'Of course we touched each other. We were wrestling. I told you.' My voice was sinking to a whisper. I was starting to sweat. 'Did you touch each other anywhere you shouldn't? Your private parts?' Evasion was no longer possible. 'Just a feel,' I said as casually as I could, to minimize the indictment.

"'Just a feel,' she echoed. Her voice dripped with doom. She knew! Would she tell? Would she tell my father? The school? The police? But nothing happened. Nothing for a week. I thought it was over, until one morning when she told me to take a bath and put on clean underwear. 'What for?' I asked, groaning. 'You're going to the doctor.' 'But I'm not sick,' I protested. 'We'll see about that,' she warned. 'Now hurry up and get washed.' I knew what it was about then. We traveled all the way to Lakewood, where her sister knew a good physician. She couldn't bring this disgrace to our own family doctor. Doom hovered above my head. I felt like Norma Shearer in a wooden cart being scorned all the way to the guillotine. The heroine within me quaked. The doctor asked lots of questions as he weighed and measured me and did the usual prodding and pinching and poking. I told him everything, determined to make a clean breast of it and be cured, contrite before my confessor even if I wasn't a Catholic, desperate to regain my mother's respect, so I could reenter the lists and joust for her love. Finally he called her in and delivered his verdict: 'Your son is normal,' he said. 'He's just been experimenting in the ways boys his age all do. And don't worry about the other symptoms you told me about.' I threw her a sidelong glance. I knew what symptoms he meant: my walk, my talk, my laugh. He finished, 'Do you want him to be a street-corner hooligan? He's sensitive and intelligent. All boys aren't ruffians.' I wanted to kiss that doctor, but that would have deflated my new image as a heterosexual aesthete. Escapes can be just so narrow, and I was going to let this

sleeping dog lie even if it took a sledgehammer. 'Thank you, Doctor,' she said. There was a note of tentative relief in her voice, perhaps a willingness to accept what she knew wasn't true, even if it meant lying to herself. My mother could use her fancy as well as she could rationalize. Who was she to question medical science? Her son was a heterosexual."

In interviews, many porn stars talk freely about their first experiences. Steve O'Donnell said he *graduated* to gay sex when he was 19. "It was with a total stranger and very unplanned," he told *Manshots*. "You know, I can't remember the first time I penetrated or who it was. I think it was my first boyfriend, but I'm not sure. That's fucked-up, because it's supposed to be one of those things you remember forever."

What Steve does remember vividly is what came next: "I went to work at a couple of bathhouses in Michigan. I was fucking everybody I could. There was a tiny little linen closet that we kept extra sheets in, and this guy on the shift before me was just getting off, and I was just coming in, and I fucked him in the linen closet for a good couple of minutes before I had to go to work. To this day I can't actually believe that I got away with it. Shit like that happened constantly."

Baths *do* provide fertile ground for graduating to greater sexual awareness. I know they did for me because I was a married man in my early twenties and had few outlets to explore this side of my nature.

In John Travis's "In Man's Country," Sonny Markham tells us that only three short years ago, he was a shy and retiring youth who hung out at the gym developing the massive pecs we now see. But it wasn't enough, says Sonny; he just didn't have any kind of life outside the gym. "I guess you could say I was fucked up," he notes.

But all that changed, he tells us in an interview contained in the video, when he turned 21. On that day, for a birthday present, his friend Adam took him to the Chicago bath house called Man's Country. Sonny and Adam voyeuristically watch a shower-stall scene between Tony Cameron and Chris Ramsey, who cum all over themselves in rather short order. Sonny gets so worked up over this that he asks Adam to blow him. Adam obliges. *Manshots* says, "The blowjob is good and thorough,

but what's best about the scene is Sonny's flair for exhibitionism. A major part of his enjoyment – and mine, too – comes from his flexing every one of his hard, overdeveloped muscles while getting his fine dick serviced the way it deserves. I just love that in a man, and you probably will, too. Sonny heaves his huge chest out, moans, and cums all over Adam's face, then sticks his wet dick into Adam's mouth for a few seconds more, after which Adam himself shoots thick white cum all over his own torso."

And speaking of torsos, hairy, beautifully built Gianfranco says he remembers when he was little there were guys who would come to fix the fence around the house. "I loved to run around and wrap my legs around them and hold on to them. Then when I was in first grade, I had a cousin who was in eighth grade. We used to wrestle each other. I would get naked and rub my crotch on his stomach. Back then I did not know how babies were made; in Iran they don't teach you about sexuality. So one day my friend asked me if I knew how babies were made, and I said no, so he said he'd show me. Well we got naked and he started putting his dick in my ass, and I told him it hurt and that I'd like to get him pregnant. I ended up fucking him, and every weekend from then on, I would go to his house and fuck him.

"He had a brother who was in college, and I just loved him. Every time I saw him without a shirt, I got a hard-on. One day I was in his room, and he came out of the shower and was like, 'I want to show you something.' He showed me an issue of *Playboy*. He asked me if I liked what I saw, and I said I did. Then he grabbed my ass and said he liked it and wanted to know if he could have some. My heart started beating because this was my dream thing. He tried to fuck me, and I wouldn't let him, and I tried to fuck him, and he couldn't take it, so we ending up just sucking each other. He had another brother – this family is taboo! – there were four brothers and I had three of them. I was babysitting him one time, and he turned around to kiss me because there was this kissing scene on TV. I French-kissed him, and that was my first kiss. They had another brother, but I never had a chance to do anything with him."

New performer Hawk McAllister, who is gaining quite a reputation as an insatiable bottom, told *Manshots* that the first

week in college, he had nothing but sex – with girls. Yet he knew he was gay. "It's like, I wake up with a hard-on, I go to sleep with a hard-on. I like sex – I'm a Scorpio. I've always been very sexual. I mean, I've masturbated since I was eight. Later on, in college, I had my first 'valued' gay experience. He came over to study. For hours, it was just like on edge, because I didn't know how to approach somebody, but I wanted it really bad. So finally we started going at it. We started kissing, and right then and there I knew it was right. And I had the best orgasm ever.

"Then in my theatrical group there was this guy named Michael. He was very outgoing, very energetic, very flamboyant. But I didn't realize what flamboyant meant. That was my second experience. My first boyfriend lived in Seattle – we had met at a bar. I had my full sexual experience with him – you know, intercourse. Hated it. He'd come over the weekends from Seattle. One time I went to Seattle with a girlfriend of mine, to surprise him. But he was really cold. So when we were getting ready to go to bed, I went up to him, and he said: 'I'd rather sleep alone.' I went downstairs and ended up crying for fifteen minutes and went back home. Tried to track him down over the years. I figure either he had a boyfriend or he was sick.

"But my true gay lifestyle started just a year and a half ago. I moved up here with a friend. On the second day, I met this guy, a famous photographer. We proceeded to do nothing but have sex for a week. I was ready for that. I was ready to go out and have fun and have sex, meet men. Went back home for awhile, came back, started to model, because this photographer said: 'Come down here – I'll make you a model!' All he wanted was to make me a whore. Make me a boytoy. I learned the lesson... Well, it took nine months. Lost my job, went down to the lowest point, and then I met my first real lover. He showed me kindness and happiness – everything I was used to back home. Which I didn't see here. All I saw was sex parties and drugs and the underground stuff – disgusting things to me now... like piercing and fisting. I'm not into that anymore. But back then, it was all new."

The exotic porn star Devyn Foster told *Manshots* about his first time with another guy: "The guy was a few years older

than me. I was scared to go to any of the gay clubs in New York. I had a fear of being seen, and I didn't know any other way to meet guys. So I picked up a copy of the Village Voice, and I noticed that they ran personals on all kinds of sex, guys with girls, girls together, everything. And I noticed there was one part, 'Guys to meet guys.' So I was like 'Wow! That's kind of interesting.' I felt like there was not a real threat of being caught. The fear had gone. So that's how I met the first guy I went out with – through the personals. He was actually a very nice guy, too. I'm very lucky. It just could have been a nightmare. I'm still friends with him. And that was five years ago." Foster thought gay sex was much more satisfying. "I felt so much better. I felt it was me. And I didn't feel guilty at all."

This was surprising because he was brought up in a strict Catholic family. "The way we were brought up, especially by my father, we were expected to go out with girls at a certain age. It was all kind of like mapped out. You had to do this at the same age. I was never really exposed to anything as far as anything gay, so it was never really something that I thought about or wanted to do at the time. I just never gave it a thought. Later on, when I was in first or second year in college, I started to find an interest in the same sex – guys."

Underground porn top Max Stone remembered his first time: "It was a very weird situation. It was with my friend; we both had chicks, and one night we were all out and got real drunk. We dropped the chicks off because they weren't giving us none. We started talking about how horny we were, and one thing led to another. The next thing I know, we started dropping those chicks off more and more.

"We started out playing around, but then the whole thing got confused, because he didn't know or think he was gay. I was into checking out the whole gay scene. He got uptight when I went running around – it got to be a very touchy situation. He ended up getting married. I ended up becoming a fag and a porn star."

Kurt Young told *Manshots* about his first time, and how it grew into a romance for the boy who would eventually go on to Hollywood with his lover, Matthew Easton, and star in "Heat of Passion," "On the Prowl," and other videos: "I love to dance. The summer when I was nineteen, I got in real good

shape. I was actually very confident of my body. And there was a big White Party or Madonna party on a Saturday night, which is all gay, and I went with the girl who first took me there. It was me and three girls. All really good friends. And that's when I first saw a totally gay society. And, uh, I got asked out a couple of times. And I got hit on a lot. Some guy chased me out of the bar when I was leaving, and asked if I wanted to do something some time, dinner or something. I was just like, 'I'm straight, though. Sorry.' (*Chuckles*) I don't know. When I would go there I'd like to be all pumped up and look my best. And I'd wear gay clothing, I guess. You know, I wore short shorts, cutoff shorts, the big socks and the boots, and whatever. Just what other people wore.

"I told basically all my friends – my fraternity brothers knew – that eventually I would sleep with a guy – this one-night stand thing – just to experiment. The end of my junior year of college, I moved in with these two girls. I found this house and moved in. It ended up being five girls and me. So, all their ex--boyfriends would come by and their boyfriends, and Matthew Easton was one of them. And I wouldn't sleep with any of these girls because I'd become too good friends with them. But they all tried. They were kind of like the party girls of the town anyway. Guys were there all the time. So they all told Matt that I was gay. And he was, but he was very closeted about it, so he decided he was going to persist. And he would come over every time we had a party, and I would see him when we all went out. And then one night, I went down to this club that we went to every Thursday. I just got really messed up that night, and he just pursued and pursued, and I decided that he was the best guy to try it with.

"But I wasn't very attracted to him. I was attracted to his personality. He was very funny, you know, like the center of attention, the hit of the party. And I liked that, figured it would be easier...

"I decided to do it when I was drunk. To do it when it was offered and to do it with somebody who was very straight acting. 'Cause that was something I had learned by going to Trax all this time was that these guys might look good, but they acted like queens. You know, I just wouldn't do that. And so, he's straight acting, he liked me, and I thought it could just be

a one-time thing or whatever. So, we did it. We did it at his place, 'cause the party was at my place. It was an after-hours party at my place. And then, in the morning, you know, he asked for a ride home, blah-blah-blah, and he initiated things. It was fun. I hadn't actually had sex in awhile. (*Chuckles*) With anybody. 'Cause I couldn't find anybody I liked. And it really didn't hit me as a very big deal that I'd done it. 'Cause I'd known that I would – I'd had about two years to prepare for it."

Lukas Ridgeston, George Duroy's incredibly hot porn superstar, told *Manshots*: "I have a girlfriend, but after my scene with Johan Paulik, I've realized that I can enjoy sex with a boy as well as a girl. I don't understand my sexuality even today. The only thing I know is that I am a very sexual person, and I don't feel any special prejudices to complicate my life. I am certainly not spending my time trying to understand it. I am just enjoying it."

For his part, Johan said of his being fucked by Lukas in "Lukas' Story:" "When I was filming with Lukas, Lukas was in the same mood as me. He wasn't any more reserved and shy. It was very easy to work with him, so I wouldn't say that Lukas was overly reserved with me."

No, Lukas didn't appear to be a bit shy about shoving it all the way into Johan. But Lukas was not Johan's first "(The first time I got fucked) at the very beginning, it hurt a little bit, but later on, the pleasure was so overwhelming that I forgot everything about the pain. I didn't really fantasize about it, because I didn't have any experience with it, so I didn't know how good it would be. I had a good day – like any other – I just had more money. I had good feeling about it. It was the first time I was ever with two boys at the same time. I thought it was more good sex than work.

"I thought it was one-time thing. I would do it, and that would be the end of it. Nobody would ever hear of it anymore.

"(In fact) it would take almost a year before I shot another scene. It was 'Lukas' Story.' The only thing I can say is that I enjoyed the experience with Lukas."

On his first video shoot, Lukas says he was more than a bit nervous. "I didn't know what to expect – I guess you would call it fear of the unknown. I lay in bed for hours that night and

stared at the ceiling. I wasn't sure I would enjoy doing it in front of people I didn't know, with cameras. I had a sinking feeling in my stomach that night, I didn't get much sleep.

"(Luckily) there are very few people around when you work for Bel Ami. George Duroy does all the camera work by himself, and then there is one assistant with him. There is a person watching the monitor, but he is always in another room. Of course there is a make-up artist too, and several boys who are guarding the area when shooting outdoors, and they leave when it's time to have sex. But directly on the set there are only two people. George is very detail-oriented and he takes as much time as necessary to do a good job. One scene usually takes about three days to shoot. And that's not including the location search, still photos, etc. We did the opening – the non-sexual scenes and parts first. Then the solo itself. On the second day we were shooting double solo shots with Ken Christy – it was the first time in my life another boy had touched me intimately, and his first time too, I believe. But there was an immediate communication and connection between the two of us. The third day we shot interplays between me and Ken and his solo. The fourth day was reserved for shooting stills. I didn't count one day we spent on location making photo and video tests. So five days altogether for my part in 'Tender Strangers.'

"It's easier to make a solo video in a deserted ranger station than to shoot an orgy with about twenty-seven boys having sex in one room, as we did in 'Lukas' Story 2.' The orgy scene was a never ending shoot with almost sixty models altogether. We shot it during a span of two months, and it took us two weeks of net time to shoot this single one scene. It was the first time I've seen George really nervous. It cost him a fortune to produce 'Lukas' Story 2.'"

Lukas says he makes a lot of money doing videos. "In one week I earn more than my father does in half a year. That's one thing. The other part I like about it is the fun. It's quite different from the rest of my life, and it's not a full-time career. That makes it enjoyable. *(Pause)* And of course it is not bad to be a star for a few days."

Johan said he first saw a hard-on other than his own when he was fifteen years old. "It was usual that during the course

of school, they would send us for ski training, because part of the curriculum in schools here is that everybody should ski. I was sharing a room with some other boys. I was sitting on my own bed, and there were three boys together, jacking off, competing to see who would come first. ...We were a little bit tipsy and it was a lot of fun. We didn't have any problem after it."

Johan lost his virginity during a dancing seminar. "We would live together and have intensive training for one week. So I met this girl. I'm still fucking her. It happened in the training room in front of the mirrors. In the night, everybody slept, and she was sitting on the table, and I was standing in front of her. I lifted up her dress. Both of us were completely dressed when it happened."

The dancing was ballroom dancing and Johan says, "it was very good for me, and I felt very good about the people. That's where I was introduced to the major things in my life, like girls and alcohol and cigarettes. I still am a professional dancer later now in my life. But I was never interested in ballet dancing."

In fact, Duroy first saw Johan when he was still working as a producer for a major theater. "I took notice of him, so later on, I needed somebody for one show to sing, 'Lollipop,' with three other boys. I needed somebody who would dance and sing it, and I remembered him from these competitions. I went there and asked him if he would like to do it. Then I was not doing porn; I was still in regular show business. That's how we met and we were in touch then, basically, all the time, and later, when I started to shoot porno, I asked him to do stills."

Johan said, "After the first photo session, he claimed that I was too thin and childlike, that I looked too young, so he couldn't shoot me. Later on, basically, George asked me about filming, about doing a solo, but I didn't want to do that much."

Finally, Johan agreed. "The primary reason, of course, was the money, but there was also curiosity of how it looks, because I'd never seen a shoot like this. So there was this state of new experience and sort of adventure in it. So that was the second reason why I did it. Same as Lukas, I didn't think about it too much. (After awhile) I was watching boys do it all the time, so it wasn't so strange to me anymore. The first person to suck my dick was either Dano Sulik or Daniel Valent, one of them, and

it was on the set of 'Sauna Paradiso.' I never did it with boy before that. Since they were doing it, I was determined to do it. As they did it, I was trying to imagine how the girl would do it. He would do it the same way. (But) I was not really thinking about sensations like that. It was basically a job, and I was supposed to do the best I could. I was just thinking about how to do it so that it would look best. It was not pleasant or unpleasant – maybe a little bit awkward because it was the first time.

"The reason I like the pleasure to work with Dano is because he's employed with the company and goes on the shoots with us and comes to the office. He's closer than other boys who come to the office, because we are quite close to George, and so we would go out. But I don't think I'm closer to Dano than the other boys."

In an earlier issue of *Manshots*, Sulik spoke for himself regarding his experience with Johan. Sulik told *Manshots*, "It was marvelous place (where we filmed 'Sauna Paradiso') and I loved it. The main thing is that I met Johan there, who is my main friend and competitor in this company. So I was the one who was teaching Johan the ropes, how to do certain things. So that's why it was very good."

Duroy said, "You know, it might be the reason why Johan decided to shoot hard core, because he had seen a lot of other people were doing it, and he was just supposed to jack off in 'Sauna Paradiso.' That was the only thing he agreed to do before the shooting. After the first day's shooting, he agreed to do the rest of it. So, after the shoot, Dano taught Johan how to do the rest of it.

"So it would be easier for Johan," Dano said, "Johan would fuck me first, and second time, I would fuck Johan. Johan made it clear that he likes it as much as I do. Because we are very similar in our attitude toward sex."

Duroy took the boys to dinner and then left them alone. Dano remembers, "After George left, I jumped on Johan, and that was it. We started to undress each other immediately. Johan was about as horny as I was, and he wanted to show that he could match me sexually. Daniel Valent (their partner in the three-way) is a very good partner for sex, even though it's not something like with Johan. It's not as close a relationship,

basically. I liked his body a lot, and I knew that I would be a top, so I enjoyed the idea of working with him. But I was more fascinated with Johan, because he looked so innocent and young."

Sulik said that Duroy's scouts found him in a disco and brought him to his office. "I was thinking about it even before they approached me, but I never thought I would do it with boys. I was thinking I would do it with girls. I like to show my body and I don't mind. So the only little bit more difficult part was when I started to shoot gay porn – I don't think about myself as a gay person. But there was this sum of money involved, too. But I didn't think about it as anything that would be wrong. Since I'd had sex with men before, it was not so strange to me to have sex with other men in front of a camera. It's basically the same thing. The only trouble with sex in front of the camera for me is that there are a lot of interruptions and changing angles, and somebody's bossing me around and telling me what I'm supposed to do. But otherwise, it's the same. There's also one small difference: in front of camera I usually fuck with boys, and in private I usually fuck with girls.

"Basically it's all the same for me. What arouses me most is when I'm fucking somebody, to see that I really, really, really arouse them. The more they are screaming, the more I see that I'm doing very well, the more hot it is for me. I really love to fuck very hard and...it doesn't matter if it is boy or girl. We say in Europe, they can't be dead in bed. They must respond. So, if they respond – and how they respond – that's what interests me.

"If I'm fucking a boy, maybe what I'm interested in would maybe be his abdominals or his ass, you know, or his muscles. That's what arouses me in a boy. I love to fuck girls in the ass, because I prefer to fuck an ass to fuck a cunt. That's probably why I like boys, because the ass is tighter and it makes it much more pleasure."

In his memoirs, *The Waterfront Journals*, David Wojnarowicz talked about the first time he graduated to seducing another man: "I finally got picked up by this one guy who used to live in Minneapolis and as we were riding along we were talking about politics and street stuff like what was going on with

prostitutes and hustlers and all that ... I told him that I didn't think they should arrest hustlers cause they weren't really doing anything fucked up and that I knew some hustlers myself and they were sensitive people. He gave me this funny kind of look and we started talkin about sexual repression and gay politics and after a while he pulled over to a highway rest stop and we both went in to take a piss. He stood in the booth next to me and stared at my face, you know gave me the eye, so a few minutes later we got back into the car and rode a while more. He said he lived in a small town just below Saginaw and asked me if I'd like to spend a few hours over at his place...

"If I wanted I could spend the night and he'd drive me up to Saginaw the next morning. I said 'Yeah,' and we pulled down this dirt road past all these broken-down farms and wheat fields and it was getting into late afternoon and the sunlight was really beautiful on the roads. We pulled into the driveway of this tiny farmhouse two stories tall and went inside. He had this dog tied up in the back, a huge dog with long black fur ... so after we get inside I'm waiting for him to like seduce me ... see I never seduced anyone in my life I always let them seduce me ... and he was much older than I was so it was awkward for me to even consider it. But he didn't make me so I started thinking maybe I had figured him all wrong, wished I had kept hitching instead of going home with him... He told me I could lie down on the bed ... he was real nervous when he said that ... I started getting a hard-on and he couldn't notice it ... Then he got all red and started to leave then said: Well, I'll leave ya alone and you can do whatever you want. I said: Hey, don't go stick around and he stood there all red in the face and looked uncomfortable ... and I surprised myself by saying: Why don't you lay down next to me? he took off his shoes and lay down next to me all stiff like a desert mummy and after a few seconds I started running my hand down his side. He did the same and I slowly took off his clothes and then my own and we made love ..."

Some guys spend most of the prime years when they should be enjoying their sexuality simply fantasizing. In the book *Farm Boys*, David Foster relates, "There were men that came to the farm to sell farm products – Watkins products: herbicides, petroleum products, seed corn – and I always found these men

attractive. The inseminator I found attractive, the milkman I found attractive. If I was home alone when the milkman stopped in to deliver the milk, I would fantasize about going up to him and saying 'Would you mind if I played with your cock? Would you come in the clubhouse with me?'

"When I was a junior in high school, I had a terrible crush on a very athletic senior. Kevin was adorable and much more mature than the other boys. He had a brown furry chest already. I wrote a love story about Kevin for English class, and I kind of put me in the character of the girl. It was about the prom – 'The Infinite Prom' – and they were killed on their prom night in a car accident. I read it in front of my English class. I used Kevin's first and last name, and had to build up my confidence to ask him to sign a document that gave me permission to use his name. I typed it up real nice. He signed it for me, so I had his autograph."

Another farm boy, Cornelius Utz, explains, "I was highly attracted to a number of guys in high school, but I didn't dare let it be known. To be a good, sturdy, non-sissy guy, you had to be interested in sports like football and basketball. I really tried to be an athlete because I wanted to emulate my brother Sam. He was the first and only other man in our family who went through college, and he was greatly admired by my parents for doing that. Sam called everybody and his dog a sissy that wasn't a high-level football player. I really hated football, but I tried to play because it would make me more of a man. The first time I had sex-play with Sam, I was on the track team in our high school. We had a track meet in Cameron, Missouri, where Sam was the coach. After the meet, he asked if I would like to stay overnight. We shared the bed where he roomed, and he initiated sex-play with me, which I welcomed. When I was in college in Columbia, he came down there on coaching business several times and spent the night with me and we would have sex-play. This was after he was married and had children. He told me that his wife was kind of nervous, like a Jersey cow.

"In college, I heard about a biology professor who was homosexual. When I finally connected with him, he took me to a very lovely place m the country, a secluded and protected woodland area. We were enjoying the birds and the view when

he put his arms around me, turned towards me and kissed me. That was the first time I'd ever been kissed by a man. He gave me a deep French kiss, which was highly exciting. We hugged each other a bit and then went to his house. He lived with his mother who was closeted in the back of the house and told never to interfere when he had guests. We went to his bedroom and disrobed and made love some more. I took his tongue in my mouth and put my tongue in his mouth. I played with his cock some, but I could never suck him without gagging. He always sucked me, and never seemed to expect me to relieve him through masturbation or anything.

"He really introduced me to what it can mean to have gay sex. It was an idyllic experience. I would feel ashamed of myself, but whenever I felt horny I would call him and ask if he would be home a little later. He always said yes. To a great extent, this took care of my sexual needs throughout the rest of college. I really think he fell deeply in love with me, but I couldn't allow myself to feel love for him, because that would make me a really full-blown 'that way' person."

In the same book, James Heckman said he was twenty-two or twenty-three when he began to masturbate and had his first sexual experience when he was twenty-five, in graduate school! Says James, "A guy approached me in the library rest room and we went to his dorm room and had sex. I loved it, but I was so scared I was shaking. The oldtime Catholic church was wonderful at teaching guilt. I went to a priest immediately afterwards and cried uncontrollably. 'Don't worry about that. It will pass,' he told me. 'It happens to a lot of guys. You'll meet a fine girl and you'll have some kids.'

"Two or three times after that, the same guy approached me. When I said I couldn't do it, it wasn't right, he tried to tell me it was okay if it was what I really wanted and if I felt okay about it. I had a couple of experiences with a married guy in graduate school who followed me into my room. I didn't like that, because he was forcing himself on me – although I have to admit there was a little bit of it I liked."

And we trust you will have to admit you'll like more than a little bit of what is to follow.

THE DRIVER:
A VIRGIN'S CONFESSION

John Patrick

On this muggy, starless night the drivers stand around outside the Spike, chatting, or smoking. Some just wait in their cabs. I watch as some boys climb into a long black limo; I wonder if they are celebrities. It is a strange moment, seeing the tallest one slide in beside the driver. A man I met earlier took me into the place with him, but he said leaving was the hard part. "Coming out of a gay club is coming out," he said, and I know he was right.

This cab driver knows about me. But, what the hell, he has *chosen* to be outside the bar, hoping for a fare. Maybe more.

"Where to?" he asks.

I look up, but it is too dark to tell anything much about him.

"The Summit Hotel," I tell him. My dad got me a room at his corporate rate.

The air conditioning had been turned all the way up inside the big old Mercury sedan, but I am still sweating. I have left the bar still a boy, only a boy, embarrassed and hopelessly confused. I will go home to Michigan having done *nothing*. But what did I expect? Did I expect New York would somehow celebrate me? I'm still feeling it in my stomach, a desire that coils around itself, knots itself up into a ball.

We stop at a light and I look for the picture of the driver that is supposed to be hanging in the cab, but there isn't any; I realize this is a gypsy cab. My father warned me, no gypsy cabs. What have I done? He'll drive me all over town and charge me double. He might even rob me! Now I'm starting to get the shakes, I can feel them coming, odd and sickening.

The driver is upright behind the wheel, staring straight ahead, but then he looks at me in the rearview. "You okay, kid?"

"Yeah, I'll be okay."

"What'd you tell your folks?" He has a heavy accent. Italian maybe.

"My folks?"

"Yeah. You're stayin' with your folks, right – at the Summit?"

"No. I'm alone. My last adventure till I go to college."

He chuckles. "And so, has it been an adventure?"

"Not really."

"Disappointing, eh?"

"Yeah." I don't feel like talking, but he certainly feels like it. He's his own best audience. It's eerie now in Manhattan. On the way uptown, everything is closed, dark, gated, locked, empty. But I get a running commentary on everything we pass. I didn't ask for a Gray Line tour, but I'm getting one anyway.

"Yeah," he says, finally, as we pull up in front of the hotel, "this is a nice hotel all right, 'cept for that fuckin' fire station next door. They keep you up?"

"What?"

"The fire trucks?"

I haven't been paying attention. "Fire trucks?" I know nothing of fire trucks. I begin to tremble. I have just realized the worst has happened.

The driver puts his arm across the seat and turns to face me. "Somethin' wrong?"

I am madly searching my pockets, although I know now what has happened. "Yes. That man – "

"What man?"

"The one who took me into the bar with him. I bought him a drink and he saw my money clip."

The driver breaks into a hearty laugh. "Dumb shit! Dumb shit!"

He really doesn't really need to keep saying that, but he does anyway. At least he finds it hysterically funny.

"I have my wallet locked in my suitcase in my room. I'll go up and get it."

"Hey, I know the score, kid. You go up there and you find out the maid fuckin' stole your fuckin' suitcase!"

"I'll just be a minute."

"Hold it!" he orders, slamming the car into reverse. He parks the car, rather sloppily, in the cab stand. "I'm fuckin' goin' with you."

"No, no. That won't do. Look, I'll only be a minute."

"That's what they all say," he says, showing his perfect teeth in a wolfish grin. "Let's go."

In the elevator I get a real good look at my driver. Yes, Italian. Not particularly handsome, but not ugly either. And, at six-two, he towers over me. He is huge; he should be working down on the docks, not driving a cab. He reeks of garlic. But I am too nervous to be repulsed.

He can't seem to stop chuckling. He looks over at me, cowering in the corner of the elevator. He shakes his head. His eyes take me in, from my new boots to my new jeans, my white T-shirt, my new haircut. I thought I looked pretty tough when I left the hotel, but now I feel puny, terribly out of place. He's wearing nearly the same outfit, but on him it looks so much better. He certainly fills out his jeans better than I do. My eyes can't leave the bulge at his crotch, and he catches me staring at it. He doesn't say anything, just adjusts it, making it loom even larger, chuckling all the while. I take a deep breath and finally pull my eyes away when we reach the 14th floor. He is still chuckling as we step from the elevator.

He follows me down the hall. "I'll bet they loved you at the Spike."

"Why?"

"That ass. You got one cute fuckin' ass."

Nobody had ever called my ass "cute" before, let alone "cute fuckin'." Now I wonder what this goon has in mind. Images of the maid finding me in the morning flash through my mind; the desperate calls to my parents; the embarrassment over the newspaper headlines: "Recent Grad Stabbed in New York Hotel Room." I fumble with the key but finally unlock the door and enter the room. I switch on the light and start to close the door, telling him I'll just be a second, but he's already pushing his way into the room.

He senses my uneasiness, rubbing my ass. "Cute fuckin' ass," he says.

"I'll get my wallet," I say, pulling away. But he will have none of that. He grabs my arm and tosses me on the bed.

"Why don't you just work off the fare?"

"What?"

"You're the fuckin' dumbest rich kid I ever met – " He

stands next to the bed, unbuckling his jeans. "But I know what you want."

I gulp. This is not what I intended at all, but – There's no denying it, I crave him. He beams proudly at me with not a word.

In a flash, he has it out, the biggest cock I have ever seen. He smiles broadly as I stare at it while he plays with it. It grows even longer. Not only am I a virgin when it comes to butt-fucking, I am a novice regarding foreskin, which I see the driver has in abundance. I am fascinated by the look of it, and he chuckles as he kicks off his boots and jeans. Sweat and hair is everywhere, and his cock is lengthening from my hungry stare. He climbs on the bed and mounts me, putting the huge thing in my face. He takes off his T-shirt. More sweat, more hair. I reach out and pull the erection to my nose and breathe in its heady aroma. The eye of the cock is now staring me right in the face. The folds of skin wrap around the huge head. A long strand of precum drips from the iris. With his calloused hands, he takes hold of the foreskin and stretches it back into the long, thick shaft.

My lips part as he brings it closer. Slowly he feeds it to me. Stretched tall above me, he groans as I work it into my mouth. He lets go of the shaft as I slide most of it in. Now he takes hold of my head and begins.

I nurse his cock helmet. It dribbles some more cum. He moves it in, to the back of my throat. I suck deep on it while I bury my nose in the fur above his hard-on.

Soon his thick thighs buckle and shudder, but suddenly he pulls out.

It's as if he has read my mind, because my own cock was aching for release. He runs his fingers over my crotch. He allows me to sit up and, in a flash, I am nude and back into position. He smiles and straddles me again. His balls swing about a foot over my face, then he drops them to my lips. I kiss them, suck them, then I slide my tongue in his asshole and he moans with satisfaction.

Grabbing big chunks of my hair, he begins to fuck my face again. He's breathing heavily in no time, then stops again. He gets up and walks across the room, pulling the long mirror off the wall and leaning it on top of the bed, which in this room is

shoved in a corner. He angles the mirror to reflect the bed's activities. He positions me where he wants me, then orders, "Lie back, babe, and suck me good and hard. Then I'm gonna fuck yer cute hairless ass."

I nod, but I know I'm not up to things going that far. I don't have time to reflect on it, however, because he aims his shaft to my hungry mouth. He fucks my mouth like a wet pussy and his balls slap at my chin. I let my eyes wander to the mirror beside me to watch this stud use me as his little fucktoy. Another first for me, watching myself while I'm doing it. His cock throbs faster in my throat. He drips sweat from every pore of his skin and soaks me with it. The cold air blowing on me from the air conditioning has kept me fairly comfortable. His moans and panting get louder as he pumps long, hard strokes down my throat. I reach down and begin to masturbate. Then, just as I am peaking with desire for him, he pulls his cock out forcefully.

"Roll over," he barks.

I follow his order as he grabs the bottle of lotion off the nightstand. I watch in the mirror as he prepares my asshole and his cock. Then he mounts me and begins. He is surprisingly gentle now. Perhaps he knows I've never done this before. I cry out when he fingers it. He lets up for a moment, but then he has the head of it in. He pauses for a second, but then doesn't stop; he keeps on shoving his hard cock into me, eventually to lower his large torso down on me in a final, sweaty lunge. His cock sweeps into me in rapid thrusts. I take deep breaths, getting used to it. He props himself over me and watches his cock going in and out. I look into the mirror myself to watch and I squirm and moan in ecstasy. I feel my cock rubbing the sheets, ready to come. As if he is reading my mind, as I am struggling for air under his heavy body, he rolls me over on top of him so I can breathe. This way, I can fuck the big cock and watch it penetrating me in the mirror. This sets me off and I come all over his hairy chest.

I keep at it, though, wanting him to come, now more than ever. God, I really like it here, him inside of me. This is the best sex I've ever had. Better than giving Jerry, the football center/hunk/moron, a blowjob occasionally – far better. I now know the kind of sex I was born to have. It is good for my

driver, too. I can feel the end drawing near. I pull my buttcheeks wider apart, helping him. Soon I am being thrashed wildly around on his cock. His orgasm is quieter than mine, but no less intense.

There is no lingering, however. No after-sex cuddling. Instead, he bounds from the bed, still full of energy, and says, "Let's take a shower." I agree it's a good idea, since I have cum dripping from my asshole.

The shower barely holds his big body and mine. He lathers me all over with soap. He smiles the whole time but says nothing. Then he turns me around to wash my asshole. Gentle strokes sooth my ravaged pucker. Slowly, but firmly he runs his hands over me. He works his way to my front, slips his hand firmly on my cock and squeezes. He works my cock in his hand, biting my neck. He is running his renewed hard-on up and down my crack. I shoot again in seconds.

I know he wants to fuck me again, but he senses I have had quite enough battering for one night. He turns me around and forces me down. I end up sitting in the tub while he fucks my face again.

Soon I am making him scream in ecstasy. He lets me take over, and my mouth fully encompasses him, my tightness holds him captive. He starts to shudder, but I keep him going, anticipating his inevitable orgasm. My eyes are closed, and in the darkness of my mind I see him enjoying this act to the fullest extent possible. Up and down I go, over and over again.

"Oh, kid," he sighs, "God!"

I don't respond, and the pace seems to quicken a bit. He is drawing nearer and nearer. Another few sucks on it and it will all be over.

"Oh, kid," he sighs again, his now voice seeming so warm and pleasant, just like his cock.

He suddenly pulls back, watching himself ejaculate in a stream, straight up in the air. The residue comes down on my face, only to be washed away by the spray of the shower. I pull him toward me again, kissing the slowly softening penis.

But he still is in no mood to linger. "Hey, I'm losin' fares hanging around here," he says, climbing out of the tub. "Back to work."

By the time I return to the bedroom, he's dressed and

combing his hair. He's put the mirror back on the wall. He doesn't look at me.

I step over to the closet, crouch down to get at my suitcase. I unlock my suitcase, pull out my wallet. I still have a hundred dollars cash and some traveller's checks. My hand shakes as I hand him the bills.

"What's this?" he says.

"I don't want you losin' fares 'cause you were hangin' around here." The minute I say it, I regret my tone, and my mimicking of his heavy accent.

But he pays me no mind. He shrugs, shoves the bills in his pocket, and returns to combing his hair. "How long you here for?" he asks.

"I have a four o'clock flight."

"We should leave by two."

I have dropped to my knees and am busy returning my wallet to my suitcase, then locking it. "What?" I know what he said but I want him to repeat it, just to make sure. "What did you say?"

"I said, we need to leave by two."

"I don't understand."

"You worked off your fare, and now you gave me enough to take you to the airport. Okay? That's not too hard to figure, is it, even for a little rich kid?"

"Okay." I smile and look at my watch. It is now four o'clock in the morning. "But what will we do between now and then?"

I look up, but now all I can see is blue denim as he takes my head in his hands and crushes my face into his crotch.

HIS NEW BOSS

John Patrick

I.

The new boss was in his office, jacket off, sleeves rolled up, working the phones, smiling wryly as his young, love-hungry assistant, Jimmy, entered the room.

Jimmy had taken an instant dislike to his new boss. The new boss was small, thin, rather fragile-looking, running on nerves, jumbo cups of strong black coffee, and the desire to get the job done – at any cost. He worked Jimmy like a dog, exhausting him.

But, after a few days, Jimmy began to look at the man a bit differently. For one thing, there was always that smile. Jimmy couldn't escape it. It was as if the new boss, who told Jimmy to call him Drew, not Mr. O'Connor, knew Jimmy's secret. Of course, Jimmy never hid the fact that he was gay, he just never made a point of it. It was awkward when a woman went after him, and he would have to reveal himself to that woman, and they always ended up being friends. But Jimmy had never had a boss who fancied him. Now there was the strange way Jimmy felt when Drew's eyes lingered over him as he talked on the phone, closing another deal for yet another new office park or condominium project.

And then Drew asked Jimmy if he wanted to go with him to take a look at a new real estate development from the air. The client, a man of extreme wealth, flew his own helicopter. Jimmy agreed to, as he said, "tag along."

Once they were in Drew's long, white Mercedes, Drew began an interrogation of his assistant that was relentless. Drew wanted to know all about Jimmy's childhood, his schooldays, his prospects for the future. Jimmy became increasingly uncomfortable. He figured the trip was being used as a pretext to get him out of the office, to put him in a place where he was vulnerable. This had happened once before, just after Jimmy graduated from high school and was working as a clerk in a travel office. He had spurned that man's advances; that man

was just a co-worker, not the boss, but now Jimmy's boss was interested in him. And, to make matters more difficult, Drew was appealing to Jimmy in a perverse way. Jimmy fancied himself as a stud, and he could picture himself fucking Drew. But while Jimmy considered himself a top man who controlled the situation, here he was being controlled by a man he could only categorize as what his mother would call "a pipsqueak." Still Drew had a cute little butt, and he was blessed with a real estate salesman's self-confidence. Plus Drew's knowledge was vast, while Jimmy, an average student, thought of himself as a bit slow. But Jimmy made up for what he lacked in intellect by being a hard worker, a man who could type very well. And his filing was impeccable.

They made an intriguing couple as they joined the wealthy man on the helicopter ride out over the ocean and down the coast. Jimmy had never been so exhilarated. No ride at Disney World could compare to this.

Later, as they were returning to the office, Drew checked his watch, announced it was too late to go back to work, and offered to buy Jimmy dinner. This was it, Jimmy thought, the beginning of the end. "Sure," Jimmy said, without looking at his boss.

"So," Drew said after they had ordered drinks, "you get along with Rogers?"

Rogers was Jimmy's old boss, who was arrested for embezzlement of a client's funds and was awaiting trial. The scandal nearly broke the company. Drew was hired, Jimmy knew, because he had been associated with one of the top developers in Miami and would add luster to the company when it sorely needed it.

"He was okay," Jimmy said.

"Terrible thing. Did you suspect anything?"

"No. It came as a shock."

"You appear to be a boy who can keep his eyes open but his mouth shut."

"I'm hardly a boy," Jimmy joked.

"You're a boy to me. Anybody ten years younger than I am *has* to be a boy."

"I'm not as young as I look."

"I doubt you're even twenty one."

"Almost."

Drew laughed. The waiter brought their drinks, and they sat sipping them, taking account of each other.

"Is it true, then?" Drew asked finally.

"What?"

"That you can keep your eyes open and your mouth shut?"

"I guess. I mind my own business."

"You're a good boy, I can tell. And a handsome one, too. I'll bet you have a lot of girlfriends."

"No..."

And it went on like that for half an hour, through a second drink. Drew would get close but back away. Jimmy couldn't do anything but play along. It wasn't his place to say, let's fuck. No, he had to wait for Drew to complete his seduction. And it *was* a seduction. It was as if Drew was selling a ten-million-dollar project. He was selling himself to Jimmy, that a relationship could be exceedingly beneficial to both of them.

By the time dinner was over and they were lingering at the table with cognacs, Jimmy was ready. Still, Drew kept up the act, talking and talking, on and on. Jimmy thought if he weren't in a public place, he would have gotten up and shoved his cock in Drew's mouth just to shut him up.

Drew had tried to impress Jimmy, even talked about his sexual exploits with girls. But Drew never considered himself a practicing homosexual. He had dated girls, and one who came to spend the night stayed for three and a half years. They were like a bitter married couple: soul mates stuck together, in love, in some strange way, but in trouble. The men he met, however, turned out to be as bad off as he was. One boy he lusted for said he was "basically straight." Another one said he was "straight with a shade of gay," and then left the next day while Drew was in the shower at the motel room Drew had rented for their assignation.

But now Drew didn't need to rent any room. He was free to take Jimmy back to his apartment. First he offered to take Jimmy back to the office to get his car. "Or," Drew amended, "maybe you'd like to stop by my place for another cognac."

"You're the boss," Jimmy said, suddenly feeling light-headed. He usually didn't drink, much less drink for two hours

straight.

Jimmy was staggering as they entered Drew's vast palace of a house on Harbor Island. Drew led Jimmy to the master bedroom, where the youth promptly passed out. Drew stood over the body, lusting for him.

For at least a year, Drew had almost no sex, no dates, and no romance. He was determined to get a lot of work done. He was promoted to vice president and making big money, but he was unhappy. Glory holes had become his only sexual outlet. It was comforting in a way, this anonymous sex, but, unlike in busy Miami, he was lonely. Just when the loneliness became unbearable, along came the offer from Landco. The new job was challenging, and he was making more money than ever, but he had found no glory holes near Gulfport. And then he saw Jimmy, his "assistant," called that because they didn't like using the term clerk at Landco. Jimmy was everything Drew liked in a partner. He wanted a hunk, but not a jock. Given their situation, Drew was in control, but he did not want to take advantage based on that. Still, Drew knew being the boss would provide the opportunity to get to know Jimmy better.

But now it had come down to a simple question of anatomy. As Drew gazed at the tall sleeping figure on the bed, he decided he simply had to remove Jimmy's clothes. By the time Jimmy was reduced to only his white briefs, Drew was hard. Jimmy, nearly naked, was even more glorious than Drew had imagined. It was obvious the youth spent his spare time at the gym, sculpting his body into a hard, flawless mass of muscle. Drew tore off his own clothes and kneeled down over the slumbering figure. He brought his mouth to the bulge in the briefs and licked it, sucked it, inhaled it.

The next morning, when Jimmy awoke sun was streaming in through the windows of the mostly white bedroom. It was so bright, Jimmy pulled the pillow over his face. Then he shook himself and looked at the clock: it was nearly noon! He pulled himself up from the bed and slowly made his way to the bathroom. His head began to clear as he splashed his face with cold water. He was in his boss's bathroom, in his briefs!

But where was his boss? He relieved himself, then set about looking for Drew. Drew was nowhere to be found. He had left

a note on the kitchen table: "Good morning. Take the day off. Have a swim. I'll be home early. -D."

Obviously Drew was not upset with his assistant. In fact, he was "coming home early" just to see him. Jimmy felt strange, still vulnerable in this situation. He could have dressed, taken a cab to the office, returned to his desk, and finished the day as usual. But he didn't. He looked about the house. It was, without a doubt, the most beautifully decorated place he'd ever seen. He realized it was important for a man in Drew's position to have a showplace of a home, but this was too much. He wandered around the place, inspecting everything as if he was thinking of moving in, which perhaps he was, all things considered, Drew was quite a catch. He briefly considered what Drew might have done after he passed out. He didn't remember anything, but he did awaken stripped to his briefs. Whatever happened, he hoped Drew had enjoyed himself.

Jimmy was lounging in the sun when Drew returned to the house. Drew stood over Jimmy admiring the view. "I see you found a pair of trunks," he said.

"They're a bit tight," Jimmy said, beaming.

Drew dropped to his knees beside him. Jimmy's muscular thighs flexed as Drew ran his fingers up to the waist of the trunks and over his lightly-furred belly.

Drew pinched Jimmy's jutting brown nipples, tweaking them as Jimmy's dick jumped. Drew buried his nose in the boy's crotch, the musky smell of his manhood filling his nostrils. Dragging the trunks down with his teeth, he rubbed his nose against the hairy base of the bobbing cock. His moist piss slit clung to Drew's nose, his balls swinging beside Drew's chin.

Drew sighed. When Jimmy's cock was hard, it was surely one of the most magnificent he had ever seen. It was easily nine inches in length, nicely cut, and thick. Drew sucked Jimmy's dick inside his mouth, coating it with saliva as it inched toward the back of his throat.

"Aren't you gonna strip?" Jimmy whispered, running his hot hand over Drew's back as he deep-throated him. "I want to see you naked."

Drew nodded as he began undressing, not wanting to allow Jimmy's dick to fall out of his hungry mouth. Jimmy reached

out and helped Drew take off his pants.

As the suck continued, Jimmy had a hard time holding still. He squirmed in the lounge. Drew was having a grand time, playing Jimmy like an instrument, knowing just when to rub hard and when to pull back and gently caress. Soon any attempt to stop the oncoming orgasm was useless. Jimmy tightened up, so close, so close, and then the hot, sweet wave rose up out of his groin and moved up his spine in a rapid, blissful sweep. Jimmy bit his tongue to keep from crying out as he came. Drew's mouth sucked every last wave out of Jimmy's cock, and Jimmy fell back, stunned.

Drew kept the cock in his mouth, licking it, kissing it, while he jacked himself off. When Jimmy realized Drew was coming, he struggled to pull himself together and ran his fingers through Drew's hair.

They lay quietly for a moment. Then Drew got up, telling Jimmy to stay and rest. Jimmy reached up, took Drew's hand and pulled him down, kissing him on the lips. Drew made the kiss brief, however, as if he might be afraid of such affection.

Jimmy watched the older man pick up his clothes and make his way to the house. Jimmy liked the ass that was exposed to him now, without shame.

In an hour, Drew was eating the grouper he had just grilled, the picture of poise and manners.

Orgasms always relaxed Jimmy and he seemed to need all of his strength just to lift his hands and finish eating his dinner.

Drew made coffee, put a plate of chocolate cookies on the table. Jimmy began munching them as Drew poured the coffee.

They hadn't spoken much since the sex, but now Drew talked about what had happened that day at the office. Jimmy had almost forgotten that there existed any world outside of this beautiful house and his wonderful, newly-found cocksucker.

Drew got up to clear the table and leaned over for a quick kiss, which turned passionate very quickly. Even though drained, Jimmy was just as much in need as Drew. Jimmy's tongue was in Drew's mouth immediately, probing and pressing against his as hard as he could. Jimmy took his hand

and guided it between his legs. The flesh of the big cock seemed on fire. Reluctantly, Drew broke away. He couldn't get to the bedroom fast enough, and Jimmy was hot behind him. But they stopped halfway for another long, passionate kiss. Jimmy came up behind him and hugged him tightly. His hands gripped Drew's asscheeks and planted delicate kisses on his neck while he began fingering Drew. Drew reached behind and grabbed Jimmy's erection, pulling him to his body.

Drew led Jimmy to the bed. Jimmy made him lie face down on the comforter and knelt beside him. Jimmy started at his neck, rubbing gently, feeling his soft skin move beneath his fingers. Gradually he worked his way down his spine, kneading the flesh around his shoulders.

Every now and again Jimmy would bend down and trace the curve of his spine with his tongue, burying deep in the indentation just above his ass. Drew sighed and begged Jimmy to fuck him. Instead, Jimmy spent a long time kneading his firm, creamy cheeks. Then he leaned down and gently tongued the cleavage between them. Drew moaned and lifted his hips to meet Jimmy's tongue. Jimmy began finger-fucking Drew. Immediately Drew bucked his hips up to push the fingers all the way in.

There was a new sensation; Jimmy's fingers were deep in Drew's ass, his tongue licking Drew's erection. This drove Drew wild and he came, his heavy load soaking the comforter under him. But still he wanted Jimmy's cock. He pulled himself up on his pillow so he could see as Jimmy's cock entered him, and it was gorgeous.

Jimmy pushed hard and Drew gasped. They started a regular rhythm. Jimmy moved frantically and began to cry out. He came violently, his cum flooding Drew's aching ass. Jimmy moaned and shivered, enjoying every last wave, pushing against Drew.

Jimmy pulled out and lay next to Drew, panting. Gently, Drew kissed him on the lips, then the forehead.

There was no question of Jimmy staying now. Drew was not about to let go of him right now.

II.

Drew wished his lover a good morning and deposited a cup of strong black coffee on the nightstand beside Jimmy. Always an early riser, Drew was dressed with his cup of coffee half finished.

Then Drew was down and working Jimmy's cock over before Jimmy even realized it. The warmth from his wet tongue radiated through his body. Drew licked his lover slowly, carefully, as if he was ice cream or a forbidden sweet treat. Jimmy could only groan and go limp with the pleasure. He let the delicious feeling of Drew's mouth take him over. Drew licked his thighs and went back to the sucking of the cock. Jimmy could have lain back and taken this for hours, it felt so good, and he often did. Drew knew it, and smiled as Jimmy gasped. Drew wanted to make him come. He concentrated on his cock now, feeling his excitement Jimmy ran his fingers through Drew's hair and pushed him deep into his crotch. Faster and faster Drew sucked him, while the boy gasped and squirmed on the bed. Finally he cried out with his release; his hips moving, he came.

Usually, Drew would let it go at that, but the suck was so exciting, Jimmy's load so heavy, Drew threw off his clothes and lay down next to Jimmy. Drew's cock was still throbbing sharply, and as they kissed, Jimmy's hand strayed to it, and Drew moaned at the first touch of his fingers. Jimmy played with him, still kissing him. Jimmy asked Drew to mount his chest. Drew slid his cock in Jimmy's mouth, and Jimmy reached up and grabbed Drew's asscheeks, and Drew was soon overcome with the sensation.

For a moment, they snuggled in bed together. It seemed as if they had spent all of their time in bed the last six months. Drew hugged his young lover tightly and told him he was bringing some clients home "for cocktails."

Jimmy's heart sank when he heard the door close behind Drew. The breeze coming through the open window had an end-of-summer chilly touch to it, and once again he was filled with the same conflicting emotions that overcame him of late. He no longer had to work in the office, but it was obvious he had a new job, providing stud service for Drew's steadily

increasing number of "clients." Some of this wasn't too bad.

Jimmy remembered how it started, after cocktails, when Drew suggested the two men, who were visiting the States from Italy, take a dip in the pool. Jimmy swam out toward Drew, following him to the deep end. The two clients, Leo and Alexander, both about thirty and attractive hunks, close behind them. Jimmy was drawn to Alexander; Drew seemed to be partial towards Leo.

When they reached the deep end, Jimmy felt a hand graze the front of his Speedo, fondling his nuts. He looked up just in time to see Drew swim by, grinning as he snatched Leo's suit off and tossed it up onto the side of the pool.

Alexander swam between Jimmy's legs, rubbing his balls before he eased Jimmy's suit down his legs and tossed it on top of Leo's. Alexander led Jimmy into shallower water, his fingers inching inside Jimmy's ass as he steadied myself against the edge of the pool. Jimmy let Alexander fingerfuck him several minutes before reaching over and touching the stud's dick. Not satisfied to stroke it through lycra, Jimmy tore Alexander's suit down and wrapped both hands around the long, thick, uncut rod.

Now Drew swam up and clamped his mouth over Jimmy's tool, tonguing him practically to the brink before releasing his grip. Leo pulled down Drew's suit as Jimmy rubbed Alexander's dick, easing his loose foreskin up and down, his cockhead playing peek-a-boo.

Drew, Leo, and Alexander huddled around Jimmy, the four of them alone in the floodlit pool. They circle-jerked. Jimmy's eyes closed as he fondled Alexander in his right hand and Leo in his left. Jimmy wanted to taste them, and he wanted to feel them inside him. With Drew, Jimmy was always the active one. Although he considered himself quite the stud, Jimmy was versatile, but Drew would have none of it. Drew said he equated fucking with women, that he had only fucked women. It was confounding to Jimmy, but he accepted it. Then Drew started bringing "clients" home. Now, Drew said, Jimmy could get what he wanted.

"Let's go upstairs," Jimmy urged, running his finger under Alexander's foreskin as he moaned.

"I fuck you here," Alexander whispered hoarsely, in broken-

English, plunging his fat fingers past Jimmy's balls and up inside his ass. Jimmy fell back against the side of the pool, still frigging Drew's dick as Leo rough-handled Jimmy's aching tits.

They climbed from the pool and Jimmy knelt in front of Drew, engulfing his throbbing knob. Alexander spread his asscheeks wide open as his tongue fiercely lapped at Jimmy's hungry hole.

Leo gleefully positioned himself in front of Drew's face, forcing his huge pole into Drew's throat. Drew seemed to be enjoying himself, slurping and sucking with abandon.

Jimmy shifted position, forcing his dick into Alexander's mouth, pinning him to the terrace with his thighs. Without waiting for Alexander to adjust, he rammed it into the back of his throat, slamming his tonsils with each thrust. Alexander sucked him a while, but eventually maneuvered his way back to Jimmy's asshole.

Jimmy felt a slight burning sensation as Alexander skewered him, inching his way inside him. He eased away from Leo, moving his mouth up Drew's hairy torso toward the two pink caps poking out of his furry pecs. Clamping down on the right one, he tweaked the left with his hand. He was soon joined by Leo, and they shared the tits. Drew lay his hands on their heads, urging them to suck harder. They obeyed, and he groaned, letting Leo's cock fall out of his mouth.

Jimmy moved off of his tit and eased his butt down over Alexander's erection. Drew rocked and moaned appreciatively. as he backed onton Jimmy's cock.

Alexander stood behind him, tweaking Jimmy's nipples while Leo lapped at his shaft. Alexander's uncut meat proved too thick for Leo's mouth, so he jerked it against Jimmy's back.

Jimmy cried out as his dick shot into Drew's twitching ass. Soon the stud had emptied his load into Jimmy's ass.

Alexander cupped his hands under Jimmy's knees, dragged him up and shoved his fat pole into Jimmy's sloppy asshole. Jimmy cried out, the incredible pain of it blinding him.

Leo moved around front and shoved his dick into Jimmy's mouth. Jimmy was being fucked at both ends by clients as his old boss, now his lover, looked on, trying to revive his hard-on with both hands.

The pain lessened as Jimmy's ass adjusted to the huge meat

Alexander stuffed in; he began bucking to meet his thrusts. He reached up and twisted Leo's dark tits, sucking in more of his cock as it expanded to its limits.

Leo's load hit the roof of Jimmy's mouth just as Alexander thrust deep inside him and began to shoot himself. Jimmy gulped, clamping down on Alexander's dick. Alexander shuddered, crying out as the sensation hit him.

As they withdrew, Jimmy glanced over at Drew, reclining on the edge of the bed. His dick had regained its full hardness. He lifted his legs. "Fuck me again, please," Drew begged.

Alexander chuckled, "Yeah!"

Leo lapped at Jimmy's cock until it was slimy, then Alexander led him over to the bed. Leo took Jimmy's erection in his hand and guided it to Drew's opening, then eased it in. Alexander and Leo jacked their cock, keeping them hard, while Jimmy fucked his lover for a few moments. Then they took turns at Drew's ass. Finally, Jimmy was back in and the clients came again as Jimmy's fucking of Drew progressed. The visitors went to the bathroom, took showers, and returned to the bedroom. Jimmy was still fucking Drew. They watched the scene with great amusement, then stealthily left the room.

After Jimmy came and the lovers lay in each other's arms, Drew thanked Jimmy for his "help" in entertaining his clients.

"You're the boss," Jimmy sighed, resignation in his tone.

Remembering the orgy now, Jimmy jacked off, then smoothed the bed, pulled on his shorts and took his coffee to the pool. As he rested in the morning sun, his mind returned to the "clients," not Alexander and Leo, but the others, the fat ones, the skinny, ugly ones, the smelly ones. And what did this night hold? He had never considered himself a whore, but that was what he had become. When thinking about it became too much to bear, he stripped off his jeans and dove into the pool. As he swam his laps, he decided he would be like Scarlett O'Hara and think about it tomorrow.

III.

Alexander leaned down and parted Jimmy's legs, then flicked his tongue against Jimmy's hard, aching cock. Jimmy's whole

body trembled at the touch and he moaned out loud. He had had his cock touched many times before, but never with such desire, such expertise. As Alexander sucked, his hands played with Jimmy's nipples. Having sex with Alexander was as if Jimmy was a virgin again, experiencing sex for the first time in his life. Never had anything felt so good, especially when Alexander was finished sucking and got down to fucking. Jimmy had never been fucked like Alexander fucked him, or as often.

Alexander moved very slowly over Jimmy's cock, devouring it, then he kissed Jimmy's thighs. Eventually he moved down to lick at Jimmy's tight ass, pulling his cheeks gently apart with his hands and kneading them with his fingers as he did. He made long laps on the lips of Jimmy's ass, and made a point of his tongue so that he could slip the tip of it into the entrance to Jimmy's hot tunnel. Everything he did seemed to feel better than the last, and Jimmy moaned loudly.

Alexander climbed up on the bed and knelt over Jimmy's face. At first, Jimmy did nothing but stare and breathe deeply. He couldn't get over how beautiful and big Alexander's uncut cock was. How good it smelled, so hot and ready, so in need of a mouth or ass to relieve the pressure built up inside.

Now it was time for Jimmy to suck. But Jimmy didn't need to really work at it; Alexander would, he knew, fuck his mouth for a while before moving on to the ass. "That's it, that's my boy," Alexander said, mangling the English language. "Suck! Just like that!"

Jimmy needed no encouragement at this point. He just worked to keep from choking on the massive member.

Jimmy's skin became alive and on fire with each touch of Alexander's brilliant fingers and tongue. Alexander was an expert at lovemaking, and it was a joy just to lie back and submit to his will.

When Alexander finally shoved his erection in Jimmy's ass, Jimmy cried out with pleasure. Alexander had somehow managed to focus Jimmy's whole body on this point, and he showed Jimmy no mercy as he fucked. Alexander kissed Jimmy and it drove Jimmy wild and he cried out for Alexander to fuck him even harder. Alexander moved faster, his cock deep inside the youth, and Jimmy's orgasm caught him by surprise. He too

began to quiver and shake, and soon it was over for the night. Jimmy finally calmed down in the loving circle of Alexander's muscular arms.

They talked for a long time, punctuated with tiny kisses.

"I love being here," Jimmy said. "There's nothing like Italy – or Italians."

It had always been thus: when Jimmy's life looked most desperate, something always turned up. Alexander called, saying he was back in town for a couple of days and wanted to see Jimmy "alone." When the offer came to leave with Alexander, "for a little vacation from Drew," as Alexander put it, Jimmy jumped at it.

Alexander was now saying, "There's no reason for you to ever change that thought."

"No way! Give me tall, dark and handsome!"

"I wish I was darker. I swear. And you know what's funny? When I was working in Rio, there was nothing like, 'He's black, he's Jewish.' I never saw that. In America there is a lot of discrimination. I think it's the way Americans are brought up, their families. It's sad. I think they've got to do something to change people's minds in your country. Being Italian, I have never experienced prejudice... Maybe because we've been brought up educated about this and that and we've never felt inferior. I think the ones that are feeling prejudiced are the ones that have a problem with themselves, and they're trying to hide whatever is making them feel bad and are pointing the finger to other people. If you are at peace with yourself, you don't give a fuck about what anyone else is doing. It's your world. Make it. Don't hurt others. If you want to hurt yourself, do it."

"The thing that gets me about Italy is the Vatican."

"Yes, I too am confused with religion. What I don't like about the Catholic church is that there are millions of kids dying all over the world and the church is so rich. And you go to Rome and you see the billions and billions of dollars and people are starving. It's sad, it shouldn't be. I also believe that you have to have someone or something to hold onto. If not, you won't have peace."

"Sex for you is so great. What's normal for you is vulgar for us. And Drew, he's so deep in the closet, he'll never come out."

"Yes, all of my life I've been very open and never hidden anything. I like both sexes, and I make no apologies for that. And I needed you. I needed someone so much with all that was going on. It was very intense. I am glad you decided to leave with me for a little vacation."

"I felt like I was 13 years old, running away from home."

"Do you miss your friends?"

"I have very few friends any more because it's very hard to trust. Now, I don't mind being alone a lot. I like this place because you have your bedroom, I have my bedroom. That's the only way I can live with someone. I love to live with someone, but I have to have my privacy."

Besides fucking him, Alexander loved taking Jimmy out to dinner and to the bars. They would walk into a restaurant and menus would be lowered, eyeglasses adjusted, and conversation stopped. Jimmy began to realize he was like a trophy to Alexander. It was as if the older man had gone to America, picked up a pretty young blond, and then brought him back to Rome to show off his prize.

But, after a time, Jimmy saw that Alexander did not respect him. He would treat him the same way Drew did. He would go off with a woman, be gone for days. For Jimmy the most important thing was respect, so he left.

IV.

Drew put his arms around Jimmy. They kissed slowly, and Drew reached under Jimmy's shirt to run his fingers around his nipple. Drew pushed his tongue into Jimmy's mouth, wanting more. Then Drew kissed his throat, the back of his neck. His skin was still warm from the sun and tasted slightly salty, as if all the ocean had swept over him. Jimmy reached into the back pocket of Drew's shorts to cup his firm ass cheeks, knowing how nice they looked naked, with his cock sliding between the cheeks, deep into his lover. They stood for the longest time, fingers kneading firm flesh, kisses planted on anything they could reach.

Finally Jimmy moved away, smiled at Drew and slowly, seductively, removed his baggy T-shirt. Drew's tongue found

Jimmy's nipples instinctively. Drew loved to suck them in, one at a time, then run his tongue slowly around each one while it's still between his lips. He bit them gently, pulling on them, nibbling at them, still flicking his tongue over the tender tip he held between his teeth. He ran his hands up and down the slim body, finishing down between his legs, sucking on the bulge in the shorts. This made Jimmy weak with desire for him. He leaned back, and he reached down to help Drew pull off his shorts. Jimmy's long cock bobbed into view and Drew fell to his knees.

How Drew had missed this cock. He humiliated himself now, making no apology for adoring this penis. He probed with his tongue and hands, and Jimmy groaned appreciatively. Drew lapped at the moist, salty erection eagerly. Jimmy held his head and pushed his cock deeper into Drew's hungry mouth. Jimmy fucks his face with it. After Alexander, Jimmy felt he was better at this than before. Having this done to him so often, he had learned what to do, how to guide his cocksucker, tease him. His hands roamed in Drew's hair, and the older man's face became wet with pre-cum and his own saliva. Jimmy would force himself out of Drew's gaping mouth and slap Drew across the face with his erection, then slam the big cock back into Drew's mouth.

Finally they went to bed and Drew got on his knees. He wanted it doggie, to begin with. Jimmy returned to Drew's hole as if he had really missed it, which he had if he dared to admit it. He began lapping with long strokes, and Drew relaxed, moaning. Jimmy reached under Drew to grip his cock; he jerked it until he felt Drew getting close, then left it, so that Drew collapsed to the bed, nearly at the edge of orgasm. Finally, after several long minutes of teasing his ass, licking, flicking, lapping. He knew Drew's responses as well as he knew his own.

Drew cried out as Jimmy entered him, sparing him no mercy. All of Drew's muscles tightened, and he came. He was very vocal, crying out, pushing Jimmy deep into him, shaking. Jimmy's cock was throbbing as he fucked every last quiver out of Drew. Know he knew exactly how good it felt; he had been fucked repeatedly – and deliciously – by Alexander.

"Tell me," Drew said, holding Jimmy close after their first

sex in eight months, "is it awful to see me again? Are you still angry?"

"I wish you'd stop going on and on about me being angry. I was never angry. I don't get angry. I thought you knew that. Hurt perhaps. But never angry."

"But you fucked me as if you were angry with me."

"Maybe *you're* angry at me and that's why you keep accusing me of being angry at you."

"Oh, no. I forgave you long ago."

"*You* forgave *me*?"

"For running off with the stud from Rio."

"He was from Rome. He was just living in Rio for a time."

"Anyway, I forgave you a long time ago."

"Very big of you."

"Oh, never mind. It's just so good to have you back – "

Jimmy threw off the sheet. "It's so warm here."

"Hot. I imagine. Compared to Rome."

"Rome was very cold, as it turned out."

"Alexander didn't warm it up at all?"

"Not very often. In fact, he became downright chilly – for an Italian."

"He had a gorgeous cock."

"Yes, he did. And he fucked very well."

"Yes, I remember. Of course, I had it only once."

"Once was enough, as it turned out."

"Well, at least you won't complain about not getting fucked anymore."

"No," Jimmy chuckled, "I may never get fucked again."

"Is that why you left? Was he fucking you too much?"

"No. Not enough."

Drew blinked. He didn't like where this conversation was headed, but he had to ask, finally: "Is that why you left, because I wouldn't fuck you?"

"No. I left because you left."

"I was only gone for a weekend, for chrissakes!"

"How was I to know that?"

Drew shrugged. He had no answers. Instead, he changed the subject. "Other than the fucking, how was Rome?"

"It's all a blur, actually."

"Drugs?"

"A lot."

"Helps, when you're getting fucked."

"Yes."

Drew became reflective again, his eyes dreamy. "Oh, he was good. Alexander was a good fucker."

"Yes, when he was there."

"People are always leaving you home alone?"

"Yes. They take me for granted."

"I never will again, I promise." Drew lowered his head into Jimmy's lap and sucked on the cock for a few moments.

Jimmy held his head while Drew enjoyed himself. "Oh, bossman, how strange it is to be here with you. As if time really hasn't passed at all."

Drew let the now erect cock drop from his mouth. "Or the time that has passed is somehow beside the point and we can just pick up where we left off?"

"Can we?"

"Yes. It's been my fantasy. In fact, you have been my fantasy."

"I am, I was, still?"

"Yes, right from the start. I was crazy to think a woman could please me anymore." He gripped the erection, dripping pre-cum. "After this – "

"You flatter me. Alexander was much bigger."

"But this cock, it is so... well, hefty. And it tastes so good. I really don't care that much for an uncut cock."

"I don't mind. An uncut cock feels good when it's in your ass."

Drew smiled, stroking the erection of his dreams. "All the while you were gone, I jacked off to what would happen when we were back together again." He brought the cock to his mouth. "When this was mine again – "

"You mean, even while you were fucking those women at the office?"

"I've never fucked a woman at the office."

"Just me, I know. But then who was she – the one you went off with for the weekend?"

"Fred Gaines' secretary."

"You mean, the guy with the helicopter?"

"Yes."

"That was fun, that trip."

"You were so excited."

"I'm excited now, obviously."

"You're so cute," Drew said, kissing Jimmy. "I can't believe you were really there with me again."

"I can't either. But I have a confession to make."

"I knew it."

"I really wanted to see you again. I wanted to fuck you again."

"So, how was it?"

"Nothing has changed."

"That's the way it should be."

"No, that's the problem. It wouldn't be different if I stayed. It would be the same. Just whenever things got going well, we'd start to fight and it would be all messy and you'd go and I'd leave and go somewhere..."

"No, I made a mistake. I should never have used you like that."

"You should never have let me meet Alexander, you mean."

"Yes, I realize that now."

"I'm sorry if I hurt you when I left."

"We could make it work this time."

"No, you'd never stop reminding me about Alexander."

"I promise I'll never mention him again."

"Ha!"

"No, I mean it."

"I don't know. It's just that you were my boss. I've never known how to say anything to you. You frighten me, you know. You always have. But you also fascinate me. There's nothing you haven't done. Nothing you haven't seen."

"But," Drew smiled, "*I've* never been to Rome..."

ONCE, UPON AN ISLAND

Rudy Roberts

I'll always have fond memories of that island: white sandy beaches, lush banks of lilies, thick hedges, clear hot skies, and tanned bulging bodies. After all, the Island is where I lost my virginity. It seems so long ago now, but it was just a few years back. And still, whenever I'm out there – a stone's throw across the bay from the city – I feel as though it were just yesterday. And it all comes back clearly to me.

I'd started jerking off back when I was thirteen. I knew that some guys got started earlier, so I was quick to make up for lost time. Before long, I was jerking off at least once a day, sometimes more. So, by the time this happened, I was a veteran at masturbation. And more than just slightly curious about boys.

I suppose when all this began was the night Chris was my waiter. It was a Friday night. I was a busboy in a busy downtown restaurant. And my waiter that night (finally!) had been none other than Christopher Barnes. Before then, I'd only ever dreamed of being his busboy. From my first day on the job, in fact, I went out of my way to catch a glimpse of him: his taut body, striking face, shimmering dimples and the unmistakable bulge in his pants. I drove myself crazy. Finally, though – after having to pay another busboy to switch with me – I found myself scheduled to work with Christopher Barnes. And later that same night, I was lying on my back, pulling on my hard-on, thinking of Chris.

And there he was, naked in my imagination, glorious and erect. I'd felt those stirrings before but had dismissed them as some sort of weird, adolescent chemical imbalance. But they'd never been out of control like they were that night. Before I knew what had happened, I'd shot off all over the place. The smell was pungent and heady. I thought that the smell alone would wake the whole house. In a panic, I cleaned myself up and changed the sheets. And I went back to bed, infinitely satisfied, exhilarated and head over heels in lust.

My best friend at the time, Ben, had made it extremely clear

that he, too, was quite taken by Christopher Barnes. We used to share stories about him, in fact. And we would often find ourselves checking him out at the restaurant. Despite all the other good-looking guys we knew either at school or at work, we knew that what we wanted more than anything was to lose our virginity to Chris Barnes. And God only knew how we were to go about doing that.

Even though Ben also had the hots for Chris, we never argued about him. We were both obsessed by him, but that never interfered with our friendship. It was, in fact, one of the focal points of our friendship (something which I only later realized was not sufficient to keep our friendship alive). We would often get together to jerk off while sharing our fantasies. Both of us wanted our first time to be with Chris. We ached to lose our virginity. Even though we knew that most of the other guys in our class were full of shit with their tales of sexual conquest, we still ached to join the ranks of what we perceived back then to be "adulthood". I'm still not sure what the big rush was. But, if only vicariously, we could at least enjoy the forbidden world of our wildly-running, libidinous imaginations. I'll never forget, though, when it actually happened. I'd always thought that Ben would lose his virginity first. But that wasn't the way things turned out.

The summer came, hot and sunny. Ben and I had made so many plans. But then his grandmother died and he had to fly with his family to England for the funeral. And they decided to stay on for about a month afterwards. So, Ben's and my plans had to wait.

The day before he left, he came over to say goodbye. And, with a wicked twinkle in his eyes, he smirked and said, "Don't go losing anything before I get back!"

"And what if I do?" I returned, equally lascivious in both tone and posture.

"Then I want to hear every sordid detail!"

Ben hadn't even been gone a week when it happened. I couldn't wait for him to return so that I could tell him about it because his excitement would have made the entire experience valid and not just an extension of my own fantasy. In fact, until Ben finally returned from his holidays, I was still somewhat in a daze over the ordeal.

The restaurant staff had its annual summer picnic coming up. And this year, the festivities were scheduled to take place on the Island. It was a large and surprisingly secluded island, dense with vegetation, dusted with clear sandy beaches and open to the public. I was always so surprised to look out across the bay, whenever I was on the Island, and see the sparkling skyscrapers against the sky, smeared across the tops with a thick, brown-yellow haze like nicotine. The city seemed so very far away out there. It became my haven. I couldn't think of a better place in the whole world.

Fortunately, the day arrived clear and hot, with a gentle breeze blowing in off the lake. We'd all gathered at the ferry docks at ten o'clock, laden with towels, frisbees, volleyballs and badminton rackets. The managers had brought hampers and hampers of food and drinks. And there was Chris -- wearing a T-shirt and a pair of cut-off denim shorts. His chest was sculpted. His legs were chiselled. And the bulge between his legs seemed even more impressive than usual, if that were at all possible. I could feel the twinges coming on strong all the way across the lake. I kept my focus on the trees across the water and waited for our arrival.

We set up the volleyball and badminton nets and then broke into teams and played hard for a couple of hours before stopping for a bite to eat. At the risk of sounding arrogant, I have to admit that I was a pretty good volleyball player, much to the surprise – and chagrin – of many of my co-workers. But what thrilled me more than anything was Chris' unusual friendliness. Fortunately, we were on the same team; we won three matches effortlessly. And every time I made a point serve, or slammed a return over the net, Chris would come up from behind me and clap his hands onto my shoulders and shake me. He was usually so serious. It was a particular thrill to see his face lit up. He had one of the most beautiful smiles I've ever seen.

And that set the pace for the rest of the day. Chris wanted me to sit with him at lunch, to team up with him for badminton and to join forces with him for the treasure hunt. It was a thoroughly exhausting day, to say the least. And Chris' constant attention didn't do much to relieve my anxiety.

As late afternoon rolled around, several of us decided to go

for a swim. Although the City had made the Island accessible to the public, they hadn't equipped it with change-rooms. So, we took off into the bushes and stripped down into our bathing suits. And there, through the bushes, I could see Chris.

It was as though all of my dreams had come true in that one moment. There I was, the true voyeur, concealed as I watched him take off his clothes. First to go were his shoes and socks. Then he slowly peeled his T-shirt off, revealing a toned and tanned, muscular chest, sprinkled with dark hair, his nipples black against his tantalizing flesh. And then his fingers went to the front of his shorts, deftly working at the button-fly, prying them open. And he pushed them down over sinfully slender hips, stepping gracefully out of them, suddenly wearing nothing but underwear.

I gulped hard, sure that he'd hear and I'd betray my secret vigilance. But he didn't seem to have noticed and commenced pulling his underwear down. At first, he had his back to me, obscuring my view of his cock and balls. His back was broad, freckled and deeply tanned. And his butt was indescribably beautiful: full, pert and round. It also seemed to be tanned as darkly as his body. And that thrilled me even further -- to know that he sunbathed in the nude.

But when he turned around, I let out an audible gasp. What I'd only up until then imagined to be a large endowment actually turned out to be a mammoth, glistening prick. I couldn't stop staring at it: the heavy balls hanging low between his muscled thighs; the thick shaft, dark and brooding; the plump head, shimmering in the afternoon sun, partially obscured by a cloak of foreskin. It was magnificent. My throat was achingly dry. My cock was painfully erect.

And then, just as he was pulling his Speedos up over those hard legs, a twig snapped beneath my foot. I froze. Chris turned his head casually and saw me standing there, staring dumbfounded at his glorious body. I almost broke into tears at having been caught in such a lecherous act. The look on Chris' face was almost angry at first; he seemed to be seething with rage. I was sure he'd beat me up. But then he just laughed and a dimpled smile effectively wiped away any semblance of anger.

But that didn't serve to make my dilemma any less agonizing. I felt as though I had to come up with an excuse as to what I

could have possibly been doing standing there staring at him like that. But there really wasn't any excuse for it. I'd been caught red-handed, staring unabashedly at Christopher Barnes' magnificent nudity. Simple as that.

"Aren't you going in for a swim?" Chris asked, adjusting his crotch openly. The incident didn't seem to have bothered him in the least, I noticed.

"Ah ... um ..." I croaked, not knowing what to say, my throat still dry, my body trembling with nervousness and fear. And I coughed, unable to finish my sentence.

"Well, hurry up," was all he said as he started off back towards the beach, a towel over one shoulder. I watched his butt swing back and forth as he made his way towards the inviting water.

I was cautious, undressing nervously, wary of any clandestine onlookers. All I could think of was how Chris would tell the others and they'd all make fun of me. I half-contemplated grabbing my things and going home on the ferry, but I didn't want to throw a scare into the managers and ruin the day for everyone else. Either way, it seemed, I'd be the source of enormous ridicule. Still, I'd seen him. I'd seen Christopher Barnes naked. And that image was burned into my mind, ammunition for future battles beneath the sheets.

My body as an adolescent was slim yet defined; it still is. I had gently-cut pectorals and the beginnings of a washboard stomach. Although I was still somewhat the gangly teenager, there was definite promise of a well-built body. I was proud of my body, in fact, and carried myself – despite my anguish over that most recent encounter in the bushes – with dignity and self-assurance.

The water was cold at first, sending shivers up my spine, waves of goose-pimples coursing across my arms and chest. But as I became accustomed to the water, wading out deeper into the lake, it felt wonderfully refreshing. I could see Chris swimming up ahead, whooping with laughter as he and several of the other waiters splashed about. I gulped hard and plunged into the clear water. I resurfaced and maintained a distance for some time, watching cautiously to see if Chris had noticed me, wary of the ridicule that was bound to follow. But nothing happened. I trod water, alone, for several minutes before

swimming around. Presently, I was joined by some of the other bussers and we had a game of water frisbee. I had soon forgotten all about having been discovered in the bushes.

The managers had begun to set up the bonfires, preparing for supper. While we were waiting, I went back up into the bushes to retrieve my clothes before it got too dark to find them. As I was pulling my shorts back on, another twig snapped. Once again, I froze, turning cautiously towards the sound, sure that a group of onlookers was watching. But it was just Chris through the bushes, gathering his belongings.

"Hey, Marshall," he said, smiling handsomely, "how's it going?"

"Fine," I replied, zipping my shorts up, reaching for my T-shirt.

"Did you have a good swim?" he asked. "I noticed you playing frisbee out there."

"Ya, it was fun," I replied, pulling the T-shirt over my head. I was still cautious, unsure of what to say for fear of putting my reputation on the line.

"Listen," he said, stepping through the bushes towards me, "I don't want you to feel bad about what happened earlier. You know." And he shrugged, smiling warmly.

I didn't know what to say. So, I said nothing. I just stared into those beautiful, dark eyes of his as he continued to speak.

"It's only natural to be curious as to what other guys look like naked," he reassured me. "I mean, hey, I like to look sometimes, too. Know what I mean?" And he winked at me, a smile curling at the corners of his mouth.

I wasn't entirely sure what he was trying to imply but my heart raced nonetheless. I couldn't believe that Christopher Barnes was confessing a homosexual desire. I just couldn't believe it.

"Well, say something," he said, as though reading my mind. "Don't just let me babble on like this."

"I don't know what to say," I replied. "I ... well, I just saw you there and before I knew it, you were naked. I didn't mean to intrude or anything ..."

"God, no, you didn't intrude. I'm not upset, Marshall. If anything, I'm rather flattered."

"Flattered?!"

"Yeah, it's sure as hell flattering when you're admired by somebody you like."

My heart leapt into my throat then. I was sure he could see me shaking. I wasn't sure, though, if I was shaking with fear or delight. "You like me?!"

Chris chuckled. "That surprises you?!"

"Well, I just thought you liked waiters – you know, guys your own age."

He shrugged. "Age doesn't have anything to do with it. I like people for what they offer and for who they are. And I like you. It's as simple as that."

"Well, Chris, I ... I like you, too."

"Good," he replied, stepping closer and laying a hand upon my shoulder, "because I think we could become very good friends." He squeezed me gently, warmly. I was sure that he was implying something much more intimate than mere friendship, but I didn't want to jump to any wrong and humiliating conclusions.

"You're shaking," he noticed, taking his towel off his shoulder and draping it across my back. "What's the matter?"

"I dunno," I shrugged, my voice dropping.

"Sit down for a minute," he said, dropping to his knees, sitting on his heels. "Let's talk."

I crouched down and sat hesitantly beside him, cross-legged, suddenly aware for the first time of the raging hard-on in my shorts. But I didn't dare touch myself, even nonchalantly, in case I was reading Chris all wrong. Maybe he was just trying to get me excited and betray myself as a "faggot". I was confused.

"Do you have any ... special friends you get together with from time to time?" Chris asked, his voice rich and warm. And subdued.

"What do you mean?"

"Well, I know you hang out with ... what's his name ... Ben. Are you and he ... well, special friends?" And he arched an eyebrow at me and snickered.

"Ben and I have known each other for years," I replied, becoming more and more uncomfortable with this line of questioning. "Is that what you mean?"

"Well, not exactly. I was referring to a special friend you

could ... well, fool around with. You know ..." And he made a masturbatory gesture in the air. "When your hand just isn't enough. Do you catch my drift?"

I gulped hard and loud. This time, he did hear it and he laughed. I just stared wide-eyed at him. There I was, after all those years of fantasizing about Christopher Barnes, sitting next to him in the late afternoon sun talking about jerking off. I couldn't believe it.

"I have a couple of buddies I get together with from time to time for fun and games," he continued. "You into that sorta thing?"

I nodded my head rapidly, suddenly aware of how anxious I must have appeared. But I no longer cared.

"I thought so," he replied. "Especially after the way you were looking at me today."

A voice came over a megaphone announcing that dinner was ready. I suddenly felt panicked, afraid that I was once more losing out on an opportunity.

But Chris assured me that nothing was lost. With a hand on my knee, he said, "Maybe we can come back up here after supper and become a little ... well, better acquainted. What do you say?"

"Sure," I said, my voice quavering, "that'd be great, Chris."

"Good," he replied, sensing my nervousness, rubbing my leg. "Hey, Marshall, everything will be just fine, you know. There's nothing to worry about. Trust me."

Yes, I've since learned to be quite skeptical of anyone who utters the words "Trust me". But back then? Christ, back then I would have believed anything he had to say. I reached over and touched his muscular arm then. He was hot to the touch, hot and hard.

"That's it," he whispered, leaning closer, pressing his lips against my cheek. "Just take it easy and we'll have a great time together. Okay?"

"Ya," I whispered back, "you bet!"

"Well, let's go grab something to eat and then we'll take off together. Alright?" And his fingers slid under the cuff of my shorts, inching up my thigh. Urgently, he mashed his mouth into mine and sent a long, shivering tongue past my lips. I was completely receptive, my body motionless as his tongue battled

inside my mouth. I was suddenly on fire. My cock ached. And I was in ecstasy.

When he pulled away, he licked his lips. And slowly, tantalizingly, he rose to his feet, ruffling my hair. "Come on!" And he dashed out of the bushes, back towards the beach.

I thought that I couldn't just follow him. I had to give him some lead time to avoid curious eyes. There was nothing that the staff liked more than a good scandal. I also had a very conspicuous hard-on that had to die down before I could make my way down for dinner. Fighting the urge to jerk off right then and there, I managed to take several deep breaths and relax. In fact, I was actually quite hungry and that focus seemed to release me – if only for a short time – from the grip of my anxious erection. After several minutes, I gathered my belongings together and stuffed them into my back-pack and headed down the beach to join the others.

At first, I thought I'd be too nervous to eat. But I was wrong. I polished off two burgers and a plate of salad, washing it all down with a Coke. I could see Chris across the way, chatting and laughing with some of the other waiters. And I wondered if any of them were his "special" friends. Smiling to myself, I turned away and went off to mingle with the busboys. But during the whole meal, I thought of nothing but Chris. And I wished I had Ben there to tell my story to. Because I couldn't believe it was actually happening.

Afterwards, when a couple of the waiters and managers brought out their guitars, people got together to chat and sing and laugh and toast marshmallows. Some others went off together for romantic interludes. Still others went off to smoke some joints or drink from their forbidden flasks. I thought I'd lost Chris at first and began to roam around the beach for any sign of him.

"Are you looking for someone?" a voice from behind me asked.

I turned to see Chris running towards me, a large towel slung over one shoulder, his back-pack clenched in the other hand.

"No one in particular," I replied, smirking now, somewhat more relaxed, "but you'll do."

"Oh, thanks a lot!" he laughed, clapping an arm around my

shoulder and steering me up the beach towards the bushes.

"Word has it that we're all heading back in another hour or so," Chris said, his voice suddenly subdued as we approached a thicket, "so we won't have all that much time. Okay?"

"Whatever," I replied, eager just to get on with it, whatever "it" was.

"Good," he said, and gave my shoulder a squeeze. "This is going to be fun."

"I sure as hell hope so!"

We listened carefully for sounds of any other people nearby and were happy to discover that we were very much alone. With one swift movement, Chris took the towel from his shoulder and spread it out full on the ground, dropping his back-pack beside it. And just as quickly, he dropped down onto the towel, sitting cross-legged, looking up at me. Patting a spot beside him, he said, "Have a seat, Marshall."

My nervousness had suddenly returned, but I was much more prepared for it this time. Without a moment's hesitation, I sat beside him. He instantly put one of his hands on my knee again, rubbing with strong fingers. I followed suit and placed a hand delicately on his thigh, feeling the heat and stubbly muscle. Instead of having a dry throat this time, I was, in fact, salivating. This was too good to be true, I thought.

"What do you and Ben do together?" Chris whispered, pulling his T-shirt up and off, his chest glistening in the dim light.

"Oh, you know, just jerk off. We're just friends." I could see the city brightly lit across the way. I suddenly felt very comfortable with this man.

"Have you ever done anything else?" he asked, helping me pull my own shirt up over my head, tossing it aside.

"No," I replied.

"So, this will be your first time, then?!"

We were sitting bare-chested in the moonlight, staring into each other's eyes, hands gently caressing each other.

"Uh-huh," I softly replied.

"Good," he whispered, smiling broadly, reaching for my zipper. "I like being someone's first time."

I sat back and allowed him easier access, resting on my palms. I was hard from the moment he'd come up behind me

on the beach. There was no turning back now. Chris soon had my shorts and underwear off in one swift tug. My cock sprang up against my belly, arched and glowing in the moonlight.

"My God, but you're one hell of a pretty boy," Chris stated, almost hissing with delight as he took in the full glow of my nude body. "So sweet," he added, fingering my aching prick. I sucked in a ragged breath when his hand touched my cock. "Marshall, this is nice. How old did you say you were?"

"Sixteen," I replied, savouring the sensations of this man's experienced fingers.

"Well, if this is any indication, you're going to have a huge cock. Mm!" And he began to stroke the length of my shaft slowly, deliberately.

"You mean, like yours?"

"Ah, so you did see it," he replied. "I wasn't sure. Well, what did you think?"

"You're amazing! I think you're absolutely beautiful! And your cock's fucking fantastic!"

"Well, I'm glad you think so because I think it could use a little attention right about now, too," he said, rubbing my chest, fingering my erect nipples. His touch electrified me. I was like one enormous raw nerve.

Fumbling with the buttons on his denim shorts, I managed to open his fly wide. To my surprise, he hadn't put his underwear back on after swimming and his abundant cock spilled out into my hands, semi-erect but sizzling hot.

"Oh, your touch is so nice!" he breathed. He raised his butt and yanked his shorts all the way off, tossing them carelessly aside, not relinquishing my dick for one moment.

There we were, finally naked, side by side, playing with each other's cock. His cock was huge, thick and long, filling with blood as I manipulated it. I rubbed a finger around the sensitive head, smearing the pre-cum that had started to flow. Then, without thinking, I laid my head against his strong shoulder and rested a palm flat against his expanding chest.

"Oh, man," he breathed, "what a sweet boy!" And he reached down my back for my ass, cupping my buttocks in his large, warm hand. "I don't want to make you do anything you don't want, you understand." (Another one of those statements you never believe any more. But back then ...?)

"You won't," I assured him, kissing one of those sun-blackened nipples.

"I want to suck your cock," he said, slipping a finger into the silken crack of my smooth ass.

"Sure," I said, reaching for his nipple with my extended tongue, "Anything you want."

I was pulling forcefully on his cock now. It was fully erect, a beautiful, thick nine inches.

"Well, for starters, stop jerking me off so hard," he said, pushing my hand away, smirking. "I'm liable to lose it too soon if you keep at it like that. And I don't want to shoot off just yet, thank you very much."

I brought both hands to his body then, feeling that glorious chest of his, filling and emptying, scraping my fingers lightly across his nipples, feeling the ridges of his flat stomach. This seemed to make him squirm deliciously and he leaned back, lying flat out on the towel, using his back-pack as a pillow. I climbed on top of him and clamped my mouth over his. With some surprise at my actions, he devoured my sloppy kiss, drawing my long tongue deep into his mouth. Our erections were trapped agonizingly between our writhing bodies. He was like a powerful stallion and I was riding him.

"You surprise me, Marshall," he said, breaking away, cupping my shoulders. "You're a little sex machine."

I chuckled. Fortunately he couldn't see me blush in the dark.

"Why don't you drag that pretty little pecker of yours up here for a little while," he said, licking his lips lasciviously, "and I'll show you a few things I like to do in my spare time."

I giggled and slowly, seductively, dragged my ass across his stomach, up across his chest. My balls rested against his lips; my cock pointed at the sky. With no prompting, he opened his mouth and my balls plopped inside where his hot tongue lashed around them. He sucked them with such tenderness. I closed my eyes, despite my incredible desire to watch as he sucked. I held onto his shoulders, savouring the sensations of those hot lips and that slippery tongue, careful not to fall over.

"You're a little tease!" he breathed, breaking away, his tongue lashing at the inside of my thighs. "You have done this before!"

"No, I haven't!" I insisted almost too much. "I've never

done this before!"

"Well, I guarantee you that you'll want to do it again," he said, his voice breathy, concealing a laugh.

His tongue was extraordinary, working around my balls, licking my thighs, edging its way closer to the slippery crack of my ass. But it was happening all too fast, incredible sensations notwithstanding. I was growing close to orgasm and, like Chris, I didn't want to lose it all too soon. So, I stood up, pulling that hot, slippery tongue away from my slick asshole.

"What's wrong?" Chris asked, propping himself onto his elbows, wiping his mouth with the back of his hand.

"You're getting me too worked up. I'll shoot." And I squeezed my pecker hard to force the feelings of ejaculation to subside.

"Then perhaps it's time for some lessons," he said, turning onto one side.

"Like what?" I asked, my mouth salivating, my heart pounding, hoping.

"Well, this baby could sure use some attention," he said, fingering his hard-on. "What do you say?"

"Are you sure I could take the whole thing?" I asked, assuming in my virginal ignorance that one had to suck the whole length of cock and not just what fit.

"Who cares?" Chris replied. "I just want to feel your hot, little mouth on this baby. Come on. It's easy. I'll show you."

I crouched back onto my knees at his side then, staring at his cock openly now. I was pulling absently on my own dick as I watched Chris peel the foreskin away to reveal that fat, dark cockhead.

"Lick it!" he breathed.

I love the lascivious sound of dirty talk even yet. I hesitated only briefly before leaning down, inhaling the pungent scent of his aroused pecker. I licked my lips, wetting the way, and grabbed the thick shaft.

"Ya, that's it! Now, lick it!"

I couldn't believe that it was happening. I brought my tongue out flat and lapped at the shaft of his phenomenal cock, upwards inch by inch to the fat head. It was hot and tasted salty. When I reached the head, my tongue instinctively became pointed, digging into the tip, tasting the pre-cum that was

dribbling freely.

"Holy shit!" Chris breathed. "You're a fucking natural!"

I almost laughed, finding those words amusing -- words that, under other circumstances, would have been misconstrued as the highest of insults. But hearing it now was the highest of compliments. And it induced me to continue without delay.

I didn't need much prompting before I had the fat head of that huge cock inside my mouth, actively slurping at it, pummelling it with my tongue, hugging it with my lips. Saliva was running down my chin. The shaft of his cock was slick with spit. I was sucking and slobbering loudly. I was in heaven.

"Oh, ya, Marshall! Suck that cock, man! Suck it!" He rifled his fingers through my hair, gently exerting some pressure to get me to take a bit more. I thought that I could handle some more, so sunk another couple of inches of dick inside my mouth.

"Just relax for a moment. Stop licking it for a moment and get used to the feel of it inside your mouth. Feel it against your throat. Ya, that's it. Take as much as you can without gagging. But go slowly and remember to breathe. Relax your throat muscles; that's it. Just relax them and you'll be able to take it all. No, don't force it. That's it! Oh, man!"

I didn't get the whole thing in my throat that first time. There were still two or three inches to account for. But neither of us cared. I was sucking my first cock. And it was the cock that belonged to the man of my wet dreams.

"Turn around," Chris suddenly blurted out, almost breathless. "No, don't pull off, just bring your cock up here and I'll suck you at the same time."

I wriggled my body around, momentarily neglecting the blow-job I was giving, and brought my dick up to Chris' face. Instantly, he almost inhaled my dick, taking the whole length of it into his mouth. He was a definite expert from the way he slurped and sucked on my cock. His hands pried my ass cheeks apart, rubbing a fingertip against my slippery and twitching asshole. I moaned, sensing that my orgasm was near. The feelings of Chris' mouth on my cock and his fingers playing with my asshole intoxicated me. My lips flew along the length of his dick, sucking with such wanton desperation. I wanted, more than anything else in the world at that moment, to drink

every drop of that man's essence.

Chris suddenly slipped a finger into my asshole. I was tight, gripping his finger. And all he did was gently caress my ass and thighs, encouraging me to relax. When I eased the grip, he stuck the finger in all the way, wriggling it about, sending electric shocks up and down my spine. My balls were churning, aching for release. I knew it wouldn't be long before I'd shoot off.

Oddly enough, it was Chris who shot off first, sending a thick spray of hot cum into my throat. At first, I gagged – a reflex action; I was somewhat taken by surprise. But I relaxed and soon found myself swallowing an ample load of thick, hot cream. It tasted salty and good. I had no idea how good it tasted. If I'd known that, I'd have been eating my own cum. No sooner had Chris shot off and I'd begun swallowing it all, then I lost my own pent-up load. My legs convulsed. His finger poked into me like a miniature dick. My cock spurted a huge load – bigger than I'd ever remembered – deep into Chris' throat. He gulped and gurgled and slurped my tender cock clean. My cock head was so sensitive after I'd shot off that his tongue almost sent me into further spasms. I can remember thinking that I'd actually discovered what it was like for a man to have multiple orgasms. But I realize now that I was wrong.

I followed Chris' lead and sucked his cock clean for several moments after he'd cum. His cock softened but remained an impressive appendage. I didn't want to give it up. But Chris pulled off my still-hard cock, giving it one final sloppy kiss. We panted together on the ground, staring into the starlit sky, soundless, caressing each other's body gently, regaining our breath and our energy.

"Well, I don't know about you," he began, reaching for my still-stiff pecker, "but I had a wonderful time. You have one of the tastiest cocks I've ever had the pleasure of servicing."

"It was great!" I reassured him, sitting up, taking his cock into my hands once more, fondling it warmly. "I love your cock!"

"For a first time," he said, propping himself up and looking into my face with tender affection, "I think you did one hell of a job. That was an amazing blow-job, Marshall."

"Ya!?" I replied, incredulous that I'd been so good my first

time. "Really?!"

"You bet!" he said, kissing me passionately on the mouth.

"That was the most wonderful experience I've ever had!" I added, breaking away, excited, tasting my own cum on his tongue.

"Well, they just get better," Chris said, tugging on my cock. "Man, doesn't this thing ever go soft?"

"Not with you around," I replied. I know it sounded corny, but I didn't care. I'd just had sex for the very first time – with the man of my fantasies. There was nothing better in the whole world right then and there.

Momentarily, a voice sailed through the night air, calling us all back to the beach to prepare to leave. I was suddenly hurled back into reality and felt, for an instant, as though nothing more than a dream had occurred. But then I looked over at Chris as he stuffed his cock and balls back into his shorts, I wante d to reach out and stroke them again. And I knew that what had happened was very real. And very important. Because from that moment on, I knew that my life would be profoundly altered. And I felt, for the first time really, that no matter where I found myself in this world, I'd never be alone.

I find myself on that ferry once again, making my way across to the Island, watching as those trees grow larger upon our approach. And I'm with my new boyfriend. And I find myself always wondering what happened to Chris.

Perhaps my boyfriend and I will get lost in the bushes together. And perhaps I'll tell him all about my first time.

STRANGE BEDFELLOWS

Leo Cardini

When I open the front door to the Jamaica Plain apartment me and Norm share and flick on the living-room lights, there he is in all his butt-naked glory, his huge, Polish sausage of a dick flopping back and forth in front of him with every step he takes as he heads in the direction of our bedroom, the afterflush sounds from the toilet announcing a middle-of-the-night piss.

"Oh, hi Tony," he says, absentmindedly tugging on his dick. "Have a good time at the baths?"

This is back in 1977 when Boston had a Club Baths, and even though I was just nineteen, I managed to get a membership card with a fake I.D. I think it helped, though, that I was wearing a tight white T-shirt, showing off the results of my rigorous daily workout at the Back Bay Health Club, and that I'd stuffed my meaty, Italian-stallion dick into tight-fitting, faded-blue 501's, dangerously worn to white in the crotch.

By "have a good time" he means to ask if I sucked a lot of cock, which is what I guess I like to do more than anything else in the world (except for getting mine sucked off at the same time, of course), as opposed to Norm, who has an insatiable appetite for dick up his ass

"I'll say, I did. Oh, and, this is Shawn," I say, introducing the tall, tight-muscled redhead I'd met at the baths.

Shawn steps in and his mouth falls opens in predictable surprise as he takes one look at Norm. To share in Shawn's pleasure, I try to see Norm through his eyes, making believe it's the first time I've ever seen that broad forehead and handsome, loverboy face bordered by his long brown hair parted in the middle, those expressive eyebrows and dark-brown, puppy-dog eyes, and those luscious lips ripe for kissing. I bask in his wide, good-natured smile before lowering my gaze to his broad shoulders, his nearly hairless, armor-like chest and his trim waist, following the thin line of hair that descends from his navel across his taut, lower abs, leading into the lush, dark-brown forest of pubic hair that bristles out in dramatic contrast to his creamy-white shin.

And then, of course, there's that enormous dick of his.

"This is my roommate Norm," I say as Norm retrieves his briefs from behind the sofa ("Whatever are they doing there?" I wonder) and bends over to slip them on.

"Oh, you don't have to dress for me!" Shawn says, desperately trying to stop him.

Norm looks up at Shawn. The two of them smile in lusty acknowledgment of their interest in each other, and Norm straightens up again, letting his briefs fall to the floor.

I know the thoughtful thing for me to do right now is leave the room, and I know what's going to happen when I do - which is OK with me. I mean, me and Norm share our tricks all the time. Sometimes at the same time, in threesomes and foursomes. Hell, there've even been occasions when we've had as many as...but anyhow, my point is, what are friends for, huh?

"I met Shawn at the baths," I explain, "and since we were leaving around the same time, and he has to take the Jamaicaway home, he offered me a lift. So I invited him in for a beer."

"I'll take one, too, Tony," Norm says and I know that's my cue to give them some time alone.

"Sure. Be right back."

But first I step into the john to take a piss. As I aim my dick at the bowl, slow-stroking my veiny, brown-shafted cock until I get a pale yellow stream of piss noisily splashing into it, I think of what a different person Norm is from the supposedly straight football jock he was when we were in high school.

You see, me and Norm grew up together in Jamaica Plain just several blocks away from where we now rent an apartment. But growing up in this working-class community on the outskirts of Boston where every one knows everyone else's business, all Norm was to me was just another neighborhood kid. That is, until junior high when he began playing football and I began to take an increased interest in my male classmates, especially in Norm as he developed almost overnight into an adolescent Hercules. It was my admiration of his physique more than anything else that inspired me to start going to the Back Bay Health Club at the age of fifteen when I was, frankly, kind of a sissy.

Well, when I saw what went on there in the steam room, the Jacuzzi and the showers, and the kind of guys who got all the action, I really got into improving my body. By the time I graduated from high school a lot of the men at the Back Bay were calling me Angelo because I look like this statue this ancient artist named Michelangelo carved of a boy named David. Except my dick's bigger than his.

But I guess I'm getting off the subject. Anyhow, four or five months ago - that would be last spring - Norm and I ran into each other by the Jamaica Pond and I brought him back to my apartment and got him stoned on this really good grass I had. It was the first time he'd ever been high, and he let me suck him off. Deepthroating all nine plus inches of his big, fat dick, it was like a dream come true, and I could tell from his low-pitched moans he'd never had his dick treated so well before. Well, if I do say so myself, I'm a damn good cocksucker.

The next weekend, he came over and got me stoned, and I let him fuck me. Like he really had to get me high first! Then the day after that I brought him to the Back Bay Health Club and after our workout we ended up in a threesome with an old classmate of ours in one of the shower stalls, where, for the first time in his life, Norm sucked some cock, and then, to my surprise, took it up the ass. Really!

Well, the rest, as they say, is history. Now he's moved into my apartment, and between all the bars, baths and discos in Boston, we've been having the time of our lives.

I shake off the last drops of piss, stuff my dick back into my 501's, giving into the temptation to leave a couple of buttons undone, and then step into the kitchen to pull three beers out of the fridge.

When I finally make it back into the living room, there's Shawn seated on the sofa with his tee shirt off, his jeans down to his ankles and his legs spread wide apart, and there's Norm down on his knees in front of him, noisily sucking on Shawn's dick while he strokes his own. I get a vicarious thrill thinking how pleased Norm must've been to discover what a huge cock Shawn has. I mean, me and Norm each have a little over nine inches, but Shawn's...well there are horses who'd be jealous of him. He's got a reddish cockshaft rugged with thick, bulging

veins, an enormous, mushroom-shaped cockhead with a long, deep groove of a piss slit open in a perpetual pout and drooling a seemingly endless stream of pre-cum, a flaming red bush of pubic hair spilling over onto his flat, pale-pink abdomen, and two large nuts encased in a furrowed, raw-red ballsac covered with long bristly hairs.

If I have any complaints at all about the time we spent together tonight, it would be the way I kept getting hairs in my mouth every time I sucked on his balls. Oh, and the first time he came - we were on the bed in the orgy room, which is where we met - I wasn't prepared for what a screamer he is. As I sucked him into orgasm, he kept going "Ohh! Ohh! Ohh!" each outburst louder than the one before until everyone else on the bed (it can hold a good dozen men) stopped to watch us in the dim light as he thrust his ass up off the mattress, ramming his enormous dick all the way into my mouth and shooting what must've been quarts of cum down my throat, yelling so loud the sound actually echoed off the walls.

But I think I'll let Norm find out for himself what a screamer Shawn is.

I step over to them, hand Shawn a beer, and Norm dismounts him to take one himself. Shawn's enormous dick flops onto his abdomen looking exhausted from Norm's enthusiastic, deepthroat attention.

"Shawn was telling me," Norm says after he takes a swig, "he got stood up at Sporter's, and that's why he decided to check into the baths. Can you imagine standing someone up when..."

With his free hand, Norm gives Shawn's ballsac a downwards tug between his legs, forcing his dick to rise from its resting position into magnificent, showoff display.

"There seems to be a lot of that going around."

"Huh?" I ask.

"The kid I brought home from Chaps?"

"What kid?"

"He's in the bedroom. Well, he was supposed to meet someone at Chaps. Lucky for me his date didn't show up, huh?"

"You've got a trick in the bedroom, and you're out here sucking me off?" Shawn asks with equal parts surprise and

admiration.

"Well, he's asleep right now."

"You guys are too much!"

Then he leans over towards me, unbuttons my Levi's and pulls out my dick, saying, "Though if I had a lover of my own I don't know if I could deal with such...openness."

"Oh, we're not lovers," Norm says uncomfortably, casting me a quick glance.

Why does everyone assume we are, I wonder briefly before I'm distracted by Shawn sucking my half-hard dick into his warm, wet mouth, watching Norm follow suit by deep-throating Shawn.

While Shawn sucks me into my umpteenth erection of the night, all the while skillfully managing my balls out of my 501's to fondle them, all I can think about is the stranger in the bedroom. Call me over-sexed, degenerate, or whatever, but I just can't get him off my mind. I mean, I've had Shawn and I've had Norm, and though I sure wouldn't mind having sex with them again and again, I can never resist the thrill of challenge and discovery of the man I haven't had, and I know if Norm brought him home, he's probably a hunk and a half, with a big dick. Not that Norm necessarily saw his dick (unless he followed him into the men's room - it wouldn't be the first time), but you can pretty well figure out what a guy's got packed inside his pants. And if they're too loose for a tell-tale bulge, well there's always his hands, his feet, the quality of his voice, the shape of his...well, I suppose you know all the signs as well as I do for discovering just what a guy's got hanging down there between his legs.

So I slide my dick out of Shawn's mouth, relishing this final cascade of twitchy cock-pleasure along my shaft, and struggle to stuff myself back into my Levi's with, "You two don't mind if I pay a little visit to the bedroom, do you?"

"Um-urr," Norm says, too greedy for Shawn's dick to dismount it as he vaguely waves okay.

"I can't believe you guys!" Shawn says with clear delight. And then, as I head out of the living room, he pushes Norm all the way down onto his dick, leaning back into the sofa with "Oh, Baby!"

When I step into the bedroom, it's all awash with silvery

moonlight and soft shadows. I see Norm's trick fast asleep in our queen-size bed. (Listen, just because we share a bed doesn't mean we're lovers!) He's lying on his side with his back towards me, his long blond hair spilling onto the pillow. Wide shoulders taper down to a narrow waist, the backside of his well-developed torso back set into graceful motion by the slow in-out of his shallow nightbreath. The bony ridge of his lower spine disappears under the sheet barely inches from his asscrack.

I quietly take off all my clothes. My dick's already hard again, impatiently twitching as it looks forward into this exploration of the promising unknown. Carefully pulling the sheet away so's not to disturb him, I check out the shadowy features of his tight, well-formed butt before making my way into bed. Leaning on my side, I slowly snuggle up next to him, cautiously draping my free arm around him until my fingertips rest lightly against the bulge of his right biceps.

I pause to savor the moment, thrilled with excitement of trespass onto the muscular terrain of this hunky stranger. It's the thrill of stealing cookies from the pantry, of watching your brother jack off when he thinks you're sound asleep in your own bed, of sneaking by the "No Trespassing" sign of an abandoned lot to shoot your load in the broken-window garage with the sagging roof and the old magazines full of naked women scattered on the earthen floor, limp and soggy with cum stains and bad-weather abuse.

Lightly pressing my chest against his back, I gently run my fingers across his chest, excited by its he-manly expansion with every inhalation. The sleek contours of his prominent pecs and the pin-pointy stab of his nipples set my dick all a-throb, pounding against him as if to beg rear-door entry. He stirs briefly, I jackknife my butt backwards to pull my tactless dick away from him, and he settles back into sleepy inactivity.

Ah, his skin is silky smooth, with very little body hair. There's a feathery patch of it in the deep depression between his pecs. I run the tips of my fingers through it and then trace its narrowing descent down his chest, crossing his tight abs, praying he's not the ticklish sort. He proves not to be, so I continue my trek down to his navel, and pause, my middle finger resting inside his compact innie of a belly button. He

takes a sudden, deep inhalation and his back expands against me. I'd relaxed my butt forward again and my dick responds with a mighty throb that knocks against him and I think, shit, this time he's gonna wake up for sure! But once more he settles back into his sleep and I ever so slowly make my way below his navel, crossing the firm, flat terrain of his lower abs until I reach the lush overgrowth of his pubic bush.

Pausing first to fully appreciate my progress, I finally make my way to the promising heap of soft meat that hangs down over his right thigh just above his slightly bent legs. Ah, so much of it, pliable and inviting. Feeling about, I discover he has a thick, rubbery dick and two large balls in a loosehanging ballsac, nearly hairless and smooth as satin. A wave of excitement washes through me. My heart pounds and my dick throbs, knocking against his backside, and I'm sure he gonna wake up now.

I caress his cockshaft, thumb on the topside, second, third and fourth fingers on the underside, gently massaging it. His dick's slow to respond, which couldn't please me more, and my hand bears willing witness the miracle of erection as his cock stiffens and thickens into what promises to be a truly enormous piece of meat.

He finally responds with a sleepy "oh" and lazy thrusting of his hips. My hand forms a fist and he slowly slides his dick in and out. The base of his shaft swells, forcing my fingers apart and his hipthrusts grow stronger as he jabs his way into wakefulness.

His dick exceeds even my expectations, nearly rivaling Shawn's, which by now I'll bet you has made its way up Norm's ass. Now that it's fully hard, with a wide, flat expanse on the underside, it's as smooth and unyielding as a piece of ivory, gracefully upcurving as if to kiss his navel, clearly capable of it.

Suddenly he moans, "Oh, Norm!" and turns over onto his back.

I slide out of his way, doing a not-so-bad imitation of Norm with, "Now, you just lie back and relax."

"Mmm" he says with his eyes still closed, a broad, satisfied smile creeping over his face as he laces his fingers behind the back of his head and sinks into the pillow. He kicks off the

sheet, spreads his legs and gives his body a long, luxuriant stretch that sets every appetizing inch of him into gently rolling motion before settling down again, his body spread out before me like a feast of carnal delights.

There is so much of him to sample! But I know where I want to begin, and I quickly reposition myself on my elbows and belly between his legs. Ah, is there any greater view of a man than this? Between the junction of his two muscular thighs, his heavy-hanging nuts nearly obscure the cleft in his asscheeks. His massive dick rests on his abdomen, listing slightly to the left and occasionally jerking upwards, a broad, sleek monster, beyond which I can see the tantalizing rolling geography of his powerful body.

I stick out my tongue and lick his nuts, jostling them about in his loose ballsac until I maneuver them into my mouth, gently rolling them around, giving them a good, thorough tonguing, marveling at the fact that no matter how big the nuts, if the pouch that's privileged to contain them is loose enough, there's always plenty of room in my mouth to give them the loving attention a man's balls deserve.

"Oh!" from above as I skate my tongue all over his nuts. He stiffens his legs and tenses his butt in an upwards thrust. I release his balls and seize the opportunity to slide my tongue below them; down, down, and down some more, forcing my way into this most inaccessible region of a man's body until the tip of my tongue reaches his butthole.

"Oh!' again, and he pulls his legs up with his forearms under the crook of his knees. His asscheeks spread open, I dart my tongue back and forth across the tight pucker of his hole. Then, encouraged by the repeated clenching and unclenching his rear entrance, I plunge my tongue deep inside with one bold thrust. Well, this gets him moaning out of control, so I give him a whole-hog, deep-driven tongue fuck until after the space of a blissful eternity he slowly lowers his legs. My tongue's forced out of his hole and his big balls fall onto my face. I lick up and beyond his ballsac, his nuts slip back into their natural resting position and my tongue ascends the endless underside of his wide, stiff cockshaft until I reach the tender triangle of pink flesh just below the flare of his cockhead. With every darting lick, his dick gives a buoyant jerk

upwards, falling heavily onto his abdomen again until I surprise him by pushing myself upwards to capture his cockhead between my lips. Ah, it's so fat I feel myself melting inside as I run my tongue up and down his piss slit set deeply within the valley of his fleshy, yielding glans.

Then I slowly go down on his dick. There's so much of it, it's a real challenge to my cocksucking abilities, and I enthusiastically throw myself into the task, impaling myself on his enormous rod until his cockhead presses against my throat. I can hardly believe I actually manage his fat cockhead into it. I tighten my windpipe around it, and then let it slip out, slowly working my lips up and down his cockshaft, appreciating every inch of it, one moment wrapping my lips around the ridge of his dickhead, the next struggling to slide them down over the thick root of his dick, burying my nose in his pubic hairs.

Now, I know you're going to think I'm really twisted, but I pause with his cock in my mouth to inhale the funky aroma of his bush, and somehow the odor brings the image of Norm into my mind. Well, after all, the smell is part Norm, since he was here before me earlier this evening, and I close my eyes to picture myself as Norm in this same position with this same dick filling his mouth. And as I inhale, my mind is momentarily flooded with images of Norm - Norm sucking dick, Norm tugging on nipples with his teeth, Norm desperately begging to be fucked, his enticing ass all a-wriggle.

And then from up above I hear "Ohh! Ohhh! Ohhhh!" and I realize that without even thinking about it, I've been working my way up and down his cock with even-paced, tight-lipped suckstrokes.

Well, I abandon my thoughts of Norm to concentrate on the present, ecstatically working on this huge, hard dick of this hunk who's name I don't even know, repeatedly plunging down on his ever-widening cockshaft, my lips stretched wide apart again and again as I relax my throat to take in the entire length of his dick.

Then I feel him rearrange. When I've just his cockhead in my mouth, teasing his piss slit with the tip of my tongue, I look up at him.

He's raised himself up onto his elbows. I'm stunned by his moonlit, angelic good looks. His wavy blond hair's parted in the

middle, surrounding his face like a halo, his gentle eyes catch the little light in the room, setting them a-gleam, and his delicately carved lips part in a silent "ooh."

And he's staring at me staring at him with my lips wrapped around his dick.

In a flash of stunned realization, his mouth drops and his eyes widen.

"You're not Norm!"

I nod no as best I can.

"Then who are you?"

I really don't want to give up his dick, so I tell him as best I can. It comes out "Oo-nee."

"Huh?"

So I gently lower his dick onto his stomach and say, "Tony. Norm's roommate."

"Oh?"

"Yeah."

I figure my best bet it to act quickly, so I waste no time straddling his chest. My hard cock, so sorrowfully ignored while I've been lavishing all my attention on his dick - whoever he is - quivers in front of his face like a diviner's rod that's detected the moist insides of his mouth.

"You don't mind, do you?" I ask.

I see the cock-hungry look on his face as he stares at my dick, and I know that any resistance he might have had is rapidly draining away. To help matters along, I will my cock into a throb that lifts it upwards, and then, easing my hips forward, I release it so my piss slit descends, kissing him on the lips before rising again into its out-thrust state of erection.

"Uh, no. I guess not," he says as I watch his eyes travel along the underside of my dickshaft.

"You see, Norm's in the living room with the guy I brought home last night. I suppose by now he's getting the living daylights fucked out of him."

"He is, huh?"

"Yeah. So I thought..."

He lifts his head as best he can to wrap his lips around my cockhead, sucking his way down onto the first few inches of my shaft. But he's in an awkward position for sucking cock, so I pull out of him and say, "Rest your head on the pillow again,

okay?"

Which he does. I grab the headboard and I lean over his face, lowering my cockhead back into his mouth. Once it's comfortably lodged inside, I slide in a few more inches. He closes his eyes and moans through the obstruction of my dick. With slow hipthrusts I ease my shaft between his lips, a little more with each thrust until he's managing the whole damn thing with expert ease.

Well, as good as this feels, I can't help thinking how good his dick felt in my mouth, and so I pull my cock out of him and go to turn around with the intent of sixty-nining him.

But he says, "Sit on my face, will ya? The way Norm does. You know what I mean?"

"Oh, baby, I know exactly what you mean!"

Let me tell you, until you've had Norm lower his creamy white butt onto your face, pulling his asscheeks apart so his pink, puckered hole's fully exposed and ripe for the rimming, well you just haven't lived! So, I reposition myself, squatting over his mouth, facing his crotch. He plants his hands on my asscheeks prying them open, and the next thing I know his hyperactive tongue's skating back and forth across the rim of my hole.

"Oh! Oh!" I cry out hoarsely.

And then he takes me by surprise by plunging his powerful tongue deep inside my ass.

"Oh, man!

And as he probes around, sending shivers of pleasure throughout my body, he releases my asscheeks to slow-stroke that over-sized dick of his with one hand while tugging on his balls with the other. Watching him work on his own cock is more than I can bear, so I fall forward, straddling him again, this time in the opposite direction, brushing his hand out of the way and deepthroating his dick.

"Whoa!" he goes, contracting his abs in an upwards thrust. He sucks my nuts into his mouth, tugging on them as he strokes my dick with one hand while brushing his fingers across the rim of my hole with the other.

All this attention to cock and my balls and my ass while I'm working my way up and down his huge, stiff dick washes over me, drowning me in a whirlpool of pleasure that sucks me

further and further in with every deepthroat plunge I take on his swollen cock.

"Mmm-Mmm-mm!" he purrs through a mouthful of nuts, the vibration of it spreading warm and honey-sweet between my legs.

It isn't long before I feel the cum churning in my balls, and I can tell this is going to be one of those orgasms that takes possession of the whole of me, flinging me into an ecstasy beyond time and space. While he milks my dick with a firm, expert grip, I cocksuck him like there's not tomorrow, his hard-on hot and throbbing with the advent of orgasm. Soon we're both on the verge, ready to come, willing prisoners of our own passion...

Then "Awww! Awww! Awww!" rudely makes its noisy way into the bedroom.

Shawn! The noisy fucker, giving loud utterance to his own approaching ejaculation.

Norm's trick suddenly stops cockstroking me. His fingers retreat from my butthole and he slips my balls out of his mouth.

"What the...?" he says.

I reluctantly give up his cock to tell him, "That's just the guy I brought home with me."

"It is, huh?" he asks suspiciously.

I wonder why it bothers him so, but before I can ask, he pushes me away, jumps off the bed, and runs out the door, butt naked with his huge hard-on bouncing up and down in front of him like it had a life of its own. I follow, gripping my own aching erection because I've learned how painful it can be when I run around with a stiff dick, but that's another story.

There, in the living room, I skid to a halt behind the sofa next to him. The bed's been opened up out of it and there's Norm on his back, stroking his enormous dick. Shawn's pushed Norm's knees up against his shoulders, sweating and straining as he butt-fucks my roommate with a thunderous roar.

"Shawn?" Norm's trick cries out in absolute disbelief.

"Ian!" Shawn manages to interject into his climactic wail. But then his orgasm overtakes him and he lets out the loudest "Awww!" yet. Every muscle of his tall, lean body tenses as he plunges his cock deep into Norm's butt with all his might,

clearly shooting a mega-load of cum up Norm's ass.

The gripping pleasure of discharge contorts his face as he repeatedly thrusts his huge cock up Norm's ass, never for a second ceasing to stare bug-eyed at my almost partner in orgasm.

And as he shoots his load up Norm's ass, Norm's trick grabs his own cock, exchanging stare for stare, and with a few swift strokes reaches his own orgasm.

"Ohhh, shit!!" he screams, and out it comes, spurt after spurt with rocket-like force, arching over the back of the sofa all over Norm and Shawn. Okay, so the old sofa's got a real low back for a sofa, but still, cum shots like that belong in Guinness!

"Awww!"

"Ooooh!"

"Awww"

"Ohhhh!"

And as the two of them noisily buttfuck and cockstroke away, draining their nuts, I step over to the side of the bed, stroking my own urgent hard-on. Norm looks up at me, furiously fisting his dick. Our eyes lock, the thrill of Norm's cum-crazed attention gives a boost to my rapidly approaching orgasm, and we shoot our loads, adding our own abundant contributions to the sticky mess of white fuck juice that's already landed on the hard-flesh terrain of Norm and Shawn's magnificent bodies.

Well, we play out our orgasms to the very end until me, Norm and Shawn have nothing left of our cumloads but a few final stubborn drops without enough force behind them to dribble off our piss slits.

Once we come to rest, Ian is the first to speak.

"I waited for you," he says to Shawn, who's just now dragging his meaty dick out of Norm, "and then when you didn't show up, I was on my way out of Chaps when..."

"Chaps!" Shawn exclaims. His dick plops out of Norm, as if to punctuate his surprise. "We were supposed to meet at Sporter's!"

"Yeah?"

"Yeah. And when you didn't turn up, I went off to the Club Baths, where I met..."

He finishes with a nod in my direction.

By now they've gravitated towards each other on the opposite side of the sofa. God, do they look beautiful standing there face to face, gazing into each other's eyes, their huge softening dicks curving downwards in front of them.

"Oh, Baby," Ian says taking him in his arms. "I was so disappointed."

"Me, too. I mean, when we met two nights ago, I thought..."

But before he finishes, the two of them embrace in a passionate kiss.

Norm looks at me and I look at Norm. I feel kinda mushy inside, just like I do at the end of a real sentimental movie, and Norm, who's a real softie at heart, looks like he feels the same.

Looking at the two of them, it's enough to make you want to fall in love.

"Gee, guys," Shawn says to us when their lips finally part, "um..."

"Yeah," Ian goes to help out, "you see..."

"Like it isn't obvious," I say, sitting down next to Norm, "that the two of you want to be alone."

"Yeah," Norm says, sitting up against the back of the sofa, cum rivering down his chest into his crotch. "In fact, you can have the bedroom, if you want. That'd be okay, wouldn't it, Tony?"

"Sure."

"Really?" Shawn says, brightening up, "Well, thanks!"

"Yeah, thanks a million!" Ian chimes in, leading Shawn into the bedroom. "You guys are the absolute greatest!"

"Well!" I say once they close the door behind them and me and Norm are all alone.

"Yeah. Well." He says back.

I dip a finger in the pool of cum caught in the hairs between his pecs, and then lick it off with my tongue.

"Umm. Tastes good," I say, and then lean over to lap some more off his chest.

Norm smiles a broad, satisfied smile and leans back, resting his head in his hands behind his back, basking in my attention as I work my way down his chest. Ah, all that salty, sticky cum, and all that warm flesh, so smooth, taut and responsive

to my every tongue-stroke.

But then I can feel it on his flesh - I'm barely inches away from his navel now - that his thoughts are somewhere else.

I drip my tongue into his navel, scooping out the pool of cum there, and then I feel Norm's body move as he places his hands under my arms, pulling me up on top of him.

"Isn't love great, Tony?"

This takes me by surprise, striking an unsettling chord inside me.

But before I know what to say, he pulls me tightly into his embrace, slipping his tongue between my lips. I fuse my body against his, I feel an odd swelling up in my chest of something nice, and I begin to realize why so many people think we're lovers.

A WILLING LEARNER

Peter Gilbert

He finished writing, waved the photograph in the air for a few minutes and stuck it carefully on to the page. Then he closed the huge loose leaf folder and put it way in the drawer and leaned back in his chair. Another of his students had passed an examination. Grade Three too. Quite an achievement after only six months training but then he'd known young Simon had potential when he had first met him over a year previously. It would be nice to get him through Grade Four as soon as possible and to aim for Grade Five on his seventeenth birthday but it didn't do to rush things. Grade Six on schedule looked a distinct possibility for Simon. The boy was certainly one of the best students he had ever had.

There had been poor students, not many but a few. One had refused point blank to take Grade Three. Several had stopped coming to lessons. There had even been two in whom he lost all interest and terminated their lessons.

But Simon was a willing learner. A nice looking lad too. He took the folder out of the drawer again, opened the page and looked down at Simon's smiling face. A cheeky boy.... a very cheeky boy. Most of his students were. He turned the pages. Tony. He certainly had a lot of cheek. Ricardo too. A thought occurred to him. Now that Ricardo had passed Grade Six, it was time he found an employer. The boy was due that evening, coming straight from the supermarket. It would be nice if he could find someone and introduce him then. He picked up the telephone and dialled a number.

"John?" he said. "I've got a Grade Six you might be interested in. Name of Ricardo. Yes, eighteen.... Yes, he's quite a hunk. He passed all the tests first time with very good grades indeed. Shall I fax the details? He's due here at seven if you'd care to come round. Good. See you then. Bye."

He took the page out of the folder, put it through the machine and smoothed it flat again. Then, taking another, much thicker folder from the drawer, he inserted it and locked both folders away. He looked at his watch. It was time for his

afternoon stroll. There were potential students out there. He'd found two only a week ago. Two kids struggling to get the carburetor back on a bike that had seen better days. They had been so grateful to him for his help. All his young men were. And, heaven knows, he thought, he had good reason to be thankful to them.

Another thought struck him. It might be a good idea to tell Ricardo's people about John. Not all about John of course. Just enough. He was actually in the street where Ricardo lived when he had second thoughts. It would be silly to rush things. John might not take to Ricardo though he guessed he would. Ricardo would certainly take to John. Holidays in John's villa; presents galore; weekend trips in John's BMW; Ricardo would be a lucky lad indeed. He knew he would miss the boy terribly. Possibly Ricardo would miss him too.

A policeman tipped his hat and smiled. He smiled back. Like everyone in the town, the police held him in the highest regard for his charitable work. Only last week he had presented a boys' home with a table football game. There were one or two boys there with undoubted potential for the future....

He stopped for a moment at a shop window and was looking at video recorders.

"Hi! Going into the video business? Could be fun." He looked down. It was young Tony, one of his most promising students.

"I don't know," he answered. "Why didn't you come round last week? I was waiting for you."

"You said I wasn't old enough for Grade Three."

"I didn't say that at all. I said you were not ready for Grade Three yet. You need regular lessons and practice. You can't just turn up and take a test. Grade Three needs quite a lot of practice. Can you make next Wednesday?"

"After school? About half past four?"

"Yes. That would be ideal. Make sure you come. Check with your mother first, won't you?"

Tony grinned. "She'll be glad," he said. "She can get an hour's overtime in if I come straight to you. See you on Wednesday. Bye!"

Tony jumped on his bicycle and rode off. He watched the boy closely as he weaved through the traffic and turned into a

side street. What did boys like Tony actually tell their parents? Probably just that they had been looking at biking magazines and helped with the restoration work. For that matter what would Ricardo tell his mother in a few weeks time? "I've been invited to spend a weekend at a villa in Spain. My air fare is being paid. His name is John...."

She would have misgivings at first but then Ricardo would explain that John was a friend of Mr. Jordan's and that would put things right. It probably would be an idea to see her as soon as possible after John and Ricardo had met.

"Hi, Mr. Jordan. Out for your afternoon walk?" It was Mrs. Bradshaw. She was dressed, as usual, in the shortest of dresses and long leather boots. He thought her a dreadful woman.

"My dear Mrs Bradshaw," he said, shaking her hand warmly. "It's good to see you! Yes, I thought I'd get a bit of fresh air. I've been stuck at home all the morning working."

"Don't blame you! You work too hard. What with your business and restoring old motor bikes. Not to mention all you do for charity. My Alan told me. I'm sorry he hasn't been to see you but what with the sailing and all that... I said ever so many times, 'Why don't you go and see Mr. Jordan?' I said. 'He's done a lot for you' I said, but you know what they're like at that age. If it wasn't for you he wouldn't have met Doctor Rutherford in the first place, but now it's sailing, sailing, sailing. Every weekend without fail...."

"I'm just glad that they get on so well," he said, interrupting her. "It was such a nice coincidence that they met and I had no idea that Alan was interested in sailing then."

"He wasn't. He didn't know a sailing boat from an ocean liner. But Doctor Rutherford is such a nice man. He's taught Alan right from scratch and now they win cups. Alan's got some in his own right. Of course it's good old mum what has to clean them!"

He laughed. "I think it's you whom Alan should thank, Mrs. Bradshaw. "You brought him up so well that it was natural that Doctor Rutherford should take a shine to the boy. It's his birthday soon surely?"

"Twenty eighth of May. He'll be twenty-five. Fancy you remembering! Oh! There's my bus. I'll tell Alan I met you." She clattered off.

Alan Bradshaw. Twenty five on the twenty eighth of May! Seven years previously the twenty eighth of May had been a Saturday. Alan had taken his Grade Six right on schedule. Possibly, he thought with a smile, it had been only a few minutes inside the actual day. They hadn't gone to bed much before eleven o'clock. The Paragon Hotel. The hotel and the resort had been Alan's choice. He always let them choose.

He crossed the road and went into the park. A bench was free. He sat down. The Paragon Hotel and the weekend of the twenty eighth of May. He remembered it clearly. "A room for my nephew and myself. A double would do."

"... You going to do it to me? It won't hurt, will it?" Of course it hadn't hurt! Alan had enjoyed it. They all did. That was the whole point of all those lessons. Alan undressing and pointing downwards with a grin. The same boy who had made such a fuss over his Grade Three.

Grades One and Two were easy enough. A question of presentation really. A pose to show a ripening denim clad butt. The big Harley Davidson was a good vehicle for that. Then another to show a tempting bulge in the front of a pair of swim shorts. It was usually pretty easy to persuade a lad who had been working hard on some dirty, greasy, component to get on the back of one of the bikes for a run down to the lake.

Grade three was much more difficult to achieve. "What? All my clothes?"

"You mean *everything*?"

"Oh, shit man. That's not my scene."

But most of them complied in the end. It was odd, he thought, that they would strip off for the Grade Three lessons but the moment a camera was produced it was a different story. And Grade Three required hard work - on the part of the boys and himself. Every boy was different and had to be posed differently to bring out all his good points at once. Alan had been a good example. Grade One had been a huge success. Alan stretched over the Harley Davidson in jeans carefully torn in the right places. Grade Two had been at the lake. It had taken two magazines and half an hour before it began to take notice sufficiently to stretch the material.

Then Grade Three. He hadn't taken a lot of persuading but

to discover a pose that set off all that he had to the best advantage had been difficult. In the end it had been on an old colonial kitchen chair. Alan, with one foot on the chair and the other on the ground, grinning cheekily at the camera while carefully placed spotlights picked out the smoothness of his butt, the glossy silkiness of his pubes and massive cock. Small wonder that Nicky Rutherford had gone overboard when he saw the prints. So, no doubt, had the readers of 'Teens and Tools.'. A video camera might be a good idea but to operate a video camera when his hands were already pretty busy would be almost impossible. A video record of Alan's Grade Four performance would be quite something. Far better than written notes.

Grade Four was an uphill struggle. Some students thought Grade Three was the end. Some even left when they realised that it wasn't. But Grade Three could be improved upon. "Let's try another pose." He'd have,.sometimes, to touch it; to get it in the right position or to oil it to make it shine. It was then that they got the message. He remembered Alan's embarrassed grin as it began to rise. "Perhaps we ought to stop there," he had said, and, with a suitable apology, his mentor and examiner had stopped – until the next lesson. It had taken three month's patience and persuasion before Alan was ready.

He had done well too. Much more than the minimum three millilitres. Not bad for a seventeen year old. He did much better in the test than he had in the lessons but he'd been warned to leave it alone for as long as possible. It had been good stuff; not too thick and milky white. His timing had been good too. It would be worth checking up when he got home but as far as he could recall, it had been just over ten minutes from the time Alan lay on the bed with a nervous smile on his face to the time when, writhing and smelling so delightful, he had gasped out, "It's nearly time!" and then "I'm coming!" He'd only just had time to clap the measuring tube over the end of it and stop the timer.

Grade Five. A video camera could be set up for that. It was at Grade Five that all the previous training came together. It took a long time to train a boy to use the muscles in his butt properly so that the instructor didn't need to move his head. Alan, of course, like all the others was already being prepared

for his Grade Six when he took the Grade Five test and a lot of those violent contractions were a spin off from their initial unwillingness to let anything, even a thin wax taper, in there.

Alan had performed exceptionally well for his Grade Five. He'd always had a nice muscular butt and he used it to good effect, thrusting with all his might and gasping as a finger tickled the spot which, a little later on that same afternoon would be the object of a lesson. Alan was a nice tasting boy too. He still laughed about the time when Nicky Rutherford had described Alan to his mother as "a very sweet boy!"

A video tape of Grade Six was out of the question. Grade Six was private. In Alan's case it had taken almost a year of training after his Grade Four but it was well worth while. The first lesson. Alan on the bed holding his legs in the air as just the spout of the oil bottle, itself well lubricated, tickled him and then, when his cock had risen to show its appreciation, insinuating itself past the first guardian ring. Then the wax taper. Just about three centimetres at first, doubling in successive lessons until, at about ten centimetres (and given a degree of luck) it touched the right spot and a composed teenager became a squirming, gasping creature squirting semen further than he had ever managed before.

After that, of course, there was no holding them back and no need to remind them about appointments. They pleaded for permission to come - and come they certainly did! They came over themselves, over their instructor, over the bed and even on the walls as week by week, vibrators of increasing size buzzed deep inside them.

Alan had been particularly responsive. It had been difficult to get him to take the first one. He didn't like the idea and had a notion that it might be difficult to remove it.

"Let me look at it. Is it clean?"

"Of course it is. It's absolutely sterile."

"It looks big. Will it hurt?"

"Of course not. Lift your legs a bit. That's right. Bit of oil going in now....."

"It feels cold."

"Is that better?"

"Yes. Tell me when you're going to put that thing in... Ow! Ah! Oh!.... Ummm."

"Nice?"

But Alan, like all the others, said nothing. He lay on his back, as all the others had done, with his legs in the air and a smile on his face and the only sounds in the room were his deep breathing and the muffled buzzing of the tiny motor.

There followed week after week of careful training. Various positions; Alan on all fours; Alan lying on his front with his legs apart - and the boy who had been afraid it might not be easy to remove a vibrator was soon pleading otherwise.

"Don't take it out yet. It feels good." He said exactly the same thing again in the Paragon Hotel at about midnight on the twenty eighth of May and again in the early hours of the next morning!

Alan had been good. Not, perhaps as good as Trevor who had been exceptional. Trevor now had a very good job in television and lived with his employer. He was, apparently, satisfactory at work but excellent in bed which was all that was really required of him. He made a mental note to look up Trevor's employer's name. He would know about video cameras.

And, most recently, Ricardo. What a boy he was! What a handful! That had been apparent at Grade Three. When he had it in his hand at Grade Four and in his mouth at Grade Five it had been difficult to believe that Ricardo was still in High School.

Other boys were always a bit nervous about their Grade Six examination. "Couldn't we do it another time?" "I feel a bit tired." "I've got a headache." "Will it hurt?" Ricardo had no misgivings. Ricardo had looked forward to it, counting the days to the weekend. If only he had a recording of Ricardo's training.

He would always remember Ricardo - especially his Grade Six examination. Ricardo undressing to expose the massive tool swaying between his legs. Ricardo lying on the bed, wincing as the cold oil dribbled into him but laughing nonetheless. Ricardo groaning, in fulfilment rather than in pain and then, when it was over, that rather slobbery wet kiss on his forehead. "Thank you for that," Ricardo said. "Thank you for everything."

He would miss Ricardo badly but the old had to make way for the new. A library of video recordings would be a good idea....

"Excuse me, Mr. Jordan."

He jolted out of his daydream. A boy stood in front of the bench. A dark-haired boy in a torn leather jacket.

"Yes."

"I'm Ken Blake's buddy. I've just bought a 1954 British Matchless 500 c.c. It needs a lot of work. I wondered if you might have time....."

"Well built," he mused aloud gazing at the young man's midriff.

"Sure is. It weighs a hell of a lot."

"How old are you?"

"Sixteen but I can handle it."

"I'm sure you can. Bring it round tonight. I've got a guy and another lad coming round at seven to discuss business. Are you free after that?

"Sure."

"How is Ken. I haven't seen him for a long time."

"He's okay. He's in the army now. Er... He told me you're keen on photography. I wouldn't mind having a go at that if you'll help me with the bike and you think I am suitable."

"Very suitable. Very suitable indeed. What's your name?"

"Tim. Tim Gorsley."

"Come round this evening, Tim. We can start stripping it down eh?"

Tim grinned. "Should be fun!" he said. "See you then."

He sauntered away. Mr. Jordan smiled. This was a boy who could certainly be exempted from Grades One and Two...

He looked at his watch. There was just time to buy a video camera.

A GOOD SPANKING

Peter Gilbert

"He wants his ass smacked," said Herb.

The boy in question had not expressed the wish but, to Herb, any boy is desirous and deserving of this treatment and my good friend is always ready to oblige.

The boy crouched at the edge of the lake feeding the ducks, despite a notice asking people not to do so. His shorts had ridden up, exposing an enticing quantity of white thigh. Apart from the two of us, he was the only other person in sight, hence he was the object of our sole attention.

"That's what he needs," said Herb, crossing his legs, "a good smacking. I'd take his shorts down and put him over my knee. I'd make him wriggle I can tell you."

Now there are a lot of things that can be done with a young man's butt. We both agree that it's an attractive feature but I don't share Herb's enthusiasm for corporal punishment. I said that I would have something else in mind: something more penetrating.

We were sitting on a bench by the lake. It had been a very successful weekend. In fact we very rarely have a total failure. Every month, we spend a weekend away. The hunting ground is chosen with great care. It has to have a lot of open space, preferably with a lake or pool and, more important, there must be a prep school or a military academy nearby. The more exclusive the school, the better. Scattered all over the States there are ivy - clad institutions which house up to a thousand boys and young men in what the staff hope is monastic celibacy. Small wonder that the boys shed their inhibitions with their clothes. The moment that expensive grey suit is removed - or the numerous polished brass buttons are undone, the hairy - legged scion of a rich family becomes a sex hungry animal. You can smell their excitement. A boy from an ordinary school will object, turn shy, have second thoughts and sometimes even go home.

That weekend had been as successful as most. Herb's secret

weapon had worked wonders again. It is not, as you might suppose, a cane or a paddle but a four foot long detailed model of the U.S.S. 'Wisconsin'. Herb served on the 'Wisconsin' and built the model himself and it is a superb piece of work.

It even has little missile launchers which send tiny fireworks fizzing into the air. We merely wait for an admiring crowd of boys to gather; Herb arranges for the 'steering to go wrong' and sends it into a mudbank or clump of reeds nearest the best looking boys. After that it's plain sailing. Thank them for their help, let them have a go at steering it and arrange to meet a carefully selected few in the afternoon. That sometimes needs a call to the school but you'd be surprised how adept boys can be at getting out of school and inventing cover stories.

That Saturday we had found four absolute beauties. Simon Rawlins, Michael Levinsky, Mark Thorogood and Crispin Read. Simon was a tall slim, fair haired eighteen year old heading for the Ivy League. Mark was seventeen. He, too, was fair haired. Michael was equally slim but very dark. He was sixteen and Crispin was a bubble butted, sixteen year old with a mop of dark curly hair.

With boys as with horses, it is a disaster to rush your fences. The Saturday afternoon is spent sailing the boat after which we take them back to the hotel. Then come Herb's reminiscences of life in the United States Navy. It was Winston Churchill, wasn't it, who said that life in the British Navy was all rum and bum? According to Herb, the lack of rum in the U S Navy is more than compensated for by a surfeit of available ass. It might be ethically wrong, as he always points out, but it's a hell of a lot of fun.

And, slowly, they get interested. You can see the front of those well - pressed pants swelling. One or two guys back at school do that sort of thing. Never any of our guests. Ha!

"Why not?" "What the hell?" "If you haven't tried something, you're in no position to condemn it." "A good looking guy like you. Why, I guess half the school has the hots for you if you did but know it...."

It works! They begin to open up. It always starts with an account of some teacher, instructor or sports coach. There seems to be at least one in every establishment. The guy who checks them over in the showers; the strange ritual

punishments; the dorm master who likes to say 'Goodnight'.... Well, yes, there are some boys who have gotten involved. By this time their peachy cheeks have gone a nice shade of pink. Time for me or Herb to point out that it's natural enough and that some young men in big cities earn a hell of a lot of money that way. Why do something for free in a place where everybody will know about it when you can do it for bucks in a hotel?

We give them a meal and make a half hearted suggestion about meeting them the following day (Sunday) and send them back to school to contemplate the possibility of a cash increase in their allowances.

"I wouldn't mind coming here again," said Herb.

"I thought we'd agreed on New Jersey," I said. It's always slightly dangerous to use the same place twice. You never know with boys. Although they have to break the rules to come out to meet us, and to tell all would involve admitting that, I always feel better when we are out of the place.

"That Michael!" said Herb, in the manner of a man talking about a good meal. "That boy's got the most smackable butt I've experienced in years. Like a jelly on springs it was."

"You didn't do so badly with Crispin either," I lied. "You were slapping him so hard I thought someone would come to see what was going on." In fact he doesn't hurt them at all. He just plays with them but he likes to be told he does.

He was still so full of his own success that he didn't comment upon my undue haste with Simon. The poor lad had squeaked like a stuck pig when I went into him.

"He came you know," he said proudly. "Came quite nicely too. Took me by surprise. I had him wriggling just nicely and his butt was turning a nice rosy shade. Then he went rigid on me and - splash - all over me and the carpet. I should have known when I saw all that hair. If we were to come again I thought you could have Crispin and I'd have young Mark."

I laughed. "I knew you were working up to that," I said. "Jealousy doesn't become you."

As so often, we'd almost given up hope when they arrived at the hotel. They're all the same. They set out, have second thoughts, set out again and get more and more nervous. These four arrived in their best school suits with beautifully knotted

school ties. They might have been arriving for a church service. We took them up to our suite. Herb got out the cards and the drinks and the usual game of strip poker began. Now one of the odd things (and advantages) of going for these lads is that they have no inhibitions whatever about undressing. Try asking a boy from a normal high school to take his clothes off in front of you and he'll go the color of a Montana sunset. Simon was the first to lose the last item of clothing. Herb was the next. Soon all six of us were naked and, more important (to me), both Simon and Mark were pleasantly aroused. Their cocks formed fleshy loops which were already twitching to a fully upright state. Both Crispin and Michael had nice cocks but their flaccid state ruled them out as far as I was concerned. I like a lad to show some enthusiasm. Herb, on the other hand, seems to have no interest in cocks whatsoever. Weird, I know, but true. You could show Herb a lad with the nicest cock in the world and he'd ask the boy to turn round. Well, I like a nicely rounded ass as well. especially when it's been tuned up by the sort of daily exercise roputine the private schools go in for but it has to be combined with something I can get my lips over.

To Herb, a few drops of the most delicious (and most expensive) drink in the world spattered onto the bed or the floor is merely a sign that his manipulations have worked. Sad really.

One look at his long, down-covered legs, his delightful little butt and that half lip cock made me decide I saimply had to screw Simon. He was the tallest, and long legs are an instant turn on for me. Mark, on the other hand, had what I would describe as a little boy's butt. It jutted out from him, creamy white and as smooth as a plum. You could tell, somehow, that there wasn't so much as a whisker guarding his entrance. On the other hand he had a really delicious looking cock with a gleaming purple head. It was easily seven inches - possibly more - and fleshy. So, we negotiated terms. I put Simon across my knee to oil him properly. That in itself was enough to silence the rhythmic slaps of Herb's hand which had already started work on Michael's butt. I didn't look up. Who would when he's concentrating on an apparently virgin asshole? Then Herb seemed to lose interest and the smacking started again. Well, as it happened, Simon was extremely tense and I had to

get Mark to hold his cheeks open for me. In the end (if you'll pardon an unintentional pun) I got enough oil into him and we put him face downwards on the bed to let it soak in. That gave me time to work on Mark. His pubes were like silk and he had the sort of balls that only a seventeen year old can have. Loose hanging and huge. So I sat in the chair and he stood in front of me with his back to Herb. It was in my mouth when I was suddenly aware of the silence.

Michael's undeserved punishment had halted. Well, I didn't think much of it at the time. Again, who would? I just carried on and managed with some difficulty to get a mouthful of scrotum. I was running my tongue over the surface and Mark tensed up as they do. Well I ran my hands up and down his backside to ease him up a bit and then let his balls plop out of my mouth. It was then that I got my first look at Herb. It was like one of those 'freeze frame' pictures.

There was Michael spreadeagled over his lap and Herb's hand raised half way between his shoulder and Michael's butt. He was staring so hard at Mark's behind that I don't think he was aware of the fact that I was looking at him at first. I was tempted to say "Get on with your work!" but there was a greater temptation in store; a seventeen year old cock already beginning to show a tear of gratitude for my labours. I pulled Mark towards me and took him in. With my face buried in a mass of soft pubic hair I couldn't see Herb but no sound came from his side of the room and I knew that he was watching Mark's ass like a weasel watches a rabbit.

Like them all, Mark warned me when he was about to shoot. His ass tensed up and he gasped. Herb gasped at the same time. I just sat there savoring it as it flowed over my tongue. There is nothing quite like the juice of a boy of that age and nothing to compare with the grace of their coming. None of the violent shoving against the back of your throat and the spurting of a more experienced boy. Just that delightful contraction of his ass muscles and a jetting flow of sweet semen. And I love "Watch out! I'm going to come!" and "It's coming. It's coming!" What do they think I have been waiting for?

By the time I had swallowed the lot, Herb had recommenced. Smack! "What a lovely butt!" Smack! "A real peach of a butt." Smack! "A nice tight little butt." Smack! "Good enough

to eat." Smack! "Nice and tender," and I had the distinct feeling that although the hand was unerringly aimed at alternate cheeks of Michael's already reddened behind, the observations were directed at Mark.

Now, another of Herb's peculiarities is that he likes the second course on his menu to be out of sight but within hearing. For this reason, Crispin had been sent into the bathroom to await his turn. There is no doubt in my mind that Mark would have liked to stay to watch the entire Simon performance but Herb had other ideas.

"There!" he said. "You're done." Although he could easily have called, he asked Mark to fetch Crispin. Michael clambered off Herb's lap with his dripping cock still standing proud. As Mark passed Herb he received a friendly little tap on his behind. "Make sure he's ready for me," said Herb. "You may as well take a shower or something. I don't expect Peter will want you again."

"He's welcome to stay," I said. It was only much later that I realised what he had in mind. Mark was going to be number three on his list. The greed of some people is unbelievable!

Needless to say, Mark emerged from the bathroom immediately, propelling a rather nervous Crispin towards his chastiser. Herb got Crispin into position and Mark helped me with Simon.

He, of course, had gone off the boil and was in that limp - pricked, anxious 'I must be getting back to school' stage but a little gentle tickling in the well lubricated region of his asshole worked wonders. By the time Mark had returned and we had turned him over, his cock was as hard as ivory and he had a slightly nervous grin on his face. I didn't actually look over to the other side of the room but I could hear Herb crooning with delight as he stroked Crispin's ass.

Every boy fucks differently. I've known sixteen year olds who take a tool as easily as a tunnel takes a train. I've known nineteen year olds who are well - nigh impenetrable. At first I thought Simon was going to be one of the latter. The moment my cock head touched the bulls eye he screwed up his face. Mark kept telling him that it would be alright and that I wouldn't hurt him but I'm afraid I did. His yells drowned the sound of Herb and Crispin. I stopped and waited. I remember

Mark asking if he was allright.

He was of course.

A few minutes later I felt him slacken and gave him the rest. He took it without demur. Soon, Mark was able to let go of his legs and I had them round my neck, feeling deliciously cool and sweaty. I took him slowly, letting him get used to the feeling. Towards the end he was lifting himself off the bed and grunting with every stroke. I was aware of Mark, sitting on the edge of Herb's bed and watching intently.

Herb was administering gentle slaps to Crispin's butt. It was as if my performance was receiving limp wristed and half hearted applause. Both Crispin and Simon were grunting almost in unison and each of Herb's remarks was answered in a gasping dialogue.

"I love a butt like yours," he said. "Ah!" said Crispin. "Ah! Ugh! Oh!" said Simon.

"A butt well into its teens!" "Ah!" Crispin gasped. "Ah! Ah! Ah!" Simon chorused.

"Lovely and soft. I'm gonna get my tongue right into you!" "Ah!" "Oh! Oh! Oh!"

I was only dimly aware of Crispin saying something and of a long drawn out sighing sound. I was too busy to pay much attention. Simon was writhing around madly. His legs kept falling off my neck and Mark had to hold him again. My cock felt as if it were grasped in a silk lined vise. The slapping noise came from our side of the room now. My thighs against Simon's asscheeks.

I remember Mark saying, "He's coming!" The first load hit my face. Then it ran down Simon's prick like liquid icing. Then I came, pumping it into him. There was a series of squelching noises and it was over. Simon lay back exhausted. I knelt quite still between his legs waiting for my cock to subside.

"Was it good?" asked Mark.

"Bloody great!" I said.

"Did you like it, Simon?" he continued.

Simon smiled. "Yeah! It's quite nice – when you get used to it," he said.

"Would you like me to do it to you?"

"What, now?"

"No, stupid. At school some time. We could do it in the old

barn."

"Mmm. All right." He turned to me. "I think I'd better have a shower if it's alright by you," he said. "Then we'd better start thinking of getting back."

So had ended a very enjoyable weekend but I was very reluctant to return to the field of conquest.

"It wouldn't hurt to come here just once more," said Herb.

That made me feel guilty about my haste to get into Simon and I almost said so, but at that moment the boy feeding the ducks ran out of bread. He sauntered over to us and, as he did so, he crumpled the empty paper bag and threw it into the water.

I think he would have walked past us had Herb not spoken.

"The proper place for garbage is a bin, young man!" he said.

The boy stopped. "Paper does no harm," he said. It wasn't the voice of a kid off the streets. Then he stared hard at Herb and then at me.

"Excuse me," he said. "Are you the guys with the model battleship?"

"It's packed up now," I said. "We're about to go home. You should have been here yesterday." I imagined that he heard about it from somebody.

"Were you in Fort Lauderdale about five years ago?" he asked.

"We could have been. We travel a lot. Why do you ask?"

"Do you remember John Maybanks and Tony Rizza?" he asked.

The names were vaguely familiar. I said so.

"I was in school with them," he said. "At Gloucester College."

"My God!" said Herb. "You're the little lad!"

"That's right. You said I was too young."

"And you wouldn't go away," I said, remembering how we had taken John and Tony down to the hotel lobby to find him waiting there for them. John and Tony had been seventeen. This one had been about fourteen. They didn't seem to mind his presence. We certainly did. He was with us in the hotel room on the Saturday afternoon. Try to get a good conversation going when a beady eyed fourteen year old is watching every move and listening silently to every word. It was almost a

disaster. However, John and Tony had knocked on the room door on Sunday as planned and everything had gone well. To find this child waiting for them downstairs had been a shock.

"So what are you doing here?" I asked. We were more than five hundred miles from Fort Lauderdale.

"My folks got together again and we live here now," he said.

Herb shifted along the bench and he sat between us.

"And do you like it?" asked Herb.

He said that he found the place boring. He had no friends there. His only recreation was to walk out and feed the ducks. His parents went away almost every weekend, leaving him at home.

"How old are you now?" asked Herb.

"Eighteen."

"And quite a hunk," said Herb. It was true. The shorts were small for him anyway. The lump under the tightly stretched material looked substantial. Herb got him and me to stand up so that he could 'assess the lad's height'. You know enough about Herb by now to know that he was rather more interested in another feature.

Neither of us could remember his name. Nor, for that matter, could he remember ours which was fortunate. We use different names for every weekend. He was Philip. We introduced ourselves.

"Boys who throw garbage into ponds need a good smacking," said Herb.

"Like Tony, you mean?" he asked, smiling.

"He told you did he?"

Tony had not only told him. Tony had shown him the marks. John had not been so forthcoming and had merely admitted that his ass hurt a bit. It would have hurt even more, I reflected, had mine been the first cock to penetrate him but John, at seventeen, had certainly been had before. He hadn't asked any of the usual questions: "What's that?" or "What are you doing?" He'd actually held the grease jar for me and when the time came, he clambered up onto the bed and got into position like an old hand.

"I miss them," said Philip. "We used to have a lot of fun together."

"What sort of fun?" Both Herb and I asked the same question.

"You know. Sort of private fun. In the dormitory and behind the out-buildings."

"Suppose," said Herb, "We were to come back here for a weekend. Would you like a bit of fun with us?"

He smiled. "That'd be great!" he said. I guess maybe I do need to be punished after all."

"And I," I said, "shall do my best to drill careful behaviour into you." I grinned. "And quite possibly something else as well."

GAME FOR ANYTHING

Peter Z. Pan

*"Before you judge me, try hard to love me,
Look within your heart then ask,
Have you seen my childhood?"*
— *Micheal Jackson*

When I was in fifth grade my goal in life was to become a "school monitor" when I entered the sixth grade. Having the honor of serving as a school monitor was my definition of "cool": the authority, the respect, the power – the way-cool shiny badge. Man, I popped a woody just thinking about it. I painstakingly worked towards my goal by getting straight "A's", earning good conduct awards, and maintaining a perfect attendance record. So when I was finally made a monitor, I was ecstatic but not surprised. Hell, I deserved it.

That proud day I stood shoulder to shoulder with my nine fellow monitors as Vice Principal Martinez assigned our commissions. What was it going to be? Hall Monitor? Cafeteria Monitor? Boys Room Monitor? Each one a prestigious assignment. "Library Monitor," I repeated in sad disbelief as my colleges snickered. I was crushed. It was like a police cadet expecting to make the SWAT Team but instead being stuck with a desk job. It sucked!

After my first week on the job, I realized that being Library Monitor was even more boring than I had imagined. My duties varied: for a grueling half hour before and after school I "shhhed" people, returned books to their proper shelves, and straightened chairs. And my taskmaster was a peevish little man named Mr. Peepers, Master Librarian. The geeky dinosaur had run the library ever since the school opened thirty years back. Mr. Peepers was a stickler for rules; he was always on my case about something or other. "Chop, chop, Mister McIntyre," he would say, "there's no room for slackers on my watch. I run a shipshape ship, Mister."

With that he'd pat me on the behind and send me on my

way. Sometimes his spidery hand would linger on my ass just a tad too long. This confused the hell out of me. Yes, it made me cringe; yet, it also gave me a whopper of an erection for some odd reason. Thinking about it gave me a headache, so I didn't.

Things began to get really strange my second week on the job when Mr. Peepers ordered me to straighten out his private reference section in the basement.

"The basement?" I protested. I didn't even know the library *had* a basement. I pleaded with him for a good five minutes – telling him that I was afraid of the dark, not to mention spiders and other bugs that hide in dark, damp basements, just waiting to jump out at little boys. This was to no avail.

"Stop sniveling like a baby, Mister McIntyre!" he barked. "Go perform your task or I shall have to discipline you!"

This sent chills down my spine. He was a dark and sinister man and I didn't even want to think about how he would discipline me. I went down.

The secret stairway that led to the basement was dark and scary. The door creaked as I opened it to go in. My knees shook as I felt along the wall for the light switch. Every horror movie I had ever seen flooded my mind. I was expecting a werewolf or a mutant to grab my arm, savagely ripping it from its socket. I breathed a sigh of relief when I found the switch.

After saying a small prayer, I turned on the lights. But there were no monsters here – just books. The small room was chock-full of books. The walls were made of bookcases that reached all the way to the ceiling. I was pleasantly surprised. The room was not at all scary. On the contrary, it was down right cozy, like an old den. I plopped down on the black leather couch in the center of the room and looked around me. This wasn't going to be so bad after all.

A large book on the coffee table suddenly caught my eye. I leaned forward to get a better look. It had a most curious title, "Puberty: A Boy's Guide To His Changing Body." Intriguing. "Fully Illustrated," it read in big letters on the bottom. Well, I couldn't stop myself, I just had to pick it up. My peter tingled at the thought of naked boys my age. My big blue eyes became even bigger as I excitedly opened the front cover. But nothing prepared me for what I found on the first page. Two young

boys were playing leapfrog...naked. Only they were *so* close to each other that it looked like one of the boy's dicks was going up the other boy's butt. But that can't be, I thought. What are *they doing*?! My small peter was so hard that I thought it was going to burst right through my pants.

A noise suddenly startled me, making me drop the book. I looked around the room but there was no one there. Yet I felt like I was being watched for some reason. It was almost creepy. However, my lusty desire to see more of the book greatly outweighed my puerile fears. I quickly picked it up again. The bogus book-jacket had fallen off on the floor, revealing the book's salacious, real cover. I was dumbfounded. Five blond boys stood over a brunette boy who was on all fours like a dog. They were peeing on him. The book's real title was: "Dutch Boy Golden Showers." I quickly devoured the book, furiously leafing through page after page of boys engaging in activities I never even dreamed were possible. They were kissing, sucking, pissing on each other. They were even doing what my best friend Timmy used to call "cornholing." Until I actually saw it in the book, I thought he was just making it up. But there it was in full color: "cornholing." I began to tremble and grunt then, experiencing a dry orgasm. That's when I heard Mr. Peepers coming down the stairs.

"Mister McIntyre, are you all right?" he queried with his high-pitched, whiny voice.

I utterly panicked, kicking the book-jacket under the couch and hiding the book under my shirt. The door creaked and I looked up.

There stood Mr. Peepers, staring at me quizzically. "Mister McIntyre, what is going on in here?" he demanded to know.

"Nothing, sir," I uttered.

"I could have sworn I heard guttural sounds emanating from down here."

"It's my stomach, sir," said I with a straight face. "I didn't have lunch."

He cocked an eyebrow, studying me for what seemed an agonizing hour. He then said, "Come child, I'm closing up."

"Yes, sir," I blurted out. I carefully crossed my arms so that the book wouldn't fall out and stood up. "Are you cold, Mister McIntyre?"

from pain or pleasure.

"Come on, Justin," Timmy egged on, "cornhole me." He fell on his sister, still fiercely humping her. "Spit into my asshole first like the boy in the book."

I knelt over him, releasing my spittle into his pink boy-pussy. Just then, I was struck with a sudden hankering to taste it. So I did just that. I lapped it up. Tasted better than his dick. Then I put my boner to his asshole and plunged it in hard, just like he had done to his poor sister.

Timmy screamed so loudly I thought the whole block was going to come running. He begged me to take it out, writhing beneath me, trying to push me off him. But animal instinct took over: I was determined not to stop till I had finished. I mounted him, my hips furiously thrusting hard into him like dogs fucking. Timmy's pain was unbearable at first, then as he gave in and eased into it, I could actually feel his ass loosing up. I felt Timmy quaver under me as he came into his sister, who in turn was having multiple orgasms. I came yet another time before releasing Timmy. We lay speechless on the floor, catching our breaths, looking as if we had just run a marathon.

But there was more to come. Timmy quickly got his second wind. He jumped to his feet and recreated the most daring tableaux of them all. He stood over Tammy and me, releasing his urine flux on us. We were both too stunned to react. Instead we just lay there and bathed in his piss.

I couldn't sleep at all that night. I knew I had fallen in love with Timmy and that scared the shit out of me. I didn't want to be a faggot. But my biggest concern was how I was going to sneak that book back into the library basement.

The next morning, I hid the book in my knapsack and waited for my accomplice, Timmy, to show up. He was going to create a diversion with Mr. Peepers while I slipped downstairs and replaced the book. We had seen something similar on "Hogan's Heroes."

Timmy showed up right on cue, faking an asthma attack. He was chewing up the scenery a little, but Peepers seemed to buy it. As he ran to Timmy's aid, I smoothly prowled into the basement. I ran straight for the couch and looked for the book jacket I had kicked underneath. But it wasn't there! Shit, where could it have gone? I was about to panic when I had a

brainstorm. I would borrow a jacket from another book. Peepers would never know the difference. I ran to the bookcase and grabbed the first book I saw: "How To Train Your Pet." That would do. I removed its jacket and was about to breathe a sigh of relief, when I saw the book's true cover and title: "Pussyboys and their Masters." I couldn't believe it. I grabbed another book at random and removed its jacket. This one was called: "Dungeon Buttfuck Jamboree." In a frenzy I looked through book after book. They were *all* S&M porno! There was one big, black book – without a jacket – that stood out: it looked fake. I went for it, but it was wedged in the other books. I pulled on it with all my might, finally it budged. Only it pulled down like a lever, making the bookcase suddenly open to reveal a secret room. I was numb by then. Like some bimbo heroine in a bad "B" movie I stepped into the ominous, secret room. It was a dungeon! A dungeon right underneath my picture-book school, filled with every torture device imaginable.

"Welcome, Justin," said a familiar voice from the darkness.

I startled back several feet, losing control of my bladder.

He then added matter-of-factly, "We've been expecting you."

My eyes adjusted to the light and I could now see who it was. Vice Principal Martinez was chained buck naked to the wall. I turned to run but Peepers was blocking the way. He was dressed all in leather and was holding a whip. He was also holding Timmy in a choke-hold. "Your diversion attempt was futile," Peepers stated smugly. "You've been very naughty. I'm going to have to discipline you both."

"I'm afraid you're going to be late for school today, boys," Martinez added. "But don't worry. I'll write you a note."

"Shut up! Slaves should be seen and not heard!"

"Sorry, Master," Martinez wailed, now reduced to a subservient child. The Master cracked his bullwhip and threw Timmy and me into the dungeon. Our lives would never be the same again.

Thirty years later, the school still stands, the library still stands, even the secret dungeon still stands. Mr. Peepers, however, wasn't so lucky: he passed away in a freak gerbil accident. Martinez is principal now, Tammy is a big ol' lesbian truck driver, and Timmy wound up my longtime companion.

As for me, I took over Mr. Peeper's shipshape ship.

FADE TO BLACK

L. Amore

The blue light from the screen was imbued with red and orange as the different images flickered and moved within the space. The light, the same light, flooded over the walls and ceiling as it escaped the rectangular white screen. The colors bled into one another without focus. The image on the screen, that was what was most disconcerting. As I watched, my feelings switched from nausea to fascination every other second. I thought back to how I had ended up here watching this. I looked over at Dave. My "Uncle Dave." He was a friend of the family, and the one who brought me *"out."* The man who had brought him *"out"* was his "Uncle Terry," so he was my "Uncle Dave." His face, which was illuminated sporadically by the light from the screen, wore a slight frown. His eyes were riveted to the images on the screen. I had to look away at times. I had seen nothing yet that would have made anyone turn away, but the apprehension of what I thought was going to happen was almost too great. Then why was I still sitting there? I didn't even know myself: Maybe it was shock. Maybe it was the need to find out if what I thought was going to happen actually would.

This two-week trip started out in Boston and ended up in Manhattan. "Uncle Dave" called me up just after school ended and invited me up to Boston for a little while. I knew he was gay and I'd always had the hots for him, so when he asked and even seemed interested in someone so young I jumped at the chance. The first week in Boston was great, utopic even. I lost my cherry, was in a big city for the first time in my life and I came out painlessly and gloriously. I was in a perpetual haze of lust. I constantly had a smile on my face and a half-hard in my pants that was serviced more than regularly. Then "Uncle Dave" got a call from a friend in New York. We decided to go down, and afterward he would drop me back home in Connecticut on his way back to Massachusetts. So we packed

up his truck and we were there in less than five hours.

If I had known what was to happen I would have vehemently protested. But the mistakes of youth happen to all, and hindsight is just that – hindsight. The apartment was nice enough. It was a large loft. One big room. bricked on one side, the rest of it offwhite, or puce, as Martin insisted. Martin was the "film producer" whose apartment it was. To say that Martin gave me the creeps was the understatement to end all understatements. HE MADE MY SKIN CRAWL! I was nice to him because it was his hospitality that we relied on, and I didn't want to cause a bad time for "Uncle Dave". After all I was his guest. Again if I had known then, a bad time wouldn't have been a problem to give him, but...

The boy on the screen was young. He had been staying at the apartment when we got there. His name was Doby. Doby was blond, beautifully featured and lithe. A Caravaggio for lack of better adjectives. The action on the screen - what was happening in that five by nine foot frame - created conflict in me. It also caused fear for my own safety. There was a black man sharing the screen so graciously provided. In my immature thinking of the time the black man symbolized evil, as I sat there and watched. He was probably picked to star for just that reason. The racial overtones not to be aware to me until later in life. This is the first time that I've been able to tell anyone. I've thought on this a lot.

Everything was cool with "Uncle Dave" and me - and even with Martin - at the beginning. Martin made porn flicks. He wanted me and "Uncle Dave" to appear in one. I had no problem with that. My only thought was that my parents might find out. But Mom and Dad seldom went to the gay flick palaces and I'd never seen a copy of *Blueboy* lying around the house. So, why not?

The black man was fucking Doby's mouth. It wasn't an act that was equally enjoyed. The black man's penis was huge. It was like half of a loaf of French bread. Again I thought that this was why the man had been chosen to play the part. This scene was darker than the others. The cinematography wasn't of the

best quality. I wasn't surprised. The room darkened with the screen. The beams of light reflected on the surroundings, it took on the lack of light beautifully. I felt as though I was in a darkened movie theater waiting for some climactic scene. It wasn't climactic, just chilling at the least and horrific in the apprehension of what I thought would happen next. Guilt and fear worked their cold fingers. It was not unlike the sensation when slowing down to see the damage of a car accident on the highway.

"Uncle Dave" thought that the idea of doing a porn flick with me was a good one. He was also a little nervous about my parents finding out. They didn't know that I was up in New York with him anyway. My father had to convince Mother that it was a growing up thing for me. A boy thing to do. To grow and explore my horizons. If they only knew. If I only knew.

The kid was visibly gagging. It was the least erotic image I'd ever seen. It stays with me to this day. The film was grainy. Those lines that you see in old movies, appearing one second then disappearing the next, were in it throughout. I tried to pay attention to those lines, abstract and flickering, but was drawn away by the image on the screen. No cuts. No angles. Just a fixed shot of the black man slapping Doby's ass. The red welts, or handprints, sprang to life amidst the graininess.

Doby, whom I had met the first day that we were there, was not there the next. I had overheard that he was Martin's "boy." I also overheard, quite by chance, that he was addicted to heroin. I'd had a buddy who was an addict and I remembered the stones that she used to tell me of her times. She would rip off Macy's and other department stores. She would need a fix, go in and walk out with a VCR. She would then sell it on the street and go see her dealer. She later became a street whore to support her habit. Doby was gone for two days at this point. Martin said that he did this all the time. That he would be back tomorrow. For the next three days he did not come back.

He was on the screen though. Right in front of my eyes.

Seemingly forced into something that he obviously wanted no part of. He was bent over and the black man was preparing to enter him. His erect cock in one hand, the other on Doby's shoulder. The right shoulder so that it wouldn't interfere with the scene.

Martin said that he had something that he wanted "Uncle Dave" and me to see. I had dread in my stomach when he said it. If only I'd known.

The black man was fucking Doby for all he was worth. Doby made a valiant effort to make it seem like he was enjoying it. It didn't play. He was probably told that if he could make it look as though he were enjoying it he would get his next fix. This thought crossed my mind and left when I saw the black man's hands. They slowly moved to Doby's shoulders. For effect, it would seem. They didn't stay there, but moved up. His large hands grasped Doby's neck and clenched it. Doby's penis was erect and it seemed as though he was nearing orgasm. The black man still continued to violently screw him.

We walked into a room. It was obviously converted into a small screening room. There were two sofas, a love seat and two free standing chairs. Martin was there, and another man who I hadn't met. And of course "Uncle Dave" and I. Martin hit the projector and light flooded the dark room. I wanted to think that it was all make believe. I didn't know what a snuff film was, never even conceived of the idea. Naivete is a wonderful thing, people say. I would have like to have known that something like this was done. That there was a market for this sort of thing. If only I had known.

The black man's hands were clenched tighter. Doby's face was red with exertion. At that time I hoped that it was from his orgasm. There was a close up of the black man's face and I went cold when I realized that it wasn't. Doby's face was also caught in the shot. His eyes bulged and there was a look of pure terror on his face that broke through the heroin-induced haze. I still see this image when I wake up in the middle of the night, a cold sweat blanketing my body, the darkness and fear

my only companions. Doby fell limp and the black man had to hold him up. The man pulled his now totally engorged cock out of Doby's ass before he fell to the floor. He was out of the shot for only seconds. The black man grasped his rigid organ with both hands and ejaculated over Doby's flaccid body. The thick milky ropes landing with deadly accuracy on his ass and the back of his upper thighs.

I looked at "Uncle Dave" and his expression mirrored my own *horror*. I couldn't see my face.

The screen slowly went black. The proverbial fade to black.

Martin was mumbling something about it only being an act. He seemed uncomfortable when he didn't get the reaction from "Uncle Dave" and I that he wanted. Too fucking bad.

I haven't talked to "Uncle Dave" since then. I don't suppose that he's talked to Martin since then either. If he has, I don't want to know about it.

AFTER THE GAME

William Joseph

Our basketball team had just won a crucial district game against Roosevelt High School. Our leading scorer, Tom Reynolds, and our point guard, Jim Grove, were waiting in Jim's Toyota when I came out of the door of the locker room and into the parking lot. Even though I never started a game and really didn't even get much playing time, Tom, Jim, and I had been friends since my family and I moved to Pennsylvania at the beginning of my ninth grade in school.

Tom lived next door, and Jim was his best friend. It hadn't been long before I started hanging out at Tom's house, mostly just shooting hoops in his driveway, which naturally meant that Jim was usually there, too. Since I did better than either of them in our English class, it wasn't long until I found myself writing most of their papers for them. I didn't mind, though. They were both incredible looking guys, with Jim having a bit of an edge of Tom in my eyes, mostly because of his extremely light blond hair and penetrating blue eyes. Tom was built a little stronger than Jim, but he was darker, and for some reason I've never understood, blond hair and blue eyes beats tall, dark, and handsome every time.

I remember clearly that first year. I tried out for the junior high team and made it, but all I could think about was how that once practice began I'd finally get to see Tom and Jim in the shower.

We had our first team work-out on a Saturday afternoon. Jim, who was first to get his driver's license, came by our street to pick up Tom and me, and we headed off to school. The work-out gave me a real opportunity to see just how good the two of them were on a real basketball court. I got stuck guarding Tom most of that initial practice, and his shooting pretty much made it a certainty that I'd be relegated to the bench.

As soon as Coach Myers told us we could quit for the day, we all walked into the locker room. I had staked out a locker right next to Jim. Tom's locker was across from ours against the

other wall. When I sat down on the bench to remove my shoes and socks, I suddenly realized I'd put myself in an awkward position, wondering how I'd be able to keep my dick from rising. Not looking at any of the other guys, I grabbed a towel, went right to the showers, tossed the towel on a hook, and faced the wall.

Jim ran in right behind me and started shampooing. With his eyes closed to keep out the sting, I looked him over. The suds were running down his perfectly shaped chest and his belly. Jim still didn't have a full bush of pubes, and I guessed his dick still had some more growth left in it, too, but the entire package was creamier than I had ever imagined those nights I jacked-off thinking about him.

When Tom jumped in beside us, he grabbed the bottle of shampoo from the shelf and soaped up. His pubes were tight, dark coils, and his dick curved slightly to the left, hanging heavy and almost fully developed.

The struggle I anticipated had begun, so I kept my back to them and to the other guys, then left the shower area first, wrapping myself in my towel, and keeping it on until I got my pants up. Tom joked about how modest I had become, and I laughed back.

In the weeks that followed, the three of us always went to practice together and came home together. Once the season got underway, the procedure continued. I helped to solve my daily shower problem by always being sure to toss off a quick one before we left for the gym. Even then, one look at Tom or Jim, and I was hurting.

When our sophomore year rolled around, the situation had only gotten worse. By the time we started up another year of practice, all three of us had attained just about complete physical maturity. Tom worked out more than Jim or I did, so he had a more muscular build. Jim stayed lean, but still nicely defined. They were both so near to perfection, I could barely contain myself. I was jacking off more than ever, but nothing seemed to help. All I could think about was how tremendous it would be if I could only touch them. But I figured that would never happen.

After the games, we'd always go to Lennie's, a local fast food place we all liked. The rest of the team usually showed up too,

along with the cheerleaders, each of whom seemed to have staked out her favorite player. Tom and Jim were at the top of the list, partly because even as sophomores they were already impressive basketball players and partly because both refused to succumb to the attention of the girls. All three of us had talked a lot about girls and dating, just like guys everywhere, and we agreed that none of us had any interest in getting tied down to one person.

Anyway, the Roosevelt game was the sixth of our sophomore season. Both the Rams and us came into the game undefeated. All those days in Tom's driveway paid off. Jim tossed Tom perfect passes all night long, and Tom made nine of twelve field goals to lead both teams in scoring. Jim got off ten points himself, and I even had two after getting fouled when the coach put me in late in the contest.

We went to Lennie's to celebrate, then headed home. Jim dropped us off in front of Tom's house.

"Why don't you come in for awhile?" Tom asked him. "My parents went to the Osbornes' house. They won't be home for a couple of hours."

"No. That's okay," Jim said. "I'm whipped. I just want to go home and stretch out."

"Yeah. I know what you mean," Tom replied. "I'm sore, too. We'll see you tomorrow."

Jim pulled away from the curb and waved to us from his car as he turned the corner. I started to walk toward our house, when Tom asked, "Where you going?"

"I thought you were whipped."

"Yeah," he said, smiling. "But I'm not ready to crash just yet. Your mom and dad are at the Osbornes', too. What's the sense in us sitting in our houses all by ourselves? Let's watch the rest of the Bulls game. It probably isn't even halftime, yet."

I figured we'd watch the game in the family room, but Tom said he'd rather get completely relaxed.

"We'll watch it on my TV," he said. "That way I can get into bed and relax."

Once we got to his room, I sat on his desk chair, the only seat he had, while he took the remote and tuned in the Bulls game. "I'll be right back," he said.

When he returned, I saw he had changed clothes and now

only had on a pair of basketball shorts. He handed me a 7-Up, then got under the covers on his water bed. For a while, we sat without comment, watching the game.

Suddenly, he said, "Are you comfortable?"

"No, not really," I told him honestly.

"Well, come over here," he said. reaching for a spare pillow. "You can lean against the wall."

I accepted his invitation, fluffing up the pillow, then sitting down. Tom lifted his legs, then draped them over mine. I was surprised, but still figured nothing significant would happen.

The Bulls were into the fourth quarter, and Jordan already had forty points when Tom spoke again.

"Would you mind rubbing my feet?" he said quietly. "They're really sore."

"Sure. No problem."

I reached down under the blanket and began rubbing Tom's feet. As soon as I touched him, I felt my dick getting hard. But he had his eyes on the TV screen, so it didn't matter.

"Feel good?" I finally asked.

"Yeah," he said in that same quiet voice. "Do my calves." Stunned, but compliant, I began working my hands up and down his calves, squeezing the tendons.

"Not so rough," he said, still softly. "Take it easy, man."

Not knowing for sure exactly what he had in mind, I just ran my hands up and down his legs gently now, feeling the soft down of his hair under my palms. Occasionally, I'd rub a calf with my right hand while rubbing a foot with my left.

"Is that better?"

"Yeah," he replied, his eyes fixed on the game. Then a bit later, he added, "Do my thighs. I ache all over, man."

My hands were trembling as I carefully ran my hands up and down his thighs. Testing him, I even ran them up the inner thigh, just inches from his balls, wanting to see if he'd react, but he never moved. He just kept watching the screen. The whole situation was so unreal, I could hardly believe I wasn't dreaming. I never worried that he might be trying to trick me. He had proved his friendship too many times. I knew I could trust him.

"Feel good?" I asked, my voice close to cracking.

He simply nodded his head, still staring at the screen. It was

as if that by not looking at me, what was happening there on his bed wasn't being acknowledged by him. I didn't care. I had been waiting forever for the chance to touch him, and now he had invited me to rub his thighs and hadn't objected once when I danced my fingers lightly up the inside. I knew he had to be hard, too. There was no way on earth he couldn't be responding to what I was doing to him.

"Is that enough?" I asked, sort of testing the waters.

"It doesn't matter to me," he said so quietly that I could barely hear him over the announcers on the television. "Do whatever you want, man."

I didn't know *what* he meant by *that* statement. Now my mind was reeling. Still afraid to take the most dangerous step of all, I contented myself by rubbing his feet and calves and thighs, always coming close to his balls, but not touching them.

"Do you want me to stop now?" I asked, afraid he'd say "yes."

"It's up to you." He never looked at me. "Do whatever you want."

This time when I ran my fingers up his inner thighs, I slipped into one of the legs of the basketball shorts and letting the back of my hand bump into his balls. I felt him jerk slightly, but he didn't say a word. He just lay there with his arms to his sides, his head tilted on the pillow, watching the game.

Once again, I bumped my hand against his balls, and he made no reaction. The next trip up, I finally touched them with my fingers, feeling the soft wisp of young hair there. When he made no response, I stayed put, running my fingers delicately over his balls, gently holding them and feeling their heft.

"Is that okay?" I asked him, my voice finally cracking.

He nodded, still looking away.

By that time, I figured I might as well go all the way. I had been playing with his balls for ten minutes, and if he found my actions objectional, he would have stopped me long before. Without asking for permission, I moved my right hand up from his balls and ran a slow trail with my finger along his dick. It was hard, throbbing. It was a beautiful cock, no doubt about it. My fingers shook.

Hearing no protest, I wrapped my hand around his dick, feeling it throb against my palm, and slowly stroked it.

"Wait," he said.

For a moment, I thought the show was over. Instead, I watched as he reached down with both hands and pulled down the shorts, kicking them off and onto the floor.

Immediately, I went back to work. There was no way to know just how far he wanted me to go, but I felt contented nonetheless softly stroking him with one hand while rolling his balls in the other.

"Not yet," he said in a near whisper.

"What?" I asked, barely hearing him.

"Take it easy," he said, finally looking at me. "I don't want to come yet."

"Okay," I replied, suddenly feeling shy.

I went back to running my fingers up and down his lower body, sometimes rubbing his feet, massaging his calves and thighs, and giving him a few strokes from time to time.

The basketball game ended, with the Bulls victorious. By then, all I wanted to do was to get to my own house and to release the pressure in my own balls; my dick actually hurt from its erection. I slipped my legs from under Tom's and started getting off the bed.

"Where are you going?" he asked, clicking off the TV with the remote, plunging the room into darkness.

"Home, I guess."

"Aren't you going to – finish what you started?" It was as if he was begging me.

"How?"

"Whatever," he said quietly.

"Do you want a hand job?"

He waited a moment or two before answering. "It's up to you, man. Do whatever you want."

I sat on the edge of the bed, reached under the cover, and took his dick in my hand. Running my thumb across the glans, I felt the stickiness there.

"Do you want to come now?" I asked quietly.

"I don't have anything to put it in," he said just as quietly.

My mind went back to my times with my best friend back in Indiana. His name was Scott, and he showed me how to jack-off right after we joined the local scout troop. We used to sleep out as often as possible during the summer months, and

we'd always find excuses to sleep over at each other's houses when it got too cold to stay outdoors all night, jacking off ourselves and eventually one another. One night we watched a porn flick we found in his brother's room, and when we saw the women giving the men blow jobs, we immediately gave that a try. We liked that a lot better than swapping hand jobs, and I'll always remember the night when we were in the seventh grade and Scott came the very first time. In my mouth. Two months later, it was my turn.

Still slowly pulling on Tom's dick there in the dark, I mustered all the courage in the world and asked, "Do you want to come in my mouth?"

My heart was really pounding now, terrified that now he knew everything.

"Whatever you want, man, just do something."

I pulled down the cover and lowered my head. Opening my mouth, I ran my tongue along the underside of Tom's magnificent dick, following the curve. There seemed little sense now in holding back. I figured I might as well enjoy myself.

Tom didn't move at all until I finally took him into my mouth. Now as I sucked, running my tongue back and forth across his glans, he started a slow, gentle fucking motion. I didn't want to hurry. Now that we had gone that far, I wanted the evening to last forever.

Unfortunately, Tom's dick had a mind of its own. He drove it deeply into my mouth and partway down my throat' shutting off my air supply. Then he erupted. I could feel the thick globs spurting out of him, hard and hot. I pulled back a little with my mouth, breathing quickly, and milking him with every swallow.

Finally I felt his ass dropping back onto the bed, and I let him go.

"How did that feel?" I asked, wiping my chin on my sleeve. "Was it okay?"

"Great," he answered, still in that same caressing voice.

I was about to ask him if he was mad at me, worrying that by doing this I would destroy our friendship, but he was clicking the TV back on, the light giving the room a blue glow.

The covers were still down by his knees. I looked at his cock where it rested against his left leg, all of it shining with my

saliva. Tom reached down and covered himself, now being shy as I had been.

"I better get going," I said, adding, only half-joking, "If I don't get home and whack off, I might have a broken dick."

Tom looked up at me and smiled. "After the next game, I'll make sure Jim's here, too. Maybe you two can teach each other a few things."

WHEREVER YOU WANT TO PUT IT

Kevin Bantan

It was as hot as a day gets around here, a scary thought considering that it was only June. I feared that it was a harbinger of unrelenting heat to come during my last summer before college. Smothering air cooked by a naked sun hung like fine netting outside my bedroom window. I spent the day in my air-conditioned room, reading mostly, daydreaming sometimes while playing with myself, but antsy, too, in a way I couldn't identify. It often seemed to be like that on my days off from my summer job. Maybe I needed to be outside to walk off my pent-up energy, despite the heat and humidity. So I decided to brave the oppressiveness and head for my favorite haunt: the old amusement park.

As a kid, I'd considered myself lucky to live within walking distance of the park. Almost every day during the summer I'd cool off in the unimaginably large swimming pool. Well, that, and I got to escape from my mother and bratty little sister for several hours. After tiring of the water, I'd walk around in my blue swim trunks, flip flops on my feet, towel around my neck, taking in the festive atmosphere. Generally, I was content to look at the various rides whirling around me. None held a real fascination, except for the train. I'd ride it every day that I was at the park, never tiring of its slow pace, or of seeing the same sights time after time, its route strictly governed by narrow steel ribbons. The ambience of the park charmed me every day that I was there. It was very different now but still as undefinably alluring as it was then. The park had closed several years ago. Grass grew tall between the rails where the train once snaked across what seemed like hundreds of acres. Weeds appeared to reach up, aching to touch the bed of the roller coaster at its lower inclines. It had been huge and terrifying to me in those days years ago. Now its rusted skeleton struck me as Erector Set-ish. Interesting how our perceptions changed as we grew up and older. I was even beginning to like my sister, but not the way I liked a couple of classmates, who lived in the same housing development as I. What I felt for them was love.

The latter still puzzled me. I knew what I was supposed to like, and lest I forgot, my father frequently spoke of the irresistible charms of girls. He would never understand that I found them abundantly resistible. My classmates, however, were another matter entirely. I'd lie in bed at night, my dick in my fist, and picture one or both of my friends as I jerked off.

Often when I came to the park, I'd consider this conundrum in the comforting surroundings of decay and overgrowth. My favorite spot for meditation was the old pavilion behind the once-manicured privet hedge set carefully along a sharp bend in the tracks. Although there were other such picnic shelters scattered throughout the park, this one afforded a real sense of privacy, as isolated as it was now by hedges and shrubs allowed to determine their own destinies.

On the way there, I stopped to stare past the battered carousel into my mind's eye to the objects of my dreams, their images indelibly embedded in my sex-charged brain. I saw Curt with his blond buzz cut and shining steel-blue eyes which always seemed to be harboring a secret; and Jerrod with his short brown hair, brown irises as big as quarters, and crooked smile, a smile that made my crotch stir when it was directed at me. I sighed, suspecting them to be the cause of my restlessness, and resumed my slow trek to the pavilion. As I walked toward it I felt a twinge of loss. It wouldn't be long before the couple hundred acres would become a shopping center or a housing development. The land was just too valuable to lie fallow like that.

An important part of my childhood would become a memory bereft of crumbling props, all of them bulldozed under just as puberty does to childhood. I remembered its onset. Parts of my body sprouted hair, my voice changed octaves without warning when I spoke, and my newly-activated dick discovered suddenly that guys were attractive, specifically Curt and Jerrod. They caused my cock do these strange new things when I thought about them. I stopped and turned to look down the midway. Everything changed sooner or later.

The idea of being gay, in and of itself, wasn't so bad, despite what our minister said. If I wasn't attracted to girls, what was the big deal? Because it was wrong to have sex with guys? A sin? I had pretty much gotten past that, Reverend Brimstone

notwithstanding. I mean, why would God make me want sex, if every time I did it I was going to hell? Being set up for a certain fall didn't make sense to me, and it was important at this stage of my life that everything did. At an age when my body was a rage of hormones barreling over the threshold of adulthood, feeling guilty about my desires was the last thing I needed. So, my musings in the park were less about my abhorrent nature than they were about whether or not either of the boys I lusted after could possibly be the way I was, and how I could find out without getting my face punched in.

Of course my deliberations at the shelter house had taken me clear through high school without finding out the answer. At least I didn't have to worry about becoming a pariah at school anymore. But it had been fun musing. Even though I couldn't devise a plan of attack, I did indulge my fantasies. Alone in the protected womb of the pavilion, I'd picture my classmates naked, separately or together in the high school locker room. Slowly I'd stroke myself as I feasted on the images of their wonderful youthful bodies, imagining what it would be like to touch the soft velvet of their skin. It never took me long to spatter the stone and concrete floor of the pavilion with my potent seed, holding my swollen, expanding rod and watching the jets of white arc high in the air before falling without hope of fertilizing anything, to the barren pavement below.

I was lost in thought as I approached my familiar haunt, so at first I thought it was my imagination. The sounds I heard couldn't be voices. No one came here anymore except for me and stray dogs. But if they weren't voices what could they be? I was at the hedge when I clearly heard the sounds again. They were unmistakably voices. In fact, they sounded familiar. "You know you want it."

"Yeah? What makes you think so?"

"Those cute puppy dog eyes of yours. They're always mooning over me."

"You wish." I couldn't believe my ears. I lowered myself to my hands and knees to peer through a gap at the base of the hedge. My eyes confirmed what my ears thought they heard. Curt and Jerrod were in the pavilion, bare-chested, their lean-muscled, tanned upper torsos glistening with sweat.

"You're just dyin' to suck it, aren't you?"

"In your dreams."

"I saw the way you looked at it in the showers after gym class. You hated it, because you wanted it so bad and you couldn't have it with all those guys there. It drove you crazy."

"Hah. There wasn't much to see to go crazy about."

Their taunting continued, but now they were making feints at each other's crotch. I watched in fascination as a kind of adolescent male sex ritual was unfolding before my eyes. And as the sniping continued, I began to get as hot as the temperature.

"You know what your problem is, Rod? You know you have a hard time taking all of me."

"What, this puny thing?" he replied and lunged for Curt, who danced out of the way.

"Don't give me that shit. You know it's big."

"More like a stubby pencil."

"More like a spear. And you know you need it. You need it bad."

"Yeah, okay, I need it," Rod said, tired of the game they played over and over, I would find out.

"Where?"

"In my mouth. Up my ass." He shrugged. "Wherever you want to put it."

And just like that they were locked in a tight embrace. My two friends were making out in broad daylight. Their hands were all over each other, their mouths slobbering together with the urgency of a bloated bladder desperate to empty. My crotch was stirring at the sight. I'd never seen two guys kiss and hug before. I mean they were hungry. It was thrilling to see the studs of my dreams getting it on. I was tempted to join them, but this was their scene, and I didn't want to spoil it. Besides, I wanted to find out what else was going to happen, just as my dick did, and we didn't have long to wait.

Rod dropped to his knees and slowly pulled down the zipper of Curt's shorts. He leaned his face into the parted fly and inhaled, closing his eyes to savor the aroma he found there. Then he undid the waist button and pulled them down as carefully as one would unroll a fragile, ancient scroll. The stone wall was just low enough for me to see Curt's crotch and the sizeable cock now jutting out from it. It was all so familiar and

tantalizing, because I peeked at him in the showers, too. A pang of envy surged through me, because I wanted to be on my knees there in Rod's place. He nuzzled up against Curt's boner, and started kissing it all over.

"I love this damn cock," Rod said.

"Yeah, Rod, that feels good. Suck on it, man. I love to see you swing on it."

And swing he did. I had a good idea of what cocksucking entailed, having listened to enough of my classmates talk derogatorily about it in the locker room, which had been another good reason to be carefully circumspect about my proclivities. Now I was getting a first-hand lesson in the art. Rod took Curt's head into his mouth, letting it rest there for a few seconds before he plunged on. He gripped the cock and balls at their base and started to move back and forth on Curt's long pole, pausing at times to let the sensations he was producing sink in. That's when Curt started to moan and grip Rod's head, urging him on. I was astonished to see the dick disappear into my kneeling friend and wondered how he was able to do it.

"Yeah, that's it. Get it good and wet, 'cause it's gonna be someplace else real soon."

I had no idea what he meant, but it seemed to excite Rod, who became a human piston. After another minute or so, Curt pulled him off and to his feet to kiss him while he undid Rod's shorts, letting them fall to the ground. He put a finger into Rod's mouth, and he sucked as greedily on it as he had on the bigger appendage. I couldn't believe my eyes when he withdrew the finger and positioned it between Rod's other cheeks. He seemed to be rubbing the tip of the finger against the opening, and Rod was loving it. I wondered how a finger messing around down there could feel good. I'd have to try that. Then Curt inserted it into my other friend's asshole. I have to admit that my fantasy life had never progressed much beyond kissing and touching and jacking off.

Rod was squirming on Curt's finger, his own erection peeking out from between Curt's legs. He pulled out the finger and turned Rod around, who planted his hands on the wall for support. Curt spit on his cock three times and spread it over his head and shaft, some strands of saliva still hanging from his

mouth. As wet as he'd made his boner, Jerrod squealed in pain as Curt entered him, hurting but sinking back on it at the same time. It was fascinating to watch Curt's shaft disappear into Rod and then reappear shiny and rock hard. Rod's cries of pain turned to gasps, and he started to encourage the assault on his ass. They were in profile to me, so I was able to see the change of expression on Rod's sweaty face. It was clear that he was beginning to enjoy having Curt's big prick in him. I unzipped quietly and pulled my erect dick from my shorts. I stroked it in time to Curt's movements, imagining myself in his place. I kept pace, matching my tempo to his until I was tugging frantically and coming at almost the same time as he. The two of them made so much noise that they didn't hear my own cry of release.

When they were finished, they didn't put their shorts back on. Instead they sat bareassed on the wall, sweat rolling down their bodies, telling the other what a great fuck he was.

"Man, we shoulda started to do this years ago," Jerrod said.

"Yeah, it's easy to say that now. What did you expect me to do? Just walk up to you on the first day of freshman year and say, I want to fuck your cute little boy ass, bend over?"

"Well, at least you finally did."

"And you love it."

"Yeah. You know what else I would love?"

"Yeah, I know, but say it anyway."

"To suck Davey off. He's got such a cute dick. Not that you don't, mind you. But that mushroom at the end. I'll bet it just swells up so big that it would turn into a ripe plum and choke me when I got it down my throat."

"Spoken like a true cocksucker. Now, me, I'd love to give his ass a good cleaning out. Those cheeks of his are just too perfect not to be speared."

They were lazily stroking themselves as they talked, and I blushed at what they were saying, in spite of myself. I got out of my shorts, so that I could be naked like them.

I also began to finger my hole. "I wonder if he's gay."

"Why don't you ask him?"

"I'm not gonna ask him and get my nose bloodied if he's not."

"He is," I heard myself say, as I pushed through the hedge.

They turned, shocked to hear my voice. I thought for a moment that they might panic and run away, but they sat, frozen in their positions, hands stuck on their cocks. The expressions on their open-mouthed faces were priceless. "Well, you wanted to know."

"Geez, Davey, you scared the hell out of us," Curt said.

"Sorry."

"You'll be sorrier if you don't get that fine ass over here. I'm gonna do something even scarier."

"Like you did with Rod?"

"You saw us? You watched Curt fuck me?"

"Sure did. Best show I ever saw."

"It's a double feature, Davey, and you're the star of the second one."

I walked up the steps of the pavilion and knelt in front of my friends the way Rod had. Feeling uncharacteristically emboldened, I didn't hesitate to grab ahold of their cocks and suck one head, then the other. I wasn't quite ready to have boy cock shoved all of the way down my throat, especially not Curt's. But I was pleased to be able to get them erect with my mouth. I moved my hands under them and fondled their ball sacs. It was a rush to finally be sucking and playing with the forbidden fruit of my friends. But they had other ideas. They got me to my feet and each fought for a piece of my mouth. We stood there for a while in a kissing threesome, which made my cock rock hard again.

Rod groped me and, pleased with what he found, said, "Your turn."

In no time at all he was on his knees, slurping on the purple head he'd coveted. He really could suck cock well, so nerve-tinglingly well that I thought that I would be in love with him for the rest of my life.

Meanwhile, Curt pushed his finger into my mouth and I slathered it with all of the spit that I could muster. It was my only defense for what was coming. His teasing my button felt much better than my own awkward attempt had.

When he nudged it into me, the finger felt like a rude intrusion, but the longer he stroked my sphincter, the better it felt and more relaxed it became. When he surmised that I was ready, he repeated his spit to cock routine.

For good measure, I added my own contribution. There was something about spitting on Curt's cock that turned me on even more. He mixed our saliva together, and I hoped for the best. He moved behind me, and put his hands on my waist and the head of his weapon nudged against my virgin hole.

Then flames erupted as, true to his word, he speared me. Despite the pain, my cock seemed to grow even harder in Rod's mouth. He must have felt it, because he mumbled something unintelligible. Curt took it easy on me once he was in, and I appreciated his trying to make me more comfortable. And the longer he was in me, the more I was. He wrapped his arms around my waist, holding our sweat-mingled bodies together as he humped me slowly but rhythmically. His perspiration rolled down his face onto my shoulder and back.

My head was spinning from all that I was feeling. I was getting both my first fuck and blow job at the same time. My two friends had taken possession of the most intimate parts of my body. I'd hit the sexual jackpot. I was on fire with pleasure, my nether nerves going wild with passion. I decided that I was in love with Curt, too. Curt rocked into me as Rod sucked back and forth on my bloated, twitching prick. It was too much. I had steadied my hands on Rod's shoulders for support, but now my fingers were gripping them hard as Rod was methodically coaxing the come from the balls he was manipulating, and Curt was using my colon to surrender his.

Rod was jacking himself furiously, as a steady thin rope of sex lubricant tethered him to the pavilion floor. He came first, moaning onto my flesh pole. Curt bucked one last time, burying himself completely in me and unleashing his second load of the afternoon. His pulsing sex drove me over the edge, and I creamed Rod's throat to his utter delight.

We collapsed onto the pavilion floor, sex-tired and dehydrated, as our slick, shiny bodies attested. We kissed each other lightly and lay talking about how great it was to have sex with each other. Jerrod's smile was positively beatific when he talked about how delicious my cock was. We regretted the fact that we would all be attending different colleges, but we determined to make the most of the summer, hot as it might be. And to be sure to bring along lots of water, whatever the temperature, because it would be that much hotter in the

shelter, for sure.

The inevitable sign went up announcing that the park was going to be redeveloped into a shopping center and apartments soon. The three of us continued to get together there, making the most of the pavilion while we still could. And did we ever.

Now, years later, Rod swears that the bedroom of the apartment we share is on the exact spot where the structure used to be. Curt thinks he's crazy, but I suspect that he's right, because our three-ways are better than ever.

WHEN BOB KISSED ME...

Greg Bowden

I guess Brian and I had been kind of goofing around during practice but so was everyone else on the team and it sure didn't seem fair that we were the only ones who had to stay after and run laps but we were. I don't know, maybe Coach Bowers was making an example of us or something. Anyway, by the time we got into the locker room everybody but the coach had left and he was getting ready to.

"Okay, guys, grab a shower and get out of here," he said on his way out. "And let's not have any more foolin' around during practice. You're in college now and you've got to lose that high school mentality if you want to survive. Okay?"

Brian started to say something but thought better of it and just nodded. I tried to look repentant but I guess it didn't work because the coach grinned at me and said, "You too, fella." He swatted me on the butt and took off.

We started goofing around again in the shower, splashing water at each other and trying to play catch with the soap. Then we had a peeing contest, to see who could pee the farthest, which I won. I mean, hitting the drain in the middle of the floor is probably some sort of record. Then we kind of got to playing with ourselves, lathering up our cocks and checking out how good it felt sliding our fists over them. It didn't take but a minute before both our cocks were more or less pointing at the ceiling.

"Oh, God," Brian said, "I am so fuckin' horny."

"Me too. Come on, let's jack off. We'll see if maybe you can shoot farther than you can pee." That probably wasn't right, challenging him like that but I was really horny and I wanted to jack off which I couldn't do if Brian didn't.

Brian pushed his dick into his fist a couple of times and sighed. "That's not gonna satisfy me. Not now."

"What'd you mean not gonna satisfy you? It satisfies everyone." Come on, Brian, I said to myself. I just got to get my rocks off. "I need something else," he said. "Something

hotter and tighter. Something that isn't my own hand for a change."

"Yeah. Sure. Like what?"

"Well, like your ass, maybe. Yeah, you got a beautiful little ass, man. That'd be just about perfect." He leaned closer to me and put his hand on my butt. "I bet that'd be really tight."

"My ass? You crazy or something?"

He moved his hand around, touching my butt all over. When his fingers slipped into the crack and touched my hole I jumped. "C'mon, stop that. It'd hurt too much, Brian."

"No it wouldn't. And if it did I'd stop. Really I would." His finger was pushing against my hole and suddenly slipped in a little. "Come on, Jeffey, please? Just for a minute?"

Brian pushed his finger in a little more and it felt really strange – almost good. But his cock? I looked down at it, measuring it with my eye. It wasn't as big as mine – I'm kind of special that way – but it sure as hell was bigger than his finger.

"Please, Jeffey? It'd feel so good in there." He had his whole finger pushed up my ass by now and it was making me feel all kinds of stuff I'd never felt before. It was also making this stuff dribble out my dick, like that slick stuff that sometimes comes out when you're jacking off only it never came out this much. I looked up into Brian's eyes, and I could see how much he wanted to do it so I sort of gave in. I mean, what the hell, if he wanted it that bad, why not? Besides, his fingers – he had two up there now – were feeling better and better.

"You promise to take it out if it hurts? Really promise?"

"I will, Jeffey. Really. I will."

"Well... okay. But take it real easy. And be ready to pull it out 'cause I just know it's gonna hurt."

Brian looked so happy I thought he was going to cry, but he didn't. He just slicked up his cock with his shampoo and moved around behind me, out of the water. Then he put both hands on my hips and eased me back until I felt his cock pushing in between my buns, looking for my hole. When it found it Brian took a real deep breath and slowly pulled me back on it.

"Oh, God, it's going in," he whispered, letting out his breath. "Is it okay, Jeffey? Please say it's okay because it feels

so good in there. So hot."

By then he had about half of his cock in me and I made him stop so I could get used to the feel of it up there. It had hurt a little, just at the beginning but once the head was in, past the part where it kind of flares out, it was okay. In fact, it was beginning to feel good in a strange sort of way; maybe like when you have to go to the bathroom real bad but you can't right then so you have to hold it for a while. Well, not just like that but... I don't know. It just felt good is all.

"Is it all right, Jeffey? Can I... I mean, I'm getting real close and ... and I want it all the way in before I... you know."

When I said okay he pushed all the way in and that felt good too, suddenly filling up with him. Or with his cock anyway. He wrapped his arms around my belly and pulled me tight up against him and then he laid his head on my shoulder.

"Oh, Jeffey, please don't move. It feels so good in there, so tight. I never felt anything like it. Never."

I hadn't either. I began to have chills or something and it was like there was this big bubble inside me and getting bigger. I could feel it all over me but especially in my dick and up my ass, too, up where Brian's cock was resting. I felt it at my hole, too, where Brian's cock seemed to be getting bigger and harder.

"Oh, Jeffey, I'm gonna shoot. I can't stop it, I'm gonna shoot off."

He did, too, and I actually felt his cum squirt out inside me. When that happened my bubble burst and suddenly I was shooting off too, way past the drain in the floor.

It took both of us a minute or two to catch our breath and then Brian slowly pulled himself out of me. "Man, that was something," he said, stepping in under the shower and soaping up his cock which was still pointing at the ceiling. "Was it okay? I mean, I didn't hurt you too much or anything, did I?"

I laughed. "I guess not, seeing how I shot off about the same time you did."

He looked at my dick which was just starting to go soft and he grinned. "I thought you did but I couldn't be sure. But I'm glad you did 'cause that means maybe we can do it again, huh?" He winked at me and went back to washing himself.

The next day, in the showers after practice, Brian was hardly

wet before I noticed that his cock was beginning to go hard. A couple of the other guys noticed too and teased him about it until he just grabbed a towel and covered it up. Later, out in the locker room I said maybe he should jack off more so he wouldn't show everyone how horny he was.

He shook his head and said, "Even if I did it wouldn't help. It was seeing your ass in there and thinking about what happened yesterday that did it. Besides, I did jack off this morning, thinking about the way we did it. It was okay but it sure didn't feel as good as being inside you." He patted me on the butt, the way Coach Bowers does sometimes. "I think you got me spoiled."

A couple of days later the coach asked for volunteers to stay late and help clean up the place because Dr. Akers, the president, was bringing some people through that might give some money to the college. Since it was Friday night most of the guys said they had things to do but Brian spoke right up and said he'd help. He also volunteered me which kind of ticked me off but then I thought what the heck, why not? I didn't have anything else to do anyway.

The cleanup only took a couple of hours and towards the end Brian seemed to be kind of dragging his heels a little. I saw why when he said to the coach that he probably wanted to get on home and we could finish up by ourselves. Then he asked if it would be okay for us to grab a shower when we were done and I knew right away what he had in mind. I was kind of glad he did because I wanted to try it again too but I didn't like to ask.

Coach Bowers was happy to go and said sure, we could shower if we wanted. Just be sure the place was really cleaned up and don't take all night.

We finished straightening up pretty quick after that and then stripped down for our shower. I could see that Brian was hard, ever before he took his jock off and he didn't seem the least bit embarrassed by it. In fact, it was kind of like he was showing off and letting me know he was really horny. I wasn't hard yet but I got that way when Brian put his hand on my ass while we walked down to the showers. I bet we looked kind of funny, walking along with our dicks flopping around out if front of us

like they were leading the way.

We didn't even turn the showers on before Brian stood behind me and let me feel his dick pressing in between by buns and poking around my hole. He held out his hand and showed me a tube of something. "I got some new stuff, Jeffey," he said. "It's real slick and won't burn at all like the soap did." He spread some of the stuff between my buns and I guess he coated his dick with it too because when he pressed it against my hole again it just slid in as easy as could be. It didn't hurt at all either, not even when the head pushed in. It just felt... I don't know. It just felt good.

Brian slipped in all the way and put his arms around me, so one hand was on my belly and one on my chest, holding me so tight against him that I couldn't move.

"Is it okay, Jeffey?" he asked, his voice kind of low sounding and sort of raspy.

"Yeah, it's fine," I said and was surprised that my voice came out just like his, raspy and low. It was kind of hard to concentrate because he began to push in and out of me and all I could think about was how good it felt. He was also fooling around with one of my tits, squeezing and rubbing it and that felt great too, almost like my tit was connected to my balls or something.

Then he went in at a different angle and hit something that sent like electric shocks into my dick and made me suck in my breath. Then he did it again and the shocks made me almost double over.

"What's the matter, Jeffey? You hurt?" Brian stopped and held himself still in me. I straightened up and squeezed my ass down on his dick. "No. I'm okay. It just... I don't know." I pushed back against him and he started moving in me again, faster than before.

My dick was dribbling out that slick stuff like crazy and I was getting pretty close to shooting off when Brian went rigid and bit my ear. "Oh, God, Jeffey, here it comes. I'm gonna..." He didn't say any more, just grunted and then let go inside me. He held on to me, not moving, for the first couple of shots and I really did feel it, his cum, squirting out into me. Then he groaned and started moving again, fast, short strokes and it felt like he shot out more cum every time he pushed himself into

me.

When he was through he pushed in again, as far as he could, and held me while he caught his breath. Then he put both his hands on my butt, squeezing my buns together and pulling out, real slow.

"Man, you are definitely spoiling me, Jeff," he said, turning on the water and getting under the shower. "I've never felt anything like that. If I had you around all the time I bet I'd never have to jack off again."

I turned on the shower next to him and got wet. My ass was still slick from that stuff he'd used and I let a couple of fingers slip inside while I washed. That felt so good I soaped up my hand and started working on my dick which was still hard from having Brian inside me.

"Wait. Don't do that yet." Brian splashed water in my crotch, rinsing the slick soap off my dick. "Come on. Let's go dry off."

By the time we got to the locker room Brian was hard again. He squeezed some of that gel stuff out on his hand and then rubbed it all over his cock. When he was all slicked up he turned me around, facing my locker and then pushed his cock into me. He pushed in fast, filling me up with himself all at once. Then he began stroking his cock in me long, fast strokes where he almost pulled out and then pushed back in so fast I hadn't yet lost the feel of his cock inside me. I grabbed hold of my dick and started working it but Brian pulled my hand away.

"No. Not yet. I'll tell you when." He did it hard and fast until I thought I was going to come anyway, without even touching myself.

Suddenly Brian sat down on the bench behind him, pulling me with him so I was sitting on his cock, forcing it even deeper inside me. "Now, Jeffey, now," he panted in my ear. "Bring yourself off and let me feel it. Make your ass do that clenching thing around my dick."

I didn't have to do anything. I barely touched my dick and it went off, shooting cum across the aisle and into my locker.

"That's it, Jeffey. Oh yeah, do that." I felt Brian start to come inside me; after a couple of shots he began thrusting against me and making me bounce up and down on his cock.

We both came for a long time, longer than Brian had in the shower. "It's what you do inside," he said when we were back in the showers. "When you come it's like your ass grabs onto my dick and won't let go. You get all tight around me and... I don't know how to say it but it sure is a great way to come."

When we left the gym Brian said he was hungry so we went to Gino's, a pizza place just down from the campus and he bought me dinner. After a couple of beers I went to the rest room and when I came back Brian had a funny look on his face. He leaned across the table and said, "You know, just watching that gorgeous ass of yours... I'd take you home and spend the night in you if my brother wasn't there." When we left Gino's, Brian patted me on the butt. "I'll ask my brother when his next trip out of town is, okay?"

On Tuesday, Brian twisted his ankle during practice and the coach told me to help him back to the locker room. Inside, Brian stopped hobbling and hollered, "Anyone here? We got an injured man."

When nobody answered he put his hands inside the back of my gym shorts and squeezed my buns. "I just got to get in your ass, Jeffey. Okay?" He didn't wait for me to say anything, he just pushed my shorts down and pressed against me so I could feel how hard he was. Then he grabbed that tube of slick stuff and before I even got my jock off he had his arm around my chest and was pushing his cock into me.

As soon as he was all the way in he pulled back, almost all the way out and then shoved himself back in. He did it again, fast, and kept doing it that way until he came, his cum gushing out inside me so hot I could feel it.

As soon as he was through he pulled out and patted my buns. "God that felt good," He laughed. "Just what I needed for a miraculous recovery." He kicked out of his shorts and jock which were around his ankles and started to take his shoes off. "You need to get yourself off? I'll watch the door if you want."

I shook my head. I really did want to get off but it would have seemed funny, jacking off with Brian hanging around waiting for me to finish. Besides, I really wanted to do it with Brian inside me. We hit the showers instead which was a good

thing because right after we did the coach came in to see how Brian was doing. I tried to hide the fact that I was still half hard but he saw anyway; he laughed and shrugged, letting me know he didn't care. When we came out of the shower Coach Bowers taped up Brian's ankle and told him to stay off it for a while. He didn't tell him to skip practice the next day though.

Brian seemed to calm down some after that, always running off to the library to study after practice. He still looked at me that sort of special way he had and touched my butt when no one was looking though, and he did put himself in me a couple of times when no one was around. Then one day, a couple of weeks later, in the locker room after practice, he said, "You got plans for tonight?"

I shrugged. "When tonight?"

He got a kind of funny smile on his face. "All of it. My brother's not gonna be home tonight and we could... you know."

I looked down at this crotch and saw he'd gone hard. "You want to, don't you Jeffey? Please?" I nodded. I really did want to. We hurried getting dressed so none of the other guys would catch us and tease us about getting hard in the locker room.

We picked up a couple of pizzas and ate them at Brian's house, along with a few beers his brother had left in the fridge. Then we went up to Brian's bedroom.

I wondered how we were going to do it -- I mean, we'd only ever done it standing up in the shower or sitting on the bench that one time – but Brian had it all figured out. He pulled back the sheet and put a big pillow right in the middle of the bed. "You lay on that," he said. "It'll lift your ass up, make it easier for me to go in. Go in all the way, man!"

"I don't know – "

"Yeah, it'll be easy. So easy." He folded a towel and laid it on the pillow so when I came it wouldn't get all over. When I was laid out, the pillow under me, he gave me another one for my head. Then he climbed on the bed and pushed my legs apart. I felt him spread the cool, slick lubricant on my ass and then squirt some inside me. "I gotta grease you up real good," he said in a horse voice, "cause I'm so horny I just gotta shove it in you and get real deep real quick. Hold on Jeffey. Here it comes."

I felt his cock rub over my hole a couple of times and then he pushed it in all the way, filling me up with his hard cock. Then he lay still for a while, I think so he wouldn't shoot off right away. It felt funny, him lying on my back but it felt kind of good, too, like he was covering me and protecting me or something. When he moved around, getting more comfortable and maybe in a little deeper I felt his balls slide over me and then rest there, on top of mine. I imagined I could feel their weight, pressing against my own balls and the bubble really began to expand inside me.

Brian groaned and told me how good it felt inside me and how he was really close to letting go. The feel of his warm breath in my ear made me shiver and then my bubble burst and I couldn't help it – my dick swelled up the way it does and before I could even say anything to Brian I came, my dick jerking around under me and shooting out cum so hot I could feel it on my belly.

When my dick let out its first shot Brian whispered in my ear, "You're starting to come, aren't you? I can feel it. Oh man... me too, just from you doing it." He held real still and didn't move until he'd let go with a couple of big shots and then he began stroking his cock in me, really fast. That seemed to make me come all the more -- until I thought maybe it might never stop.

Brian didn't pull out after he was through, he just relaxed, pressing me down into the pillow with his weight. "You mind if I stay in you a while, Jeffey? Just until I go soft?"

I said okay. I loved the feel of his cock up inside me and somehow it was even better with the feel of his body pressing down on mine.

After a while he started moving again, pulling back just a little and then pressing in, doing it real slow and gentle. "Is that okay, Jeffey? I mean, just poking around in there? I feel so damn good, inside your ass. It's so warm and slick in there." He moved a little faster, building up speed until he was slamming into me and pulling back as fast as he could. Then he let out a yell and came, switching to fast, short strokes until he was finished and collapsed back against my back.

"Oh, Jeffey," he breathed in my ear, giving me goose bumps all up and down my arms, "I couldn't help it. I just had to

come again. You mind?"

"No. It's okay. I... It doesn't hurt or anything."

Brian sighed and I think maybe he dozed off for a while and I felt his cock shrink up a little bit; he never did go all the way soft. I slept too, a little, and woke when Brian started doing it again, this time with long, slow strokes, sometimes even pulling all the way out and then gently going back in until he was pressed tight against my butt and his balls were back resting on top of mine. He was so slow and gentle that I guess I drifted in and out of sleep some and that bubble built up inside me so slowly I hardly noticed until it was ready to burst. When it did I came for a long time. Brian came too, starting just after I did and that made it better, feeling him shooting off inside me again.

Afterward neither one of us said anything. We just kind of let ourselves drift back to sleep and then, sometime in the middle of the night, Brian finally went soft and let himself slip out of me.

In the morning Brian woke up hard again. "I suppose it's just a pee hard-on but let's see, okay?" I guess I was still slick from the night before because he put his cock against me and it just slipped right in. He talked to me while he moved, whispering in my ear how good it felt to be in my ass and then a little later how he was getting close and had to back off for a while.

"You know what I like best, Jeffey? When you come. God, when you come it always brings me off. Like last night. I wasn't anywhere near ready but when I felt you start to shoot off I went off too, just like that." He started moving again, nice long strokes. "Can you come now, Jeffey? And bring me off with you?"

I knew I couldn't. I had to pee and my dick wasn't even hard under me. I told him that and he said, "Damn. Well, I guess I'll just have to do it myself." He pulled back until just the head of his cock was in me and began working it in and out of my hole, pulling at my ass muscle with every short stroke. That felt really good and I started to get hard but then he came, shooting off just inside me and even pulling back a little so some of his cum hit the outside.

When we were cleaning up in the shower Brian said, "You know what I said? About you bringing me off when you come? How about if we get someone to bring you off while I'm inside you? Like, say, someone's blowing you – you know, someone sucking your cock while I'm doing it to you?" He started getting hard, just talking about it and when I thought about it so did I. What would that feel like, someone sucking on my dick while Brian was...

"Come on, Brian. Who'd want to do that?"

Brian cocked his head and winked at me. "A guy I know. You want me to ask him?

My dick was so hard by that time that it hurt. "Yeah. Ask him."

He nodded and then put his hand on my butt, turning me around. "Think how it's going to feel," he said, pushing his soapy cock into me. "A hot mouth on your dick while I'm inside you, doing this." He was doing it with long, fast strokes and it only took me a minute or two to bring myself off with my hand and when I did Brian started shooting inside me.

Afterward, while we were drying off he said, "I'll try to set it up for next week, okay? I think my brother will be gone again so we'll have all night."

Several days later Brian stopped me outside my Ag Machinery class. "Friday. Eight o'clock. Okay?" he swatted me on the butt and walked off without even waiting for me to answer.

When I got to Brian's Friday night the other guy was already there, a big, beautiful blond guy I'd seen around campus a few times. Brian said his name was Bob and we all sat around drinking a beer and trying to think of stuff to say. Finally Brian put his beer down and said, "The hell with this. Let's just go do what we all want to. Okay?"

Bob stood up and shrugged out of his tee shirt. "I'm game. Where's the bedroom?"

I was kind of embarrassed to take my pants off because I was already hard and even leaking a little of that slick stuff but Brian and Bob didn't care; when they took down their pants there were both as hard as I was. Bob reached out and took hold of my dick, smearing the slickness over the head with his

thumb. "Nice," he said. "Very nice."

We all got on the bed and I wondered how this w[as going to] work but Brian had worked it all out. He told me t[o get on] my hands and knees and then he got on his knees behind me. Bob slid in between our legs. I thought I'd be embarrassed for someone to watch, to see what Brian did to me but I forgot all about that when I felt Bob's warm, wet tongue slide over my balls. Nobody had ever touched me there and it felt so wonderful I guess I let out a groan.

Brian stopped pushing his cock into me. "You okay, Jeffey?"

Bob sucked one of my balls clear into his mouth and I groaned again but I pushed back on Brian to let him know it was okay. He put his hands on my hips to steady me and pushed all the way in. I could tell he was close to shooting off already because he held himself still in me and he was breathing really hard.

I felt my ball slip out of Bob's mouth and he moved around a little between my legs. Then he... well, I guess he just swallowed my dick – all the way down. I let out a yelp and came, right in his throat. Brian came too, just as soon as I did and he began sliding his cock in and out of me, fast.

Bob started making this funny noise and I was afraid maybe I was choking him but he didn't try to back away. Then I realized he was coming too and that made me shoot off some more.

When we had all settled down Brian pulled out of me and got off the bed. "Jesus, Bob, what'd you do, come on my back?" He brushed himself just above the butt and then sniffed his hand. "Shit, you did, didn't you? All over my damn back." He headed for the bathroom. "Now I gotta take a shower."

Bob looked at me with a grin and shrugged his shoulders. "I guess I wasn't too careful with my aim -- but then I was kind of busy, wasn't I? That's one hell of a slab of meat you're packing there, you know it?" I guess I blushed pretty good when he said that. I mean, I know my dick's kind of special and all but no one's ever said anything about it. Not out loud like that.

"Hey, don't get embarrassed. If my dick was as big and pretty as yours you can bet I'd be showing it off." I looked down at his stuff and I didn't think it was so small. Probably

bigger than Brian's but I didn't say anything.

"You want another beer, Jeff?" Brian came out of the bathroom with a towel still in his hand. I nodded and Bob said, "Yeah, me too," so Brian went downstairs to get them. When he came back we sat on the bed and talked football. Brian seemed surprised that Bob knew so much about it but Bob said, "Hell, being on the varsity team all the way through high school and the first two years of college, you learn a lot about the game."

While we were talking Brian slipped his fingers down the crack between my buns and when I looked in his crotch I could see that the farther he went, the more his cock started to rise up. Bob noticed too and he slid off the bed to go in between Brian's legs. When he took Brian's cock in his mouth I could see he really liked it and I wondered what he felt, sucking on another guy's cock. Brian put his hand on Bob's head and pushed it all the way down. "Oh, yeah, cocksucker, take it all." At the same time he pressed his other hand against my ass, telling me what he wanted to do. I got up on the bed and kneeled like I had before.

"Okay," he said to Bob. "Come off it but leave it wet and slick so I can put it where it belongs." The next thing I knew Brian was kneeling behind me, shoving his cock back into me.

When Bob started to move in between our legs Brian said, "No. Not that way. I don't want your slime all over me again. Come in the other way."

Bob moved around to the head of the bed and pulled me up on my arms so he could wriggle in underneath me. I closed my eyes, concentrating on the feel of Brian's cock and waiting for what Bob was going to do to mine. When he took my dick in his mouth I gasped and Brian told him to be careful and not bring me off too fast. It felt so good in my ass he wanted to stay there a while.

When I opened my eyes I was looking right down into Bob's crotch. His bush I saw was really thick and kind of wiry looking and his dick was laying off to the side, like it was really heavy and full. While I was looking it moved, stretching out and then pulling away from its resting place. Before long it was standing almost straight up and Bob took it in his fist, working it the same way I do mine.

Brian was using his long, slow strokes and he kept hitting that place up inside me that feels so good. Along with that Bob was doing something to my dick with his tongue which was making the bubble inside me grow up pretty fast. I tried to hold it back by watching Bob jerk himself off, concentrating on it but it didn't help much. It just felt so good, my dick in Bob's mouth and Brian moving in my ass that I just couldn't stop it. And when that bubble burst it exploded.

Then, I don't know why, while I was coming, I ducked my head and went down on Bob. I mean, I just sucked his dick into my mouth and went up and down on him and made him come in my mouth. And all the time I was coming in his mouth and Brian was bucking around in my ass, shooting his stuff inside me.

When it was over Brian pulled out of me, still hard and yelled at Bob to get dressed and get out. When I got up too he pointed at me and told me to stay. Bob asked what the hell was going on but Brian would only say for him to get out.

When Bob was gone Brian wouldn't look at me. Finally he said, real sad like, "Why'd you have to go and spoil it, Jeffey? Why'd you have to turn out to be a cocksucker like him? Shit. I thought you were a regular guy, just like me and now... Shit!" He reached out and put his hand on my buns, letting it rest there for a second before he moved his fingers into the crack. "No. I can't anymore. Knowing that you're... a queer." He took his hand away and wiped it on the bed sheet. "You better get dressed and go too, Jeff. It's a damn shame, too, because I really did like doing it to you."

I never said a word. I didn't know what I'd say so I just pulled on my clothes and walked out, down the stairs and out the door. I was sorry but I did it.

Bob was standing on the sidewalk outside. "I waited," he said, falling into step with me, "to see if you were okay. What was all that about, anyway?"

"I don't know. He said he couldn't, you know, do that with me anymore because he thinks I'm a queer now. I guess because I did that to you."

Bob stopped and stared at me. "Wait a minute. He's been fucking you for all this time and he thought you were straight?"

"Not fucking. I mean we were just sort of playing around, helping..."

"Fucking. What I saw tonight was fucking, Jeff. Plain and simple fucking. And in more ways than one."

I thought about it for a bit and I saw he was right. Brian had been fucking me all along -- and I had been liking it. "So I guess maybe I am a queer then, huh?" I could hardly look at him but he just grinned and put his arm around my shoulders, starting to walk down the street again.

"Not necessarily. But maybe. Does that bother you?"

"I don't know. I... I don't feel any different than I did before – well, before Brian started..." I said the word because it was true. "Started fucking me. How do you tell if you're queer?"

Bob laughed. "Hey, man, damned if I know. But why don't you come home with me and we'll see if we can't figure out some sort of test, okay?"

I passed the test an hour or so later when Bob kissed me and I kissed him back because it felt so good – and I thought maybe I was falling in love with him.

MAKING ENDS MEET

James Hosier

It all started at dinner one night when I just happened to mention that my allowance might have covered my expenses at one point but no longer.

"Woomph!" The volcano erupted. The initial bang was my dad slamming his knife and fork on the table. Then we had the long sticky lava flow of 'Count your lucky stars' containing nuggets which had been buried for years like the holiday in Europe, my model railway and the microscope which I had hardly used. That was followed by the threatening rumble of "making ends meet."

What came out of all this was that my dad's firm (they make built-in kitchens and cupboards) does a lot of direct mail campaigns. If I cared to deliver the letters, I could earn money. Have you ever heard anything so mean? He could have taken out his wallet there and then and my problems would have been over but no, "James must learn the value of money."

Now if you think you're going to read one of those stories about the innocent getting seduced, or one of those stories which end up with the main characters swearing to love each other through thick and thin until they die, forget this one. Turn over a few pages and try the next one. And Michael hasn't promised to finance me through college or given me a gold watch to remember him by - though I sure do cost him a lot.

I had him sussed out the moment he opened the door. What happened was this. It was a really hot day, so I was in shorts. I parked the bike at the end of the block, took the bundle of letters (each one marked BY SPECIAL MESSENGER) and set off. It was a block of small, newish houses, originally surrounded by one big communal grass lawn but humans being humans, each family had planted some sort of barrier to mark off their pathetic little bit of it. So I did the first house, stepped over a flower bed, did the next, jumped over a two-foot-high row of cypress seedlings to do the next and so on. Then there was a rose bush. It wasn't very high and I certainly hadn't forgotten that roses have thorns. Somehow or other, my left leg

landed a bit too soon. I felt the thorn dig in. I swore and managed to pull it out. It started bleeding badly.

Well, I did the next few houses but the blood was becoming a nuisance. Every time I wiped it away, some of it got from my fingers onto the letters. You don't buy fitted furniture from a firm which soaks its advertizing material in blood. Something had to be done so, at the next house I came to, I rang the doorbell.

And that's when I first met Mr. Turner. He was twentysomething, profession uncertain, perhaps a teacher. Dark hair, tall and with the sort of eyes which stare at your crotch while he is talking to your face.

"Mr. Turner?" I asked, handing him the letter.

"Yes."

"I'm sorry to trouble you," I said. "Do you have a sticking plaster? I tore my leg on a thorn."

Like I say, I knew right from the start. Any other guy would have said, 'Sure. Wait there. I'll get one,' not wanting a trail of blood drips on his floor. Not Michael M. Turner.

"Come on in," he said. "Poor old you! How did it happen?"

I explained that I'd been taking short cuts. He made some sort of weak joke about short cuts and, before I knew what was happening, I was lying on his sofa and he was running up the stairs. He returned with enough stuff to stock an accident clinic. There was a bottle of some sort of red fluid, bandages, plasters, a pair of scissors - all laid out on a tray.

"It's a nasty one," he said, glancing at my shorts again. I suspect that the opposite was going through his mind. "It's a nice one" - which, if you're keen on cock, I suppose it is. Nobody's ever complained.

The thorn had gone into the side of my leg just below the knee. Blood had dribbled down to my sock so that had to come off. Then began the process of washing the trail off and it's then when I had no doubt whatsoever of what he had in mind. First he stroked it with a cotton pad, damped in cold water. Then another pad; then another. The first was pretty messy; the second came away slightly pink. By the time he'd gotten to number five they were being discarded as white as they were when they came out of the packets. But he was enjoying

himself and I didn't mind. Lying on a sofa sure beats delivering letters in seventy-eight degrees though, of course, they would have to be delivered.....

"There!" he said, triumphantly as if he'd just taken out a brain tumor. He dabbed the place with some of the red liquid which stung slightly and then put the plaster on as carefully as a man restoring some old master, smoothing it down at the edges.

"You really ought to have a tetanus jab," he said. "I could run you to the hospital."

I said that it wasn't necessary and that my arm was a pincushion anyway. I'd just had my vaccinations updated.

"They don't put tetanus in your arm," he said, smiling. "It goes in here." I'd given him the excuse he'd been wanting. He slid his hand under my butt.

I said I was sure it wasn't necessary, thanked him and went to put my sock on.

"You ought to have something to drink," he said. "You may be in shock."

I ask you! A tiny little puncture from a rose thorn. I never even had shock when I came off the bike in the snow. But it suited my purpose and it was a very hot day so I said 'Thanks' and he went over to the drinks cabinet and concocted a mixture of Coke and whisky.

"I guess I ought to read this, considering you've taken the trouble to deliver it," he said and tore the envelope open. You only had to look round the place to know that there was no way this guy could afford the 'Bavaria' fitted kitchen with its teak-faced ice box and ceramic cooking surfaces. No way he needed one, either, but he studied that pamphlet like it was a matter of life and death. If my dad had been there he'd have gotten even more swollen-headed than he is. It was "superb," "brilliant," and so well-designed.

There's a coupon on the back of the pamphlet which people can fill in and get information about the other products. He filled it in. That took time. Time to find a pen. Time to find something to rest the paper on - and all the time he kept looking at my midriff. I grinned encouragingly.

"How old are you?" he asked. Aha! A cautious one.

"Sixteen," I replied.

This amazed him. By now it was all I could do to stop myself from laughing. I'm a swimmer and diver. I'm the guy who never has trouble getting a beer. A fraction under six feet tall and he couldn't believe that I was sixteen! I had to show him my driving license which, of course, gave him my name as well.

"Sixteen eh?" he said. "Dating?"

"No," I lied.

"I should think the girls are lining up for a guy like you," he said.

I said that I wasn't that interested. The swim pool was more fun than a disco.

There was a long pause. I thought I could read his thoughts, "Where do we go from here?" Well, it does no harm in making them wait. I said I ought to be getting along. He wondered if it might be possible for me to bring the publicity material about the other products personally. I said I would. On the way between his house and the next one I bent down to untie and then re-tie the lace on my right shoe. Give him a good look at the target. He stood at the open door until I was out of sight.

Three days later I was at the pool. So was he, with eyes popping out of his head. Yes, I agreed, it was an amazing coincidence. I wondered how many times he'd been there already waiting for me to show up.

We sat on the pool - side. "You've got a superb body," he said. In fact he wasn't bad himself. Still reasonably slim and all the bulges were muscle. Except one. He crossed his legs. I think I must have blushed.

"Society is strange," he added. "I can say that a girl's got a good body and she's delighted. Say it to a guy - like you for instance - and he thinks I'm gay."

"I never said anything," I replied.

"You probably thought it, eh?"

"Why should it worry me?" I paused. Make him sweat for a few more days or start earning the big bucks immediately? "There's nothing wrong in being gay," I said.

ZING! You could almost hear the strings breaking! I was the most intelligent person he had ever met. To find a sixteen year old with such an open mind was a real revelation. I just lay back and let him continue. The usual spiel. Ancient Greeks,

Michaelangelo, Leonardo da Vinci, Tschaikovsky. A half hour of that made me hungry. I chose Roberto's. It's the classiest place in town. My folks go there and occasionally drag me with them so I was pretty certain to get a good steak - which I did.

I had to award full marks for originality at the end of the meal. I was expecting an invitation to listen to music or see some pictures. Maybe even an 'interesting' video. Michael (He told me to call him that) wanted me to hold one end of the rule so that he could measure up his kitchen - just in case he decided to order a 'Bavaria'. Totally unnecessary. If you order a kitchen, guys come round and measure up for you. It says so in the brochure which he had read so carefully but I wasn't going to tell him so. Thirty minutes later I was kneeling on a tiled kitchen floor, holding one end of a tape and writing down measurements on a pad.

One hour later I was back on the sofa and he was back on his favorite theme. He felt sorry for gays because they had to keep their affairs so quiet, especially if they fell for somebody young. And it was risky. They never knew whether the young guy would shoot his mouth off. That would be death to somebody in a profession. That's when I guessed he was a teacher.

"No young guy is likely to do that," I said. "It would be death to him too. Imagine. 'Hi fellers. Guess what happened to me last night...'"

He laughed. I looked at my watch. Nine o'clock. I sure as hell wasn't going to make the first move. That was his job. I switched on my mental video - usually used in bed. Sandra Rawlings, the girl with the big tits and the pouting lips.. holding her real tight... feeling them up against me.... her mouth pressing on mine. 'Do it to me, James. Do it to me!' It worked. My cock woke up. Michael spotted it pretty quickly. It spared me the ordeal of looking at his photograph album. He stood up to get it and then sat down again. Sat down with some difficulty. He was really aroused.

"I can't get over your build," he said. "Do you train every day?"

"Most days."

"I can believe it. You're all muscle. Real hard muscle." He put a hand on my thigh and squeezed. I smiled. The hand

moved up my leg. "Is this muscle too?" he asked.

"What do you think?" I asked.

"I'd say you had a cucumber in your jeans,"

"Don't like cucumber."

"A marrow then. It sure feels like a marrow. I guess it's nice and ripe too. It feels like it."

"You should know," I said. He was squeezing it thru my jeans.

"Only way to tell is to look at it," he said, in a husky voice.

"Then you'd better get it out, hadn't you?" I said.

The guy who invented jeans was no fool. If I'd been wearing the shorts I had on when I first went there, they would have gotten torn. He couldn't wait. He undid the belt, yanked the zip down and put his hand in. He fumbled around. I did nothing to help him. If a guy can't get a cock through a large triangular opening, he doesn't deserve any reward. Finally, after a struggle, he managed it.

"It's beautiful!" he said.

If there is one thing a cock is definitely not, at least to me, is 'beautiful'. Useful, I grant. Big, in my case, I modestly agree to. The guys in the swimming team make jokes about it and they've never seen it as it was then. All eight inches of it, sticking up out of my jeans and looking strangely white against the denim background, but certainly not beautiful. But one thing I have learned from occasionally helping my dad in the showroom is that if a customer likes a product, you don't disagree and you certainly don't point him elsewhere. Phil Clay - he's on the swimming team - has a cock that makes mine look pretty small.

"Really nice," he whispered. "Do you mind me doing this?"

'This' was his hand, slowly wanking it.

Naturally enough, I didn't answer. 'I hate it' would not have been completely true. 'It's okay' wouldn't have been the enthusiastic response he was after and 'I love it' would have given him the go ahead for more than I was prepared to offer that evening. So I just lay there. He bent his head over my face. I wasn't having that and pushed him off so he diverted his attention to my middle again. I lifted my butt so he could slide everything down and get a real good view.

I wasn't actually prepared for the licking and sucking bit. His tongue went everywhere and I do mean everywhere! There are places which I wouldn't personally savor but the customer is always right and it wasn't doing me any harm. In fact, strictly between you and me, it was a great feeling.

On the order forms in my dad's showroom there is one all important section. It's headed 'Method of Payment' and the sales assistants are told that unless that is filled in, nobody carries anything away - least of all, I thought, themselves - and this guy was really carried away. I wasn't doing too badly in that direction myself. The moans and groans of delight had been artificial at first but he was really getting me going and I hadn't even mentioned the all important payment clause. Some businessman!

It would have been entirely the wrong moment anyway. Even if I had been able to talk, he certainly wasn't. His mouth was full of cock and he was enjoying it.

I tried to think about Sandra. It didn't work. The circumstances were wrong. His hands were under my butt, lifting me so that he could cram as much as possible into his mouth. It felt warm and wet. My balls began to ache and I realized that, with my jeans round my ankles, there was no way I could grab my handkerchief to catch the flood when it came. I remember gasping something about 'a tissue or something'. He didn't seem to hear. At least he took no notice. He just carried on sucking it like a baby on a comforter.

The usual feeling swept over me. The feeling that I usually get in bed. My heart thumped. Sweat ran down my forehead and face. "I'm.... coming!" I gasped and it happened. It was considerably less messy than the sticky fingered, sodden handkerchief bedroom business but I felt guilty about Michael. I need not have been. Believe it or not, he just sucked away. It all went into his mouth. Jet after jet. I saw him swallow. Some of it appeared at the corners of his mouth. He sucked even harder and then let it go. He smiled.

"That was great!" he said and wiped his mouth on the back of his hand. "Do you want to do me?"

Ha! No way! I was annoyed with him for even asking. What the hell did he take me for? I said something about having to get home and swung my legs over the edge of the couch to pull

my clothes up.

"When shall I see you again?" he asked. I said that, if it wasn't for my fiscal problems, I could come any time - which is just about true. Once I had sat next to Phil Clay on a school geography field trip and managed it on the bus under my coat.

I explained the problem. That my mean parents paid me very little and that I had to earn enough to live by delivering advertising pamphlets. That wasn't true, I admit. There had been just one route so far. When you tell one lie, others have to follow. Every day after school, rain or shine, I said. I halved the amount Dad had actually paid me. Michael was shocked and for a moment I was afraid he would call my dad and accuse him of employing slave labor.

But it worked. Fifty bucks a time and he would help with the delivery. All I had to do was leave the ones in his area with him and lie back and enjoy it. Not bad. I suggested a three times a week routine. Dad was thrilled to see me 'take an interest in the firm at last.' Michael was terrific. He got three people to ring me at home and place orders for kitchens.

So, here I am sitting at my new computer writing to you. Seven hundred dollars in the bank already. Since I got over my hang up about touching him, the money has gone up.

He wants to take me away for a weekend soon. I am to choose the place. Florida is favorite, I think - and it won't be a cheap hotel. I know exactly what he wants. His tongue has been in there enough times. I've been getting a bit of practise in at home with a soapy finger. I shan't let on of course. I guess it's just human nature to want to go where no man has gone before. For that reason I won't tell him that Phil Clay has the same goal in mind. I have told Michael about Phil, though. He wants to meet him. I guess that could be arranged – on some sort of percentage basis.

BRADY'S CROTCH

Jack Ricardo

"The sight stopped Dennis in his tracks. Brown, lean, and youthful as Jasper was, nothing could have prepared him for the boy's nether parts. The buttocks were so round and white, they might have been carved out of the new-fallen snow. They practically invited rape.
And that cock . . . Thin at the base, thickening as it extended outward, and curling deliciously leftward near the tip. It was a cock with personality. Dennis imagined he could spend hours just perched on his elbow talking to that cock."
– Robert Rodi, from his comic novel "Kept Boy"

I've been a trucker for some thirty years, driving everything from a pickup to an 18-wheeler, shipping everything from lava lamps to computer chips. I've racked miles up in every state in the union except for that one in the cold north and the other one in the South Pacific.

The first time I got laid was in a truck. The first lover I had was a trucker. I've had more wild sex at truck stops that any man could imagine. I've been sucked off while driving a rig, and I've sucked other truckers off while they sat behind the wheel. I was a damn good cocksucker and a damn good trucker. Was is the key word here. I still consider myself a trucker but now I'm sitting behind a desk and dispatching other men to haul the loads. And I still consider myself a cocksucker, but I haven't been doing much of that lately either. I'm damn near ashamed to admit it, but I haven't had a stiff dick between my lips in over seven years. Crazy, huh? But I got two reasons for this. The damn diseases breeding out there, of course. And the fact that I'm aging and it's showing. My graying hair was confusing me, my wrinkles were intimidating me, and my expanding waist was discouraging me. But Brady set me straight, so to speak.

I have fourteen men and four women working under me, sending each on their way with correct bills of lading. Brady was the last man I hired. His application said he was 21 years

old, but he looked much younger. My eyes told me he was about five-eleven, had green eyes, brown shaggy hair, and a wiry body set comfortably in a pair of well-worn Wrangler jeans. I wouldn't call him handsome, I couldn't call him ugly. He was somewhere in between, and one sexy hunk of man. South Dakota experienced an unexpected blizzard. My entire crew was out on the road. Brady was the last man I sent out.

Once the snow started falling, I began fretting about every single one of them. About ten-thirty, Brady pulled his rig into the lot. He rushed into my office, stomping the snow from his boots. "I was about thirteen miles south of here, Boss, and knew I couldn't make it."

"Smart move, Brady. This fucking weather is gonna get a lot worst before it gets better."

Brady was standing next to the space heater I keep at the side of my desk, rubbing his hands together and hopping from foot to foot to break the chill from his bones.

"I don't even know if my pickup's gonna make it home," he moaned. "Those roads are building up fast. Can I stay here for the night?"

"Sure, son," I said without hesitation. I care for my truckers and I've shared my back room more than once. Just the room, not my single bed.

"Thanks, Boss."

The back room is not big but it's comfortable. And it's warm, verging on hot, thanks to a Franklin stove I keep stoked during our long cold winters. It's also kind of a pig pen, with laundry all over the place and enough dust to coat the Mojave. I told Brady to go inside and get warm and I'd dig out one of the canvas beds. I found a cot in the store room.

After I shut the office lights, I went back to the room. And I was floored. Brady had shucked off his hat and coat and was standing in front of the stove. The fiery glow from the burning wood was the only light. In his hand and under his nose was a pair of my discarded briefs. When he turned to me, my face turned beet red. It wasn't from the raging heat of Mr. Franklin, either.

I sputtered, "Here's...here's...here's..." I turned away, set the cot down, and muttered, "This place is kind of a dump."

Why, I was asking myself, was I so flustered? He was the one sniffing my shorts not me sniffing his. Hell, I was the experienced one here, wasn't I? Yeah, jerking off my dick with a wet fist. My balls weren't exactly busting with confidence. Brady tossed my shorts back on the floor with the rest of the crud and didn't think nothing of it. Maybe he was just wiping his brow or blowing his nose, I decided. "Some hot coffee'll warm you up," I said, grabbed a couple of mugs and filled them from the ready pot on the stove. We sat on crates around the broad wooden spool and talked about rough roads and long rides.

It was getting damn hot in that close room. And not only from the stove. Dribbles of sweat were leaking from my armpits to my rib cage. The small talk petered out into a staring match. My brow was beading with sweat, my heart was racing, my balls were itching. I had about all I could take and told myself, *what the hell,* and said, "It's hotter in here than Nevada in August."

I unlaced my boots, slipped off my shirt and tossed my jeans on the floor. I sat back down in my shorts and socks. Brady's eyes never left me for one split second while I was stripping. He hugged his mug with both hands, brought it to his lips, and sipped. A bare hint of a smile broke through his lips before he followed suit, tugging his boots off, unbuttoning his shirt, unzipping his jeans. My tongue was probably lapping at the floor. Brady's briefs were the same brand as mine. The white cotton hugged his cheeks, creased his crack, and had me breathing deeper and louder than a hound in heat. The front of his shorts was outlined with a cut cock set atop a set of balls that filled his pouch and made you want to get down on your knees and thank God for snowy weather. Brady may not have been the handsomest guy I'd ever seen, but his crotch was downright beautiful!

A familiar tingling I thought was long dead was resurrected. My nuts churned and damn near boiled over as I felt a spurt of juice ooze from my dickhead. I inhaled, got up, moved to my bed and sat leaning my back against the wall and dangling my feet on the floor. I downed my coffee and set the mug on the crate next to the bed. A heartbeat was pounding my chest louder than a big base drum.

Brady stayed on his seat, his ankles linked together yet his legs spread-eagled, his eyes warm. The thin line of dark where the legs of his shorts didn't quite meet the flesh of his inner thighs seemed to give off an enticing aroma of sweat from a set of hairy balls sneaking through. The thatch of brown hair that centered his chest shined like holiday icicles. The hairy brush that grew at his belly button and slipped into the elastic of his shorts was a waving red flag. I lifted my legs onto the bed and hugged my knees, cradling a beautiful cock that had grown to full mast and was pulsing. Brady's eyes were staring into mine when he dropped a hand to fondle the sack of his shorts, then brought that hand to his nose and sniffed. If that wasn't an invitation, then all those long-gone years were wasted and I didn't learn a fucking thing. My insides were as hot as the iron stove, my cock was as hard. I unfolded my legs. My cock was throbbing unashamedly and stretching the white cotton of my shorts all to hell. I wrapped my fingers around the shaft and formed a dick-headed tent. A dark splotch oozed at the peak. I slid a finger over the slime and brought it to my lips. I licked.

"I've been sitting out front and working my ass off all day," I said. My voice cracked. "These shorts I'm wearing smell a helluva lot better than those." I squeezed my cotton-coated cock and nodded to the laundry on the floor. The snow brushing against the window echoed like trickles of sparks on tin siding.

Brady inhaled deeply, rose from his chair. He again was fingering his shorts as he took the three steps to my bed.

I sighed from the exertion of bottled-up anxiety.

Brady dropped to his haunches at the side of the bed, and set both hands on my knees. The touch of his fingers on my skin were lapping flames. He bowed to my shorts and nudged his nose between the outlined shaft of my cock and the bulge of my nuts, then started sniffing around, grunting quietly, contentedly, happily. My mind was spinning. Too many years had passed since the last time a man buried his face in my lap. The feeling was almost too much to bear. Brady was licking, wrapping his tongue over my cotton shaft, licking at my hidden balls. I was twisting my fingers through his hair. Forgotten thrills began flowing over me like hot water on a freezing day. I was shifting my hips in a rhythm that Brady encouraged as he

devoured my shorts, slobbering over the soppy material, gnawing my cock through the cotton, salivating. My cock quivered and vaulted. I was drowning in agonizing blissful sensations. Prickles of chills zoomed through my body. My insides were quaking.

I couldn't help it; I began moaning. The pent-up juices in my balls were churning too quickly and bubbling to a point of no return. I grabbed Brady's head and pulled his face up. His eyes were bright, his mouth was open, his breathing was harsh, his lips were shining. I brought his face to mine and kissed those succulent lips. Our tongues became partners in combat as he grabbed my face with his hands, clutched it, and crushed his lips to mine. We began to devour each other. I slipped my hands under his armpits – the sweat and dank hairs sending a torrent of sensations to my brain – and hauled him up between my legs until the crotch of his shorts was joined with the crotch of mine, until the hairs of his chest were merging and searing with the hairs of mine, until I was able to wrap my hands around his back and hang on like a caring dad with his loving son. The memories of past and almost forgotten torrid nights flashed through my mind but was discarded by the man, the very real man I was holding here and now. By Brady. We both began mumbling unintelligibly into each other's face, groaning, grunting, pressing our shorts and our flesh into each other, our mouths two tunnels of fire bringing us to the brink.

Brady broke away in the nick of time. He pulled off and stood up, muttering, "Wait, wait..." huffing, trembling. I was damn grateful for the rest. It gave me a chance to air my lungs. The simmering in my nuts slowed. The embers were resting... though not extinguished. Young Brady was standing in front of me, his eyes wild. My eyes ached and my insides turned to mush just watching him. He closed his eyes, stretched his neck backward, lifted his arms, ran his fingers through his hair, and was gasping for air. The outline of his firm cock was quivering against the white of his shorts, his chest was expanding, contracting. The tangy smell of the sweat from his pits was an aphrodisiac. The sheen of perspiration on his chest built up a radiating heat that scorched my innards.

I was just as heady, just as sweaty, just as rushed. The cock in my spit-soaked shorts was trembling as recklessly as his. My

chest was heaving just as rapidly and just as heavily. Brady dropped his hands from his head and sexclaimed, "You are something else, Boss! You know how long I been jerking off dreaming of doing just this?" He swept his fingers over the swampy hair of his chest. "Picturing that rugged body of yours in my head...licking my lips over your face, just being with a man who knows what it's all about and smelling the sweat in his shorts and sucking his cock and...and...and...I...I...I..." He caught his breath. "You are one fucking man, Boss..."

I was listening to his words but my eyes were streaming over his sleek body, over his straggling head of hair, over the spiny hairs of his chest, his legs, his biceps, over his underwear packed with the potent aroma of sex. I sat up and reached out, fondling the tantalizing pouch of his briefs, moving my fingers down the thickened shaft, fisting it. Remembering, luxuriating, loving. His cock fought back, slamming into my hand.

Brady shifted his feet and spread his legs. I cupped his balls and leaned down to run my tongue over his pulsating cock. My fingers slipped into the legs of his briefs and prodded his bare balls. I shivered, ached with passion, and was soon sucking on Brady's shorts, his cock, relishing the smell and the taste of his rank sweat, thrilled with the juice seeping through the peehole of his cockhead and through the cotton, ecstatic to be gnawing a cock again. Brady's cock. I grabbed his hips and groaned into his shorts, nudging my nose lower until I was able to lick and snort and sniff my way to the cloth sack of his balls. I swallowed his nuts, the cotton harsh inside my mouth. Brady mooned quietly grabbed my head and shifted his fiery crotch, crunching his shorts into my face while I ate them, ate his cock, ate his balls and pigged-out in remembrance.

Brady leaned forward. His hands trailed over my back while I strained to keep my face plastered to his cock. I measured his cockhead with my tongue, nibbling the crown, suctioned his slimy juice straining through the cotton. His fingers found the rim of the back of my shorts and poked inside, sliding downward, as he stretched his back over mine and began licking the perspiration from my skin.

Brady's crotch broke from my face as he fell back on the bed, taking me with him. We flung our legs, our arms, struggled. His crotch slammed into my face, he shoved his face between

my legs. I wrestled my arms over his thighs, pulled them apart, and stuffed my nose in the leg of his shorts until I was able to lick the hairs and suck up his bare nuts. I moaned, Brady moaned. He was chewing my cock through my shorts. We lay on our sides. My legs were clasped over his head as he began sucking my cock in a way I could never imagine – earnestly sucking me off through my shorts. I let his balls fall from my mouth and returned the feeling, gobbling down on the cock still packed in the pouch of his briefs. I rammed my hands in the back of his shorts and began to knead and fondle the flesh of his firm little ass. His cock began quivering uncontrollably between my lips. Along with my drenched shorts, Brady had my entire cock in his throat. One of his hands was inside my shorts and tugging my nuts while fingers began tickling my crack before one finger dug into my hole. I stiffened and clamped my legs firmly around Brady's head, slammed my hips forward and swallowed as much as Brady as I could get in my mouth. I was rewarded with a gush that began shooting from his cockhead. I lifted my mouth; his cum was seeping through the cotton. I rubbed my face round and round the shooting cock, his thick juice oozing over my face, my cheeks, my chin, my neck. My nuts exploded and spit out spurts of cotton-strained cum that was coating Brady's mouth. His finger slid deeply into my hole until I felt his knuckle stop further penetration. I found his hole and shoved my finger clear up his ass. Brady yelped, his mouth full of cock, full of cum, full of underwear as his ass muscles strangled my finger. I became a blob of contentment as his load weakened out, leaving my face white-washed and overjoyed.

    The only sounds in the night was the snow slashing against the window, the only light was the flickering flames from the stove. It was a full ten minutes before we had the energy to entangle ourselves from each other. We got up and stripped naked. I grabbed a blanket and we both hit the sack. We cuddled in warmth and snoozed in each other's arms till morning.

    I was the first one up. I wrapped a blanket over my bare ass, fed and lit the stove, and made a new pot of coffee. A snow drift covered most of the window. By the time Brady woke up, the room was fired again.

He joined me, and pecked me a kiss. I poured him a mug of steaming hot coffee. Clutching the blanket over his shoulders and blowing off the steam from his mug, Brady said, "You know, Boss, you're like nobody else I ever been with."

"Yeah, huh," I said, my ingrained cynicism showing through. "I was here that's all."

"Hey, man, don't put yourself down. You are one hot fucking man. You been around the block. It's written all over your face like a map of the Black Hills. You got what it takes. You know, most guys my age just don't get it. They just wanna take it all off and slam, bam, see ya around. But not you. You really get off on being with me. *Me*," he emphasized, "not just another hard dick. Me and my underwear. And you and yours. We got some stuff in common. Thanks, Boss."

No, I thought, thanks to you, Brady. You brought me back.

BURT'S TRUNKS

Terry McLearn

For as long as I can remember I've been getting excused from gym class. Having had asthma as a child, my doctor signed a note at the start of each term and that has always been that. I'm not happy or unhappy about it; it's simply a fact.

But now, in my senior year, I return to find the swim coach has quit and been replaced by someone named Burt, with his big dark eyes and his handsome boyish face – the kind of face one might expect of a hometown hero returning from battle. Probably no more than twenty-nine or thirty, he's given me a reason to *want* to be in gym class. Burt, his short hair just beginning to recede. His tennis shirts pulling across the hard round muscles of his chest and these short, skimpy trunks that hug the tops of his hairy legs. How I love his legs. The way the huge thighs took shape when he runs up and down the stairs, usually scaling two or three steps at a time. Or the way his over-developed calves pulse and flex when he jogs laps around the baseball field. And how I loved those trunks. I assumed he wore Speedo-type swim suits before they were ever the fashion. He has a seemingly perpetual bulge beckoning from within the skin-tight fabric, and I know he's seen me staring at the sight.

He calls me in his office. He sits behind his desk and twirls a yellow whistle around his finger. He says he's looking up everyone's file and asks about my excuse. I say little. He tells me no one gets off without paying their dues. If I can't swim, and he isn't buying that at all, then I could help out and support my team in other ways. Keep time at the meets or clean up the locker room. Maybe hand out towels.

"Don't you want to be part?" He stands up from behind his desk and walks toward me. His legs at this close range looking better than I'd ever imagined. Arms folded, his biceps big and straining at the thin knit of his shirt sleeves. "What's the matter?" He just about barks at me. Can't I speak? Am I some spoiled little fairy who can't do anything more than stand there in silence? I don't answer. I look at those trunks. Those unbelievable purple trunks and that warm round bulge, full and

exaggerated, too big I'm sure for even both my hands. Then I just stare to the floor. Maybe I am, I think to myself. Maybe I am.

I give in. I do keep time for the swim team. I carry a stop watch and clock in records of the events. I hand out nose plugs and towels and then collect those same towels and dirty trunks at the end of every meet. In no time I am nicknamed T-boy, short for towel boy. I like it, though in my wildest dreams I never thought I would, just as I like working with the team. Most of all I like working with Burt. At all the meets I watch Burt. I'm sure everyone does. I notice the girls as they walk by. They stop and their eyes fall to his cock. They linger. Perhaps longer than they should. Burt notices too. He loves it, I know he does. He smiles for them and they giggle. It's easy to see how much Burt likes making teen-age girls giggle.

After practices sometimes I swim. With Tim McAlley or Billy Chance. They are kind to me and encourage me. We do push-ups and sit-ups on the smooth tiled floor. We lift weights in the rec room, to build upper body strength. Sometimes I even swim with Burt himself. Just him and me. My favorite times. My own cock straining at the stretchy nylon of my small swim suit, no where near as big as Burt's, but then not many are.

The year stretches on. I become closer to the team, but not to Burt. He is always quiet and aloof, seeming to be in a constant state of personal thought. I try. I stay after and take more time than usual to clean up the locker room. Sometimes after a swim, I bring him a towel before he showers. A big towel, he always tells me, not one of those skimpy-ass ones. He stands before me in his jock. The shower running behind him and soft hissing clouds of smoke steaming up the glass doors. His chest just right for touching, firm and hairy and his waist narrow and small. I try not to look, but that's impossible when it comes to Burt. I wait. He takes his time. Then as always, just before he gets into the shower, he wraps the towel around him, the jock falls to his feet and he looks my way.

"See you tomorrow, T-boy," he says. He salutes me with a casual flip of his hand. "Good work today." And sometimes he gives me a smile. Not everyday, just sometimes and I love his

smile. I wait for it, disappointed when I don't see it, but making the times he does give it to me, all that much better. I think about him all the time. I have at least a hundred sexual scenarios that I rerun over and over again in my head. At night before I fall asleep.

And in the morning when I wake. I shower and jerk off everyday, my father pounding on the bathroom door screaming that I'll be late. I pay no attention as I shoot oceans of cum to thoughts of Burt in his sexy little trunks. I don't go into much detail. I'm only seventeen and inexperienced, and it is a much simpler time than today. In my dreams I do touch him. I put his imaginary cock, huge and fat to my mouth and suck on it, mimicking the stories I overhear the boys on the swim team tell about their nights parked at the drive-in with their dates.

April passes. The swim meets are almost over. There are still practices, but no where near as many as before. I spend even more time at the gym. Burt never questions it. He just keeps calling me T-boy and every once in a while he smiles. May comes and friends and I celebrate my birthday. I'm eighteen. Legal in my state and we drink Jack Daniels and Ballentine ale. Much too much I'm sure and I'm sick and miss school on the last big meet of the year.

I go to the gym the next day and explain it to Burt. He seems to understand. He smiles a lot today. "Legal," he just keeps saying over and over again, shaking his head and snickering. I start to clean up the locker room and he tells me to leave it. He says the janitor can take care of it and then invites me for a swim.

"One last swim, T-boy," he laughs, and I like the way he says it. We swim together and he talks. Not about anything in particular. Every now and then he jokes about my being "legal." Asks what I intend to do when I leave school. I answer as best I can. I'm not sure myself. We finish our swim and Burt wants to do some weights. I follow. I spot him and he spots me. He stands behind me as I lie on the bench press and his cock hangs over me. I study the hair line of his thighs and deep elastic marks those tight purple trunks I love so much have imprinted into the flesh under his cheeks. Every once in a while he puts his fingers there. He adjusts the leg band and

then the pouch where his beautiful cock lay nestled and I watch, my eyes like metal being drawn irresistibly to a magnet. Two girls happen by.

"Hi, Burt," one of them says. She tilts her head for him as she speaks and puts a finger to her lips. She twirls a thin string of gum around a shiny coral nail.

Burt smiles. The girls watch for a minute and then slowly walk away. Burt and I finish with the weights and go back into the gym. He holds up one of his arms, sculpted and big. He sniffs under it. "Whew!" He shakes his head. "I need a shower. Bring me a towel, T-boy. One of the big…"

"Ones, not one of those skimpy-ass little ones," I finish his sentence for him. I've heard it so many times and know it so well. Burt laughs. He keeps laughing. "You've finally found a sense of humor," he says as I toss him the towel. He jokes with me. "Must have come along with being legal." He is standing in front me in his jock as he has a thousand times before and I am thinking. I don't know which I love more. The sight of him in his jock or in his purple trunks. "Those were some pretty little girls out there today," he says, distracting my train of thought. "Those two are always sniffing around looking for something. A man can get himself into a shitload of trouble around here if he's not careful." Burt hangs the towel around his neck. He looks at me. Something is different today, I think but I don't know what it is.

He pulls at the waistband of his trunks and seems to be studying me. I think I should leave but before I do I want to thank him for all he's done for me. I want to say a proper goodbye. "You don't like little girls, do you T-boy?" he asks suddenly. His voice is plain and straight and I stand there not knowing how or even if I should answer. "Why is that?" he keeps on. "A good lookin' young kid like you. I should think you could just about have any girl you set your cap for."

Before I open my mouth to speak, he slips out of his jock and kicks it across the floor. Now, after all this time, I finally get a look at him naked, his glorious cock every bit as magnificent as I had imagined in all my fantasies.

"Talk around the locker room is that you really don't go in for girls," he goes on but I'm not listening. I'm trying with no success at all, not to stare. "Talk is you like other things," he

chuckles. He picks up his big fleshy cock in his right hand and shakes it, and as he does my heart just about stops. "Talk is you like this," he says and shakes it harder. "Do you like cock, T-boy?" he whispers but to me his voice is as loud as cymbal crashing. He takes two steps toward me and stops. I'm barely breathing and I wait, certain that this can't be anything more than a dream.

"Come on, T-boy," he says softly. "Come on and show Burt how much you like his cock." My hands start trembling and I'm becoming light headed. I breath to slow my pulse down but it's no use. Something inside me tells me to run but I don't. I just keep looking at Burt, perfect and naked there in front of me. He continues to stroke his cock and it continues to grow. Each inch sending a new wave of fear and excitement throughout my body. He takes his foot and stretches it toward me, gently touching his toe to my cock, now three times it's normal size and aching with a relentless stiffness inside my own snug suit. Then he picks up his trunks from the floor and wipes the sweat from under his arms with them. He puts the stretchy purple fabric to his nose and then reaches it out to me.

"Come on, T-boy," he coaxes, like one would coax a puppy with a toy. "I know how much you want it. I've always known. Now is your chance to show me." His smile is confident and crass. "Come on and show me."

And, of course, I do. I fall to my knees and grab hold of his cock. With both my hands I savor it. He puts his purple trunks, strong and scented with his sweat to my nose and I inhale. I'd never imagined that it would excite me so but it does. Maybe because that's what queer little boys like me are supposed to like or maybe just because it's Burt. I keep the swim suit there and put his cock to my mouth. I hold it greedily and lick up and down on the shaft.

It's a fat cock, hard, and *so* big, yet I swallow it whole. I take more than I ever thought I could, and it slides along the back of my throat. I suck on the head, full and swollen and put my tongue to the narrow slit. I look up at Burt, smiling down on me and I love it. I feast on his cock. Up and down, savoring every inch. I use my tongue instinctively and listen as Burt softly moans. I push the huge muscle so far into my mouth, that my nose is pressed up against his black mass of pubic hair.

This is my first time but I know how good I am. Better than in any of my made-up scenarios. But then I have to be. This is the real thing and this is Burt!

The coach takes the trunks from my hand and I reluctantly let go. He then puts them to his ass and I watch. He slowly runs them along the dark crevice and returns them to my nose.

"If you liked them before, T-boy, you're gonna' love them now," he says. "Come on and get a good sniff of old Burt."

I take a deep breath of the strong man smell and it fills my head. It makes me crazy and I go insane on Burt's cock. I suck it. I wipe my face with it. I lick his balls and the tops of his thighs.

"Oh, shit!" he screams at me, grinding his cock further into my mouth. "I always thought you might be a wild one but not like this." He takes his cock from my mouth and pulls me to my feet. I grab him and hold him tightly and he lets me. I put my face to his cheek and suck the sweat from his neck and chin. Then I rub my face along his chest.

Soft tufts of black hair over those hard round muscles caress my face and he wraps his arms around my head and holds me there. Caught like in the jaws of a vice he squeezes. I lick his flesh and his nipples. I drink up the beads of sweat as they trickle down his arms.

"You're good at showing me how much you like it, T-boy, damn good." His voice is warm and resonates through my head as my ear is pressed up against his chest. "But tell me. Tell Big Old Burt how much you love it."

"Oh, yeah, I love it!" I moan between gulps of him. "I love it all. There is nothing I wouldn't do for you, Burt. Nothing."

He pushes me hard and turns my back toward him. Then he hunches me over his desk and pulls my suit off me. He slaps my ass hard and it stings. Then again and again.

"Nice little ass you got there," he chuckles and slaps it once more and I can feel the flesh grow red under his big hand. "I always thought you might have a sweet little boycunt," he tells me. "Just by the way you walk around here. Now, why don't you show me what a nice boycunt you have? Spread your cheeks." I take my hands and pull my ass cheeks apart. I lay over his desk and expose myself there in front of Burt.

"That is a nice boycunt," he repeats. He reaches into the top

drawer of his desk and takes out a jar of Vaseline. He puts a dab on my finger and then tells me to finger my hole. "Fuck that tight hole with your finger T-boy, and if you like it I'll give you something better."

I do as I'm told. I insert my finger in and out of my asshole while Burt watches. I wiggle my ass for him and keep my cheeks spread wide open. Then he moves around the desk and returns his cock back to my mouth.

"Suck it some more," he orders and I obey, of course. I keep my finger up inside me while Burt fucks my face with his long thick cock. I suck his balls and lick the underside of his shaft. I do whatever I can to make him feel good.

"You want me to fuck you, T-boy?" he teases me. "You want to get fucked by this?"

He hits me hard in the face with his cock and rubs it all along my lips.

"Yes, Burt," I pant. "I want you to fuck me."

"How much?" he keeps teasing.

"I need it," I say.

"You need it?"

I swallow his cock again and nod my head. "You need to get fucked," he says, pushing in and out of my mouth. "You want it?"

"Yes, Burt, please," I beg, letting the monster loose for a moment. "Please fuck me. Please!"

"No," he says quietly. He pulls his cock from my mouth and smiles down at me. "Burt doesn't fuck just anybody T-boy... And not just any time, but when you've hung around here a while longer you'll know that. I might fuck you one day and then again." He pauses and strokes his cock for me. "I might not." He pulls down a Billy-club which he keeps hanging on his wall. Sometimes he threatens the boys from the swim team when they misbehave or miss practice but I've never heard of him using it. He holds it in his hand and strikes it hard against his palm.

"You want to get fucked?"

I'm panting and out of breath and I nod my head like a dog begging for a piece of meat. "Then fuck yourself on this while I jerk off and watch."

He puts the Billy-club to my ass and I swallow it up. I moan

as he thrusts it in and out and watch Burt as he pulls on his fat cock. I turn to face him and squat down on the floor. I ride the club for him and I can see by the look on his face that he loves it. I pump faster and faster and I can honestly say that I've never felt anything like it. I push it as far in me as it will go, pretending it's Burt, certain that his wide hard cock would feel even better. I stick one of my fingers up inside me along with it, which really drives him wild. I grab hold of my own cock, aching and rigid and begin to stroke it. Burt starts to moan and tremors pulse up and down his body. I know he is close. I move toward him keeping my mouth open still fucking myself with the Billy-club. "You want my cum?" he growls at me. "You want it?"

Before I can answer, he grabs his purple trunks from the floor and shoots a fountain of hot white sperm into them. I watch like it's happening in slow motion, as his thick beautiful cock erupts in a frenzy into the soiled purple fabric. Then I shoot. I cum faster, wilder and more furiously than I ever have before as he takes his sperm covered purple trunks and puts them to my mouth. "Lick it up, T-boy," he says breathlessly. "Have a taste of Old Burt."

And, of course, I do. I lap up every drop of cum from those purple trunks I love so much while Burt watches.

When I'm done, he crouches down to the floor with me for one second. He sits next to me. With his finger, he wipes up a drop of cum that has dribbled down onto my chin and then puts it to my lips and I happily clean it off. He smiles at me. I put my head to his chest and feel his frenzied heart still racing. He holds me for a moment, then gets up to take a shower. He says nothing, but then there is nothing to say. I know this by the look on his face. Before he's finished with his shower, I am dressed and gone.

This is my first time. Not just with Burt, but with anyone. And I will never forget it.

. . .

Over that summer, after my graduation, Burt and I had many more times together, each one wilder than the next, but then as I confided in him so many times, he had a way of making me

do things that was sure, nobody else could.

Come September, as I was getting ready to leave for college, Burt told me that he'd accepted another coaching job. A small school somewhere in the Pacific Northwest. The last time we were together, he was somehow more tender than he'd ever been before. He gave me a small gift. He told me not to open it until I'd left for school and was settled into my dorm. I didn't question it. As always, I did as I was told. My second week of school, I took the gift out and opened it. Wasn't I surprised to unwrap the cheap dime-store tissue paper only to find Burt's cum-stained purple trunks.

NOVICES

Ken Anderson

Sept. 26, 1969

Everything was silvery from rain, and when Kevin stepped onto the terrace that night, Ron was on his way out to greet him. Kevin was wearing penny loafers, khakis, and a pastel-pink tennis shirt with the collar flipped up; Ron, old track shoes, faded jeans, and a torn T-shirt, just as Kevin had fantasized.

They shook hands, and Kevin said, "Your hand's cold."

"Low blood sugar," Ron replied, holding his hand. "Need to eat." They squeezed each other's hand, and Ron said with a wink, "You have a grip like a vise. Using one of those hand-strengthening devices?"

Kevin smiled. He did not know if Ron intended a double-entendre. Ron pulled him into an embrace, a brotherly hug, as Kevin thought of it. When they let go, Ron mussed his hair.

"Looks better without the tonic," he said.

Inside, there were four leather and suede sofas, two against walls, two back to back at a slant in front of the fireplace, with a long parson's table between them. The sofas were heaped with suede pillows and grouped with small, polished-steel cocktail tables. Roehm, the German shepherd dog, got up as if to give Kevin a seat on the one facing the fireplace, but a money belt lay where Kevin was going to sit. Dieter tossed it into the bedroom.

Dieter was a German industrialist involved in the manufacture of security systems, among other things. Thus, there were a number of advanced electrical and infrared gadgets around the house. There was a twenty-year age difference between Dieter and Kevin, and Kevin knew that Dieter had a lover, Sasha, but Kevin and Dieter had been tricking for about a month, playing what they called sex games: in the boulders behind the house, in a boat on the lake, on impulse in the hall to the wine cellar. Dieter had hired him to be caretaker of the house and to landscape the island, but Kevin did not know just

how much Sasha knew. Ron and Zane were the other "boys," really young men, in Dieter's entourage.

"Have a seat," Dieter said. "I'll pour you some wine."

Ron followed Dieter into the kitchen to pop popcorn, and Sasha and Zane were watching "A Hatful of Rain" on television, Sasha sitting cross-legged on the other end of the sofa, Zane lying on the floor with a pillow under his head. Dieter was wearing slacks and a blousy linen shirt, Sasha a pair of skin-tight shorts and a tank-top, and Zane a pair of overalls, which on him looked like a costume. Sasha was wearing a pendant on a thong, a chunk of amber. Roehm was sporting a leather collar with metal studs.

Eventually, Dieter took a seat between Sasha and Kevin, and Ron supplied everyone with a bowl of popcorn, then pulled a chair to a cocktail table. Once settled, the group smoked half a joint, and Kevin's nostrils, mouth, and eyes dried up.

He went for a glass of water, and when he returned, stepping in front of Sasha and Dieter, Sasha said, "Heard your pigeon died," meaning one of Kevin's pets, Tristan and Isolde, or Trist and Salt as Kevin liked to call them.

"Thanks," Kevin said, sitting. "They're doves."

Everyone stared at the screen, sipping wine and eating popcorn. Don Murray needed a fix and was cramping and shivering.

"In Athens," Dieter said, "the temple of Aphrodite Pandernos was purified by the sacrifice of a dove."

"Does that mean his sex life's going to improve?" Sasha asked, absently rubbing his thighs.

"Perhaps," Dieter bantered.

Ron had bent over to unlace and slip out of his shoes, dropping them aside. He turned the chair slightly, then propped his feet on the table.

He smiled at Kevin: "It already has."

After the movie, Sasha turned off the TV, clucking when he hit the button on the remote. Everyone shared the other half of the joint, and Kevin sprawled in a corner of the sofa, watching the thin line of smoke trailing from the roach in the ashtray. In his altered state, it looked as if a ghost were about to materialize. Ron got up and put on the rock group Fast Fashion's "Lie to Me," then pulled Zane from the floor to slow-dance with

him. As far as Kevin could make them out, the lyrics seemed to be about not only gay sex, but also kinky sex. He had never heard lyrics like that, music like that, especially for a slow tune, which he thought of as romantic. Dieter took Kevin's wine glass to the kitchen, and Sasha set up a projector on the parson's table, then a movie screen in front of the fireplace. Roehm ambled into the dining room and lay on his side on the hardwood floor.

While everyone was moving around, Kevin felt absolutely immobile and inconspicuous, what he thought of as a heightened sense of alienation due to the grass. He could have been, as far as he could tell, a fly on the wall, a police plant spying on the decadent nocturnal habits of a flock of vampires. At the end of the number, the volume dropped mysteriously, as if Ron had willed it, and he and Zane resumed their places. Dieter returned with another glass of wine for Kevin, and Sasha turned off the lights and switched on the projector.

The movie was a scratchy silent film whose Portuguese title Sasha translated as "The Lay Brother." It took Kevin awhile to realize that what he was watching was the foreplay of a skin flick. What threw him was that it actually seemed to have a plot. A rain-drenched Latino knocked on the door of a monastery at night and proceeded to be seduced by one masked, barefoot monk after another. Rope belts slipped from waists and onto wrists, robes fell, rumpled, onto the floor, but the masks stayed on, black hoods with the eyes cut out. Kevin had to sit up to hide his erection.

"Look at the size of that one," Sasha exclaimed, referring to a well-endowed character.

Sasha was kneeling on the sofa behind Dieter.

"Reminds me of the boy in Pompeii," Zane said.

"Pompeii?" Kevin asked.

"He means Naples," Ron explained.

Kevin looked at Ron to see if he were aroused, to see how he was responding to the situation, but when he did, Ron caught him staring and smiled, "I know what you're thinking."

Kevin blushed, then looked away, first at the athletic socks crumpled around Ron's ankles, then at the slow crescendo of sadomasochism on the screen.

"Dieter," Sasha asked, "how 'bout some champagne?"

Dieter rose, and when Kevin, like a zombie, rose as well, Sasha said, "Sit down, Kev. Dieter can find it."

"Besides," Ron joked, "Sash wouldn't want you to miss this masterpiece of erotic art."

Kevin came to, like a sleepwalker, suddenly aware of the hot, dusty smell of the projector, of the conspicuous bulge in his pants. He smiled to himself, then sat, embarrassed, shaking his head as if to clear it. He did not know why he had stood.

Zane smiled at Kevin and said, "Kev hot?"

At that point, the monks were leading the novice, elbows-bound, to an altar in front of a large statue cut in stone. The idol was sitting with its legs crossed, its hands on its knees, and everything about the oversized head was oval – the hairline, the eyes, the nose, the mouth. The monks placed the novice face-down on the altar, spreading his legs and tying his feet to corner posts. Then they began flogging his buttocks and masturbating over him. The first climax set off a chain reaction, spattering the novice with glistening semen.

Then the monks stepped back and bowed as the statue cracked open, like an egg, revealing, in flickering light, the pagan god of the film, a muscular Latin-American Indian. He had stark, carved features, like a mask, and was wearing nothing but moccasins with leather straps twined around his calves and a headband with feathers trailing down the mane of his hair. He mounted the novice, then wrapped a rope around the novice's neck. He wrapped a loop of the rope around a stick so that when he turned the stick, the rope tightened. Then he rode the novice like a horse, holding on to the stick, like a bridle, with both hands. Occasionally, he would twist the stick tighter so that at the peak of his frenzy, just as he was about to come, the novice, back arched, was coughing violently. His features swelled, his eyes bulged. He was obviously choking to death.

Kevin could not believe what he was seeing. Surely, what was happening was just a scene in a film. Then the herbal-vinous cloud in his head parted, and standing up, he experienced a sudden, pellucid sun-burst of horror. It was as if some stern chord had been struck on a pipe organ. His whole body hummed with the blast.

"How could you show me something like this?" he asked.

He stuck his fingers into the spokes of the reel, then pulled it off the arm and tossed it aside. Roehm jumped up, and Dieter was just coming up the stairs as the reel was trundling across the floor, unwinding film. The screen flashed blinding white, the projector was clicking, and a strip of film continued sliding like a snake through its mechanisms. When the film slipped out the back, the back reel began spinning and slapping the projector.

"What happened?" Dieter asked pleasantly.

Kevin trembled, Sasha snickered, and Ron and Zane sat up. Ron looked irritated, Zane blase.

"Sasha's slipped in a snuff film," Ron explained.

Dieter stared at Sasha, who backed away. Then Dieter wistfully smiled at Kevin.

"I'm afraid your innocence is lost on Sasha," Dieter said, switching off the projector, "that is, your spiritual innocence. Your body, I'm sure, is another matter."

"Spiritual innocence," Sasha laughed. "You're about as interested in Kevin's spirit as the Pentagon is in peace, as Hitler was in freeing the Jews."

Dieter set the bottle on a table and stared at Sasha.

"It was just a joke," Sasha claimed, stepping back. "I can't believe you're so defensive about the little bugger."

"May I speak to you in the bedroom?" Dieter asked.

There was nothing irked about Dieter's tone.

"Dieter!" Sasha blurted, smug. "You act as if I *made* the film."

Sasha smiled to himself, then apparently gave up, reporting to the room, like a punished child.

"I'll be only a moment," Dieter said.

When the door shut, Kevin sat, but Zane reached the remote and, to Kevin's surprise, turned on the sound in the bedroom.

"Sorry you had to tear yourself away from your new groom," Sasha said playfully. "Or is it bride? Have you popped his cherry yet? Have you plighted troth?"

"What a fine pair of newlyweds, Little Miss Cherub from Harrisville and a – "

Zane switched off the remote, and Kevin faced away, staring at the large globe in a corner of the room.

"Thanks," he whispered glumly, but at times everyone

could still pick out what Sasha was saying.

"He'll have hell to pay," Zane remarked, getting up.

He replaced the remote, then picked up the bottle and strolled to the kitchen. Ron just sat there, apparently intent on and amused by the exchange in the other room. Kevin grew restless and got up, strolling to the terrace. He was leaning on the balustrade when Ron approached, in his sock feet, with two champagne flutes.

"What'd you expect?" Ron asked, handing him one. "They've been lovers for years." Then he added, smiling, "Think you'd just walk in here and Sasha would pack up? If you want to see Dieter, don't force the issue with Sasha. Do what Dieter says."

Ron propped himself against the balustrade, facing the house, his emerald eyes glittering with sadness, even depression, Kevin thought, as well as charm.

"Ron," Kevin smiled. "I am doing what Dieter told me, and he told me Sasha wasn't jealous. Is that what this is all about?"

"Hmm," Ron brooded, sipping champagne. "Who knows what sets Sasha off? Half the time his moods are driven by drugs. Maybe it *was* just a joke." As Kevin was about to speak, Ron corrected himself, "A sick joke. He gets a hard-on only one way: S and M, whips and welts."

Ron glanced at Kevin mischievously.

"The only problem is," Ron said, "he's an S *and* M. He doesn't care who's getting it, just as long as someone is. That's what the cuffs are for, toys and games."

The first night that Kevin had stayed alone in the house, he had slept in Sasha's room and discovered the handcuffs, but Kevin could not recall talking about them with Ron.

"I really don't understand why anyone would want to be bound like that," Kevin remarked, sipping champagne.

Ron thought, then said, "Well, for one, it frees you of inhibitions. The slave can't stop anything, and the master has complete power, which, of course, is a very powerful aphrodisiac. And speaking of power, sex, often, is just a brawl to see who's head ape."

Since Ron had glanced at Kevin when he said the word *often*, Kevin felt as if Ron were qualifying the statement just for him.

"In an ape pack, one male has to dominate the others first, then fucks who he wants. With two men, the dominated and fucked just happen to be the same."

"Still," Kevin mused, "I can't imagine *willingly* putting your life in some crazy stranger's hands."

"No?"

"Unless you have a death wish," Kevin said, glancing at Ron. "Seems as if you'd really have to trust someone, the way, for example, Zane trusts you."

"But if you trust the person, where's the thrill?" Ron smiled knowingly, then said, "Pleasure, pain, beauty, repulsion, love, hate, life itself – life isn't just a bowl of anuses. Of course, now Dieter can hurt him by threatening him with you."

"Which means they're going to have really good sex tonight," Kevin speculated.

"Hang around. Find out."

"But that just doesn't sound like Dieter, not the Dieter I know."

"What?"

"S and M."

Ron smiled thoughtfully, then asked, "You sure?"

"I don't wanna hurt Sasha," Kevin claimed. "But I'm certainly not afraid of 'im."

"Guess he wouldn't be interested in *you*," Ron concluded, but Kevin had sensed that Sasha was.

Despite what Dieter or Ron had said, Kevin felt that Sasha wanted to hurt him in the sense of getting rid of him, of frightening him away, and if Sasha were, in fact, an M, as well as an S, then he wanted Kevin to hurt him, too. He wanted Kevin to be sucked to the lake bottom of his kinky bond with Dieter. In short, he wanted Kevin.

"Nothing better than grief," Ron observed.

"Grief?"

"Trouble," Ron explained, draining his glass. "Love triangles. Nothing more – entertaining. Except maybe love squares or pentagons, hexagons, heptagons...."

Kevin laughed subtly, exhaling through his nose. He drained his glass, then handed it to Ron.

"Bye."

"But, Kev, babe," Ron grinned, gesturing with the glasses,

"the night's young."

Kevin strolled down the steps into the dark, through the light filtering down the yard to the wharf, where he lingered, hands in pockets, leaning against the bathhouse. He stared at the moon glade dancing like a candle on the water, at the moon itself. The sky was so bright around the moon that it looked encased in glass, like an artifact, a moon rock in a luminous paperweight. He closed his eyes and imagined that Dieter, in tails, had joined him, gazing across the quiet channel. Slowly, detail by detail, the image faded.

. . .

When Kevin opened his eyes, reality emerged. Dieter was, in fact, standing near him, not in a tux, though, a terry-cloth robe and leather slippers. They embraced.

"You smell so clean," Kevin whispered, smelling the soap.

"You smell so sweet," Dieter replied.

Kevin could also smell the toothpaste on Dieter's breath.

"It fell into Sasha's hands," Dieter said, referring to the film. "Someone gave it to him. I'll destroy it."

"Why didn't he warn me?" Kevin asked, his forehead on Dieter's shoulder.

"Things like that exist," Dieter said, stepping back, holding Kevin's forearms. "In a sense, it's best you know. You're right, of course. He should have warned you. He should have warned us all. You know Sasha. He likes you, believe it or not. The man in him likes you."

"I haven't given him a reason not to, have I?"

"No," Dieter said, releasing him. "Perhaps he read something in the cards."

"What do you mean?"

"Nothing, just a thought."

Dieter reached his lighter and a joint from a pocket and lit up, passing the joint to Kevin. They stood in the dark, passing it back and forth.

"Everyone has to be awake around Sasha," Dieter said in a very business-like tone of voice. "Even Sasha, if you follow me."

"He's schizo."

Dieter chuckled, then said, "Perhaps <u>spontaneous</u> is a more precise word. Actually, playing along with him, at times, can be a lot of fun. Knowing him has been quite an adventure."

When the roach was almost too small to pass, Dieter refused it, and Kevin snubbed it out on the bathhouse, then swallowed it.

"You've turned into quite a little pothead."

"Can't be as bad as booze," Kevin remarked, all light and keen.

Dieter slipped his arm over Kevin's shoulder, leading him toward the steps. Kevin hesitated. All at once, he had an uneasy feeling, as if the rules had changed in whatever game they were playing, changed like stepping into a canoe or twilight cooling to dark. He felt the disadvantage, but was not afraid. Wasn't losing just the flip side of winning? When they started toward the house, Kevin saw that the lights were off.

"Ron and Zane have gone for a swim," Dieter remarked.

When they reached the terrace, Kevin noticed Sasha sitting at the table, leaning forward, elbows on knees. They strolled over and stood directly in front of him. From his posture, he seemed to be sulking. There was an odd, musky smell about him which Kevin could almost name.

Dieter stepped behind Kevin, wrapping his arms around him, resting his chin on his shoulder. They seemed to be waiting for Sasha to say or do something. Kevin felt the stubble on Dieter's chin, the warmth of his breath on his neck. Sasha slipped to his knees in front of Kevin, but when Kevin started to resist, Dieter held him.

"You'll be all right," Dieter whispered. "I'm here. I'm holding you."

Kevin could tell, from his tone of voice, that Dieter was already going off into his own voluptuous world. Kevin was just the axis of it.

(Kevin's Diary Sept. 27)

Sasha blew me last night, but it was difficult to sort the physical pleasure from a sense a disloyalty to Dieter, though Dieter had obviously put him up to it. Dieter was standing behind me with his arms around me. He kept kissing my neck and ear, tonguing my ear lobe. He kept sighing and whispering, "You

feel wonderful, smell wonderful, taste wonderful." He slipped his hands under my shirt, squeezing my pecs, playing with my nipples gently, then harder, twisting them.

    Sasha unbuckled my belt, then unsnapped and unzipped my khakis, peeling them down my thighs. He just knelt there awhile, holding back as if surprised or teasing me, the way Dieter did the first time he blew me. Then he wrapped his hands around my knees, as if to get a good grip on me, and buried his face in my crotch, all the way – his nose mashed in my pubes, his chin in my balls. He started slowly, then gorged on my cock as if starved, choking me down, like a dog. I got real hard and leaned forward, letting him have all of it.

    "Oh, man!" I groaned. "What a load."

    I can't imagine a cock harder than mine, a throat hotter than his, a load bigger than the one I kept shooting down it. He kept sucking me off like a pump. For a second, my mind was all starry black and bright moonlight. Guess I've entered phase two of my sexual education: a threeway.

(Adapted from the author's forthcoming novel "Someone Bought the House on the Island")

NIGHT SCHOOL

Edmund Miller

I noticed him first from behind on the first day of class as he strode in wearing an exotic leather cap cocked to one side. I was pleasantly surprised when he took a seat up front, facing me. The jockeying for position usually goes on for the goofing-off seats in the back row. He turned out to be a real beauty head-on too. Although he did not take off the cap, he lowered his long eyelashes slowly, then opened his violet eyes wide and his rose lips just a crack. It was a look of rapt attention. Unfortunately I had to start teaching the class as whole.

He turned out to be a good student, always on time to class, assiduous in his note taking, ready with surprising insights when we had a discussion going. But he was never the first one to talk. And he always seemed to have a little bit more to say that he could not quite get out. His contributions always ended, "And . . . ." Then his mouth would just hang open for a moment until he waved his hands as a signal that he was unable to go on after all.

We went along this way up to the middle of the term. For a midterm exam—for a final too—I always give an open-book essay exam. There is no point in just checking up to rediscover that students have no academic work ethic nowadays. Of course, most students think an open-book test means one they do not have to study for, so they came in completely unprepared. They adopt the attitude that their job is to earn course credits by figuring ways around the teacher's requirements without ever letting any of the course content land in their minds even for a moment. But Violet Eyes was not one of these. And he did really well on this exam. He had obviously read the plays—the course was Shakespeare's Tragedies and Romances—and he had paid attention to the lectures and the discussions. But—best of all—he had some ideas of his own. Some of these were not plausible because he did not know enough about the period. For example he thought that real horses might have been a staging option in Shakespeare's day in that curious episode in *Macbeth* when

Banquo and Fleance are waylaid on foot as they return from a horseback ride. But he also came up with some good insights on his own. He taught me a thing or two. For example, he pointed out how the whole character of Malcolm in that same play is summed up in the icy cold way he responds to the discovery of his father's murder with the words, "Oh, by whom?"

So he more than earned his A on the exam. But then he disappeared.

However, I did not forget him. Every time I walked into class I looked for him, and sometimes I thought about him when I was not in class or at school at all. Late one night I was having trouble getting to sleep. Strapping myself in with a cock ring (black leather with metal snaps) and leafing through my extensive collection of gay magazines seemed to be working at least some of its usual magic. At least, the hard round asses had gotten me up fast enough. And pretty-boy faces were giving me something to stroke off over. On the other hand, so to speak, although I had been whacking away for a good half hour, it had begun to seem as if I was never going to get off.

Then I thought I heard something—somebody pounding on the door to my apartment. It should not be possible to get into the building without using the intercom from the entry hall, but somebody or other is always letting strangers in. The lateness of the hour did not surprise me much either since I have a number of nocturnal friends. I felt my way out of bed and groped my way through the bedroom and on through my foyer and entry hall to the door. "Who is it?" I heard myself saying through the door as I squinted into the peephole. And there he was, Leather Cap. He focused his violet eyes on the peephole and inclined his head a bit to the side but said nothing.

Somehow the door got open, and he walked straight in and past me still without saying a word. As he moved by me, I turned to look after him in the dim light shining in from the hall behind me. He seemed to be moving with a purpose and and going directly to the bedroom, as if it were the most natural thing in the world for him to know the way. I followed, again groping in the dark since I had shut the door and—suddenly conscious of my nakedness—not turned on any lights. As I moved along I stumbled more than once over

strange terrain: he was discarding pieces of his clothing along the route to the bedroom!

When I had followed him inside, I found that a little moonlight coming through the bedroom window illuminated a form on the bed. He was crouched over into a hard, smooth ball and was almost prayerfully still. He was naked too now, and the whiteness of his ass was the brightest thing in the room. I got up on the bed and knelt behind him. I put my hands against the sleek surface of his skin and found it cold to the touch. I could feel the outline of his spinal cord and the deep indentations of each gluteus maximus, which I leaned over and kissed, first the right one and then the left. They were cold on my lips. I went back again and left a hickey as a sign that I had been there.

Then I raised myself up to full size (for a kneeling position) and began doing what had to be done. His asshole opened to my cock as if greeting an old friend and pulled me in, making me grow even larger as I sank into its spacious depth. As I slipped lazily forward and back, forward and back, in his warm interior, with both hands I held on to the hard, cold smoothness of his sides. I do not remember how or when it began, but suddenly I was coming, pouring myself out into him. I came not with screams of urgency but in a dreamy, slow way that seemed to go on forever. Afterwards we rolled over into spoon position, and I drifted off into sleep while I was still in him.

I woke suddenly to my morning alarm going off, instantly aware that he was no longer there and only gradually aware that he had never been, that it had all been a wet dream, the evidence of which was encrusted in various places about the bedsheets and my person. He was still not in class the next day.

But just a few days before the end of the semester, he came to me during my office hours with a sad and complicated tale of getting into trouble over some fraternity prank and having to work extra hours to pay for damages and having to drop most of his classes. Since he said he felt unprepared for the final and had not begun the termpaper, I told him that I would give him an incomplete and let him make up the missing work over the summer. He said he was greatly relieved to hear this; on the

other hand, he was still visibly distraught. In fact, he was shaking. Impulsively—and maybe quite foolishly—I reached across the desk and took his two hands in my two, saying "Calm down. We've just worked things out, haven't we?"

Well, we had worked things out. At least, he knew what he had to do for the termpaper. And he knew I was not kicking him out of class or failing him. But he still did not start coming to class again. Naturally, I started wondering whether he had maybe read too much into my taking his hands into mine to try to calm him down. And as the semester ended without his having returned to class, I also started to wonder whether I had not maybe been doing more by taking his hands and if I had not in fact driven him away from class.

After driving myself crazy for a few weeks imagining terrible repercussions, I found his termpaper in my mail pigeonhole one day. It was excellent—better than that, it was obviously his own work. I recognized the style, and both the range of ideas and the limitations of historical knowledge were plausibly his own. I could be sure he was being straight with me and could believe I was being straight with him. He had attached a note saying he was sorry for not coming back to class and saying he wanted to show me he could do the paper even if I was fed up with him and was no longer willing to let him make up the final he had missed. He asked me to call him.

Since I had already given him the incomplete anyway, I called to give him some substitute final exam questions. It had been an open-book exam anyway. I did have one thing that needed to be checked out, of course. I said, "You know I was a little afraid that at our meeting in my office I might have said something—or done something—that added to your troubles."

My guilty conscience cleared up right away, however, when he said, "Oh, no, you were great! You helped a lot. I was just trembling because I knew I wasn't playing straight with you. I wasn't going to come back to class. I'd taken on work assignments because of this money problem, so I realized I was conning you." Then he took a long pause before adding, "I owe you one."

Well, the final showed up in my mail a week or so later. And it was up to his usual fine standard. I submitted the change-of-grade form and gradually forgot all about the incident.

Then about four months later, he called me. At home. At about 10:30 in the evening. He thanked me again for having been so understanding when he was letting his personal problems interfere with his academic performance. He said he had something he wanted to give me by way of thanks. I told him he did not have do to anything like that. He alluded again to the idea of owing me something. I started to get turned on all over again and launched into giving him details about my office hours so that I would be sure to be there to get this little thank-you present in person.

"No, no," he said, "I think it would be a little awkward to give you this present in your office." Then I found I was the one leaving the little conversational pause hanging in the air, as I calculated the odds—and the ethics. I reasoned that he was no longer my student and that this had all been his idea—if indeed it was not all just in my mind even now. And he had earned the A on his own merit. I may have bent a few rules for him, but I do that all the time for students with no sexual attractions, even women. And the quality was there in the work. And the work was demonstrably his own. "Would you like to come over here?" I heard myself asking.

It turned out that he was happy, even eager, to do so. He asked if right then was a good time, and I said it was the usual time for such things before correcting myself to say that I seldom went to bed before 2:00 a.m.

To that, he answered, "Well, maybe you will tonight," and laughed. And I suddenly realized that the sexual implications of this conversation were not all in my own mind.

So, shortly after 11:00 there he was on my doorsill, still in the leather cap but carrying a dozen roses all just the color of his lips. So there was a present after all, and I had to start to disentangle myself from the idea that we were going to have sex.

He followed me as I went into the kitchen to put the roses in a vase. I was yammering away the whole time one inane thing after the other. He stood very close to me as I fiddled with the flowers. His brick-hard thigh touched against me as if by accident. I said I was sorry.

As soon as I had set the vase down on a table in the living room, he took my two hands in his and said, "You're

trembling. Calm down." But he did not let go. Instead, he yanked me forward so that I fell into his rose lips. And before I knew what was happening, we were tongue kissing.

"Do you," smooch, smooch, "really want to do this?" I asked.

"Look," he said, "I'm an escort. I do what we call `private parties' to put myself through school. You obviously have the hots for me. You're a nice guy and a great teacher. And you did me a favor. Let me do one for you." With that he started unbuttoning his shirt. What came out of it was hard and smooth with sharply defined contours in all the right places. Then he reached over and unbuttoned just one button on my shirt before flicking my chin as I looked down at what he was doing. Then he went back to undressing himself, popping the metal buttons on his jeans one by one and then giving the jeans a little shove so that they would go down.

"Help me off with these, will you?" he asked, falling on the sofa in a twisted vulnerable heap. I pulled the boots out from underneath and then helped him slide the jeans off. He was wearing a jockstrap, and as I looked up he fluffed out the already substantial bulge, outlining the contour of his cock with his finger. "Professional secret," he said, dipping the waistband down a little to show that he was wearing a cockring and then quickly covering up again. "Or maybe I can interest you in something in a smaller size," he said, twisting around suddenly and arching his back so that his ass was practically in my face as I knelt there on the floor.

Almost involuntarily I reached out a hand to touch the smooth round surface. As I did so he reached back with both hands to spread his ass cheeks wide, and I found myself tongue kissing him at the other end. I could still smell the roses scenting the room.

After a bit more of this, he suggested we adjourn to the bedroom, where he promptly fell face-down spread wide across the bed. When I just stood there looking at him for a while, he said, "Why don't you give me a backrub to begin with? Got any baby oil?"

Well, it just so happened I did. I went and got it, stopping along the way to strip down and slip into pajama bottoms. I got astride him and started working the oil into his back, not quite

knowing what I was doing but aware it did not much matter. Then I skipped down to his legs, noticing for the first time how enormous his thighs are—at least in proportion to his small frame. I ran my thumbs through the ridges of muscle. I finally gave in to his ass, which turned out to have a little malleability to it despite the hardness and the curvature. I ran my finger through the trough, and he gave me a little muscular spasm in return. I went back to rimming him, and he grunted a little. Baby oil was the only scent in the air, but I was thinking about roses.

I got off him and reached up to the headboard where I keep my supplies. I put on rubber gloves, carefully pressing the fingers all the way down. Then I squirted a bit of K.Y. on my fingertips and, leaning one elbow into the small of his back, spread his ass cheeks a little while the index finger of my other hand started playing with his rosette. I switched to the middle finger still with its original supply of lubricant and slipped inside, where it was warm and comfortable. I eased in and out gently, then turned round a bit and wiggled back and forth. More grunts from him. I pulled back and put the index finger in to make wider circles. Then I slipped both fingers in together. "Ooh, ah," he said, arching up slightly before subsiding again. I flipped the fingers over sharply, then eased them back and forth to clear the way. I added a third finger, thrusting slowly until I was all the way back to the base. Then I pulled out and shoved in again and started dancing my fingers around one another. I pulled all the way out and watched his hole pulsate in apparent dismay for a moment. Then I plunked in my thumb. I alternated thumbs for a while and then did both thumbs together, stretching the little entrance wide between the two of them. Then I did the same thing with the two index fingers.

Finally I was ready. I pulled off the gloves and the pajama bottoms and slipped on a condom. I lubed it up and knelt over the hole. It was still winking away at me. As I had my cockhead just in position for the final exam, I thought I heard a sound from him. I pulled back to listen. Unfortunately, I had heard correctly. He was snoring. I fell back on the bed to contemplate this new ethical dilemma. While I was deciding that I indeed had his full consent, my cock was busy deciding

that I had no interest in a sleeping beauty. So I unwrapped, put the pajama bottoms back on again, and went to sleep myself.

In the morning he was all in a rush with barely time to get to his day job again; he was still doing extra hours there. On his way out the door, he apologized several times for falling asleep. He seemed not to realize that I had had a great time anyway. But if he wanted to think he still owed me one, that was okay, too. He has just called back, and he should be here any minute. Oh, the doorbell just rang.

CLASS ACTION

Chad Stuart

"Hey, stud, wanna fuck my tight ass?"

Since I think I'm alone in the schoolroom, I almost jump a good three feet, straight up, before turning around.

Judd Baxter, buck naked from his waist down, his stiff pecker in hand, stands there. I didn't spot him right off because he's partially behind the open door. The blind on the door-window, usually open to allow Principal Morris to check on classroom activities, from the hallway, during any school day, is pulled.

"Jesus, Judd!" I complain. "What if I were someone other than one of our gang, for Christ's sake?!"

"No one comes to these things early," Judd says. "Not even our little group, unless previously arranged. How many of these little meetings have we had now? Three. When did anyone get here even half an hour early? Usually everyone, you and I included, is late."

"You're here. I'm here," I remind. "We're early."

"Yea, but I'm early because you told me your mother had a hot date and would drop you off early."

No denying his boner gives me one. The always respectable bulge my cock provides the crotch of my pants, presently aimed downward along my left thigh, grows noticeably in both length and circumference. Nevertheless ...

"This is really foolhardy, you know?" I argue.

"Foolhardy to want the feel of your impressive dick rammed to its heavy balls up my tight behind? Naw!" Judd disagrees. "How can it be foolhardy to want something that feels so damned good pumping my asshole?"

Somewhere -- the third floor -- Mr. Crankshin, the school custodian, starts up some machine, maybe the buffer. It gives me a nervous start.

"You're needlessly paranoid, stud," Judd says. "Nobody here but you, me, and the janitor. Nobody scheduled to be here, except us, for at least the next half hour. I got it straight from Mr. Crankshin, when he unlocked the front door, that

he's waxing and buffing floors all this evening, starting up top and working on down. So that as much as removes him from the picture."

All well and fine. At least, as far as it goes. But what happens if, this night of all nights, my cock rams to my balls up Judd's tight ass, and someone decides to show up early? Not Keith, or John, or Mitch, because they'd each end up with a boner and want to join in. I'm talking Mr. Keel. He shows up early, and it could royally fuck our plans.

"I know just what you're thinking, stud," Judd says and gives his big dick a loving stroke that yanks his uncut foreskin up to an almost completely snouting of his cockhead. "You're thinking, 'What's Judd have to lose by getting caught, here and now, during a homo-fuck? Nothing! He's never made any bones about his being gay. Not to Mr. Keel, nor to anyone else, faculty and/or student body.' While you're still pretty much in the closet, at least as far as Mr. Keel is concerned."

"It's just that I don't want to blow this evening," I insist.

"Would you like to blow this, instead?" His hand, on its downward journey, that strips his loose outer cockskin toward his balls, completely unveils the bulbous head of his impressive erection.

"You know what I mean," I counter. "Mr. Keel shows unexpectedly, finds us fucking, and he goes ballistic. That's not what we plan."

"Even if he does come early, he'll get a thrill out of our rutting. You and I know all homophobes are gays, only so deeply in their closets they don't even know they're in there. Besides, he's not coming early."

Judd's free hand unbuttons his shirt. His athletic body is suddenly even more on display. The perfect squares of his pectorals are covered with a faint fan-pattern of hair. His washboarded abdominals are hairless except for a straight-line run from his serrated cleavage to his pubic bush.

No doubt, Judd is sexy, in a thoroughly masculine way. Except by his having made it perfectly clear, from the beginning, that he's gay, it's not likely anyone -- Mr. Keel, included -- would guess it by looking. Judd has no stereotypical limp wrist, lispy voice, or swish. He looks perfect, all-American stud. That he's so openly gay is a route I fear to take, as far as

my own sexuality. Even more scary is how Mr. Keel actually flunked Judd, scheduling Judd not only to miss graduation with the rest of us but, also, to go to summer school, all because Judd is gay. Well, not officially for that reason. Officially, Judd failed an all-important exam.

From the very first day of Judd's arrival, at the beginning of our senior year, a select, knowledgeable few of us tried to tell him Mr. Keel is homophobic, but Judd doesn't listen. Or, he listens, like now, but refuses to heed our warnings.

"Come on, stud." He invites farther by turning his bare ass in my direction. A lovely ass it is, too, made sexier by its scar in evidence of the genuinely nasty gash that once extended, as a result of the bus accident, from his asscheek to the back of his knee.

He bends at the waist. His well-muscled asscheeks are so well-mated, along their mutually shared crack, they're easily mistaken for a couple of Aztec-hewn wall blocks that keep even the thinnest piece of paper from slipping between.

Upstairs, Mr. Crankshin turns off the buffer, and I prepare to use that as my excuse to say no to what Judd proposes. It's only a quick second of silence, though, before the distant sound effects begin again.

"I'll keep my ear propped against the door," Judd says, "while I've got myself bent over and my butt extended for servicing. I'll hear anyone coming, like I heard you coming. Your coming not the kind of coming I really want to hear from you, but ..."

"You don't figure my fucking you to climax will make either of us less able to perform later?"

"Come on, stud!" he chides, out of his temporary bend and, once again, aiming his cock in my direction. "You know how fast I am on recovery. Old Never-Soft! Isn't that what you've called me on more than one memorable occasion? Best butt-fucker of our bunch you may very well be, but even your talents will only calm me down and make sure I don't prematurely ejaculate later. As for your reputation for quick repeats ..."

"I don't know, Judd." I'm still not convinced.

"I'm really all excited about what we plan for later," he says. "All that camaraderie and help-a-shat-upon-friend. Same kind

of turn-on I remember from rolling around with you guys in some of those big dog piles on the football field."

There has been none of that since the bus accident, at the first of the year, which temporarily disabled Judd, with his gashed buttock and leg, disabled me with a broken arm, and laid up numerous of our classmates. Jeff Polynard ended up dead, Guy Preston permanently crippled. So many of us jocks were made damaged goods, there wasn't one intramural varsity team our first or second senior semesters at John Gramacery Prep.

I check the clock on the wall. I want to shift my still-hardening dick into a more comfortable position within my pants.

Judd watches like a predator eyes his prey.

"See. Plenty of time," he assures. "Even for the seemingly could-fuck-all-night antics I've often had from you in the past. And don't tell me you're not tempted. That a sausage in your pants, or are you just happy to see me?"

"Both." Finally, I adjust, into a more comfortable alignment, my cock along my thigh.

"Come on, then, stud," he encourages. "Can't tell me you didn't bring a rubber, not with what we plan for later."

"Maybe, less confident of my endurance than you, if and when, I only brought one."

"You with just one rubber?" He doesn't believe it.

"I said, 'Maybe'."

"Well, if that's the case, which, by the way, I don't believe for a minute, I'm the better Boy Scout." His hand to his shirt pocket produces a condom packet which he tosses to me. Reflexively, I catch it.

"Look, Judd ..." I begin, but he interrupts.

"Time's a wasting, stud. What say we get the show on the road, even though there's no one here to appreciate the sheer beauty of it but you and I?"

I check the clock again. I calculate time-needed, based on other nighttime meetings like this one. Not even the lawyer ever shows up before five-minutes-before-the-hour.

"You see the possibilities, don't you, stud?" Judd guesses. He has a nice smile that tugs his dimples deeper. He has two dimples, one dead-center each cheek. They're not the kind of

dimples that now crease the whole side of his face, in later years to become giant wrinkles. They're precise punctuation marks that'll have women and men falling all over themselves for Judd's affections, probably until he's long into his eighties.

"You hear anyone coming, and I mean anyone, I expect you to abort, whether you're on the brink of creaming your load, or whether I am," I hammer out the guidelines. "The rest of this evening gets fucked up, and I'm not the one out my sweet revenge, am I?"

"No, sir, you are not," he agrees. "And, all that considered, I still want you to fuck my ass, here and now. No dick up my butt ever able to get me as hot and as horny as your dick up my butt. Which says one helluva lot, since my rectum has been stuffed by quite a few very fine cocks in my long career as a sexually active queer."

"By your reckoning, you've had so many cocks, I'm surprised fucking you isn't like fucking a Carlsbad cavern."

"Of my very many fucks, few have been by cocks the size of yours, or my butt might very well have reached the point of deterioration to which you refer. In fact, your cock is the first and only exception I've made to my avoid-big-dick-at-all-cost rule. Yours always was and remains too much of a temptation for me to resist."

The greater temptation is my resisting his ass. He knows it, too. He's known it from the first time he bared his butt and aimed it in my direction, with an accompanying invitation to go as deeply as I could in exploring its his funky depths.

I intend just unzipping, tugging out my dick, fucking my boner up his butt, with all my clothes still in place. In case we're interrupted, I want every opportunity to get presentable. Except, my cock is way too stiff to get out that way. I have to unzip, unsnap, unbuckle, and drop my trousers and undershorts down around my ass. Even then, I have trouble prying free my dick without more completely dropping my pants."Might as well pool all your clothes around your feet," Judd provides his solution.

Which is what I end up doing and simultaneously realize he's still concealed by the open door, while I stand in full display for anyone who happens by.

My duck-waddle to his spot of better concealment is more

laugh-provoking than sexy, but Judd is too busy turning his butt in my direction, one more time, to do more than chuckle.

"Madness," I define what we're doing. "Pure, unadulterated madness."

"Such insight," Judd says, his hands on his knees, his bare ass mine for the taking. "No wonder Mr. Keel gave you a B."

"I'm going to give you a B-as-in-Big-Dick," I tell him. My hand is on his ass and pries open his crack in a way that will provide my dick an easier passage to his sphincter.

"Ahhhh, yes, you have found the target, gunner," he says when my fingertip finds his pucker. He jiggles his ass, with a slight back-thrust that puts my finger into his butt to my first knuckle. As many times as we've done this, I marvel at the tightness of his asshole. It could well be cherry. Except, it's not cherry. Judd knows it's not. Mr. Keel knows it's not, which is why, homophobe that he is, Mr. Keel flunked Judd.

I was surprised, but only momentarily, that Keel didn't flunk the whole lot of us. Not because he suspects we're all gay (not one of us, besides Judd, ever publicly admits a penchant for male cock and ass), but because we're all so chummy with the class queer. Then again, flunking more than one of us is easier said than done. Most of our parents look upon Judd's failure more as Mr. Keel's failure. Schools, like John Gramacery Prep are supposed to have teachers who, for the price-paid, can cram the basics for prestigious college admission into even the dumbest rich man's son.

I sheathe my dick with a rubber and put the result to Judd's target area. My cock wedges its way into his buttcrack, like an arrow shot through rock-walled chasm. Against the bulky head of my cock, his pucker is no bigger than my cock's pisshole; although I can't see my cockhead or his pucker. I see only the lower extremities of my drawbridge erection, from my curly pubic bush, to my cock, disappearing into the tight hug of Judd's buttcheeks.

"Feed my hungry asshole," Judd says. "My hungry, hungry, asshole."

Luckily, the rubber on my cock is lubricated, or my invited entry would rip his asshole for sure. As it is, my cockhead pushed inside him, it's as if I have a clothespin suddenly clamped to the end of my dick. Yes, his asshole is that damned

tight!

His hands prop against the wall, and his extended arms lock their elbows. His ass back-thrusts and gobbles up another good inch of my dick.

"You know what I want," he says, and it's not a question. He rocks his hips to stir my cock inside him, like a swizzle stick twirling inside a cocktail.

My fingers curl his hipbones and take hold. The slight ridging of his scar is sexily evident. By pulling on his hipbones and exerting pressure to the heels of my palms, I spread his twin buttcheeks along their mutually shared crack. Widening the crack, however, doesn't make his asshole any bigger. His asshole remains a tight, painfully pleasurable fit as I drill even more of my cock into it.

It's not an easy slide I'm attempting, from my cockhead to the roots of my stiff dick, up his butt. Even with my lubricated rubber, my dick only makes real progress when I commence a slight pull and push, pull and push, each pull surrendering a bit of his asshole previously claimed, each push managing to probe a bit more of Judd's hidden anal depths.

My hands slide the sides of his torso, beneath his shirt, over his muscle-striated ribcage. His flesh doesn't have an ounce of excess fat, and it's firm but velvety. My hands flatten over his pecs, his nipples hard against my palms. I rotate my hands, in place, managing small circles that drill his pin-prick nipples into my hand, even as I feed his asshole more of my erection.

My cock pulls back slightly: easier than pushing, in that previously covered ground remains slicked with lubricant left by my rubber. My hard dick pushes, more forcefully than ever before, in this particular fuck, and, suddenly, there's only one lone inch of my cock left to go. It's the thickest part, and it seems impossible for something so big to be pushed successfully into something so small, no matter how stretched Judd's asshole already is. No matter, either, that my boner has made the trip before. It only takes another slight withdrawal, then a follow-up push to bury all of my cock as far as I can go.

"Oooomph!" Judd says. He's an air-filled man-doll, my cock the pin that pricks and suddenly releases all of his air.

I grind my lower belly against the firmness of his asscheeks. My pubic hair presses curlicue designs into the resilient and

receptive globes of his muscled butt.

One of my hands leaves the ever-hardening stab of his nipple and slides down the scalloped ridges and crevices of his highly defined abdominal plain. My fingers reach his sexy navel. His belly button is neither innie nor outtie; it's almost indistinguishable when viewed as part of the total washboarded surfaces of his belly. What points the way is how the fine line of hair, that spills through the serrated indent between his pectorals, progresses in its straight line to his thick pubic bush, except for the slight parenthesizing of hair at his navel; the swirl of an otherwise straight river around a low-lying island.

His pubic hair is familiarly crinkly as my fingers comb over and, then, through it. Farther progression of my caress is stopped by the outward jut of his penis.

I leave his stiff dick alone, more interested in his two cum-filled balls that hang in their hairy bag from the base of his cock. Like his line of belly-hair bypasses his navel, my hand bypasses his cock and drops before conversion into an upward cupping around his thickening and hirsute scrotum.

My hand has been here before. When Judd is less stimulated, his scrotum actually overflows my impressively large hand. Now, however, it's pleasure-compacted to tennis-ball size and is just a fuzzy.

Unlike a tennis ball, though, Judd's scrotum contains large nuts which my fingers roll into a collision course.

"Oh, yes, manhandle my gonads, you sexy, sexy bastard!" Judd encourages.

Instead, I desert his balls, lean my body into a more complimentary curve of his body, and I fish for and find my scrotum dropped low by the weight of my nuts. Defying the pleasure that will soon have my sac as tightly tennis-ball compacted as Judd's scrotum, I stretch my hairy sac beneath the overhang of Judd's cock-plugged butt. My nuts meet his. Our scrotum hair mingles, like the snakes atop Medusa's head.

"Yesssss!" Judd hisses; I moan in harmony under the pure pleasure of his nuts rolled against mine, my boner jabbed deeply up his asshole.

Once I release our nuts, there's no reclaiming them. Our scrotums are suddenly too compact. His immediately tugs so tightly against the base of his erection, it's as if his nuts have

returned to wherever it is from where they'd dropped at puberty. The elevation of my cum-rumbling nuts isn't all that different or far behind.

"Fuck me," he says. "Fuck me ... fuck me ... fuck me."

"Oh, yes," I agree. I've come into this screw fearing the dangers of discovery, but I've since accepted the inevitability of fucking him to his climax and to mine. Someone coming down the hall, even entering the room, will probably distract my concentration, but I've reached the point, in my spiraling enjoyment, to doubt any finish to this butt-fuck short of dual eruptions of our hot and heavy cum.

My cock withdrawals to its pulpy head, easily achieved on the slideway provided by my rubber's lubricant now veneering Judd's asshole. My cock's return trip, over the same moisture-dewed corridor is, for the very first time, accomplished in one long, sensuous, and uninterrupted glide.

His hand fists his cock. My fingers fist as much of his fist as they can. His hand and mine ride the full length of his stiff dick, from his bulbous cockhead to his thick cockroots, then back again. The pumping milks his dick of its first oozes of preseminal lubricant. Some of the stickiness smears my fingers.

"You were made for fucking me," Judd compliments.

"And you were made for the fucking," I say and begin the coordination to have me fucking in cadence to the suddenly swift pumps of our fists over his erection. In no time, my cock glides in and out, in and out, as his cock gets masturbated down and up, down and up.

On each complete insertion of my dick up his rear, there's a slapping sound, of hard bare flesh against hard bare flesh, as my naked belly collides with his naked ass.

Somewhere upstairs, oblivious to sexual fun and games in this room, Mr. Crankshin buffers away as I royally wax Judd's ass.

I know better, but I still can't believe my cock, on each inward dive up Judd's asshole, doesn't actually push all of the way through him and out his crotch at the other side -- into his fist and into mine. Sexily, it's as if I fuck asshole and fists at one and the same time.

"Like it ... like it ... Jesus, love it!" Judd chants.

He has this marvelous ability to make the lining of his

asshole flutter. It seemingly enables my cock to claim even more anal territory than is possible with just the normal dimensions of my erection. When the rippling effect continues, while my cock withdrawals, it causes increased friction. The increased friction increases my pleasure.

I would grunt like a pig if I wasn't making a conscious effort to keep from it.

There is definitely something to say about the extra edge-enhanced pleasure had from fucking in a place where you can be discovered at any minute. However, there's an uneasy balance between that extra charge gotten from risking discovery and the fear generated by the same. In this case, the former dominates just enough so that I don't lose my boner and will to continue. Nonetheless, the former keeps me keyed to such a state of apprehension that there's a paranoia to the building ecstasy that is more than a little disconcerting. My body tells me I want to do this, and there's pleasure in the doing. Somewhere deeper, though, I'm reminded that there can be dire consequences.

I'm not prepared to prolong the fuck any longer than necessary. Not that my rush to orgasm, here, behind the door of the schoolroom, will allow me the control I might otherwise display, were the site a little less public. With each passing second, our chances of being come upon by someone less than understanding, I'm thrust closer and closer to ejaculation.

"Good, fucker!" Judd proclaims his own enjoyment.

It is good. I can't deny it. My perplexity is my need to judge whether that goodness is better, or worse, than ecstasy experienced in more secluded, more private moments. My decision, made haphazardly through the sensual blur of approaching blastoff, is that it's neither better nor worse. What it is is different, thereby giving it a novelty that is pleasurable in its own right.

I'm a fucking jackhammer but not nearly as noisy. I want to scream, to shout, to moan, to groan, but I'm afraid someone might hear, maybe even Mr. Crankshin, over the continuing burrrrrr of the buffer.

I try to isolate the sound of the buffer, up three stories. It's not only hard to do, in my steadily deteriorating mental state that has me gone positively hyper, it's impossible. My world

and all my senses have been compacted to include only Judd, me, and the sex we're having in that small area behind the still-opened school door. My world shrinks even smaller, more and more concentrated at my crotch, as the fuck progresses.

"Make me cream! Make me cream!" Judd commands me.

"Shhhhhh!" I want him to be quiet. I don't want Mr. Crankshin to come running. I don't want Mr. Keel to hear us, somewhere out on the street. What in the hell have I let Judd talk me into? This is pure madness. "Mad ... ness!" It comes out a two-part grunt.

His asshole makes wet sounds as its suction rebels against each outward slide of my dick, then exalts in each return of my stiff dick to anal depths. In accompaniment, there's the slap, slap, slap of my belly against his butt, both belly and butt gone sweaty in constant, staccato collision.

My hand still rides his hand, over his cock, up and back, along the seemingly expanding trunk of his erection. My free hand returns to his nuts. At first it's hard to find them, they're so far elevated into their pocket at the base of his dick. By probing that pocket, however, I locate both of them. I scratch at them with my fingertips, rather than with my fingernails, the latter likely to cause damage. Then, I pet them, one finger at a time, one finger after another, as if my hand becomes a giant caterpillar walking across the roots of his big dick.

"Jesus!" His voice is breathless and throaty, less loud than before.

I glance to the clock, but I can't seem to find it. Whether because it's concealed from me by the open door, or whether because my world has so thoroughly shrunken to exclude the timepiece on the wall, I don't know. All I can be sure is that I'm bounding speedily down the speedway to orgasm.

I know I'm close to creaming when I don't give a fuck whether or not the whole world comes suddenly streaming through the door to see what Judd and I are about.

"Let 'em come!" I say. I mean the world, but it's my cock and Judd's cock that respond, each, simultaneously, pulsing release of streamer after streamer of hot, soupy cream.

"Yes! Yes!" Judd says appreciatively.

His fist and mine are soaked in those quarts of his cum not already forcefully splattered against the wall.

His asshole exerts a suction more powerful than any mouth, seeming to expand for one brief fraction of a second only to collapse against my pecker with such force that my prick is actually able to define the bulge of his prostate against it.

Whatever cum I've left in my dick is milked from it by Judd's asshole and added to the reservoir now held by the cyst-like ballooning of rubber off the tip of my cockhead.

"I can't believe we just did this," I say, and my fear of being found out is back in the forefront, no longer obliterated by the rumbling of my ejaculation.

"Mmmmm," is Judd's only response, made as I remove my dick from his asshole with very little ceremony except the care necessary to be sure my rubber doesn't slide off to cascade his butthole with my cum.

I don't know how many of my pubic hairs get tangled in the rubber as I roll it free of my cockbase, but I pull them out by their roots, rather than risk taking the time to free them, one by one. The resulting pain returns me one more step closer to normality.

While I tie off the open end of the cum-filled condom and hoist my pants and underpants in a quick effort to hide all evidence, on my part, Judd continues to be unconcerned. My pants are buckled, snapped and zipped up, the used rubber stashed in a pants pocket, and Judd is still naked from the waist down, his shirt still unbuttoned, his handkerchief leisurely clearing up the mess on his fingers and cock.

I hear something over the continuing hum of the upstairs buffer.

"Jesus, Judd, someone is coming!"

Except, it's no one. It's only my own heartbeat and heavy breathing. I'm on the verge of hyperventilating.

"Calm down, stud," Judd soothes. "We've done what we've done, and no one caught us, or is going to catch us now and make any heads or tales out of any of this.

I notice, though, that there's still his sticky cum trailing the wall like the leftovers from garden slugs.

Of course, he's right, in that it's another good fifteen minutes before anyone else arrives. By then, all visible evidence of our sex is wiped away.

The first to arrive is only Mitch Jensen who would probably

have liked being present for my fucking of Judd. Likely, he would have eagerly joined in.

Mitch and I have done a lot of fucking around together in our time. His rugged, dark good looks genuinely appealed to me at an early age. Back when we were freshmen, I already had a boner for him by the time he picked the desk next to mine in which, that first day of school, to plop his muscled butt. If his looks make him a favorite sexual fantasy of every girl, and a lot of the boys, in class, Mitch doesn't mind at all. He's the only truly bisexual I think I know. I don't think he'd turn down fucking a pigeon's ass if the bird only went so far as to hint at an invitation.

"Yo!" Mitch greets and joins us at the back corner of the room where we've decided to hold court. "I see your parents, like mine, have decided to forego all this once-again bullshit."

The parents to whom he refers are Judd's mom and dad, and my mother. My father died even before I'd enrolled in John Gramacery Prep. He'd spent so much of his time at the office, earning the big bucks needed to maintain our big house, our big car, and our big chance to enroll me in a prestigious prep school and get himself membership in the exclusive Galleatean Golf and Country Club, I never really missed him as much as I probably should have. Certainly less than I thought I would. It was easy to imagine him merely at work, where he'd usually been, instead of dead and gone. Especially since he'd left us enough money for our lifestyle to continue pretty much uninterrupted.

By the time the school room contains almost everyone who's coming, there are only three parents in evidence. All of the others have opted for a hey-kid-report-anything-new-back-to-me approach. My mother only had to hear once from our lawyer, Gaylin Justin, of Justin, Justin, and Justin, that this kind of litigation, the class-action lawyer, Tillison, talks about, can be held up by the courts for years, before my mom pretty much washed her hands of any active participation. I usually continue to show, like now, because it gets me out of the house and with my friends.

"As usual, Mr. Keel looks as if he walks around with Judd's big cock stuffed up his butt, and is not liking it one bit," Mitch says. Mitch's black hair is thoroughly attractive in its tousle that

bangs so far over his forehead that it gets tangled in his as-long-as-any-girl's eyelashes. He brushes his hair out of his eyes now.

"Naw!" Judd disagrees. "He looks as if he's dying to get my big queer dick up his butt, disappointed because he thinks he doesn't have a chance of a snowball in hell."

I check to see if anyone eavesdrops, gratefully confident the only receptive ears appear to be those of our immediate group. I return my attention to Mr. Keel, the cause of Judd's scholastic dilemma and the subject of our proposed vendetta.

Genuinely, Mr. Keel is one handsome dude, especially for a man his age. Too handsome to be all as straight as he pretends. A bonafide closet queer, to be sure, unable to accept his homosexuality that begs him for hard dick and tight male asshole. His homophobia is his way of battling his love-that-boy's-dick and love-that-boy's-asshole mentality that exists, albeit undiscovered, deep within him.

Whatever scars he has, as a result of the bus accident, they're concealed. He never was in the hospital, like Judd, or had a cast on a broken arm, like I did. The rumor says his injury was to his back; although, he doesn't seems to have trouble walking, standing, or sitting. Mr. Keel may merely say it's his back, thinking to cash in whenever the case is settled, however many years up the line.

The last to arrive, five minutes late, are Paulie Sventon and his dad. Mr. Tillison, the lawyer who's officially in charge, is having a last-minute tete-te-tete with some other briefcase-carrying dude who has showed for the meeting.

"Don't any of these ever start on time?" Mr. Sventon complains. "I've another appointment this evening."

His appointment is probably with his lawyer. Sventon Associates has financial trouble. Anyway, that's the scuttlebutt. That Sventon is here, now, is possibly because he holds hope of seeing this lawsuit bring in a bit of money to offset his company's impending bankruptcy. From what our family lawyer tells mom and me, though, Sventon's chances of any bucks, any time soon, as a result of his son being a victim of the bus accident, are few and far between. More likely Paulie's kids -- if and when -- will most likely benefit.

Actually, the class-action concerns one-hundred-ten bus accidents, ours just one, that have occurred cross-country over

a period of five years. This meeting to inform us there have been two more, one in Boston, one in some backwater Washington State burg, Sprague. Both the latest accidents are traced to the same brake system as the one on our wrecked bus, and on all the wrecked buses involved. Our chances of a favorable settlement looking up, although no checks are in the mail.

We're introduced to the other briefcase-carrying dude who's another lawyer, Mr. Sparks, coming aboard. Mr. Sparks, being brought up to speed, prefers getting up-close and personal.

"I feel it important to put faces to at least some of you victims," he says. He has questions, regarding some of our affidavits.

"And," adds Mr. Sparks, "recent testing of the brake system infers a loud grating before complete failure. Do any of you remember any such sounds before the accident?"

I don't, but Mitch raises his hand, as do four others.

The whole meeting takes a couple hours. Mr. Sventon leaves after the first hour, apparently deciding what's happening isn't going to save his ass, money-wise, any time soon.

Our post-meeting plan requires Mr. Keel, as usual, to leave last. We base our assumption he will on other such night meetings called by lawyer Tillison. The schoolroom is officially Keel's, insofar as he uses it for the majority of his classes, during the day, even has his desk in one corner, and his excuse for always being last-man-out is likely his need to make sure everything is left in order for the coming day.

Since discussions of the accident, by its victims, have become old-hat, there's usually no incentive for anyone else to hang back.

That Judd, Keith, John, Mitch, and I hold back, this night, isn't for small-talk. That John, alone among us, funnels out the door, on the tail of most everyone else, is for him to make sure we're warned if some non-conspirator should decide to return, for whatever. Mr. Keel, true to form, examines his desk as if expecting to find it rifled by one of us, prior to his arrival.

Before Mr. Keel realizes we're not leaving with everyone else, Judd, Keith, Mitch, and I grab his sorry ass.

"What the fuck!" he says, his arms locked behind him. It's enough said for me to get the gag not only wrapped around his

mouth but between his lips and teeth. Only, then, reality strikes home, and he really puts up a struggle. Not that his attempts get him anywhere. He might be in good condition, from his regular workouts in the school gym, but he's no match for four high-school jocks whose musculature, due to physical therapy sessions, since the bus accident has us pretty nearly back to the prime specimens we were before the bus brakes failed.

John returns just as we successfully wrestle Mr. Keel belly-down over one of the student desks.

"Everybody, as usual, out of here, like a bat out of hell," John reports. "Mr. Crankshin still upstairs and dancing with his buffer."

Keith has brought, in a plain paper bag, the wrist and leg cuffs, with permanently attached linchpins that act as locks and keys, that we use to attach Mr. Keel to the desk. The cuffs are lined with sheep fleece and are part of an extensive collection of dungeon paraphernalia belonging to Keith's parents and discovered by Keith during our sophomore year at John Gramacery Prep. Often, since, incorporated in our sexual fun and games, they, and the make-shift dungeon, also, found in Keith's basement, behind a secret door, hint of his parents practicing some pretty inventive sex, although none of us can really imagine Keith's mom strung from chains, Keith's dad fucking her up her asshole.

Our original plan called for hauling Mr. Keel's ass off to Keith's parent's basement dungeon, except there was the realized danger of being spotted getting him from the school to the car, from the car to the house. All that made moot, because Keith's parents refused to oblige by going somewhere this evening. I only hope they don't miss the cuffs we've borrowed from them.

We affix Mr. Keel to the desk and make damned sure he won't get loose by merely tipping the desk and slipping one end of each cuff off the desk leg to which it's secured. Judd sits in the desk seat, his weight keeping the desk stable as our examination is completed to everyone's, but Mr. Keel's, satisfaction.

Mr. Keel is thrust belly-down, over the desk, from front to back, and his face is positioned pretty damned close to Judd's

crotch. If Mr. Keel isn't completely disoriented, from his ongoing surprise and panic, he can't miss the bulge Judd's stiff cock makes in my classmate's trousers. Just in case he does ...

"Want to see what I've got here, just for you, up close and personal?" Judd asks. His hand goes just-so, over the impressive length of his erection, so his fingers can better press his hard-on into higher relief beneath his stretched denim. The ridge made by his peeled-back foreskin, at the spot where his cockhead attaches to his cockshaft, is readily visible beneath the strained material.

Mr. Keel mumbles something totally indecipherable. It's not likely, "Damned right, let me see that stiff dick of yours."

"You ever see hard queer pecker?" Judd asks. "If not, why not, since you've wanted to see it, and have it, for the longest time now."

Mr. Keel's mumbles are accompanied by another futile attempt to get free. Even with Judd's weight anchoring the desk, Mr. Keel wants to tip it, maybe even could, if not for the rest of us, placed on either side.

Judd unbuckles, unbuttons, and unzips. His ass lifts slightly and his jeans and his undershorts peel right on down, beneath his ass, all of the way to his knees. His giant cock, once free, springs to an upright position before Judd's belly. It misses Mr. Keel's face by a whisker, only because Mr. Keel's reflexes successfully jerk his head back in time.

"Jesus, Judd," says Mitch, "that hard cock of yours is really obscene -- as usual."

If anything Judd's dick is given additional bulk by the irritation of the jack-off his and my fist delivered to it earlier in the evening. It's certainly impressive enough to make Mr. Keel's eyes go buggy.

"Want a lick?" Judd asks Mr. Keel. His hand fists his dick and moves the loose outer layer of cockskin up and down over his cock's harder inner core

Unbeknownst to Mr. Keel, his licking of Judd's big cock is the last thing we want him to do, because, while we've tried our best to research the ins and outs of DNA testing, it's still pretty much Greek to us. We know all sorts of things can be determined by the traces of semen left behind, even little traces of preseminal leakage found in violated cunt and/or asshole, but

we're uncertain whether or not saliva and/or gastric acid destroys such evidence on contact. Not knowing means we're not about to take the chance.

The purpose of the exercise, although Mr. Keel can hardly know it, and isn't expected to know it, isn't to fuck his mouth, or his ass, but merely to have him fearful of getting fucked, fore and aft. Without creamy evidence left up his cherry rectum, and/or in his virgin mouth and throat, he'll have a hard time convincing anyone he has been attacked by the five of us. Likewise to our advantage, John Gramacery Prep isn't exactly a ghetto school where teachers walk around scared for their personal safety. None of us are slum children who would rather push crack than learn Latin. Well, maybe Latin isn't such a good example, because I truly do hate that subject and almost flunked it.

"Why don't you lick Judd's dick?" John suggests, his father a respectable stockbroker, his mother a professor of ecology at Bernhalin Tech.

The sons of respectable parents, like we're the sons of our respectable parents, don't upturn their teacher's butt over a school desk and threaten it with hard dick. If there are, occasionally, exceptions to rule that even children from good families can behave badly, the Menendez brothers immediately coming to mind, no parent of any of my classmates will believe any of us did any of this. Hell, even I find it hard to believe, and the suggestion we do it was mine; the joke having taken on a life all its own.

Mr. Keel will be hard-pressed, without substantiating evidence in back-up, to convince anyone that even Judd picks this particular kind of revenge for Mr. Keel having flunked him. Especially not with four of us prepared to give Judd an alibi that says otherwise.

Mr. Keel struggles a bit more but doesn't go anywhere. Watching him squirm against the desk, helpless in his cuffs, I'm struck by just how vulnerable he is, just how easily we've made him that way. He really is at the mercy of our merest whim. If we truly want to make him suck our teenage cocks ... if we really want to make his asshole take on our teenage cocks, to our cum-bulged teenage balls ... he doesn't have any say in the matter.

"Why don't we check out Mr. Keel's ass, bare as the day he was born?" I suggest. "I'll bet it's every bit as muscled and cherry as it looks with his pants on."

I hoist the tail of Mr. Keel's suit coat and tuck my hands under and around his waist to locate his belt buckle. Actually, I've seen his naked ass before, although it's doubtful Mr. Keel knows when and where. He'd been using the coach's shower, the only one in the gym with a door for privacy, but he'd stepped out just as I rounded a bank of lockers. Surprisingly, he looks even better naked than Coach Riley who daily grows considerably thicker around his gut.

Judd's cock remains uplifted before Mr. Keel's face.

"Think of my boner as an ice-cream cone that begs to be licked," Judd says. "As a lollipop that begs to be sucked. As a piece of lint, you the vacuum cleaner."

Bent over Mr. Keel, my arms around waist, its almost like I'm fucking him. Actually, were my cock out of my pants, it would be laid out, like a wiener in its bun, because that's how it is now, except his pants and mine are barriers in-between.

I get his belt and his fly unfastened. My fingers, beneath the waistbands of his trousers and shorts, tug. His pants and underpants slide from between his belly and the desk like a tablecloth yanked by a magician from beneath a eight-place table setting.

Another tug, and his clothing, from his waist on down, peels over his butt and down around his legs.

"Mitch, John, Keith," says Judd, "why don't you boys pull out your dicks and give Mr. Keel a better peek at just what we've got in store for him, as far as this evening's entertainment. You, too, stud," he includes me, speaking over Mr. Keel's naked ass. "What you guys have, by way of enormous contributions, will really put the thrill of God into this closet cocksucker."

Mitch, John, and Keith immediately unzip for viewing. I'm too occupied with the marvels of Mr. Keel's bare butt to fish my hard cock out of hiding.

If I've seen his butt before, I've never seen it this close. A fine line of hair appears where I've hoisted his shirttail and suit coat. The hair continues into the crack where his buttocks swell sexily from the base of his spine. Most of the hair disappears

into the crack, but some fans over the exterior of his buttcheeks. It's not crinkly, pubic hair, but the fine hair of a baby's head, only grown on the pate-like domes of Mr. Keel's ass.

My finger follows that line of hair, down his spine. My fingertip dips into his asscrack, like my toe tests the water of an outdoor swimming pool on a cool day. The inner slideway of his buttcrack is tacky and sticks to my finger like two cum-glued pages of a one-hand reader.

Can the police get my fingerprints from Mr. Keel's skin? As if I touch a hot spot, I pull back my hand.

Mitch, John, and Keith have their cocks on full display.

Mitch's cock is the most impressive. Perfectly circumcised, its scarring choker is the same color as the rest of his cock. His whole erection is a sleek rocket, only slightly thicker at its base than at the point where it begins its gradual taper to its blunt tip. His pisshole is wide and deep, as if Lizzy Borden's ax found its mark and cleaved deeply before being pried free.

In a butt-fuck, though, it's John's cock that, despite its smallest-of-the-three size, is the hardest to take. It has this funny, but sexy, little bend, about two-thirds of the way up its shaft, like a finger, once broken and improperly set. His cockhead looks like a miniature butt, its twin globes mirrored across the crease of his pisshole. Having his dick up your asshole is a unique experience, I can tell you, from personal experience. So can Mitch. So can Keith. So can Judd.

"You're really going to love John's prick up your butt," Judd says. "Your prostate hasn't really had a workout until John's bent prick provides one, his hairy balls slapping against your behind."

Keith's cock looks like one of those individual juice cans that come in six-packs, but without the logos and nutritional information. His dick isn't long, but it's stubbiness is so fat none of our fingers can't meet around its girth. What's more, its pisshole looks exactly as if a snap-top metal tab, once in place, has come free, leaving a key-hole hole.

Between the five of us, we prove cocks come in all kinds, shapes, and sizes.

Meanwhile, I've seen enough television, and movies, where authorities lift incriminating fingerprints, to suspect there's

probably none to be had from human skin. Cops do marvelous deductive reasoning from telltale bruising, but my hands, now on Mr. Keel's butt, have no intentions of taking hold with nearly enough force to do damage. Cops do marvelous deductive reasoning, when someone's ring punches human flesh, but I'm not wearing any jewelry.

I drop behind Mr. Keel's sexy bare butt. My hands glide his buttocks as if molding wet clay. My hands continue to the backs of his knees.

I touch the metal cuffs at his ankles and immediately regret doing so. I use a handkerchief, from my pants pocket, to wipe first one cuff and then the other. We don't plan to leave the cuffs behind, but I'm paranoid about the possibility of fingerprints on any of them. My paranoia extends to the cuffs at Mr. Keel's wrists, and I wipe them as well.

"Come on, stud," Judd coaxes me. He's less interested in my erasure of possible evidence than in continuing to give Mr. Keel a good scare. "Mr. Keel, here, sees everything offered but your cock, and your cock is the biggest of all. Let the bastard have a look."

I line up with Mitch, John, and Keith. They pump their dicks, in simulation of fucking Mr. Keel's ass or mouth, and I unzip. As earlier, with just Judd in the room, I'm quickly at an impasse. There's no way I can pry my too-stiff dick out of my open fly; the breach in my trousers just isn't large enough. I have to unbuckle, unbutton, unzip, and drop my pants and underpants all of the way over my ass.

"Will you take a look at that, Mr. Keel!" Judd marvels. "You ever see a boner that big in all your days of secretly yearning for gay cock? Did you ever dream that once finding it, it was all yours?"

Mr. Keel says something. Only he and God know what. His voice is completely muffled by the now spit-soaked gag with which I've stuffed his mouth.

"Mr. Keel is duly impressed," interprets Judd.

"We're all impressed," says Mitch, "and we've seen that juggernaut before."

"What did you promise the guy who passed out cock?" John asks me, for not the first time. His legs bend slightly at their knees, and he scoops a hand into his open fly, at the base of

his extended dick, and ladles out his admittedly impressive balls.

No one there, including me, not even Mr. Keel, whose impressive scrotum is visible to anyone taking a look at him from the rear, can match the two tennis balls hanging from John's cock. You want enough cum to expand a rubber to a possible explosion, and John's balls are the ones to supply the deluge. It's unbelievable, the amount of cream he squirts during just one orgasm. We had him measure it once, and it came in just short of a quarter cupful.

"Bet you'd like to suck one or both of John's heavy nuts, wouldn't you, Mr. Keel," Judd says, and it isn't a question. "Well, you're going to get your chance."

John moves closer, gives Mr. Keel a better look, and says, "We're here to fulfill your wildest fantasies, teach."

I'm fascinated by Mr. Keel's up-close butt, and I duck-waddle, my clothes at my ankles, in a return to it. I'm genuinely tempted to pry open his asscrack, locate his hair-haloed pucker, and fuck my cock so far and so deep that Mr. Keel thinks his throat is plugged with my cock from the inside-out.

I see no reason I shouldn't make my fantasy a reality, as far as seeing what Mr. Keel's sphincter looks like. God knows, I won't be in any more advantageous a position to do so at any time in the near future.

Facing his butt, I clamp his buttocks, my thumbs sliding into his asscrease and pulling his twin globes outward from his crack, as if I've an apricot that wants splitting.

His butthair plasters the walls of his crease, his sphincter a pinprick pucker, like a miniature mouth primed and ready for my cock to give it a soul-kiss.

I kneel for a better look, distracted by his scrotum as viewed from behind. I reach between his hairy legs, beneath his hairy ass, and clamp onto his hairy nuts.

Mr. Keel moans. Since I've not vised his balls with nearly enough force to hurt him, I assume his response is something other than pain. Is it his surprise at having his nuts stoked? Is it his unadulterated pleasure in having one of his students fondling his balls?

I lift my hand so his scrotum overflows my fingers, his two

balls nestled, side by side, within my palm. It's my extended fuck finger that makes the startling discovery that ...

"The bastard's got an erection!" I tell everyone.

I'm scared out of my wits by the sudden, accusatory, "Jeffrey, you goddamned lying, sonofabitch'n, hypocritical, two-timing bastard!" that's bull-horn bellowed from the still-open doorway.

No matter my name isn't Jeffrey, I let go of Mr. Keel's scrotum, like a rat letting go a sinking ship. I come to my feet with such an uncoordinated effort that I almost trip over my clothes pooled at my ankles.

We're all frozen to the spot: one of those tableaux, usually of famous pictures, that use real people.

It's the custodian, Mr. Crankshin, standing in the doorway. His impressive physique dwarfs the space it occupies.

When did I become so caught up in the game being played that I completely forgot Mr. Crankshin and his buffer? How had the five of us been so goddamned careless as to get too turned on not to notice when the buffer got turned off?

"'Oh, my ass is way too tight for a cock your size, Phillip,' isn't that what you tell me, Jeffrey?" asks Mr. Crankshin.

Someone, somewhere, sometime, told me, I think, Crankshin's first name is Phillip. And Jeffrey?

Mr. Crankshin continues: "Yet, here you are, Jeffrey, butt-up for some kid whose cock is twice the size of mine."

Jeffrey – Mr. – Keel? By God, yes!

"'Can't we somehow manage to persuade at least one of the handsome little bastards in the school where we work to join us in some sexual fun and games?' How many times have I asked you that, Jeffrey?" Mr. Crankshin wants to know. "How many times have you told me, 'I can't fuck around with the kids where we work, and neither can you. It's not safe. It's not ethical. It's not done.' And, here you are, not only with everyone-knows-I'm-a-queer-Mr.-Studly but four of his buddies. How long have you been getting teenage smorgasbord and leaving me out in the cold?"

Doesn't he see Mr. Keel is cuffed, arms and legs, to the desk? Doesn't he see Mr. Keel is gagged? Doesn't he hear Mr. Keel's reply, all muffled and indecipherable?

Not only does he see it all, and hear it all, but he has his

own explanation for it.

"I always knew you wanted bondage and discipline, Jeffrey," says Mr. Crankshin. "I never could figure, though, why you so adamantly resisted my every suggestion that I tie you to our bed. Seems the answer is that you're getting that kind of service elsewhere, you selfish sonofabitch!"

Mr. Crankshin steps farther into the room.

"Well, don't think you're talking yourself out of this one, Jeffrey," he says. "No moaning and groaning about the dangers of my splitting your don't-even-try-to-tell-me-it's-cherry ass. I've heard it all, anyway, and you're more attractive with your mouth stuffed and gagged."

"So, Mr. Crankshin, how long you and Mr. Keel been an item?" Judd asks. Inquiring minds want to know. I want to know.

"I'll bet the bastard hasn't mentioned me, even once, has he?"

Simultaneously, we all shake our heads.

Mr. Crankshin rubs the bulge his cock makes in his faded jeans, and it makes me even more horny than I already am.

I used to fantasize sex with Mr. Crankshin all of the time, imagining how he'd look stripped down and naked. That he was gay never crossed my mind. He was a much too stereotypically straight stud, complete with rugged jawline and obviously hunky physique. Where Mr. Keel always looked like someone trying too hard to pull off the very same role but not doing it nearly as well.

"Jeffrey and I have been diddling each other for about a year and a half now," Mr. Crankshin says. He's worked his cock to an sizable extension along his left thigh.

I've never seen Mr. Crankshin naked. His work hours are mainly after I'm off the premises, although I've seen him arriving and leaving plenty of times.

"There was a water leak in the ceiling of the locker room," Mr. Crankshin says. "Some water damage that a good buddy of mine at Renleu Construction thought he could probably fix on the cheap. I had my trusty Polaroid to snap a few photos to give my fiend an idea of the problem he was going to find. I find Jeffrey down, among the lockers, snarfing some student's, maybe even one of yours, discarded jockstrap and whacking his

own meat. I snap a picture of his self-abuse, and the flash clues him that he's no longer alone. He gets all wall-eyed and excited, offering me money to hand over the photo which, by then, has come out of the camera in perfectly colored detail. What I tell him I want, instead of money, for the picture, is a blow-job."

"Mr. Keel gave you a blowjob?" Judd expresses some of the disbelief we all feel.

"It was what I wanted," Mr. Crankshin reminds, his fingers back to massaging his already stiff dick. "I was always a little pissed by how butch Jeffrey tries to come off. I figured his giving me head would be the best thing for getting rid of whatever the stick he perpetually seems to have jabbed up his ass. Turns out, it wasn't a very good blow-job, but he's a fast learner. The latter something you guys probably already know."

"But you've never fucked his ass," Judd wants confirmation.

"Kept telling me it was cherry, that my cock would spit it from his asshole to his balls."

"It is a tight one," I say. If it's cherry and Mr. Crankshin is hung like a horse, which his bulged crotch gives every indication he is, the last thing I want to be part of is causing even one asshole of a teach, like Mr. Keel, any permanent damage.

"You got a big dick, Mr. Crankshin?" Judd asks and knows, as well as I do, that being a part of any ripping of Mr. Keel's virgin ass isn't going to play well.

"As big as yours," Mr. Crankshin boasts, "although nowhere as big as his," he nods towards me and my erection that still juts out and into my hand. I'm surprised Mr. Crankshin's unexpected appearance on the scene hasn't softened my dick to pabulum.

"Why don't you let us check out this dick of yours before you do the honors with Mr. Keel?" Judd suggests.

I figure Mr. Crankshin will merely unzip and pull his dick out, like Mitch, Keith, and John. At the most, maybe he'll drop his pants and underpants around his feet, just like Judd, Mr. Keel, and I.

He surprises by first unbuttoning his flannel shirt and stripping that material off over his massive shoulders to reveal

his chest, his arms, and his belly, their well-delineated musculature evident despite the fact they're covered with a thick matting of black hair.

"You boys don't mind if I get buck naked, do you?" His smile reveals a small dimple just to the right of his full lips. "I always feel more comfortable out of my clothes than in them."

"Be our guest," I encourage. I'm really turned on by his thick matting of hair where it disappears beneath the waistband of his trousers. Unlike most hairy men, Mr. Crankshin doesn't have visibly furry shoulders, back, or upper arms.

For not the first time, Mr. Keel says something, but no one can tell what. With Mr. Crankshin doing his strip, nobody gives a damn, anyway, about any asides Mr. Keel might be making.

Mr. Crankshin props one foot up on a nearby desk, unlaces its work boot, and peels off his sweat sock. He repeats the process with his other foot. Even the bastard's big feet are sexy.

When he unbuckles his belt, unsnaps his pants, unzips his fly, it's obvious, through the sudden breach of denim, that he's not wearing any underwear. That's confirmed when he unceremoniously drops his pants and kicks them to one side.

"Looking real good!" Judd compliments.

No lie!

Mr. Crankshin hasn't lied about his cock. It's just about the length and bulk of Judd's cock, only circumcised and a tad more streamlined. Mr. Crankshin's circumcision scar provides his tapered cockhead with a collar hardly noticeable. His cockshaft becomes fatter and fatter, the nearer its attachment to his lower belly, but the increase in size is gradual. It's one of those cocks perfectly designed for entering asshole smoothly and easily, causing the least amount of difficulty and/or damage. It provides no bends, bumps, or any other inconsistencies, to give any virgin ass any major problems.

"Here, you'll need this," Judd says and tosses Mr. Crankshin a lubricated rubber which the man catches with an ease that could well insinuate, if I didn't know better, its expected arrival.

"Much obliged," Mr. Crankshin says and tears the aluminum packet with his teeth.

"Funny that Mr. Keel never mentioned you," Judd says, playing right along. "Then again, maybe not. You've

mentioned how he likes to pretend he's so super straight? At times, he comes across downright homophobic."

"Which is what turned me on about him," Mr. Crankshin admits. He places the soppy rubber atop his dick, the condom's nipple an extension of his boner.

"Even has some of us convinced he flunked me just because I'm gay," Judd says.

"Except you, and I, and certainly Jeffrey, know he flunked you because your exam paper was a fucking screw-up, don't we?" argues Mr. Crankshin whose fingers are sticky with lubricant as he rolls the wet condom down the length of his dick. "I saw that final exam of yours, kid, and you messed a whole lot of the easiest questions."

Which has Keith, John, Mitch, and I casting curious glances in the direction of a truly embarrassed Judd.

"Yea, well .." is about all Judd can come up with.

I realize I'd never gone over Judd's test paper for quality of answers.

"I'm glad to see you took your flunking like a man," Mr. Crankshin wrongly interprets Judd's presence. "I mean, still ready and willing to show Jeffrey a good time, even though you'll be spending most of your summer in school."

"Well, Jeffrey does have a damned tight ass," Judd reinforces Mr. Crankshin's ongoing misconception. "And you've obviously taught him a good deal about cocksucking since he first swung on your dick in the locker room. It's kind of easy for me to overlook mere flunking when Jeffrey, here, has so much to offer by way of a consolation prize."

I'm definitely pissed at being there under false pretenses. If Judd actually flunked his exam, not graded down by a homophobic Mr. Keel, well ...

"When I'm through with Jeffrey, he'll know a helluva lot more about butt-fucking than he does now, too," Mr. Crankshin promises. "Not to knock your techniques as cocksmen, boys, but I've been around the block a few more times than any of you, and I've fucked a helluva lot more asshole."

"You will be careful with his asshole." That's about as far as I go toward pulling out of, or aborting, the session. The idea of seeing hairy Mr. Crankshin fuck his cock to his hairy balls up

Mr. Keel's cherry ass is just too much a temptation to spoil. It's not as if Mr. Keel is a complete virgin to male-male sex, what with what we've learned about Mr. Crankshin and him. It's not as if Mr. Crankshin's cock is so large it's likely to do any lasting damage. If Mr. Crankshin is the cocksman he boasts, and I see no reason to doubt his word, Mr. Keel is only going to thank us for allowing his own graduation into the farther joys of homosexual sex.

His rubber rolled all of the way down his uplifted dick, Mr. Crankshin pats down the latex hugged firmly to the base of his erection.

I duck-waddle, pooled clothes and all, to one side, in order to give Mr. Crankshin my position at Mr. Keel's ass. I'm going to move farther, but Mr. Crankshin reaches out and grabs my dick. The contact of his large, callused hand around my thick boner is so pleasurable a shock, I'm surprised it's not enough to have me creaming, right then and there.

"Don't go too far, kid," he says and holds on to make sure I've stopped all momentum. "Jeffrey's ass isn't the only one around here that can appreciate a cock the size of yours." He gives my stiff meat a hardy squeeze in additional invitation.

Mr. Keel begins another useless struggle to get free. I read it as a please-no reaction. Mr. Crankshin, though, reads it as something else again.

"Yeah, Jeffrey, you do want my cock up your ass, don't you?" Mr. Crankshin says.

Mr. Crankshin releases my cock but keeps his hand within easy distance until he's sure I'm staying put. Then, with a wide smile that indents his small dimple all the farther, and a lick of his lips to make his full mouth all the more sexy, he puts both of his ham-like hands to Mr. Keel's upturned butt, and he pries the twin globes open along their shared crack.

I've got a ringside view as his cock is put on target. A good half of his dick disappears into the crack before any actual penetration of Mr. Keel's tiny pucker. The visible length of Mr. Crankshin's boner forms a bridge anchored, at one end, at the janitor's hairy lower belly. Beneath the base of his extended dick is hung his hairy scrotum whose contents droop, one lower than the other; both of his balls move, this way and that, as their contracting sac begins to hoist his gonads more closely

to the base of the man's hardy erection.

Mr. Keel registers verbal protest, and I'm tempted, once again, to clue in Mr. Crankshin that Mr. Keel isn't exactly where he is on his own volition. While I'm still wondering if and how I should say something, Mr. Crankshin pushes a good inch of his dick up Mr. Keel's cherry behind

Mr. Keel's muffled groans are louder, and the cuffs on his wrists and ankles bang against the portion of the desk to which they're fastened.

"Yea, real tight!" Mr. Crankshin agrees. If he sounds surprised, it's probably because he's wrongly assumed my far bigger cock has already broken in the territory, at least a few times previous to his present stuffing.

"Easy, Jeffrey," Mr. Crankshin says and gently, lovingly, strokes my teacher's hair. "Believe me when I tell you you're going to thank us all for the ride I plan to give you this evening."

Mitch, John, and Keith have second thoughts. Anyway, they're into a combined, slow, but steady, progress toward the open door. I'm no more anxious to be around when Mr. Keel breaks the news to Mr. Crankshin that this teacher and students haven't really coordinated for these fun and games. I would ease slowly toward the door if not for two things. One, Mr. Crankshin might reach out for my cock and stop me. Two, I too much enjoy the slide of Mr. Crankshin's cock up Mr. Keel's virgin asshole to do anything, at the moment, but play voyeur.

A slow pressure, exerted by Mr. Crankshin's forward thrusting hips, dimples that man's hairless asscheeks, even as his cock slides into Mr. Keel's butt all the farther.

"I told you my cock is made for your ass, Jeffrey," Mr. Crankshin says. "Feel what you've been missing." He feeds my teacher another couple of inches.

"Good, isn't it, Jeffrey?" asks Judd who speaks to Mr. Keel's closed eyes.

Whether it genuinely is good for Mr. Keel, or whether he has just accepted the inevitability, he no longer struggles. His grunts and groans have deteriorated to purrs that last only for the duration of each additional inch of cock rammed inside him.

I'm so engrossed by the increasing nearness of Mr.

Crankshin's hairy belly to Mr. Keel's hair-fanned buttocks, I'm surprised Mitch, John, and Keith are no longer in the room. If anyone else notices their successful departure, no one says. Of course, some of Mr. Keel's grunts may be, "Where in the hell are those three cocksuckers off too?," but I doubt it.

There's this funny little sensation, somewhere in the region of both my balls, that says my prostate releases an oozing of preseminal goo. A firm upward stroking of my cock confirms and wets my fingers with clear liquid. Immediately, I veneer the outside of my dick.

As I do, Mr. Crankshin feeds the last of his cock up Mr. Keel's asshole. As I'd suspected, and hoped, there's no visible damage. Were Mr. Keel's asshole split from his balls to his pucker, or even subjected to far less damage, Mr. Keel would be doing more than just lying, so calm as he is.

"Maybe not so far up your butt as this studly to my right," Mr. Crankshin says and indicates me by providing a sexy smile and nod in my direction. "But I can safely promise you a genuinely good time."

He pulls his cock out until only his cockhead remains held by Mr. Keel's gripping pucker, then, he pushes his cock back inside. By now, the anal pathway, traveled by Mr. Crankshin's erection, is well veneered by lubricant left there by the condom. In all likelihood, Mr. Keel and Mr. Crankshin are due for smooth sailing. Which is my cue, if I have any sense, to begin my slow exit. Except, the pleasure of watching continues to glue me to the spot.

Mr. Crankshin grinds his hairy belly firmly against Mr. Keel's ass. His scrotum thickens even more, the lower hang of his one nut no longer noticeable in the more compact packaging.

"Now, studly," Mr. Crankshin says to me, his hand back on my dick and threatening me with ejaculation. "It's time for you to put your cock to better use than mere display. Ask your brags-to-the-world-he's-queer friend if he has another rubber handy. Preferably lubricated, because even my experienced butt needs all the help it can get when subjected to the likes of what you have to offer."

"Your wish is my command," Judd says and scoots out of the desk to pull up his pants, and underpants, to better access his condom supply cached in one trouser pocket.

"Feel free to make it a daisy chain," Mr. Crankshin invites. "The more the merrier."

Mr. Keel seems to be having a better time than he probably ever expected; his eyes remain shut, and there's actually a grin on his lips.

Mr. Crankshin turns loose of my cock only when Judd produces a lubricated rubber and begins, personally, to roll it down over my dick. Judd's silly-silly-ass grin is all ain't-this-the-most-fun-you-could-ever-have-imagined?

I'm still pissed that Judd flunked Mr. Keel's exam, on his own lack of merits, and not because Mr. Keel decided to take the teacher's indicated homophobia out on the class queer. Nonetheless, Judd's playful hands, sheathing my dick for a proposed thrust up Mr. Crankshin's until-now-only-fantasized ass, makes me genuinely forgiving. That I might have graduated John Gramacery Prep without having known our studly custodian is not only gay, but willing to be fucked up his ass by my cock, would have been too much a chance missed to accept lightly.

"How about it, stud?" Judd asks; my cock is all raincoated for Mr. Crankshin's ass. "You mind if I climb into your asshole for a tandem fuck?"

I should say no, just because he's brought me here under false pretenses.

What I say, though, is, "The more the merrier."

I can't wait to tell Mitch, John, and Keith what they missed by turning chicken-shit and running scared while Mr. Keel is still sufficiently bound and gagged to keep from letting the proverbial cat out of the bag.

My thumb hooks over my cockshaft, the weight of my hand pushing my cock to less than its upthrusting vertical. The head of my stiffy aims towards the floor, and my cock feels as if it's going to snap under the strain. I step in and put my cockhead underneath the hang of Mr. Crankshin's sexy ass. By releasing the downward pressure I still exert on my cockshaft, my erection, under its own impulse to return to vertical, springs upward into the crack of Mr. Crankshin's ass. Every inch of my cock's climb upward, along the crease, is punctuated by gentle thrusts of my hips to pinpoint the studly custodian's pucker. My first efforts result in nothing but flattening my bulbous

cockhead into the hair-lined valley of his crack. Finally though, my dick locates potential quicksand and succeeds in an actual roll-open of his tight sphincter.

"Yes, kid!" Mr. Crankshin verifies I'm on target.

I'm surprised at the ease with which my cock sticks completely into place up his butt. With nary a pause, my boner is sunk so deeply inside him that my pubic hair presses indents into both the muscled globes of his ass. More surprising, after I'm in, is how the resulting tightness of his anal hug, around my pecker, belies the ease with which I got there. The corridor of his ass masquerades as way too small a container for having had my meat so easily and successfully placed inside it.

"Sweet Jesus!" I say as his ass clenches and makes his asshole hug my cock even more securely.

Mr. Crankshin is to his balls up Mr. Keel. I'm up to my balls in Mr. Crankshin. Judd wastes no time feeding his rubberized erection up my willing behind.

"Agghrrrh!" I groan as the head of Judd's cock bounces into my prostate and his cockshaft drags right on by.

My hands slide Mr. Crankshin's torso, through the hair sexily matting his chest. My palms splay, then flatten, over his nipple-punctuated pectorals. He leans over Mr. Keel, and thrusts his butt even more fully over my erection.

For the enjoyment of all involved, Judd and I have participated in daisy chains before. This one could have been extended by Mitch, Keith, and John, and still been successful, considering the practice my four classmates and I have put in over our shared stay at John Gramacery Prep. It's Mitch, Keith, and John's loss that they've checked out early and left Judd and me to sample the fun and games offered up by Mr. Crankshin's experienced and by Mr. Keel's inexperienced assholes.

The trick to daisy-chain fucking, unless there's enough of you to form a complete circle, is to let the last man move first. Judd doesn't waste any time assuming his lead. In no time, he draws his prick out of my butt and leaves only his cockhead gummed by my sphincter.

I roll my asshole back over Judd's dick, simultaneously withdrawing my erection from Mr. Crankshin's asshole to where, since my cock is the biggest, not only my cockhead, but three inches of my hard dick, remain shot through Mr.

Crankshin's sphincter. Mr. Crankshin takes his cue and pushes his asshole back to a total engorgement of my prick, immediately unsheathing most of his cock from Mr. Keel's asshole. Mr. Crankshin's cock slides back in Mr. Keel's asshole, followed by my cock up Mr. Crankshin's asshole, then Judd's cock up my asshole. The whole procedure is, then, repeated again ... and again ...

Despite our combined experience in man fucking man fucking man fucking man, it's not without a couple of glitches before we completely master the best fucking rhythm. Like when Judd's dick pops free of my butt, and we all calmly wait for its re-placement. Like when Mr. Crankshin is so anxious to have all of my cock bucked up his rear, his prick flips free of Mr. Keel's asshole.

In the end, though, we get where we want to go, and butts get fucked with the same automatic skill that tells a centipede which of its legs to move, and when, in order to manage successful walking.

Against my palms, Mr. Crankshin's nipples are hard as the points of thumbtacks. By kneading my hands, over his pectorals, I massage his nipples to even greater hardness.

Judd's hands clamp my hips.

Mr. Keel moans and groans like sixty, and his soundings come across as anything but protest. The fucking of his cherry ass has obviously become just as pleasurable for him as he's probably always feared it would be. His fear of the pleasure having made him keep Mr. Crankshin's cock at bay until tricked into taking it.

The way I figure, either Judd or I is likely to cream first. Mr. Crankshin has a few more years of fucking butt, and Mr. Keel may or may not automatically orgasm with just the feel of Mr. Crankshin's inches working his behind; Mr. Keel's cock fucking thin air unless, of course, Mr. Crankshin, in his lean over Mr. Keel, has provided Mr. Keel's cock a fist to fuck. If Mr. Keel does have fist to fuck, his chances of coming out of this with his own bout of heavy creaming increase tremendously.

As well as the four of us fuck together, I can't imagine any equally well-coordinated mutual orgasms in finale. It has been my experience that someone is always quicker on the trigger, especially in a daisy chain, than any one or other of the

participants, and I see no reason this should be an exception. That only one of us may manage a climax up asshole, the rest destined, in the inevitable loss of coordination, during the first guy's orgasm, to finish off in our hands, doesn't distract from the pleasure of fucking a fucker while being fucked up the ass. Quite to the contrary.

I make no concentrated effort to control my recognized rush to orgasm. If any of us is to blast off first, it might as well be me. The idea of getting off up Mr. Crankshin's sexy butt is too much a temptation to have me think of anyone's pleasure but mine.

Therefore, I'm surprised by how my need for an increased fucking cadence, spurred by my rising passion, doesn't throw either Judd or Mr. Crankshin off rhythm. The three of us, having become one, progress to a faster, then faster, jab of cocks up assholes. Of course, Mr. Keel has nothing to say about it. Laid and cuffed over the desk, Mr. Keel's movements remain pretty much limited.

"Big cock up my tight ass, big cock up your tight ass, Jeffrey," says Mr. Crankshin.

"Like my cock, buddy? Like it? Like it?" Judd chants, leaned so close to my ear, from behind, I not only hear but feel his hot breathing.

"I do like your cock up my butt," I compliment Judd. "I do like my cock working, working, working Mr. Crankshin's tight rectum."

Mr. Keel moans, partly from the now-obvious pumping of Mr. Crankshin's right hand, somewhere beneath Mr. Keel's belly.

The four of us are a runaway train suddenly brought to an abrupt stop by collision with a brick wall. My cock falls into Mr. Crankshin's ass; he rams Mr. Keel's ass; Judd's dick rams to his balls up my asshole.

"I'm cuming!" I say over my rumbling pleasure and over Judd's animalistic grunts in my ear.

Even as my cock lets go to fill the rubber thrust so deeply up Mr. Crankshin's ass, there's the ballooning of another rubber pressed deeply up my rectum.

Mr. Crankshin's "Jesus fucking Christ!", and the sudden vising ripples of his asshole around my erupting dick says his

cock is in explosion up Mr. Keel's cherry asshole

The miracle of at least three simultaneous orgasms (I can only hope Mr. Keel joins us by spewing his own sticky load to Mr. Crankshin's obliging fingers), only make my final shudders more intense and enjoyable.

Luckily, the composition of the daisy chain provides Judd and me the possibilities of an easy escape from it, once our orgasms are done. Were one of us fucked in between Mr. Keel and Mr. Crankshin, our breaking the chain might not have been as easily accomplished.

Getting the hell out of there is quickly Judd and my prime objective. Neither of us wants to be around when the gag and cuffs come off Mr. Keel. Mr. Keel may have enjoyed the fuck, as much as the rest of us, but it's doubtful, his own pleasure over and done, that he appreciates the process that has brought him to this moment of Mr. Crankshin's exploded dick up his ass.

Judd wastes no time removing his cock and cum-filled rubber from my ass.

I move quickly, too, but I'm interrupted by Mr. Crankshin's massive hand reaching back and clamping my ass.

"A few seconds, more, please," Mr. Crankshin requests. "Just a few seconds."

I can hardly deny him his request. To do otherwise is to risk leaving behind one of my asscheeks in his talon-like grip. However, the first indication his grip relaxes, and I take the advantage to slip free.

Judd is already at the door with a better-hurry-it-up look on his face, even as he finishes zipping his trousers.

Mr. Crankshin, hardly aware of what compels Judd and me to discard the mellow pleasures to be enjoyed in the aftermath of a good fuck, makes no move to come unattached from Mr. Keel's fucked rectum.

I hurry to remove my rubber, tie it off, and put it in my pants. I'm made clumsy by my need to get out of there. It's only my accidental glimpse of Mr. Keel's cum, splattered on the floor beneath the desk, as well as its webbing of Mr. Crankshin's fingers, that tells me just how much pleasure Mr. Keel really ended up having from the experience.

"Mighty, mighty fine," Mr. Crankshin mumbles against Mr.

Keel's back. Mr. Crankshin's sweaty cheek makes a damp impression on the cloth of Mr. Keel's hoisted suit coat.

Judd and I say not a word as we're out of there, like two bats out of hell. Neither of us appreciates the thunder-like quality, with accompanying echoes, like rain on a corrugated tin roof, that accompanies our each and every hurried-to-a-run footstep as we head on down the hall.

"Jesus, was that a trip, or what?" Judd says only after we've exited the building and are on the sidewalk outside.

The sudden reappearance of Mitch, Keith, and John scares the hell out of the both of us.

"Goddamn!" I accuse the chicken-shit trio.

"Where are the cuffs?" Keith wants to know. "Didn't you get the cuffs?"

Is he kidding!

"My parents find them missing, they're going to shit bricks!"

As if Judd or I had been about to wait around to ask for the cuffs after Mr. Keel is released from them.

"I wiped them clean of all prints," I say, like I'm quite the expert at destroying state's evidence. Have I really wiped them clean, or does my memory play tricks on me?

"What happened in there?" Mitch moves right along.

"Could we get a little farther away before I give you the blow-by-blow, or is it fuck-by-fuck-by-fuck-by-fuck?" Judd asks and heads for Mitch's car parked conveniently at the curb.

We're safely driven down the block and around the corner before John echoes Mitch's earlier request for details.

"What happened?" Judd repeats, playing parrot. "A miracle, my boy. And you missed out on it."

All the rest of that night, and into the next day, I'm paranoid. Judd looks just as ill-at-ease, decidedly less cocky and exuberant, as we join up for graduation rehearsal in the school auditorium.

"Seems Mr. Keel has a sudden and very bad head cold," John whispers as he hurries by to assume his prescribed place in the crowd.

Which takes my heart out of my throat only for as long as it takes Mrs. (please no cracks about the one-time English Prime Minister) Thatcher to come over to tell me Mr. Crankshin, the school custodian, wants to see me in his basement office.

"You been up to some kind of mischief?" she asks me. She says it with a smile and only in passing. It's doubtful Mrs. Thatcher could easily imagine me with my cock up Mr. Crankshin's asshole, his cock up Mr. Keel's butt, Mr. Keel's cock fucked up Mr. Crankshin's fist, my butt stuffed with Judd's big boner. Besides, Mrs. Thatcher has other things on her mind, like how to get all of us through the paces for tomorrow's graduation. "Try not to be too long," she says and hurries off to give assistance with a public-address system that's suddenly wailing like a banshee.

I cast I'm-off-to-the-slaughter glances in the directions of Judd, Mitch, John, and Keith, but they're completely hemmed in by classmates and don't even see me get up to leave.

Feeling very much alone, I exit to the hallway.

All the lower classes are still in session, and will be for the rest of the week, but the building seems completely deserted.

There are two stairwells, and each extends from the subbasement to the third floor. Mr. Crankshin's office is in the basement, directly across from the locker room. He waits for me, though, where the stairwell narrows for its final drop to the subbasement. He sees me coming and walks down to the landing that commits the narrowed stairs to their final u-turn descent to the locked door at the bottom. I pause.

"I thought you might like your cuffs back," he says. "They look as if they might be expensive."

I can tell him they're not my cuffs, they've been ripped off from Keith's parents who, thank-God, apparently haven't yet missed them, but I don't say a thing. I'm concerned about his leading me to the locked area at the bottom of the stairs. Very few students, not even unauthorized faculty, are ever allowed into the guts of our school's heating and cooling systems.

"Don't worry, kid, I've no intentions of locking you behind closed doors and jumping your bones," he says. His smile, dimpling his small to-the-right-of-his-mouth dimple, is designed to prove his sincerity. "Not unless you want your bones jumped, that is." His smile widens. "No need to worry about Jeffrey, either. You may have heard he's down with a bad head cold. Actually, it's not a head cold at all. It's merely his way of dealing with the ethical problem he sees in having fucked around with five of his students; well, actually, with only two;

well, actually, it was only my cock up his butt at the time, but ..." He shrugs. "Not that Jeffrey didn't have a good time, despite himself. It's because he had such a good time that his conscience bothers him as much as it does. I predict a complete recovery as soon as you're all graduated and out of here."

He proceeds down the last leg of the stairwell to the locked door. I proceed only as far as the landing he's just deserted, and he already has the door unlocked and held open.

"I didn't want the cuffs lying around in the open for anyone to see," he explains. "Why invite unwanted questions that have answers people don't really want to hear? Plenty of hiding places down here, though."

I'm reluctant, even a little fearful, but that doesn't keep my cock from going stone-hard in my pants. My heart picks up its already rat-a-tat cadence. My hard prick pulses as I flash memories of it stuck up this handsome custodian's tightly muscled ass.

"Come on," he invites. The spider inviting the fly into its parlor?

"Can't you just go get them and bring them out?"

"Sure," he says. "I can easily do that. You want me to? Really want me to, I mean? Realizing this is liable to be the only time you and I will probably find ourselves together, with a bit of privacy, before you graduate to fucking college studs and forget all about prep-school janitors?"

My feet move, although I don't remember asking them to do so. I join him at the bottom of the steps. He widens the access made by the unlocked door, and he motions me on through. When we pass, face to face, his hand brushes my crotch. No way does he miss the hard cock he finds there.

I enter the maze of pipes and ducts that are the major ingredients of the subbasement decor, and Mr. Crankshin slips by me and takes the lead. I follow right along: an filing caught by the powerful force of a magnet?

It's easy to lose direction in the labyrinth, but I try to memorize the route back to the stairwell door that, although once again locked, can easily be unlocked from this side.

I'm still waiting for Mr. Keel to jump out at me, from behind every door, or appear around each and every corner.

Mr. Crankshin and I end up in a space near the boiler. It's a

space that seems no different from the countless passed to get there. That is until I follow his glance to one pair of missing cuffs draped over a length of sturdy, well-supported pipe.

"How about the matching pair?" inquiring minds want to know.

"Here," he says and nudges a brown paper bag at his feet but mainly concealed by more piping. "I don't see where we'll need them, for what I have in mind, for the moment, though."

He starts to unbutton his shirt. When he finishes, providing me a sensuous peek at his hairy chest and belly, on the other side of the breached material, he slips off the shirt completely and puts his torso on full display.

He's just as sexy as I remember. I'd figured my memories had made him better than he really is, but I was wrong.

"What do you think?' he asks and unbuckles his belt, unsnaps, then unzips his pants. As before, he wears no underwear. When his pants drop, there's a complete viewing of what he offers me, once again. His cock is stiff and extends outward and upward.

"What I think is that you have to be the studliest man I've ever seen."

"Flattery will get you anything your little heart desires. What do you say?"

He wears moccasins, no socks. He leaves his shoes beneath his pile of dropped trousers when he steps out. He reaches for the handcuffs hanging above his head. He slips one cuff around one wrist and secures the linchpin. He slips the other cuff on his other wrist.

"Need a little help securing this one," he says.

I step in and use its linchpin to lock the fleece-lined manacle in place. Mr. Crankshin's naked body emanates heat and odor I can feel and smell. My so-assaulted senses titillate my building desire.

My hands descend his uplifted arms, and run through the tangles of sweaty hair beneath his armpits. My fingers come to rest on his hips. One of my hands explores his belly and his crotch to take firm hold of his stiff dick.

"What say you give me the genuine treat of seeing you stark naked, this time?" he asks.

I'm reluctant to let go of his dick. It feels sexily velvet,

nestled firmly against my palm. Nevertheless, I release it, watch it rock from side to side as if a phallic metronome. Then, I oblige his request, and I strip to my birthday suit.

"God to be so young, so goddamned handsome, and so hung like a horse," he compliments. Except, he's the one who's about as perfect a male specimen as they come. Youth usually overrated, in my humble opinion; enormous cock usually overrated, too. His cock, on the other hand, just the right size for eating, just the right size for easy fucking. Not everyone, John included, can swallow all of my cock. Not everyone, Keith included, can take all of my cock up his butt with genuine comfort or pleasure.

I'm tempted to wrap Mr. Crankshin's perfect dick in a rubber and suck it to climax. Maybe sit my asshole over it with a force that'll slap his balls against my butt.

"I've several condoms in my shirt pocket," he says. That he's brought more than one gets me additionally excited by my prospects. Except, how long do we have before Mrs. Thatcher, or someone else, comes looking? Will that someone have a key to the subbasement?

Mr. Crankshin reads my mind. "We'll hear anyone coming," he promises. "With plenty of time to make ourselves perfectly presentable."

I know he'll have a viable excuse for our being in the subbasement, too.

I want to make every minute count, and I quickly locate his stash of rubbers. They're conveniently lubricated, and one feels cool and slippery as I roll it down the entire length of my erect cock.

I'm still tempted to detour for a bit of fun and games with Mr. Crankshin's just-right boner.

"Stuff your big cock up my tight butt, stud," he says and proves what I've always heard: in any b&d session, it's really the bottom-man who leads the parade; although, Mr. Keel, butt-up and leaned over the desk, might have been an exception.

"Yea," I confirm. What I want, too, is a renewal of that ecstasy had with my cock thrust to my balls up his asshole. His cock, and the pleasure possible from it, will have to wait.

From front and back, the hang of his body provides an even

more pronounced than usual v-shape to his torso. He has a surprisingly small waist that, from the rear, swells into his not-too-large, not-too-small, just-right buttocks.

His pinprick of a pucker is ready, willing, and able as I prop open his asscheeks for a look-see.

"Hard and fast, stud!" Mr. Crankshin instructs when the rubberized head of my dick is pushed on target.

I doubt hard and fast is achievable, what with the size of my cock that – if possible – is even bigger than usual; I remember the tightness of his asshole. Nevertheless ...

I'm into my balls in one impressive forward thrust of my hips. As before, though, his obliging asshole belies the ease of my complete entry by immediately clamping down on my cock with a force that, I swear to God, makes my dick thinner but longer in its placement up his butt.

"Jessssussss!" I hiss, run my arms around his chest and hold on as his ass attempts to gum my cock off at its base.

"Mmmmm," Mr. Crankshin purrs. The sound is sexy, and I hear it through his shoulders against which I press one whole side of my face.

After awhile, the discomfort of his hugging asshole becomes exquisitely bearable, and I marvel how I haven't already squirted a rubber-filling load up his asshole.

"Fuck me!" he says. "Yeah, fuck me good."

I do what he asks. If I still expect Mr. Keel to appear suddenly, maybe grab me from behind and fuck his dick up my ass, even hope that'll happen, as I screw Mr. Crankshin's hanging body, my pleasure is no less intense when it doesn't happen. My orgasm, when it comes and feeds my ropy streamers of steamy jism into the rubber up Mr. Crankshin's butt, and Mr. Crankshin's explosion when it comes and feeds his pearly ropes of cum into the thin air in front of his dick which I've obligingly fist-whipped, is just about all of the enjoyment I can possibly take at any one time.

JUNIOR CUM LAUDE

Chad Stuart

My hands hold his head. My fingertips, at the nape of his neck, have combed his cut-short and thinning brown hair to get there. My thumbs press his cheekbones. My palms partially cover his ears. My hips provide the easy backswing that slowly draws my cock out of his mouth to where his lips tightly hug the groove my cockhead makes in its flare from my cockshaft.

He's kneeling. His left hand has crawled up the back of my right leg and is anchored to a spot just above the back of my knee. His right hand cups my balls, his fuckfinger jabbing under and back to tap out indecipherable, but thoroughly sexy, Morse code against my sweat-sticky sphincter.

A forward motion feeds my dick, once again, full-length, into his face. If he has tonsils, they part for my cock passing through them.

When he sucks, his mouth and throat are a thoroughly snug cuff for my erection. He sucks with such force it makes my cock gain an extra inch in length, as if my dick were fucked into one of those sex machines that boasts, "Make your cock bigger or your money back."

He knows my cock and knows what to do with it to make me groan, squeal, mewl, and talk dirty.

His tongue curls around my dick, like a python around its prey.

I can't control my low murmur of appreciation. I've tried for such control, on other occasions. Some guys get through a whole fuck without a sound, but I never do. I feel pleasure and automatically go verbal.

Most people like my being so helplessly noisy. It makes them feel they're accomplishing something.

Calvin, who likes to make me squeal, coasts his mouth back up to my cockhead, slobbering slippery goo as he goes. His hand squeezes the back of my leg. His other hand squeezes my nuts. My testicles ache, in collision with his fingers and with each other, but not so much that the resulting pain overpowers my escalating pleasure.

"No one eats my meat, like you do, Calvin," I compliment and jab my cock back inside his face with a force that has choked tricks unfamiliar with it.

It's Calvin's turn to moan, and he does so. His sounds vibrate the submerged length of my dick.

My cock comes almost out, pauses, slides back in.

I fuck Calvin's face, but how would it be to fuck Mr. Clacker's face? Not because Clacker is more handsome than Calvin, because he's not. Clacker and Calvin are probably the same age: mid-fifties. They have the same mousy brown and thinning hair, although Clacker has even less to comb, from right to left, beginning at his too-low part just above his right ear; such tortured hair looks ridiculous in its feeble effort to disguise, up and over, pates destined to go bald as billiard balls. Nor do I imagine Clacker gives better head than Calvin. After all, Calvin knows every inch of my cock, doesn't he?

"That's it, Calvin," I encourage. "You know just how to do it, don't you?"

I'd be more realistic to imagine my sucking Clacker's fat and stubby cock. A cock I've seen but never touched. One evening, Clacker's cock and going-to-seed hairy-back body were in the high-school shower room; Clacker exhausted from playing handball with Mr. Davis. Now, Davis is something else again. It's hard to believe Davis a teacher of dull Advanced Math. Geometry seems more suitable, considering his perfectly squared jaw, his perfectly rectangled pectorals, his perfectly triangled chest-to-waist. His abdominals are muscled Gordian knots. As for his big, thick, juicy cock ...

I shake my head to clear it. Davis has no place in my thoughts these days. He's already told me I'm getting an A. Not much else he can do, since math is so cut and dried. A math question has but one right answer. Get it right, and the teacher is obliged to give you an A. Clacker, on the other hand, teaches Creative Writing. There's less right and wrong in that subject. There's only murky territory wherein teacher ends up playing God, interpreting what's right. Yes, Clacker is my chief worry at the moment. Although imagining Davis' big dick and studly body will get me hotter, faster.

Calvin pulls free. Had my mind not been occupied elsewhere, I could have prevented him his freedom by holding

tightly to his head and force-feeding my cock back down his throat.

"Anything wrong?" Calvin asks. It's so dark, among park trees, I hardly see his face. I've known him long enough, have seen him in good lighting often enough, to picture his expression: mouth slightly pouted, eyes curious, brow knitted in obvious concern.

"Wrong?" I echo. "Only that, for whatever the reason, you've cut me off mid-suck. Tease me for too long and that handful of my nuts you're holding will turn blue for sure."

"You seem ..." He searches for the word. "... distant," he decides finally.

How is he able to sense that from merely sucking my cock? What is my stiff dick: a transmitter that whispers, "You may be eating this hustler's cock, Calvin, but his mind is a thousand miles away?" It's not the first time Calvin has pulled something like this. Earlier in the year I had that slight disagreement with Mrs. Prockmire, over a history grade, and Calvin sensed that, too. ESP shit makes me more than a little uneasy.

Calvin decides to put the blame squarely on his shoulders and on the rubber that wraps my cock. "I can never manage to make it as good as in the days before condoms-always-required."

Maybe so, but what do I know? I've never had one-on-one sex without a rubber. Not from that very first time, earlier this year, in this very park, not more than a few yards from this very spot, when I first discovered I could get money for sex. I'm not likely to know better head than Calvin-swinging-on-my-rubberized-dick.

"Come on, Calvin, you were doing just fine," I encourage. He prides himself on his skills at eating cock. There are guys, even among those who pay, who are better looking, better hung. Calvin needs something to offset all his minuses. He needs that as much as I need an A from Clacker. "No one gives head like you do, Calvin. No one. You want to hear me beg for it, you sadistic bastard? Okay, I'm begging: Please suck my cock, you cock-sucking genius, you. My dick needs your mouth wrapping it. I've two nuts so hurting with cream-to-be-exploded that if you don't coax my balls to flooding, soon, my testicles will explode under the pressure."

"God, I wish I could swallow each and every gallon of your cum, junior" he says. He'd like to be rid of my rubber, but he never comes right out and asks. He knows what I'll say. Although I'd probably be in little danger, from his swallowing my load, I don't like even those odds. I've plans that don't include even the risk of any sexually transmitted disease.

"You want to swallow something, swallow my dick," I tell him. "It's made for your face. It's made for your mouth and your throat."

"I'd rather have your cock up my butt. Can you do that for me, junior?"

"Sure, Calvin."

Sometimes, he gets off by beating his meat while sucking. Even now, his cock is out and ready for a pounding, although he's too quick on the trigger to take hold until I let him know I'm about to explode. Sometimes, though, he wants it up the ass. He has a surprisingly tight ass for someone as old as he is, his poop-shoot having passed God only knows how many giant turds. Not to mention however many cocks, besides mine, which have been thrust up his butt in his lifetime. Last time he asked me to fuck him, it was when I had that problem with Prockmire. Maybe Calvin figures I pay him more mind when I fuck his ass, as opposed to when I fuck his face. Do I?

"You want my cock up your butt, it's yours," I tell him. "No mouth gets me off better than your mouth, though, Calvin."

"Really?"

"You're a genuine talent, Calvin," I compliment. "I've a long list of customers who swing on my dick, and you rank right at the top." I'm an expert at bullshitting clients and letting them think they get their money's-worth, but if Calvin were younger, better looking, took better care of his body, his sexual skills could easily see him a seller, at this meat rack, rather than a buyer. How did he manage, in his younger days, before his hair thinned, before his belly sagged, before his tits became almost feminine in their hang from his ribcage?

He takes me at my word and returns to my dick in so well orchestrated a move that he immediately has my full attention. Even my concerns over my Creative Writing final grade are filed for future reference.

I'm determined to stay focused. I'm here to forget the pressures of school. Calvin deserves services paid-for. He shouldn't be short-changed just because Clacker may well hold my future in the mere stroke of his pen.

"Mmmmmm, yes," I say. It's more a loud purr: one of but many spontaneous sound effects from my extensive, reflexive, repertoire.

Have I always made so much noise during sex? No. It began when I got off with the first man. Before that, I could be as quiet as the next guy, even beating my meat to silent climax, beneath the covers, while my parents slept fitfully in the very next room. I hardly squealed when Betty McDaniels slipped a hand down my trousers and webbed her fingers with my suddenly exploded slime. I can still keep my mouth shut while beating my pud. I probably could do likewise should another girl play my dick to climax; although I've not given too many girls that opportunity lately. Straight sex not only seems less enjoyable, these days, but it's decidedly less lucrative. There are women who pay for stud services, but it's a helluva lot easier, and a helluva lot more fun, to carry out business with the endless line of paying customers available in the park.

"That's it, Calvin! Jesus, you know how to get me hot and horny and keep me there, don't you?"

His lips gum the base of my stiff dick. His nose butts my lower belly. My small patch of pubic hair is his mustache and beard.

He prepares to do something only he ever manages to do. I marvel at how he can do it; because, not bragging, my cock is bigger than average. I'm not just talking long but bulky and big around. I've had guys back out of sessions for fear they'll either choke on it or see it split their assholes all of the way to their balls. Not Calvin. When he's a mind, like now, he can successfully suck up not only all of my cock but both my balls, at one and the same time, too.

His hand moves my nuts into position, tugging them forward, his fuckfinger momentarily leaving my sphincter.

"You really know what gets me even hotter, don't you, Calvin?"

He sucks up one of my nuts and mashes it deliciously against the swallowed base of my cock. As my other nut joins in, he's

a boa constrictor dislocating his jaw in order to swallow a prey-fattened python.

No cockring does for my cock, as far as stiffening it and keeping it that way, what Calvin's lips around my cock and balls do. When he gums down on his mouthful, my cock pulses longer and fatter.

"Yes, goddamn-it, yes!" I congratulate. A reflexive backswing of my hips stretches my scrotum to the point of ripping, but my balls stay right with my dick within Calvin's moist saliva which washes them. I surrender with a forward buck of my hips that releases the stretch of my scrotum and eases the pain in my balls.

There's a marvelous rippling along the length of his throat and around my submerged inches. That snake, with prey now swallowed, works diligently to coax its meal deeper. If I'm to be made a eunuch, there's no more pleasurable way.

Except, Calvin enjoys my cock and balls too much to deprive me of them. He does what he does to show his talent, as a cocksucker, no matter his less than attractive packaging. No doubts: Calvin is cocksucker supreme! I'm lucky he's leeched, once again, to the very base of my belly, that I've sprouted his head, neck, torso, arms, hands, legs, feet, cock and butt from my crotch. I'm luckier still to be paid for it.

My balls, ejected, one by one, through a tiny slideway between his pursed lips and my hard cock, are squashed painfully but pleasurably, and my scrotum is awash with his spit. My hairy sac feels cool as his saliva begins to evaporate into the night air. Calvin is hungry to have my cock and drink the cum-cocktails contained in my big balls.

His face slides up my dick and lingers at its top. His tongue caresses a particularly pleasurable spot on my cockbelly where my cockshaft attaches to my bulbous cockhead.

I groan my appreciation, much as always: loudly and spontaneously. My hands clamp harder against his face and hold him where he best works his magic. He and I know he can get me to orgasm merely by concentrating some furious sucking of my cockhead. He can get me there even faster if, along with his sucking of my lollipop dick, he provides my cockshaft with some hearty up-and-down hand strokes.

Calvin, though, wants more of my cock than just its head.

His hands clamp to the muscled cheeks of my ass. His mouth swallows my uplifted cockshaft, his forehead riding against my muscled belly most of the way down. His throat squeezes my cockbelly, where it meets my cockhead, with almost as much resulting pleasure as when his tongue and lips perform the service.

"Jesus, Calvin, eat my big dick!" I command. How it comes out is, "Jeeeessus, Caaallllllvvvinnnn, eeeee iiiiiii big dick!"

"We've been through this enough times to avoid rough transitions. Smooth and easy, he face-fucks my dick, up and down, up and down again. At the same time, my hips take up a forward-and-back rhythm. Every downward slide of his hungry mouth, over my burgeoning dick, has my hips feed my cock into his face. Every time he pulls back up, my hips pull my cock out to its head. Together we're faster and more graceful than on our own.

I'm not the only one making sounds, although Calvin's are wet, where mine are animalistic. I purr and mewl, grunt and groan, manage a decipherable, "Eat me, eat me!" He sloshes, slurps, sloppily blows bubbles from his drooled spit. An animal, part cat, part dog, seems caught in a washing machine, unable to get out.

My cock really pumps his obliging face, and, as enjoyable as that is, it can't last forever.

"I'm pretty far gone, Calvin!" I warn, and I'm so far gone it sounds as if I'm speaking through a saliva-sopped rag.

My scrotum, long dried of that veneering of spit obtained when sucked, with my cock, up Calvin's mouth, is provided a new deluge of Calvin's spit that clings to my hairy sac in translucent beads. Calvin isn't decorating my nuts to make them look like Christmas. His clinging globes of saliva rupture beneath the roll of his fuckfinger that steals their goo. His fuckfinger, wet, shoves beneath my pleasure-shrinking scrotum and jabs to its first knuckle up my asshole.

"Oho!" I exclaim, my butt now stuck even as my cock gets sucked. I take a wider stance to provide for a more pronounced entry of his finger. Calvin obliges and jabs even deeper.

The hustler Jerry, who initially showed me the ropes as regards the park scene, wouldn't approve of how far I'm letting Calvin go. To Jerry, a hustler's ass is sacrosanct. Let a trick

violate your butt, even with his finger, and you step over some invisible line that labels you queer forever. Jerry, up until his disappearance, suddenly, and without explanation, considered himself straight. He considered me straight. Therefore, he'd emphasized, "You don't kiss 'em, and you don't let 'em anywhere near your ass." Except, if those were the criteria separating straight from gay, I was gay from the very first time Calvin tapped Morse code on my sphincter and I invited his finger, in no uncertain terms, to go exploring farther and deeper.

Calvin has as much perfected the finger-fuck as he has the head-job and the cock-gobbling of his ass. His finger drills my asshole, torques outward, drills again, all the while crooked to milk my prostate for all it's worth.

Fed pleasure from both ends, I'm not destined to hold out much longer.

"I'm about to cum, Calvin," I warn. My words are indecipherable, even to my own ears, but Calvin has heard them enough times to know what they mean.

He fists his dick, jutted from his open fly since almost the beginning. With complete coordination, he sucks my cock, beats his meat, and finger-fucks my asshole.

"Agghhhrrr, ah, ah, agghhhhgrrhhh!" I provide sound effects. His harmony is all foot-being-pulled-from-the-mud.

I try to hold off orgasm, but I'm the little Dutch boy trying to stop the leakage from a mere hole when it's the floodgates that are open wide.

A forceful buck of my hips, and a downward dunk-shot of his head over my orgasm-primed erection, and my cock is locked in place. His finger-fuck of my asshole keeps right on going, like sixty, until one massive shock wave after another shoots through my body. My butt clamps so tightly that Calvin's finger becomes a coal miner caught in a cave-in.

I feed my cum through my cock and into the rubber I've cock-crammed deeply inside Calvin's throat.

My balls work overtime to geyser my super-heated cream up and out, up and out, up and out, with no letup of the exquisite pleasure set loose inside me.

I make more of the sounds I always make during orgasm. They're loud and sexy sounds, but this time, as usual, all I hear

is what I assume must be a whole crowd of orgasming onlookers cheering me on.

My massive squirts aren't enough for Calvin, and he follows up with additional sucking: my cock a giant straw through which he coaxes each and every sperm presently manufactured by my cum-producing testicles.

I clamp my forefinger and thumb to the base of my cock. Not to keep Calvin's final hearty suckings from vacuuming my cock loose from my lower belly, although it does feel he'll succeed in just that. Rather, it's to be sure my cum-greased condom doesn't slide off my dick like a raincoat caught in the updraft of a tornado and suctioned from a helpless victim of the storm.

"Jesus, Calvin!" I'm back to knowing what I say. "You've not only sucked up all my cum but every bit of marrow in my bones."

To be sure, he gives a final suck of my cock as his finger gives a final prod of my prostate. I'm afraid the vise-like compression of his throat will burst the bubble of cum sprouted from my cockhead like the bulbous nose of an elephant seal. However, when Calvin finally pulls free of my cock and of my butt, my cum is safely contained.

I peel off my condom without pulling out too many pubic hairs. I tie off the open end of the rubber and pull up my pants. I put the used condom, with its cum, into my right front pocket. Like the animals I sometimes sound like, during a fuck, I have an inbred instinct not to foul my own nest. Some people are genuinely turned on by sex among discarded rubbers, but I'm not.

"Feel like a cup of coffee?" Calvin asks. He so swiftly gets his cock wiped free of its mess and stuffed back in his trousers I only catch a fleeting glimpse. Not nearly as large as mine, his cock, nonetheless, has a nice streamlined taper from its pulpy head to its thick base.

"I'd like a cup of coffee," I decide. Jerry, the straight, helpful hustler, once told me that, after being sure a trick doesn't kiss me or fuck me, I should never get up close and personal with one. "Fucking a queer and getting sucked by one is one thing," said Jerry. "Getting all chummy with one ..." He never spelled out the consequences, but I never doubt, even for a moment, that he feels the dangers are real and frighteningly

dire.

During Calvin and my stroll to the edge of the park, we get a close-up view of what others are up to. I'm so thoroughly drained from Calvin's sucking that not even the usually cock-hardening performance of Gerald, whose forte is being sandwiched between two hot-and-hunky guys, provides rejuvenation for my poor pecker.

Lers Hut is a coffee shop and all-night diner a couple of blocks away. For a long time, I thought the place owned by someone called Ler, until Jerry provided his don't-be-so-dumb insight: "Rearrange the letters, they spell Hustler. Guy who owns the joint is Gerbetti. 'Big' Dick Gerbetti. And I do mean big dick."

I've never seen Big Dick Gerbetti, or Big Dick's big dick. I've only met Alice (please-don't-ask-me-if-I've-ever-owned-a-restaurant!), and Christian (please-don't-ask-me-what-a-Christian-like-me-is-doing-in-a-place-like-this!).

"So, you want to talk about it, or what?" Calvin asks over the steaming cup of brew Christian leaves before leaving.

"Talk?"

"About what's wrong."

"You brought me here to ask for a refund?" I know better. Calvin has this sixth sense that invites me for coffee whenever something is troubling me. Actually, we originally met in the coffee shop, not in the park. He brought me coffee, then, too, then asked how much I'd charge to let him give me a blow-job. I'd said I'd just been tapped out of fresh cum by some asshole, literally, in the park. He'd promised me another hard-on and more cum in no time. He hadn't lied.

"School?" he divined. Not much of a brainer, because most of my problems were school-related. Not the problems of a kid who doesn't give a damn about education and thinks himself better off fucking, sucking, or smoking dope. Quite the opposite. I learned, at an early age, my only chance to make something of my life was education-dependent. Hustling was fun, and lucrative, while it lasted, but not even a stud like me can expect to be fresh meat forever.

"Highest grade point, at the end of the year, gets the Grailman Scholarship." Not much, just a couple thousand bucks, but, along with the money I'd saved from selling my

cock in the park, it would give me a year's college tuition.

"I thought you were pretty good in the smarts department," Calvin says. Originally, he figured me some kind of jock. Not bragging, but I look the part. My physique, and even I admit it's a damned good one, is more the result, though, of good genes (thank my otherwise deadbeat old man for something!). I manage quite well in most any sports arena, never the last one chosen for any team, but I'm not a natural at game-playing. No way do I get into college that way.

"I'm good, but Steven Grailman, Junior, is good, too."

"Steven Grailman, Junior. Grailman Scholarship."

"Bingo! Three Grailmans in the old high-school since great granddaddy Grailman set up the scholarship. Two got the scholarship, and Steven's dad expects him to be number three. Right now, Steven and I are just about neck and neck, me with a slight edge because of some teacher, not won over by Steven's suck-up charms, having given him an A- instead of an A, back when we were sophomores."

"You've projected final grades and see Steven pulling ahead in the last minutes?"

I notice a certain something in Calvin's eye that I intuitively connect to his hand beneath the table.

"Are you whacking off, Calvin?" I change the subject.

"Never you mind, junior," he says and smiles a caught-in-the-act that's all Alice-in-Wonderland Cheshire. "I get turned on just listening to you."

I almost ask if I should charge him for the good time, as well as let him pay for the coffee, but I don't. Calvin is a good guy. Actually – sorry Jerry, straight hustler, wherever you are! – I like the guy. What's more, I need someone to talk to. Dad's never sober long enough to process any thought except how he'll get his next shot of whiskey. Mom is too busy just trying to hold the family together and make ends meet. There's never been any I'd-like-to-thank teacher to take me under his wing. Mr. Tanburn, in ninth grade, might have been, but knowing he was slightly effeminate warned him away from any personal relationships with his students, me included. As for school chums, I don't have any in a system that draws such a definite line between jocks and nerds and can't fit me comfortably on either side. I play sports too well to be a geek, and I'm way too

smart for most of those Neanderthals forever towel-slapping bare ass in gymnasium locker rooms.

"About this Clacker," says Calvin and brings me back to the here and now. "You ever think of waving your big dick in his direction? Maybe he sees that dick of yours, up close and personal, and you see an A in his Creative Writing course."

"Clacker, if he likes boys, and there's nothing but unsubstantiated rumors to say he does, likes them prettier and far less butch than I am." Steven Grailman, Junior, is pretty and fine-boned; as is his equally pretty and fine-boned father, Steven Grailman, Senior.

Under the table, I slip off a shoe and extend my foot in a direct route for Calvin's crotch.

"Jesus!" he jumps about a foot when my foot touches down. Had he jumped any higher, everyone would have seen hot, fist-bunned, wiener not on the diner menu.

I laugh. I can't help myself. He looks so funny. He even manages an attractive blush that subtracts virtual years from the way he looks.

"See." I touch my foot down again, having reflexively pulled it back when he'd made his reach for the ceiling. "Just me."

"We were talking about your problems with Mr. Clacker," he says and begins a slow peel of my sock from my foot.

"Did I mention that my Waterloo is a Creative Writing final tomorrow afternoon, fifty percent of the course grade riding on it?"

"I suspect an imaginative young man, like you ..." He pauses and puts the length of his erect cock against the sole of my now-sockless foot. "... is a whiz at writing creatively."

"I am, if I've the right subject. I just have this gut feeling that tomorrow, for finals, Clacker isn't going to say, 'Okay, give me fifteen-hundred words about some guy, with a foot fetish, fucking your foot in a twenty-four-hour diner whose name unscrambles to spell Hustler.'"

Lots of eye contact, almost flirtatious, between Clacker and Steven lately. Does Clacker want responsibility for the first Grailman heir, up for the Grailman Scholarship, coming away empty-handed?

Calvin humps my foot in earnest. His hands are under the table and clamp his cock to the sole of my foot.

I sip my coffee. Calvin's ain't-this-grand expression works miracles on my cock which noticeably stretches its impressive coils within the crotch of my pants.

"You'll do fine," he encourages. He keeps one hand beneath the table and uses the other to drink coffee.

His cock feels good, pressed so firmly against the sole of my foot that there's heat from the friction caused by its jiggling. I imagine one of those exotic, Oriental foot massages that uses a wooden dowel instead of a woody.

Calvin stops for a moment and locks the head of his cock between my big toe and my toe immediately adjoining, as if attaching his oar to an oarlock. So hooked up, he puts both hands on the table. His fingers drum the tablecloth.

"If you were in my Creative Writing class, I'd give you an A, if I had a Creative Writing class."

"Don't believe me when I tell you it's the thought that counts," I say with a can't-help-myself grin.

I sip more java. I squeeze my toes together and curl them slightly. My garroting his cockhead makes his eyes go positively dreamy. I see the chill of pleasure whip through him. He and I have obviously tapped something new, by way of fun-and-sex games. My cock continues its resurrection.

I'd get harder, faster, if I concentrated more on the pleasure-at-hand and less on my jealousy over the ease with which Steven Grailman, Junior, gets his good grades. I sometimes have to sweat blood to achieve the same ends. It's as if he gets good grades not because of hard work but merely because he is who he is. Does Clacker feel Steven deserves an A because Steven is who he is, Steven's father is who he is?

I'm depressed. Which is why I was at the park in the first place. I'd be even more depressed if I hadn't fucked Calvin's mouth and didn't now have Calvin's prick locked to my foot.

Christian refills our cups.

"Cream?" I ask Calvin when Christian leaves.

"Don't mind if I do," Calvin says. He doesn't reach for the cream pitcher, though, but for his cock and my foot under the table. He renews his more heated rubbings of his dick against the sole of my foot.

He's quiet about it; something I wouldn't have been able to pull off. About now, I would have been grunting, groaning,

moaning up a storm. I would have had people asking if I were all right. Someone would manhandle me from my seat and perform the Heimlich maneuver.

The only blatant evidence that Calvin plays his cock to climax against my foot is the glassiness of his eyes. His eyes, dark blue, are possibly his best feature.

When he speaks, "Good thing you aren't ticklish, junior," his voice isn't so breathless as to notice.

"You're giving me a hard-on, you bastard," I say over my coffee. I shift my ass and drop a hand to my crotch to better align my cock for more convenient swelling within the snug confines of my trousers.

"You're always quick to get a hard-on," Calvin says. "That's one of the reasons you're so attractive. Of course, it helps that you look so young I'm not the first to mistake you for jail-bait."

"Calvin," I scold, "you never told me you had a thing for chicken."

"Look like jail bait," he reminds. "The last thing I want is trouble with the cops."

"Well, Calvin-who-likes-chicken-look-alikes, you perform a wicked foot massage. Maybe you ought to go into the business."

"Maybe ... maybe ... maybe." His chant corresponds to his hand movements and with whatever else goes on between his hand, my foot, and his erection.

I stiffen my leg and more thoroughly lock my knee to press my foot even more firmly into his crotch.

"Mmmmmm." That's all he says, as if he's in a coffee commercial, thoroughly approving some special blend.

It's not what he says, even how he looks, that tells me he's popping his rocks. It's the splash of his blasted wet-and-hot cum against my ankle, against the top of my instep, against my bare toes.

"Jesus," he allows himself finally, "who would have guessed?"

"No previous suspicions of this foot fetish?" I smile and sip more coffee.

"Not until your foot came along." He pulls several napkins from the dispenser on the table. He wipes up the mess under the table; at least, he wipes up whatever the evidence on his

cum-webbed fingers, on my cum-laced toes, and on the rest of my foot.

He puts my sock back on my foot. I put my foot back in my shoe. Christian asks if we'd like more coffee.

"I've really got to get going," I tell Christian and Calvin.

"Me, too," Calvin says.

Christian leaves our tab on the table. Calvin pulls out his wallet.

"I think, junior, you deserve something more than just the coffee. He thumbs some pretty large-denomination bills, and I'm tempted.

"Consider this time on the house," I decide to be generous. "It's not everyday I graduate to new sexual horizons."

"I accept your generosity, only because you'll profit in the long run." He smiles. He has a nice smile. From what I can tell, he still has all his own teeth. "You'll see me twice as often now that I find your foot, as well as your big cock, so enticing."

I think briefly of returning to the park, a shame to waste my so impressive a woody on my hand, but it's a school night, and tomorrow is Creative Writing final. I won't get extra points for falling asleep during the test. So, I nurse my unrequited boner on the bus ride home.

It's only sheer chance I pick the bus route, one of the three available, that goes nearest my high school. It takes thirty minutes of riding before I spot the school a block away. There's a meat rack closer to my school, and to where I live, than the park I frequent, but I've never been. I don't like the increased odds of running into someone I know who might carry tales about what I do in my spare time.

Spotting Steven's new car, his early graduation present from his old man, isn't hard to do. If he wants to be inconspicuous, this bright red auto isn't the way, even if he manages to park it within the deeper night-shadows of a large tree.

I push the 'ding' bar that brings my bus to a halt at the next stop. My curiosity, as to what brings Steven here, at this time of night, overcomes my urge to get home and beat my stiffy to manageable softness. Steven's present parking spot is more convenient to my house than his. Who does Steven pal with who lives nearby? Randall Max lives just down the block, but

Randall is a die-hard jock who wouldn't be caught dead with a nerd like Steven, not even if Steven drove even fancier wheels.

The quickest way to my house is through the school yard, and I head in that direction, all the while checking for the little rich boy. His vanity license plates -- SGJR -- confirm the car, indeed, is the property of Steven Grailman, Junior.

"So, what brings you out to play, at this time of the night, in this area, Steven?" I ask the night.

There are lights on in the school, but the only car in its official parking lot belongs to Mr. Conner, the custodian.

I take aim on the football field and figure to cross it on the diagonal. No way am I prepared to rattle school doors and ask a disgruntled Conners if he's seen Steven Grailman, Junior, anywhere about. Conners is a big-as-a-house ex-marine who saw duty in Desert Storm. He keeps to himself, and it's doubtful he'd appreciate my intrusion.

Maybe Steven's car merely broke down and is awaiting the friendly neighborhood tow truck. It would serve the little prick, and his father, right, for not buying American, but I'm grabbing at straws. More likely Steven is pulling an all-nighter with some chum from school.

I'm in the shadow of the bleachers when walking any farther, with my hard dick in my pants, becomes too much a bother. I lean against a metal support pole that's no less stiff than my cock, and I pull out my boner through my unzipped trousers. Who would know my cock has so recently been made flaccid by its workout in the park with Calvin? What has there been about Calvin rubbing his cock to climax against the sole of my foot that is so damned sexy?

I fist my cock, give it a couple hurried pumps, and have no intentions of prolonging my masturbation any longer than necessary. I figure the resulting sounds are some of my usual reflexive gutturals. Except, I'm not all that noisy when beating my own meat. Even if I were, it's a little early for me to be quite so vocal.

My fisted cock juts like a drawbridge before some castle wall. My erection, and getting it soft, are suddenly not my primary concerns.

Sounds. Definitely sexual. I've spent enough time, in the darkness of the park, across town, to know what I know from

hearing what I hear. I have this knack, too, for pinpointing origin; sometimes, in the park, I want to give guys their privacy, other times I want the turn-on of watching.

It's probably a football jock fucking a cheerleader in a final farewell, before graduation. Can one of my classmates, pumping his stiff hose in and out of some eager cunt, turn me on? It's been so long since I've given any genuinely serious thought to straight sex, I'm curious to find out. Certainly, the idea of jock-fucking-cheerleader doesn't immediately soften my boner.

I explore the maze of metal support poles under the bleachers, drawn ever closer to the sounds and to whomever makes them. I have to be careful I don't whack my still-jutting seeing-eye pecker against a pole and get my dick soft that way.

It's not any jock I know. His ass is too flabby. An unattractive pale white, in the bargain. His asscheeks don't dimple on each thrust of his penis; instead, they jiggle like jelly. My fist detects a definite draining of starch from my erection.

It's likely some local daddy who has spirited his old lady out of the house to fuck away from the kiddies.

I stuff my gone-limp-from-the-display dick back in my trousers and zip up. I detour for home, made to pause by some of the couple's sexual sounds that reach my ears ungarbled.

"Tell me how badly you want my cock," says the one. Male.

"I want it. I want it," says the other. Male.

I'm given no raging hard-on by the idea of watching two past-their-prime men tripping the light fantastic, under the high-school bleachers, late at night, but it's at least of more interest than some hubby drilling his wife.

"Fucking little tease, aren't you?" says Mr. Ass-as-white-as-a-sheet. "All year long, flaunting your cherry ass. Five days a week. Had me thinking of you even during school holidays."

"Fuck my cherry ass! Fuck it!"

Stealthily, I move for a better look.

It's Steven Grailman, Junior, getting his ass skewered by Mr. Clacker's stubby dick, but I'm the one really getting screwed. I'll feel it tomorrow, sitting in Clacker's classroom, as he calmly announces, as if he's not been bought and paid for with a few frantic motions of his hard cock up Steven's cherry ass, that we're to write our final paper on ... On what? I try to think of

some subject at which Steven excels. Probably something about animals. Not the human animals who fuck under high-school bleachers, but the fuzzy-wuzzy non-human variety. Clacker went absolutely ape-shit over one syrupy story Steven wrote, mid-semester, about a goddamned cat's fur-ball that ends up cozily wrapping the nestlings of a robin the cat has been out to eat for dinner. I got an A, too, about a rabid dog who gets his comeuppance from an equally rabid raccoon, but Clacker called my story a little too dark for his taste. He would have docked my grade if he'd remembered to tell us, at the beginning, he wanted us to write cuddly; I'm not good at cuddly.

"Sexy, sexy, sexy," grunts Clacker. His ass gives an earthquake shudder that would topple buildings. It's obvious he's really into pumping his cum like crazy.

Steven holds tightly to one of the support poles, like Tarzan – or Jane? – holding to a jungle vine. His pants are around his feet, his shirttail hoisted above his belly and ass. His cock is limp and has been the whole time I've been watching. He's either already gotten off, or he endures the fuck just to get a good grade.

I can rush in, scare the living shit out of them, make accusations, even threats. No doubt I'll have them promising me the moon. Later, though, they'd come to their senses and know it's my word against theirs. My word against the word of a rich man's son and the who-me? word of a well-respected teacher. Not even my unimpeachable scholastic record will likely tip the scales in my favor.

Besides, despite my drawing the short stick, I'm impressed by Steven's determination and success. Had Clacker been more inclined toward someone butch, or been more needy of his ass getting plugged, rather than his stubby cock doing the plugging, it could have been me fucking Clacker's pasty jello-like ass under the bleachers, instead of Steven's cherry butt getting fucked. I would have even offered up my own cherry-from-cock ass to Clacker had I ever thought he'd be even vaguely interested in a deal. On that, you can bet the wife and two kids.

I head home. Already, I've crossed off the Grailman Scholarship as any source of tuition revenue: no one ever says I'm a poor loser. I'll come up with some other way, between

now and college first-quarter, to find the cash lost by this temporary setback.

I'm almost on my doorstep when the car pulls a little ahead of me and stops. Its window rolls down as I come abreast.

"Kind of late to be out on a school night," the guy behind the wheel says. He's nothing to write home about, but he doesn't have to bag his head. He wears a nice suit, and he drives a nice car.

"There some kind of curfew?" I'm wise-ass.

"Actually, I'm happy as hell to see you," he says. "I began to wonder if I was going to have to wait around and catch you headed for school, come daylight."

"You figure that long a wait worth it?" I ask and calculate the possible money to be made. Does the fact I'm suddenly in need of more money offset whatever the disadvantages of tricking so close to home?

"I have a proposition for you," he says.

I walk in closer and give him a better view of my cock-bulged crotch before I lean down against the sill of his open car window.

"Do you now?" I give him the sexiest smile I can muster.

"Why don't you get in, and we'll talk?"

"You see any late-night traffic honking to get on by?" I've never been picked up by anyone in a car before, preferring the wide-open spaces of the park. Had I wanted to try the scene, there are a couple of roadside meat stands, none of which exist on the street where I live.

"Come on, kid, get in." In farther temptation, he adds, "You'll certainly find it worth your while."

This close to home, I can use a bit more concealment than the obviousness of discussing business through a car window. Granted, the guy could be mistaken for someone asking for directions, but ...

I walk around and climb in. The car interior is spotless and smells vaguely of new leather. Can a driver's personal hygiene be determined by his upkeep of his car?

"What can I do for you?" I ask. The idea is to make him spell it out. He doesn't look like a cop, but neither does that handsome piece of shit who busted two hustlers in the park a couple of weeks before.

"It's what I can do for you," he says.

I don't necessarily plan to keep my ass cherry from cock forever, but this guy doesn't look at all like Mr. Right.

"I think you have the wrong kid for what you have in mind," I tell him.

"Maybe," he gives me the benefit of the doubt. "Then again, take a look in the glove compartment."

What the hell ...?

"Now take out the manila envelope and take a look inside."

The damned thing is stuffed with enough hundred-dollar bills to make me whistle my surprise.

"You want me your toyboy for life?" I finally manage. Maybe this guy does possess the lucky boner to make my cherry-from-cock ass cherry no longer.

"Toyboy?" He looks genuinely confused.

"Buy exclusive use of my asshole so only you get to fuck it until it's too loose to give even a freight train a tight fit."

"Jesus!" he says, usually the first indication someone is turned on by my talking dirty. However, there's something about his nose all wrinkled as if I've just farted a really foul stinker. "I thought you were some kind of scholar."

Scholar? This guy out for a mind-fuck?

"The money has nothing to do with your asshole," he says. He's doesn't look at me but through the windscreen. "It has to do with you pretending to be a little less smart than someone ..." Obviously not him. "... apparently thinks you are."

"Who?" That's what I want to know.

"The gentleman prefers to remain nameless."

"You're kidding, right?"

"I'm quite serious." His look says he's netted a mongrel when he's been led to expect a pedigree. "The money is yours if you play it a bit stupid on a certain final you're having at school this afternoon."

"A test final ... at school?"

"No need to play it a whole-lot stupid," he qualifies. "Maybe you get a B instead of an A. No one wants this to look as if you foul out on purpose."

I want to ask why Steven Grailman, Senior, doesn't know his son has already paid the price, elsewhere, with cherry ass. Is this a case of the right hand, Senior, not knowing what the left

hand, Junior, is up to, and vice versa? There really should be more communication between fathers and sons, in this day and age. It could have saved a kid his virgin ass, or save his father a decidedly large outlay of cash.

"The money is double the scholarship," the guy says and looks as if he wishes to hell he were out of here. He's failed to put a name – Grailman – to the scholarship. When Steven, Senior, told him not to mention his name, this guy must have taken him dead-seriously.

"If I get a B and, say, a certain someone flubs and gets a B, too, do I suddenly have someone banging on my door asking for a refund?"

"You and I know a certain someone isn't about to get a B, anymore than you would if not otherwise persuaded."

Someone has more confidence in my ability to second-guess Clacker than I do. Then again, neither this guy, nor Steven, Senior, has seen Steven, Junior, affecting Clacker's grade curve by pulling down his pants and getting his cherry butt stuffed with Clacker's fat dick.

"Okay," I agree. Hell, this guy, or Steven, Senior, or Steven, Junior, if they only knew, could have my never-had-by-cock asshole for the price being paid for an already done-deal. There's no way I lose on this one.

I take the money and get out of the car. I head for the house.

"Don't try to pull anything funny," the guy warns, somewhere to my rear. "My client wants what he pays for."

Mom has left on a night-light. For me and/or for Dad, either of us apt to show up at odd hours. Mom has long tired of trying to get us to change our ways.

I lock my bedroom door, waterfall the money from its packet onto my bed. I shuck my clothes, every last stitch, and fall amongst the money. I roll around like a pig rolling in its own shit.

On my back, I lift my ass and grab a handful of crushed bills to spill onto my belly and crotch in a tenting of my suddenly rip-roaring erection.

I grasp several bills in the same fist that claims my hard cock. I pump my cock like holy hell, all the while grinding my butt into the crushed cash beneath it.

I prop the pillow higher behind my head, because I want to

see my hard, hot cock getting jacked off amid all that green, cold cash.

I'm flogging my old hog but, in my mind, I'm fucking Steven, Senior, and/or Steven, Junior (suddenly, I can't separate the one from the other). I'm giving them both their monies worth for Grailman cherry ass and Grailman dollars sacrificed on the altar of Grailman family pride.

My mind flashes Clacker's under-the-bleachers bare ass, but his butt seems less fleshy, less pasty, less formless jelly. Suddenly, it's not his ass but mine. It's my cock fucking the cherry ass of Steven, Junior. Nor is the cock of Steven, Junior, soft while I give his cherry ass the kind of working over old Clacker couldn't have managed even in his prime. The cock of Steven, Junior, is rock-hard stiff, willing, and ready, for my hand to reach around his cock-stuffed body and take hold.

I bend my legs at their knees, my feet flat on the bed. I fillet my thighs on the bedspread. My free hand slides through the hundred-dollar bills on my belly and dips along the inside of my thigh to turn upward in a cupping of my balls.

"I'm fucking Grailman asshole," I whisper, pleased I'm still capable of a muted fist-fuck when the fist is mine.

I roll my nuts and stretch their containing scrotum toward my asshole in search of my sweaty sphincter.

The paper money squishes more between my fist and my dick and scratches, but the irritation only increases my high. My fingers twist around my dick, pump up, pump down, and the crinkling sounds of hundred-dollar bills get me all the hotter.

This is better sex than with Calvin. This is better sex than my very first time. This is better sex than any sex I remember.

I poke a dry fingertip up my asshole. It's tough going, with no obliging slideway of lubricant, but the difficulty makes it all the more pleasurable. I jiggle my butt and work its hole farther and farther over my ass-sticking fuckfinger.

My scrotum loses all looseness and coverts to hairy a lump at the base of my fist-pumped erection. It ill-disguises the movements of my cum-bulged nuts within its pleasure-thickened casing.

"Ugggh!" I grunt as my fuckfinger hits paydirt; I hoist my ass higher, and my fuckfinger crooks up my asshole to re-poke

my prostate.

I milk clear and gooey natural lubricant from the mouth of my dick. My hand spreads that oiliness over my cock and onto several crumpled hundred-dollar bills.

"Yes, yes, yes!" My whispered mantra matches the pump of my hand over my cock and the drill of my finger within my asshole.

I squirt my load. Soupy streamers of my pearly slime leap free. The first wetly plops its comet-head into the crater at the base of my throat, splats its tail onto my upper chest, and strings its long unbroken linkage of cum in between. The next gobs form a descending line from my upper belly to my navel. The final mess oozes my fingers and feeds Ben Franklin, who's on each of the hundred-dollar bills, multiple facefuls of undammed-by-condom cream.

For the final exam of my Creative Writing class, Clacker instructs us to write something Walt Disney-ish. Something about animals with human characteristics. He looks directly at me when he adds, "Something amusing."

I write about a dog that finds a cure for cancer and sets out to communicate that long-sought-after answer to humans. He doesn't succeed. In fact, one scientist locks him in a cage and uses him for laboratory experiments that give the dog the disease. When the dog escapes and cures himself, he decides to share his secret only with other dogs.

What Clacker is bound to argue is that he gives me a low grade because he emphasized the exam assignment be amusing. I'll argue irony as a valid expression of humor. I won't win the argument, but I'm not supposed to.

Clacker catches a man burglarizing his apartment and is hospitalized by a nasty blow to his head.

All of our Creative Writing test finals are trashed during the robbery. Even if they had survived, Clacker's headache is too great for him to grade them. His substitute teacher announces our final grades, in Creative Writing, are based entirely upon grades earned before the final.

"By which, I end up with the Grailman Scholarship," I conclude, to Calvin, in our regular booth, at Lers Hut, after hot and heavy sex in the park.

"Well, don't you luck out!" says Calvin and smiles. "All that

bribe money and the cash from the scholarship, as well."

"Unless Grailman wants his bribe money back."

"He can hardly blame you, can he? According to Clacker's blow-by-blow, you'd have to be a master of disguise, familiar with all the tricks of theater makeup. Have access to a wig. Know spirit gum attaches fake mustache and beard. Know about fake noses, fake ears, fake ... whatever".

"Nonetheless, he probably figures himself on the short end of our deal."

"Well, should he decide to renege, show him this." Calvin fishes into a back pocket of his pants and tosses a snapshot across the diner table. "Tell him you have a friend who has several more."

"Jesus, Calvin!" It's a picture of a buck-naked Steven, Senior, fucking a stark-naked woman dog-style.

"The lady playing bitch isn't Mrs. Grailman, by the way, but Marianne Rothkline, the wife of a very prominent investment banker. Her unknowing husband can cause Grailman all sorts of problems, not the least being the grounds by which Mrs. Grailman can file for a very messy and costly-for-her-husband divorce."

"Where in the hell did you get this?"

"At the Grailman house."

"You know the Grailmans?" To say I'm surprised is a gross understatement.

"Never had the pleasure."

"Then ...?"

"It's what I do for a living, junior," he says. "Clandestinely visit other people's homes and find where they hide their valuables -- and secrets."

"The Grailman house?" Then, since I don't have to be hit over the head twice, "Clacker's apartment?"

He smiles.

A wig? Spirit gum attaching a fake mustache and beard? Fake nose? Fake ears? Fake ... whatever? "Christ, Calvin, you could have killed old-man Clacker."

"I'm a pro, junior," he chides. "You think I don't know the difference between giving someone a headache for a few days and dispatching him permanently into the Great Beyond?"

I don't know what to think. He's caught me completely by

surprise and it's readily evident in my good-God expression.

He laughs.

I'm speechless.

He's having an extraordinarily good time. "Why not let your sexy toes do the talking?"

I slip off my shoe, extend my foot under the table, prop my heel against the seat between his open thighs.

He peels off my sock.

He tugs his hard cock from his trousers and aligns it with the sole of my foot.

Neither of us says a word as he humps my foot to cum-splattering orgasm.

When he's done, looking very pleased with me and with himself, he says, "Did I remember to wish you a Happy High-School Graduation!?"

AN ABUSE OF AUTHORITY

Dan Veen

"Get that Private Fuckhole over here."

Crouched in his darkness of the tiger cage Private Dennis Curry stiffens to his Master Sergeant Desmond's command. All the tactically sensitized points of Private Curry's body prick – like a dog's ears – to attention.

Like other recruits in the SIR program before him, Private Curry is immediately treated like a bonafide prisoner of war. "It is essential," Desmond briefed all his eager volunteers, "to replicate exactly the grueling containment camp situation."

SIR (Survival – Intimidation – Resistance) was originally designed to accustom men to the hardships of an enemy camp.

Private Curry hears the groans of his fellow participants in the Program. Other boys's climaxing sobs echo through the ancient barracks. Sequestered for two days in his dark cage, Curry has only his hard-on for company, and his future humiliation to anticipate. Inside this cramped darkness, Private Curry fantasizes. What is being done to the boys? Their howls sound so oddly like howls of pleasure. Curry hears, and he envies, and he fantasizes queer fantasies he has never before fantasized. Curry hungers for strict sweet discipline. He craves the firm punishments, the demeaning indecencies lavished upon the other boys's pliant volunteering bodies. Two days with his demanding unhandled hard-on goads Curry into almost doggish devotion. A latent canine desire emerges, the desire to fetch and roll over and beg. He is anxious – very anxious – to please.

"Get that Private Fuckhole over here, Lupini!"

Private Curry's 'special training' starts at 1700 hours. The young man is hustled from his cage to appear before the two-man Initiation Committee. Today, Sergeant Desmond's assistant is Corporal 'Pony Boy' Lupini. Desmond maintains several discrete 'assistants' like Lupini who gladly induct new recruits into the SIR program. Lupini holds a camera that takes instant pictures.

Lupini's first photo looks normal enough:

Private Curry stands before them now. Erect and obedient, every inch of Curry is rigid with expectation.

Curry's fresh burrcut outlines a sleek, somewhat hollow, cranium. His thick-columned neck crowns large crescents of power-pumped deltoids. His spotless white T-shirt, biceps bunching the armsleeves, shows the segmented flatness of the youth's midriff tapered to a twenty-eight inch waist. Curry's buttock-cheeks look vacuum-sealed inside his skintight fatigues. The damp seam pinches the boy's asscrack. The boy's hard-on is obvious. It lumps his crotch. The hard-on acts like a small magnet. It juts up, pointing north, stuck up embarrassingly, unconcealable in his tight pants. A stiff quivering iron widget.

Poor Private Curry is very gung-ho and, yes, kind of dumb. The unsuspecting boy prides himself on being 'goal oriented' and a 'people person'. In high school Private Curry was a top-seeded wrestler and varsity All-Star quarterback. The Curry boy is a 'go-getter', a 'self-starter' motivated to network his way to the top. He is forever joining projects that will make him more popular. Junior Achievement. Eagle Scouts. Young Republicans. That's why Curry thought this SIR training program would do him good. It is 'an advancement opportunity'. A gold star by his name in the roster. Brownie points for initiative.

It is this wholesome all-American subservience of Curry's which gave Master Sergeant Desmond the idea to try Curry in the SIR program.

Private Curry's dogtags rattle. The bare lightbulb hanging in the deserted World War II barracks makes his eyes blink. The incandescent fixture glares like an interrogation lamp. The three men stand in its arena of light in the middle of the barrack's darkness. Like a spotlight.

It makes Curry feel like he is going to put on a show.

How Lupini relishes this kid's puzzlement! Sweat beads the private's thick brow. The stupid cheeser's bottom lip hangs open slightly in thick pout. Funny, Lupini thinks, the stupider the kid looks, the more fuck-able he looks. Ignorance, Lupini sneers tenderly, is bliss. Lupini can't help but take another picture of this sheepish lamb. This Curry kid is a model grunt. An uncommon incarnation of bred-to-service military architecture. Perfect raw material for the SIR program, Lupini

thinks, licking his chops. Lupini's camera just eats up Curry's innocent beefiness. Photos of this big lunk will look good in Lupini's personal album.

"Remove your uniform, private." Desmond orders the young 'inductee' Curry standing before him.

"Sir?" Private Curry blinks like a deer in the headlights.

"Remove your entire uniform. Every stitch of it. Fold your clothes. Place them on the floor. Now that you're a prisoner here, you won't be needing your clothes. Your hands will be bound. You can't amuse yourself with your usual jerking off. Wanking your worthless pud-weenie ten or fifteen times a day." Desmond's methods might be unorthodox, brutal, some say, but his methods prove highly effective in instilling unquestioning obedience in strapping young boys like Curry. "If you are allowed to masturbate at all, it will be for our amusement. Not your own. And it will be when, where and how we dictate. Is that clear, Private Fuckhole?"

Private Curry's mouth gapes dumbly open. Masturbate? Amusement? Fuckhole? What the heck has he volunteered for? Yes, trembling in the overpowering presence of Master Sergeant Desmond, Curry wonders: Has he done the right thing? Has he made a wrong move? Maybe he's gone too far to be a popular guy, a people pleaser.

Or is this just where he belongs?

Beneath his white T-shirt, Curry's stiffening pectorals secretly respond.

"I said, Is that clear Private Fuckhole?" Desmond barks.

The boy jumps. "Sir, yessir. That is clear, Sir."

"Well?"

"Sir?"

Coldly, Desmond invades the confused recruit's face: "When I give you an order, I expect you to obey it, Fuckhole!" Wadding up the boy's T-shirt in his fist, Desmond rips the shirt off the boy's body.

Curry's naked chest prickles with goosebumps. Two big pink self-conscious nipples dot Curry's pectorals like proud medallions. Dogtags drape over his collarbone; they jangle like a chain and suddenly feel just as heavy. Otherwise the kid's glossy bare torso gleams porcelain-white. Not a mole. Not a freckle. Not a tattoo. Curry shivers in his brand new nakedness.

It is a nakedness he has never felt before. As if he has never in his life been as naked as he is now. His plated abdomen ripples down to a navel which peeks just above his polished belt buckle.

Desmond barks again, circling, threatening: "Well?"

Curry gets the idea. "Sorry, Sir!"

Sergeant Desmond wants him naked – now.

Quickly Curry unbuckles his belt. Shoes, socks; his pants are efficiently discarded.

Curry is left standing there in his briefs, peekaboo swaddling for his milky buttocks. But those briefs don't last.

For just a moment's hesitation, Desmond fingerhooks the snug elastic band. He stretches the young private's briefs. Stretches it tight so it gives the kid a wedgie. Gooses the young man's ass. Constricts Curry's cock as if it's shrink-wrapped in cellophane. In a split-ripping-second, the fabric shreds off Curry's fine wrestler body like a cheap striptease act.

Curry's pink penis flaps between his legs.

Lupini smirks; snaps a picture.

Curry instinctively covers his jangling wee-wee with his hands.

Desmond smacks them away.

"What did I tell you about frigging, boy?"

"But I wasn't – "

"Don't smart off to me, Private Fuckhole! The only kind of jacking off you'll do around here is jumping jacks. Now hop to it. I'm going to put you through your paces. Two hundred of them, right now, Private Fuckhole."

Straightaway Curry spreads his thighs. He knows better than to not obey and obey quickly. His arms lift. Wisps of strawberry blond hairs tuft his perspiring armpits. Like a good naked soldier, Curry counts his jumping jacks aloud:

"One-two-three-ONE...One-two-three-TWO!".

Curry's bare muscles thicken with the calisthenics." O n e - two-three-THREE!"

His fluttering dumplings are windmilling red yo-yos. His sprig of boyflesh hardens as he splays open his legs. His puffy shrimplet boings in mid-air, wiggles at his groin. Pre-cum sputters out Curry's pee-pee. Dick-slime tinsels Curry's red-gold pubic hairs. Finished, Curry's flapping tab dangles out like a

startled wet worm.

"What's this?" Desmond thumbs the boy's sticky spud. He dabs pre-cum beading out from Curry's miserable meatnub. "Does being naked in front of two guys get you hot, Private Fuckhole?"

"Sir, no Sir." The poor boy's expression looks conflicted. His pesky erection – it just won't stay put. And the more he thinks about his doohicky, the stiffer it gets!

"Oh no? I'd say it excites you plenty, Private Fuckhole." Desmond invades the young man's face. "Judging by that pud of yours it looks like you're awfully excited to be shaking your bare butt and baby balls in front of us." Desmond's words register deep in Curry's puppy soul. "From the way that puny tadpole's spitting, I'd guess it's probably been some lifelong dream of yours."

Private Curry sniffles, almost grateful for any human attention.

This isn't him. This can't be him. Yet it mirrors a dark fantasy which germinated like mushrooms while Curry stewed two days in caged darkness. Curry couldn't get Desmond out of his mind. Desmond's lecherous flesh-appraising look now feels almost flattering. Curry is grateful Desmond deigns to look at him. Never in his life has Curry considered the size of another man's penis. Yet, there in the dark, with his constant hard-on, Curry's mind reverts to Desmond's crotch. How full it looks. Potent with meat. A full-force package. Then Desmond's boots, and Desmond's magnificent big-fleshed physique that towers over him. Curry feels privileged, honored, grateful, to grovel naked before such a man.

"You want to get naked for some guys. You want them to treat you like shit." Desmond recites aloud the secret journal of Curry's mind. "Treat you like the sorry-assed fuckhole you are. The fuckhole you want to be."

Private Curry grows thrillingly self-conscious of his bare exposed little anus. His asslips tingle. They itch like a mosquito bite.

"You'd like to be a fuckhole, wouldn't you? Isn't that why you joined the army in the first place?"

"No sir, I mean – " The inner aperture of Curry's asshole dilates. The fleshy rosebud needles and swells. The heatsunk

crater within Curry's sweaty naked buttocks implodes.

"You love to be ordered around. You need to be told what to do. You don't want to think for yourself. You need to be ordered to accept your fate. Does it arouse you to take orders from guys, fuckhole?"

"No. I mean yessir, I mean – " Curry's burning asshole transforms insideout into pure pussy. It mutates. Into a cunt. A quim. A butt-beaver. A fuckhole. It opens. It becomes...a hole.

A hole that needs to get fucked.

"Two hundred push-ups now, Fuckhole! And that's an order! I want to see that baby ass of yours pumping double-time -- move! And keep that worthless dripping pin prick of yours outta the way! Stick it between your legs. Hold it there. That's it, wad it up your ass for all I care."

Lupini snickers at Private Curry's submission to training. Most kids crave some father figure to boss their lives. Someone to make them obey.

Lupini takes a picture of the kid's upraised butt. Between the cheeks of the hot full rump mounds, he glimpses Curry's virgin fuckhole: a pink button winks at the apex of Curry's straining hams.

If Private Curry ever saw the photos in Corporal Lupini's top secret album, the poor doofus would shit his diapers. If Curry only knew he would soon be like the healthy wholesome boys captured in Lupini's pictures.

Corporal Lupini's album of before-and-after photos is scandalous evidence of what behavior modification can do. Some nights Lupini spends hours whacking off looking at his obscene photo albums. All of them raw recruits 'conditioned' by the SIR program.

The All-American boys in these pictures are changed boys. Their slimed, disheveled hair and glazed red faces make them look like newborn chickens wobbling out of their shells. Carnal and wanton boys. Depraved bestial fuck-obsessed boys. Dumb bantam Bubbas – redneck studboys just like Curry – lewdly shaking their purple dicks for the camera's delectation. Their wills warped, these boys volunteer their fuckable juvenile assholes to be photographed – slutty whores eagerly splaying

their just-fucked ass-beavers for centerfolds. Shameless boys now brainwashed with one desire. One need.

Cock.

Sure, some bucks resist. Some more than others. The boys balk at first, unwilling to accept their own irresistible degradation. But with proper coercive techniques (and lots of mind-fucking), Lupini and Desmond always get these boys exactly where they want them.

Or where these boys really want to be.

Lupini remembers how each once-proud indignant boy is eventually licking his lips. Each subject salivates like Pavlov's dogs. Begging to be fucked up their raw pussyholes. And geezus how they get fucked! Dicked dozens of times. Lupini loves dicking these former-straight boys most of all.

He loves dicking straight boys like this Private Curry. Straight boys always try to be such 'men' about getting fucked -- even when they're getting a man's big dick screwed up their tight cute little straightboy assholes. Sure, they're macho at first. Like tightlipped jocks getting steroid shots, they lay back. They stoically spread their legs. Doing their patriotic duty. Accepting their fate as Lupini's cum depository. Resigned to playing barracks cunt to Lupini's ramrodding cockmeat. But even the butchest rednecks come around. They can't maintain calm about Lupini's butt-splitter cock, once they see it. Once they feel it, they grow very fond of it. They come to like Lupini's cock as it drills farther up into the virgin strata of their bowels. These boys begin to love the idea of having a cock up their asses. Before you know it, they're whimpering, then howling like wolves. Their log-size haunches strain and shimmy beneath Lupini's thrustings. When his dick works up into their tight straightboy assholes, Lupini holds it up there in them. Very very still. Up inside their fleecy pooters. His newly-cored pussy-privates fidget irresistibly. Their impaled butts yield, impregnated with Lupini's foreign object. Lupini's fist-fat nightstick of a cock enflames them. His cock's mean ballooning length lodges up inside their bloated rectums. Alive. Pulsing. It lays planted up in them. His solid oaken throbber radiates up into the rupturing channels of their hugging guts. And they love it. Their helpless prettyboy mouths form wide imploring ovals. Arching their backs convulsively, their tongues flick the

wet red rims of their lips as if to taste the fuck.

Sometimes Lupini snaps a picture right there with their surprised cute fuck-me-please-sir faces. Or he pulls out from their asses just an inch, documents his prick fucking this straight stud's fresh-busted cherryhole. Shame turns the guys on even more now. They love being degraded. Now the boys start twisting their own tits. The boys's hands roam around their renovated bodies. They turn into churning fuck engines. The slutty boys massage their beckoning cock-spitted butt-cunts.

But Lupini waits.

He waits and soon they are dithering in a ravenous fuck-frenzied cock obsession. He waits. Lupini's long cock slides gradually out of the boys's jittery meat-enraptured asses, teases it out endlessly, ever-so-slowly withdrawing his cock's length to it's plummy hard knoll-head. Their private pussies gasp open for cock, reluctant now to release the head of it. He tests their eagerness for cock. They writhe and flail and try to lunge up for his cock to fit his iron boybuster back, back up into their newly punctured ass-slot. Then –

Then, always, the words come.

Lupini loves it when the words come.

Almost as much as when their pricks spasm all over their bellies, Lupini relishes their outpouring ejaculations of words.

Imploring. Pleading. Guttural.

Nasty words that straight boys like Private Curry never mouthed before in all their straight lives.

Words they did not know they could say.

Words they don't want to say, but have to say.

They pant, squirmy, skewered like butterflies by Lupini's dick:

"Fuck – " they gasp, "Fuck ... fuck ... fuck...me!"

Gibbering, their hot insisting asses hunch hard against Lupini's meatpole. Hungry to be hardballed by his sadistic dick.

"Fuck me! Fuck me! Fuck me!" Horny straight boys tweaking their tits. Spreading their butts. Boys begging to get fucked by Lupini's cock. "Please fuck me up my ass! Put it in me! Fuck your dick up my hot ass!"

Hell, most of the time Lupini can't pull'em off his cock once he's done ramming their holes. When he cums he pulls out of

them so the boys can spit-polish his filthy cock with their tongue like it's a Medal of Valor, all the time wagging their butts and begging him to please fuck them again. Once these straight boys get 'inducted', they make the most satisfying gutterfucks around. Most of Lupini's pussy-fied privates would gladly march the perimeters of the base with Lupini's cock crammed up their tight asses. Nice thing is, any time Lupini wants one of his Private Cumcatchers, they are slavering to give him a piece of their ass again. Their legs practically salute him! Pony-Boy Lupini is never hard-up for some crewcut-pussy.

One-hundred-seventy-three....

Private Curry's pumping neck-muscles strain into his cantilevered arms. His expansive backside, buttressed with bull-sinew, strives at his push-ups. His buttocks are quivering. His meaty hindcheeks are clenching with tension. Testicles suck into his groin. Curry is struggling in his own slick of perspiration and pre-cum. His tool dangles. It won't keep clamped between his thighs. It springs loose. His donghead fobs the cement slab floor. It aches numbly. His buttocks lift; strands of his pudjuice trail to the ground.

Lupini sprouts a hard-on when he sees what Sergeant Desmond is holding.

The yardstick in Desmond's hands is ordinary enough. But both officers know what it is for.

It is to help Private Curry measure up.

Strong as he is, try as he might, Private Curry's gym-crafted body can't summon two hundred push-ups. At his one-hundred and seventy-fifth push-up, the naked beefboy collapses with a gasp. He sprawls bareassed on the floor like a beached dolphin.

"See this, Fuckhole?" Desmond brandishes the yardstick beneath Private Curry's nose. "For every push-up that you didn't make, you get one spanking from this."

Desmond takes the yardstick and saws it between the boy's creamy butt cleft.

Curry moans.

The yardstick's thinness runs between young Curry's plump buttery asshalves. Its slicing cool metal edge razors the private's deepset asslips.

The private's buttocks clasp at it reflexively.

With the flat of the yardstick, Desmond pats the young man's dimpled buttcheeks, pats them oh-so-gently.
Tap.
Curry's waiting baby tush contracts.
Tap. Tap.
Wet hammy taps, like raw meat patties.
Then – Crack!
The young naked private howls.
His butt stings – blisters – sizzles.
The private sprawls, seized with rich crackling spasms.

"Up, boy, up!" Desmond laughs, a sadistic lion tamer snapping his whip. "Up on your knees, fuckboy! Attaboy! I'm going to swat your sweet rump twenty-five times. That's for all the push-ups that you didn't do! This will help you to measure up from now on! Dance! Shake that ass! Crawl!"

Desmond's yardstick lightnings the air like laser fire and nicks the kid's startled rump. Crack! Private Curry's two flayed buns jiggle and tremble. His knees bicycle the slick floor. Turning everywhichway. Chasing himself. "Wag that tail, boy! Stick it up for another!"

Each whip-smack nearly rockets the boy across the compound. But his tits are hard kernels. He sticks his butt up. His dick shows – hard and slobbering.

"That's it, fuckhole, put on a little show for us! Show us that sweet little ass-snatch of yours! Stick that bitch butt out so I can hit it good and proper! Stick out that big pussy so I can smack it, boy!"

Curry scrambles for dear life, screaming real screams and crying real tears and coming real hot quids of cum, a flinching, begging, quivering wad of pink plastic need.

Desmond pauses. The boy is barking and sniveling at Desmond's boots, seeking relief at the very source of his torment. Desmond admires his yummy blithering handiwork.

Hot pink stripes criss-cross Private Curry's fat tenderized baby nates. He whimpers. Snot comes out his runny nose. Curry's red babyface bawls with tantrums of anguished humiliation. He wets himself. The boy's doggie yelps now grow almost expectant. Not responding to the last stroke, but clamorous for another. His balls waggle mincingly between his legs with every smack. Spastic ropes of his cum is dribbling to

the cement floor. Lupini snickers. Through it all, the kid's foaming dick rubs rigid against his belly.

"You want my cock bad, don't you?" Desmond says when the squalling boy finally modulates to mewling primordial whinnies, madly humping his Master's legs.

Curry hears Desmond unzip his pants.

Desmond stands there with his fly open, lording it above Curry, with his hands on his waist, looking down upon this naked crawling fuckhole.

Curry can't help but drool from every orifice.

"Look at you. You are one hungry fuckhole. Two days of thinking of nothing but my dick." Desmond sounds disdainful. "You want to be told to kiss my dick. You need to be ordered to suck it. Well, take it out, you dumb cum-hungry fuck. Stick your tongue in there. Get your face in my fly. Suck my dick out." He smacks the boy's butt one more smack. "Suck my dick out with your cocksucker mouth!"

Curry's eager face disappears into Desmond's open fly. The heat of Desmond's cock sizzles upon his tongue. Curry feels the superior heft and rank of that sergeant's cockmeat. The cock uncoils out of his sergeant's fly.

Desmond's cock is a stunning heat-seeking missile of incredible meat. It protrudes from its filmy steel casing, nearly knocking Curry on his butt.

Desmond's cock is a long foreskinned cock, pendulous with its big head. His cock bobs like a ripe suckable fruit bending its knobby branch towards Curry's face.

Curry's eyes open wide.

"Yeah, it's big, idn't it?" Desmond's cock hangs so near Curry's waiting face that Curry goes cross-eyed. "This the first cock you ever seen this close? You never sucked a cock before in your life, straight boy? Never even thought about sucking a cock before? Now sucking cock is all you can think about, huh? Well say hello to your new life, straightboy fuckhole. You're going to be spending a lot of time swinging on the end of this cockmeat. Go ahead. Say hello to it. Tell it how fucking glad you are to see it. Tell it what you'd like to do to it."

Desmond's huge and wanting cock waits at Curry's lips. The beige boner and its wire-haired pendulums loom towards him. The weighted gonads pulse in their sacking.

Say hello to it? Curry looks up at Desmond, through the enormous cock fanning his face. Desmond is serious. Curry looks Desmond's cock straight in its moist red eye. Curry stutters to the cock. "H-Hello."

Lupini laughs aloud.

Curry continues: "Hello. I'm – I'm a...fuckhole and...and I'd really like to suck on you...." Curry hears his own desperate voice babbling.

"That's it, Private Fuckhole. Make my cock feel at home. Don't you think you ought to kiss it now?" The cock juts teasingly toward Curry. "After all, you guys are going to be friends for a good long time. Go ahead. Pucker up, fuckhole."

Curry's lips purse together, puckering to a point so that he looks like a flirting girl blowing a kiss. He leans forward. He obediently presses his lips to the very piss-slitted tip of Desmond's oozing prepuced cock. Like kissing a warm egg.

He tastes the cock's saline pre-slime. Musky goo flavors Curry's palate like an erotic elixir. Curry's tongue delves like a hummingbird to sample more of Desmond's dick nectar. Desmond drops his pants. His balls hang before Curry's nosing face. "Kiss them." he demands.

Curry kisses each of Desmond's balls. His lips smack as he mouths the pink grenades, glad to get closer to Desmond's cumsacs, wishing they would detonate in his mouth.

Until he tasted Desmond's cock, Curry never thought of another man's cock. Until he tasted Desmond's cock, Private Curry fancied himself a lady's man. Curry always considered his own average penis as something that slid pleasurably up between a woman's legs and made them squeal until he unloaded his sperm. Now Private Curry is learning what all their squealing was about.

Desmond's tasty cockmeat changes Curry's mind about lots of things. Why, down here between Desmond's legs there's a whole masculine underworld which Curry can't wait to explore.

"Yeah. Take it in the face." Desmond feeds the boy cock.

The smooth-round popsicly fullness of Desmond's dick in his throat feels comforting to Curry. It tastes like his future.

"Hmm. He's got some tongue on him!" Desmond thrusts. "He's a topnotch peter-eater!"

Now Lupini whips his cock out. "Do you think this ass is

ready to be dicked?" Lupini leers, palms the hot halves of the boy's buns. He runs his cock over the blond fuzz of the boy. The crewcut rubs Lupini's fat balls.

"Feels like this'un's ready for anything, Corporal." Desmond poles into Curry's slobbering noisy throat. "Look at this cumcatcher suck me. He's got the whole thing down his throat! Go ahead, put your dick up in him. Dick him."

Lupini garnishes his cock with an army-issue rubber. He testshoves the cock between the boy's striped burning buns. Lupini's cockpiece tantalizes. Its hardness tickles the lozenge of meat at the fuckboy's very core. Curry moans. His slot opens. He wants Lupini's cock. He needs Lupini's cock in his hole. He rocks back on his haunches. He cocks the globes of his ass and widens his hole. He's gotta get it stuffed in him.

"He's opening up that ass real nice for ya." Desmond leans over and probes, "Prime freshmeat fuckhole. Look at him take my finger. Look at him suck it up." Desmond's cigar-sized finger explores the crevice of Curry's widening ass, trenching the moist loam of his shithole. "Yeah. Fucking ready for some breeding! It needs something hard and hot up it. Yeah, he wants it. He wants to be rode. Dick him good and hard, Lupini."

Desmond twangs the rubbery gasket of Curry's hole. Curry moans. His pelvis cants upward. Curry grows incensed with his ass's hot emptiness. "Make him feel you, Lupini. Let's see if he can beg for it with my cock in his mouth. Stick that big ol' head up there. Widen him out. This stud's hole is gonna have to sit on my cock all night long."

The thought of getting screwed by Desmond's monster meat makes Curry's moist buttlips shape a natural hot receptive socket. Lupini's pushing fat-headed cockhead plugs into the mitt of Curry's ass.

"M'm...nice hot fudgey insides! C'mon!" – Lupini slaps the boy's rump – "Open up that hole! Suck my big fucking meat up your pussy butt! That's it. Take that big head! Take my meat all the way, bitch boy!"

The kid's arm-muscles quicken. His butt tenses. Sucking and groaning, Curry braces himself. A wince of constipated pain reddens the boy's face. Lupini's up-thrusting cock splinters Curry's sphincter. The soft target offers pleasing resistance

before it gives. Lupini's cock begins to bayonet into his fuckhole. A resilient hole shaped for his pleasure. Halfway up into his hole, Lupini fingers the boy's own hapless hard-on, twiddles the crinkly naked pods between the boy's legs. Ratchets up his drive, driving the boy over the edge.

"This one's got the best butt yet, Sir," Lupini humps it into Curry's shit tunnel like an arm through a sleeve. "That whipping really gets them bucking good."

"Yeah, excavate that ass!" Desmond plugs Curry's throat. Curry's mouth is caked with curds of Desmond's pre-cum and glazed with dick-hairs.

Desmond and Lupini pin the fuckboy between them, practically hoist him off the ground with their dick-thrusts. Private Curry doesn't know which he likes more now – getting fucked in his mouth or his asshole. He's just grateful for both cocks – happy to have their manly muscular dicks plunging up inside him. Cum spews out Private Curry's cock in constant drizzles of spunk. His ass constricts around Lupini's buttpumper. It ripples its contours gratefully when Lupini shoots a big buttload of Curry's first mancum. Curry's ass milks the dick for more. Lupini grabs his camera in time to get Curry, hollow-cheeked and sucking, throating spuming cumloads out of Desmond's cock. Desmond hoses the kid good. Shoots cum all over him. The kid looks like he's suckling a pacifier. Cum globs his face. "Congratulations, Fuckhole." Desmond pipes the boy more cum. "For excellence in the line of duty, you've been promoted to Chief Cock and Ball Washer!"

"Thank you, Sir!" Curry blubbers through his jism-basted face. He knows his future is here. Being a hot eager cumhole for Uncle Sam!

Curry nuzzles deeper into Desmond's crotch. Bubbles of Desmond's cum exude from Curry's lapping mouth. He is happy to serve both their cocks in both his holes all night.

Desmond's spent tubing of cock dislodges from Curry's gloryhole throat, leaving Curry noisily slurping air. Desmond turns around. "Now show us what a good ass-kisser you are."

Lupini gives the boy's head a shove: "Service the target, shithead!" Lupini crams the boy's face hard into Desmond's ass and holds it there, forcing him to inhale straight from his

sergeant's ripe shitpipe. Curry, the natural brown-noser, the cheeser, is ready now to jump through flaming hoops to pleasure his Master Sergeant Desmond. Gladly he wedges his nose up into Desmond's dark furrow. Curry's lubricated face fits into it like a muzzle. His lips kiss the sergeant's fur-lined fundament. He inhales. Desmond's funky masculine tang intoxicates the boy.

"Ah." Desmond pats Curry's burrowing devoted head. Desmond lights up a stogie. "Yeah. Looks like we've found ourselves another barracks slut. A cumcatcher the whole platoon can use for R & R. Once we get done with him."

Private Curry's face grazes rapturously in his Master Sergeant's raunching butt. Private Dennis Curry. Wrestler. Varsity football quarterback. Junior Achievement. Eagle Scouts. Young Republicans. Now, naked on his knees, Curry can imagine no better promotion, no higher military honor, no nobler way to serve his country, than to suck Desmond's cock and eat his ass and let Desmond and every other superior officer, dick his ass.

Curry hopes and prays that all his voluntary 'special training' will get amply rewarded.

But what Private Curry doesn't know, fast in the throes of his new fuckhole servitude, what Curry never will know, is that five years ago the SIR program was officially discontinued.

Rumors of "procedural irregularities."

Something about an abuse of authority.

Lupini snaps another photo of Private Curry dutifully volunteering to swab Desmond's cum-plastered balls. Desmond's balls dangle there. Just above the boy's mouth. Curry's tongue reaches up to lick...

Corporal Lupini reloads his camera.

Private Curry's special training is just getting started.

A DAY AT THE BEACH

Jimmy D.

My friend Brad and I had been plotting it for weeks, trying to pick the perfect time to have outdoor sex at a nearby beach. Unfortunately, our conflicting schedules kept this thrill a dream until just last Monday, when the planets must have aligned or something and we finally made it to the beach together.

The sun was just beginning to set as we approached the sand dunes.

The setting was perfect – not too windy or cold, and basically deserted...except for one person wandering aimlessly. Could it be a patrol officer, we wondered hesitantly. It was Memorial Day after all, a perfect breeding ground for some straight cop to bust two gay boys having too much fun.

"Oh well, let's open that bottle of Merlot, anyway," I said.

"You got it," he whispered back, and took the bottle clutched between his thighs and popped it open. I felt a chill run down my spine in anticipation of what was for dessert, basically this beautiful man sitting next to me. At this point the sun was settling into the Pacific, and casting a warm glow on his soft face dusted with a five o'clock shadow, his lips wet from the wine. His long brown hair caressed his broad shoulders, and his open shirt revealed a lush fur chest.

Suddenly the wine began to tingle throughout my body, and I felt my loins shiver with excitement. At that moment I could think of nothing else except burying my face in his chest, and feeling our naked bodies pressing into each other.

"Let's head to the bushes," I said with determination. "Besides, that stranger is getting closer, and he does look like a cop."

As we were walking toward the labyrinth of bushes I kept noticing his lovely ass in front of me, teasing me, inspiring me to keep walking fast. And before I knew it we had arrived at a small secret clearing.

"How's this?" he asked.

"Perfect." Besides, I was getting hornier by the second and didn't care where we were, I wanted this god before me and I

was ready.

"Take off your shorts," I demanded.

As he was slipping them off I removed my cumbersome garments as well, and allowed my stiff penis to breathe the salty air. There's something really erotic for me about being naked outside, to feel the wind wrap around my thighs and shoot up my crotch – it's downright electrifying.

I turned to face Brad, grabbed him closer to my body, and felt his stiff member poke into my belly. We looked into each other's eyes and laughed. It did feel a little silly to be here now and finally indulging our fantasy. The sunlight was fading fast, and I thought there was not a second to lose. I knelt down on my knees and greeted his erection at eye level, mesmerized by its beauty. I gently opened my mouth and welcomed it in, savoring its soft flesh. I felt his hips writhe in pleasure and enjoyed his soft moans echoing above me. After a while I stood up and brought my mouth to his, sharing our sweet saliva. He then spit on his hand and started to jerk me off.

"Ooooohhhhhhhh my fucking god," I yelled.

"How's that, big boy?" Brad asked.

"Don't stop... Don't stop... whatever you do, don't stop," I managed to utter.

Suddenly I started to have a fantasy of the stranger, possibly a cop, watching us in the bushes. This made it all hotter, to think of being on display for some curious straight dude. I spit into my hand and reached down to find Brad's penis, and started to stroke it softly, then furiously, and softly again. We were getting into a pretty intense moment, losing all sense of reality, and then I felt my cock expand in his hand and explode onto his hairy chest, my knees wobbling out from under me.

At that moment, Brad heard a rustle in the bushes. "What was that?" he whispered.

As I was gathering my bearings, I looked around, embarrassed, to see if in fact there was a figure in the darkness watching us. "I'm not sure what that was," I spoke, my heart beating a mile a minute.

And then we turned and looked at each other and giggled softly.

"Maybe it was an animal or something."

"Who knows," he said.

As we were finding our way out of the maze and walking back to the car, I kept thinking that whoever or whatever it was they sure got a show.

"Do you mind driving?" I asked as we approached the car. "My legs are still a bit shaky from that orgasm".

"Not at all," he said, then continued, "actually, do you feel like doing me a favor?"

"What do you have in mind?"

"Have you ever given head in a moving vehicle?"

"Well, yeah, but not in a really long time," I said. "But I'd love to."

As I was brushing off the sand engraved in my body, he took off all his clothes and got in the driver seat. Immediately I felt a slight quiver in my groin again. He looked so hot there, touching himself, with the moonlight coming through the window. I jumped in the car, and off we went. Once on the road and cruising comfortably, I crouched down on the floor, and twisted my body to face his lap. His arms were resting comfortably on my shoulders at this point. I took a few deep breaths to prepare for the descent onto his manhood, and gobbled him up with my mouth.

"That's incredible, James," he said almost breathlessly.

I was too busy to return his comment. I was literally losing myself in ecstasy. I felt myself reverting into infancy sucking that pink pacifier. Calming sensations were overflowing me now, and the sound of the engine was just a distant hum. I was able to look up and see the stars through the moonroof. I felt as if I were in some twilight zone space, unaware of the real world passing by at sixty miles per hour. Unfortunately, the thought did jump in my mind that if we were to get in a head on crash I was basically history. Somehow the sudden danger made this moment all the more thrilling, more erotic. I figured that if I was going to perish that I should at least go with a lovely cock in my mouth.

I crouched down even farther into my cubby hole abyss and continued sucking away diligently and with purpose. I wanted Brad to come and shoot all over my body...

"Aahhhh," I heard somewhere through the black hole in the car.

I pulled away and sat up to face the blinding lights coming

at us. Brad reached down and grabbed his penis, moaning in pleasure. In a few quick strokes his body jerked and squirmed on the seat to the trembles in his groin.

"Woooowwww! What a rush that was," he said.

"I'll say. I could feel the energy oozing out of you."

Still breathing heavily, Brad kept his hand on the wheel the whole time and drove us home safely...

I'll certainly never forget this little diversion up the coast and probably will never look at oncoming headlights the same again. You just never know what exotic thing is happening in the darkness.

OLD HABITS

Mark Anderson

My favorite time of day is that one hour prior to sunset known as the witching hour, or my quiet reflecting time. Lost in thought, waiting for the blue green flash telling me the sun has truly gone. I then applaud, an old Key West habit.

Today, all alone on the beach beside the National War Memorial on Kuhio Beach, I sipped from my thermos of martinis and munched peanuts, aware that a smile has creased my winter tanned face. I was reasonably happy. While packing up and brushing sand from feet and shorts, I caught a movement on the beach under the banyan tree near the cement walkway. Having thought I was alone, I felt invaded, spied upon and robbed of my personal moments.

Then I noticed how young the man was sitting there motionless, just watching me.

Not a street person, I realized, noticing lightly tanned legs. Probably just another lost tourist. In passing him, my mild interest was rewarded in hearing a deep melodious voice call, "Haven't seen anyone do that since Florida."

"Do what?"

"Applaud an old man sun for his day's performance," he said, rising and falling into step with my slowed pace.

Nice height and build, I thought, immediately warmed with the sudden companionship, my own memories of Florida. At ease, I smiled at him, encouragingly, drawing out his story of spring breaks in the Sunshine State. While he talked I was amazed at the maturity of one so young. His tee shirt though not tight emphasized the conditioned chest and flat stomach. His casual manner was relaxing. Discovering our mutual affinity for Southern Florida was the path our conversation took. We laughed of March days spent on the beach at Fort Lauderdale.

"Did you know the Marlin Beach Hotel, with it's Poop Deck restaurant is gone?"

"Yes," I returned.

"Ever been to the beach past the Marriott Casa Marina on Reynolds Street near the Key West International Airport?" he

asked, changing his tactful way of dialogue.

Aware the groundwork had been cleverly mapped out, and that we were fast approaching the congested hotel strip of Waikiki Beach, I asked him, "Would you like a beer? My condo's just two blocks up from here on Walina Street."

"Cool," was his only reply.

"No view," I stated, as we approached the apartment.

Walking into the apartment I stowed my beach things and cooler holding the leftover cocktail things.

"The condos with a view in this building go for double the price of this one," I explained to him, adding, "a friend of mine, Rique, told me about this one being available, so being in the right place at the right time, I jumped at it, and got it. Always wanting to be in Hawaii the plans just fell into place. Just lucky I guess."

"Bud or Bud Lite?" I asked.

"Lucky would be too crass," I heard him say behind me as I fiddled with the damn screw caps, trying to avoid ripping my hands on the sharp metal edges.

"But lucky just the same," he said much closer. I suddenly felt heat radiating from his body on my back, then his arms slid under mine moving up to mould over my pecs, as he gently pulled me against his hard body.

"Lucky," he whispered, as his hot moist breath moved below my ear followed by tender brushes of his full lips against my neck.

Holding me tightly, in his massive arms, I realized this young man was a lot more muscular than I had thought. A moan escaped from me as his tongue moved in a slow sensuous way down my neck. At the same time, fat, thick thumbs flicked tantalizing back and forth over my nipples, bringing them to a standing hardness beneath my white tee shirt.

"Slowly, slowly, please" he whispered, taking control of the moment.

Withdrawing from me, he ran his thumb down my back, and I could hear him saying quietly, "Nice, so nice," as he traced my vertebrae to their end. His palm then rolled over, around my ass, smoothing, caressing and kneading the hard twin globes.

Stopping for a moment, the thumb traced again, exploring

the fabric of my shorts where a crease and fold dipped into the valley between my clenched butt.

"Nice, nice," he said continuing with both hands while I stood paralyzed by manipulation of practised hands.

As he turned me to face him, I was pulled into the depths of his sincere eyes, as they locked into mine, while his fingers continued their torturous dance with my nipples. Flicking, rolling, and gently pulling the nibs, I let out another moan.

"I've found your weak spot," he said, his face breaking into a smile that set fire to my soul. Reaching for my tee shirt, pulling it up, I saw it float down to the tiled floor. Exposed now, my flesh to his fingers, I was at his mercy standing with my arms at my side to signal my vulnerability. Tits sensitive and hard, I flexed them, offering him total control of my pectorals. Over my chest his hands roamed, while he sighed how great and defined the development was.

"Not yet," he cooed when my hips automatically tilted forward outlining my fully trapped arousal for him to take. "So very nice!"

Looking down, I was mesmerized watching his clean, freshly manicured fingers trace patterns similiar to the titillating fondling I practise when jacking off alone at nights. Cupping, lifting and tweaking oversensitive flesh, he was lost in his own world. His concentration, never wavering was pulling both of us forward to a higher level of lust.

Glancing past his hands finally, I saw his own nibs pointing from round white mountains of his polo shirt. God, his chest was well-muscled. Huge shoulders, bulging biceps, thickly massed arms covered in a dense layer of soft light brown curly hair. The back of his hands and even the fingers were covered with hair. Watching his hands move, palms down upward over my chest to my neck and shoulders, massaging and kneading my muscles, I caught a glimpse of bushy armpit hair trying to escape from the rolled up armband of his shirt. Upward my questing eyes flew noticing for the first time the mat of hair sprouting, standing, and signaling to me from the loose collar of the shirt. Soft and luxurious, a mane of hair lay still hidden from me. I had to see it!

I was afraid to speak, lest the huskiness of my voice betrayed my excitement and rising lust. Shit, I couldn't wait any longer.

I reached for the shirt at the waistband of his navy shorts. Surprised at how easily my trembling hands followed my anxious brain commands, the shirt lifted from him in one fluid movement.

Leaving his arms above his head after the tee shirt was removed, he watched me gasp at the vision before me. My dick began to twitch painfully in my shorts. Smiling at my reaction, he bent his arms placing and resting his hands at the back of his head.

"Lick my armpits," he ordered me, seeing how my eyes were riveted to the twin bushes that he presented.

Abundant would not describe the forest springing from his underarm. A quirk of mine was always watching, lusting after and checking out guys armpits. So this was a fantasy come true. Groaning aloud, I bent and burrowed my face into a forest of clean smelling fur. Forehead resting on biceps, chin on rib cage, I set my tongue and lips to the task of worship. His sudden gasp alerted me to our mutual idiosyncrasy. Sucking and slurping, face coated with my own saliva, I worked first one pelt, then the other, till they were both wet and plastered darkly to his arms.

"Now my tits man. Do it!" he hissed, driven to the same plane as the one I was on.

Gasping for breath, taking air in ragged chokes, I pulled away from him to survey my next area of assault. He stood waiting, arms still raised watching my eyes caress his torso hungrily. How masculine, I thought. What a prize had been given to me, and only minutes ago, I had been watching the sun go down all alone or so I thought.

Bringing his arms down to his side, the stretched pectorals resumed their full, rounded shape, covered in matted curling pile. The hard mass standing from the rib cage had the fullness of a woman, but was solid like a man. The areolas, taffy-brown in colour and silver dollar sized, stood puffed from the pectorals with their own unique identity. Baby-fingered in size, the nibs stood from brown saucers. I knew from experience they were not natural, but had attained their size from years of hard play. Below his rib cage, down the flat planes of his stomach he was barren of hair. Only a thin line from between the deep-etched cleft of his pecs, travelled in a straight line down, around a

belly button to disappear below his waistband.

"Look at my nipples," I heard him say as I looked up into an agitated and frenzied face.

Tasselled silky brown hair, and that of his chest framed his square masculine face. A large flat brow cantilevered heavily over deep-set wide-spaced eyes of the darkest brown flecked with gold. Cheeks flushed and brown stood full either side of the wide straight nose. Upper lip curled in the centre, white teeth were just visible and a full moist bottom lip, balanced the symmetric jaw that was almost as wide as his neck. I watched the lips pull back into a gentle smile.

"Suck my nipples," he ordered.

Shaking fingers would not respond, so my mouth assumed their task. As I bent forward, two erogenous zones connected. Lips to nipple, nipple to lips. So sweet and so clean I thought as my lips suctioned the complete areola into my hot cavern.

"Oh yeah," he said, while the other nipple entertained my fingers. "Wow!"

Shorts tented like mine, brushed, then rubbed against my belly, while I chewed on him. Moving to the other pectoral, my hand dropped, cupping the mound protruding at the front of his shorts. Surprised at the fullness my hand encountered, I squeezed what I could. He whimpered.

Reluctant to leave the sensitive elongated nib, I gave it a gentle nip to feel him twitch involuntarily. Sinking to my knees before him I took one last glimpse upward to see his head thrown backwards in ecstacy. Tracing the line of hair down to his flat belly, I clutched each side of the elastic waist band of the shorts and pulled them down. Snow white briefs faced me with their swollen package. Gasping, I halted for a second, appraising the cock.

"Please release me," he groaned, my clue to proceed unwrapping this fabulous gift bundled before me. "Please."

Reaching for the sides of the Fruit of the Looms I edged forward till my nose touched his testicles.

Breathing deeply, his freshness was intoxicating, and his radianting body heat almost burnt my face. I could wait no longer and pulled the underwear downward, freeing the cock. Springing upward, arching then righting its ridged form, it settled before my face.

My God, was all my stunned mind could come up with. It wasn't the length that took me unawares, but the thickness of the shaft that had me. It had to be thicker than his fore-arm I thought, almost afraid to touch it. The head of the dick sat atop a ridged crown standing out further than the white shaft like a ripe plum. Unexpectedly it twitched filling out completely so the stretched skin took on a sheen of pure marble. It darkened to a deep red before my eyes. I was delighted when a bubble of clear precum rolled from the elongated urethra opening, held there for a second then travelled downward in a thin thread to the beige tiled floor. Looking back up at the girth I noticed his scrotum pulled up tight against his shaft. Each testicle to either side, so they rested and supported the shaft independently, both vying with the knob for greatest size, in their almost hairless sac. Above a halo of soft fine brown hair complemented and framed the masterpiece.

"Suck me. Suck me now man, please," was his insistent command.

Planning my assault on the weapon, I was fixated with the urethra opening, that had just oozed seminal fluid. The meatus and glans had engorged on either side of the urethra opening so much that they had opened the slit to bisect the knob. To test my discovery, I pointed my tongue, quickly scooping up the second drop of precum and dipped at the opening. Looking back at it, I saw a deep darkening tunnel and again pushed forward entering the slick channel tonguing into his cock. Downward my pointed tongue travelled as the wide opening expanded. How far could I go I wondered, stopping only when my lips came to rest on solid flesh of the hard knob. Suction cupping myself to it I let my tongue piston in and out of the slit, greedily sucking his precum till I felt him shudder, moan, and pull me with a popping sound from his dick.

"You're just too much man. Now, my turn."

Standing before him, I watched as a few teasing bites were taken at my nipples prior to letting his hot wet tongue slide downward to the hidden line where my pubes ran into my shorts. A quick pull and my shorts and underwear disappeared leaving me naked and aroused before him.

"Nice, very nice," he mumbled cupping my pendulous shaved balls in one hand while my cock was vacuumed into

and down his throat to the root.

Gasping aloud, I grasped his solid shoulders while I looked at his head bobbing up and down my shaft. No instructions were needed. I felt him pull gently on my nuts, then tug to increase the pressure. My sighing signalled to his brain, and his fist tightened about my nuts.

"Ahhhh," I moaned, and he responded by pulling my balls down harder forcing my cock from it's arched position, outward perpendicular to my groin. Taking my dick in those thick hot lips he worked me till I realized I was standing on my toes and pumping with long thrusts into his mouth. I could see his penis bobbing, dripping with precum between his straining thighs.

"Turn," he instructed and I obeyed, enjoying being the instrument of his pleasure. Large hands rolled over my firm butt, pulling, slapping lightly, relaxing me till 1 was arching forward extending my butt for his full concentration. My nuts swayed hitting against my thighs, stopping only when his fist encircled the flesh above and pulled, forcing me to squat to relieve the insistent tugging of his fist. In return, I opened my ass for him. Clever man, I thought, feeling hot breath at the centre of my ass.

"Yes," I grunted, grabbing both cheeks of my ass pulling them apart to allow further access for his flickering tongue. "Oh yeah," I moaned bending forward balancing myself with my hands on the floor, raising my butt into the air. I was open and panting for him and he worked me harder. We were moving, building, enjoying together as one.

"I'm going to fuck you, boy, and I know you can take it."

"Yeah, do it."

I responded by opening and relaxing, I wanted that monster girth inside me. Hearing him pull his shorts from the floor I heard the rip of the condom package opening. Snap, it was in place, then the lube and the greased finger teasing my hole in anticipation of things to come. Then I felt it! I was opening, opening, and I was about to panic, when he bent and stroked my belly, telling me that it was alright, he would take his time. Slowly, I calmed, trusting him, feeling his massive yet tender spirit surrounding me, coaxing me. Yes, I wanted him and needed this. The enormous head popped past the sphincter to the rectal passage. Breathing deeply to get used to the width of

his cock, he waited for me unmoving.

"Oh, great, man, you're just too much for me. Don't move a muscle or I will cum."

Composed now, I was the first to move, backing up, pulling him deeper into me, wanting it all, now! That is when I first felt his large corona brush over and past my prostate sending electrical signals to my brain. His thickness had a sponginess which instead of tearing, massaged me. Working him back and forth over my sensitive gland had me panting, and causing me to clutch at him from within.

"I can't hold back!"

"Neither can I, man," I screamed at him, feeling orgasm building, helpless to stop it.

"Awwwwww," he screamed popping the massive dick from my ass and showering his scalding semen over my back.

Joining his vocal outburst, I let my cum fly in fast spurts to the floor. Enjoying the adrenaline rush and subsiding climax alone, I abruptly felt his arms tugging at my stomach, pulling me upright, turning me and drawing me to his body so the last spasms of orgasm were enjoyed together. Catching our breaths, hearts still pounding against each other we hung on to our dreamland. His lips sought and covered mine pulling them inside his mouth, letting his teeth nibble on them. Two pairs of hands roamed freely discovering, and reacquainting flesh newly met.

I could have stood like that forever, but reality set in. He finally moved his head back smiled at me, and said those fateful words.

"It's getting late, and I have to go."

"You are welcome to stay," I mumbled, trying not to sound like I was pleading.

"Thanks, I'd really like to but I have to go."

"Sure," I said trying not to sound too disappointed. "Why not give me a call, and we can get together again."

"I would like that, but it's impossible."

"Why, may I ask?"

"Because I'm on my honeymoon, and the only reason I was out tonight was because my wife and I had another fight."

My face must have shown surprise, because he started to laugh. He went on to explain that not only was he horny,

bisexual, and had a wife that suddenly would not let him near her, but that they had not even had sex yet on this trip.

"And I thought I had problems," I offered, which cracked him up. "The offer still stands," I told him letting him out of the apartment, making sure he had my phone number.

A couple of days passed and just when I thought I would never hear from him again he showed up and rang from the lobby. Excited, at the prospect of seeing him even though it was late, I was erect by the time the elevator deposited him at my floor. Noticing when he walked to my door that he was in the same erect state as I, we both broke out laughing.

"Another fight?"

"Yeah, but I started it when she got drunk and started coming on to me in the restaurant. I then took her back to the hotel."

"What happened then?" I asked putting my arms around him.

"Well I used the same line she uses on me. Not tonight darling, I have a headache! Then I left her."

"Well," I said looking in his eyes, "Let me help you with your headache." I slowly reached down to the head of his dick asking him if it hurt there.

"Yes, painfully," he chuckled.

"Let's see if I can make it better," I said, adding as I walked him, to the bedroom: "You just might have to stay the night this time."

"Might just be right about that," he said turning around and planting one of his all-consuming kisses on me.

IN ANGELO'S ROOM

William Cozad

In high school Rod and I were good friends. He lived across the street from me, so we walked to school together. By the time we were seniors, I began to think differently about him. It happened in the locker room after gym class. I started looking at him a lot when he showered and dressed. He was medium height but thin. Brown hair and brown eyes. He had a fat circumcised dick that swung between his legs, and big balls. He had sparse hair on his chest but thick hair on his legs. Every night when I went to bed with a hard-on I thought about Rod, his naked body and equipment, and I jacked off.

Girls in school seemed to like me, but I was shy and didn't date. I wasn't much interested in the opposite sex. But Rod was. He said that he knew a slut who lived on the other side of town. I was a little jealous because I wanted Rod myself. I wanted to play with his dick. That was out of the question. Besides, if he knew how I really felt about him he might tell everyone, and end our friendship. I couldn't take a chance on that. When I pressed him for details about the slut he knew, he was kind of vague. Except that he told me she gave good head. I got a real boner when he described how she licked and sucked on his dick until he came in her mouth. She even swallowed his load. Some Saturday nights Rod and I went to the cinema in the mall. Just sitting next to him in the dark theater gave me goosebumps. When his leg accidentally touched mine I got a woody.

One night Rod and I left in the middle of a boring movie. "Whatcha wanna do?" he asked. "It's still early."

"I'm horny. Why don't you call that slut and fix me up," I asked.

Rod hesitated. "She's probably got a date," he said.

"C'mon, I'd do it for you, buddy," I coaxed.

Rod finally relented. At a phone booth he took a matchbook cover with a number on it out of his wallet and dialed the number. "Angelo, it's Rod," he said. "I got a horny buddy, the one I told you about. Could we come over? Yeah, he knows

the score. Okay, see you soon." He hung up the phone.

"What was that all about? Angelo? The score?" I asked suspiciously.

"Gotta level with you, buddy. It's not a girl, but some queer. He gives free beer and great blowjobs," Rod said matter-of-factly.

"A queer? You mean a fruit? A fairy?"

"Whatever. Best damn blowjob, man. Still interested?" Rod stared right into my eyes as he said this.

"Oh, wow, I dunno." I was plenty interested but I didn't want Rod to think so. "Where did you meet him?" I asked.

"In a gas station toilet near my old high school. He used to suck off guys. He gave me his phone number when I moved out of the neighborhood. Sometimes I call him and go to his room." He spoke evenly, without emotion.

I was shocked. My best buddy let a queer suck his dick! "Is it safe?" I asked.

"Sure, he's cool. You game?"

Just thinking about getting a blowjob made my balls tingle. "Let's go," I said.

Rod and I got on a bus and went to the seedy part of town. He told me that his mom had married her boss, and that's when he moved to our neighborhood and transferred to my school.

The little deli appeared to be closed for the night. Rod yelled out and the man came down the stairs to open the gate. He was a slender Latino guy around thirty and grinned when he saw Rod.

He led us to a room that was small with little furniture and a mattress on the floor. Angelo was friendly and served us cans of beer. He kept staring at me as Rod stepped over to him. Angelo ripped open the button fly of his jeans and hauled out Rod's cock.

"God, you got a big cock, Rod. You are my favorite," Angelo said.

Seeing Rod's big stiff dick gave me a boner. I'd never seen his dick hard before. It was even bigger than I'd thought.

"And you show my buddy here what a good cocksucker you are," Rod said.

Angelo was drooling. His huge brown eyes were riveted on

Rod's dick. He scooted over between the kid's legs and gobbled up his dick. Something I'd dreamed of doing myself.

"Suck it, you *puto*," Rod said. Angelo not only bobbed his head up and down on Rod's dick, but he opened his robe and stroked his own dark, stubby, uncut cock. I couldn't believe this was happening right before my eyes. I watched the man suck my buddy's dick. I was tempted to take out my own dick and jack it. I was so hot. But I was too embarrassed.

"Like to suck cock, doncha?" Rod said. "Deep-throat it. Yeah, that's it. Do a good job and I'll let you suck my buddy's dick. He's got a big one too. This could be you lucky night, you fucking queer." Rod's verbal abuse didn't bother his cocksucker. In fact, he seemed to be getting off on it; he slurped and slobbered all over the teenager's big dick.

"Aw fuck, it's gonna shoot! That's it, cocksucker. Sunk it. Drink my fucking load! Don't you dare spill a drop. Oh, shit, that feels so good." Rod let out a loud moan.

When Angelo let go of Rod's tool it was still stiff, red and slimy. I wanted to do it to my buddy myself. I'd gladly take seconds. I spread my legs and grabbed my crotch.

"Take out your dick. Let the cocksucker blow you," Rod ordered.

Angelo crawled over to me, with his robe open, his dick dangling. "Go for it, Angelo. Suck my buddy's big ol' dick!"

Angelo unzipped the fly of my jeans and freed my cock. It was hard, sniffing the air.

"Do it, boy! Suck it dry, you cocksucking pig!" Rod barked.

Angelo had no more than fastened his hot, wet lips around my crown when I felt the cum churn in my nuts. My cock exploded, blasting jets of hot cum into the man's mouth.

"Holy shit! Oh Jesus! Never seen a cock go off so fast. Got a hair trigger buddy," Rod yelled.

Angelo slurped up my balljuice that dripped down his chin, then he got up and went to the fridge.

Like a good host, he brought us each another beer. "This whore ain't just a cocksucker," Rod said.

"What kind of work do you do?" I asked.

"He's a busser at the Top of the Mark, for chrissakes."

"But that ain't what I'm talking about," Rod said. "Show him, Angelo. Show him that hot brown butt of yours."

Angelo sort of mooned me. He had a fat butt. "You wanna fuck me, Rod?" the man asked.

"Maybe. Let me finish my beer." Rod chug-a-lugged his beer, then stood up. "Get on your belly, you fucking bitch. Spread those buttcheeks."

I watched bug-eyed while Rod dropped his pants and kicked them off. Now he was wearing only his T-shirt and shoes. Angelo lay prone on the mattress on the floor with his robe bunched up on his back, spreading his buttcheeks. I left my own soft cock hanging out.

Rod mounted the man, slapped butt. "Got such a big hole. Can hardly feel anything."

"Fuck my ass, Rod," Angelo said.

"Beg for it, you slut."

"Please fuck me. Oh, please," Angelo begged.

I couldn't believe this scene. Rod's cock was hard again. He slapped it against the man's buttcheeks. He had complete power over the man, it seemed. And he got abusive again. "You're pathetic. Cocksucking scum. Why should I give you my dick? Why should I waste my cum on you?" Rod snarled.

"Because I love you, Rod. You know I do. You're my favorite boy," Angelo said softly.

"Don't talk shit to me in front of my buddy. Don't want him to get the notion that I'm a fucking fag." Rod slapped Angelo's ass.

"Oh, god, stick me, Rod. I need it bad," Angelo screamed.

"Bet you been fucked a dozen times since I last fucked you."

"Oh, no! You're the only one I let screw me," Angelo said, clawing the mattress like an animal.

"Lying bastard! Maybe I won't screw you after all. Maybe I'll just beat off."

Listening to Rod's power trip and looking at his fat pecker slide in and out of Angelo made me own asshole twitch. I'd only fingered my butt while I masturbated, but I knew I'd like Rod's meat in me. But I didn't dare tell him. He'd be mean to me like he was to Angelo.

"Oh, please, fuck me. I need it," Angelo moaned.

"Not bad, bitch. But I know your real story. Had me pimping my buddies to you at that gas station shithouse for smokes. Used me. Lucky the cops didn't bust your ass." Rod

whacked Angelo's ass again.

"I'd do anything for you, Rod. You know that. Just fuck me." Angelo was shaking he wanted it so bad. Rod was brutal, the way he rammed his cock up the man's butt. He rabbit-fucked him. Angelo was screaming and crying but they were sounds of joy, not torture. "You're the best Rod!"

Rod closed his eyes as he battered the man's butthole.

"Oh, oh, oh," Angelo cried as he jacked his own cock.

Rod grunted and collapsed on top of the man on the mattress.

I squeezed my cock, wishing Rod was shooting his cum up my own rump.

Suddenly Rod pulled his prick out of the man's butthole.

"You're next, pal," Rod said.

"Can he take anymore?" I asked, kinda feeling sorry for the man.

Angelo looked over his shoulder with glazed brown eyes. "Yeah, fuck me, baby. Put your big dick up my ass!"

I took off my pants and mounted the man's ass. It wasn't so much that I wanted to fuck his fat ass as I wanted to rub my dick in Rod's cum that was inside the man.

"Fuck the whore's ass," Rod said, popping open another beer and gulping it.

I eased my cock up the slimy, hot hole and pumped away. Just looking at Rod's exposed crimson cock that was covered with cum and assjuices, I was close to getting my rocks off. That's when I got the surprise of my life. Rod started patting my butt. Soon he was rubbing it and fingering me.

"Man, you got a nice butt, buddy. Real tempting. Beats the hell outta this slut's flabby ass."

"Fuck that punk's ass while he fucks mine," Angelo said.

"That's the best idea you ever had, bitch. Yeah, that's what I'm gonna do." When Rod mounted me and slapped his hard dick on my butt I felt jolts of electricity through my body. He was really going to do it. Then I was stunned when Rod started to lick my ass. He ran his tongue into my crack and licked my pucker. My whole body tingled. He nudged the crown of his dick into my cherry butthole and stayed still while my ass-ring expanded. It hurt bad but my mind was taken off the pain by having my dick up the other man's asshole.

Rod began humping my butt. In turn, I humped the man on the bottom. I was the middle of a fuck sandwich. And I loved it. Especially knowing that it was Rod's huge dick sawing into my ass. But I was not about to let him know it. Even though the pain was gone, I cried, "Oh, no, please no."

Rod ignored my protests. "Oh, yeah, that's what an ass is supposed to feel like. It's so hot and tight. I love it, buddy," Rod moaned.

The three of us began fucking like a well-oiled machine. I didn't want it to ever end.

"Oh, shit. Fuck! Cumming up your ass, buddy," Rod yelled. I felt his sperm squirt into my asshole.

At the same time I got my nut and shot my load up Angelo's ass. My hole clenched around Rod's cock until he pulled out of me. Then I pulled out of the man on the bottom. Angelo turned around and started licking the goo off my cock that had been up his ass. I grabbed hold of Rod's cock and licked it, spit-shining it. Amazingly, his cock stayed hard. So while Angelo nursed my cock I gave Rod a blowjob.

"My god," he gasped, but he made no effort to pull away. His cock was so big I nearly choked, but I was determined to get him off in my mouth and taste his cum. I had to grip his shaft and suck on the crown, tonguing the ridge below it, but I eventually got him off. His cum tasted real sweet and creamy.

Angelo tugged on my balls while he slurped on my dick, and I shot my second wad in his mouth. After that, we all lay silent for a while. We drank another beer. Rod looked at his watch. "Gotta go. Fucking curfew," he said.

And what started in Angelo's room ended up in my room with me sucking off Rod and him fucking me whenever we got the chance, which was quite often, until I went off to college.

HOTTER THAN HELL

Rick Hassett

As Cody and Sean left the Mexican restaurant in Sedona, Arizona – internationally famous for giant rock spires the color of blood and shaped like erect penises – Cody said, "It's hotter than hell, man."

Sean blinked as Cody pulled his black knit shirt over his blond crewcut before he revved the engine of his bright yellow Sidekick. Sean wasn't a queer but he felt an urge to tug his gay buddy's gold nipple ring anyway. He resisted the sudden temptation by playing with the silver crucifix he inherited after his father's death in a plane crash.

Cody's bare shoulders, broad and brown, began to sweat. Droplets trickled down his caramel-colored flesh along a trail of light hairs that started above his navel but sank out of sight at his waist. At a stoplight in the middle of Sedona he smiled, rubbing his forearm, and the red air made him seem like Lucifer himself to Sean. "Yeah, hotter than hell," Sean muttered.

Sean had agreed in Los Angeles to visit Sedona with Cody, to share a motel on summer break from college, but made it plain he didn't want to be seduced. More tired than he thought, drowsy after the wine he downed at the cantina where Sean talked about buying a newer vehicle, he used Cody's shirt as a pillow. He drifted asleep in the desert warmth but it seemed like only a minute had passed when he felt a hand on his beefy left thigh.

"Wake up, Champ," Cody said, using a nickname that started last November after Sean dashed ninety yards untouched with seconds left on the clock to score the winning touchdown for UCLA against favored rival Southern California. "I spotted a showroom with new vehicles. Let's go look."

Sean crawled out of the Sidekick, yawning, and headed toward the glass building.

"That Jeep's real nice," Cody said, pointing at a turquoise one with a pink designer stripe.

"They're not cheap."

"Girls like guys who drive Jeeps, Sean. Hell, guys like guys who drive Jeeps."

"Then when we get back to L.A. I'll buy a new Jeep – just for you and the girls who want my bod," Sean said, half dead from the heat. He'd become a recognized sports celebrity at nineteen after that football victory, gorgeous cheerleaders finally taking notice, but he was still a virgin waiting for the right woman to come along.

"Good, Sean. You might have been raised a strict Catholic in south Boston, but you need to loosen up and enjoy yourself more. Okay, dude?"

Sean nodded at his lanky friend's remark before they hauled ass back to the Sidekick.

"God, it's so *hot*."

"Not half as *hot* as you are," said Cody, a business student making a sales pitch on their final night in Sedona.

"I know you want to suck my cock, or have me fuck your butt so hard that it hurts for a week, but we have a deal over this trip."

Cody smiled like a sheepdog.

"You can't blame a guy for trying. I've noticed you wearing a jockstrap at the motel, your fiery red pubic hairs sneaking outside, and it's been driving me to drink like a fish. You might dig sex with yours truly."

"Sorry, buddy."

Partway up Oak Creek Canyon, Cody acting dizzy while driving through what tourist brochures called the largest ponderosa pine forest in the world, a red light flashed behind them.

"Well, well," a bow-legged highway patrolman in a brown uniform said after he pulled them over onto a narrow gravel shoulder and swaggered forward chewing a toothpick. "California boys."

"What's the problem, officer?" Cody asked him, playing innocent.

"Drivin' under the influence judgin' by your weavin'. Yup, kid. I definitely can smell liquor on your breath. Step out."

"Why should I?"

"Because *I'm* sayin', boy. I'm a state trooper."

"A poor excuse for one," Cody said, mad as a bee.

"Get out now and take the test."

"What test?"

"A sobriety check. Standard procedure."

"Okay, okay," Cody told him. "I'll take the test."

Cody followed the cop's instructions, touching his finger to his nose easily and walking a straight line heel-to-toe without any problems, but Smokey said he'd failed.

"You're a fucker," Sean said, watching from the vehicle.

"And you're a fuckee," the armed officer shot back, suddenly handcuffing Cody against the Sidekick.

"What're you doing?" Cody yelled at the top of his lungs.

"I'm teachin' you a lesson."

Smokey dragged Cody toward his cruiser and forced him into the back seat. Then he strolled forward, scratching his necklace of collarbone hair through an undone button, and circled to Sean. He rested his left palm on Sean's right knee as though they were football buddies.

"You're under arrest also," he said, pulling another set of cuffs from a back pocket.

"What for?"

"Obstructin' justice."

Sean started to resist but the patrolman managed to catch his right wrist. He pulled it behind Sean's back and began to snap the metal ring around. Sean's left hand flew back to help and he got that one too.

"Verbal abuse is grounds for arrest," Smokey told him, king of the hill.

The powerful jerk walked him back to the flashing light, opening the opposite door, and shoved him inside with a disheveled-looking Cody.

"Sorry, Sean. I got you into this. Forgive me."

"It's not your fault."

Smokey got in the driver's seat and turned on the ignition.

"We're goin' for a little ride," he said.

Silence filled the interior until Smokey swerved off the winding highway onto a dirt road leading into dense trees near Oak Creek itself.

"What's the deal, man?" Cody asked.

"We're gonna have some rootin'-tootin' fun by ourselves in this little grove I know."

Sean glanced at Cody nervously.

"There's the place. Pretty and quiet. Drenched in moonlight."

Smokey shut off the custom engine, stepped outside and came around to Sean's door.

"Out, boy," he motioned. "You're it."

"Forget it. I'm staying."

The tanned officer grabbed the nape of Sean's neck and yanked him outside with the strength of a sasquatch.

"Take me, man," Cody said. "Leave him alone. He's not gay."

"I prefer redheads," Smokey stated while he slammed the door behind. "Straight's even better."

Sean began to sweat after Smokey began to smile.

"You're scared, aren't you, good-lookin'?" the cow-eyed cop asked, grinning broadly at the bulge in Sean's light blue denims.

"Hardly."

Smokey undid the buttons on his beige shirt, removing it casually, and tossed the garment onto a nearby boulder.

"These are real muscles, boy, so don't you struggle."

"I can see."

"I'm gonna do nasty things to you tonight."

"What kinds of things?"

"Indecent liberties, we call 'em, in Arizona," the strapping body builder replied, absent-mindedly playing with a bronze nipple point.

Sean gulped hard.

"The best part is that your queer buddy's here to see us."

Smokey raised his right elbow and propped it high against the rough bark of a stout pine trunk six feet away from his car's hissing radiator. Relaxing before starting, sticking the fingers on his left hand into the visible waistband of his white boxers, he remained silent. Sean figured the handsome but arrogant son-of-a-bitch was probably trying to decide where to begin on this steamy night in the mountains as he scratched his underarm.

"Turned on by wet armpit hair, Red? Step over and sniff my manly scent."

"What did you say?"

"You heard me okay."

"It smells bad," Sean said. "You've got B.O."

"Don't describe it for me. Just take a big whiff of it."

Sean sniffed from a distance.

"Not like that, kid. Put your nose in."

"You've got to be kidding."

"Move your ass now and put your damn nose way down into my pit. Where it's real hairy and stinky. I want your blond friend there to watch you sniff me like a puppy."

Sean didn't like the idea, but Smokey lost his patience.

"Rank, isn't it?" he taunted after pressing from behind so Sean's nose was smack against the pungent area. "I've been workin'."

Just when Sean thought the smelling was over, finally released slightly, Smokey came up with a brand new project.

"Lick the hair," he said.

Sean couldn't believe his own ears as he stared in a trance at the bushy clump, half the black strands poking up to his great bicep and the other half running downhill.

"You're gonna taste my sweat whether it appeals to you or not."

"That's gross."

"Stick your tongue out right now, boy, and sponge bathe my whole armpit."

Sean started at the bottom, where hairs ended, and worked his way higher.

"That's real good, kid. You're a skilled pit licker. Must like it okay. Now the left needs some lovin'."

Smokey lifted his forearm to provide direct access, making Sean sniff his bunch for a while like the first time around.

"Let go, man, let go!"

"Red digs my pits," Smokey lied, raising his voice to make sure Cody could hear inside the cruiser. "He reminds me of an Irish setter lapping up every drop. I can't make him stop."

Sean stopped then despite Smokey's hold.

"Kneel on the ground," the lawman ordered him without delay before unzipping the trousers of his uniform. "Resist and you'll suffer."

Sean sank to his knees.

"Turn this way so your pal can see your face."

Sean twisted to his right a little in the haunting moonlight, already ashamed, as Smokey freed his limp penis from the bottom of his shorts.

"Big, huh?" he asked.

Sean could smell the musky aroma from where he knelt as if in church, noticing Smokey gloating overhead, but dwelt on the extreme width and obscene length of the thing as it swelled.

"Give me some good head, boy, or I'll blow your head off."

Sean thought of biting a chunk out of the whopper when it touched his lips, sealed against entry, but figured Smokey was actually unstable enough to carry out his threat.

"I'll lick the skin, man, but I won't suck."

"Yeah, punk," the earthy cop oozed as Sean began to tongue the front of his organ under the ridge.

"Don't, dude," Sean started to protest after Smokey gripped himself, semi-hard, and pistol-whipped a cheek to achieve complete erection. His captor took quick advantage of Sean's open lips and stuffed partway inside. He placed his left hand behind Sean's neck, fingers spread, and pulled him closer so roughly he almost gagged. Sean hadn't bargained for what was now happening and he didn't like the situation one bit.

"Look at that, Blondie! Your redheaded straight buddy's eating a foot-long Polish with relish. He just went down on me. Think he'll enjoy sucking dick?"

Smokey didn't wait for genuine sucking, knowing it wasn't too likely, but fucked his mouth instead.

"That feels nice," the officer crooned, watching Sean rocking. "You look funny with those cheeks puffed out. Blow that horn!"

Breathing proved difficult as Smokey pumped his thickness into Sean's tonsils, making him retch, in a steady machine rhythm that seldom missed a beat.

"This boy's already a pretty good cocksucker, Mister Crewcut. With more training he could earn a scout merit badge."

Smokey shoved the blunt point in much faster without relief until Sean's nose was buried in coarse pubic hairs an inch deep that spilled outside the front of his stinky boxers.

"A-a-a-h-h-h," the cop said at last, head back, when he came in gushes.

Scalding hot semen coated the back of Sean's bruised throat

in an untamed river.

"Like my jism? My waitress friend says it tastes great. Sweet as honey."

Smokey withdrew the entire length of his organ, which sprang higher, and lifted Sean easily so they stood facing.

"I need your belt for what comes next," the smirking patrolman disclosed, removing it quickly before turning Sean around and pressing his stomach against the cruiser.

"What's that?" Sean asked, quaking like an aspen.

"Don't worry, sport. You'll love it."

Smokey secured Sean's left calf to the bumper, took his own belt off and tied the right calf in the same manner.

"Ever take a dick up that cute little butt?" Smokey inquired before lowering Sean's jeans to mid-thigh.

"Never, creep," Sean spit out.

"Then tonight's your lucky night. I'm gonna break you in."

"You can't be serious. Your prick won't fit."

The officer just snickered.

"Wanna wager? A hundred bucks I'll succeed. Betting closed."

"You'll split me apart!"

"I reckon you'll stretch – further than any restroom condom – after I'm properly introduced."

"You turd."

Smokey hooked his fingers inside the waistband of Sean's jockstrap, testing its elasticity before letting it return with a sting, and then cupped naked buttocks as though frisking a suspect.

"These white melons are moist," the cop let Cody know. "Fresh and plump. Like summer produce at your local grocery store."

"You fucking bastard!" Cody shouted from his prison.

Smokey parted the melons to inspect Sean's fuzzy crevice.

"Please, mister. I'm straight."

"Give it up, boy. You can't con me."

The lawman found Sean's hidden orifice with his index finger.

"Maybe you're right, good-lookin'," he said, rubbing the button until it quivered. "It's only the size of a dime so I'll bet it's new to this. You haven't let your queer buddy over there

enjoy heaven on earth?"

"No, sir. I told you I'm not gay. Untie me."

"Sorry, Charlie. I'm gettin' into that twitchin' little asshole tonight come hell or high water if I have to use magnum force. Mighty temptin'."

Sean's heart began to pound.

"Give me a hand," Smokey requested, rubbing his growing boner against the flesh of Sean's upturned palm and metal cuff. The stiffer it became the stronger he pressed. Within moments it felt like a bloated monster, an American version of Godzilla, capable of breathing fire and flattening whole neighborhoods.

"Poppin' your cherry is gonna be paradise," Smokey said, stepping much closer and teasing Sean's groove.

Sean felt the knob at his back door.

"I forgot lube, kid, but I'm spittin'."

The trooper promptly attempted to penetrate, Sean clenching his sphincter muscle instinctly, but he couldn't overwhelm nature's defenses. Sean's fears eased in the dark--maybe this fucker would give up. Smokey cursed before he suddenly pitched forward again, pressure amazing, and plowed right through the ring like a raging bull.

"Holy shit!" Sean screamed to the heavens.

Smokey laughed.

"You lose. Where's my hundred? Cash only."

"Take it out, man, take it out!"

"Your manhole's even tighter than I imagined," the cop said as he sank to the hilt.

Sean lurched forward trying to escape, despite his restraints, and Smokey began to forcibly sodomize him.

"Pull it out! Pull it out!"

"Sore already, cowboy? I'm ridin' in your saddle until the trail drive's over in Abilene. So just relax."

Sean continued to squirm, bucking higher than a rodeo bronc, but couldn't dislodge his rider.

"I enjoy it when you fight. It gets my juices flowin'."

"Ah...ah...ah."

Sean's eyes met Cody's over the hood then, a huge cock deep in his butt, and he felt like a wimp from the pain.

"He's velvet smooth inside, Big Eyes. Getting jealous? You're missing out on preemo stuff."

"Jesus Christ," Sean gasped. "You're hurting."

"If it hurts now it'll hurt real good when I get all the way in."

"I'm dying here! It's killing me!"

"Your boyfriend's lovin' every second, Romeo. He's whisperin' sweet nothings in my ear."

"Oh...oh...oh."

Sean saw stars but not in the sky.

"You're my homeboy," the patrolman declared.

"It's bad, man, it's bad!"

The tearing of delicate rectal tissues that was taking place couldn't have been worse, Sean thought, if a giant saguaro cactus had been jammed up there instead.

"Push and pull," the cop said then, "push and pull."

"Man...man...man."

Smokey's fingers slipped under Sean's loose shirt as he fucked the living daylights out of him.

"Hope it's okay to pinch your tiny boy's tits."

The trooper started to breathe much heavier, panting with passion, and twisted Sean's nipples even harder.

"You move the way my girl does when I butt-fuck her," the asshole stated. "She hates me when I poke in but loves it in the end."

Each stab into Sean's guts hurt more than the last one.

"Ouch! Ouch! Ouch!"

Smokey bumped Sean's prostate for the umpteenth time, sending lightning bolts through his system, and nonchalantly asked Cody if he could see his friend's body experiencing spasms.

"Red likes it up the ass," the lawman claimed.

Sean looked straight at the windshield, noticing the insects squashed against the glass, but couldn't detect Cody's present mood. Smokey went into high gear then. He drove into Sean's tunnel like a sixteen-wheeler, hormones on overdrive, at what must have been sixty-five miles an hour. Sean felt like a rag doll on the warm body of the car. The officer jumped onto the bumper without losing contact, changing angles swiftly, and started plunging into Sean from directly overhead. The sensation it produced was indescribable. Smokey balanced himself then on Sean's back as if a gymnast, feet in the air on

both sides, and allowed the force of his weight to propel him deeper.

"Jesus...Jesus...Jesus."

"Fuckin' like this probably takes endurance," the acrobatic guy speculated, puffing loudly.

"Shit, dude. I can't take any more. Come, man."

"I'm almost there, good-lookin'. Just a few more minutes."

Gravity assisted Smokey's straight vertical motion, suction strong, until he reached places Sean didn't know existed.

"Oh my God...oh my God...oh my God."

"See my dick, blondie? This is for you. It all fits in."

There wasn't any doubt in Sean's mind that Cody was watching the athletic position with undivided attention.

"Hang on, Sean!" Cody yelled in support. "Hang on, bro!"

Nailed from above, face flat, Sean began crying.

"He's losin' it," Smokey stated as if talking on a police radio. "Guess he can't handle twelve inches. I'm still goin' strong."

Several minutes passed in silence except for grunting and groaning, Smokey grunting and Sean groaning, that could have been heard miles away in sleepy Sedona.

"I'm comin', boy, I'm comin.'"

Smokey fired several bullets into Sean, but not from his gun, before telling him it was bitchin'.

"For you," Sean said, "not me."

The officer kissed his backside and climbed out of the box canyon.

"Gettin' your socket plugged the first time couldn't have been too awful," the perspiring rapist concluded. "You were moanin' louder than a Vegas whore for fifteen minutes."

Smokey walked to the closed door by Cody, opened it tiredly and then motioned him forward with his weapon.

"I want to see you fuck Red in the ass real hard now too," he said. "I hate to see two boys with such hot bods not have any fun."

When Sean awoke at the motel on the day after, hugging his college buddy's solid chest from behind, he thought about the pleasure he felt that second time. Midway through the gentle screwing Smokey jumped into his cruiser without speaking and tossed the keys to their handcuffs out the window. When Cody finally quit fucking on that smooth boulder, and Sean called the

Sedona Police Station from a nearby pay phone, they learned that "officer" was actually an escaped prison convict. He'd killed a young trooper earlier, stolen his uniform, revolver and vehicle and started to terrorize tourists passing through sunny Arizona. A female dispatcher working the graveyard shift informed Sean that the scumbag who assaulted him was still on the loose.

"I guess things aren't quite the same today," Cody said when he woke up, feeling Sean's wet tongue licking the blond tuft in his right armpit, his large hand jacking him off strongly and his thick penis sliding into a waiting, amazingly compliant ass.

They kissed then with a sudden passion that made a July heat wave seem frigid by comparison.

JONAH'S ISLAND

Jarred Goodall

The sky was clear, the air was warm and the two boys had been on the trail since early morning. They had stripped off their shirts, and Jonah, whose turn it was to follow behind, felt thoroughly in tune with the pair of idiotically smiling have-a-good-day socks which swayed and jiggled drying on the back of Dan's back-pack. They came to a bridge and stopped and mopped their faces, sniffing the cool air of the little trout stream below.

"Let's eat," Jonah said.

"Is cock all you think about?" Dan turned around and grinned at him, a big, wide-mouthed grin. "Come on!"

They scrambled down to the stream and sat beside it munching the sandwiches their mothers had prepared. A solitary hiker came by. Dan raised a stick as though it was an imaginary gun and pulled the trigger on him. "Pow! Pow! Another environmental polluter bites the dust!"

"Come on, Dan, they're just like you and me."

"Not so. Our shit don't stink, our piss is sweet as rain-water. We belong here, Jon-boy, like the Mohegans."

"If you say so."

A troop of Boy Scouts came by, weary and homeward bound. Two stragglers walked with their arms around one another.

"I bet those two zipped together their sleeping bags," Dan said.

"What do you mean?"

"You know, real buddies."

They reached the lake in mid-afternoon and found it deserted. But the obvious campsites had a well-used look, with rings of blackened stones and half-burned rubbish in their centers. They decided on a small island in the middle of the lake, little more than a granite knob rising some thirty feet above the water.

They stripped to their undershorts, inflated their air mattresses, piled one on top of the other and their backpacks on top of that and launched their make-shift raft, kicking it

slowly and carefully over to the island.

Amazingly, only the air mattresses got wet. They crawled out and inspected their domain. Near the top of the island a solitary pine had managaed to thrust its roots into a network of fractures, and on the west side of the island was a birch grove and a bouldery shore rich with driftwood for their fire. On the other side was a little sandy beach.

That's where they were standing now. Dan flexed his muscles and said, "I'm king of the island."

"Hell you are!" Jonah said. They met and wrestled, not very seriously. In a moment they relaxed, Jonah on the bottom, Dan on top. "Man," Jonah said, "this is a hell of a way to celebrate our eighteenth birthday!"

"It's too hot to fight," Dan said, suddenly disinterested.

They rolled apart. "Just think," Jonah said, "nobody's around for miles. We could do anything we wanted and nobody would know it."

"Like, if there a girl."

"That would spoil it."

"Okay, two girls."

"Nah, you'd never get a girl out here hacking around and getting wet and dirty and stinky. They don't go for this backpacking bit."

Dan laughed and grabbed Jonah around the neck. "I guess we just got each other!"

Jonah stood up, vaguely uneasy. "Let's take a dip."

"We just did."

"I mean a real dip, where we can splash around."

"Bare ass, right?"

"Yeah, bare-ass."

"Okay, buddy. You're my real buddy."

"What's all this real buddy business?" Jonah asked.

"Don't you know?"

"Nope."

"If I was your real buddy," Dan said, grinning, "I would do this!" And he grabbed Jonah's penis and gave it a quick pull.

Jonah gasped, colored and Dan bent over with laughter. Jonah socked him on the shoulder, and Dan fell backwards into the lake.

They fought, shouting, splashing, spitting water, then

decided to swim around the island. When they got cold they crawled out and climbed to the top of their island and flopped down on their backs to dry in the sunshine.

"That was great," Dan said.

"Yeah. Lake water's so fresh and sweet..."

"And it feels so good flowing around your balls." Dan grabbed his cock and moved it about. "Big Fat Dan here doesn't get to greet the sun very often."

"Mine neither," Jonah said, but when he touched his own penis he found it instantly began to fill.

Dan noticed. "Getting a hard-on, eh?!!"

Jonah started to roll away, but Dan put a hand on his shoulder. "Big Fat Dan is always showing off that way, too. It's a pain - back home anyhow."

"Yeah."

"Especially when it happens at the wrong time, like the show's over and you gotta stand up and there's always these chicks looking at you and you come out of your seat bent over like an old man."

"And you got to run to the can to bring it down."

"I hate that," Dan said. "I always feel so, I don't know, empty and conned out of something afterwards, don't you?"

"I guess so."

"Of course sometimes, if you don't wave it around or anything, it can turn on someone you like."

Jonah didn't say anything.

"Not that it gets you anywhere half the time. It's usually my luck to get a chick that just wants to tease you. And tease you. And talk about love. So pretty soon it's all over, inside your skivs."

"Man."

"And then she's mad at you 'cause you aren't interested any more."

By now they both had hefty hard-ons, and Jonah suddenly realized he didn't care. It felt good. He wanted to share a hard-on display with Dan.

Dan laughed a little nervously. "What a couple of creeps we are - two buck naked guys with boners and not a chick in a hundred miles."

"I guess it doesn't hurt."

The sun dropped. Shadows of the pines pressing upon the lake cast longer and longer shadows over its breeze-rippled surface. They didn't bother to set up their tent, the sky being clear.

They brought out their casting rods and caught one black bass each which they later cooked and ate along with some freeze-dried potatoes. Afterwards they built up the fire into a big, cheerful blaze and Dan sprawled out in front of it leaning against the tree.

"Hog," Jonah said when he came back from washing his plate and fork in the lake. The tree was the one backrest they had.

"We'll share," Dan said, spreading his legs and patting his chest. Jonah dropped to his knees, scooted over and leaned back against him.

For almost a minute they just stared silently into the fire. Jonah felt a great sense of peace flooding through him. "This is the life," he said, knowing it expressed only an infinitessimal part of what he felt.

"Yeah," Dan agreed. "My best birthday yet."

Jonah had known Dan all his life, and Dan had been his best friend for most of it. For a few years in high school they had drifted apart, when Dan had gone out for sports, but recently their common interest in environmental issues and enthusiasm for backpacking had brought them together again.

They talked quietly and lazily, about everything and nothing - how sweet-scented the night was, how bright the stars were, how the lapping of wavelets on the granite knob sounded to Jonah like gamelan music.

"What's that?" Dan asked.

"What they play on Bali."

"I hear the girls there are beautiful and dance sexier than anywhere else in the world."

"I don't think I'd trade Bali for this," Jonah said.

"Yeah, this is pretty nice... for now."

After a while they grew stiff and a little cold. They got up to fix their sleeping bags, then taunted each other into plunging into the lake for a starlight swim. The water was surprisingly warm and in its blackness just a little mysterious. "We're in an alien kingdom," Jonah said.

"Watch out that some brother of those basses we just ate don't come up and nibble your balls."

They got out and slung the water off their bare skin in front of the fire. Jonah gazed at Dan's body: so familiar through all its changes over the years, now so sturdy, spare, hardy and well-proportioned. His eyes fastened on the rounded buttocks and, in front, the springy bush of pubic hair from which hung the large, pendant penis. Dan's legs were lightly brushed with dark hair, now wet, and he stood easily upon them, feet slightly apart.

When they were dry at last and enjoying the fire's radient heat, Dan turned to Jonah and said, "I'll wrestle you."

They grappled and fell down on their sleeping bags, again fighting only half-heartedly. Soon they were stalemated again. They rested, lying against each other.

"Okay, I guess we're warm," Dan said.

But something was happening to Jonah. A deep, plangeant joy was stirring through him, especially where his skin pressed against Dan's. The feeling was new and yet it seemed very, very old, too, as though it had ancestral roots, was inherited from those dim races which hunted great woolly creatures in the mist and rain before the retreating glaciers.

And it was remembered from his own life, too, from years before, when something had happened crawling over wet grass, climbing trees, and later in the contentment of his own bed. Something forgotten but now recognized as infinitely precious.

Once again his cock was hard, and it was pressing against Dan's leg.

"Okay, okay I give," Dan said. "Let's turn in."

But Jonah continued to hold him. He moved his cock, ever so slightly, along Dan's leg.

Dan stiffened. Their eyes met in the unsteady firelight. "Quit it," Dan said slowly, meaning it. He broke Jonah's grip and got up.

But a minute later he turned to Jonah and said, with his old enthusiastic smile, "I'm going to catch a bucketful of fish tomorrow and we'll eat bass till we smell like otters."

Jonah gulped with relief, and when he crawled into his bedroll a few minutes later, it seemed no time at all before dawn was awakening them into a new day.

Jonah and Dan did go fishing and brought back enough bass for a big fish-fry that evening. By then it was hot and they went to the beach and stripped off their clothes, and Jonah found himself once again admiring Dan's body. Dan grinned at him. "I know about guys that are always staring at your dick."

Jonah pushed Dan in the water and they wrestled there, splashing and ducking each other and getting slippery half-nelsons around their necks. They climbed out, lay down on the warm granite, arms touching.

And then, inexplicably, they started to wrestle again, this time fairly earnestly, struggling for position. Ultimately Dan pinned Jonah on his back, as both of them had always known he could if he set his mind to it. The full weight of Dan's body rested heavily upon him.

"Say uncle," Dan said. His face was red and running with sweat.

"Why should I?"

"'Cause you lost."

Sweat fell on Jonah's cheek. Suddenly all the mysterious feelings of the night before were back, and doubled. Blood rushed to Jonah's penis which slid in its expansion in their comingling sweat. Dan suddenly released his wrists. Their eyes met, just as they had met the night before, questioning, evaluating.

Dan started to say something, but then he frowned and shook his head. Jonah tightened his grip around Dan's back, holding him in place. The ancestral memories were coming back, the mists clearing away. Jonah started to move his prick, back and forth, back and forth, sliding in their sweat.

Now Dan was definitely saying something, but Jonah wasn't listening, couldn't listen. He tangled his fingers in Dan's hair and brought Dan's head down until Dan's mouth was pressed against Jonah's shoulder, threatening to open, threatening to bite. With his other hand, Jonah grabbed one side of Dan's buttocks, tucking his fingers into the crack and drove Dan's narrow hips down hard against him.

Dan's resistance began to crumble, as somehow Jonah had always known it would. Dan, too, was hardening up, his cock pressing into Jonah's stomach. Jonah sighed with relief: it was really going to happen, something that had always been too

vague and misty to even dream about. Although he'd ever done anything like this before, he was confident, and, in his confidence, full of joy.

Now Jonah cupped both of Dan's buttocks with both of his hands and pressed down and forward, making Dan's cock start to move, slide against his stomach next to his own. Jonah let go of Dan's ass now and thrust upwards with his hips against Dan, feeling Dan's cock slide back against his, feeling Dan's balls drop into the cleft between his thighs.

Now Dan responded on his own and thrust back, digging his hips down onto Jonah. Jonah's hands started moving all over Dan, over the strong back, muscular shoulders, neck, head, fingers tangling in the sweaty, sun-bleached hair. Jonah felt Dan's arms slide underneath him and tighten, Dan's mouth lock onto the place where his neck and shoulder met and bite.

The motion was strong now, spontaneous and natural. There was nothing more Jonah had to do. Everything was happening all by itself. The feeling in his loins rose, brightened, tightened, becoming all the time stronger and more magical, until it blotted out every thought, every sensation, memory, hope, fear, except for his terrific closeness to Dan.

And still it rose, like a great tidal wave, like a star exploding, and peaked with excruciating beauty and declined with gigantic pulses that seemed to empty his soul.

Dan was sitting up, his back turned. Jonah reached over and put a hand on his shoulder. Dan shrugged it off, stood up and went down to the water and waded in. He could hear Dan splashing himself.

Jonah pulled on his cut-offs and walked to the other side of the island and sat down and dangled his legs in the water. He knew what had just happened was incredibly important, but he wasn't yet prepared to think about it. He needed a few minutes alone, simply to exist, without feeling or reflections. Dan was rigging his casting rod when Jonah returned to the camping area. He grinned sheepishly and said, "You know, that was pretty queer stuff we just did."

"I guess so." Jonah avoided Dan's eyes. "Are you mad?"

Dan shrugged. "Naw."

"I liked it, sort of - while it was happening, I mean. Didn't you?"

Dan bit off a leader and tied it to the line. "Sure," he said. "Have you ever done it before?"

"Hell, no. And I don't think we better do it again, or else we're liable to turn into a couple of queers." Then he smiled conspiratorially and nudged Jonah with his foot. "Just imagine what it would be like doing that for real, with some foxy girl!"

That evening they fried up the bass and cooked some beans and built up the fire until it looked like a signal flare that made the night all the darker.

Watching it die down, they dragged their sleeping bags over to its windward side and Jonah opened them facing each other. Dan stared at them doubtfully for a moment, then went down to the water's edge to wash. Jonah walked to the other side of the island, opened his cut-offs and threw a strong, warm stream into the still waters of the lake. He held his cock proudly, full of anticipation, filling his lungs with the piney air.

When he came back, Dan was sitting on his sleeping bag, staring into the fire. Jonah came up behind him and grabbed him in a bear hug.

Dan didn't respond. "I'm too tired for that," he said. "Besides, we'll get our sacks all messed up."

But Jonah wouldn't let him go, and wrestled Dan down until he had him pinned under him. Dan wasn't to be tempted into anything but defensive resistance. "I guess you better get over on your own sack," he said. And then, when Jonah still didn't release him, "Come on, Jonah."

"Do you think you can lick me?"

"That's not the point. I remember what happened this afternoon."

"So do I."

"We decided it wasn't going to happen again, remember?"

"I remember you saying something like that."

"And everybody but you knows that sort of stuff's just not right. It just isn't."

"Dan, we left everybody back at home." Jonah made a first thrust downward with his hips.

"Goddamnit, Jonah, quit it!" Dan tried to rise up but Jonah held him down. Already his hands were at Dan's neck and had found the zipper.

"Leave my jacket alone!"

"Are you going to sleep in your duds?"

"No."

"I think you're getting a rod on."

"Jesus Christ, get off!"

"Okay." Jonah sprang back and began to strip.

Dan rid himself of his jacket, pulled his sweater and T-shirt over his head in one smooth manoeuvre, revealing once again his fine back flickering red in the light of the dying fire. Now he looked back over his shoulder and frowned at Jonah as he removed his Levis.

By now Jonah was completely naked, with his cock hard, raised and pointing half way between Dan's head and the top of the pine tree. With the blood singing in his ears, he grabbed Dan about the chest, pinned his arms to his sides.

"Quit it!" Dan shouted, but Jonah had found Dan's cock and was pumping it up to rapid and full erection.

"Come on," Jonah whispered, his lips touching the hard tendon at the top of Dan's shoulder. "You know this feels good!"

"Guys aren't..."

"Fuck that!"

"So I got a hard-on. Guys still aren't supposed..."

"Forget about `supposed'. There isn't any `supposed' out here."

Jonah could feel Dan wavering. "Jo, aren't we crazy to be fooling around with this?"

"Nobody's got to know. Just remember what this afternoon was like. This is going to be even better."

"Okay!" Dan spat it out, then pried Jonah's fingers off his penis. "Just this once!"

Jonah opened out Dan's bedroll and climbed in, Dan moving over to make room. They lay on their sides facing one another, hard cocks meeting and smearing each other with their exuded slime.

Jonah put his arms around Dan, ran his fingers through Dan's slightly curly neck hair and breathed a great sigh of pleasure.

"This is just the nicest thing in the whole world," Jonah whispered into Dan's ear. "It makes us..." But he couldn't finish because just then Dan's fingers closed around his cock

and all he could do was gasp.

"That feel better than pulling on it yourself?" Dan asked slyly. He took Dan in hand now, smeared the pre-cum oozing out of the knob all around and began to caress the whole length and breadth of Dan's penis. How beautifully it snuggled into his hand, as though it belonged there just as Dan's friendship belonged to him, warm and probing and absolutely right. With his other hand he was exploring the skin of Dan's face and neck and chest and stomach, as though he was getting to know Dan for the very first time in his life.

Jonah had never before touched, or tired to touch, another person like this. He could hear his own heart beat fast, getting faster, loud, heavy and commanding.

Then suddenly he found himself bending double, his hips spilling out the side of the sleeping bag and his mouth seeking the knob of Dan's cock.

Dan gasped. "Jo, Jonah, for God's sakes, not that!"

But Jonah hardly heard him. The soft/hard velvety tip of Dan's penis was right there pressing against his mouth. He licked his lips, opened them and felt Dan slide in, as instinctively he tongued the loose skin where he knew the best feeling for Dan would be.

"Yikes!" Dan cried, and then seemed to give himself over to the automatic thrusting which drove that hard cock in and out, in and out of Jonah's mouth, as hard hands came to Jonah's head, tangled in his hair and demanded more, harder and deeper plunges, until, at last, he felt Dan's body racked by gigantic shivers. Soon sperm was shooting out into the back of his mouth, bubbling up into his nose, intensely smelling of Dan and his vitality, stinging, and then he realized that almost at the same moment he, too, had erupted and was dripping his own load onto the ground.

Jonah woke up at dawn. It was starting off to be another clear day. The western sky was red. A couple of birds were chattering in the branches of the island tree.

Dan was still sound asleep in the other bedroll, snoring slightly with his mouth open and the quilting drawn up to his chin. Neither of them had bothered to put on any clothes after their lovemaking and Jonah had slept a little cold.

Now he crawled in beside Dan and draped an arm over

Dan's chest and snuggled up spoon fashion. Dan stirred a little, then lay still. Jonah sought and found Dan's penis and held it without making any motion. It slowly filled in his hand.

"It's tomorrow already," Dan mumbled a few minutes later.

"Yup. And it's cold out." Jonah brushed his lips against the back of Dan's neck.

They heard a fish jump in the lake and Jonah lifted his head to see bright, broadening rings on the water.

"There goes breakfast," Jonah said.

"You know, this is a whole new way to wake up."

Jonah breathed in all the intimate smells of Dan's body: the warm skin, perspiration, hair, the slightly sharper scent of waking breath. Nothing had ever been this perfect in his life; nothing could ever beat it. He licked his fingers and the palm of his hand and brought it back to Dan's cock and gave it a gentle squeeze. They moved around so they were lying face to face. "I wish I didn't have to go away to college next week," Jonah said.

One of Dan's hands grabbed Jonah's neck and gave it a roughly affectionate squeeze. "Don't think about it," he said. "What's wrong with now?"

"Nothing," Jonah said. He gathered their two cocks into his spit-and-pre-cum-lubricated hand and started thrusting against Dan's. And that sent them both into the full, deep current of lust's most basic satisfaction.

Afterwards, they dozed and awakened and, as the sun climbed up into the sky, made love one more time.

"I'm starved," Dan finally said. They got up, washed at the lake, and returned to start the breakfast fire.

Soon the two boys were sniffing hungrily at frying bacon and bubbling coffee. Dan bent down to blow on some flagging coals.

"Jeez, I'm going to miss you," Jonah said, heart suddenly full of pain. "I wish you could come to college, too."

"Me with all that book work? No, thanks."

"I just wish... I don't know."

"Look, there'll be girls there, Jo. Girls are a great invention, take my word for it."

"I suppose so."

"Boy," Dan exclaimed, "that making out makes a guy

hungry. Talk about salivating dogs!"

"You gonna write?"

"Sure."

But he wouldn't, Jonah knew. He felt almost like crying.

Dan raised his eyes and squinted through the smoke at Jonah. "Besides, in the next week we ought to be able get in an awful lot of thrills."

SPANISH SUMMER

David Laurents

I was sitting on a bench in the plaza below the street which led up the hill to the Alhambra, when a man sat down next to me. It was a long climb to reach that red Moorish castle, and I wasn't yet ready for it. The walk across town had exhausted me, from the heat more than the exercise itself. However, the Alhambra was the coolest place to be in the city, because of the water gardens of the Generalife. The entire hill was covered with greenery, watered by the run off from the countless fountains and pools.

I glanced over at the man who'd sat next to me, and realized he'd been staring at me. He met my gaze boldly and smiled at me, and suddenly I knew what was happening. I almost laughed. The heat had driven away almost all thoughts but finding someplace cool, and it had been so long since I'd been cruised – by a man, at least. Spain, and especially Granada, was a culture which was so thoroughly based on heterosexuality – it even colored the language itself, with its masculine and feminine endings to words. The family I was staying with, and all my teachers and fellow students, were loudly homophobic, so I'd had to be very careful of what I said around them.

But now, it seemed, I'd stumbled across another gay man – or rather, I'd sat there and let him stumble across me. I looked around us, wondering if anyone else had noticed our brief interaction. I looked away from him, knowing I'd already decided to go home with him, or wherever – it had been so long since I'd felt another man's cock, my fingers itched to reach out for him, my mouth and ass yearned to take him in, even though he wasn't what I would normally find attractive. There was a hotel behind us, and as I thought about it, things suddenly fell into place – that this might be a queer cruising grounds. It was a place where many foreigners would pass through, almost everyone who came to the city made a pilgrimage to see at the Alhambra, and thus every gay tourist had to pass through it, too.

I was living here for part of the summer, so I didn't feel like that kind of a tourist. But I was playing a typical role in many ways. Europe seduces college students to come visit, with special tickets offering unlimited train travel and hostels at every step along the way, not to mention our own wanderlust. It's almost impossible to resist this siren call – no matter how tight your budget is, it's affordable – so I didn't put up a fight. The summer between my junior and senior year at college, I enrolled in a 6-week language program in Granada (which meant, because I was earning college credit, that it was covered by my scholarship – including air fare). I'd spend two months in Andalucia, surrounded by Spanish men, and then would spend the final month traveling, my international gay guidebook in hand, wherever my fancy took me.

Well, that *had* been the plan. It was only when I got here that I realized it wasn't so easy finding Spanish men who were receptive to the idea of sleeping with other men, and hardly any who would identify themselves as gay. Even the most flamboyant queens – who I only saw when I was with straights and therefore couldn't cruise or talk to them about where to go to meet men – were closet cases.

It was my first time traveling alone. I'd gone on trips with my family, around the States, and even to Europe twice before – England and Scotland when I was thirteen, and Paris when I was fifteen. But traveling on my own was going to be different. For months I had the most vivid dreams of various encounters I might have, with beautiful men, exotic and alluring, seducing me with liquid eyes and lilting accents, a mixture of romance and unadulterated carnal lust. We'd kiss at twilight in deserted parks, making out beneath overgrown statuary, and have sex in their apartments late into the night, then wake to sit all day in streetside cafes drinking and smoking.

I knew things wouldn't really go as smoothly, that these were all fantasies, and also the myth of Europe, from movies and books, not the Europe I would really find. But I hadn't expected to feel so isolated, by my being gay more than by my being a stranger in a strange land. I was more a foreigner to such rampant heterosexuality, and I longed for the comfortable gay sub-culture of college life, all of us full of young rage and rebellion, our support groups and monthly dances. My Spanish

wasn't good enough for me to read the gay press – if there'd been any, and I couldn't help realizing how lucky we had it, with three little weekly queer newspapers given out free in the bars, and all the gay porn magazines that were available at nearly every magazine rack.

It had taken me days to find a kiosk which sold Spain's equivalent of gay pornography, and I then hesitated for two more days before going out late one afternoon with my backpack and walking clear to the other side of town to buy an issue. I didn't bother to flip through it as I might've if I were in the States – a little nervous, perhaps, at being seen by friends, but otherwise unconcerned. I thrust it into my pack and hurried away. I couldn't go home right away, but wandered all over Granada, pretending to sightsee, although I don't recall anything at all. Everywhere I looked I saw, superimposed, the scantily-clad cover-model.

I wondered what the pages between would contain as I roamed across the city. I had a suspicion the magazine would be fairly vanilla solo shots of men posturing in the nude, their hands far from their half-hard erections, lest they appear to be jerking off, and certainly nothing with another man in the scene! But right then, I was so desperate to see any cock, hard or soft, cut or uncut, I didn't care.

I sat down at a restaurant, even though I was so nervous at being discovered with a gay porn mag, and so anticipating getting a chance to actually read the magazine and jerk off, that I couldn't eat anything. But I wanted to use the bathroom, and that meant ordering something. "*Churros y chocolate*," I told the waiter, when he finally arrived. And, as he went off to bring the donuts and hot chocolate, I took my bag and went into the rest room, locking the door behind me.

Alone at last!

I sat down on the toilet and tore open my bag. The magazine was named MACHO, and I eagerly ripped off the shrink-wrap that prevented the curious from sneaking free peeks. I was hard before I even had the magazine open, my cock straining inside my jeans with the anticipation. I undid my fly with one hand as I flipped open the magazine in my lap. There before me was naked flesh: swarthy Mediterranean boys like I'd dreamed of, with long drooping cocks peeking out from dark folds of

foreskin. I was shooting all across the pages in less than a minute, I'd been so worked up from the long weeks of fantasizing without any privacy or source of release.

I leafed through the entire magazine, memorizing every naked body, and left the magazine in the bathroom, afraid that it would be found by my host family when they cleaned my room. A bit expensive for a quick hand job, but worth every peseta. Those naked boys filled my fantasies and day dreams for many days to come.

But now, at last, I would have sex with another man again, not merely in my mind. I hardly knew the vocabulary to follow-through on the pick-up with the guy sitting next to me, but he understood that I would go with him. I tried to undress him, mentally, as we walked along streets that were half-familiar, but my mind kept going back to the image of the cover model from MACHO, the curve of his cock lifting up towards his navel, the dark ball sac hanging below, shrouded in wiry hairs.

The man I was following was in his mid-forties, I imagined, not unattractive, I guess, but not my type, either. He was showing his age, thickening everywhere, although he sported muscles from a life of working manually. I wasn't proficient enough with the language to tell much about him by the way he spoke, just that he was Andalucian through and through and characteristically swallowed the ends of his words, making him even more difficult to understand.

But we managed to grope our way through the encounter. He tried for a pretense of civility when we got back to his apartment, but his heart wasn't in it as he offered me a drink and tried to make small talk: what we both wanted was to get it on already. He sat very close to me, and I could understand only every third word he said, so to shut him up and get things moving I finally leaned forward and kissed him. He was taken aback a little bit, and pulled away, but then he started kissing me with a violence and fervor that surprised me. His hands were suddenly all over, pressing into my groin, clawing at my back. My hard dick throbbed beneath his fingers beneath the cloth.

I reached for his own crotch, feeling for the size of his own cock. My fingers curved around its shaft and it was as if my hand orgasmed, the muscles themselves so joyed at again

feeling cock. With my other hand I started to undo my fly, thinking we were to have sex right there on the couch, but he stopped me. He was a traditionalist, it seemed, and wanted us to move to the bedroom. There was no foreplay for him, he just started undressing himself. I always think there's something really hot to having sex in partial clothing, and to undressing someone slowly, teasingly, but he just stripped right down, even took off his socks. He wasn't finicky about his clothes, like some queens I've had sex with, who need to fold everything neatly or even hang things back in the closet before they climb into bed and turn their attention to having sex. He let his clothes fall where they dropped, and crawled under the covers to wait for me to undress myself.

I watched him as he stripped, playing the voyeur at least, if I was going to be denied the pleasure of undressing him. It was a very short show, but my neglected dick was aching the entire time. His body was nothing special, pretty much exactly as I'd imagined it, but it was naked and in front of me, and that was something wonderful. His cock was a pleasant surprise, being shorter but thicker than I had imagined. I thought about going down on it as I stripped out of my own clothing, and my saliva started to flow as I imagined the taste of his cock's flesh, its weighty solidness between my lips.

He lifted the covers for me join him on the bed, and I crawled in beside him. He was all over me, roughly kissing my neck, and chest, his stubble rubbing my skin raw, his arms kneading my ass, his cock pressing up against my belly as he wrapped his legs around mine, pinning me to him. I felt half-suffocated, but I yielded to him, and to the sensation of being surrounded by his masculinity. It was unpleasant and yet I wanted every minute of it.

I pushed him away enough to catch my breath and to let me take control of the situation. I wanted his cock, and I rolled him on his back and began licking his nipples. He pushed my head down towards his crotch and I worked my tongue down along the trail of hairs leading to his cock, teasing him. He didn't seem to understand, and kept pushing my head more forcefully towards his cock, lifting it up for my mouth with his other hand. So much for foreplay, I realized, and went down on him right away, taking the head between my lips and lowering

myself onto him. I pumped up and down a bit, then pulled off to lick the shaft and his nuts. He grabbed my hair and pulled me back onto his cock, grinding his hips so that he was thrusting into my mouth.

Nothing fancy, then, just the pure hydraulics of sex. I still went into almost a trance of cocksucking, so focused on his dick sliding into and out of my mouth. I thought of nothing else, just that meaty organ pumping between my lips, the feel of his cockhead sliding over my tongue, the tickle of his pubic hairs on my lips and chin, and was therefore surprised when I felt his own lips clamp around my cock. He'd swiveled around on the bed so we were locked in a sixty-nine, and I slowed my rhythm to match his. (There was no way he'd have noticed enough to match mine.) His mouth was hot and wet, but right then I was so focused on sucking cock, I probably could've come, without even touching myself, just from sucking him.

Suddenly he had a spit-lubed finger up my ass. I hadn't even noticed that he'd stopped sucking me, but I relaxed into his finger and thrust my ass upwards a bit more and kept working on his cock. Soon he had a second finger up inside of me, and I was pushing back against his fingers as I worked my lips up and down his cock. He thrust a third finger inside of me, and started saying he wanted to stick his cock in me. I asked for a condom, which he didn't have, so I told him no. He tried to convince me otherwise, but I refused. He was disappointed, and thrust my face back onto his cock, grinding his hips upwards so he was fucking my face.

His finger fucking had brought me close to orgasm, and I licked one palm and began fisting myself as I sucked on his cock. I slipped my tongue between the foreskin and the cockhead, tasting the strong stale scent of him, then taking his whole thick cock down my throat, as far as my gag reflex would allow, and just sucking, like I could suction the cum out of him. I was dragging my lips up and down his shaft when I came, squirting lines of jism across his legs and the sheets. My lips locked around his thick shaft until I was done, and then my mouth began pumping once again. Soon I felt his balls tighten, ready to explode, and I pulled off and began fisting him. He kept trying to push my head back onto his cock, but I just kept fisting his thick tool in one fist and a moment later he was

shooting streams of cum up onto his belly. He didn't have much range, but he made up for it in volume, the white liquid drenching the mat of dark hair that coated his lower torso.

As soon as the sex was over and he'd caught his breath, he jumped out of bed and started putting his clothes on. He didn't clean himself up or anything, just pulled everything on right over the jism, which soaked into his shirt right away, leaving a large damp spot. He was trying to act as if nothing happened, although he also kept inviting me back and telling me he had American porn videos if we wanted to watch one, and things like that. I thank him but told him I ought to be going. The awkwardness was making the whole affair seem sleazy in some way, but I resisted falling into that line of thought.

He wrote down his phone number and address, and I stuffed it in my backpack when I was out on the street, but I doubted I'd be calling him again. I'd needed him right then, and maybe I'd need him again, but I now knew where to find men.

The city was as hot as ever as I walked across town, but I didn't care. I was riding high on sex and being queer. Besides, the taste of cock was lingering in my mouth and that was enough to make me forget all else.

I walked to the plaza beneath the Alhambra, and sat down again on a bench in front of the hotel. It was barely one o'clock. There was sure to be another wave of tourists after lunch. Already my cock was beginning to stiffen in my pants as I waited.

And as soon as the siesta was over, I'd buy myself a box of condoms.

STRANGERS ON THE ROAD

David Laurents

Two men converged in a yellow wood,
And horny from their travels both,
One sank to his knees where the other stood,
Went down on him as far as he could,
His own cock brushing the undergrowth.

They made a very handsome pair
And soon the man who was standing came
Upon the grass – a full pint, you'd swear!
Then the man who'd sucked declared
He'd like his new friend to do the same,

And both that morning equally lay,
First one, then the other, upon his back,
And was fucked on that forest highway.
They arranged a tryst for next Friday,
When each had dressed and shouldered his pack,

And continued on, each with a sigh
And a final, awkward, backward glance.
Strangers met in a wood one July,
On a path with no other passers-by,
And that made all the difference.

FLEXIBILITY

Cory James Legassie

He wants to fuck me.

Well, he hasn't really come out and said as much, but I'm pretty sure.

I'm a guy. And he's a guy. I mean, we both are. So you'd wonder what the hell's up with that. I don't really know. But I know he likes me. He gave me this note one time. It was a love letter, really. One of the scary more-than-friends kind. At least that's how he put it. He told me that I'm special. Guys like me don't come around every day. He says I'm a beautiful person - that he's attracted to my personality as well as my body. He admires me. He thinks I'm very mature for a freshman in college. He's a senior, and I think sometimes that he's totally thwacked. But I like him. Well, not like that. I don't think.

I catch him sometimes gazing at me in this kind of wishful way, like my butt's made of pure cane sugar and he'd like to run his tongue all over me. What's up with that? I wonder what it is about a guy his body that can turn another guy on. I wonder what it is about my body that turns my buddy on. It could be just my face. Or my athleticism. I know I'm in good shape. I'm a gymnast, high flexibility, if you know what I mean. He asked me once if I could blow myself. I told him I could. Or maybe it's just all of me put together. Sometimes when I'm around him I even pose a little, like I know he's checking me out and I want to turn him on. I mean, I tried to imagine what it might be like for him. Say, if he were a girl what would he be thinking then. Would I be attractive in all the same ways? He says it's no different than liking a girl, if that's the way you are, but I don't know. Truthfully, I'm not sure I've ever liked anyone like that. I mean, not in his scary more-than-friends way.

I had sex once. With a girl I mean. It was back in high school, my junior year actually, and she was a friend. I guess it was really kind of an experiment more than anything else. She didn't really turn me on. We grew up together in the same neighborhood. Our parents used to have these barbecues, one

weekend at our house, the next at theirs. On like that, you know. It went on for at least ten years, which is about as far back as can remember. I know plenty must have happened in my life before that, but the ol' hard drive is just empty. With no backup. That part of my memory is hollow, like turning the page of a book and finding the next one ripped out. It's really pretty weird, but I can't explain it. Maybe I've been traumatized. What is it they say? Maybe I was toilet-trained too hard. Or is it too early? I don't know.

But back to Sandee. Yeah, if I didn't mention it before, that's her name. My first fuck. My only one, actually. She's a gymnast too. From the same team. Our high school used to be top-ranked in gymnastics, but when I graduated, I stopped giving a shit. I'm not even sure what Sandee's doing now. I think she was accepted at Bowdoin in English Literature or something like that. A real poet and don't know it, as Pee Wee would say. I don't know about literature, but she sure knows how to screw. Well, OK, I guess I wouldn't really know the difference. It's not like I have anything to compare the experience to. But I ought to give her credit. She got me to consent that one and only time. She was totally into it.

It was on the way back from a meet, nothing big, just one of those friendly competitions at another school, and Sandee and I were sitting in the backseat of the darkened bus. It was snowing outside, I remember, and we were drawing these monster mega-penises on the frosted window. The two of us always sat together; I mean, nothing up with that, it was just natural. You know, with the barbecue and all that. All I know is that I had just drawn the granddaddy of all dicks - I mean, this one had all the modern conveniences, and then her hand is on my crotch. I didn't say anything, but I could hear her kind of chirping softly in her throat as she pulled back the elasticized band of my sweats and touched me. Down there, yeah, she grabbed around it and tugged a little bit. I was scared, really. Then she bent over slowly and touched me with her lips. All nibbly and stuff. I looked around the bus, but everybody was pretty much sleeping. And coach was yakking with the driver. When we got home, the snow had stopped. We walked into my house together, past my parents, and went upstairs and did it. It was nice, but I don't care if I never do it again.

Not that I'm asexual. I just don't need anything like that right now. And I can't think of one single girl I could trust like that.

He says I could trust him like that. Well, he never really came out and said it. But it's pretty obvious. Last semester he took this sex class, on attitudes or something and he showed me his journal. The one they had to keep and then pass in to the professor. It was confidential I guess. He had to do this exercise where you draw a picture of yourself naked from the front. Then you rate yourself as a whole person and as a sexual one. Then you do the same for the partner of your dreams. We're there, in my room over pizza, and he pulls out his picture. And it's me. Holy shit, you should've seen the equipment he drew on me. I was pretty flattered, I guess. It was a total ego boost. But I didn't know what to say. What do you say when your buddy pulls out something like that? You smile. You say thank you. You change the subject. At least, that's what I did.

Actually, it really pisses me off. I mean, if he came on to me, I could tell him to go screw. No thanks, I'm not interested, you know? But he has to go and be so goddamn nice about it. He's a good friend. I know he cares about my feelings. But that's what makes it so hard. I guess I don't know what's up with my head. I don't know my own feelings. I mean, I don't know how I feel about *him*. He's really cool. He was the first upperclassman I ever met at the university. We hit it off. And he's always been interested in what's up with me.

Maybe I'm just like him, only I don't know it. I have never said anything about my feelings. I've never brought up his, either. I hate that. I can discuss almost anything else. But feelings are a private thing, you know? I can read him, no problem. Why doesn't he try to hide what's inside? Sometimes I wonder why I can't be more like that. Mostly I'm glad I'm not.

He told me once what it was like for him when he found out he liked guys. I think I remind him of himself at my age; like I seem kind of confused, too. He was twenty, a little over a year older than I am now. He said it was slow. First he just kind of fantasized about it. Then he told a gay friend about it. Then he told all his friends. It was hard. I don't know if I could do that. I mean, you can't care too much what people think, but

that's pretty big. You can't take it back. He says he doesn't really want to.

But he seems so sad. That's the thing that gets me most, late at night when I'm lying in the dark and I wonder what it would be like. I don't want to break his heart. If that's possible, I mean. I'm not even sure I believe two men can have that kind of love. Religion always makes it out to be all lust and sin. But what if there was more? What if it's all really true, that love is just love? I wonder if he's in love with me.

I had this crazy, fucked-up dream about him last week. I don't know where it came from. The details aren't important, but let's just say we got together. And he kissed me. Right on the corner of the mouth. It was warm and wet, and I remember the way his tongue felt. Feathery, like.

Then when I woke up, I had this strange feeling inside me all day. It was in the back of my mind. And when I saw him, my stomach got nervous. What do you think's up with that?

We've kind of grown apart in the last few months. I used to hang with him and his friends, but now I have my own crowd. I eat lunch at his table in the cafe sometimes, but when I don't, he always knows where I'm sitting. I can feel him looking. When I walk across the room his eyes are on me, like hands. I guess I like it. I can't stop thinking about him. I try to put him out of my head. I go out with my friends. I laugh at their jokes, and watch a shitload of TV. I do my homework, I listen to tunes, I go to the gym and life weights till I'm weak. But he's always right there. I don't think he knows it, though. He's shy as hell. Every once in a while he'll call me and leave me odd little messages on my answering machine. He calls me by my middle name. I don't mind.

I wish I knew what to call what I feel for him. If I could name it, I could deal. But right now it's just this faceless thing I have inside me. I need to know what it is. I need to know who I am. I want to ask for his help, but I can't. I'm afraid, but at least I'm alive.

It's like he says. You only get one chance at that.

THE NEW PAGE

Edward Bangor

I was starting my first job. Actually I suppose it was my Uncle Mike's job more than it was mine. You see, at that time, the man I called Uncle did the accounts for one of the travelling shows that were so popular in the late, seventies.

The attraction I joined was a medieval jousting troop, quite a good one, actually. (This was long before the modern theme park was constructed up along the M6 motorway, near Preston, where King Arthur's Camelot was meant to have been.) Anyway, they always used a local kid as part of their act and that's where I came in. I'd never fancied the idea of playing a Page before, but Uncle Mike volunteered me. Still, I was going to get paid and have to admit, in those days of my budding interest in Heavy Rock, I'd do just about anything for a couple of quid to buy some 12-inch loud vinyl. The job, as it turned out, was little more than following the actors around and, there was even another kid - Bryan - to do the more difficult stuff with all the broadswords, axes, horses and such like.

The week before I started work, Uncle Mike had to go and see the Jousting Troop in their previous encampment and using my not inconsiderable, boyish, charm I managed to wangle a free trip to check the job out. (Uncle Mike could never refuse me anything if I joined in his exercise routines.) I had to be sure the job was right for me, or I'd pull out, I told him that straight. There was no chance of that however, not once I'd seen the costume I was going to wear. Even on the girl, who then wore it, it looked wonderful: Brown, furry boots that came halfway up the extremely tight tights. I was really into tight clothes at the time of flairs - with one leg in white and the other in black-and-white vertical strips. A green shirt somewhat clashed with the tunic hidden behind, a wonderful gold shield embroidered on the front and mirrored on the back. No ordinary hat sat on her head. Made of a brilliant blue cloth that trailed down the back of the girl's neck and held in place by a thick rolled band across her forehead, it looked like a cross between a skull cap and a bank robber's stocking mask. How

could anyone resist?

The first day we drove in Uncle Mike's distinctive car - painted with the insignia of his favourite football team - down to the fair site. My bad nerves ended the near endless chatter Uncle Mike enjoyed so much but, if my mouth was quiet, it had nothing to do with inactivity inside my head. There, questions rained down on each other in an endless torrent: What if I was too small to do the job right? What if I was too young? Or, not strong enough? What if I was bored? What if I made a pig's ear of it? What if I upset my uncle and embarrassed him? Then what? The end of one of the best uncle/nephew relationships I had ever had the privilege to be part off and something that I would always try to copy in my own adult dealings with my "nephews."

Once we arrived at a muddy field I will never forget as long as I live, disaster overtook us. One of the enormous, smelly, and deafening diesel generator powered rides was broken. This meant one of the more successful attractions on the site was out of action and wouldn't be running again until my Uncle granted permission for its repair. No sooner was this explained to him, by the harassed foreman, than Mike was charging off across the mud, leaving me in the charge of a Steward.

He was a nice enough old man, the Steward, but not really firing on all cylinders, if you know what I mean? I wasn't too sure when he put his arm around my shoulder either, but in those days, kids didn't think about such things, not like now when the slightest touch of someone they don't know, causes the Child Protection Agencies to leap into action. Times, will, I guess, change but not always for the better.

Anyway, the old bloke and I trudged from the thrilling rides and towards the fenced off arena where, later, horses would thunder down either side of a short wooden fence aiming great long lances at each other.

Twin tents guarded the arena entrance with colourfully decorated canvas, in either red or blue, and small flags fluttering from their summit baring one of the two shields scattered around the arena. A sign hung, loop-sided, over the left-hand tent said 'KNIGHTS-PRIVATE'. The old Steward shoved me towards this and vanished, like Merlin, in a puff of

smoke. Inside, I discovered Bryan. At least I assumed he was the other page-boy as it was a hard to tell seeing as he didn't have a stitch of clothing, modern or medieval.

"Can I help you?" he asked completely unselfconscious about the effect his exposed body had on me.

Bryan was thin and I don't mean boney, I mean skinny, like he hadn't eaten for days. Back in those days I wasn't a third the size I am now and would remain the thinnest boy in my school, until a growth spurt hit me with a vengeance a year or so later turning me, almost overnight, into the incredible bulk but I had nothing on Bryan.

There was something else about Bryan that made his thinness seem so odd. I couldn't put my finger on it at first but, eventually, it dawned on me. It was his bum. It stuck out, even when he stood up straight it poked out a mile with two intriguing dimples on either side of his cheeks whenever his buttocks flexed. Then there was his genitals or, rather, there wasn't.

By this time, I'd become something of an expert on this area of male anatomy but I'd seen nothing like Bryan. Still haven't. The boney chest, with each rib clearly marked, led down to the slightly rounded belly that, in turn, led to the penis. The four-inch long dropped penis was skinny as the rest of him, but with no testicles, not even the slightest sign. Lots of hair though. He can't have had more than a couple of years on me, even if he wasn't that much taller, yet his loins were covered in the stuff. I just couldn't help staring, a fact that was soon noticed.

"Can I help you?" Bryan, repeated.

"Page," I tore my eyes away from his swaying groin, "I'm the new Page."

"Well, that's more like it." Bryan looked me over so closely I shivered with embarrassment as if I was naked and he wore the flowery shirt and bell-bottom jeans. "Better than that damn girl we had in the last place. Thought she owed me she did, just cos her dad owned the land what we was camped on."

I kept my mouth shut. Bryan seemed capable of doing enough talking for the two. "All she wanted to do was show me dick to all her stupid, giggling friends, cos it was the biggest what they'd never seen, like." He gave a small hop. His prick

flipped up so the tip slapped his belly and, then, down to slap his closed thighs. "Maybe I should get a stand on one of the side-shows. Something like 'Elephant boy and his Magic Trunk,' what do you think?"

Shit, what could I say? I just stood there like the cat had got my tongue.

"Anyway," Bryan said to my silence, "We'd best get you kitted out. Plenty of time for a chit-chat later." He started to unbutton my shirt.

To say I was surprised at this development would be to severely understate the matter. Sure, I'd been stripped by other boys before as part of some game or other and this was a long way from the 1976 school camp with my then mate, Mark Douglas.

As soon as Lights Out was called Mark and I would start trying to get the other's clothes off before our own were removed. No rules. No guide-lines. Anything went as long as neither of us got hurt and our clothes weren't damaged, the fighting only ending when one of us was completely naked. That wasn't the end of the game though. By some sort of schoolboy logic the loser then had to be humiliated further by having him lie down full stretch on his belly for the other to smack his bum. The spanking never got out of hand because, the next time, the victim would always have the chance of retaliation the following night. Mark and I were pretty much evenly matched, as far as Strip-Smack went.

While I remembered that fateful final night at school camp, I absent-mindedly pulled the tails of the hideous '70s shirt out of my trousers, actually helping towards its removal, completely ignoring the current situation and the naked, skinny boy stripping.

Both Mark and I knew what the final night of camp meant. Whoever won that bout would become the supreme winner, as there was no way the loser could gain revenge back at school. As we clambered into our small tent Mark noticed the four pegs I'd hammered into the corners with the loops of twine attached, just as I noticed the tub of grease Mark had hidden under his bag.

We were so worked up by the time the shout came that nothing would have stopped us. Within a few seconds our

outer clothes vanished. We'd both taken the extra precaution of adding few extra layers and the belt on my second pair of shorts gave Mark some serious trouble but, just as I loosened the triple knotted draw-string on his swimming trunks we were both dragged out into the open by our ankles. Seems the rest of the camp had been about to go on a midnight feast in the woods when they'd heard the noise we were making.

Rapidly, Mark and I were stripped and then, naked, carried off into the woods. Out of sight of the teachers we faced each and were made to kiss. Even though it was on the lips, this wasn't so bad, but worse was to come.

Some bright spark - I'm not sure who - suggested using some sticky tape to bind Mark's prick to mine. Now, this wasn't too bad either, at first. Then the same bright spark decided the only way to stop us from peeling the tape off was to whip our arses and soon they had us jumping about all over the place like a couple of march hares. It didn't last long through. After a couple of minutes Mark went all weird, pushing his little ram-rod prick against my belly as if he was trying to drill a hole through my navel. Then he let out a blood-curdling scream and fell over. He nearly pulled my willy off as he did which gave me the strangest sensations all over. It was from that moment I became interested in, what I would later learn was called, bondage.

I never spoke much to Mark after than night, or rather he never spoke to me. The late 1970's might have been an enlightened time in some respects but when it came to telling boys about puberty, it may as well have been the dark ages. I mean, what's the point of telling a fourteen-year-old about erections, wet dreams, and ejaculations? It's a bit bloody late by then. My sexual education happened, not in a classroom, but in a small tent at the end of a muddy field.

My shirt was gone by the time my fourteen-year-old mind had travelled back from 1976. I was barechested and had hardly felt a thing. Now the naked boy turned his attention even lower and was unzipping my bell bottoms. I caught him just as the double waist buttons were freed.

"Come on, don't be shy." Bryan said. "There's no need to be bothered about the size of my prick. It's what you does with it, what matters, just ask the bloke what plays King Arthur."

I was looking down by this time – down at the hands holding the front of my jeans open that weren't my own and, down at the penis, curled in a perfect quarter circle between the Page Boy's slender legs.

"All the kids we has here are bothered at first, but they gets used to it. So will you." explained Bryan. "Sometimes I even lets them touch it, if they lets me do them after. All but the Girl that is. I wouldn't let them do nowt. They don't know how to treat it right, they don't. I wouldn't even let that last one do it after she locked me head and arms in them stocks we got. That got her, that did. She left me alone after that. Didn't let me go mind. Left me there, she did, with me tunic up and me tights down with me bum stuck right out, like. King got me out in the end, but not before he'd given me a right good going over that was right close to more than I could handle. Almost as good as the mace handle he were. Almost, but not quite."

As the Bryan chatted on, I dropped my guard and he dropped my trousers. Now I was in my underpants, somewhat large and not particularly tight or flattering underpants but still underpants.

"You ever do that to yourself with the handle of owt?" he asked, "Stick it up your bum? I've tried just about anything what I can get me hands on round here: bog brushes, candles, bits of the horse's gear, even the leg of a broken stool once. You name it, I've tried it."

Bryan's hands went to my hips and gave a tug on my pants. I was still tying to work out just what the heck he was talking about. Was that why Mark Douglas had the grease in our tent back in '76? Was it why he spent so much time in the senior boy's toilets at school afterwards? My underpants moved. Bryan kept talking:

"The mace handle is the best by miles, though. It's the knobbly bits what does it. All over the handle they is. King says it's to help the Knights grip but I knows what I uses them for? They tickle, that's what they does. You know what I mean?"

As he continued to speak, slowly but surely, Bryan bent from the waist and, with his elbows locked dead straight, took my underpants from me. One of my arms flew sideways, not to stop what was happening, but to grab a clenched fist full of tent cloth to stop myself from falling over, in the mud.

"I bet you knows all about it, don't you? I heard you go to one of them boys- only schools, where the big lads always does it to the good looking ones, like you."

Suddenly Mark's new life made sense to me. No wonder he hadn't needed me over the last couple of years, not if he'd had four dozen well-hung sixth-formers at his beck and call. I, meanwhile, had been left on my own trying out my bondage experiments. You see, Uncle Mike never did anything sexual with me. In fact he did nothing more than his athletic type training and wrestling 'exercises'. Often in the past I'd wished he would, but he never did. Not that I got the chance to explain any of this to Bryan. He was still talking.

"Don't know if I'd like that or not. No time for me mace, see? No way I could handle being without that for long."

Laughing at his own joke, Bryan's face came level with my boyish groin. His mouth a fraction of an inch away from everything I held dear. His breath brushed the soft, hairless surface, gently blowing my penis from side to side as my underpants sailed right past my knees. My eyes looked down Bryan's bent back, along his curved spine and down between the surprisingly fleshy valley of his buttocks.

"I tried it once with an older Page what we had here, one time. Tried it proper, I mean. Big lad, he were. Much bigger then me. Built like a brick shit-house, but his prick. His prick were the size of a baby flea's pube. I couldn't feel nothing. Like throwing a marble up a train tunnel it were."

Finally my underpants came off and went the way of the rest of my clothes. Still talking Bryan took my hand from the canvas and led me to the back of the tent where the bundle of our discarded clothes formed a mattress of sorts. On this he had me sit. A firm boney hand, with quick bitten finger nails, tipped me onto my back.

"He got real mad, the big kid did, when I told him he weren't no good at it. He stuck the mace handle right up me, he did. It hurt like bloody hell. Blood and everything there was. But, I had the last laugh that time cos I told King on him and got the bast'd booted out on his big, fat arse."

It may sound strange and, somewhat naive, but only after he said this did I start to get the idea of what Bryan was intending to do with me and only then because he played with my

smaller prick, gently wanking it.

"Then there's the Black Knight. You'd better watch for him. The slightest excuse and he'll do his 'Whipping boy' speech and you'll have a sore bum before you know what's happening."

We were both erect within seconds under Bryan's expert fingers, none of which were bigger than my penis and no where near the size of his prick which hadn't got that much bigger, at least not around. It was as skinny as the rest of him and rather long. I can still see it now, all these years latter. About the length of a new pencil, pale and golden all at the same time, snaking out from his nearly non-existent testicles and small forest of pubic hair like a worm seeking food. The tight looking foreskin pulled right back behind the head and slotted in out of the way in such a way that I couldn't do then and still can't now. Then, as he still talked, he somehow - and don't ask me how - managed to coat the entire thing in gallons of spittle.

"I'll never forget the time I dropped the Black Knight's broadsword and the bast'd pulled me hat down over my face. Shit, did the crowd jeer him for that, but he loved that, don't he? Just loves it."

One by one Bryan folded my legs back over my chest. My arms curled around them as Bryan shifted onto his knees. His skinny matchstick legs parted. His penis pointing down between them, towards my upturned bum.

"Really loves himself, does that Black Knight. Still, what no one knew but me and him was that he'd had jammed the head-band into me gob so I couldn't say nothing. Not a damn thing. Couldn't do nothing, neither, cos I sure ain't no match for him and you'd be less of one. Big bast'd he is, that Black Knight."

With his hands still on my shins, Bryan's skinny hips lowered his spittle wetted prick down towards the stretched open target of my virgin arsehole.

"The jeering only set him off again, didn't it, and he slaps the flat of the broadsword on me bum and set the crowd off yet again like mad at him, or something. Hissing an' all, they was."

For the first time, Bryan actually paused for breath to allow guidance to his glands. I jumped. He was so hot. I'd never

expected that to be amongst the various things I hoped for, but it was. Almost too hot, like a poker only it didn't hurt. Tickled really, especially when he finally had it positioned correctly in the centre of my warm crack. He re-found his voice and pushed down.

"Next thing the Black Knight does is reach up under me tunic and pulls me tights down to me boots and shows the mark of the sword right across the two parts of me bum. A matching set, like."

Ever so slowly I felt my body open up. It parted as the skinny boy's even skinnier prick sunk into my virgin behind. Feeling my body engulfing his length was - and still is - one of the most wonderful feelings I have ever had the pleasure to experience.

"Only then does the King come to me defence and do something about it and, I's meant to be his Number One an' all. He didn't do nowt but shout for the Black Knight to bring me over to the throne."

Bryan's body continued to sink into me. His feet slipped in the mud, jarred me, and that hurt, but the pain soon passed, the sudden shift having gained just that final bit more of penetration. The entire length of the slim young penis went right up inside my smaller body.

"The Black Knight sticks his hand back under me tunic, not to slap me arse no more. In his other hand he grabs the collar of me tunic and lifts me clean of the deck, no messing."

Bryan rested on me before he started to withdraw and let himself sink back in again. He rippled through my innards in way that cannot be described to anyone that has yet to experience it. Only those people who have been in that situation can appreciate - no matter how good the writer - the feelings that shot throughout my tender body that day. Nothing, like that had happened to me before that magical day in a small tent and I loved it. Even with the distraction of Bryan's story.

"It weren't no ordinary hold what the Black Knight had. Don't rightly know how he managed it - maybe he'd had his finger in some horse grease or something - cos he got his biggest finger rammed right up my bum. All the way too, no half measures for Black Knight, that's a cert. And it stayed up

me bum right until he tipped me arse-over- bollocks into the King's lap."

"Very gently Bryan's hips started to increase the pace with which he moved his slender penis in and out of my bent double body. In my mind's eye I could see his buttock dimples contracting as he exercised his remarkable control of movement.

"The crowd was the best what we'd ever had for any show. But they soon changed when the King gets me sat on his lap. I was so mad that I chucked the first thing what I could get at the Black Knight and I hits him too, right at the back of the head. It were only a bread roll - stale mind you - but I felt better than if I'd done nothing. Still, I weren't keen on the way what the the crowd went 'Argh' like I were a cute baby or something."

As far as I was concerned Bryan was anything but a baby, cute or otherwise. His continuity slipped a couple of times as he speeded his fucking up. His slight weight taken by my bent legs and his own elbows beside my ears, was face inches from mine, yet it gave no sign at all of what he was doing. It was just as if we were having a chat, or rather he was having a chat as I had hardly said two words in the short time since we had met. So short a time and yet here he was performing the most perfect act of loving one boy could ever give to another.

"What the crowd didn't see - because of the table - was that the King hadn't let me pull up me tights before he'd sat me on him and, in fact, I weren't sat on his lap at all. When he'd lifted me up it weren't so I could take no bows from the crowd and the White Knight who was fighting for me honour, but so he could get his prick in me. All the way up, just like... what... I am... in yours."

That was the first mention Bryan made of anything he was doing to me. All though the stripping and the sex he'd said nothing about me, now so close to the end he mentioned it. Maybe I wasn't dreaming after all.

"And when I was twisting and turning about in so-called gratitude it was really cos, cos the King was, was pumping his, pumping his stuff up, up me, up me bum."

Suddenly Bryan stopped. Stopped talking. Stopped moving. Stopped everything. He was done. I was done. It was done. I was a virgin no more. For the first time I had that delightful

feeling of freshly spilled semen seeping into my veins. My little bum was well – and truly – fucked.

. . .

As you can guess, I really enjoyed the rest of that holiday job. Bryan and I worked well together, helping the King - who was a nice man - and teasing the Black Knight - a bigger bastard than even Bryan could have made out. And then when we weren't working, we tried everything, every way up and in every combination imaginable, plus a few you couldn't even dream off.

We had our periods apart but I still see Bryan now. Uncle Mike paid for the pair of us to go to our collage, me technical and Bryan agricultural, and while the days might have separated us, the nights didn't. How we qualified, with honours, I'll never understand.

We share a house now, but Bryan's often away running his animal shows. It keeps him away from home a lot, but that's life, I guess. Still it does make for great reunions, especially when Bryan brings a stable-boy, or two, home.

So, what was your first sexual experience and, be honest, can it really match mine? And, have you the nerve to send it to a publisher? The ball is in your court, so to speak.

WILD IN THE WOODS

Rick Jackson, USMC

"He went through the wet wild woods, waving his wild tail, and walking by his wild lone. But he never told anybody."
— Rudyard Kipling

I hadn't been hiking since my seminal days in the Boy Scouts, but that last week of August was so warm and, even down in the city, the air smelled so fresh that I pulled out a map and scouted around for someplace both close by where I could find nature, and far enough from the city that I would have no troops of noisy children and obese bikini-clad matrons behind every tree. The Skedaddle Mountains up by Susanville mainly caught my eye because of their name, but seemed upon reflection to be just what I was looking for. They were close enough to San Francisco to be convenient, but far enough from Gray's madding crowd for me to think I could find a trail to hike up and lose civilization behind me.

I was more right than I had hoped. I left my car and hiked about five miles up a steep and twisting trail before I saw what seemed to be a deer track leading off into the trees. I had only passed a few people in the previous couple hours, but I was curious whether the track might lead me to something resembling real nature. I stripped off my shirt so the mountain air could lick the sweat from my chest and followed the path into adventure. The track broadened slightly away from the main trail and led me around the flank of a hill and into a vale that was half Shangri-La and half Sherwood Forest. Now and again I caught a sparkle of sunlight glinting off water and followed the twisting track down through the trees to find myself at the edge of a magical clearing that was silent and serene as an enormous green cathedral.

The trees stood tall and close together around a space of perhaps five or six acres. Half that area was taken up by a shallow green pond I have since learned is called Woodpecker Lake. Moss covered the banks and the flanks of the trees and green algae carpeted the bottom of the pond. The air was clear

and pleasantly warm and completely still but for the buzzing of huge dragonflies and the easy swish of the breeze through the pines. A grassy bank sloped gently down to the water and was bounded by two enormous fallen logs that stretched from the dense forest far out into the pond. For many minutes, I stood lost in awe at the edge of the clearing and had the uncanny sensation of being out of time, as though I had wandered accidentally into a Mesozoic wonderland.

The water eventually drew me down to its edge. Somehow I knew just from looking at the way the dragonflies were darting about that the jade-colored pond would be warm and welcoming as bath water. I kicked off my shoes and socks and dropped my shorts onto the mossy bank and splashed into the pond like a giddy four-year-old. My easy frolic took me out into the middle, where the water came up to my chest, and I floated about in the warm sunlight, feeling every inch a child of Nature. After a time, I even had the uncanny sense that Nature was watching, perhaps approving of my return to the fold.

When I stood up on the soft, green bottom again, I discovered that it wasn't exactly Nature watching, though if anyone looked the image of Father Nature it was Chuck. My brain was so far in neutral that I thought at first he was a Sasquatch, though more was big about him than his feet. Then I felt sheepish being caught skinny-dipping and mildly resentful at having to share my special place with an intruder. When I splashed closer in answer to his smile, though, his sleeping bag and other gear laid out behind a log implied that I was the trespasser. A moment later, I got a closer look at Chuck and my mind slipped back into neutral.

The guy was about 6'2" and built big. He looked to be about 30 or 35, but had an ageless quality about him that was hard to read. Gigantic arms and shoulders swept down to a belly that looked fat at first glance, but was really layer upon layer of muscle in the fashion of those burly Russian weightlifters. His whole body was covered with a thick mat of curly brown hair that all but hid his stiff dick from view — and for a good reason. The thing was built like a beer can, incredibly thick but no more than five or six inches long. Two huge hairy balls hung low between equally hairy thighs as thick as oaks. When I managed to tear my eyes away from his crotch, I noticed his face

matched the wild-man image: round cheeks, feral brown eyes, a button nose, and a brown beard that drooped low to blend into the curly pelt on his chest.

The funny thing is I don't remember how I got out of the pond and over to Chuck. He must have mesmerized me with his woodland wiles or something. All I know is that one moment I was in the pond; the next, my hand was trying to stretch around his monster-thick dick and failing. I couldn't resist playing with his knob — only slightly larger than the rest of his shaft — and the floppy foreskin that hung off its end. My other hand found its way to the thick mat of fur on his chest and fumbled about running my fingers through his soft curls on the way to his fat, firm tits.

My mountain man didn't say a word. He didn't have to. His body shivered slightly as I squeezed his dickhead and wrapped my other fist around his right tit and all the fur that kept it hidden away from the world. That was nothing compared with my reaction as his massive hands slipped around my waist and up my flanks to grab my tits for a good squeeze. Once I had barked out in pain, he eased down fore and aft until his right hand parted my butt for a good feel and the other started stroking my nine hard inches of San Francisco treat.

I paid him back in kind, reaching around to cup his hairy ass in my hands. I liked what I felt and was just starting to pry those massive glutes wide for some real Nature loving when he gurgled deep in his throat and popped over to his sleeping gear. After a moment's rooting around in his bag, he was back with a couple of gold-foiled rubbers that looked as though they might even fit his sequoia stump-sized dick.

Old Grizzly Chuck had misread my clues if he thought there was a chance in hell I was going to let him shove that leviathan woodland log up my tight city-bred ass. I wasn't even sure how much of his dick I could do more than lick, but, as he rubbered up, I parked my knees onto the forest floor to do my damnedest.

I started off with his nuts, licking the fur around them and sucking one after the other of those boulders into my mouth to give them something mean to think about. Chuck grunted and growled and twisted his crotch around against my face, but I wanted to do more. He gave me the chance — and thrust

greatness upon me.

His hands had long since locked onto my head, but no matter how hard he pushed, I couldn't force my mouth wide enough to get any more of that latexed dick than its tip into my mouth. Mercifully, my wild man knew all about the limitations of civilized cocksuckers and didn't seem too disappointed. In fact, the harder I sucked and worked my tongue along the underside of his stripped-back dick, the more his randy hips poked me in the face and made me gurgle. If I hadn't had my hands wrapped tight around his clenching, grinding powerhouse of butt, he'd have fucked my face backwards and my ass into the dirt.

That apparently wasn't his plan, though. After he had gotten his dick sucked the way he wanted, he lifted my face to his and used his lips and tongue to rape my mouth. A guy doesn't get to be 28 in a place like San Francisco without acquiring a past, but I had never felt anything remotely as savage or ruthless or unrelenting as the way Chuck gnawed on my tongue and forced his far enough down my throat to change Zip codes.

His hands were everywhere at once — sliding along the back of my neck and down my spine, coasting across my biceps and down my flanks, holding my dick hostage to his lust, and, especially, prying my glutes wide enough to satisfy any sylvan exhibitionist asshole. His lips and hands and the dick grinding against my belly were so overpowering that I suddenly felt all wobbly in the knees. When I collapsed against him, he pulled me even tighter and gave me a great, sloppy bear hug with so much good will that it threatened to squeeze my guts out through my ears.

The next thing I knew, I was lying on my belly, bent over a mossy log. The moss felt rough on my chest and arms. Just as quickly I was back with the program enough to straighten up and find that thick, stubby dick of Chuck's was helping me out again — by being slammed up my ass with enough power to rip me apart.

For a moment I was confused again. I had been done deep work enough to know my ass had company, but I also knew there was no way my butthole would stretch wide enough to accommodate anything as massive as Ayers Rock or Khufu's pyramid or Chuck's huge woodland shank. Then a second later,

those few nerves I had still working flashed my brain the bad news, and every muscle I had rebelled against the impossible. One wave after another of searing pain shot up my spine and ripped a scream out of my mouth that is still probably echoing around those mountains today.

I felt his hands on my shoulders, so there wasn't any point in trying to launch myself off his dick. I didn't stand much chance anyway with my legs spread wide, my body pounding into one log while the other reamed my city butt wide. Mostly though, I stood no chance because, deep down, I needed his dick up my ass almost as much as he needed it there. As the remnants of my brain fought hard to find order in the chaos, I realized that Chuck's mutant meat was sizzling quietly away for the moment. I felt my ass strain vainly to find room for that fierce woodland beast, and then noticed it hadn't screwed me much past the shattered gates of my outraged virtue.

Before that thought was fully formed, Chuck reared back and jerked his tongue up my butt, and the top of my head flew off. Once he started seriously rimming, though, the guy tried to take care of me in more ways than one. His brutal dick cut me no slack whatsoever, but he proved he could be delicate as the flutter of a dragonfly's wing with the feel of his lips on my neck and his hands coasting down to worship my flanks — on the way to taking a fresh, firm grip on my hips.

When Chuck found his rhythm, all I could do was hold on to that mossy log and hope both my butt and the skin on my chest and belly would eventually recover. That huge dick reamed me raw with a hungry fury that was at first steady and then grew more desperate as my ass yielded to his brutal onslaught. Now and again his knob would pop all the way out of my hole. Then I could hear his shank slam up against his furry belly, doubtless splattering my ass-juices across his pelt, before he rammed his way back inside my once-tight shithole and took up business where he had left off.

After a bit, I heard him groaning and snarling as his pelvis pounded into my butt and he stabbed me in the back with his classic blunt instrument. Something about the tone in his growl turned me on even more and helped bridge the gap between chronic agony and limitless ecstasy. I still couldn't do much but keep my ass in the air and hope for the best; but from that

point on, the harder he reamed my hole, the warmer it glowed and pulsed with the kind of raw, savage life we domesticated fucks so seldom feel. I had long since stopped screaming and now heard myself moaning like a chastened puppy in perfect counterpoint to his woodland noises.

Chuck kept on reaming away, harder and faster with every furious, feral fuck-thrust until I was sure my butt was about to go up in flames — and I was all for it. Then, suddenly, his strokes went all jerky and I felt his nuts slam up against my ass for the first time. His beard tickled my back and I felt his savage teeth lock hard around the nape of my neck as though he were a mountin' lion and I, just some tight little pussy he had trapped in the wild.

After fifteen minutes or so of looking at nothing but a few feet of forest humus while my butt received the reaming of its young life, I was stunned when the forest flashed past my eyes. Chuck had snatched my body off that log and up tighter against his stubby colossus, as though I were no heavier than an impure thought, and gave me another bear hug that took my breath away. This time around, though, I was facing away from him. I couldn't see the delirium of rapture contort his face, but from the way his body was humping away at my hole and his soul was gurgling up and out in howls of primal frenzy, I knew what was happening well enough.

Chuck wasn't content to take my ass and use it for his pleasure. He wanted me to enjoy the experience. At least, I suppose that's why his gigantic paw slipped down to lock around my nine inches of stiff city dick. Maybe the guy just needed a handle to hold on to. In any event, he used it hard — slamming my body forward to rip my dick up through his fist and then heaving his hips backwards to jerk my knob back down to shake his hand. My feet dangled off the ground — not because he was that much taller, but just because he had fucked my legs to jelly.

Suddenly his head reared back and a howl of ancient and manly triumph reverberated about our forest glade, putting the seal of rapine conquest on my ass and proclaiming my surrender to all the world. His dick stopped slamming in and out and, instead, seemed almost to twirl about as though in need of a good exorcism, forcing his cruel fucker to new depths

of cruel despair and breeding heights of absolute ecstasy. Chuck's grinding, heaving, butt-humping dick was more than good enough, but that hand yanking at my crank was too much for mortal man to endure without rupturing.

My balls burst wide with hand-pumped pleasure, spraying my white seed out across the fertile forest floor in arc after nacreous arc of whirling globs of glory that caught the sunlight and shimmered as they splashed to earth. The harder Chuck reamed my hole in his own selfish frenzy, the harder that hand pumped my load out to gush across the landscape and make me truly one with Nature.

By the time Chuck had run dry and dropped my feet back to the ground, I only had a blast or two of jism left, but I whirled about and let it fly straight at his matted, sweat-covered chest. My cream quivered there briefly before I went after it with my tongue — and backed his furry forest butt into the pond by the time I was finished sucking his pelt clean.

I kept Chuck splashing around and treading water until I was ready to pump out another load — this time up his tight little hairy behind. After that, the silly bastard ran out of rubbers and we needed to hike back down the mountain to civilization. Chuck climbed onto his Harley and followed me as far as Susanville, where we rented a room for the rest of the weekend. He still lives in Reno, so now and again we make arrangements to rendezvous up at our lake for a few days. My asshole can't take more than that. But you can be sure that I never head out without several of his special, jumbo rubbers!

NAKED SKATEBOARD BOY

Frank Brooks

The wrestling mat was so slick with sweat that it felt like oiled skin under Corey's jockstrap-clad body as he struggled under Tim, his opponent. The cubicle-like wrestling gym, hardly larger than a handball court, roared with the hoots, squeals, and catcalls of sixty testererone-crazed teenagers and the bull-like bellowings of Coach Moore as four two-minute matches went on simultaneously on the over-sized mat. It was the last match of the gym class and, as usual, Corey found himself naked except for his jockstrap, and flat on his back, struggling to keep from being pinned. Tim, shirtless and barefoot, but still wearing gym trunks over his jockstrap – he'd lost fewer matches than Corey and hadn't been required to take off as much clothing – Tim seemed to be riding Corey instead of trying to pin him, as if he were enjoying the struggle and wanted the match to go on until the last possible second.

The small gym felt like a steambath. Being the wrestling team's workout room, it was kept over-heated on purpose, so the wrestlers would sweat off their last grams of extra fat. Now, with a gym class of sixty sweaty, hot-blooded boys packed into it, the temperature had to be over ninety degrees, and the combination of heat, noise, and the lack of air had Corey in a dizzy, almost hallucinatory daze. When Tim's wet armpit pressed to his face, he lost his mind, floating in another world as he inhaled deeply the young-male scent, then sucked at the blond, salty tuft of armpit hair. Tim pressed his armpit harder against Corey's mouth and Corey almost passed out with excitement.

"Fight!" Coach Moore bellowed. "Anybody who gets pinned is a worthless pussy!"

"Pull off their jocks!" the onlooking boys chanted. "Show us their pussies!"

Corey and the other three jockstrap-clad boys had each lost all their matches during the gym class. All competitors started the class session in jockstrap, gym trunks, t-shirt, sweatsocks, and sneakers. When a boy lost a two-minute match he had to

remove an article of clothing, starting with his sneakers. If he lost his next match, he had to remove his socks. T-shirts came off next, then gym trunks. Those who ended up in jocks alone were the class wimps, and Corey was always among them.

As Coach Moore counted out the final seconds, before his whistle ended the match, Tim pinned Corey. As the class hooted and descended upon the losers, Corey found his jock being ripped off. Somebody draped it over his face like a mask and voices taunted, "Pussy! Pussy!" Seconds later the bell sounded, ending the class, and a traffic jam of whooping boys fought its way through the gym doorway, those in the rear throwing back taunts at the four naked boys left lying in pools of sweat and wearing jockstrap masks. Tim, lingering behind, helped Corey to his feet.

"Good match," Tim said. "I almost didn't get you pinned." He tugged at the pouch of Corey's jockstrap and uncovered an eye. "Cute mask. You oughta wear it to classes and thrill the chicks."

"Sure," Corey muttered, pulling off the jock. He felt humiliated and embarrassed. He wondered if Tim had felt him sucking at his armpit. He didn't know why he'd done such a thing. What had come over him? Temporary insanity maybe.

"Catch you later," Tim said, a glint in his eyes.

He felt me doing it, Corey thought, flushing. I was sucking his armpit and he felt it. Who's he going to tell?

By the time Corey had gathered up his clothes and got down to the locker room, it was nearly deserted. At the end of the school day most boys skipped their showers and fled to freedom as fast a possible. Corey was set to do the same. He'd throw on his clothes, grab his skateboard, and hit the streets. Skateboarding would clear his head after the prison ordeal of school and gym class. Naked in front of his locker, he was about to slip into his jeans when Tim, also naked, swaggered past him, a long, fat hardon wagging from side to side. As Tim disappeared around the end of the row of lockers, heading for the showers, he glanced back at Corey and winked.

Corey flushed to his toes and his heart began to pound. Suddenly, jeans dropped, towel in hand, he was heading for the showers. It was as if Tim had just invited Corey to come and look at his hardon, his big, fat, notorious, ever-present

hardon. Since Tim had started going to school here, nobody had ever seen his cock soft in the locker room or showers. Corey found Tim's parading around with a hardon both shocking and enviable. Since his first day as a freshman, Tim had been the perpetual target of taunts about his hardon, taunts by now numbering in the thousands, but Tim had never seemed to be bothered by them. In fact, he seemed to enjoy them, even to intentionally provoke them.

Corey found two other boys in the showers with Tim, both of them eyeing Tim's hardon and exchanging smirks.

Tim flexed his cock a few times as if for their benefit. "Eat your hearts out, dudes. You're looking at a piece of meat that's been inside every pussy in this school ten times over."

"Bullshit!" said one of the boys.

"Sex-crazed bastard," muttered the other one. "I'm getting outa here before he starts doing something with it that makes me puke."

"Or before you get too excited," Tim called after them as they left.

Corey, with his back to Tim, and not wanting to appear too obvious, stole glances over his shoulder at Tim's cock. There it stood, the most looked-at, legendary cock in school. The legend was that Tim had fucked every female in school, including all his lady teachers, and half the women in town as well, both single and married. Corey believed it.

"What're you up to after school?" Tim asked, soaping his erection with jackoff motions.

Corey swallowed. "I'm going out skateboarding," he said, surprised that Tim was being so friendly. It was the first time in the nearly four years they'd gone to school together that Tim had paid him any attention.

"I've seen you ride that board," Tim said, his hand moving faster on his cock. "You're good at it."

Corey wrapped his hand around his own cock, which was as rigid as Tim's, and began to soap it. He was trembling. We're going to blow our loads together, he was thinking. He couldn't believe it.

Just then, Coach Moore padded into the showers, his muscles flexing, his enormous cock flopping from side to side. Corey instantly released his cock and turned so the coach

couldn't see it. He always got butterflies in his guts at the sight of the muscular coach, who both terrified and fascinated him. He'd certainly die if the coach caught him jacking off in the showers.

"Incredible!" the coach said, staring at Tim's erection, which Tim had released and was rinsing off. "Don't that thing ever go down? You should maybe see a doctor about that piece of wood. It ain't normal."

"It's just natural, coach," Tim said. "It has a mind of its own. Know what I mean? I mean, what can I do about it?"

"You've got sex on the brain, you horny bastard," the coach said. A bar of soap squirted out of his hand, hit the floor, and slid between Corey's feet. "Hey, dude, shag me that soap."

Corey was so shaky with nervousness as he bent over to pick up the soap that it slipped out of his hand a few times before he got a grip on it. Without turning around, he handed it back to the coach.

"Thanks, dude." The coach closed his hand around Corey's for a moment as he took the bar.

Tim, whistling, strode out of showers, and Corey, ready to shit at the thought of being left alone in the showers with Coach Moore, rinsed off in two seconds and trotted after him, keeping his hardon out of sight of the coach as he fled.

Tim lingered in front of Corey's locker. "You gave coach an eyeful, dude. I thought he was gonna lose it."

"Huh?" Corey said.

"Huh," Tim mimicked. "You know what I'm talking about. You rubbed your boy-pussy in his face, and you know it. Picking up that soap the way you did, waving your horny little butt at him. I thought he was gonna stuff you right there."

Corey stood there open-mouthed, flabberghasted by what he was hearing.

"Better watch out now," Tim said, grinning. "He's got your scent, boy. No telling now what he might do. That horse-dick of his was sticking straight out like a fucking log by the time you gave him the soap. The man's a sex pig once he gets the scent. Yes sir, coach thought he was gonna get himself a piece of grade-A boy-pussy right there in the showers. But you ran away on him. Now what's he gonna do? The bastard's probably having a fit. I bet he's hosing down the showers with his load

right now."

Corey swallowed, still not believing what he was hearing, but both thrilled and scared to death by it.

"Yes sir, you better get a move on, Corey boy. Coach comes out here and catches you all by you lonesome, there's no telling what he might do."

His heart pounding, Corey started to dress, stumbling into his jeans.

"Why don't you come along with me?" Tim said. "I've got a buddy who'd like to meet you. I know you'll like him and you can even make some bucks."

"Bucks? For what?"

"You'll see. Easy money. And fun besides." Tim patted Corey's ass. "How about it, Corey-boy?"

"OK," Corey said, his mind in a whirl.

Minutes later, Corey, dressed in his jeans, a baggy, checked long-sleeve shirt, sneakers without socks, and his baseball cap, worn backwards, was riding his skateboard down the sidewalk. Tim, in tight jeans and a torn-up, shoulderless t-shirt that showed off more of his smooth torso than it hid, jogged beside him. A small shell necklace circled Tim's neck and a small gold earring was anchored in his left ear. On his bare left shoulder CHERI was tatooed above an arrow-pierced heart.

"How far is it?" Corey asked. "Where're we going?"

"Not far," said Tim. "We'll be there soon--after we make a pitstop."

"Pitstop?"

"So many questions," Tim said. "Trust me, man."

Corey was starting to get nervous. He didn't like all the mystery. Tim had a reputation as a pothead as well as a sexual dynamo and Corey feared he was going to get involved in a drug deal or something. Just as Tim always had a hardon going in the lockerroom, he also seemed to have a perpetual high look in his eyes.

"Why don't you tell me where we're going?" Corey said.

"It would ruin the surprise," Tim said, patting Corey's rump. "Trust me, cutie-pie, you'll love it. You'll even love our pitstop."

Corey flushed at being called cutie-pie.

A few blocks from the beach, Tim led the way into the

vestibule of a stuccoed apartment building and announced himself through an intercom.

"Give me two minutes," said a woman's voice.

Corey followed Tim up to the third floor, where an apartment door swung open before Tim could knock on it twice. A giggling woman, dressed only in a gauzy, see-through negligee hauled Tim inside while grinding her ample tits against him and kissing him. She was a long-haired blonde of about 30.

"Timmy, where have you been? You've been neglecting me, honey."

"I've been busy," Tim said. "Hey, me and Corey've only got few minutes – we've got an appointment up the beach – but we decided to stop in for a few minutes and say hello."

"Only a few minutes?" the woman said. "For the two of you? Why are you young studs always in such a hurry?" She reached over and stroked Corey's cheek. "So, you're Corey. Cute name for a cute boy. Tim honey, where ever did you find such a cute one?"

"School, as usual," Tim said, unhitching his jeans. "Me and Corey've been classmates all through school. Corey's a skateboarder."

"Ooh, I like skateboarders!" the woman said.

Tim pulled out his hardon and shoved it up under the woman's negligee. As he lifted her right leg, he pushed his cock inside her.

The woman's eyes rolled back. "Stud! Oh stud!'"

Corey thought he must be dreaming. He stared, open-mouthed, groping himself through his jeans as he watched Tim fuck the woman. He'd seen people fuck before only in photographs. Tim's cock made squishy noises in the woman's pussy as he rammed up into her faster and faster, making her gasp with each thrust, and Corey was tempted to crouch down and watch Tim's cock close up as it fucked in and out.

"Honey!" the woman gasped, kissing Tim's face and clawing at his back. "Stud!"

Corey knew now why Tim's shirt was all torn up. Undoubtedly, women had ripped it to shreds as he'd fucked them. Corey squeezed his legs together, gripping his cock fiercely. He was ready to squirt cum in his pants.

The woman started to shriek, the toes of her uplifted leg clutching. Tim grunted, ramming upward as if he wanted to fuck her right through the ceiling. Boy and woman shuddered, and, after several seconds of frantic motions and fierce panting, Tim slipped his cock out of her and they separated. Tim's cock looked even larger than usual and was shiny, as if oiled. A few drops of pearly jism oozed from his pisshole.

"Fantastic!" the woman sighed. "Darling, you're such a good one! Is your cute boyfriend as good as you are?"

"Try him," Tim said, pushing Corey toward the woman.

She pulled a string and her negligee fell off. Her naked tits looked enormous. She crushed Corey in her arms, kissing him, feeling up his cock through his jeans. "Ooh, it's so hard! Fuck me, skateboarder, I can tell you're ready." She yanked Corey's jeans open and gripped his naked cock. "Such a cute one--and so hard."

"Fuck her," Tim growled in Corey's ear, his finger sliding up and down Corey's asscrack. The tip of his finger tickled Corey's asshole. "Fuck her, boy."

The woman lay back on the carpeted floor and pulled her knees to her tits. Tim pushed Corey down on top of her and reached down between his legs to guide Corey's prick inside her. When Corey's cock was anchored in the hot tunnel, Tim swatted Corey's ass and Corey started to hump, as if he were a sex-doll whose motor had been switched on by Tim's slap. The woman started to squirm and coo.

I'm dreaming, Corey told himself, his eyes closed as his body undulated and his cock pistoned. How could this be happening for real? He'd never imagined doing such a thing, had never actually felt the desire to fuck a woman. As the woman clung to him, whimpering with the sensations he was giving her, her loins rising to meet his thrusts, her mouth sucking at his downy cheeks, Corey recalled the image of Tim fucking her and the image excited him. The realization that his own cock was now where Tim's had been and that it was greased with Tim's freshly shot jism excited him even more and he started to ram. "Way to go!" Tim said, caressing Corey's bouncing ass, wiggling a finger between Corey's asscheeks. His finger found Corey's asshole and slipped insaide it. "Boy-pussy," he whispered in Corey's ear.

Corey gasped. He'd never felt such exquisite pleasure. A cyclone of orgasmic sensation overwhelmed him and he yelped as he exploded up the woman's twat. The woman moaned, her cunt clutching as her own spasms hit. Tim finger-fucked Corey until his orgasm subsided, then pulled him off the woman and hauled him, dazed and wobbly, to his feet.

"Zip up," Tim said. "We gotta split."

"Don't go!" the woman whined, still lying naked on the floor and catching her breath. "We're just getting started."

"Catch you later, babe," Tim said, pushing Corey out the door. "Thanks for the fuck."

"How was it?" Tim asked when they'd stepped out into the sunshine. "Was she tight enough for you?"

"It didn't happen," Corey mumbled, "did it?" He was still dazed.

"You're cute, you know that?" Tim said. " Stevo's gonna love you."

Only a few blocks from the woman's apartment Tim led Corey up a side street off Beach Boulevard. They went down an alley and entered a rear door of what appeared to be an old warehouse. Corey's stomach tightened. This was where the drug deal would take place, Corey was sure of it. After they'd tramped down a maze of hallways and up a flight of wooden stairs, Tim knocked at a door.

"Who is it?" came a man's voice from inside.

"Who else?" shouted Tim.

"As usual, you're late," said a tall, strikingly handsome man as he swung open the door. "Incorrigible as ever. Come in." The man was deeply tanned, his square pecs and rippling abs peeking from his half-open Hawaian shirt. He wore snug-fitting shorts and was barefoot, his muscular legs shaved. He was either a competitive bodybuilder or a pro wrestler, Corey decided.

"We had to make a pitstop," Tim said.

"Pitstop, huh?" the man said. "I don't want to hear about it. Unsavory dealings with the unmentionable, if I know you. You always show up here smelling of it. I swear, you do it on purpose just to spite me. I don't know what you see in that--that other gender. But tell me, who is this young gentleman? A skateboarder, no less. This is inspiring."

Tim introduced Corey to the man and, as they shook hands, Corey glanced around what at first appeared to be a large studio apartment, but, on closer inspection looked more like an apartment on a movie set. Spotlights and cameras were positioned here and there around the large set, with chairs, tables, couches, and bed apparently as props. This was a studio for photography or film-making.

"Charmed," the man said, holding tight to Corey's hand. "Another of Tim's schoolmates, I presume." The man's name was Steve.

Corey nodded.

"Well, do I get a big bonus this time?" Tim asked.

"I'm doubling your finder's fee for this one," Steve said. "Why can't you bring me dolls like this every time? And a skateboader, no less. You've outdone yourself, Tim."

"I knew you'd go for him," Tim said. "So does Coach Moore."

"Coach Moore?" Steve said. "Who's Coach Moore?"

"Later," Tim said. "Let's get working, I'm in a rush today."

"When aren't you in a rush?" Steve said. He held Corey's chin between his thumb and forefinger and looked him over. "What a cutie you are! Tell me, darling--and be truthful--are you gay or straight?"

Corey swallowed, blushing. He'd never been asked such a question. He'd never considered such a question. How could he answer?

"Gay," Tim said. "He's got FUCK MY BOY-PUSSY written all over his ass."

"I knew it," Steve said, stroking Corey's cheek. He tweaked Corey's freckled nose and pecked him on the lips.

Corey flushed even deeper. No man had ever kissed him before. He felt faint and sat on the couch.

Steve picked up a magazine from a pile of them on the desk and handed it to Tim. "How do you like it, coverboy? It came out only last week and already the editors have forwarded letters to you here from about 200 admirers. Men all over the world are beating off day and night drooling over your pictures." Steve tossed Corey a copy of the magazine, which had FOR MEN ONLY printed on the cover under the title and above a closeup of Tim's smiling, dreamy-eyed face. In the

photograph, Tim was wearing his shell necklace and his ripped-up shirt. A caption under his photograph read: YOUNG, HUNG, AND FULL OF SPUNK!

"They got that right," Tim said, having read the caption out loud.

Both boys turned magazine pages. Corey had seen a few PLAYBOYs in his life, but never a magazine like this one, devoted not to tits but to cocks and balls and the young-male body. The pictures of cute, stark-naked boys with roaring hardons made him tremble. His own hardon wanted to split open his jeans and he found himself panting like a steam engine. Maybe Tim was right about him. Maybe it was time to admit his real desires and call himself gay.

Tim, in the magazine centerfold, was stretched out on his side, raised up on one elbow, the tip of his hardon pecking at his navel. His other arm was raised to show off his blond armpit. In another shot Tim wore his school jockstrap, the one he actually wore to gym class. In another, he leered at the camera over his shoulder as he pulled apart his asscheeks and displayed his pink anus. Corey licked his lips and almost creamed at the sight.

"You like my magazine spread?" Tim asked, smirking at Corey.

Corey gave Tim a shy smile.

"You can take it home and jerk off over it if you want," Tim said. "That's what it's for--gay guys like you. You like my big cock, Corey-boy? I can tell you do. Look at that big thing, huh? That baby's fucked a lot of pussy."

"That's not all it's fucked," Steve said. "You've had your share of ass--male ass--even if you swear up and down you're straight."

"Yeah, so what?" Tim said. "Like they say, variety is the spice of life. Hey, I don't have much time."

"Okay," Steve said, "Let's take some shots and show Corey how it's done. Corey, why don't you kick off your sneakers and get comfortable?"

Corey kicked off his shoes and wiggled his bare toes, wondering what was going to happen next. He was tempted to ask Steve where the bathroom was so he could lock himself in with the magazine and beat off over Tim's pictures. He was also

tempted to bolt for the door and run for it. The anxiety and excitement he was feeling were almost more than he could handle.

Steve switched on spotlights and began giving Tim directions and snapping pictures of him. Grinning, leering, pouting seductively, Tim posed. Steve took closeups of Tim's small nipples peeking through the rips in his shirt. To make the nipples larger, Steve sucked on both of them and photographed them wet. Tim took off everything except his shell necklace and earring and Steve licked the boy's armpits, then photographed them. Tim bent over and pulled apart his tight buttocks. Steve, kneeling behind him, licked out Tim's moist crack and wiggled his tongue up the boy's asshole, then took closeups of the wet, winking pucker. He turned Tim around and started sucking Tim's cock.

Corey rubbed his cock through his jeans. Was what he was seeing for real--one guy sucking on another guy's cock? He'd imagined sucking cock countless times while jerking off, but he had never been quite sure that such a thing was actually possible. Now he knew. He watched Tim stretch luxuriously, sliding his big prong in and out of Steve's mouth. He noticed a huge tent in Steve's shorts. Steve's man-cock, sticking straight out with excitement as he sucked Tim, had to be as long and as big around as a Coke bottle.

Steve licked and sucked Tim's hairless balls, then took close-up shots of Tim's cock and balls from various angles--above and below, from the side and head-on. As Steve positioned Tim this way and that and took dozens of shots of Tim gazing seductively at the camera, Tim talked: "That horny Coach Moore, he almost got hold of Corey's ass in the showers today and the baby almost lost his cherry. You are a virgin, ain't you, Corey-boy?"

"I guess so," Corey mumbled, and Tim laughed: "I thought so."

Steve snapped a few shots of Corey half-reclining barefoot on the couch and Corey almost creamed in his jeans at the lustful looks the man gave him. Steve was a handsome, muscular god and it was obvious that he wanted Corey. What exactly does he want to do with me? Corey wondered, trying to imagine what was still almost unimaginable for him.

"That Coach Moore," Tim said, "he has us play strip wrestling, which is like strip poker, except when you lose a match (instead of a poker hand) you have to take something off. Shoes first, then socks, t-shirt, shorts, until you're finally down to your jock. The young cute ones--the ones the coach goes apeshit over--always end up in nothing but jocks, their bare butts up in the air half the time so everybody can see their assholes and Coach Moore's eyes almost pop out."

Tim turned his ass up close to Steve's camera, asscheeks parted, and Steve mumbled, "Jesus!" groping himself with one hand while trying to control his camera with the other.

"And then today in the showers," Tim continued, wiggling his ass, "in comes the coach and intentionally on-purpose drops his soap so Corey has to bend over and pick it up. Corey turns his butt up real cute and just about rubs it in Coach's face. The man's crowbar stands right up. I got the fuck outa there in a hurry--before he lost it and started fucking everything in sight."

"Including you," Steve said.

"Including me," Tim said. "Cute-assed, virgin Corey got outa there just in time, too. Hey, you've took about five hundred pictures. I've gotta split soon. Got an appointment."

"Just a few more," Steve said. "I want to get a few of you and Corey together."

"Sounds like that could be fun," Tim said. "I'll give you a few more minutes."

Steve came over and started snapping pictures of Corey, who was barefoot, but still dressed in his shirt, jeans, and baseball cap. Corey blushed sheepishly.

"Gorgeous," Steve said, leaning close to snap pictures of Corey's face. He had Corey rest his bare feet on his skateboard, curling his toes over the edge, and he took several closeup shots of Corey's feet and toes. Then he crouched low and started licking Corey's toes. He held up Corey's feet one at a time and kissed them all over.

"Wild!" Tim said, stroking his cock as he watched. "You like them dirty boy-toes, Stevo? You're a kinky dude, man."

Steve unzipped Corey's jeans and pulled out his cock, then photographed it sticking out of the fly. "Beautiful dick. It's not that big, but it sure is pretty," Steve breathed. He leaned over

and licked off the lubricant that was oozing from Corey's pisshole, then engulfed Corey's prick completely and gave it a few good sucks before releasing it and snapping closeups of the excited young rod, shiny with saliva and throbbing away.

Corey was shaking. He thought he was going to shoot off in the air, no-handed.

Steve pulled Corey up off the couch and kissed him, then pushed him, reeling, toward Tim. "Kiss each other, sweethearts."

Corey was stunned as Tim wrapped his arms around him and pressed his hard prick against Corey's. "Let's make this look real good," he growled in Corey's ear, and he covered Corey's mouth with his own and slipped his tongue inside it. Corey sucked Tim's tongue and drank his saliva, moaning, grinding against Tim and never wanting to release him. He was staring into Tim's blue eyes and madly in love. He'd never felt such thrills in his cock. Steve kept saying, "Beautiful! Beautiful" and his camera whirred.

"All right," Tim said, breaking their kiss, "you've had enough tongue, dude, now how about some cock?" He pushed Corey to his knees and shoved his entire cock into Corey's mouth.

Corey felt Tim's hot cockhead rubbing in his throat. He was surprised by how big Tim's cock felt in his mouth, and how hard, and how good it tasted. He sucked greedily, as if he could never get enough. He wanted to suck Tim's cock forever. I want it! he kept thinking. I want it!

"Beautiful!" Steve whispered, taking one closeup shot after another of Corey sucking cock. "The kid's a natural cock-sucker. Yeah, baby, suck it!"

"Aw fuck!" Tim moaned, pushing his cock in and out of Corey's face. "I wanna fuck his ass, but I can't stop fucking his cute face. Aw man!"

Steve slipped a finger between Tim's asscheeks and wiggled it up Tim's asshole. Tim gasped, his cock flexing hard in Corey's mouth. Suddenly, hot jism was spurting down Corey's throat and Corey choked on the force of the ejaculations. Steve pulled his finger out of Tim's asshole, yanked on Tim's hips, forcing him to pull his cock out of Corey's mouth, and photographed Tim's jism splashing across Corey's face as

Corey, tongue stuck out, begged for more jism.

"Fuck!" Tim said, milking the last spunk out of his cock onto Corey's tongue. "I wanted to plough his ass."

"Next time," Steve said. "Next time we'll make a video of you two and we'll call it, BOY FUCK."

"Cool title," Tim said. "But hey, time to pay up, Stevo, I gotta split. Remember that big bonus you promised."

As soon as Tim had left, Steve took off all his clothes. "Alone at last," he said, massaging his enormous nut-sac, which was shaved like the rest of him. His hard cock looked as large and powerful as the tusk of a rhinoceros, and Corey stared at it. He'd never seen one so huge – it had to be eight, maybe even nine inches long – and not only that, but it had foreskin half covering the knob. Corey was as awe-struck as he was excited.

Steve grinned at him and started snapping pictures. "You're so adorably cute with that baseball cap on backwards and that boyish hardon sticking up in the air. You're a shoo-in for a coverboy. Stand on your skateboard. Beautiful! NAKED SKATEBOARD BOY – I can see it on the cover now."

Steve kept interrupting his picture-taking to stroke his cock. The realization that he was turning the man on thrilled Corey and he started flashing seductive facial expressions at the camera – as he'd see Tim do – and posing his willowy figure in seductive ways that only his bedroom mirror had ever seen before. The slit at the tip of his pink cockhead was open and oozing lubricant, a trickle of which slid down his nearly vertical shaft.

"Adorable!" Steve said as Corey balanced on his ass on his skateboard and jack-knifed his legs to display his pink asshole. It was as if he were offering himself to be fucked on his skateboard. "Christ, you're driving me crazy!"

Steve put down his camera and crouched on all fours to lick Corey's ass. His tongue slurped up and down the moist crack, then probed the pink pucker. He snaked his tongue inside Corey and Corey gasped, an electric thrill shooting through his asshole and cock.

Steve lifted Corey off the skateboard and lay on top of him on the floor, kissing him, grinding his massive cock against Corey's silky-smooth stomach. Corey had never felt so small

and frail. Steve was at least twice his size. Steve stroked Corey's forehead, knocking off the baseball cap, and reddish-blond hair fell forward into Corey's eyes.

"Christ, you're cute! I can't get over it." Steve shoved his tongue into Corey's mouth.

Corey squirmed under the man, moaning, quivering from scalp to toes. He'd never in his life felt so hot. He clung to the man, sucking his tongue, grinding up against him. He opened his mouth as wide as he could so Steve's tongue could slide down his throat and lick his tonsils.

"I'd love to fuck you, boy," Steve panted. "Would you like that?"

"Yes," Corey said, totally out of his mind.

With Corey still clinging to him, Steve stood up and walked over to a table to pick up a container of Vaseline. Man and boy were face to face, Corey's arms around Steve's massive neck, his flat chest pressed to Steve's bulging pecs, his legs around Steve's waist. The top of Steve's massive, tusk-like cock lay along the length of Corey's asscrack, throbbing powerfully, and Steve started greasing it with Vaseline. Corey wiggled his ass, going crazy with the idea that he was going to get fucked.

"You want it, don't you, honey?"

"Yes," Corey panted, a throbbing, itching ache in his loins such as he had never before experienced.

Steve slipped a greased finger up Corey's asshole, then two more fingers, and Corey churned his ass in circles, moaning, wanting to feel his asshole stretched even more. Steve pulled out his fingers and pressed his greased knob to Corey's part-open orifice. With one easy thrust, Steve's hugely swollen fucker slipped to the hilt up Corey's asshole.

"Ohhh yeahhh!" Corey sighed as he felt the cylinder of man-dick fill him. "Oh Steve!"

"Yeahhh!" Steve moaned as his dickhead probed Corey's depths, every inch of his fucker buried inside the squirming teenager. "Does it hurt, honey? Is it too much for you?"

"Feels great!" Corey sighed, sure that his tight little loins were going to split in half. But he didn't care, he was getting exactly what he wanted.

"You're a natural, kid," Steve said, his big hands gripping Corey's asscheeks, his cock slipping in and out of Corey's

clutching hole. He gazed into Corey's eyes as he fucked the boy and he shoved his tongue into Corey's mouth.

Corey was in heaven. His toes curled and pointed as the big man juggled him like a weightless doll and fucked him. Each thrust of the armlike cock into his skinny body sent such a jolt of sensation through him that he almost came. His rigid cock, bubbling pre-cum like sap as he fucked it against Steve's smooth, rock-hard abdomen, had never before felt so saturated with pleasure. He gazed into Steve's eyes, as madly in love with Steve as he'd been with Tim, and Steve went into a humping frenzy.

Steve's eyes rolled back. His cock swelled in Corey's asshole and flexed again and again. The massive cock shuddered and a stream of liquid fire burst into Corey's guts. Steve grunted, fucking out torrents of man-spunk. The electric current of Steve's orgasm saturated Corey's loins and suddenly Corey was in eye-popping ecstasy, daggers of an exquisite orgasm torturing his cock and balls and asshole as spunk spewed repeatedly from his cock and greased Steve's belly.

"Ohhh Steve!" Corey groaned. "Ohhh God!"

Steve shot so much jism that by the time he was finished the cum was leaking out of the Corey's asshole and running down Steve's balls. His cock slipped out and he set Corey down. "What a fuck!" Steve said, catching his breath. "I love fucking boys in that position, but they're usually too heavy to lift comfortably. You're just the right size: light and compact. You were made for fucking, Corey."

Corey laughed, blushing. Steve was right, that's what he was made for. No doubt about it now.

Before Corey left that afternoon, Steve, besides taking a lot more pictures, fucked Corey twice more, once from behind, standing up, and once lying on him face-to-face, with Corey's legs hooked over Steve's shoulders. Between fucks, Corey sucked Steve's cock and managed to get him off once that way and taste his jism. Steve had thicker, richer, saltier cum than Tim, and Corey savored it as he swallowed. Steve snapped pictures of Corey's cock-stuffed face as he was shooting off into it.

"That's it for today," Steve finally said, "I'm fucked out."

Corey, although he'd creamed five times himself, was still

hard.

"Do you think Coach Moore reads this magazine?" Corey asked as he was leaving. Along with his school books he was carrying a copy of the magazine that featured Tim as coverboy. He'd be jacking off with his nose in it as soon as he got home.

"If the coach is as crazy about young ass as Tim claims he is," Steve said, "I wouldn't be surprised if he reads it."

"Then maybe he's seen Tim's pictures in it?"

"I wouldn't be surprised. Hey, are you worried that he'll see yours?"

"Nah," Corey said, his guts twingeing with sudden anxiety. Truthfully, the thought of Coach Moore seeing naked pictures of him terrified him – terrified him as much as it excited him. Then the coach would really want to fuck him, Corey realized.

"How long before the magazine comes out with my pictures in it?" Corey asked. He was hoping it would be soon.

THE BIRTHDAY PRESENT

Ken Smith

It was a sunny but crisp day and, to all intents and purposes, it was to be like any other. Morning coffee and cereal had been cultivated and consumed, and the day's mail read but not answered. Then came a knock on the door. I was expecting no one, especially at nine in the morning, on a Saturday.

Then I saw him: Vispa was clearly visible, though distorted, through the bubble-glass door; and I wondered what he was doing here.

"Good mornin', Mr. Chips," he greeted, as I swung the door toward myself.

"Hello, Vispa," I smiled, surprised, yet delighted to be greeted by this vision of beauty.

"I've brought you somethin'," he said, grinning and handing me a square, flat box wrapped in brown paper, with a white envelope attached. Written on it, in large gold letters - TO MR. CHIPS.

"Come in, Vispa," I offered. "I've just percolated some coffee."

Vispa moved past me, releasing a smile which I can only describe as cunning, or maybe suspicious - definitely one I had not observed before.

"What are you up to today, then?" I asked, passing him a black, sugar-free coffee; his usual preference.

"Nothing. Just thought I'd come and say hello."

"Well, that was nice," I thought. Then again, it was always nice to see, Vispa. Always nice to observe him working in the garden in his white shorts, and wonder what lay beneath the cute, cotton-covered bulge between his muscled thighs. I often wondered why I had never discovered the answer to that question. Perhaps I thought it too dangerous a desire to discover. Yes, I had known him since the age of ten - my paper-boy. And from the age of twelve - my paper-boy and gardening-boy. And, now, as a strapping youth - my gardening-boy and handy-boy. But, no, I had never once attempted to get him to divulge the contents of his denims. Not

that I wouldn't have sold my entire family's souls to the Devil, in order to have that question answered.

"Going to open it?" Vispa questioned and smiled again, nodding to the brown package on the conservatory table.

It was a classical CD - Mozart - and a rude, albeit, pleasantly rude, birthday card. "Thanks, Vispa. You shouldn't have spent your money on me," I scolded, but in a kind and grateful way.

"Want any work done, Mr. Chips? I'm not doing anything," he offered.

I hadn't any work which needed doing that I was aware of, but I guessed he needed the cash to pay for my gift. And I'd be lying if I said that I would rather have spent my birthday answering letters, watching tele or some other task, than watch Vispa at work.

I conjured up a job - cleaning the jungle-of-a-conservatory - aware that the tropical heat within might at least lead him to remove his 'I'M A BAD BOY' T-shirt. Even so, observing his buttocks bending beneath dying banana bushes and inquisitive ivy, would be reward enough for the extra payment I intended to give him.

However, as I already said, Vispa appeared to be in a strange mood and before he'd even begun his chores, his T-shirt was tossed onto the wicker lounger beside me. It smelt of boy-sweat - musty, with a hint of sweet deodorant - and I wondered if, indeed, he'd ever been 'A BAD BOY'.

He was definitely up to something. What? I had yet to discover. But I lay back and began a reply of one of my letters - a task, I must admit, which became impossible.

There was something about a boy who was of mixed race which I always found appealing. And watching Vispa's toffee-coloured chest glisten and glow in the warmth of the conservatory left me in no doubt that the letter would get no further than the first paragraph. In fact, it stopped after three lines.

I wanted to embrace this half-naked youth. Feel his moist chest against my face, against my own nakedness. Wanted to slip his snug-fitting, white jeans over his buttocks and push my face into the scent of his boyish bulge hidden, hopefully, beneath a pair of pure white Calvin's. Instead, I returned to the kitchen and poured myself a stiff scotch over ice - ice that may

have been better used in my underpants.

I cannot be sure, but I do believe I turned the heating to the conservatory, full on, before returning to my observation of buttocks, bulges and well-defined, brown-nippled pecs. Within minutes, I guessed that I had because I was sweating profusely. What with the scotch I'd consumed and a biteable bottom just a breath away, I was turning into a human volcano. Vispa, however, looked fairly cool, although the dampness around the crease of his jeans, separating the cheeks of his buttocks, made me aware that he too was warming up.

"Are you warm, Mr. Chips?" Vispa inquired. "You should take your top off."

That casual remark stunned me. Never before had he asked me to remove any part of my clothing, and I was tempted to say, "Only if you remove your pants!" But, instead, I suggested that I turn the heating down.

"There's no need, Mr. Chips," was the reply I didn't expect but one which I delighted in. And obeying my house-boy, as he continued hacking his way through the jungle, I pulled my sweatshirt over my head.

"You see. Isn't that more comfortable?" was accompanied by a flash of white teeth and a smile that almost melted the ice in my scotch, but definitely caused a minor eruption in another volcanic part of my anatomy.

It may seem strange, but I didn't even know if Vispa knew I was gay. I certainly had no idea if he was. But surely he must have known? He'd worked in my house when I'd had the occasional lover stay over. He'd seen my collection of books, almost all of which were gay. And although I wasn't camp, some of my antics and strange habits, must have given him an inkling. Even so, Vispa was obviously happy and comfortable working for me; and his politeness was almost disturbing. The times that I'd requested him to call me Tom were too numerous to mention. And to this day, he still called me Mr. Chips. Perhaps it was his way of keeping a distance between us. I really had no idea.

"You're sweating, Mr. Chips," commented Vispa. "You can wipe yourself on my T-shirt if you wish. It's got to be washed. Save you getting a towel."

Was that a strange thing for a boy to say? An erotic, sexual

thing to say? Or was it just an innocent offer? Doing it, however, was erotic, was sexual and far from innocent, and almost sent my heart into spasm!

The underarm odour of this youth's body was simply stunning. And I rubbed the area of his T-shirt which had been closest to his crotch, into my face - and how sensational that smelt! - and wondered: would he suggest the same with his underpants?

Thank goodness Vispa couldn't see inside my underpants, I mused, for he would have found them super-glued to my stomach.

"Feel better, Mr. Chips?" he seductively grinned.

Did I answer, Oh yes? I really cannot recall.

By lunchtime, the conservatory no longer resembled a jungle, and as I fed Vispa a chunk of Cheddar and fresh, crispy bread, I contemplated what other task I could conjure, in order to keep him tormentingly naked and within arms reach.

Together we sat in the hot, sunny jungle, naked to our waists. And still Vispa had an aura of naughtiness exuding from his every pore - whilst I had neat scotch exuding from mine.

Perhaps he could start on the bathroom? I considered. And when he was beneath the shower head, I could accidentally set it off and observe those tight, white jeans absorb the fine spray and soak into that tantalising tuba buried in the undergrowth of his jet-black pubics - for they would surely be that - black and bushy as his coal-coloured curls.

"I have to go now, Mr. Chips," was not the statement I wished to hear. But the promise that he would return in an hour, was.

Vispa pulled his 'BAD BOY' T-shirt over his succulent body - sadly, he'd been anything but. At least my body odour and fluids were now hugging his. Somehow, I found that satisfying.

Closing the door behind such a cute behind, I was tempted to head straight to my bedroom, but the promise of his return led me toward the bottle of scotch. I wished myself a happy birthday for the third time and downed another.

Mozart was sent spinning beneath the laser head as I tried to prevent my brain from doing a similar thing inside of mine. So much scotch before midday was not such a good idea, I

guessed.

What was Vispa up to, I wondered? But I wondered, more, what was up inside those jeans? Suddenly, my scotch-sodden brain went haywire, and I shot into a world of fantasy. Did Vispa wear jockeys, briefs, boxers or nothing? Was he passive or active? Was he a passionate, rough boy or a gentle, kiss and caress youth? But, more importantly, was he?

The sound of the front door colliding with the Tibetan chimes hung above, brought me from my thoughts. Vispa, as promised, had returned. I'd given him a key, just in case the scotch began to win the battle and returned me to my bed.

Was it to be the bathroom ploy or could I magic another cleaning act that might require the removal of more of his clothing?

In he strolled, not cocky and arrogant, as many youths found it necessary to be these days. It was more a glide - gently floating toward my tortured body.

He'd changed T-shirts - hopefully, not because of my body scent - which now read, 'I'M A VERY VERY BAD BOY'.

Was Vispa trying to tell me something?

"Mr. Chips. How are you?" he greeted.

That was strange. It was almost as if it was the first time he'd seen me this day but I didn't reply, "I'm tipsy." or "As horny as hell." or any other such truthful statement, but simply told him I was fine.

Mozart continued to seduce my ears, whilst Vispa seduced my eyes and I was just about to try the bathroom ploy when Vispa told me not to get up but to close my eyes tightly - he had another surprise for me.

I have no idea why I obeyed this youth, but I kept my eyes firmly closed for what seemed an age, and, then, just when I had almost fallen asleep, serenaded by strings, a soft, deepish voice, with a hint of Indian, said, "You can open them now, Mr. Chips."

Gingerly, I lifted the lids, then popped them wide open - very wide open! Before me stood Vispa, naked as the day he was born! "Oh, my word!" didn't leave my lips, it remained jammed in my throat, and I took another gulp of scotch to help release it. "Vispa!" I whispered. "What are you doing?" My eyes focused firmly on his soft, lazy dick lying over two tight

balls. Above them, I noted, a tuft of black curls, so few, I think I counted all thirty from where I sat. "Vispa!" I whispered again, and began to rise - that is, I began to leave my seat.

"Don't get up, Mr. Chips. Please close your eyes again," he ordered, in a voice that slid over my whole body like a palm of lavender massaging oil.

I obeyed without hesitation. Without knowing the consequences of my action. And what would those consequences be? Would I open them to find a naked Vispa sitting on my lap - on my face? Or would I be greeted by that curly coal-coloured crown buried into my crotch? Or maybe to his full erection, tantalisingly and titillatingly teased to its full potential for my pleasure.

"You can open them now, Mr. Chips," came the long-awaited command.

I opened them very, very slowly - teasing and torturing myself. I closed them quickly. Opened them again. Closed them again.

I was drunk. I was asleep. I was dreaming. I was all three. I opened them slowly. I was in shock!

Before my bulging, blue-grey eyes stood naked, Vispa - sadly, without an erection. Next to him stood naked, VISPA - also, without an erection. Vispa had a twin. A scrumptious, sensational, sensual, perfect identical self.

I think I wet my pants!

I couldn't move. Couldn't take my eyes from the sixty pubic hairs and the joint six inches of soft cock, or the four balls held tightly into their groins.

I definitely wet my pants!

Both boys grinned, the sunlight catching those perfect white teeth, almost blinding me. "Vispa?" I questioned, looking at one, then repeating it, looking at the other.

The boys remained silent and grinned again - they weren't letting on - and began to glide toward my aching body.

My heart stopped - it actually did - then gave an enormous thud, almost breaking two ribs, then raced like a galloping horse toward the finishing line. "Vispa?" I queried, addressing them both a second time. They remained silent, slowly being drawn toward my dissolving body.

Beside me now, two loving, slender palms gripped both my

hands, and with a naked youth attached to each, I was led toward my bedroom.

An easy chair was slid to the base of my bed, and in a dazed state, I was requested to sit. Vispa and Vispa moved away, one either side of the bed, and were re-united in the centre of the mattress. Nestled into the multi-coloured duvet, they looked like two exotic chocolates waiting to be wrapped. Both, I noticed, just before they climbed onto the soft centre, had semi-erections - strangely at the same angle and of the same length.

Patiently, but excitedly, I waited for the show to commence - for this was indeed a show. Entertainment of the highest quality. Whether I was to come on as an extra, I had yet to discover.

Not a word left their lips as they mirrored each others movements, and I wondered if they had done this all their young lives. Hands glided over thighs, chests, nipples, more thighs, then firm young cocks - firm, young, heathly six-inch cocks. Their hand movements were in unison as foreskins were rolled back, just the right distance, then brought back over the head, then rolled back again. Gently, ever-so-gently, they caressed their cocks, and I was sure that if I measured the distance their tender, loose flesh rolled back, there would not be a millimetre of difference between them, such was their togetherness.

It was when mouths met mouths, tongues tickled tongues, and lips moistened lips that my cock exploded in spasms of pre-cum. I wanted to join in. How desperately I wanted that!

I began to remove my clothing. I wasn't sure if that was permitted, but I would surely die if I didn't. But a brief break from boys feasting on boys, and a glance from each as I disrobed, confirmed that I hadn't broken any rules. And I slumped back into the easy chair - naked, sweating, and so stiff I could have drilled a hole through eight inches of concrete.

Who choreographed these boys, I wondered, as they slipped silently head to tail. I guessed this was the big one, and my shaking body raised itself as two sweet cocks were sucked, and sucked, and sucked.

I began to caress myself - how could I not? And then it happened. A hand raised from each boy and beckoned me onto

my bed. And even as they did that elegant gesture, their mouths continued to work.

I was suddenly struck with a strange guilt - like it was a crime to interrupt such a beautiful union, but my guilt was quickly swept away when Vispa on the right, reached toward me with a condom and lube - still savouring Vispa on the left, I might add.

I hadn't been to the same Dancing School of Sex as these two boys, and I began to wonder how I would fit in without interrupting their rhythm but began by kissing the brown boyish bum, then working my way up the voluptuous body of the boy who I thought was Vispa. I really hoped it was. But did it really matter? They were identical!

Vispa's legs parted slightly. Both boys ceased sucking, turned and smiled, and with a nod from each, indicated that I should commence lubrication. My shaking fingers tore open the sachets, first the condom, then the lube, and within seconds I was probing deeply into the depths of the softest sphincter I had ever serviced. My sex soon followed, and with sensationally slow strokes, keeping rhythm with the sucking boys, I slid deeply in and out of his soft, smooth cheeks.

It was their first sounds, their emissions of pleasure, that almost brought me to the point of coming, whilst I delighted in the vision of delicate dicks disappearing then re-appearing. And as I drove my dick deep into Vispa 1 and was about release a joyous gasp and jettison my juices, Vispa 2 passed me a second condom and lube.

I moved to the other side of the bed, thinking, these boys must be psychic. They knew precisely at which point to stop.

I commenced Act Two in a similar fashion to Act One, savouring as much skin of Vispa 2 as I was permitted, before being instructed to proceed.

They are the same person, I thought, as I entered the second pair of juicy buttocks, because as I drove deep and hard into my second Vispa, I'm sure my first Vispa was recieving an equal amount of pleasure, as if it were he that I was fucking.

Hungrily, I watched as Vispa 1 sucked on Vispa 2 - desperate to do that myself - when their delightful moans re-appeared. This time both boys would surely come into their respective mouths, and I would release enough of my own to fill a

tankard. But, no. There was an Act Three!

My head was spinning and my balls ached!

The condom was removed and I was tissued clean. A Vispa each side of me now - it was kissing time. Was it kissing time! Tongues, sweeter than boys dicks, darted in and out of my mouth, whilst feminine fingers foraged and fondled.

I was writhing in ecstasy. Wriggling like a hooked worm. Controlled, caressed and almost crying from the euphoria my head was swimming in. Jesus! It couldn't get any better! It COULD?

A pair of lips on mine, another slipping, sliding and slurping over my cock. A pair of lips on mine, another slipping, sliding and slurping over my cock. A pair of lips on mine, another, then another! Each boy was taking it in turns, sucking, slurping or kissing.

'OH LORD, PLEASE LET ME COME! PLEASE LET IT STOP!' I inwardly screamed.

But it didn't stop.

Vispa 1 sucked hungrily on me whilst I sucked on Vispa 2, and then the reverse. Vispa 2 had sixty-nine with me whilst I was screwed by Vispa 1, and then the reverse. Every possible sexual combination was explored and re-explored.

They were torturers - beautiful boy torturers!

Again I almost came. Again I was prevented. It was time for Act Four - the final act. It had to be the final act. The boys brought themselves together into a seesaw position so that their balls touched and their cocks stood proudly together. Another seductive smile from each and I moved my head over both sexes, swallowing them to the base. Crazy for their cum, I crammed my mouth into both tufts of pubic hair. Feasting like a famished child, I worked my mouth wantingly over their youthful weapons - all the while running my palms over tightening stomach muscles.

Both boys gasped and raised their bodies, slamming their lips together and locking naked chests with arms. Then, with a final tightening of solid, smooth, stomach muscles, sent salvos of semen swirling around my sucking mouth.

Crazily, I captured their creamy cum, concentrating on their cock-heads for the last droplets, before consuming the lot.

With the taste of their cum still lingering in my palate, both

boys dived between my legs. I departed to another universe when the boys began working. Two mouths sucked in rapid sequence - Vispa 1, Vispa 2, Vispa 1, Vispa 2 - not a micro-second without a marvellous mouth manipulating. My body tightened and arched toward their working mouths. Who was to get the liquid torpedo loaded in my tube? I wondered. But these boys were brilliant blowjob bunnies. And when I released that final scream - I really did! - somehow, both boys managed to savour an equal amount of cum, swapping it between their mouths as the kissed their final kiss.

I lay on my bed, semiconscious. Slain by sex. The boys returned from the lounge, each dressed in their respective 'BAD BOY' T-shirts and holding scotch. Passing me a measure of the much needed liquor, both boys raised their glasses.

"HAPPY BIRTHDAY, MR. CHIPS!" they saluted.

THE SHOOTING CLUB

Peter Gilbert

I never really disliked Mike Mitcham exactly. I found him amusing and his strange stories had a certain fascination but he was...well, odd. In a sense, I guess we both were. We both liked the boys. At gun club meetings he always sat with me and the air rifle boys after shooting was over for the evening. He never sat with the other men even though he was an ace shot and his rifle, a Mannlicher, was the envy of just about everybody.

He never said anything out of place. He never bought plates of French fries or drinks for the boys as I sometimes did. If he spoke at all, it was about ordinary things; shooting or football. The lads accepted him, probably, I think, as a friend of mine.

I was the only person who was interested in air rifle shooting and got the job of teaching the kids - which suited me perfectly. It wasn't only shooting pellets into a target that they learned from me.

Of the eight or nine kids round that table, two had passed my private test with flying colors. The first had been Steve; he was the oldest. Then there was Gerry.

Mike knew about my preferences. He didn't know names of course. Not until one night when Steve stood up. He was the last of the boys to go. "See you Sunday afternoon," he said. I nodded.

"Big lad that," said Mike watching him go out of the door. "Why the Sunday meeting?"

"Oh... er, I help him with his homework," I said.

"Looks like he's got a pretty substantial cock on him. Nice ass too," said Mike. "I'm not a complete fool you know."

I think I must have blushed. "The one you ought to be going for is that little blond," he continued.

"What? Martin? He's far too young!"

"Just right. God, that kid would fuck well. What an ass!"

To be perfectly honest with you, I'd had the same thought. Watching Martin shoot in the prone position was extremely enjoyable even though he rarely managed to hit the target.

There had been times, too, when he stood up again to stretch his arms and it was obvious that it wasn't only his limbs which had stiffened.

These however, were private thoughts. I snapped back something about not wanting to end up in jail and Mike said no more.

I'd already summed up Mike as one of those characters who is all talk. He kept on and on about Martin and I did nothing to stop him.

One Tuesday evening, shooting had been cancelled for some reason and he suggested that I should go round to his place for a drink. He collected me and talked about Martin all the way there. I don't think there was a single square (or curved) inch of the boy which hadn't been described or hypothesized by the time we got to Mike's house.

I'd been anxious to see the house for some time. It had been built for old man Bateman, at that time wheelchair bound. Towards the end of his life he'd been paralysed and looked after by two male nurses. The house was said to be full of labor saving devices. Certainly there were ramps where other houses have steps and an elevator but that's all I noticed at first visit.

We sat in the lounge, looking down on the valley through the huge picture window.

"What you need to do," he said, "is set a definite date and fuck him. It's the only way. He's ready for it, God knows. I saw the looks he was giving you the other evening."

"Was he?"

"Too right he was. He can't wait. Why should you?"

"Patience is a virtue," I replied.

"So's chastity but you've thrown that one overboard. If I were you, I'd get my cock up his tight little ass as soon as possible."

It was amusing really. There was I, regularly obliged by Steve and Gerry and there was Mike who never even got a whiff a boy and contented himself with talking about them.

"What business are you in, Mike?" I had to interrupt him to get the question in. He'd started at Martin's blond head and got as far as his knees.

"I'm in export," he said.

"What do you export?"

"Oh, various things. Have you noticed the curve of Martin's calf muscles?"

I had of course. In fact there were very few curves on that boy which I hadn't contemplated with pleasure and dreamed about afterwards.

"He's the most perfect boy I've ever seen," he said. "It would be such a waste...."

I had not the slightest intention of letting Martin's talents go unappreciated but I had the advantage of a lot of experience and I wasn't going to rush my fences. Boys, as I am sure you will agree, need to be led along gently. It had taken a long time to persuade Gerry and Steve. Even so, they amused me. Gerry always said he hadn't got much time; a few minutes at most. Fortunately his conception of time was as elastic as his ass muscles. Both could be stretched provided one did it gently. Steve, on the other hand, was invariably 'not really in the mood' but changed his mind as soon as his cock was in my hand.

"All boys want it really," Mike continued.

"They most certainly don't," I replied. Like everybody else in this world I'd had my fair share of failures. I'd watched cocks swell under denim in the car as their owners told me about their gay acquaintances and agreed with me that there was nothing wrong with it. Then, as soon as my hand reached over, they changed their opinion dramatically.

Even Gerry had told me to keep my hands to myself on the first occasion. I had quite a struggle to get his fly open to bring it out into the open air. It was just as well I did. He shot his load seconds after I'd got my lips over his cock - head.

Steve was more amenable. He enjoyed looking at the magazines I'd shown him and even asked if I had any 'smut videos'. It was while we were watching the highly unlikely adventures of a young sailor that Steve said he had a friend like that and, within seconds of saying it, discovered that he had found another.

I knew somehow that Martin wasn't going to be as easy. Visual aids were not the way to his ass. Unbeknown to Mike I'd found that out already. Martin succumbed, to a certain extent only, to flattery. He'd been happy to strip off his shirt and show me his well developed chest and arms. I remarked upon

his underarm hair. It was blond like that on his head and remarkably long. When his arms were at his sides, it poked out in front and looked as if he had a couple of brushes secreted in his arm - pits.

"My mum said my dad was the same," he said.

"I'll bet you've got a lot somewhere else too, eh?" I said. He blushed slightly but didn't answer. He wasn't very keen on showing off his legs but, after a lot of persuasion, pulled his jeans down to his ankles and stood in front of me like someone in fetters. I said I had never seen such strong legs on a boy of his age. He modestly agreed that they were pretty strong and said that he was keen on swimming. I said he had a powerful butt too and put my hand on his boxers. Soft flesh suddenly went as tight as a drum. He got dressed again pretty rapidly and we spent the rest of that afternoon talking about air rifles.

I was rather enjoying these private thoughts and Mike seemed to have an unlimited supply of Bourbon. There must be more money in the export business than there is in real estate, I thought.

"That's what you ought to do," he said. "Set a date, invite him round, get his clothes off and screw him."

"You make it all sound delightfully easy," I said, looking down on the valley. "There are quite a number of boys down there who would accept an invitation to call but precious few who would go along with anything else."

He chuckled. "I don't give them a chance to say 'No'," he said.

"And how do you manage that?"

He got up out of his chair and went to the drinks cabinet. I thought he was going to pour himself another drink. He'd already had far more than I could handle. He took out a little cylindrical plastic box, took off the top and emptied the contents into his hand.

"These," he said.

They were little yellow tablets, tiny little things.

"One of those in a Coke knocks a kid right out in less than ten minutes," he said. "It's quite funny to watch. A boy sits here, often in the chair you're in. He sips his drink, tells me all about his girl friend and before he knows what's happened the glass is on the floor and he's out like a light.

"And then?" I tried not to smile.

"Bundle him in the elevator, take him upstairs and give him a bath."

"Why? I'd rather smell boy than bath soap any day."

"Not with these you wouldn't. I pick 'em up in the Corrall."

The 'Corrall' is the town eyesore. Old man Bateman when he was alive did all he could to have the tin shacks knocked down and the inhabitants rehoused. Since his death the Corrall had gotten even bigger, populated in the main by illegal immigrants from over the border. It was definitely a no go area. The thought of a well heeled guy like Mike even driving through the Corrall in his smart car and coming out unscathed was comical enough. Actually picking up one of the filthy, shabbily dressed teenagers who lived there, bringing him back to the Bateman house and still be in possession of one's wallet was ludicrous.

"I imagine it's quite difficult to undress a boy and give him a bath if he's unconscious," I said. I began to think that Mike was an over - imaginative psychopath.

"Put your drink down and come with me," he said. We went up in the elevator, along the landing and into the bathroom. The bath was not the sort of tub that most people had. It was more like a miniature swimming pool set onto the floor with a wide marble surround. Over it, projecting from the wall was what I can only describe as a miniature crane or derrick. You'd have taken it for a gallows had it not been for the fact that the cord terminated in two, leather padded nooses instead of just one. It had obviously been installed to lift old man Bateman from his wheelchair and into the bath. Mike took the hand control to give me a demonstration.

"Get his clothes off, get the loops under his arms, press the button and up he goes," he said. "Press the other button to swing him over the tub. Easy as that. Then he gets the first really good scrub and soak in his life. You should see the water afterwards. It's like soup!"

"I can imagine," I said, and thought 'so can you'. We went downstairs again. He helped himself to yet another drink.

"Nicest sight in the world," he said.

"What is?"

"A kid hanging, dripping wet with his cock and balls

dangling in front of you."

"And presumably so unconscious that he's unable to get a hard on," I said. "Doesn't that rather dampen things?"

"Some can. It's surprising. But their asses! Sheer paradise! Slap one and it's like smacking a jelly. You don't need any lubricant. They're so relaxed."

"It must be rather difficult to screw a boy who is suspended on the end of a rope, surely?" I said.

"I take him into the bedroom for that. Lay him on the bed, open his long brown legs and hey presto I'm in! Beautiful!"

"And afterwards," I said. "When it's all over? You dress him again and drive him back to the Corrall. He wakes up again with a sore ass and goes back to Mummy."

"Who said anything about them going home?" said Mike.

I began to feel that this little fantasy had gone on long enough. Certainly the image of a boy dangling in the bathroom had been a turn on but then, so were the highly imaginative stories in some of my magazines and video tapes. I didn't believe a word of them either.

"So what do you do with them?" I asked, despite myself.

"I told you I was in export, right?"

"Right."

"Well, in a certain Gulf country there are three of four princes who enjoy a nice soft Mexican butt and a Catholic cock. I ring my contact in the embassy when I've got one. They collect him, and a few days later Jose becomes Faisal with a passport to prove it and on the next plane out."

By this time I really had had enough. It was getting late anyway and I had to be at the office early in the morning. It was, as I said, okay for rich exporters of boys to stay up late; not for junior partners in a real estate firm. He offered to drive me home but he'd drunk far too much. So, for that matter, had I. I almost fell over on the ramp by the front door.

I had a pleasant stroll home, thinking with amusement of all I'd seen and heard. The bathroom winch intrigued me. One could have a lot of fun with a thing like that. I determined to look them up in a catalogue in the office. With pleasant thoughts of Steve or Gerry, suspended but fully conscious and smiling happily, I opened the front door. A piece of paper had been stuck between it and the door-post. It had been torn out

of a school notebook.

"I came to see you but you were out. Martin."

I went to bed thinking what a nice kid he was. Leaving a note was thoughtful. None of the others would have done that but then none of the others had Martin's concern for other people. To Steve and Gerry I was just an eccentric who helped them get good scores, provided occasional snacks and drinks and who helped them get their rocks off. It would do them good to be suspended above a huge bathtub, lowered into the foamy water, washed lovingly, raised again. Steve's cock, thick and a bit stubby projecting out of his dense clump of pubic hair... Gerry's much longer and more aesthetically pleasing member, stiff as marble and already weeping the first drips. One after the other... Steve first, then Gerry.

"Aren't you going to let us down again?" That would be Steve.

"Not yet. Game's not the only thing that improves by hanging. When you're ready I'm going to fuck your asses. Let me see. Who will be first?"

Swinging them round, feeling the soft flesh of their butts. Steve was bigger than Gerry. More powerful too. He had a grip like a vise. Gerry was softer, slightly easier to get into and infinitely more active when you'd achieved it....

The inevitable happened. I wiped myself dry and went to sleep dreaming about Arab princes who lived in pyramid shaped apartments with picture windows.

Saturday came round. I did the usual shopping, Elsie showed up to do the weekly cleaning. I shut myself in my studio to escape the din of the vacuum cleaner and her dreadful whistling. The phone rang. It was Gerry.

"I shan't be able to come round this afternoon," he said.

"Oh! That's disappointing. Why not?"

"Various reasons."

"What about this evening?"

"Not really, no. I may see next Saturday."

It was on the tip of my tongue to suggest Sunday but that was Steve's day. It would be just my luck if Steve cancelled and Gerry could have made it. Kids! If only they realised how much I looked forward to these sessions. I was really disappointed and am sorry to say that poor Elsie got the brunt of my bad

temper.

Sunday. The morning free. Mike rang to ask if I would care to come round. I said I was busy.

"With Steve?" he asked.

"Maybe. I don't know yet."

"It's Martin you should be after but have a good time."

Two o'clock. Steve was due at two - thirty. I got ready. A towel on the bed; rubbers and cream in the drawer. I was as horny as hell. I usually am but it was worse that day. Gerry's non appearance I guess.

Two thirty. Two forty - five. No Steve. Three o'clock. They were all the same. On Tuesday at the rifle club he'd say 'Sorry about Sunday' and make some feeble excuse and I would have to say 'That's okay'. But it wasn't okay. It was thoughtless, inconsiderate and almost rude. It might even be worth while to buy one of those winches and a stick; one of those whippy canes. 'This is to teach you to keep appointments. Hoist Gerry up first... Running my hand over his butt; feeling the smooth skin tighten in anticipation. Standing back to take aim. Hearing the cane swish through the air and land with a thwack. That would teach him! He'd whimper a bit at first. By the time the third stroke had landed he'd be crying out, pleading with me to stop and promising to keep appointments in future. And Steve? Steve would be snivelling in fright waiting for his turn. I had never thought about things like that before. Amazingly, the more I did so, the more I was being turned on. I lay on the sofa, reached down to undo my belt - and the door bell rang.

Doing myself up as quickly as I could and trying desperately to hide the evidence of my strange daydreams, I went to the door.

"Sorry I'm late," said Steve. "I had to wait for Martin."

There they were. Both of them. Steve tall and smiling and Martin standing beside him.

"Oh.. er.. come on in."

For sheer idiocy, I thought as I went into the kitchen to get drinks for them, Steve took some beating. There may have been some good reason for bringing Martin. In fairness I didn't know the full story. The chances were that they had met accidentally. Martin would have asked Steve where he was going. Steve would have told him. Martin probably insisted on coming too

and there was no way Steve could tell him not to. That would have made the kid suspicious. It was annoying, but at least I had company. Spending a weekend alone is not my idea of fun.

"How's the shooting going, Martin?" I asked, handing him a Coke.

"Oh, okay. I did okay the other day."

"Good."

There was a period of silence.

"Dating already I guess."

Steve laughed. "I wouldn't have brought him with me if he was, would I?" he said.

Surely not. He couldn't mean that, or could he? "What's that supposed to mean?"

"I thought we could all three have a bit of fun."

"You mean...?" He nodded.

"And what does Martin think of the idea?"

"I don't mind," said Martin. "It's something to do, isn't it?"

I'd often wondered how much, if anything, Steve or Gerry said to the others. It was pretty obvious that Martin, at least, knew everything. A worrying thought at any other time but I would have given Steve a medal if I'd had one to hand. I didn't but I had something else. Just one look at the ripe bulge in Martin's jeans was enough. I sat next to him on the sofa.

He actually opened his legs a bit to let me have access to it; a thing Steve never did. I suppose I must have fumbled a bit. "Let me," he said. He fished inside his fly and the most delectable cock I'd seen in years sprung out. It wasn't huge. I'd give it about five and a half inches in length and about an inch in diameter. He sighed softly as I put my fingers round it and gently retracted the skin. There is something about a boy's cock which they seem to lose at about the age of eighteen. They seem, somehow, to look eager and have a delightful scent which sends me into ecstasies.

"Let's have a look at yours," he said.

"We might as well all get stripped off," said Steve. There is no romance in that lad at all. My clothes came off in double quick time. Steve attended to himself and then we both set to work on Martin. As far as I recall, all Martin did was to take off his trainers and his socks. He giggled as his tee shirt, jeans and boxers were peeled off and lay, still giggling looking up at us.

I'd been right about his bush. It was slightly darker than his underarm hair but so dense that it looked like a bundle of brass scrubbing wool stuck on to him.

"You've got a big one," he said; a compliment entirely undeserved. Mine, if the truth is told, is very little bigger than his.

"You going to suck him or shall I?" asked Steve, manipulating his own rigid cock.

"Both," I said. "You go first."

He knelt on the floor beside the sofa and got down to work. I contented myself by stroking up and down in his furrow whilst his head moved up and down and Martin, eyes closed and mouth open, began to gasp.

"My turn," I said as gasping turned to panting. Reluctantly, he gave way and I took his place. It had been a long time since I'd had a boy like Martin. I licked his balls, lapped in and out of his bush and then set to work on the hard shaft. Unlike Gerry on his first occasion, Martin took a long time but he didn't mind waiting to shoot to load. On the contrary, he enjoyed every moment. He was wriggling around and gasping like a steam locomotive on a hill. I could feel Steve's fingers playing on my back as I took as much cock as possible in to savour its taste and relish in its hardness.

"I'm... I'm...." he panted and pushed himself upwards. My mouth filled with warm, sticky sweetness. Carefully, I let it go, stood upright and swallowed.

"Good eh?" said Steve.

"Sure is," I said, wondering how many of Martin's ejaculations had ended up in his gullet.

"You going to fuck Steve now?" asked Martin.

"If Steve agrees. Unless you..."

"He can't do that yet," said Steve. "Gerry tried yesterday and couldn't get it in."

So that was why Gerry had cancelled his appointment with me! I could hardly blame him. Faced with being screwed or having access to Martin's ass I know what I would have chosen.

We went into the bedroom. Steve got in his usual position, on his back with his legs in the air. Martin watched with the intentness of a medical student. I managed to insinuate a well greased finger and Steve's sphincter tightened on to it. He

moaned.

"Can I try that?" asked Martin. For a moment I thought he was volunteering his cherry. Sadly, it was only his finger. He dipped his ginger into the pot and I showed him how to go about it.

"Like this?" he asked.

"That's it. Push a bit harder. Feel it?"

"Oh yeah. Gee, it feels warm in there!"

"Nice eh?"

"Yeah."

"Now push a bit more. Let him feel all of it."

Steve writhed and arched upwards. "Now try two fingers together. Make sure they're well greased," I advised.

Martin was a quick learner and I was enjoying my role as teacher. Slowly, Steve's usual inhibitions vanished. His cock stood upright and the head gleamed with dampness.

"Is he ready?" asked Martin.

"Yeah!" Steve gasped.

I got into position with his legs on my shoulders. For a moment I forgot Martin. Steve's soft lining enveloped my cock. His muscle ring gripped it tightly. He groaned again. Then, to my surprise, Martin climbed up onto the bed, knelt down and took Steve's cock in his mouth. That really turned Steve on. I've never experienced anything like it. He's always good. That time he was superb. He was actually shoving his crotch against me, desperately trying to get as much as possible inside him. It was incredible. I had no doubt at all as to the moment of his coming. I felt him squeeze my cock in a sudden spasm and semen streamed down from Martin's lips into Steve's bush and onto his thighs.

I came a few seconds later. Steve and I were panting. Martin was retching slightly and the smell of semen seemed to fill the room.

"I don't like the taste much," said Martin.

"It's acquired," I said. "You'll like it better next time."

"Can I come next week too?" he asked.

Steve laughed. "You can come as often as you like," I said.

"I don't know what to tell my mum," he said, doubtfully.

"Tell her it's a shooting club meeting," said Steve.

"And tell her you're an ace shot," I added, licking my lips.

"And not a bad target either," said Steve, stroking Martin's neat little butt reflectively. "There are at least two people who want to shoot into it."

Just four days later, on Thursday, June 19th, Martin disappeared. He was last seen at school, as happy and carefree as ever according to his teachers and classmates. Nobody saw him get on the school bus. He was never seen again. The police were thorough. They even came to see me. I said he had been round to my place once or twice to talk about shooting. That satisfied them.

They never visited Mike. There was no reason for them to do so. He left town some months later. His story to me was that one of the princes had taken a fancy to white skins and had asked him to move to Europe.

My firm got the job of selling the Bateman house which wasn't easy. The only people interested were an elderly couple from California.

"You may want to keep this or have it dismantled," I said, showing them the winch. "It was used to lower Mr. Bateman into the bath from his wheelchair. It operates like this." I pressed the button, the winch swung out and the cords descended. That's when I saw it. Caught in the stitching of the leather padding was a tuft of golden hair.

A LONG HARDNESS

John Patrick

He straddled my legs and began to massage the large bulge in my jockstrap. I felt at once enraged, rebellious, hurt, but, finally, coddled – and hard. Jerry whispered that he was going to make me feel *very good*, then started to rub his face all over my cock and between my thighs. Then he eased himself farther down the lockerroom bench so that his face was directly over my quivering cock. Then he nuzzled the sweat-soaked cotton of my bleached-white jockstrap and asked me if any of my girlfriends had ever sucked my cock before.

"Almost. Last summer, this girl who was working here as a counselor started blowin' me in the equipment shack, but some idiot kid came in right when she was about to start sucking on my rod, and then she was too freaked to ever try it again."

"Well, now it's *this* summer, and *I* am the counselor, and here we are, and we won't be disturbed."

I stopped resisting. This was going to be interesting, I told myself. I'd been here four weeks and it took Jerry that long to get around to it. I'd given him all kinds of opportunities because, somehow, I just knew he wanted it. And, somehow, he knew I wanted it.

Now he promised, "I'm gonna give you a blowjob you'll never forget." He gingerly peeled my jockstrap back with his teeth, pulled his body back and nestled his face against my swollen cockhead. Then he slowly drew his tongue up the shaft and around, carefully covering every millimeter of my nine-inch boymeat. Then he went down lower and sucked on each of my balls, and, as he did, the rest of the dick balanced against his cheek, bouncing against his face like in the pictures of the cocksucking cunts in my dad's girlie mags I had so often used when I jacked off. He drew the tip of his tongue up along the bottom of my cock until he was at the head, on which he placed a sweet little kiss which made me want to face-fuck him; naturally, I refrained. He slid his lips around the head of my cock so excruciatingly slowly that I had to restrain my hips from thrusting into him.

"Man, what a big, hard dick you have, baby! You're bigger than most grown men. I bet you'd like to stick that big dick in my hot mouth, now wouldn't you?" he asked.

Well, I would, yes. I wondered briefly whether silence or a response would make him continue, and opted for the former: "Yeah, I guess."

"You want me to take your big prick down my throat? Is that right?"

"Yeah."

With that, he took the entire head in his mouth, drew the air from within his cheeks, and swirled his tongue around it while he began to suck. I wanted to slam my whole shaft down his throat – hard – but he held me down.

Nothing in my young life had prepared me for his deep-throat artistry: he grazed the top of my cockhead with his teeth before suddenly swallowing all of it down his throat. He closed his eyes as he had me there, all the way to the balls, and he had me moaning like crazy every time he wrung it with his lips. Holding back was excruciating, but I wanted to enjoy this as long as I could. He looked up at me, measured my need, and smiled as if he owned me. He then went back to his sucking. He started moaning, and smiling, all the while holding me down with the slightest pressure from his index fingers. He allowed my cock to slide slowly out of his mouth, and smiled down at me as he began to mount me, like an equestrian, with me as his steed. He pushed my legs together so that the shaft stood straight up. Pre-cum oozed all over the head, mixing with his saliva. As he straddled me, he lightly grazed the head of my cock back and forth with the lips of his ass. Then he moved up to my face and I spread his ass, so that I could see the inside of the man-pussy I wasn't fucking. His ass was pink and smooth on the outside, and a deeper rose color on the inside, which was coated with a slickness. I stuck a finger in and he groaned. While continuing to give me a blowjob, he began contracting the walls of his ass for my benefit – alternating a slow, thick, cock-sucking motion with more rapid, squeezing movements.

"You want to fuck that, don't you, stud-boy?"

"Oh, yeah," I replied, a bit too hastily I feared.

This turned him on even more and he quickly mounted me, hovering over my cock, which was so hard I could have fucked

through steel. He lifted himself back so that his ass was arched above my tortured cock. He took my cock in one hand and smiled as he slowly swallowed my whole cockhead inside him, and though I quivered with the intensity of the scene, I was reluctant even then to give myself over completely to my desire. Then, in the same way he took the whole of my cock down his throat, he slid down my shaft until – amazingly – it disappeared completely inside him. He closed his eyes and moaned deeply, and I put my hands on his smooth hips, started thrusting, and finally eased into the act as if I'd been doing it for years.

I could hold back no longer. He took all I had, as blast after blast of my pent-up cum found a home deep inside him.

But he wasn't finished. He got on his hands and knees, and soon I was told to start thrusting my cock into his tight ass. My dick had only been semi-hard when I entered him, but he reached back and spread his ass open for me and I was fully hard by the time I was all the way in him again. I grabbed his hips like they were handles and plowed his ass like a jackhammer. I kicked his legs apart, mounted him, and held his body down with my weight, while I pinched his nipples with one hand. I grabbed both his thin wrists in the other while I tore into his tight ass.

All at once, his ass became thick around my dick. I released my hold on his wrists and he reached forward, grabbed my sweaty jockstrap, began biting on it; his body heaved up in jerky movements underneath me. I reached down to feel the stickiness on his cock.

But I was far from done with him. I turned him over while I was still inside him, put his ankles on my shoulders, and regained the momentum of seconds before. I grunted with every hard thrust into him. He received me with his entire body; his hips tilted upward, his legs wrapped around my back, and he sucked my dick tight inside his ass until we were both dripping with sweat and our bodies were sliding across one another. Finally, my cock swelled until it blasted once again inside him. He took a deep breath, threw his head back, and I felt his ass start to vibrate with another orgasm. I took his prick in my hand and brought him off.

"What a stud-boy you are," he said.

I pulled out of him and caressed his thighs. "That was great."

He smiled. "Let's take a shower," he said, scrambling to his feet.

He couldn't keep his hands off me. He spread my legs and he parted his lips. I pushed his head to my cock, wet and sore from the fucking. He exhaled, closed his eyes, and sucked me like it was all he needed to survive. "Ohhh...what a cocksucker you are," I said as I stroked his hair and arched my back for him.

The hot water pelting my body, I eased into a peace in my submission. The muscles in my legs strained with the urge to come again, but held back. For several moments I stood lost in the rush of water and forbidden teeange lust that poured down on my nakedness.

Suddenly I heard someone come into the locker room and I was overcome with the shame of what we must have looked like, the shame of having my body taken like this, of its willingness and pleasure. Jerry pulled off and stood. He stepped away from me, not touching me for the first time, and I missed his touch. I knew that his touch, no matter how unaccustomed I might be to it, was what I wanted, what I had been seeking. He knew it too.

We stood motionless, speechless. We heard someone pissing, then flush. There were footsteps then the slam of the door.

Jerry chuckled, tugged at my now limp dick. "Tomorrow night," he said.

I gulped. Tomorrow was the final day, the big picnic dinner on the water's edge. I had no idea what he had in mind, but I was game.

"Okay," I said, as he released my cock.

. . .

I watched with appreciation as his sinewy body prowled past the bonfire, those eyes practically glaring at me above the licking flames. Then he turned away and I swallowed hard as I eyed the place where the swimsuit hugged his ass, leaving little to the imagination. My imagination was running wild. I

could practically feel my cock up his ass, and as he disappeared in the shadows, I forgot all about the picnic and felt compelled to follow the counselor. Once inside the lean-to that served as our sleeping quarters, my eyes had to adjust to the dark. My pulse quickened as Jerry beckoned me with his hands. The farther I crept back into the cramped space, back to where he slept, behind a flimsy privacy curtain, the more aware I became of my own fear. What was I doing, after all? Common sense began to filter in, and I told myself to turn back and rejoin the others. What if we were disturbed once again?

But he groped me, found me semi-hard. What was I doing? I asked myself again, but I damn well knew *exactly* what I was doing. I wanted his touch again. A hard body was pressing against me, causing a quick intake of breath before I steadied myself, standing perfectly still, prepared for anything. Warm breath tickled my ear before cool lips found my neck. Light, lingering kisses followed by nibbles that turned quickly into biting and sucking. This was too much! I should have pulled away, but I couldn't. I was too overwhelmed by the sensations that enveloped me, and the secluded safety that I knew the darkness held. His sure hands circled my waist, tugged at my swimsuit. Those fingers showed no mercy as they found my cock, their touch anything but gentle as a groan was forced from my throat and my knees began to buckle. Smoothly, he was reaching down, stroking my dick. His other hand caressed me everywhere, intoxicating me, drowning me.

As he sank to his knees and began licking my cock, I was consumed by a sudden, breathless longing. Never, never had I felt like this before. I wanted to look into his eyes, but the darkness hid his features. My hands caressed his back, stroked his hair, and I pulled him tight against me. He gave a small murmur of pleasure and deep-throated me.

Before long the top of my head was lifting off. Between my legs the throbbing became an unbearable, joyous agony. Fireworks blazed behind my eyes as my body erupted, and I slammed my cock deep down his throat. To him I gave it all, or at least, what I thought was all. But he wouldn't let up on my cock. He just kept sucking. I wanted to fuck his hot ass, the way I had the day before, but I knew that was impossible. The other guys would be back soon. Too soon. But the thought of

how sweet that ass was got me going again.

I yielded to the insistent mouth sucking me, surrendered to the strong hands pawing at me.

"Oh, Jerry," I whimpered.

As his lips and tongue enveloped my cock and worked it strongly, I yanked at his hair so hard I know it must have hurt him and brought tears to his eyes. I uttered a strangled scream, then started to shudder. He paused, but didn't let go. I tried to speak, but couldn't get words out. I held his head there another minute until I had finished coming. Then I released him and he rose to take me in his arms. I clung to him, pulling his face down to mine and kissing my own cum from his lips.

. . .

Even with the rush of the new semester and football practice, I couldn't get the memories of summer camp and Jerry out of my mind. Nearly every night I would jack off remembering what a great cocksucker he was, and how tight his ass was that one time I had it. It was our own secret, of course, I could never tell anyone. But I wanted to, I wanted to talk to someone, anyone, about it.

And then Jerry wrote. He was at the University and hated his roommate. In fact, he pretty much hated everything at the school. He longed to get away, if just for a weekend. But how could we work it? It was then I noticed a bulletin tacked up in the lockerroom about a famous coach who had retired and written his memoirs. He would be speaking at Jerry's university. I could go for the show – and stay overnight for the fun! And my dad would pay for all of it! Of course Jerry was delighted. He wrote back saying he had already bought the tickets and reserved a room, in dad's name, at the Motel 6.

Jerry was standing near the main gate when the Greyhound pulled into the station. He was even more beautiful than I had remembered. I had jacked off to his image every day since we parted, and I was delighted when he said there was time to stop at the motel and get "freshened up."

Jerry sat on the edge of creaking bed and reached out for me as I came out of the bathroom. He was naked, and he had an

erection. He stroked his cock, which was as long as mine but not as thick. It had a funny curve upward when it was really hard. I stood before Jerry as he began to make love to my cock once again. His sucking was a expert as ever, and I was loving every minute of it. I let him maneuver me onto the bed, and he got down next to me with his head in my crotch. As he returned to sucking my cock, I encircled his hardening cock with my hands and began stroking him. Before long, I brought the head to my lips, and a savage heat seemed to enter the skin. And my mouth was everywhere at once. I was feeling a strange, familiar, exciting, new touch on my lips, parting them. I was touching another cock for the first time, so different and so similar to my own. The cock filled with pumping blood. I was no match for Jerry, but I sucked as best I could.

Jerry seemed to enjoy what was happening, but he could not hold back his amazement. He pulled his mouth off my cock and stroked my erection, wtaching intently while his cock slid between my lips and into my mouth. Something shattered inside me.

"You really want it? You *really* want it?" he growled, his voice breaking and crashing into its lower register.

With one glance up into his sparkling blue eyes, I told him everything I knew and everything I felt. I brought my hands to his ass and pushed, sending his cock all the way into my throat. I began sucking slowly and silently. I pressed my body against his and we gasped together, the pressure creating a mutual awareness of my transformation. I too had become a cocksucker.

But Jerry was the one who couldn't stand the suspense any longer. His hands pushed me away, saying he wanted me inside him. He dropped between my legs and began sucking me, preparing me. Leaving my cock sopping, he backed down on it. I cried out with the pain, with the intense pleasure of it, as his hips surged down and his ass swallowed me completely for the first time in so many weeks. I was swept upon a wave of incredible desire, pushing into him, feeling myself grow bigger and bigger, trying to reach his very center. I could not hold back; I came, and Jerry felt me coming and bucked up to press himself harder against me, and he jacked himself off.

. . .

I don't remember the coach's speech. I don't remember the food that followed, only being lost in Jerry's smile, the graceful movements of his hands as he picked at his meal. I could not remember being as thoroughly aroused since, well, since camp. As we left the banquet hall, he smiled a closed-mouth smile that was pure wickedness, and batted the long lashes of his twinkling eyes.

I was on new ground, and he knew it, and it was exhilarating. I wanted to suck him again the minute we got back into the motel room. He was wild, thrashing and surging under my mouth, and the moan that came out of his throat when my fingers grabbed his hips to push his cock all the way in was so loud it frightened me. I uttered a low growl of my own as I tasted his precum and moved my head back and forth, at first gently, then with increasing force. His fingers wound tightly, almost painfully, in my hair now as he held me hard against him. His breath was coming sharper and the moans had changed to small cries. I slowed my attack and began licking at him with long firm strokes that traveled from the tip of his cock to his balls. Then I began to suck on his balls mercilessly, stroking his cock as I did. As his cries grew more desperate, I realized this wasn't what I wanted. No, I wanted him in my ass.

A long hardness – Jerry's cock – was soon pressed against my buttocks. I felt his cock sliding, lubed and sheathed, in between my cheeks, rubbing against the sensitive skin. "Please, be careful," I begged, but my body was crying out for him to be as aggressive with me as I had been with him. I thought I might not be a very good cocksucker, but I did fuck him pretty good. He pressed his hands hard against my hips to still me. Slowly he spread my cheeks and I felt the head of his cock nudging against the one remaining entrance into my pleasure centers, clenching and releasing with fear and delight. I jerked backward and impaled myself upon him. He begged me not to come, to hold off so that I could fuck him. I let him come inside me, then he got on his hands and knees in the middle of the bed and I entered him. I was so horny I came almost immediately, but I kept my cock in him for a moment, hugging

him to me.

"Too long," he said in a voice that was almost a sob. "It's been too long."

Slowly I pulled out of his ass, then got one arm under his head and turned onto my back, pulling him after me. He put one arm across my stomach, pulled one knee up to rest against my thigh and lay his head against my still heaving chest. He was falling into sleep quickly, but, after kissing my nipples, managed to say, "We still have tomorrow."

He began to breathe deeply. I smiled a very satisfied smile, laid my cheek against his hair and said, "Many tomorrows. I promise you."

And I soon followed him into sleep.

NEW YORK AVENUE

In the soul of this city
lies a sinful view
Full of potholes and pity
and skies black and blue
The world isn't pretty
on New York Avenue

Boyish teens
lean boozing
outside of gay bars
Homeless toys for old men
cruising by in their cars
Back and forth, forth and back
They survey the merchandise
Wondering who is worth
their time of day,
risk of attack and price
Some noses are broken
Some front teeth are missing
Two huddle coking
One begins pissing
Another is toking
While two more are kissing
Then a comic starts joking
as the rest stand and listen
But their laughter is mute
and the jest is on who?
Life isn't cute
on New York Avenue...

- Daniel Robinson

HE HAD NO IDEA

It felt so good
The boy couldn't help
Putting his hands
Around the base of his cock
As the young man sucked.
He had no idea
He would squirm and sigh
When he decided to let
Himself be blown
For the first time.
Or that after he came
He would lay sprawled
In such pleasure,
For a few moments
He couldn't move
Or speak.

– *Antler*

Illustration on preceding page of Jim Darley and Greg Brookes courtesy Suntown Studios, London.

How desperate can you get?

HUSTLING THE BONE IN ATLANTIC CITY

A Novella by
THOM NICKELS

STARbooks Press
Sarasota, Florida

"Straight boy? Look, Cody Foster rolls over and holds his own legs in the air. I mean, I've fucked the gay ones, and they're whining, 'Oh, I just did legs, I just did this, it hurts.' I tell them to shut the fuck up. One guy whined the whole time about his legs. But Cody: Cute, nice butt, straight blond boy, no bitching, no nothing. We did it in two positions, and he's saying, 'Let's do a third.' And the director was saying, 'I think we've got enough.' And I'm like, 'Give it a rest, kid.'"
— Porn stud Dino DiMarco

I.

When I was seventeen I walked out on my family because my adopted Dad was always beating me and his wife, Joan, was always on my case.

Do I miss them? Sometimes, but it's not the kind of missing that makes me want to go back, though I did call them recently I'm shamed to say.

It was Christmas and my landlord wanted to kick me out because of unpaid rent. I told them I had a wife and two children and couldn't afford to be on the street. I called Joan after not speaking with her for ten years. I told her I was in a fix, that I needed money for rent and didn't want to be homeless at Christmas – even if I lived in Florida where the weather is warm. Joan turned the phone over to my brother William when I brought up the money question. William is the expert when it comes to money. He always knows how much people owe and what things cost, and who should get what.

"How much do you want?" he said, his voice colder than ice cubes.

"Two thousand in a cashier's check, if you don't mind."

"That's a lot of money."

Which was bull. Joan had over a million, not counting the stocks and bonds and the big farm in upstate New York. She spends more than that on her pet dogs.

"I'll pay it back in installments. I'll sign a contract," I told my brother. My brother likes promises in writing even though he said no way to the idea of a contract. Still, he said he felt sorry for my kids and didn't want them to be homeless at Christmas. "I'm doing it for them," he said. "Not you. If you had no children, I wouldn't be doing this. I'm doing it for your children. Get that?"

I asked him how he was doing but he didn't say much. "Gettin' closer to Mama's big bucks, heh?" I added. Maybe that was being a smart-ass. Maybe my approach should have been softer. He didn't like that comment. To change the subject I told him that my feet were still nice – the way he likes them – with

soft undersides, long toes and high arches. The kind he likes to suck on. I thought I'd get a laugh out of him but I felt him stiffen up, like he was remembering something good but turning it into something bad. Like he was trying not to remember all the times he tickled my feet.

    I left them right after high school graduation. I took a train into Philly and hopped a bus to Atlantic City. I didn't know where I was going or what I was doing. I only knew that homosexual men loved the way I looked. My body was pretty near perfect. In high school I played soccer and football and everything was tight. Girls loved me, begged me to take them out. They loved the way my hair fell over my forehead, the way my butt looked, snug and tight and boxy, my huge cock which was always ready. I was never without a girlfriend then and when I lost one there was always another one waiting to take her place.

    I'll tell you how I knew to go to Atlantic City. One time my fake parents took my brother and me there for two days. It was in my junior year in high school and we stayed at The Claridge. Joan always hated the ocean and she was unhappy being there so she took it out on us by doing a lot of complaining. My brother took after Joan so he didn't let himself get too excited about the ocean either. But Leo, my Dad, was feeling pretty good, and he talked about getting up at sunrise and walking the beach or going surf fishing.

    That first morning he took my brother and me for a walk on the beach. He was in a good mood because the ocean always put him in a good mood – we never had to worry about him yelling at us when he was near salt air or the sound of the waves. He was always happy and became a different sort of man.

    So we were walking on the beach counting all the dead horseshoe crabs and jellyfish when this man passed us. He looked like a professor because he was wearing small wire glasses. There was also a big box tied around his neck; it was filled with seashells and things from the ocean. When Dad said hello to him, he nodded back. My brother wasn't looking at the man at all but I was curious about his box and so strained my neck to sneak a peak. When I did, he tipped the box and

showed me what he'd collected. There were sea horses, shells and red slimy things I'd never seen before. Dad and my brother walked away as the professor told me what some of the things were. I was in my red bikini bathing suit with no shirt, a sight the professor must have kinda liked because he kept staring at my nipples. Then I saw him slide his eyes down to my navel and fixate on my crotch. He soon turned red and began to stutter. He also picked up one of the red slimy things and explained what it was as he rubbed his thumb over it in a caressing motion and then used his other hand to jerk it back and forth.

He told me if he kept doing this some sea fluid would come out even though the creature looked half dead.

When he said sea fluid I got hard and knew what he was hinting at. That's when I wished I was alone on the beach so he would take me somewhere and pretend that I was a slimy thing.

Miracle of miracles, he said: "If you want to learn more, come back and meet me under the boardwalk at noon." At that point my Dad was waving me on. I remember it was a beautiful morning with the sun reflecting off fishing boats on the horizon. I felt happy for the first time in my life knowing that a professor or whatever he was wanted to see me under the boardwalk and that there was a real life away from them.

All morning long I thought of the professor: even when Joan fixed breakfast I was distracted, so much so that she asked me what was I dreaming of, insisting that it wasn't like me to be so quiet. She was right. I was thinking of the professor and trying to keep my boner down. I imagined him stroking me...

When Dad said he wanted to take us to a Marine museum at eleven-thirty, I panicked because that would interfere with the meeting. I knew if I wanted to see the professor I'd have to run away for a while, so that's what I did, aware that when I returned Dad would beat me and Joan would give me the cold treatment.

Though it was a lot of work, I managed to get to the boardwalk at the appointed time. The professor was laying on a beach blanket in a big white hat and looking through his box of crustations. He had flip-flops on his feet, his legs whiter than Comet cleanser... not a hair on them at all, at least as far as I

could tell.

He pointed to a spot on the blanket where I should sit. Then he started talking about the history of shells. I was already hard, thinking of the way I'd seen him stroke the red thing. Of course, old people have this waiting period thing where they like to talk or ponder before doing what they really want to do, so I sat with my legs spread and leaned back against the pier so he'd have access to me whenever he decided it was time.

It didn't take too long, really – I guess because my boner was so obvious. He sat down alongside me and stretched out while flipping through a shell catalog. I was flat on my back and staring straight up through the cracks in the boardwalk, on top of which was a closed-off pier so we were alone for the most part. He talked about how things from North Africa could float all the way to Atlantic City and wind up on this beach. By now my boner was hurting and I was wishing he'd shut up when all of a sudden I felt his hand on it, squishing, squeezing, grabbing. I opened my eyes and saw him looking at it as if I had just floated in myself.

Then he started rubbing it the way he rubbed the red thing, using my pre-cum as a lubricant. I was afraid I'd cum so I crossed my feet and thought of Joan but before I knew it lots of warmth came flooding in. When I looked down, his mouth was on me as he yanked my bikini down around my ankles and tried to get the whole thing in his mouth, which he could not do. He'd stop every so often and look at me, then start up again, then do it again.

"You're one beautiful boy," he kept saying. "Where did you come from?"

I didn't know what he was talking about, so I just smiled. That's when I realized that my cock was a life support system to him, that he needed cock to survive. I thought: "If there's one of him, there must be more, and if my cock is such a prize, it would be a prize to many. I can make money this way." This was my first vision of hustling. It was like climbing a mountain and getting an answer.

In no time I was squirming like a worm and didn't care what kind of beating Leo gave me when I got back. I thought about how I wanted to spend the summer here and not go back with them. I was getting close to cumming when I noticed the black

inseam of a woman's bathing suit through the cracks of the boardwalk. It was a bird's eye view of the crack between a woman's legs...she was standing straight over us on the pier that we were under, up high that's true but I saw enough of her to focus on, her black bathing suit material seeped into her cunt crack – just the kind of prop I needed for a good blowjob.

I spasmed big time. When I looked up the professor's glasses were gooey and he had a dripping mustache. I thought of a shaving cream can exploding all over the place. I was embarrassed, thinking he'd be angry but he was smiling. He was even pumping me for more but I had to tell him to stop because I was feeling ticklish and couldn't take it anymore.

Then we stretched out for about half an hour, him talking about shells and how I should visit him if I ever came back alone.

He gave me a conch shell with twenty dollars in it and his business card, which read: Professor Siegfried Deusch, scientist. When I said good-bye to him I didn't expect to see him again.

Back at The Claridge, Dad and Mom were fit to be tied. Dad said he'd punish me when we got back home but he was not ruining his vacation by doing anything now. The rest of the vacation was spent touring the fishing docks by the bay and then going to a seafood house where another man, a fat man in a horse Derby hat, kept winking at me from across the room. At first I didn't know what he was doing. I thought he had an eye twitch but then I realized he was trying to get my attention. I twitched back but Mom noticed it and asked what was wrong with my eye. I said nothing, as the man, I swear it, made his way to the men's room. He tipped his hat at me, then nodded for me to follow into the quarter slot bathroom. He must have been crazy because there were all sorts of people crammed into that restaurant, families with babies, children, grandmothers, and there was a long line of traffic near the rest rooms – busboys with trays, waiters, cooks.

I didn't know what to do, though my boner kept saying "Do it!" The thought of more money made me want to take a chance. Just as I was about to stand up Dad got up himself and went into the bathroom. I kept looking for the man in the Derby hat to come out but he never did so I guess he met

somebody or decided to set up camp in one of the stalls.

When we got home, Dad beat me and confined me to the library where he gave me a book to read. Sometimes when he punished me he gave me a book to read and then later he'd give me a test on what I was supposed to read.

II.

When I returned to Atlantic City a year later, I looked for the professor but couldn't find him anywhere.

I went to the address listed on his card, a little red cabin three blocks from the beach, but no one was home. The thing is, I was in A.C. for just a day and was starting to feel scared because I didn't want to be alone. I knew that back home Dad and Joan had probably already sent out a searching party, so finding the professor was necessary. I even went to the boardwalk where we had sex but there was nothing. Then I thought that maybe he moved away or had taken a trip somewhere to collect shells. I was so stupid I even went to the seafood restaurant where I saw the fat man in the Derby hat, thinking maybe he was a regular and would be there again, but he wasn't anywhere in sight either. I went into the bathroom there and was surprised to see large holes between the stalls.

I spent the first day walking the boardwalk. I'd taken Dad's French sailor hat, one of my brother's fluffy pirate shirts, and fifty dollars from Dad's wallet. I figured if he can beat me, and if Joan has a million dollars, they could afford to lose a lousy fifty bucks, especially since I wasn't planning on coming home.

I ate lots of cotton candy and candied apples and looked for men who were looking at me. There were lots of them, especially near New York Avenue when I'd sit on the boardwalk facing the ocean. It was fun sitting there, smelling the ocean and watching the waves. I liked looking at the colorful striped beach tents people rented so they wouldn't get sunburn. I liked the idea of going into a tent and closing the door and being cozy in a dark space with the sound of the ocean in the air. I was hoping I'd see the professor among the tents; I always had one eye out for him even as I was looking for other men and looking at the girls.

A man came up to me out of nowhere. I didn't see him walking behind me or approach me from the side. He just appeared and started talking. "My name is James. Where are you from?" he said. He looked like he had had a hard life. It was also plain that he didn't take care of himself. He stood beside me with his hands in his pockets as the wind blew up parts of his hair that covered the bald spots.

"Nice day," he said.

"Yeah."

"But do you know that yesterday a boy drowned? He went out in the early morning before the lifeguards went on duty. Tide swept him out to sea, way out there by the fishing boats. Now the sharks have him or he's still floating – to Africa or China or wherever. What a beautiful way to die," he said, eyeing my crotch and licking his lips. The man was a creep but at least I was making human contact.

I didn't know why he was telling me that, especially since he said it like he was licking his chops after eating a steak. And there is no beautiful way to die, that's for sure.

"I love to swim in the ocean. I would not have gone out far if that had been me," I told him. "You have to respect the forces of nature." This was my father's learning coming through. It was one of the things he taught me that made sense and that I liked repeating.

"You wanna make some money?" Jim said.

When he smiled I saw brown spots on his teeth and gums and I didn't want to think of him sucking me. I don't know what happens to adults when they get old but all kinds of crazy things, like big moles or black teeth start creeping in. Compared to the professor, he was a worm, looking over his shoulder the whole time he was talking to me like he was afraid somebody was watching him. "Doing what?" I asked, not used to guys being so blunt but knowing what he wanted just the same.

"Suckin' your cock. Over there, under the boardwalk, or in the Fun House. Have you ever visited the Fun House?"

I'd been to the Fun House with Dad and Joan. It was full of mirrors, secret passageways, cobwebs, hanging gobblins, skeletons, witches, and recordings of wind storms. The Fun House was cheap looking, with lots of black velvet and barbed wire cased around not-so-scary dummies and headless corpses.

Leaving the Fun House was the scariest part. You had to climb up a rickety ladder and duck under this small tunnel, making you feel like you were burrowing beneath the ground. When you reached the opening at the end you came to a black conveyor belt that was really a moving sliding board which transported you 200 feet down towards the exit. The ride was soft and quiet. Finally you were able to see the light at the end of the tunnel and you were home free.

Jim wanted to take me in there because he said it was the only place he could get off. He said he was the assistant manager and it was his day in charge. All he had to do was open a closet behind one of the barbed wire skeletons and we could have sex behind the cobwebs. He said he would give me ten dollars and ten free tickets to the house in case I wanted to come back and ride the conveyor belt. He also said I could bring other tricks in there as long as I gave myself to him whenever he wanted me. But of all the things, the conveyor belt was the biggest thrill because it came after you climbed the ladder and crawled through the dark, tight tunnel. When you did this dark forms shot out from the walls and you got the feeling that the tunnel was closing in on you and you'd suffocate if you didn't get out of there fast. Some people were so afraid of the tunnel they turned around and left the way they came in.

I took the free ticket and handed it to the woman in the glass booth. She was a fat woman with red hair who looked at me over the tops of her glasses and smiled a toothless smile like she knew what was going on.

Jim said he'd be in the House behind the skeleton with chattering teeth. "It's the second skeleton you'll see. He's up high on a niche. Wait in front of him until you hear from me. I'll be behind the trap door. I know when people are coming but when the coast is clear, you'll see the skeleton cage move and they'll be a space for you to walk into. Just walk in there as fast as you can and don't say anything. Okay?"

"Sure," I said, wondering what I was getting into but terribly excited because the whole thing seemed so dangerous and cool.

I walked past the stuffed witches till I came to the Hall of Mirrors. There I was, all 1,000 versions of myself, taller than a

Beanstalk in some cases and fatter than a house in others. In one mirror my head was stretched up high while my body was normal; in another, my ears protruded straight out like Dumbo's. For fun I took my dick out and flashed it around to various mirrors until one magnified it 100 times. It was a whale with the slit on the head looking like a giant eye. I didn't hear anybody coming so I got it hard: it became a Good Year blimp, fat, long, the eye opening and closing as I jerked it back and forth. In a few seconds it was bigger than any of the mirrors could handle.

"Suck on that," I said out loud.

I heard somebody coming so I zipped it up, amazed that it went into my pants so easily. They were kids, a guy and a girl, necking. I slipped down the dark corridor, passing the first skeleton, a hanged man with rope draped over his bones. I felt my way down the corridor, the sound of rustling wind and a woman's screams bringing me to skeleton number No. 2 with the chattering teeth. He was strung up on a huge pole.

I waited there till I heard the knocks, then a red light went on and the skeleton cage moved. The whole thing moved around until I saw Jim inside a dimly lighted room. He waved me inside, pressed the button again, and the front began to close. Before I knew it I was in a control room lighted by a bare bulb, Cracker Jack boxes on the floor. Jim was in his underwear, sniffing something he held against his nose. He sat on a folding chair and said we had to hurry – the manager would be back in fifteen minutes. He asked how fast I could cum. I said real fast if he did it right. Then he stuck the bottle up to my nose and told me to inhale. I breathed in and felt my mind take off; it was like part of me was on the ceiling; I was coasting into space and running away from myself until at last it felt like I had no feet.

Before I knew it, my pants were down around my ankles and he was blowing me with his black teeth and sore gums. He was doing it real fast and he nicked me every now and then. Every so often he stopped to look at me and sniff from the bottle. He wasn't as good a sucker as the professor because he kept stopping to sniff the bottle and I like a steady pace that doesn't give up or take stupid breaks.

"Where'd the hell you come from?" he asked, which got me

thinking about the professor again.

Then he took a really strong whiff from the bottle and began sucking me like crazy. He was going a mile a minute, moaning but grabbing too tight until at last it hurt and didn't feel good at all. I was getting soft because the whole thing was turning me off when he dropped the bottle. Stupid fuck! It broke and within seconds the room flared up like sour socks and apples. With each breath I felt as if I didn't have any feet again as Crazyass Jim began to whip himself with my dick, telling me to piss on him, saying that he wanted to eat me outside and in. I didn't know what to do so I whipped it against his face. He said harder so I whipped it again until his cheeks turned red. I was so high I would have done anything he asked me to do, except kill him – I couldn't do that. I couldn't believe this could feel good to him but he got more and more excited until he was begging for more. "Punch me," he said. "Do it right. Let me have it."

Crazy-ass jerk.

The more he talked the more excited he became. He stopped sucking me and got on the floor saying he wanted me to jump on him. Everything became wilder and wilder.

"Tell me you're the beautiful boy swimming," he said. "Tell me how you stepped into the ocean at the crack of dawn, letting your bathing suit drop as you ran into the surf and dove over the breakers and headed out to sea. Let me see your body in the waves, your bare butt, the hole for sharks and my tongue."

I didn't know why he was talking about the dead boy, but it scared me. I didn't want to play a dead boy or pretend I was bait for sharks, no matter how beautiful he said I was. I didn't know what this had to do with sex. Anyway, I raced out of there without waiting to be paid. It was hard going out because the House was crowded. I dreaded crawling through the tunnel and waiting my turn at the conveyor belt. Lucky for me, no people were near the exit, so I was able to split, the whole time wondering whether the whole Fun House smelled like the bottle.

I raced across the boardwalk and headed to the beach where this crazy black woman in a sandwich board was walking in the surf. She had wild hair and yellow eyes. "Jesus is coming!"

she screamed, pointing to the horizon where I could see fishing boats and white sails. I sat by the surf, feeling the waves wash over my sneakers as I watched her pass. People ignored her. "Jesus is coming! Gather your boats and prepare for the launch!" she screamed again and again.

I hunched up like a crab to let her pass since she was walking close to me. "Crazy bitch," I said. She didn't say anything but made a wide angle and stepped way out in front of me. Then she looked at me with her yellow eyes. "Jesus is coming."

"Crazy bitch," I said again.

She didn't say anything but walked on by. I figured that she was probably used to insults and could just shrug them off. I didn't mean to be mean but what could I do? I was pissed. It was late and I hadn't made a dime. Where was I going to sleep? How was I going to eat?

Just then I had an urge to swim. The late day's sun was casting golden rays on the water and I wanted to go in there bad.

I took off my shirt and shoes and left them in a little pile on the sand. I walked into the surf while little kids played with buckets or flopped over small breakers. Everybody seemed happy and in a minute I lost my own worries and got into the feel of it, liking the splash of waves on my chest before diving into a roller and then coming out on the other side. In the deep area I floated on my back over more rollers. I had a good time until I began to think morbid thoughts of the boy who was lost at sea.

I wondered how he felt when he was drowning and what it would be like to die in the ocean, twirling around in currents and watching the shore get further and further away. Maybe it was like being thrown up into space, just you and all that emptiness.

I was thinking this when I spotted a figure on shore around my pile of clothes. The figure was male and was looking at me. I couldn't make him out because when you're in the ocean the distance seems further than it is when you're on shore. I let a big roller glide me in and then I had a much better view: it was the professor in a wide-brimmed hat, a shoulder bag and camera around his neck.

I did a stomach flop and let the breakers bring me in. Then I was on my feet sinking into the sand and taking forever to get to the beach when he gave me a wave.

He aimed his camera at me and took pictures as I walked on the hot sand.

"Fancy meeting you here. Are we alone?" Click, click. "Wow!" he said. There was another click of the camera.

"I've been looking for you. I went to your house, the address you gave me. A crazyass woman said Jesus was coming, are you Jesus?" I joked.

"Maybe," he said, then, "Where are you staying?"

"I have to find a place. Can I stay with you?"

"We'll talk about it. Are you hungry?"

I'd only had a cheeseburger and fries at a McDonald's and a slice of pizza on the boards but I was very hungry.

"We'll cook dinner at my place," he said, putting his camera away.

He brought me back to his little red house three blocks off the beach. The house was decorated with lots of paintings, books and good furniture. The kitchen was big, with many cabinets. He started cooking right away and didn't try to have sex with me, even though my boner was poking through my shorts. I was horny as hell and wanted to get off and then have dinner but for some reason he was taking the slow approach. He made steamed clams, corn-on-the cob, cucumber salad and sweet brown rice mixed with vegetables. He opened a bottle of white wine.

"Eat and drink up," he said, "don't be shy."

I ate everything, came back for seconds and thirds, and drank more wine than I should have. By the end of the meal I was buzzing but not in a sick way, just flying high. Sigfred then gave me a tour of his house, namely the upstairs which was filled with blue lamps and large statues of dead people. He lay down for a while in his brass bed, and then it was like the first time: his mouth all over me, kissing, squeezing, only this time he was doing more holding, clenching me to him and spending less time on my dick. I felt warm and tingly and glad to be with him in his house. I kissed him with passion and lost myself in something strange. It was the wine.

Later, he excited me with tales of the Canary Islands, Spain,

and the history of Atlantic City. I got hot from hearing his mind work. I wanted to fuck him but had to make do with straddling his chest and slipping into his mouth, where I came in no time. I wanted to come again but he said we better call it quits and go to sleep.

I thought maybe that's how it is when you get old, sex as a one-shot deal.

The next day I woke to the smell of fresh coffee and bacon smokin' up from the kitchen. That's what I miss now, special smells like that. Anyway, I went downstairs where I ate in jockey briefs, my long hair hanging over the plate and my feet in a pair of thongs Sigfred said he bought in a flea market. He talked about a bike ride to Wildwood Crest, so an hour later we were off, his Comet Cleanser legs getting burned as he peddled his bike like Elmer Fud. He looked stupid in the hat he was wearing but I couldn't tell him that because it was a good trip. He bought me lunch, blew me in a wooded area behind the sand dunes, and then bought me this cool dinner in a wharf restaurant where we could see the waves break on the beach. I couldn't believe my luck: he said I could stay with him as long as I let him teach me things, about shells, about art, about life. Mr. Wizard, I called him. He always had an answer for every question. In the Fall, he said I could find a job or consider going to school. I could live with him, he said, as long as I didn't turn into driftwood.

For a month we shacked up, you know, every day an adventure, fishing in the bay, eating clams, meeting his buddies, heading down to Philly or to New Hope for art auctions and flea markets.

Then one night relaxing on his brass bed looking at all the old paintings, I started to feel trapped. I felt so trapped I even had trouble breathing. It was the same feeling I felt at Leo and Joan's, the feeling of being in prison, of somebody shutting me out with a pillow over my face.

I needed to get out, walk the boards, meet new dudes. I liked his blowjobs and the food but hated how everything was becoming like a machine. It was no longer new. So I snuck out one day when he was off in Cape May on business. I wore the sailor hat and cut-offs and went to the extreme end of the

boardwalk, away from the stores and amusement piers.

I sat there till I saw, of all people, Fun House Jim. He was walking with a new boy, somebody he found on the beach. I know he was bringing him back to the House... I know he saw me looking at him but he turned his head the other way. Just like a crazyass coward. I guess he felt bad or something. He was wearing big sunglasses and a large hat, a creepy disguise. The boy was skinny with stooped shoulders and he walked with a limp. Jim was talking to him with his hands and pointing out to sea. I figured he was going on about the drowned boy and saying how beautiful it was--the shark butt hole thing and that craziness. Pretty soon they got lost in the crowds and I couldn't see them anymore. I know he was going to have the boy sniff the bottle and beat him with his dick. Maybe the boy would freak and go running out, but maybe not. Some boys like that kind of stuff, though this kid looked like a scared rabbit.

I took my shirt off and draped it over my shorts to feel the sun on my back, and tied my hair in a pony tail. I knew it was only a matter of time before the sun turned my hair blond... already I was getting a tan and looking pretty good. People were looking at me, especially girls. Sometimes if a girl was with her mother, her mother would look like she thought I was cute too. The people on the boards were boring, tourist families with small children, or lovers walking hand in hand, not many single men, homosexuals, who might want my body. Then again I don't always know when somebody is looking at me. Sometimes I get my signals crossed. Like the time this guy said hello to me while walking with his wife. Was he a bisexual?

I started following them, thinking that's what he wanted me to do, careful not to follow too close but pretending to hang around a soda stand whenever they stopped for a soda. When they went into Resorts International I had to follow close behind because there were too many people. I followed them for a good hour maybe, and when the husband went into the men's room I went in after him. I was at the sink washing up when he finished his business at the urinal and came up to me. I didn't know how he knew I was following him because I thought I was being careful.

He said, "You've been following my wife and me for over an

hour. Do you have a problem or shall I call the police?" He was a super-paranoid, anal dude, real square-cut, maybe a cop or somebody like my Dad.

I mumbled something about coincidence and said that nothing was wrong. Then I high-tailed it out of there and went back to the boards to do more waiting. I thought to myself, "Where are the fucking homosexuals?"

Then I spotted this red haired dude walking like he'd been on the boards for 10 years. He was a little older than myself, maybe 24, but he looked worn out. He had his own shirt tied around his waist and he was sunburnt to a crisp though he was turning tan around his face. When I looked at him closer I could tell right off that he was looking for homosexuals too. I said hello and right away he asked me where I was from. From that point, everything happened fast...it was as if we could read each other's minds. "Make any money?" he asked.

"A little." I told him about the professor but didn't go into detail. I also told him about the Fun House guy.

"Whipped dick in the face, huh?" he said.

We both laughed. He said he stayed with the Fun House guy the whole time, whipping his dick in the guy's face till it was swollen. He said he was made to tell the story of the drowned teenager, which got the guy off. "A cheap whacko!" Eric said.

Eric seemed kind of whacked too, like he'd done too many drugs or been thrown in jail too many times. He said he usually hustled in Philly, where the pigs are always arresting hustlers. He said there were no cops in AC who went after hustlers because the scene on the boards was too jammed – who could tell who was doing what? Everything was a big freak show. Still, hustlers have to hang somewhere, so it was usually by the old gay section, near New York Avenue. That's where he said I should go if I wanted to make money.

Eric was really whacked. The whole time we were talking he'd stop and stare at passing men, even those walking with women. He would say: "What's up?" He had trouble balancing and his body would wave back and forth. I knew I couldn't hang out with him long, even if he did show me a spot under the boardwalk where he slept and showered under a fresh water shower that used to be for bathers before the casinos came. It was a shower they forgot to take out...it still worked,

though the water was only a trickle. Other hustlers from Philly slept there when they weren't with tricks. Eric said they did it for protection and company. A few brought girlfriends there, drank beer, and shot up.

It was a cool place under the amusement pier and way out on the end of a jetty. The jetty was man made with rocks and logs and Eric's camp was on the tip, way out beyond the rollers where the ocean was deep.

Eric said I could sleep there but that I should watch my valuables. He said that some of the older hustlers sometimes came around and robbed the younger guys after they tricked. It was the same game they played in Philly, he said. The old ones knew homosexuals wanted young guys so they kept an eye out on newcomers and then stalked them until the time was right. Many left because they couldn't take being robbed all the time, or they found sugar daddies or regular contacts and didn't cruise the boards at all.

III.

"Want coffee?"

I opened my eyes and there was Eric, holding a paper cup. He looked like a faun or some kind of hurt animal, all hunched up like a crab with sand on his hands. There were bags under his eyes, but he looked happy. Happy he was: he said he had scored twice: a man who fucked him for $75 and another man who paid him $20 just to sniff his sneakers and tickle his feet on the ferris wheel.

He had a Danish pastry wrapped in wax paper that he was offering me. He'd already eaten half of it but I didn't mind. "Thanks dude," I said. Suddenly I didn't feel so lonely, though I knew the professor was probably looking for me, him as well as my bogus parents. I hoped the professor wasn't too mad. I intended to go back but I have to be me. When, I didn't know – sometime in the future is all I know. I needed sleeping by the ocean, waking up near seagulls, and seeing Eric's whacked face and sandy hands.

"How many times have you taken it up the ass?" I asked him.

Eric, defensive, tried putting on this macho act and started talking gibberish, but I knew it was his favorite thing, something he couldn't live without. I knew he'd do it even if he weren't paid for it. He was even walking funny, like the guy he had was too big or something, and I kind of thought that he was careless, you know, didn't care if somebody stuck their dick in there without a rubber. He just didn't care...he just wanted to get fucked and be done with it. He was too whacked out to care.

I knew I'd have to make some real money and stop screwing around, so I told myself I had to concentrate on making big scores. Eric said to hang around the Taj Mahal and I'd be okay. I just had to be patient. Homosexuals don't gamble like heterosexuals, he said. Anyway, Eric said he was taking the bus back to Philly to see his mother in Port Richmond, a trip he makes twice a month or so when he scores enough cash. When in Philly he heads to 17th and Pine Streets, even though he risks arrest every time he visits. The pigs know who he is...his red hair sticks out. They love to haul his ass into the paddy wagon. Eric's always comparing Philly to Nazi Germany. I guess he should know, he's been arrested enough.

I went to the Taj where I stood under the golden arch, propped on the rim of the boardwalk fence with my shirt off and wearing a pair of shades. It was so early I didn't know if the homosexuals would be walking around, but sure enough, there was a guy in a baseball hat who said he's been up all night dancing in the clubs. He just wanted to talk, so I let him pass.

I didn't meet anyone that day, but after that things kicked in. I was sleeping in Eric's camp every night, waking up to the sound of the ocean and then giving blowjobs all over the place. The money piled up but I had no place to hide it so I spent a lot. I gave some to Eric, who wasn't always so good at scoring. Eric was a fixture on the boards while I was new. Plus, word had gotten out that he had AIDS. I don't know whether he had AIDS but he was beginning to lose a lot of weight. I told him it was because he was getting fucked in the ass all the time and not caring whether the men wore a rubber. He only shrugged. "It's too late now, man! Who wants to live in this fucking

world anyway?" he'd rant. Some days he'd wake up coughing; other times he'd stay under the boards all day and not go anywhere. He was always complaining of being tired. I'd bring him things, sandwiches, sodas, coffee, piles of vitamins. He'd eat the sandwich and then I'd make him take the vitamins.

A Latino boy joined us whose name was Candido. He was from Philly and men liked him because he had a ten-inch dick. Candido was a thief but he stuck to small thefts like wallets, watches and rings. He did not carry a knife or gun and he was never violent. He always stole when a person was asleep or going to the bathroom. He thought he was hot because he had a beeper. The beeper was always going off. Gay white men from Philly were always calling him, guys stuck on Latino boys like some people are stuck on drugs. These white guys always had a hard-on for him. My dick was as big as Candido's but because he was Latino he was considered special. Maybe it's because he had a face like a girl's. It was pretty, though Candido was no sissy. Some guys wanted to have a relationship with him and put him up in their house like Sigfred wanted to do with me. Candido stayed with these guys only for a short while, then he said he had to go home and take care of his grandmother. But he always kept a door open so he could walk back into a person's life. He had several white men like this, each of whom thought they were the only ones, and he'd go from one to the other.

Because of this he wasn't under the boards very much. He'd work the boards when things got too suffocating, when the white man he was with started to watch his every move and treat him like a piece of property. Everybody wanted to own his cock. Then he'd slip out, saying his mother was dying of cancer or his grandmother had fallen off a stepladder. The white men had to let him go if they wanted him to come back. The sex was that good with him. He told me the white men said he tasted like walnuts.

But there were a couple of white men he worked this way, and after they got wind of his tricks they wanted to kill him. Or if not kill him at least teach him a lesson he'd never forget. He said he had at least three of these types looking for him, so he was careful when walking the boards to be on the lookout and

watch for suspicious characters. It was a foul way to live but he'd gotten used to it and didn't seem to mind. He lived on danger's edge.

A couple of times he brought boys he called his "cousins" to Eric's camp, all of them cute with big dicks but trained to lift wallets and watches. Whenever the boys stayed with us they would lure white men to our spot and then while they were having sex another cousin would pick through the man's clothes. It was always the same set up. If the man caught them in the act, the boys would scream that they were innocent children and threatened to call the police. When the white man heard this he usually forgot his stolen valuables and just got out of there as fast as he could.

The cousins had to split because they turned on each other, stealing money or food until there was a war with everybody acting like a crazyass. Candido said they'd have to learn how to be more "slippery," to do things "like a snake, real quiet and quick and not making a sound."

"It's all about self-control, amigos," he'd say. "Ever see a dude work a puppet? He has to know how to pull the strings. That's what you have to do."

Sometimes I thought that Candido's dick was a little bigger than mine. When he took a piss into the ocean it looked like a beer can. White men called him a sex machine because he was always hard. Even when pissing he'd get hard, standing there under the boards with his boner standing straight up in the air. He was always kidding me about sucking it but I told him I don't suck for free... I only get sucked. Plus, I knew if I tried anything with him (he asked me to fuck him once), that would give him an excuse to get slippery and start robbing me. Sex and robbery went together with him. He couldn't have sex without robbing someone. He knew I'd beat the hell out of him if he tried anything like that so he kept his distance, or at least he respected me some, which is more than he felt towards Eric.

He fucked Eric whenever he could, even when Eric was sick and sound asleep on his stomach. Candido, always horny, would take out his cock and yank down Eric's pants and just stick it in. Twenty or thirty thrusts and it would be all over. He loved fucking Eric this way; he loved a partner who was out-of-it or doing something non-sexual, like doing a crossword

puzzle. This turned him on. With Candido it was always: "How many times can I fuck Eric?" Eric would fight him off but it was not a real fight because I knew he wanted it. Eric liked the feel of Candido's big dick, and he loved the way Candido surprised him and just stuck it in his ass.

When Candido was finished fucking Eric, he'd zipper up and leave. He never used a condom, never, but always came inside him, once, twice, sometimes four times a day – this while taking two and three tricks a day on the side. Skinny Eric with his red hair and small white butt always made Candido want to fuck him.

One day Eric was really sick, vomiting and coughing and having big headaches. He was spread out on his stomach, running a fever when Candido came in from tricking. Candido talked to me, then saw Eric lying there. I could tell what he was going to do, even though I told him that Eric had thrown up all over himself. I thought this would turn him off but instead it had the opposite effect. Candido knelt over the boy, a crazy look on his face as he unbuckled his pants and yanked them below his knees. Candido then spit on his huge dick and rammed it in Eric in one take. Watching him fuck Eric turned me on even more than usual.

He humped like a gerbil or jackrabbit, going ten thousand miles a minute, his little melon ass bobbing up and down like kids bobbing for apples.

"It's you who should be fucked, dude," I thought, stroking my cock and thinking, "Well, what would it matter if I stood up and stuck it in him..."

So that's what I did, though the little bastard turned and told me to fuck off. But there was a look in his eye that told me he wasn't serious, that the fuck off was only a game, a macho thing. He was too pretty, this Candido, with long eyelashes and a girl's eyes, I just knew he'd take to being fucked. He just needed a trainer, that's all, someone to force the issue, to demand that he do it. Of course, the minute I was hard and began ramming it in his little behind, I knew I was a goner: he'd be after something of mine to take, anything, a shirt, a dollar bill, a shoe.

Candido couldn't have sex with anyone without taking something in exchange. But I didn't care. Watching that little

olive brown ass go up and down was just too much. In my head I heard the sound of flamingo guitars, and that game in Spain where people all run from the Bulls – sights and sounds were getting mixed up as I slid inside him, his rose-hole puckered tight and squirming like I was sticking him with needles and pins.

How tight he was is something I can't forget, and the hotness of it was like those tropical places where all the boys are like him, brown-skinned and rose-holed.

We humped, the three of us, like some snake or new strange animal crawling along the earth, and I didn't mind the jerks and slip-outs that sometimes happened. I was back inside him as soon as possible, fucking deep, listening to him whisper fuck off and then grunt like he was in heaven. After all, why should I care? It seemed that the sicker Eric got, the hornier Candido became.

Candido came first. When this happened, his asscheeks contracted like he had a motor in there and all I had to do was just lie quietly and let the motion of the contraction rotate my dick and bring it to my own peak, a gush of myself I emptied in him in what I swore was a quart of cream, my stuff in his little brown ass, no more virgin, that's for sure.

When we were finished, he got up and punched me in the nose, little bastard that he was. He socked me on the left cheek, grazing it, then landed square down so I thought that it was broken. But no, it was just bleeding, blood gushing out like I was Eric and on the beach dying, or a soldier wounded in war, and this runt, the same runt who rams it in Eric night and day and never takes no for an answer, all of a sudden he is real uptight about things. So I returned the compliment with a head-on pounder, knocking him over the sand till his little body went rolling towards the ocean.

"You pay for this!" he screamed.

I knew he was talking about his little cousins, the guys he'd pay to come get me, but I paid this no mind. Deep down I knew he liked what had happened and that he was fucking Eric in front of me all along just to get me to do something to him. I'd played the gentleman too long and finally got the message, but he still felt he had to play Pac Man.

"You loved it, man."

"Nobody fucks Candido without paying. You pay me $20," he said, sitting his ass down in the ocean and letting the waves lap up my cum.

"I'll give you something when I get something," I told him, wantin' to keep the peace because I don't like having to watch my back. That's one of the reasons I left home. "Just wait till I get my extra cash, and don't steal nothin' from me or you'll be sorry."

When Candido was finished being angry, he walked to the end of the pier, knelt down by the water and let the waves wash the rest of his cock.

Then he sat there looking out to sea while Eric went back to sleep again. It was a cloudy day and there weren't many people on the beach, but there were lots of seagulls swooping down all over the place so there must have been plenty of fish in the ocean. I think a storm was blowing out at sea. The waves were rough. I sat for a while not saying anything when I heard Eric make a noise. It wasn't a good noise. I was getting worried. He hadn't been up and walking around for two days or so. I was mad at Candido for just fucking him like that, and promised myself I'd stop him if he tried to do it again. I knew we'd be in for a fight because this was what turned Candido on the most, somebody who was defenseless and at his mercy.

IV.

On the boards, I met Tory, an Italian from South Philly who was down for the summer making money for his wife and daughter. I met Tory outside Taj. He was pacing real slow in front of the casino and checking his watch when he caught my eye. He nodded in my direction, then came over and asked if I was "working."

I said yes.

Tory could have any job he wanted because he's smart and he's been to school but says he can't take the bullshit in the work world. He told me Candido was shit, that he was out to find a rich daddy to manipulate so he could stay in this country.

"Illegal alien?" I asked.

"Illegal and a petty thief, maybe more dangerous than that. He gives us a bad name."

"He stays under the boards where I am. He has this guy Eric under his power. I don't know what he does to Eric when I'm not there. I don't want to know."

"Well, where I am is this weird place called Seaside House. Rooms are cheap. The manager gives me half off if I let him blow me once every two days. So that's what I do. He gives me the best suite. It's nice, it looks out over the water. Better than Philly, anyway. In Philly the cops are bustin' ass and lockin' everybody up. The police are on bikes and they come speedin' out of alleyways and up behind you before you know what's goin' on. Only cops here as far as I can tell are guards in the slot houses. Hey, maybe you should try Seaside House to live..."

"I can't leave Eric. I like the outdoors," I said. Tory looked at me as if something was wrong. "No, I really like being close to water. But I'll see. Meet any babes here?"

"Yeah, one. She does house cleaning at The Claridge. She cooks me dinner and packs me lunch – see..." Tory held up a brown paper bag with a wet bottom.

"Why is it wet?"

"She don't know enough to dry the lettuce before she puts it on the bread, so it soaks up everything. Sometimes the fucker

falls out and I have to get a pizza at Romagnoli's. Listen, you want to stop by Seaside House and see what I mean?"

I decided what the hell. He seemed like a regular guy.

As we walked off together, he pointed out all the things he said I should know about – like the fortune teller who picked his pocket after she jerked him off and read his palm.

We stopped at a liquor mart for beer, and then headed off the boards a couple blocks till we came to a big old house with a wide porch around it. It looked like something from the 1800s, with stained glass and fancy columns. It was pretty much rundown. The manager, Mr. Miller, was walking around the porch in his flipflops. He was older, chubby, and he had a bald head with hair around the sides like a circus clown.

"Is this the guy that sucks you?" I asked Tory.

He said "Uh Huh."

When Mr. Miller saw us he came over and said hello. Tory introduced me as his cousin from Philly...he said I was hustling and needed a room, and could we work up a deal like the one that he worked up with him, blowin' him and all.

I couldn't believe it. I'd just met the dude and here was Tory talking about blowin' dicks and special deals. I didn't like Mr. Miller at all. He didn't say anything but I just didn't like the way he looked. He gave me the creeps. I especially hated his thin wire glasses that blew up the whites of his eyes like giant white marbles. He looked like a fuckin' serial killer!

I forced a smile when we shook hands, and I waited for him to smile but he didn't. He looked me up and down and then frowned as if he saw something he didn't like. I hate when people do this. I didn't do nothin' to this man, and here he was, passing judgement on me like my father.

"How long you gonna be in A.C.?" he asked.

He had real knobby knees and gray hair on his legs. The end of his nose was sunburnt and there was a kind of scab on it that he kept scratching. His lips were real thin, like paper.

"The summer, maybe longer."

"You can't stay here. You need reservations to stay at Seaside House. Tory knows this – " Here he shot a mean look at Tory. "But...if Tory says it's okay, you can spend one or two nights with him, no more. His room has a double bed. Also, before you bed down tonight, I suggest you check with Tory

about our little philosophy."

After he said that, he waved his hand and said, "Have a nice day!"

Then, as we were getting ready to enter the house, he called Tory back in a whisper. I waited for them in the living room, which was very dark because the curtains were closed, though there was one guy on the sofa rubbing suntan lotion on his legs. In a minute, Tory was back. "Mr. Miller asked about your dick," he whispered." I said you had big meat, you do I hope..."

I said I did, but why did Mr. Miller want to know? I knew the answer myself but didn't want to believe it. Before I could say anything, Tory said, "I think he wants to suck you. Don't be surprised if you get a nudge in the middle of the night. That's, like, the little philosophy...if you don't do it, you're out on the street. You gonna do it? If you don't, don't come cryin' to me, dude. You have to put out."

We went upstairs to the best suite. It was at the end of a long hall with lots of other rooms on all sides. Since it was daylight, everybody was out swimming or playing the casinos.

"Back here," Tory said.

When we were around the corner, he started making fun of Mr. Miller. "Having sex with him is like having sex with Bozo the clown...especially when you grab both sides of his head, grab a hold of his hair, and ram your cock down his throat. He takes his teeth out before he sucks dick, which is a trip. He doesn't gag. That guy can breathe through his eyelids. I can thrust and move all I want and he feels nothing. Teeth take up so much room. If he blows you, tell him to take his teeth out...you're in for a ride when you do that..."

Tory unlocked the door and I saw the room. It was painted sky blue and had lots of white wicker furniture. Pictures on the wall were of old sea captains with white beards, big ships, mermaids, and ocean waves breaking over scared- as- shit surfers. Tory's stuff was in three duffle bags. The bed wasn't made. There were two bottles of poppers on a table, a pipe, and a plastic bag filled with white powder, probably crack coke. On the bed, was a pile of dollar bills and a nudie magazine with nothing but Asian girls inside.

Tory grabbed the money on the bed. "Money from last

night. Some Chink wanted me to fuck him. He was fat... smelled like Wanton soup, little, tiny dick about yea big," he said, holding his hand up and measuring about two inches with his fingers. "Fucking faggots all want to get fucked. I tell ya, there's nothing like fucking real pussy – these guys think they're better than women when they roll back and put their legs up. That guy, he wanted me to do him for twenty, and he had me wear two condoms. At first he said three and I said, "Look, if anyone's diseased it's you, because you get fucked...I can't feel anything with three."

The room was pretty nice all in all, and I sat down on the bed, watching Tory straighten things up a bit when I heard a sound coming from the closet.

"What's that?" I said.

"Where?" he said.

"In the big closet."

"Hey, Henry, it's almost two in the afternoon. Better get your ass up, little man!"

With that, the closet door opened and out walked this kid, blond hair falling in his face, pug nose, Mick Jagger lips, white as a ghost. He was in his underpants with nothing else on, nipples the size of quarters. He looked lost, or sleepy, or drugged, and was rubbing his eyes like he was trying to see.

"Who's that?" I said, thinking it was Tory's brother, or somebody family related. But he told me, "Henry...that's Henry. Henry was homeless in Philadelphia. I ran across him living in a box in Washington Square across from Independence Hall. So I adopted him as my little brother. He follows me everywhere..."

Henry stood about five two, a miniature stallion in every respect. He looked strange but not ugly at all, just different, almost as if he was from another planet. His eyes were the strangest part. They were deep and set very far apart. He moved very slowly and when he looked at me he kept his eyes on me for a long time. It made me nervous but I also felt that, during the stare, he was the boss, the king, the manager of everything.

Inside the walk-in closet he had his sleeping bag, his collection of sea shells, and what looked like buckets of sand.

For a little guy he had some really big feet with a man's veins and long toes that went on forever.

"He likes living in the closet," Tory said. "It reminds him of the box. He spent a long time in the box. Mr. Miller knows he's here. He doesn't charge Henry anything because he stays in the closet. He doesn't use any sheets and likes to shower in the outside stall showers guests use to wash the sand off when they come back from the beach. I wanna teach him to hustle but I'm scared as shit. They'd eat him alive out there. Just look at his cock, at that little body...they'd swallow him whole out there. Isn't that right, little man?"

Henry looked at Tory and turned red. "He doesn't know what he wants, or what he wants to do. But he lives on poppers. He lives, eats and sleeps poppers. I tell you, man, I can't keep enough poppers in this room. He goes through them like nothin'. Morning, noon and night – he unscrews the caps and sticks them up his nose. Before he has breakfast, before he gets dressed, before he does anything, it's always poppers..."

"Except for sucking, I think he's a virgin...

"He did tell me that a man used to come around and blow him in the box in Philly. And a few times he went to Tomcat bookstore and caused a commotion: every dude in the place wanted to blow him. They were all chasing him up and down the aisles, trying to force him into a booth, fighting one another to get to his pants. Wherever he goes, man, he creates a riot.

"In the box, he let the man blow him only if he brought him poppers. Poppers and hamburgers. Look, I've been meaning to extend his horizons, but I just haven't had a chance. You're the first person besides that Chink to come in this room. Mr. Miller isn't interested in him because he's allergic to poppers. Poppers make him wheeze and blow up to twice his size, like what bee stings do to some people. But Henry can't do anything without poppers. Like now, the only reason he came out of the closet is because he thinks I have a box full of them. I think it was the Philly box. That box did something to him.

"Hey Henry," Tory said, holding up a popper bottle. He came over like a little robot.

"Does he fuckin' talk?"

"Deaf mute."

"Then I guess he writes everything down, or – "

"Yeah, he explains with his hands. He's shy, but not when he sniffs. He grunts. I can understand his grunts but nobody else can."

I watched Tory unscrew the bottle and hold it up to his nose. Henry breathed in like it was his only hope. He kept breathing in and breathing in. Soon the room filled with popper aroma and I was getting aroused. I always get a hard-on when I smell that stuff. Henry, too, was turning into another person. His cock got rock hard and he started to take another look at the room, especially at Tory and me.

That's when I saw Tory get a sex glaze look in his eyes. Without telling me what was up, he started sniffing himself, and then he passed the bottle to me. I refused at first but then I went for it, sniffing and getting real high till all three of us were real glassy eyed and leaning sideways and playing with ourselves. It just kind of happened.

Tory took off his clothes, never taking his eyes off Henry's big dick which pointed straight out like an exercise bar. The kid had this really white skin that looked like coffee creamer, and he had these tiny, pointy nipples that had turned real red. His ass was shaped like a melon and kind of bouncy looking with plump cheeks that reminded me of a great big pair of tits. This Henry was massaging his own cock with his pre-cum and standing at the foot of the bed, both his legs spread far apart and just waiting and looking at Tory, who started fingering himself and then laying back on the bed. Tory didn't have a big cock at all...he was little, and maybe that's what glued him to Henry, watching him and then slowly picking his legs up until his ass was propped up like a pillow, waiting for Henry to fuck him, which is what the kid did, grabbing hold of the base of his cock and slipping it in and then swaying back and forth with his hands clasped behind his back like a Mattel toy, keeping a steady pace till Tory was crazy with moans.

I felt left out, so I went around behind Henry to watch his little melon ass move in and out. That ass got to me. I touched the crack and ran my fingers inside it some and then took my hand out to smell my fingers. It was like the sap smell from trees near Joan's house, warm and wet like a pussy. I stuck two fingers in and worked them up and twisted them round to test what I could do, and he backed up into me, forcing them inside

him further till I was way up inside. The whole time he kept fucking Tory, the same pace, you know, that big cock of his sliding in and out of Tory as I opened him some more and stuck the popper bottle up to his nose.

The room was in a whirl but I wanted to get inside him. His hair was curly in the back and these fucking ringlets flowed down around his neck. I then forgot he was a dude. His skin was like satin, and I kissed it though I couldn't believe what I was doing, being straight and all, but he was different, so hot, and bending over so I could ram it in him further, so tight – like a clamp, and warm, a small oven on ivory snow skin...damn that little prick. I went in all the way and for a second he broke his pace. Then he spasmed out, coming in Tory in one long stalled pump, just standing there not moving his cock but I could see the root throb and shake and overflow cum spill out of Tory.

I let loose inside little man in the best fuck I ever had, the best fuck, including pussy, though it beats me how this happened.

Tory was shit-faced after Henry fucked him, all embarrassed, not saying anything but wiping himself clean and looking gloomy-eyed and trying to work his manhood back. Henry was still horny, still hard, and still sniffing poppers – what a freak.

In other areas of the house, I could hear people moving about. I knew they were upset and nervous because they'd heard the shouts and the bed springs creak. They wanted in on the action.

Then the door opened, and who should peek in but Mr. Miller, his Bozo the clown hair sticking out and his face all red. He was nude except for his flip-flops, jerking off with a jar of vaseline in his free hand, poking his nose through the door to test the air for popper aroma.

"It ain't clean," Tory told him, meaning the air.

"Tell him to come here," Mr. Miller said, standing back and showing off his dick like an A-1 stud.

"He wants you," Tory said to me.

I had already fucked Henry, and my dick was shrimped over, limp as a noodle. I needed at least ten minutes flex time while Mr. Miller looked like he was gonna explode any minute.

Already he was on the floor on his knees, his thin lips open, waving me over. I went over, and I remembered what Tory had said. "Have him take out his teeth." So I made the request, and he took them out, the full plates, and set the big clam on the night stand, diving down on me deeper than anyone had ever done before.

As he sucked me, I stared down on his bald head and lost myself looking at it. I noticed that he had tiny blue veins all over his head, like a map of the Middle East or a drawing of rivers and streams stretching out across the planet. I wondered where he got all the veins, and what they meant, and why getting old has to do this, making a mess out of heads and changing the body like that. He sucked real good, and his gum hold on my cock was the best, but I held back for a while, wondering what he looked like when he was my age, and how he can live like this, being fat and bald with blue veins crisscrossing his head. I hoped that I wouldn't end up like this, with veins and bumps on a sweaty bald head that Tory says he held and rough-fucked so many times.

Before long, I was getting close to coming, and I know I must have been shooting pre-cum because Mr. Miller was speeding up his pace and getting close to coming himself. He was breathing real hard, and making all sorts of moaning and slurping noises, as Henry came round and watched from the sidelines, jerking himself off and sniffing from a popper bottle.

I remembered what Tory said about Mr. Miller's allergy and I grew afraid. He was so into the scene he didn't see Henry sniff the poppers and I just knew that the popper aroma was making its way into Mr. Miller's nose. Nothing happened at first, but right on the verge of coming I saw him begin to blow up, his face expanding like a balloon and the blue veins on his head becoming thicker until they widened out and covered his white head like a blue funk umbrella.

Finally, I shot into him, and he came too, both of us making all the noise we could. By now, Mr. Miller was having trouble breathing and he was getting fat in the chest, his skin a scarlet red and his cheeks all blown out like Santa Claus. Finally he couldn't take it anymore, so he got up and ran from the room in a mad dash, wheezing and coughing, and Henry, he just moved back and kept jerking himself off while in the

background Mr. Miller was making sounds like he was dying.

When I cleaned myself up, Tory was already in the shower and Henry was back in the closet. I didn't know what to do. I had to wait my turn in the bathroom, so I just hung around the bedroom, looking at things. On the bureau was a picture of a girl I guessed was Tory's girlfriend. I don't know why I did this, but I started opening drawers and saw collections of rings and watches. There were wedding bands, small diamond rings, watches with Roman numerals on them, all expensive. Then I came across credit cards, and a stack of IDs, like driver's licenses, library cards, passports.

Tory was a real operator...the licenses had names of people in New Jersey and Pennsylvania, most from Philly. I checked my own pants pockets for the twenty dollars I had stuffed in the back pocket, and found it gone. That sucker had ripped me off somehow because I know I had twenty when I walked in there, and now it was gone. I looked on the floor and checked near the bed but didn't see anything. I knew I had to hurry because Tory had already turned off the water and was stepping out to dry himself, so I did what anyone would do, I went back in the drawer and took the first ring I put my hands on. I didn't know what it was until much later, when I left the place and was outside walking back to the boards, away from Tory and Mr. Miller's house.

When Tory came in from the bathroom, he acted as if nothing was wrong, asking me how I liked Henry, and if I wanted to spend the night, though he'd be going out to the casinos. I said no thanks, and pretended like I knew nothing. I feared he'd look in the drawer where the rings were, so I skipped a shower and told him I'd swim myself clean in the ocean and shower at a friend's house. I had no friend, really, but I knew it was only a matter of time before Tory checked the drawer.

"Eric is sick, dude, I gotta be travelin'. Besides, I'm all blown out, if you know what I mean..."

He looked at me crooked, like he saw through me. I already had my clothes on and was ready to move. "Catch you later," I said, slapping him on the shoulder like everything was okay, and shouting "yo!" to Henry. I expected him to catch on and

come chasing me, but I was down the steps and out on the porch before I heard him shout "Jesus Christ!" at the top of his lungs and come racing after me. I knew he'd spotted the missing ring, and I also knew that the ring I'd taken must have been a winner, the big prize of the lot because as I ran up to the boards I could still hear him carrying on like someone had murdered his mom.

I knew enough not to stop and look at the ring until I was way on the boards, lost in the middle of hundreds of people, a long way from Seaside House. I went over to the railing facing the ocean. The sun was real bright and the ocean real blue when I took it out and saw, like, this huge diamond, big and sparkly, not like any diamond I'd seen before.

. . .

B.C. Jewelers is near Romagnoli's Pizza. The man there put the diamond under a microscope and did a few other things and said it was probably worth $20,000. "It's from the 1920's," he said, "very unusual...where'd you get it?" I told him it was a gift from my grandfather but I don't think he believed me. He said "Um hum," then looked me up and down like I had 'thief' written across my face.

But Tory is the thief. Whoever he stole this from is long gone...I was only trying to recap what he'd taken from me and accidentally struck it rich. It was luck. But I knew he'd be after me something fierce, so I planned a disguise. I decided to dye my hair platinum blond, grow a mustache and goatee, and wear thick sunglasses. Even that was a risk because Tory knows my body type, and since there aren't many hustlers in A.C., he might catch on real fast.

I took the diamond back and showed Eric, but before I did that I dyed my hair in the bus station. The dye was a woman's dye, since men's dye doesn't have platinum blond.

It's a good thing there was hardly anyone in the men's room when I mixed the packages and rubbed it in my hair, though the stuff stank up the whole room. Anyone who came in would have noticed it but at least it was better than the smell of piss and stale body odor that place usually smelled like.

So I rubbed it in my hair, and waited for forty minutes in one

of the stalls, sitting there with this stuff on my head smelling like a chemical plant as guys came in the stalls to shit.

I was in the middle stall, reading the dye directions and looking at the diamond, when I see this guy tap his foot in the stall beside me. I didn't know who he was, I just saw the shoes, Doc Martens. He also had jeans on. I tapped back because he wouldn't let up. Now, I'd never been in that bathroom cruising, though I wasn't cruising, just waiting for the dye to work, but all of a sudden I got horny. Then I saw his hand come under the stall and wave me over to his side. Then a finger on his hand pointed down towards the floor, like he wanted me to kneel down and stick my cock under.

I didn't think there was any way, not with dye on my head and the dye stinking up the place, but since my cock wasn't being dyed, I crouched down and stuck my boner through to him, snuggling in as tight as I could so he could reach my balls and all. He started to go down on me and I was coastin' real nice, feeling the buzz really big when some people walked in and ruined the whole thing, stupid college kids all laughing and pushing and right away yelling: "It stinks in here! Who the hell is making that stink!"

Stupid, fucking jerks— if I had had a gun I would have killed all of them right there.

I sat up and hunched over forward, thinking if they looked over the partition I'd really let them have it, but that didn't happen. They were such goofballs, like it was their first time in A.C. They reminded me of the guys in Joan's neighborhood – assholes. Then one of them goes into the only remaining stall and begins to take a shit, farting and letting loose this huge dump that went on and on, like he hadn't taken a dump in months, and all the while my hard-on is going down and the guy who was sucking me is making fidgeting noises like he's thinking about leaving.

This kid, I guess, something in him got curious and before I knew it he was moving one foot over in my direction. I couldn't believe it because his friends were so close, and unless they were all seated quietly outside waiting for a later bus, there was nothing we could do.

But there he was, anyway, his foot tapping and sliding under close to mine, as the man who'd been sucking me made good

on his first claim, sliding his foot way under and bringing his hand around too and pointing all his fingers this time, demanding that I kneel down and get it over with. I suppose he was afraid I'd go to the other guy, but since I knew what to expect from him, I knelt down and let the college guy – he brought his hand under – play with my ass as the first guy sucked me, slobbering and making more sound effects than I thought safe in a place like that.

The poor college dude was acting like he'd never touched a guy before because his hand was shaking like a leaf.

When I came, the college dude grunted too, and the man on the other side went into big spasms until the whole bathroom was like one big exploding dick.

Afterward, when they had both left, I left the stall and walked out and saw myself in the mirror. The dye on my head was like a foamy helmet, but when I washed my head under the sink, rinsing and rinsing under the faucet like the homeless guys I'd seen do in Philly restrooms, I came up with pale hair which was just like the color of the diamond.

V.

Eric told me the lifeguards found the body washed up on shore. It was a skinny white boy, about 17, in a T-shirt. He said the boy went out too far and got caught in the tide. They found him washed up on the beach in the early morning, a bunch of horseshoe crabs draped all over his body like a design. He was blue and bloated and his skin was wrinkled and his body looked like a toy, he said. He said the cops called it an accident before they did an autopsy. The boy had semen in him. His picture was in the *Atlantic City Press*, Eric said, right on the front page.

After that I picked up a copy of the paper and checked out the mug. I knew the face, that's for sure. It was that nerdy kid, the scared rabbit I saw Fun House Jim with on the boards.

I couldn't believe it. That guy made the kid swim out to sea or got to act out his fantasy and then something went wrong. I was with him myself in the Fun House and God knows what

might have happened if I hadn't gotten out of there in time. Maybe it was coincidental, but I don't think so. I knew I had to call Siegfried.

When I went to a pay phone to dial Siegfried's number, I got a recording saying that the line had been disconnected and that no further information was available. I hate when that happens. I dialed again to make sure and got the some recording. I was so mad I kicked the stand under the telephone. Then I walked the distance to Siegfried's house and was shocked to see a Real Estate sign out front and a SOLD sign plastered on the front of it. He never told me he was going to sell his house, never said a word. What gives with people? I went over and looked in the windows and the rooms were empty. Everything looked naked without the paintings and rugs. I looked in the kitchen window, where Siegfried cooked me dinner, and everything was empty. Like he never was, gone, disappeared.

I was starting to feel scared. I mean, I always thought he'd be there, always thought I could come back when I had had enough out here. I never counted on this. This was the very last thing I expected. Then I thought that maybe Siegfried was out looking for me. He found me the first time. He must have known I was still in A.C. He should be looking for me at least.

VI.

I wasn't thinking of sex when a man in Bermuda shorts approached me in Romagnoli's. I was sitting there eating a slice, thinking of Siegfried when he came up with his slices and asked if he could join me. He told me I looked like a young man in search of something to do, a boy without a purpose or a "fixed idea." That's what he called it, a "fixed idea."

"You need a fixed idea," he said, shaking garlic powder over his pizza, his enormous diamond rings flashing in that little greasy joint I'd gone to many times in the last three months.

When he said "fixed idea" I thought of the lady with the Jesus sandwich board. She had a fixed idea. Candido had a fixed idea: it was fucking Eric and stealing. Jim in the Fun House had a fixed idea: he wanted boys to swim in the ocean

and drown. Even Eric had a fixed idea: he wanted to kill himself, only he was taking the slow ride out. Even Candido's cousins had "fixed ideas:" stealing watches, rings and wallets and inventing new ways to get over.

"I have a fixed idea," I told the man, who was Italian, heavyset, but very rough and masculine. "I want to make money getting my cock sucked."

"That's not enough," he said, putting more garlic on his pizza.

"What do you mean?"

"You need a goal. This money that you get from getting your cock sucked. What do you do with it?"

"I use it to live on."

"That's what I mean. You're floating around in space with nothing fixed. You need something more detailed. Have you ever thought of becoming a lifeguard?"

"Isn't that for college boys and jocks?"

"Mainly. But I can help you there. I train the lifeguards here. I also recruit local talent. You look strong and healthy. Of course, you can't be a good lifeguard without being a good swimmer. Are you a good swimmer?"

"I whip ass in the water. Butterfly stroke, backstroke, freestyle, sidestroke..."

"Look, I know what you do, okay. I'm not blind. Every day I walk the boards I see you working your routine. How long have you been here? Three months now? Well, maybe at this point you're okay. But give it another five months, or even another two, and I bet you have a drug problem, or get caught up in petty crime. Maybe that Candido what's-his-name you hang with will lead you into something...I don't know, but something bad will happen. It always does..."

"You know Candido?"

"Everybody does. He has cousins and brothers and second cousins and he sends them all over to do the same thing: to get over. Candido's on the downhill slide. He's burned too many people. But he'll do himself in before anyone lays a hand on him. People hang themselves with their own ropes. Myself, I'm the father of two grown boys. Yeah, they were lifeguards for a season but they moved on." He was silent for a minute, and then he said, "So whad'ya say?"

"What do I have to do?"

"For starters, fill out this application." He opened his briefcase and took out a form and a pen. "You can do it here. Don't worry about a home address. I gathered that you're a runaway but that doesn't matter. Use a friend's address if you like, even if they just left the area or something like that. We just need something official sounding on paper, something for the records. Would you like another pizza?"

He bought me another slice and a soda. I filled in Siegfried's address, and for references I wrote Siegfried's name as well as Eric's, only I made up a last name for Eric, knowing that Ralph said that things just had to look official.

"Oh," he said, after I'd finished, "don't worry about a contact number for yourself. I know where you're living. Just meet me here tomorrow at noon, and we can start training. I'm sure you'll be approved. The men on the board are my friends, and I doubt whether there will be a problem. If you're approved, and I'm sure you will be, you can come live with me and my business partner. You can take my son's room. That's where I put up lifeguards-to-be who haven't a place to go, or who can't afford apartments. But I have to warn you: it's a tough program. You won't be free to roam the streets like you do now. But the money is good, and the rewards many: you'll meet lots of people, girls, boys, men, women. Sometimes Hollywood sends scouts out here...you might even find yourself in the movies one day. So if you're ready to settle down a bit, this is for you. If not, tell me now so I'm not wasting my time."

I told Ralph it was okay, that I'd meet him in front of Resorts tomorrow at noon. I was sure it was okay. I was tired of Candido, and afraid of what might happen to Eric and what I might see in that regard.

"One thing though," I asked, "Can I bring Eric along? He needs a place to stay. He's sick. Candido is abusing him. I don't know what to do."

"We'll take care of Eric. He has to be protected for his own good. Once you're settled in, you can bring him around and we'll see."

Back at the pier, Eric was showering as a john was putting on his shoes.

Candido was gone. The man, probably a rich businessman, seemed happy because he was humming a tune. Eric was also feeling good. The man said hello to me and then Eric waved to me from the shower. I was glad the mood had picked up. "Hey," I called out, "I have good news! This dude wants me to be a lifeguard. I can make a million bucks, meet girls and get my cock sucked every day of the week."

The man getting dressed looked at me, then glanced at my crotch. Eric was washing his ass real hard so I knew he had just gotten fucked. "Nice hideaway you guys have here,' the man said, buckling his belt and getting ready to go. I told him yes. He slapped me on the back. "Good luck, pal," he said, waving good-bye to Eric. Eric grinned and stuck his butt out and wiggled it at me.

"This man I met says you can come visit or stay with us. You won't be left out, isn't that cool? But first I have to establish myself. They're going to train me. I know I can swim. I can beat anybody. This man says he's been watching me and knew all along that I had talent. He even knows about this place; and he knows about Candido. Small town, really. Anyway, I filled out this application and he promised to meet me tomorrow at noon. Fromthere I'm going to his house where he's going to put me up in a room. Then I'll begin training."

Eric didn't say anything though his mood changed very quickly. He turned his back to me as he switched off the water. I must say he looked good all wet, his skin fair and smooth like a woman's, his long red hair matted against his ears. I asked him what the matter was but all he would do was look at me.

"Look, the man said you could be a part of it too, only after I'm there for a time. That could be two days. I'll talk you up, I'll spot you. Don't worry. I'm not just going to walk out of here."

He still seemed pissed. Maybe he can't be blamed for that. After all, he didn't even know where I was going or where I'd be staying. He'd have no way to get in touch with me. I couldn't give him an address.

"I'll come back and get you. If Candido goes berserk, tell me. Hunt me down by one of the casinos, maybe Resorts."

I didn't know what I was saying... the more I talked the sillier I sounded. I got the feeling that Eric had been through something like this with other guys and that he saw me as one

of many. Soon I figured I could do nothing right so I just shut up. Eric would have to come around on his own.

Night fell and we went to bed. It got very cold. A wind was blowing in from the ocean and we didn't have enough blankets. Eric was curled up like a baby with Candido's sleeping bag on top of him for warmth.

The waves were coming in so rough I didn't want a freak wave to wash us out to sea so I moved us back under the pier where it was really dark. We were closer to the main beach, and people would see us there in the morning. That was a good risk compared to being close to the crazyass water. After the move, I fell asleep till I heard Candido cursing about the sleeping bags. By that time the ocean was quiet and Candido didn't see why we had to move. He blamed it on Eric. He was also pissed that his sleeping bag was being used as a blanket.

I was afraid he'd start fucking Eric, so I covered my ears and buried my head in the sleeping bag. For a while it was quiet and I thought he'd gone to sleep when I started to hear fucking noises. I peeked through the bag and saw Candido, butt naked, fucking Eric. He was holding Eric's arms down in the sand, which seemed weird because Eric was lying still. Usually Eric makes some kind of movement when Candido fucks him but this time he didn't do anything. I figured he was so used to Candido's surprise fucks he didn't feel them anymore.

The fucking went on a long time. Candido had been drinking so it took him longer to come. He was making all kinds of grunting noises and I was afraid that the people on the pier would hear him. But nothing happened. By now I'd lost most of my respect for Eric, too. I mean, at some point a man has to stand up and defend himself but Eric never moved, never did anything to fight him off, never said no in a way that you knew he meant no. He must have been getting off by having Candido dog him.

VII.

It was almost noon and I was seated in Romagnoli's Pizza Parlor waiting for Ralph when I started wishing that I never walked out on Siegfried. Now I was getting involved with somebody I didn't know, starting over again, not knowing what was up ahead! I felt scared, something I don't like to feel. The feeling of being scared came out of nowhere, just like it always does. Part of me wished that Ralph wouldn't show. I didn't feel right about leaving Eric with Candido around. I knew Eric didn't stand a chance, especially as he was getting sicker by the day. Maybe Candido would go back to Philly and work 17th Street, leaving Eric under the boards until the surf washed him out to sea. That's what Fun House Jim would want. He would want to find Eric washed up on shore, all purply and bloated. Then he could jerk off. What a sicko!

When Ralph showed up, he was with another man, a skinnier guy with light hair who carried two shoulder bags. He looked like Liberace, and he had lots of rings on his fingers. Ralph said his friend's name was Joseph. Joseph looked at me funny till his eyes aimed at my crotch. Then he seemed a little nicer.

"Ready for your new career?" Ralph said, smelling like Brut and folding his hands on the edge of the table.

"I'm ready," I said.

Joseph smiled and our eyes met for an instant but then he started looking off to the side and his face took on a serious look – like he was thinking of an airplane crash or something. I got the feeling I wasn't supposed to act happy. Joseph made me nervous. I couldn't shake the feeling that he had a secret I should know. I wanted to open his head and see what was inside.

"You're going to enjoy your new home. It won't compare to living under the boardwalk," he said.

They were in a hurry to show me my room, so together we went to their car just off the boards. I sat in the back seat where every so often Joseph would steal a glance at my crotch. I figured I'd make things better if I got it hard for him so I

squeezed it a couple of times until it was stiff. When he turned around again he saw it sticking up through my shorts and he had a surprised look on his face. His face turned very red as he looked at it a long time, at least till Ralph looked at him and made a face. There was no more staring at my crotch after that. We drove for about fifteen minutes and then we pulled up to a house off by itself near a private beach. The house was a long rancher with a large white fence around it, just off the ocean but on a hill so it'd be safe from high tides.

Joseph showed me my room, a clean space with a single bed and bureau. It faced the ocean and a little lighthouse they had in their backyard. From the window I could see the skyline of A.C. – we were on a peninsula and there was only one other houseway down the beach.

They said I could relax, so I got on the bed and rested. I didn't know when training was to begin, or what I was supposed to do after the nap, but I told myself not to worry. I knew they'd tell me what to do. I fell in and out of sleep, waking up to see Joseph walking the halls. One time I thought he was peeking in on me. Another time I thought I saw him standing by the bureau. I must have been really tired because I can't remember whether this happened or not.

I woke up once and thought I was in Siegfried's house. I even called his name. I dreamt of the boards, and of Eric getting fucked by Candido. The Candido/Eric part was awful. Candido was fucking him so hard Eric was sinking into the sand until it looked as though Candido was fucking the sand.

"You want dinner?" It was Joseph, his hand on my crotch, his smiling face close to mine. I could see one of his gold fillings his face was so close to mine. He seemed so horny I knew he was about to burst. There was alcohol on his breath. He squeezed my dick and started rubbing it up and down real fast. I was about to say hands off when I thought better of it. I could tell it wouldn't be cool to say no. I got the feeling looking at him that he wasn't happy with Ralph, that he was even afraid of Ralph. Ralph controlled the purse strings, Ralph controlled everything. Ralph was like – God. How I knew all this just by looking into Joseph's eyes I don't know, but I did. I felt sorry for him. Maybe at one time he was a good looking dude but now he was old with nothing to show for it except

what Ralph let him have.

Pretty soon he had my pants down and he was blowing me. He was doing such a good job my cock was standing straight up. It looked bigger than usual, the dome big and purplish and reminding me of the sky over the ocean – and for some strange reason of Eric sleeping by the waves and dying of AIDS. Joseph was acting nutty – slurping, licking, yanking, sniffing – while blowing me. But I noticed he began looking at his watch a lot and kept checking the door. It seemed he was afraid Ralph would come in.

"How fast can you come?" he said, wrapping his right hand around my shaft and sliding it up and down as he sucked the head with a loud "Yum!"

"Fast – if I think hard."

"Think hard. Concentrate. You'll be doing us both a favor. Would you rather I blew you standing up?"

"Standing takes a little longer. Keep doin' what you're doin' and I'll blow. Don't change anything... That's it... Yeah!"

When he was finished drinking me he asked if I had any more. I told him I needed twenty minutes between sucks but I could go on forever as long as I had twenty minute rests. He said, "There's no time for that," and walked out, leaving me to clean myself up. He was a cold fish.

I made a promise to myself that if he ever asked to blow me again I'd tell him to go to hell.

I went back to sleep, and when I woke up I heard loud voices in another part of the house. Ralph was screaming at Joseph. I couldn't make out what he was saying but it sounded like they were talking about me. I heard my name mentioned anyway. Somebody was pounding their fist on a table.

Then I heard, "You ruined it! You went ahead and did it. You know the rules!" Soon I didn't like the sound of it at all and got up and crept closer to the door so I could hear more. Ralph was really putting it to him. Joseph was crying, saying he was sorry and making all sorts of promises. Then I couldn't hear anything...I think they must have gone into another room.

I crept out into the hallway to try and hear more but there were no sounds until I heard a yell from outside. I went down the hall to the window and saw Joseph running on the beach,

Ralph trailing behind him and chasing him into the water. Joseph kept turning around to see how close Ralph was. He stepped into the surf, then ran down the shoreline, with Ralph chasing him.

Alone in the house, I started to look around. I knew I only had a limited amount of time, so I went into their bedroom. There I saw many photographs of them with different boys, blond boys, dark haired boys, Asian boys, Black boys, geeky boys, all types and in different poses, some in foreign countries, in Egypt near the pyramids, in France near that tower, in England by that clock. One wall of the bedroom was covered with framed pictures, close-ups of favorite guys. There was a redhead with freckles who wore an elf's hat. The picture said: "Dublin, 1980." One picture showed a whole row of butt naked boys standing with their arms around each another. Other pictures showed boys asleep, boys playing with their hard-ons, boys peeing into toilets, boys with hard-ons doing push-ups, boys with hard-ons building model airplanes, boys sucking their own toes, naked boys playing volleyball.

Then I saw something that freaked me out. I saw a picture of Eric standing between Ralph and Joseph on the boards. Eric was smiling and his red hair was sticking straight up like a wind was blowing in off the ocean. The two men had their arms around him. The picture was named: "Getting Sandwiched by ERIC, 1984."

When I saw Eric's picture my only thought was to get out of there. It made me mad because I knew they must have promised to make Eric a lifeguard too. It was just a scam to get him to live with them.

On Ralph's bureau top there was a collection of rings that I just scooped up. I also opened every drawer I could lay my hands on till I found some cash. In one drawer I found condoms, morepictures (Mexican boys on donkeys), sex lotions, and a roll of twenty dollar bills. I didn't count the bills but stuffed them into my pocket.

I looked out the window and saw Ralph sitting on top of Joseph in the surf. He was sitting on Joseph's chest, holding his hands down in the sand and looking into his face. I thought this was a good time to escape, so I hightailed it out the front door and down the driveway where they couldn't see me. Then

I took to the road, running straightaway towards A.C. Central. I didn't care if they followed me... traffic was thick and there were other walkers, so I knew I was safe. I couldn't believe I'd been stupid enough to believe them about the lifeguard thing.

I crossed a bridge over the swampy part of the bay and made my way into town. I'd counted two hundred dollars in cash, which I rolled up and put into my shoe. First thing I did was buy groceries and then I headed out to the amusement pier where Eric was.

When I came to the camp, Eric was eating a sandwich and throwing bits of it to the gulls. When he saw me he didn't say anything, though I saw a smirk cross his face, like he wasn't surprised, like he was thinking "I told you so."

I didn't want to talk about it. I just crawled into my old sleeping bag thinking again what a jerk I'd been to believe a scam artist like Ralph.

Before I drifted off, I took out the wad of twenties and flashed it to Eric. He smiled, and I slept for a little while.

I woke up to the sound of Eric getting fucked by a small fat man in a golfer's hat. This guy must have been a regular contact because he knew where to find Eric. Usually guys who knew Eric just walked into camp and started fucking him. They were all learning to do what Candido did. The golfer had Eric up against one of the pier columns, his hands tied with rope above his head. The golfer's Bermuda shorts were down around his ankles. He had a fat ass, as white as Siegfried's Comet cleanser legs, and when he fucked his ass flab shook like a Jello mold.

I went back to sleep and when I woke up again the man was gone and Eric was resting, his butt propped up in the air for the next taker.

Later, Eric told me he found out Candido had gone into Philly with his little cousins. The trip was to teach them hustling in the big city: how to avoid the pigs, how to steal a wallet before a man takes you home – stuff Candido knows best. Eric was too weak to walk to the boards, so I said he should stay under the pier and I would go out, score, then bring back more food. I don't know why I felt this way. I didn't know Eric really well, and he meant nothing to me really but I

wanted to take care of him.

"Look, don't you think you better go to a doctor and take this ATZ shit and all?" I said. He got real mad when I said this. He spit at me, then kicked a pier column. I knew the doctors would send him away and put him in a sanitorium or charge him an arm and a leg for the ATZ. Then they'd lecture him about hustling and try and talk him into working at McDonald's for five dollars an hour. I didn't question him anymore after that. I just went out and scored.

I cruised the tents on the European beach in my bikini briefs. I met two gay lovers who paid my sixty dollars to lick and tickle my feet. They put me in a hammock with my feet sticking out the net holes. One of them sucked my toes for an hour while the other one, a muscle man, tickled my feet with a feather.

Now, I had always thought that feet, and specially my feet, were disgusting. When I was little Dad would sit with us in the living room in his bare feet. He had big feet and long toes and when he sat there with us watching television he'd stretch out his legs so that his feet would be in our faces. After a long day's work, they stunk, but that didn't prevent Dad from putting one leg on top of another and rubbing them together like they were special items.

I don't know why he didn't wear bedroom slippers, because sometimes Joan would joke and say that something stank. "Whew! I smell feet!" she'd say, and then make a face and look at Dad. Dad would just smile. He wasn't about to put slippers on just because Joan said his feet stank.

Sometimes he did, though this wasn't too much. Since I sat on the floor when we watched TV, I usually sat closet to Dad's feet, and all through the show I'd hear him rubbing them together. When I'd turn around to talk to him, he'd be wiggling his toes, drinking his whisky and water and looking so content. My own feet I'd pick as we watched TV, tearing off bits of skin and leaving them in the carpet or putting them in the shirt pocket of my pajama top. Or sometimes I'd flick a piece of skin across the room, like my brother did with his boogies. It was just things kids do. Dad hated it when I picked my feet and he always told me to stop, but sometimes he pretended not to see me do it, which I never understood. Sitting there barefoot

myself, I hoped my own feet didn't stink, at least not like Dad's, and to avoid that I poured talcum powder over them before watching TV with the family.

Now that I think of it, maybe Dad wanted Joan to massage his feet and all. He always did seem to have them in her face, whether it be on a foot stool or in the summer when they were on the patio together and he had his feet propped up on a patio chair, close to hers. Like before, he was always rubbing them together and making that sound that two feet make when they're rubbed that way.

I picked my feet real bad, though, sometimes pulling off pieces of skin so big I made them bleed. When this happened I'd have to get a napkin or some toilet tissue to stop the bleeding. If I went too deep, I'd have trouble walking the next day. There would be this stinging feeling and maybe I'd hobble along with a limp. Then for days I wouldn't touch my feet, and each night I'd test how they were healing, adding iodine or first aid cream when I had to. A week later, they were ready to be picked again, and I'd start from scratch.

It was more fun to pick after a short healing because the skin was more like a scab and came off like flakes without making a new injury. So I could pick to my heart's content.

When I went roller skating with my brother, I'd come home with puffy white blisters along the sides of my feet. These sacs were filled with water and sometimes they were like little balloons, so you could press on them and feel the liquid inside. Watching them cave-in was cool: sometimes I'd pick around the edges till I'd puncture the puffed up part, and then watch as the whole thing crashed. The water would then run over my heel as the white puffed-up part lay all broken up in little bits. This I would pick off until it hurt. I had to be careful with blisters because if they were picked too much they'd affect my walking for days.

One day a gym teacher in school saw the condition of my feet and said he wanted to talk to me.

"Don't you know that feet are the most important part of a man's body," he said, pointing at my blisters and torn skin areas. "You have beautiful feet but you are destroying them with your ignorance. It's better to take up smoking than attack your feet and ruin a beautiful thing."

I told him it was a nervous habit I was trying to get rid of. "Try as I may I can't keep my hands off them," I said. "When I feel jittery, I always go for them and start to pick. It's something to do, and way before it starts to hurt, the picking is fun."

"But look at what you've done," he said, putting his hand on one and giving it a squeeze. "An infection can happen overnight." Then he took out a first aid cream and started rubbing some on my right big toe. There was menthol in it and the feeling became hot as he started rubbing the whole foot, going between my toes with his fingers, then sliding his hands underneath as he pressed and rubbed, sliding up to the toes again, swooping down and up, sometimes fast, sometimes slow, all the while adding ointment and another cream until I sat there like I was paralyzed. He was explaining the muscles and the arches, and doing both feet at once. They were propped up on a gym bench as I slouched back and felt a tingle near my balls and a hot sensation flooding my prick till I shot up with a hard-on that made a tent of my gym shorts.

I don't know whether he saw that, though I think he did. He kept rubbing, telling me how he was making it better for gym class, how the medicine would work, and I didn't want him to stop. He must have seen my eyes bulging out and my cock shifting sideways in my shorts, plus the drops of pre-cum soaking the shorts so that a big wet spot showed loud and clear. I closed my eyes while he kept rubbing, sliding both his hands up and down my feet like he was jerking off two giant cocks. Inside me the tingling grew and I felt cum starting to gather inside and get ready to shoot straight up into my gym pants, my legs shaking like crazy as he talked about feet.

"We're gonna get your feet back into shape, boy," he kept saying, and before I knew it I shot and tried to muffle any noise though my body bucked and jerked upward, my face real red and tears at the corner of my eyes.

Now I have respect for feet, and after that I took care never to pick again, but wash them and cut the nails straight across in a careful way. Of course, after the massage, the gym teacher pretended he didn't see what happened, and gave me some cream to take home. Sometimes I think he didn't know what I was feeling and would have been surprised to know that I came

when he rubbed me, though I do know he didn't once touch me on the cock or say I should touch myself, or make one sexual remark. He just rubbed my feet, that's all, in the name of high school health and science, and in the name of being a good role model. Which he was.

In the hammock, with the two men sniffing my feet and sucking my toes, I started to feel the same dizzy feeling, my cock harder than it gets when I jerk off. I was so excited pre-cum was oozing out in a big way. Both guys were sucking my feet as they jerked themselves off, and so I jerked myself off too, wiggling my toes in their mouths and rubbing the bottom of my feet over their faces and saying to them, as they wanted me to, "Suck my feet, smell my feet, suck them toes."

Then they put this foot stockade over my ankles so that my feet stuck out through two holes. They screwed down the top of the stockade till it pinched my skin though the feeling gave me a buzz. They said they'd never seen such beautiful feet, such beautiful smelly feet with long toes and curvy undersides, and I thought back to my gym teacher, and all the times my feet weren't nice.

One thing about getting your feet sucked and stroked, it makes for a tingling feeling that creeps into your balls, a feeling that rises up and sends big tingles through your cock. As I jerked off, this feeling came flooding in. My legs were board stiff and sticking straight out on the hammock like they'd been pulverized and my feet were pointed and strained into their mouths. It was like they were trying to swallow me feet first, sending more shivers through me the whole time. When I came I came more than if they had blown me, more than if I'd fucked them, more than if I'd fucked an Asian girl. That crazy damn foot thing gets me all the time and these guys really had it going. It was also the easiest seventy-five dollars I ever made.

Next day I went swimming in the ocean and noticed that the diamond ring wasn't on my finger. At first I thought one of the foot-fetish guys took it, but then I remembered that I was wearing it the whole time I was with them. When I got back to Eric, I took it off to show him, then put it on my pinkie to pretend I was a queen.

Then we started drinking wine: one of Eric's tricks had some

red, and I downed a lot. I remember taking the ring on and off my finger so I could look at it, then flipping it in the air and seeing how the diamond shinned at night, under the stars and near the ocean.

Candido was not there, but at some point I fell asleep, wasted by the wine and sleeping deep till morning when I awoke to find it not on my hand and not remembering anything. Since Eric was dead to the world, I knew it wasn't him, but Candido came by and I figured it was him who took it, so I made a promise to myself that if I ever saw him again I'd fuck him up real good, just like Tory was going to fuck me up for taking the diamond in the first place.

For two or three days I walked on the boardwalk and looked for him real heavy, staring at every Puerto Rican face I saw. I knew there was a good chance he'd gone back to Philly, or that one of his white boy lovers took him away somewhere. I went to B&C Jewelers and asked if they saw a Puerto Rican with the ring I came in and asked them about, but they said, "We see a thousand Puerto Ricans a day," which is true in a place like Atlantic City.

I walked under the boardwalk and checked the people there, mostly homeless guys from Philly or crazy crackhead hustlers the cops there were always chasing. Nobody had seen Candido, though some had seen him or heard about him and his little cousins. Then one guy told me he'd been killed, but I found out later that he was confusing Candido with another Puerto Rican.

I got over losing the ring because, after all, it wasn't even mine and I paid nothing for it.

Another night, after Eric and I ate, I asked him if he ever told the guys he has sex with that he was HIV-positive.

"It don't matter with rubbers," he said. "They're straight...they don't think they'll get it. They're fucking me, I'm not fucking them."

Later that night, after we drank a few beers, Eric got a spurt of energy and wanted to hit the boards. I was feeling good too, so off we went. It was a damn good feeling to be up and about and walking among people at night. At first we were going to go to the Fun House and get on Jim's case but then we decided

to take a ride on the ferris wheel. That ferris wheel is the largest wheel in Jersey. It goes up fifty stories and has as many lights as a spaceship. When you're up top you can see way out over the ocean...it even looks like you're way out at sea.

We climbed into our seats, which had a cage around it, and waited for the wheel to turn. Eric started rocking our cage so we'd go up swinging. In the cages around us I saw families with little kids sticking their noses through the wire netting and boy and girl couples getting ready to feel each other up. When the on button was pushed, we jolted forward and started to lift way up over the boards. We kept going up and up in a gliding manner until we were way over the ocean in the dark of night, the lights of A.C. getting smaller. Pretty soon everything we'd been through was below us. We were now different and away from it all. Up there, you can see your past and consider how your life is going. Mine wasn't going nice but up there it didn't feel like your life at all.

The wheel stopped turning when our cage was on the topmost section. Eric then began rocking the cage with his body so that we swung to and fro. People in other cages looked over at us. They seemed afraid that we would drop. Some of them were afraid because the wheel had stopped moving.

"Up here you don't have AIDS, I still have Siegfried. Life doesn't suck," I told Eric.

Eric was acting goofy, trying to open the cage door and stick his head outside. He did this to attract attention, not to jump. When he opened the cage door, a woman in another cage called out for him to stop. He only laughed. He'd been fucked by men he didn't even know, plowed into the sand by roughnecks, by crazy-ass Candido and a thousand little-dicked men in geeky golfer hats, and here was this woman getting on his case because of this one little thing.

EPILOGUE

I stayed out while Eric entertained some married guy. When I saw the guy leave, I went back and I was smoking reefer and looking at the waves. Then I got to wondering why Eric wasn't saying anything. I looked over at him. He was just lying there like he always does, only this time something seemed different. I called his name, then threw my sandal at him. I started to feel very strange. I walked over and looked down into face. His eyes were wide open but still and glazed looking. I knew what it was. He had just slid away without a sound.

The only thing I could do was stare into the dark ocean. I couldn't see a thing but I could hear the waves crashing in and smell the salt breezes. It was like Eric had stepped into the black. I wondered where he was and whether he could see me now—or whether he was just like a burned-out light bulb. I sat with him all night, not moving but sitting there listening to the waves till at last the sun came up.

In the sunlight, his hair was just as red though the look in his eyes seemed further away than ever.

A man came up...one of Eric's regulars. I saw him walking towards the camp. For a second I wanted to test him and see what he'd do if I didn't say anything, just let him find out for himself and see what happens, whether he'd do it, if he was that desperate, whether he had any respect for the dead. But I couldn't put myself or Eric to that test. I told him: "He's dead."

He looked at me as if I was crazy. He took a few more steps, head stretched out like a bloodhound. He got real close.

Then I saw his eyes get real big. He turned white as a sheet and raced out of there like there was no tomorrow. Stupid-ass coward, I thought.

In the past, he'd fucked Eric I don't know how many times and now he just turned around and left him there without so much as a kiss or asking how it happened. For all he knew I could have murdered him.

Sure, I called the pigs, and they came and took Eric away. I was asked a few questions but they let me go. They knew

who Eric was and where he'd been.

After that, Atlantic City just wasn't the same place for me. I tried to hustle but it didn't work. The ocean was telling me it was time to move on.

Y'all come on down...

In the Presence of Innocence

Memoirs of
A Lusty Early Life
Down on the Farm by
Thomas C. Humphrey

STARbooks Press
Sarasota, FL

> "These images, these fragments ... are a few motifs of a life, the seeds from which the rest grew."
> – David Rees, "Not for Your Hands"

PROLOGUE

The farm is gone now. Dwarfed by a cluster of towering oaks, two crumbling red brick chimneys keep lonely sentinel over the remains of the rambling clapboard farmhouse. Where the front porch should begin, a rose bush blossoms an anemic pink in the weed-choked, exhausted soil, and a few patches of verbena flower among the thick Johnson grass, reminders of how transitory were the attempts of Mama - and Richard's mother before her - to bring a small measure of gentility to the harsh, unyielding, often cruel Georgia countryside.

I wade through hip-high crowfoot grass across what once was an undulating green sea of corn framed by white crests of open cotton bolls. I grapple with a thick undergrowth of elder and bramble along a rusted barbwire fence, and trudge the broomsage-covered pasture until I reach the pond where Richard taught me to swim that first summer.

Settling beneath a gnarled beech tree near the edge of the pond, now diminished by thick cattails and lilies, I wonder, as I do each time, why I have come back, why, after nearly fifty years, I keep returning periodically, hoping to recapture - or at least recall - what it was that I never had or that I lost too soon here.

There are huge gaps in my recollections of family and school and community, but as I drift back, some resurrected memories are as vivid and complete as if they were of yesterday. The voices of Richard, Travis, Ellis, Brett - sometimes in solo, sometimes in unison - resound through the deserted countryside, like the refrains of half-forgotten songs. As memories of them come alive one by one, I am convinced - without knowing exactly why - that this rural childhood was the most important period of my life and has molded everything I have done and become.

ONE
NEW TO THE FARM

"What's the matter, Jody? You never seen a rooster fuck?" Richard asked.

We were strewing chicken feed in the back yard for the flock of Plymouth Rocks when a hen squawked in terror behind me. I turned to stare as the big Rhode Island Red rooster clamped down on the cowering hen's head with his beak and beat the air with his wings and danced around behind her for a few seconds before he turned her loose and strutted off. The old hen shook her head a few times, fluffed up her feathers, and went back to pecking up grain as if nothing had happened.

I had been on the farm just a few days, but already I hated that rooster. He chased after me every time I walked close to him, advancing and posturing and threatening, and Richard had pointed out the sharp, thorny projections on his legs and warned me, "It hurts like shit if he spurs you with one of them."

When I turned at the sound of the hen squawking, I thought the rooster was just fighting with her. I didn't know whether I was more shocked at the discovery of what he actually was doing or at Richard's use of the naughty word to describe it. That January in 1944, I was going on nine, and, until Mama and Vernon got married, I had always lived in town. I had only a glimmering of understanding of the dirty word Richard used, and I never had seen the act performed, by animal or human. My new stepbrother was almost thirteen and knew everything. I viewed him half in admiration and half in terror.

"I wouldn't mind being a rooster," he mused. "They don't have to do nothing but fuck any time they feel like it. But I'd rather be a bull."

"Why?" I asked in all innocence.

"Cause they got a big dick, stupid. You ever see a bull's dick? Bigger'n your arm. Mine's starting to grow, and I hope it gets that big, too." He scrutinized me for a few seconds. "You want to be like a rooster or a bull?"

"A bull, I guess," I said, really just wanting to be like him. I had never thought about it before, and I didn't see why it

mattered. You could pee okay no matter what size it was.

Richard was always exposing me to new things and shocking me as we went about our chores around the farm. I tagged after him every day, sometimes blushing over things he talked about, his conversation littered with four-letter words, sometimes just studying the way his body moved as he went about his work. Although we were still uncomfortable with each other, he always took time to explain things about this new life that I was struggling to accept.

It was midwinter, and we didn't have to work in the fields, but there was still plenty to do. We had to split firewood and lug in armfuls every day to heat the drafty old farm house that wasn't nearly as nice as the two-story one with tall white columns in downtown Wilkinson we had lived in before Daddy was killed and Mama and I moved in with Aunt Bessie.

Richard tried to teach me to use the ax, but my swings were wobbly and weak, and, most of the time the base of the handle jammed into the log, shooting a stinging pain nearly to my elbows. Even worse, then Richard would laugh at me.

After a few tries, he gave me a hatchet and let me cut kindling wood while he did the heavy work. If it was warm enough, Richard would shed first his coat and then his shirt. I would watch with a peculiar growing excitement as he poised the heavy ax above his head, set his legs, and sent it rushing downward, the rope-like muscles on the sides of his bare back bunching at the impact and then relaxing, his grunting, "Huh!" melding with the solid "chunk" of the ax burying itself in the yielding wood, the pieces parting and toppling almost in slow motion.

Every morning we herded the cows out to pasture, the frosted grass crunching like thin glass tubing beneath our heavy brogans, our breath steaming in thick white swirls before us. We retrieved them after school and forked down peanut hay from the barn loft after Richard finished milking.

I could not get used to him squirting my face with a sudden jet of warm milk when I least expected it, and I flushed with embarrassment every time he tried to teach me to milk and I could not get a flow. "A tit's just like your dick," he said once. "You have to pull on it slow and steady until it gets to feeling good and the cow gives up her milk."

I didn't know what he was talking about; I never had to pull on mine to pee. But I knew it was dirty talk, grown-up talk, and it excited me, even if I did flush scarlet to the roots every time he talked that way.

When he bent down and took one of the cow's teats in his mouth and sucked it one day, I was speechless. "Here, try it," he insisted. "It tastes good."

Grimacing with reluctance, when he shoved my head down, I dropped to my knees and took the teat partly in my mouth. He squeezed and tugged at it above my lips, and a stream of warm milk flooded into my mouth. I quickly withdrew my head and swallowed. "Feels good, huh?" he said, grinning at me. "Probably like giving a blow job." I didn't know what a blow job was, but I wasn't about to expose my ignorance by asking.

Tagging after Richard was about the only thing that made my new life bearable. I had retreated into some deep, private well of unhappiness after Daddy was killed. It was as if all my boyish exuberance for life had drained out of me and flowed into the dark red earth as Daddy was lowered to rest. Then Mama and I had packed up and moved in with Aunt Bessie, a stern, humorless old maid who always made me feel that she was afraid I was going to break something in her house. I tiptoed around her, too scared to do much besides sit in my room and read for most of the year we lived with her. Just as I was beginning to adjust to the twin traumas of Daddy's death and living with her, Mama took me out to the farm to meet Richard and his little sisters, and she and Mr. McCluney told us they were getting married.

Right after New Years, Mama and Vernon were married in Aunt Bessie's parlor. Since the War was on and gasoline was rationed, they just drove to Atlanta for the weekend, and Monday Vernon loaded our possessions on his old pickup and we moved to the farm.

It was only after we started unloading things that I found out I had to share not only a room, but a bed with Richard. Actually, it was hardly a room, just an unheated, shelled-in place with unfinished walls and exposed rafters that had been added on when the McCluneys got indoor plumbing.

After Richard ordered me to stay over against the wall and not pee the bed, I was terrified to sleep with him. Night after

night, I hugged the wall and refused to move until my arms and legs were numb. Most nights I soundlessly cried myself to sleep long after Richard's breathing had become deep and regular.

The weather changed all that and changed Richard's and my relationship forever. In early February, it sleeted and turned as cold as it ever gets in central Georgia. Water pipes burst, and icicles a foot long hung from the eaves of houses. The red clay earth froze and spewed up several inches high along roadways, and pine saplings snapped from the weight of the ice. Richard's and my little room was frigid, and the wind whistled through cracks around the windows.

"It's cold as a witch's tit," Richard said as we hurried out of our clothes.

"Yeah," I agreed, through chattering teeth. I hugged my arms across my chest, dreading to hit the cold sheets.

Despite having so many quilts piled on we practically smothered, our bed was a cake of ice, the chill penetrating our heavy union suits. As I lay curled up with my whole body trembling, I could feel the bed move from Richard's own shivering.

"Scoot over this way," he said, and I backed right up against him. He huddled up close against my back and put his arm tight around my chest. Almost immediately, I began to warm up. In no time I fell asleep, secure in the protective warmth of Richard's embrace. All during the night, we became each other's heater and kept turning at some unconscious signal to warm each other's back.

During the several days that the cold snap lasted, we started whispering and giggling and sharing secrets as we lay huddled against each other every night before falling asleep. After the weather warmed up, we kept whispering and huddling, and we developed a kind of friendship - and, eventually, more.

One night I was almost asleep when Richard began pushing and rubbing against my butt. I didn't know what was going on, so I just lay still and pretended to be asleep. Richard shoved the covers down and unbuttoned the flap of my union suit. I shivered from the sudden rush of cold air against my bare buttocks and then relaxed as his warm body pressed tight against me. He slipped his dick high up between my legs and

slowly pushed in and out. His dick was hot and wet, and it tickled almost more than I could bear when it rubbed right up behind my balls. I shifted slightly to relieve the agonizing stimulation.

"You awake?" Richard asked.

"Yeah," I said, "What're you doing?"

"I'm tired of jacking off. I want something different tonight," he explained.

"It's all right; I don't mind," I said, under the spell of a vague, nascent excitement.

"You can play with yours while I do it," Richard said.

"How?" I asked. My peter got hard once in awhile, especially sometimes when a friend of mine and I wrestled around and rubbed against each other, but I always ignored it until it went down.

"Here, I'll show you," Richard said. He unbuttoned the front of my underwear, reached in for my little peter, and started moving his wet fingers up and down on it, squeezing and rolling it around. Almost immediately, it got hard. Richard took his hand away. "Keep doing it like that, and it'll tickle real good," he said. He went back to pushing between my legs.

It didn't tickle before Richard quit that night, but next day in the toilet, I kept at it until it felt so good I closed my eyes and quit moving my fingers and just held it tight for awhile. Richard started pushing between my legs almost every night, and sometimes I could make mine tickle before he was through.

Neither one of us ever said a word the next day about what we had done the night before. Richard never warned me not to tell, but somehow I knew even that first night that it was a mysterious secret that we shared only in bed, a secret nobody else could ever know about.

Richard quickly became bolder. Soon he had me handle his dick, which was about as big as a weenie, and play with his balls while he instructed me on how to jack him off. My balls, nestled tight against my body, were about the size of the agate I used to shoot marbles, but his were closer to the Bantam eggs we collected, and they hung down lower than mine. He had wispy hair growing around his dick, and I was fascinated by running my hands through it while he lay groaning and squirming.

When the weather opened up, we shed first our union suits and then our drawers and started sleeping naked. Once in awhile, Richard would lie facing me and hold me tight, his stomach grinding into my hard little peter, while he slid between my legs. Before we started, he would have me spit on his dick and get it good and slippery.

Toward the end of that first spring, a warm, sticky fluid was on my legs when Richard finished. "What is that stuff?" I asked.

"It's called come," he said.

"Is it because of all the milk you drink?" I asked.

He broke out laughing. "No, dodo, it's what makes babies if you do it to a woman and come inside her."

"Why doesn't it come out of mine?" I asked.

"You're not old enough. I'm just starting to do it. When I'm older, there'll be lots more of it, enough to make lots of babies," he said.

I was fascinated by this new ability of his, and I persuaded him to leave the light on sometimes and let me jack him off until it came out of him. I enjoyed the experience as much as he did.

Richard spent most of his time with me in the afternoon after we finished with chores. He dug out a couple of old baseball gloves, and we played pitch until it was too dark to see the ball. We tramped the woods together, and he pointed out all kinds of plants and trees and taught me their names. He showed me where to locate a big black walnut tree and some bullace grape vines. We romped around playing War, taking turns being the Japs or Germans. When it got warm enough, he taught me to swim in the pond out in the middle of the cow pasture. Some Saturdays, we hiked for miles to the Ocmulgee and camped out, cooking catfish we caught from the muddy red river over an open fire, and sleeping close together in a pup tent. With all this attention, I developed a strong case of hero worship. I would have done anything to stay in his good favor.

Not too long after he had started to come, one night as I was playing with his balls and getting his dick good and hard before he put it between my legs, he said, "Let's play cow and calf."

"What's that?" I asked.

"I'll get on my hands and knees, and you crawl under me

and suck on it like a calf does," he said.

"Uh-uh. I can't put my mouth on it. It's dirty," I objected.

"You know I just took a bath," he said. "Come on, Jody, let's try it. It'll be fun."

He straddled my chest, on hands and knees, and I scooted down until his dick was just over my head. When he kept insisting, I raised up and took his dick in my mouth and sucked on it. He began pushing in and out, and in no time, the warm sticky fluid, tasting faintly of Clorox, streamed into my mouth.

After that night, Richard wasn't satisfied rubbing between my legs; he always wanted my mouth on it. Only we didn't play cow and calf anymore. As we got started, he would just say, "Suck it, Jody," or push my head down firmly without saying anything. It was weeks before he told me this was called giving a blow job.

One afternoon, after we had swum in the pond awhile, we got to fooling around on the soft grass that edged the pond. A few minutes into our routine, he pulled out of my mouth.

"Let's play bull and cow," he said.

I was pretty sure what he meant, but I asked anyway, my heart pumping with a growing fear.

"Spit all over it and get me good and slippery," he instructed after he had explained what we were going to do. I slicked him up, and he said, "Get on your hands and knees."

I obeyed, but as he kneeled between my legs, the realization of what was about to happen almost panicked me. "I don't want to; It'll hurt!" I protested.

"No, it won't. Just hold still. I'll go in nice and slow," he said, stretching me open with both thumbs. The spit-slickened head of his dick slid in, stinging like fire.

"Take it out! It hurts!" I cried out, twisting and shrinking away from him.

He just kept pushing in deeper, putting his weight on my back and following me down until I was flat on my stomach. Without ever saying a word, he hunched away, ignoring my whimpering beneath him, until he got the good feeling he was after and collapsed on my back.

"Let's go swimming," he grinned at me when he finally got up.

"That hurt," I complained.

"You'll get used to it," he said, dragging me to the water. He was in the best mood I had ever seen him in, and he roughhoused and teased with me more than usual. I knew that it was because of the new way he had just done it to me.

He started doing it that way most of the time, and I did get used to having him inside me, even when his dick became huge almost overnight in a rapid spurt of growth. As with our earlier game, he never referred to bull and cow after that first time, but simply muttered, "Turn over," or tugged at my hips and flipped me onto my stomach any time he decided he wanted to do it that way.

As much as I worshipped him and enjoyed being around him and learning things from him, I knew from the beginning that we did not have much in common, aside from our secret activities, which were enjoyable to me mostly because I liked being close to him and doing things to please him.

Richard was not dumb, but he had no interest in school and would never have thought to read anything he didn't have to. His interests were more physical, and, as he matured, he developed a big, muscled body and athletic skills to go with it. By his junior year of high school, he was the star of the football, basketball, and baseball teams, and was one of the most popular boys at school.

Occasionally, I dreamed of having a body and skills like his, but, although I was not fragile and held my own in rough-and-tumble play with other boys, I had very little athletic ability and even less interest in organized sports. I had little more interest in cultivating friends, preferring to spend my free time reading. Before I reached high school, I had read everything of interest in our sparsely stocked small-town library and was spending what little allowance money I got on a membership in the Doubleday Dollar Book Club.

Whenever Richard had to give a book report in high school, I coached him on plot details of a novel he never bothered to read and wrote the report, requiring him only to copy it in his handwriting. He was hopelessly lost when he had to take algebra, and I mastered it years ahead of schedule so I could teach him enough for a D in the class.

As he got older, Richard had more and more friends his age out to the farm on weekends or went to visit them. He made it

obvious that he didn't want me hanging around when he was with them, and I spent less and less time with him. The only thing that did not change right away was our nights together in bed.

About the time Japan surrendered and the war ended, when I was ten, Richard became best friends with Travis Peavy. That fall, they both started ninth grade and played football. They were always together. Richard sometimes spent the night with Travis, and, a few times, Travis stayed over at our house, sharing the bed with Richard while I slept fitfully on a pallet in the corner. Whenever they were together, all they talked about was girls, and the size of their boobs, and which ones they would like to do it with, and what their chances were. As their friendship intensified and Richard took up less and less time with me, I became jealous and resentful of Travis, but also vaguely excited around him.

Of course, I had known who Travis was for years; in our little town, everybody had at least a passing acquaintance with everybody else. Travis' father owned Peavy's Drugs in downtown Wilkinson, a favorite hangout for kids because it had the only soda fountain in town. Even before he became a teenager, Travis worked at the store, sometimes dipping ice cream or making chocolate malteds.

When he came to the farm, he pretty well ignored me, except to tease me about spending all my time reading. Once in awhile, when Richard was getting dressed or something, he would talk to me, and I soon found out that he liked to read, too, though he never let on about it around his friends.

When I was about twelve, the American Legion sponsored a teenage baseball team, and Vernon, a baseball fanatic, was named manager. Of course, Richard and Travis were the star players.

Although baseball bored me, I got drafted as the team's statistician. After Vernon showed me how to mark each play in the scorebook, Saturday after Saturday, I would pile into the back of Vernon's pickup with some of the players and take off for Gordon or Deepstep or wherever and then sit on the unshaded player's bench out in some cow pasture, sweltering in the relentless July and August heat, eyes squinted almost closed against the glaring sun, and keep score. I always prayed

for a pitchers' duel, so the game wouldn't drag on forever.

As much as I disliked baseball, I was always vaguely excited during inning changes, when Richard and Travis and the other players crowded around the water cooler at the end of the bench beside me, smelling more and more of sweat, their jockstraps molding a neat mound in the crotches of their tight, damp uniforms. They stood with their legs spread and held soggy cuds of Beechnut or Day's Work tobacco in one hand while, one after another, they swished and rinsed and spat, the foul juice staining the powdery red earth in dark splotches beneath their feet, before they took long draughts of cool water from the communal tin cup. Then, especially if we won the game, I would ride home silent and somehow content among them as they jubilantly replayed the game, told dirty jokes, boasted about their sexual activities, and made other man-talk.

Back at home, if Richard and Travis were going out for the night, sometimes Travis would bathe and change clothes at our house and stay for supper. I always found a reason to be in the bedroom while they peeled off their sweaty uniforms and individually went to take a bath. Seeing Travis fully naked became an obsession for me, but he always stripped down only to his jock strap and took his underwear with him to the bathroom.

One afternoon, as he lounged on the bed and flipped through the bra and panty section of the Sears, Roebuck catalog while Richard took his bath, I sneaked looks at his crotch, where I was sure I saw him slowly tightening and swelling beneath his jockstrap. My breathing became short and labored, and my own crotch tightened.

He caught me looking. "Wanta sniff my jock?" he asked, cupping the pouch in his hand and tugging up the side enough to reveal a few wisps of pubic hair.

I flushed down to my toes and quickly turned back to my model plane, my heart pounding, my erection shriveling.

"I don't mind if you look, Jody," he said through a teasing laugh. "I might even let you touch sometime."

I was saved further humiliation by Richard coming back in. Travis turned and smirked at me as he went for his bath.

For the next couple of years, he occasionally teased me like that, but mostly he called me a sissy and even a fairy

sometimes when we were with other guys and Richard wasn't around. Despite this torment, I was drawn to him by some magnetism I did not understand, and I arranged to be around him whenever I could.

Just as I was detecting the first hints of approaching puberty and my times with Richard were beginning to excite me in a way unrelated to my desire to please my hero, Richard became madly attracted to Shirley Quinn. For weeks, that's all he talked about, and, while he thrust inside me at night, he would tell me how much he wished it was Shirley and what he would like to do with her. As he approached climax and began coming, he would be whispering her name, as he had never whispered mine. I began to resent Shirley's intrusion on our times together and to wonder why he wasn't satisfied with me.

One night he crawled into bed smelling of beer and woke me out of a sound sleep. As was my habit, I wordlessly reached between his legs, but he pushed my hand away.

"Not tonight, kiddo," he said, his voice dancing with happiness. "It finally happened! And, man, it was something!" he said, bouncing onto the mattress, hands locked behind his head.

"What was? What happened?" I asked.

"I finally did it with Shirley! You wouldn't believe how great it was, Jody." He leaned up on an elbow. "I popped her cherry in Travis' back seat, while he was trying to get beyond first base with Mary Beth in front. God, we made a mess, with blood all over, but I got her cherry! And I lost mine. I ain't virgin anymore!"

From then on, he just lay in bed and talked to me about what he had done with one girl after another before we went to sleep. He did not initiate anything with me anymore, unless he came in about drunk and in need after a fight with his current girlfriend. Once, out of desperation, I groped for his crotch, hoping he would be interested, but he turned on his side.

"Go to sleep, Jody," he said. "I don't need none of that kid stuff anymore."

Without even having a name for what I was feeling, I cried myself to sleep that night over a tremendous sense of loss. In the following weeks, I realized that it all had been a mere interlude for Richard, that I had been nothing more than a

marginally satisfying stand-in until he could achieve what he really desired.

I retreated inward again, not recognizing the irony of the fact that, just when our relationship was assuming an importance to me of such magnitude that it eventually would have led to self-recognition, it had become completely meaningless for Richard.

TWO
ABANDONED BIRDS' NESTS

> *"Hope is the thing with feathers*
> *That perches in the soul..."*
> *– Emily Dickinson*

After what seemed like hours of sweating over the pile of Sunday dinner dishes, I finally rinsed and dried the big blue roasting pan with the white specks in it and put it away and hung up the drying cloth. It had been a particularly onerous chore because - as usual - Richard wasn't around to help, and my stepsisters had to hurry off to a birthday party. Throughout the ordeal, I fumed that I probably was the only thirteen-year-old boy in the county who had to spend all Sunday afternoon washing dishes. I was in a hurry to meet my new friend, Ellis Goddard, at our special place in the woods, and I kept fretting that he would have given up on me and found something else to do by the time I got there.

Rubbing my prune-wrinkled fingers on my pants legs, I eased onto the front porch, where Mama and Vernon and Aunt Myrtle and Uncle Roy rocked and fanned in unison with little funeral parlor fans as they reminisced about a square dance in Devereaux when they were young.

"I'm all through," I said, barreling into the first gap in their conversation. "Can I go see Ellis?" Not waiting for an answer, I hurried down the steps before anyone could think of something else for me to do.

"You behave yourself, Jody," Mama reminded me, as she always did when I was going to be out of her sight for more than ten minutes.

"Yes'm," I answered by rote, crossing the yard.

As I cut around the house, Vernon's, "You be home in time for chores, boy, y'hear?" echoed in my ears. Then I was free.

On the way to meet Ellis, I trotted through the corn field, shielding my face and bare chest against the rasp of coarse, broad leaves with my forearms, my bare feet stinging from the heat of the sun-baked earth of the middles. On the other side of the field, I followed the little branch that flowed through Mr. Hargrove's farm, consciously luxuriating in the dark coolness of

the huge oaks canopying its banks. Anxious as I was that Ellis would have given up on me and left, I stopped a minute to poke at a dead dog that lay partially in the water, its stomach bloated, its blank eyes staring at nothing.

I didn't know why I stopped; things like that didn't bother me anymore. Like the overnight bursts of spring wildflowers in the meadow or the patchwork of sweetgum and maple quilting the hillsides in fall, cruelty and suffering and death were natural occurrences on the farm. Vernon said it was the same everywhere; it was just part of the human condition. I had gotten so I didn't even flinch anymore at hog-killing time when Vernon - or, as he got older, Richard - stuck the rifle between a hog's eyes and pulled the trigger and the hog squealed and kicked and flopped a little before it lay still. It had been a long time since I'd woke up with a bad dream about the time Vernon had clubbed old Queen's newborn litter to death because we couldn't afford any more mouths to feed, even if old Queen was a good hunting dog and their sire was one of the best in the county.

About the only thing that bothered me anymore, though it excited me, too, was a young mare's frantic pacing and twisting at breeding time when the stud was brought in, and her terrifying scream when the stud finally mounted her. Dogs were mostly quiet when they mated, except that time Vernon tried to pull a stray off one of his bitches and the male got turned around backwards, and Vernon kicked at them, with them stuck together and howling and crying, until he finally kicked them apart.

Lately, all kinds of sexual thoughts intruded at the oddest moments, and sometimes I wondered if I was the only person in the world who spent so much time thinking about sex. In all the years since Richard first started with me, I had never been much concerned about what we did together. It wasn't anything I particularly looked forward to or thought much about afterward; it was just something that had been happening since I was nine. But as I started my own physical development, it was accompanied by an actively emerging fantasy life which dominated my attention more and more.

From years of church-going and revival meetings, I knew all about spilling your seed and lying with another man, and now

I was embarrassed and self-conscious about the rapid changes in my body and the urges I couldn't resist satisfying. I started to think that Mama and Vernon and every other adult could tell exactly what I did with myself almost every night before Richard came to bed. I would swear off forever and manage about a week before I gave in when I wasn't strong enough to resist the temptation and kept tossing and turning in bed, unable to go to sleep.

More and more, my thoughts at such times turned to Ellis. About a month before school let out for the summer, we had become good friends, and my desire to be with him had become so strong that I was spending a lot of time figuring out ways to be around him.

I had known Ellis most of my life; I had known everybody most of my life. Nobody moved in or out of Wilkinson, they just got born or died. Everybody went to Liberty Creek School until they were bused to the county high school when they started eighth grade. Some of my teachers had taught Mama and Vernon when they were young. Everybody went to church at New Hope Methodist or Bethel Baptist - or sometimes both, if their parents were members of different churches, as mine were.

Sitting around on porches in summer or in front of fireplaces in winter, everybody expressed the same opinions and voiced the same complaints about the Republicans and vowed that the communists were taking over the country. Every Saturday night, everybody huddled in front of the radio listening to the Grand Ole Opry, and whenever they got together, the men told the same hunting stories over and over, or talked about the same drought or big freeze. Nothing ever changed much, and everybody just took it all for granted.

Which is what I had done with Ellis, until a year before, when I was turning twelve. Late that spring, for the first time in my life, I had started skinny-dipping at Liberty Creek with a bunch of boys after school, if there wasn't plowing or other chores to do. It gave us a chance to escape the watchful eye of parents, to eat watermelon which we filched from old man Sherrer's field and cooled in the creek, and to smoke cigarettes and talk about sex, which suddenly was on everybody's mind.

Most of the boys were older than me, thirteen or even

fourteen. Because I read so much, I was more knowledgeable than most of them, though, and I gained instant acceptance when I brought along a dog-eared copy of *God's Little Acre* and read aloud some of the more salacious passages.

As we frolicked in the shallow pool, we did a lot of physical comparing and a lot of teasing about whether we all played with ourselves. Several of the boys were fully developed, with underarm hair and everything. At first, I was self-conscious about my child's body, but nobody teased me, and I soon relaxed. Toward the end of summer, as we were horsing around and dunking each other, Bernie, the oldest and most aggressive of our group, stood up in thigh-deep water, exposing a full erection. He stroked it slowly a few times and then challenged us all to get out and do it along with him. After a lot of hesitating and embarrassed laughter, everybody agreed.

From then on, it became something of a ritual every time we went swimming. It wasn't always exactly the same group of boys; at times some of us couldn't make it for some reason, and occasionally a new boy would join us. But somebody must have talked to the new ones ahead of time, because they were always ready to join in the ritual when it started. It was all casual fun, and after the initial excitement of seeing them with hard-ons and discovering that I wasn't the only boy in the world who spent a lot of time thinking about sex and who played with myself, I was only mildly interested in it, preferring my own uninterrupted fantasies in the privacy of my own room.

A week or so before school started, I went to the creek by myself a little later than usual. As I walked down the narrow path toward the swimming hole, an unfamiliar voice cried out, "Ow, you're hurting!"

Curious, I crouched down and sneaked through the tall broom sedge beside the path until I could see the clearing where the creek made a turn to form the swimming hole. Nobody was in the water, and only two people were on the bank, naked. One was Bernie; the other was Ellis, who had never been to the creek with us before. Ellis poised on hands and knees, and Bernie kneeled behind him, holding his hips with his hands. Just about the time I was sure of what I was seeing, Bernie backed away from Ellis and stood up.

My face flushed with embarrassment, and I felt bad about

spying. I eased myself back to the path without a sound and then whistled a loud tune to warn them before I walked on down the path. Even so, I got there in time to see Ellis take off for a running dive into the creek.

"Hey, Jody; you're late," Bernie said, coming from behind some bushes shielding himself with his hands, his eyes guilty and evasive. "I thought I saw a snake crawl in here," he added, poking halfheartedly at the bushes with his bare foot.

"Was it a moccasin?" I asked, going along with things.

"Naw, I think a black snake," Bernie said.

I got out of my clothes and we swam a little, without the usual bantering and horsing around. We climbed up the slippery clay bank and stretched out on a patch of grass in the sun. Ellis dug out a Camel he had turned up from somewhere, and we passed it around, me taking little puffs and coughing and sputtering each time. As we lolled on the grass, our damp bodies tingling from the cool wind rustling through the towering trees, I was excited by Ellis, as I had never been by Bernie and the rest of the gang, and I kept sneaking glances at his body. Too soon, Ellis stood up and said he had to be going, and Bernie said so did he. As we got dressed, I was sorry that Bernie hadn't suggested our usual ritual.

Ellis never showed up at the creek again, but when school started, I found out he was repeating seventh grade, after having already failed an earlier grade. We were in class together every day, and I became more and more conscious of him as months dragged by. As we got to know each other better, every once in awhile when I was in bed at night and couldn't sleep, it was as if a Kodak picture would flash through my mind, and I would see Ellis' body just before he hit the water that day at the creek.

By late winter, when Ellis was going on fifteen, I noticed how fast he was growing, and I was intrigued by the soft hair sprouting on his upper lip, which he shaved every once in awhile. He talked a lot about girls, and just before summer vacation, he was always teasing Judy Proctor and trying to feel her tits, which were bigger than most girls' two years ahead of us in school.

A long time before, I had decided that Ellis looked like the Phantom, which had become my favorite strip in the Sunday

comics. Ellis had the same straight nose, high cheekbones, thin lips, strong chin, and compact, tightly muscled body. I did not really know why I liked the Phantom so much or why I thought of him every time I was around Ellis. But that spring, I started sneaking the comic page to my room after supper every Sunday and lay exciting myself with fantasies of living in the Skull Cave with Ellis.

When we actually were together, we didn't ever do much, just poked around looking for snakes under rocks and logs in the branch, or slid down pinestraw-covered hills on pieces of cardboard, or swung across a dry gully on a rope we had climbed way up a big oak tree to tie to a limb.

The day before, we had hacked and tugged at kudzu vines that had completely shrouded another big oak until we made a small dark cave at the base of the tree where all the grass was dead from lack of sunlight. As we huddled close together in our narrow hideaway, thighs touching, and shared a cigarette which Ellis had lifted from his grandpa's pack, my pulse inexplicably raced; my chest felt suddenly tight and full, and I experienced a kind of ineffable excitement, almost painful, which was completely new to me. I wanted to reach out and touch Ellis, maybe put my arm around him, but something, some innate shyness, some confusion over these strange feelings, stopped me. I just sat unmoving, watching Ellis in the faint light filtering through the kudzu until he broke the spell. He stabbed the cigarette butt into the soft dirt and crawled out into the open air. I silently followed, my whole body trembling.

As I hurried to meet Ellis on that hot August Sunday afternoon, my pulse again raced and my chest again tightened in some vaguely defined hope that whatever had transpired the day before would be renewed and maybe farther advanced that afternoon, although I did not know specifically where I wanted it to go.

When I reached the curve where the path sloped down to the rope swing across the dry gully, that hope faded. Ellis was not by himself. Jack Switzer, who was about twelve and lived up the dirt road from Ellis, was swinging back and forth on the rope. As I walked on down to where Ellis sat, his bare back against a tree, I attempted to will Jack into going somewhere else and leaving me alone with Ellis. But, of course, Jack just

kept swinging.

Ellis had filched two Luckies from his grandpa. He put one aside for later, and lit up the other one. We passed it back and forth, after Ellis warned Jack not to nigger-lip it the way he usually did. When we finished smoking, Ellis reached into his hip pocket and turned to me with a big grin on his face. "Look what I got," he said, handing me a thin booklet printed on cheap paper.

Richard had shown me a few of these books. One I remembered was a crude comic strip of Mickey and Minnie Mouse, with exaggerated body parts, engaged in various sex acts. The one Ellis handed me featured Popeye and Olive Oyl, with the same exaggerated anatomy, in the same crude poses. As I disinterestedly flipped through the pages, Jack crowded against one shoulder and Ellis the other, both ogling the drawings.

"Damn, Popeye's big as a horse," Jack said.

"And look at them knockers on Olive Oyl," Ellis added. "They're bigger'n Judy's. Man, I'd like to get my hands on them. I can't get nowhere with the girls around here, and I'm so hard up I can't stand it."

I closed the booklet and handed it back to him. "I know what you mean," I agreed, "but there's not much we can do about it."

"Me and Ellis used to do things together," Jack blurted out. "We used to cornhole each other."

"Shut up!" Ellis lashed out.

"Why? We did used to," Jack said.

"Shut your damned mouth!" Ellis yelled, standing up.

"What are you getting mad about?" Jack said. He stood up, too, and backed away slightly, but he didn't have sense enough to keep his mouth shut. "We did used to; you know we did," he insisted.

Ellis' face underwent a complete transformation. He flushed deep red, his eyes blared, wild and scary, and a vein pulsed in his neck. In the dappled light beneath the trees, he looked like some crouching savage. "I told you to shut your goddamn mouth!" he hissed between clenched teeth. He grabbed Jack, roughly twisted one arm behind his back, and pounded him in the chest several times with his fist.

"Ow!" Jack screeched, trying to squirm away.

"I told you!" Ellis said. "I told you!" He hit Jack twice in the stomach, hard.

Jack doubled over and collapsed to the ground, whimpering in pain. Ellis stood over him, both fists balled up. He let Jack lay sniffling for awhile, and then he started kicking him in the butt.

"Get up and go on home," he said. "And don't ever talk that kind of queer shit again. Real guys don't do that stuff." He gave Jack one final kick. "Now drag your ass home and don't come hanging around again."

Jack hobbled down the path, bent over in pain, clutching his stomach with one arm, wiping away tears with the other. Ellis paced back and forth, too mad to stand still, and glared after Jack until he was out of sight.

I sat anxious and confused. I could not understand why Ellis had exploded in such raging fury. As I thought about it, two Kodak pictures flashed into my mind: the familiar one of Ellis diving into the creek with his erection sticking straight up, and almost on top of it, a second one of Bernie pulling out of Ellis and letting go of his hips.

I did not know how to interpret what was on Ellis' face while he was beating Jack. I just knew that it was something primitive and ugly and terrible, something that had changed my feelings for Ellis forever. With a sensation almost palpable, something burst out from deep inside me, leaving a hollow that I knew would never be completely filled.

Then, as quick as a cloud passes across the sun on a hot day when you're praying for shade, Ellis' face shifted, and the terrible ugliness was gone.

"Come on, I want to show you something," he said, starting down the path.

"What?" I asked, not really interested.

"Come on!" Ellis urged, his voice boyishly eager. "I'll show you a bird's nest. We'll have to climb way up in a tree, but it still has two real pretty blue-speckled eggs in it. Come on!"

"Not now," I said. I started down the path the other way. "I've got to get going; I've got chores."

As I slouched down the path toward home, I felt as if Ellis had punched me in the stomach, too.

THREE
AT BIG RUBY'S

Of course, I knew all about Big Ruby. By the time we were nine or ten, all of us boys in Pelham County knew about her, and where she lived, and how she supported herself and her son, Adolph. She was the only one in town, so most guys eventually got around to knocking on her door, since the girls didn't give up anything, unless maybe you were a good-looking football star like my stepbrother, Richard, or drove around in a big new car like his friend Travis.

I suppose somewhere in the back of my mind I always took for granted that I would pay Big Ruby a visit someday, too, an assumption about as conscious as the awareness that I would grow old, and maybe become fat or bald, and eventually die. A month shy of my fourteenth birthday, I was experiencing some strong, but confusing, urges, with no really satisfying outlet for them, but as I sat squeezed in between Travis and Johnny in the front seat of Travis' Olds, on the way to her house, with Rhett and Benny and Pete and Chuck leaning over from the back, guzzling beer and practically frothing at the mouth with excitement, I was sure I wasn't ready for Big Ruby, and almost as sure I never would be.

Big Ruby was just what her name said. She was fat, and her enormous breasts jiggled when she walked, even though she had them strapped down. Her hair was dyed so red it was almost purple; her big mouth, which dominated her face, was always covered with bright red lipstick, and her cheeks were heavily rouged. She had to be at least ten years older than Mama and Vernon, and, except that she was fatter, she reminded me of Belle Watling in *Gone with the Wind*, which I'd seen in Macon after reading the novel.

She and Adolph lived way down on the south of town, where the Central of Georgia railroad crossed over Liberty Creek, and you never saw her downtown unless she was shopping. Then she scurried around like some night creature who's been flushed into the light, but she scurried with her head held high and her eyes straight ahead, even when Mama and the other ladies turned their backs as she passed. Once,

before Mama married Vernon and we moved out to the farm, we were in a store with Aunt Bessie when Ruby came in. As she walked by us, Aunt Bessie spat out, "Hussy!" as sharp as a whip crack. Big Ruby hesitated in her step and hunched over, as if she'd been hit between the shoulder blades, then quickly straightened her back and kept walking without turning her head. Mama grabbed me by the ear and snatched my head around so hard she nearly tore my ear off when I kept watching Ruby go down the aisle.

The older boys joked that some of the wives had cause enough to hate her, because they were so ugly a good part of their husbands' wages wound up in Ruby's hands. They also said she just lay there eating peanuts and timed them with a clock while they did their business, but Richard told me it wasn't so, at least not when he'd been to see her.

As we got close to her house, I prayed for time to turn back fifteen minutes, to just before the point where I had been fool enough to get myself in this predicament. Usually, when Travis started tormenting me, I ignored it as best I could, or just walked away from him if he kept it up. That night, though, when he started in on me around a group of guys outside the picture show, I didn't have sense enough to keep my mouth shut.

Travis and Richard had been best friends for years, and Travis spent a good bit of time out at the farm. From the beginning, I was always nervous and keyed up around him, and when he occasionally slapped me on the back or punched my shoulder playfully, just his touch gave me goosebumps. Since he was four years older than me, though, he had always pretty well ignored me, except for a few snide remarks about me always having my nose in a book. When I started high school and didn't go out for football, though, Travis started teasing me about being a sissy. As the year progressed and I didn't try out for basketball or baseball, his goading became more vicious, and he even got to calling me a fairy when Richard wasn't around, and suggesting what I could do for him. For awhile I worried that maybe he knew about Richard and me, but then I decided there was no way he could know anything.

That night, I was just standing outside shooting the bull with

Rhett after the movie when Travis screeched his Olds to a stop in front of us and got out to talk to Rhett. I could smell beer on him as soon as he walked up, and I saw the others in the car swigging on their Blue Ribbons.

"We're going to Ruby's for a piece of ass," Travis said to Rhett. "Want to come?"

"Got more beer? I'd have to get tanked up before I could plow through all that fat," Rhett said. They both laughed, and Travis slapped him on the back.

"Yeah, we got plenty. We'll ride around a little to let you catch up," he said. Then he noticed me. "Want to come, squirt? Naah! Fairies like you wouldn't know what to do with it," he said.

"Shut the fuck up! I'm not a fairy," I surprised myself.

"Well, you sure got me fooled," Travis sneered. "But come on to Ruby's and prove what a big man you are. I'll even pay for your first piece of ass."

"Yeah, come on, Jody. It's time to pop your cherry!" Rhett said, clamping me on the shoulder and steering me toward the car.

At Big Ruby's, after everybody had paid their money and she moved to the bedroom, Travis wanted to shove me in first, but Johnny bought me a little time by saying he didn't want seconds from a little shit like me. When he came out grinning and tucking in his shirt a few minutes later, though, Travis pulled me to my feet and I knew there was no way out of it.

As I closed the bedroom door behind me, I almost panicked and ran back through it. Big Ruby lounged on the bed in a scarlet terry cloth robe which she hadn't bothered to gather around her. Her fat hung in layers, blue-veined and fish-belly white. "Well, drop your pants and come on over," she said in a deep throaty purr. "Let's see what I'm gonna get for your money."

I fumbled with my pants and crossed toward her. I stopped beside the bed, just out of her reach. My heart was pumping like crazy. For some reason, Sidney Carton's "It is a far, far better rest I go to" speech flashed through my mind, and, as terrified as I was, I almost laughed at the absurdity of it all. There I stood with my pants open, all shriveled up, quoting the execution lines from *A Tale of Two Cities* to myself, when any

other boy would be all hard and rearing to go.

"Come on, honey," Ruby encouraged. I took another step, and she reached out to help me with my pants and pulled my underwear down. As she dipped into a washpan for a rag with some kind of mediciney liquid on it and started to wash me off, she looked up into my face, and then just gently fondled me.

"You don't really want to do this, do you?" she asked.

"No, ma'am," I muttered.

"Ma'am!" she said, laughing softly. "Ain't nobody ever called me ma'am in this room before." She dropped the smelly rag back into the pan. "I'll tell you what. I've already got your money, so you don't have to do nothing you don't want to. It'll be our secret. Besides, it'll give me a little breather before them other wild Indians charge in. How does that sound?" She reached to light a cigarette.

"All right," I said. It really sounded heavenly.

"Then pull your clothes up and set a spell. Some of you young bucks just try to prove yourselves before you're ready. After awhile, you go out fixing your pants, with a big smile on your face, and everything'll be fine."

"Yes, ma'am," I said. I sat gingerly on the edge of the bed, not too close to her.

"You're Vernon McCluney's step-boy, ain't you?" she asked. "What's that crazy Richard doing with hisself? He ain't been to see me in a long while."

She sounded really interested, so I told her. "He's mostly spending time with Nadine Mullins over by Dry Branch."

"I might have guessed," Ruby said. "That silly girl ought to've made him put a ring on her finger. That boy ain't ever going to buy the cow when the milk's free."

I couldn't think of an answer, so we sat quiet for awhile. Then, stubbing out her lipstick-stained cigarette in the overflowing ashtray on the table, Ruby said, "You'd best get on out there; lingering too long's as bad as leaving too quick." As I stood up, she winked lewdly and added, "Come see me when you've growed a little more."

When I opened the door, Travis was standing there, naked, with an erection even bigger than Richard's, which had always seemed huge to me. I had to force my eyes away from it so he wouldn't catch me staring. "How'd it go, squirt?" he asked.

"Never you mind, Travis," Ruby scolded. "He did just fine. Now get on over here and let's take care of that big thing for you."

I knew I couldn't just sit there with the other guys, so after I'd smiled and said, "Fine," to their questions, I went outside across the junk-strewn dirt yard and sat on the front fender of Travis' car, my knees drawn up under my chin. The sweet aroma of wisteria washed over me from the creek bank, and chuckwill'swidows courted softly across the night breeze in the huge oaks. At that moment, I felt completely hollow and inadequate, without knowing why. I wanted to cry, but tears would not come.

"Hey, Jody," a voice startled me. I turned and saw Adolph standing at my shoulder. He had crept up so silently I hadn't heard him.

"Hey, Adolph," I said, disinterested.

Although he was three years older than me, Adolph and I had been in the same class for awhile in grade school, before he quit altogether. Even then, he had been almost a complete stranger. Nobody knew anything about his father. One story had it that he wasn't a bastard at all, but that Ruby had married one of her clients, who later got killed, but most people figured he was an accident that Ruby hadn't caught until it was too late.

Of course, none of us kids were allowed to play with him, or to do more than speak at school. The teachers picked on him in class, and older boys tormented him at recess. When he dropped out, nobody even noticed.

Since then, he'd hung out around town, occasionally getting into trouble with the police, but mostly tinkering with old cars, which cluttered up his whole yard. Tall and skinny, he had straight black hair which looked like it was plastered to his head with motor oil from one of his cars. He had little narrow-set, weasel eyes, a weak, receding chin, and a swarthy complexion that made him look like he needed a bath.

"Got a smoke?" he asked, sidling close enough to brush my shoulder.

"Naw, I don't carry 'em," I said.

"Couldn't get it up with Ruby, huh?" he asked.

"How do you know?" I said.

"I got a peephole in my closet. I watch sometimes, especially when new ones come in." His talk made me feel dirty, and I shrank away when he moved closer and rested his hand on my shoulder. The thought of him watching his own mother with all those men turned my stomach.

"Maybe I can do for you what Ruby couldn't," he said, sliding his hand off my shoulder and down my chest and then up my thigh to my knee, which was still tucked under my chin. He gave my leg a squeeze and moved his body right up against me. "I bet I can give you the kind of good time you really want," he said, something in his voice making my skin crawl.

He was so close he was breathing on my neck and down my collar, and his body heat was almost more than I could bear. I wanted to move away, but I just sat there, my whole body trembling, with strange spasms tightening my stomach, making it hard to breathe. His hand inched back down my thigh and rested in my crotch. He started a rhythmic squeezing and whispered right into my ear, "I'll take care of you if you'll buy me a pack of smokes."

"There's a new pack of Luckies on the dash," I croaked hoarsely, dropping my legs off the front of the car, giving his hand more freedom.

"Get 'em and come on," he said, giving me one more squeeze and stepping away.

More excited than I'd ever been, with curious new feelings churning inside me, I reached in for the pack of Travis' cigarettes and followed Adolph around the side of the house. He grabbed the Luckies and stuffed them in his shirt pocket, and then opened the door of an old car without any interior lights. He pulled me close, unfastened my belt, and slid my pants and underwear down, freeing my erection, as urgent as the one I'd witnessed on Travis earlier. "Yeah, you really want this," he said, tantalizing me with his fingers. "Lay down on the seat."

I stretched out across the worn fabric, and my nose protested against the pungent smell of decay. My mind recoiled from the sordidness of what was happening, but my body, quivering with expectation, was in control. Nobody had ever touched me like this, except that one time years before, when Richard had shown me how to play with myself while he thrust away

between my legs in the double bed we shared after I moved out to the farm.

Adolph tugged my pants down to my ankles and positioned himself on the floorboard beside me. When his moist, warm mouth suddenly took almost all of me in, it was as if an electric charge ran through me and arched my back clear off the car seat. "Don't; it tickles too much," I complained, shrinking away and pushing at his head roughly. He grabbed both my hands and shoved them away while he continued his manipulations.

Every movement of his lips or tongue created a distinct, acutely pleasant stimulation, more heightened than the last. "So this is how it feels to Richard," I thought. Then I closed my eyes and floated out of myself and swirled in a fevered, mindless, eddying void of pleasurable sensation.

I was brought back to earth all too soon by an involuntary flexing in my buttocks, which was lifting me all the way off the seat and driving me deep into Adolph's mouth. He clung to my thighs and matched my thrusts with his bobbing head until I clutched frantically at his greasy hair and cried out loud as a surge of release swept all through me and peaked with more force than my body had ever experienced before. I held onto his head possessively long after I quit coming and sagged back onto the seat.

He broke my grip and sat up to spit out the door. "You liked the shit outta that, didn't you?" he said, his voice hard and mean, as he got out of the car. "You ever want it again, it's gonna cost you some bucks. You ain't gonna get it any more for a pack of smokes. I got my business same as Ruby, and I'm better at all kinds of things than she is."

He walked away, and I lay there awhile, not wanting to move, my pants around my ankles, a warm satisfaction still in my groin, and breathed the mildewed decay of the old car mingled with the cloying sweetness of wisteria and listened to night birds call among the trees. I no longer felt empty or inadequate.

I never went back to visit Ruby or Adolph, and I never gave either one of them much thought. But for weeks and months afterward, my memories of that night were dominated by the image of Travis standing naked in Ruby's doorway, and from

that night on, every time I was around him, a peculiar, demanding excitement stirred in the pit of my stomach.

FOUR
A DEBT TO NORAH LOFTS

"Here, Jody. Have another swig," Richard said, shoving the Mason jar under my nose.

Ignoring Mama wrinkling her nose in disapproval, I took a small sip of the lightning, which hit my throat like a hot coal.

"Atta boy!" Richard said, slapping me on the back. It was still hours before he had to catch the Trailways bus in Macon, but he was already wearing his dress uniform with the sharpshooter medal pinned on his chest and was more good-looking than ever. He was pretty well along toward being pie-eyed. I had already taken a couple of sips when Vernon first pulled the jar out of its hiding place. The shine, which had scalded all the way down, sat heavy in my stomach, and a warm glow seeped all through my body.

Mama, a staunch Baptist, hadn't said a word or given one of her withering looks when Vernon first passed the jar around, although, except for her and Vernon, nobody was old enough to drink. She hadn't even said anything about Richard keeping Black Label in the refrigerator the whole time he'd been home on leave from the Army. After all, he was on his way to Korea, and even Mama reasoned that, if he was old enough to fight and maybe get killed, he was old enough to drink a few beers.

Nobody had really talked about it, but I knew that his going off to fight was on everybody's mind. President Truman had just relieved General MacArthur from command, and things weren't going too well for our troops. Richard had made light of the whole thing around the family, but I had learned to read his moods better than anybody else, and I knew it had gnawed away at him the whole time.

It was mostly what was making him so grumpy around Betty Sue now, and causing him to keep shoving the Mason jar at his best friend, Travis, after taking a good slug himself. Betty Sue, who was losing hope that Richard would give her an engagement ring before he left, kept putting mushy songs like Patti Page's "All My Love" on the record player and coaxing Richard to dance with her.

Travis, pretty high from the shine himself, trapped me in a

corner to tell me how much he was going to miss Richard. While we talked, he absently draped his arm around my shoulder and left it there. Although he seldom teased me or called me a fairy anymore, I got nervous every time I was around him, and his touching me and breathing on my neck made me uncomfortable. While I was figuring out how to escape from him, I could see Betty Sue whispering urgently in Richard's ear, and she almost broke down and cried when he walked away from her in the middle of a song and went to join some other guys in the kitchen.

Travis finally took his arm off my shoulder and followed after Richard. As they got louder and louder, with what I knew was forced jollity, and as the living room heated up more and more, though it was only the first week of May, I got to feeling a little queasy from the shine, so I went out on the back porch for some fresh air.

The farewell party was turning into one big unhappy occasion, but I refused to succumb to the darkening mood. Despite being a little sad about Richard heading to Korea, I had had a good time while he was on leave, even if I had had to share the double bed with him again, just when I was getting used to having it to myself.

Richard had always seemed like two different people to me. Around the rest of the family and especially around his friends, he was cold and distant and mostly ignored me. After we got to know each other, though, especially after he started fooling around with me in bed at night, we were good friends when we were alone, and he talked a lot and shared very personal feelings with me and went out of his way to do nice things for me.

While he was on leave, he let me drive his Studebaker around town, showing off to my friends, even though I wasn't old enough for a license. He let me drive all the way to Macon once, where he bought us supper at the big S and S Cafeteria on Cherry Street and then paid for a movie. I wanted to see *Sunset Boulevard*, but Richard said a talky movie like that would bore the piss out of him, so we settled on Broken Arrow, with James Stewart and Debra Paget, which was all right.

He wouldn't let me drive home, because it was dark, and when he pulled off the road to a rocky bluff on the Ocmulgee,

I expected him to want me to repay him for treating me, but he just lit a cigarette and leaned back in the seat and talked.

"You're a damned good driver, Jody," he said. "I'm going to tell Daddy to let you use the car all the time when you turn sixteen. And I'm putting it in writing that it's yours if anything happens to me, okay?"

"Nothing's going to happen. You'll be back in a few months," I said.

"You never know, kiddo. One of them gook bullets might have my name on it," he said. "But I want to go. I want to get out of Wilkinson and see some of the world and do something with my life. I don't want to rot on a wore-out farm like Daddy."

He inhaled on the cigarette and stared out at the slow-moving river awhile. Then he flipped his cigarette over the bluff and started the car, and we drove on home, mostly in silence.

Richard hadn't treated me like a kid at all the entire two weeks of his leave. He seemed to want to spend time with me, as if he could let me see his real self and not have to pretend. We went fishing together several times, and he started teaching me to shoot pool at Sammy's Billiards, although he warned me not to tell Mama, because the pool hall sold beer and Mama said it was a den of iniquity.

At night, except for the trip to Macon, Richard stayed so busy with Betty Sue that he crawled into bed every morning sometime before dawn, usually smelling like a brewery, and went to sleep immediately. He had left me alone the whole time, which suited me. After I'd discovered something of what it was really like one night outside Big Ruby's, I had become more and more resistant to his completely selfish demands. By then, though, it was a six-year-old habit that Richard never gave up altogether.

Even after he started dating regularly, and all we did most nights was talk about how he did it with Shirley, and then Nadine, and, finally, Betty Sue, sometimes he would come in half drunk and desperate on a Friday or Saturday night after a fight with his girlfriend. I hated those nights, because he was rough and took forever, but I never reached the point of trying to stop him.

Sitting there on the top step, chin cupped in both palms, I kept thinking about Richard and me as I looked vacantly beyond the dilapidated barn and other outbuildings that I had come to know so well, and on out to the sedge-covered fields, no longer under cultivation since Vernon had taken a full-time job and gradually closed out the farm. As my thoughts turned to the war, I was suddenly afraid for Richard.

Just about the time this fear became conscious, Richard came out and sat on the step beside me.

"You having a good time?" I asked.

"Yeah, but after all that booze, it's going to be a hell of a rocky bus ride to California," he said.

"What's the matter between you and Betty Sue?"

"Aw, she's on the rag and being a real bitch. And I'm so hard up my balls are gonna explode." He didn't look too happy. All at once, he tugged at my elbow. "Come on," he said.

We walked beyond the chicken coops to the outbuildings. Richard pulled me into the smokehouse and closed the door behind us.

"Come on and take care of this for me," he said.

In the faint light seeping through a few cracks that hadn't been chinked, I saw his erection swelling out against the left leg of his uniform pants. The smell of the shine clung heavily to him. I was afraid I was in for a pretty rough few minutes, as I was every time he was this drunk. I sat on a little bench near the door, and Richard stood in front of me, fumbling to drop his pants. I reached for him and took him in my mouth.

There was still a ham and a couple of slabs of bacon hanging, and the smokehouse smelled of hickory and curing spices, one of the unforgettable aromas that made the farm home. Maybe it was because of the shine I had drunk, but I got a sentimental feeling about Richard and started to think about him maybe getting killed in Korea. I wanted to make this last day good for him, maybe something, like the smell of the smokehouse, that he could hold onto while he lay bleeding in the jungle somewhere around Inchon. Close to tears, I tried hard to do everything he had ever instructed me to do to heighten his pleasure.

I was surprised that Richard just stood there with his legs

spread and ran his hands lightly through my hair. He wasn't choking me and making my eyes tear over, like he usually did when he'd been drinking. "Oh, god, yeah! That feels so good, Jody! Keep doing it that way!" he whispered one time.

I really got caught up in it then. As I tried even harder to intensify his pleasure, I opened my own pants to stroke myself. Much quicker than I expected, I knew it was about over, from the way Richard's thighs had begun to tremble. I sped up my hand, hoping to come at the same time he did.

Just then, the door burst open, and I was blinded by the bright sunlight slanting in. I jerked my head off of Richard, just as I heard Travis' voice. "Well, I'll be damned! I was right all along! I saw y'all sneak in here and wondered what y'all were up to."

"Yeah, you were right," Richard said. "Come on in and whip yours out for him, too. Jody likes big dicks, don't you, Jody?"

I started crying and burst past them out the door, not bothering to tuck myself back in and button up until I was halfway to the house, with Richard's drunken laughter pounding in my ears.

I rushed past the people in the kitchen and down the hall to our room. I locked the door behind me and collapsed across the bed, crying uncontrollably. More than anything else, I wished I could just disappear. I did not see how I could ever face anyone again, after Travis got through spreading his talk, as I was sure he would be eager to do. I wished that Travis was going off to get killed in Korea along with Richard. I hated them both.

Knowing that nursing my hatred would do no good, but knowing also that I could not go back to the party, I dragged Richard's duffel bag into the hallway and locked myself in the room. Then I did what I always did in times of stress - I picked up a book. It was one I had started and then had to put aside the night before when Richard came in early from his date and wanted to go to sleep, a new Doubleday Book Club offering by Norah Lofts about Richard I of England, *The Lute Player*.

At first, agonizing thoughts about what had happened in the smokehouse kept breaking my concentration, but eventually I became totally absorbed in the story. Then, all at once,

something happened that would influence my life forever. I got to the part where Richard's mother walks in on an intimate scene between him and his companion, the lute player, and makes a shocking discovery about her son. As I read on, I experienced my own shock, so strong that it made the hair on the nape of my neck rise up and sent tingles of excitement through my whole body, a wondrous shock of recognition: Richard the Lionhearted had been a fairy, or, as the book put it, a lover of boys.

It was the first time I had ever seen anything about it in writing, except for the dreadful admonitions in the Bible. Until then, I had just heard the cruel comments and snickers of other boys, but, despite my activities with Richard and that one time with Adolph, I had only vaguely applied any of it to myself. Now, there it was, printed in a book, and I accepted as if by revelation that it applied to me, too, that Richard the Lionhearted and I were kindred spirits.

I was interrupted by Richard jiggling the doorknob and then pounding on the door. "Come on, Jody. Open the door. It's time for me to leave," he said.

"Go away," I said.

"I want to talk to you," he pleaded.

"Go away," I repeated.

"Please, Jody. I'm sorry about awhile ago. Come and tell me goodbye, at least," he said.

I did not respond.

"All right, be that way," he said. "But remember, I am sorry. Write me." His footsteps resounded down the hall.

I went back to my book and, with mounting excitement, read on through the other knocks on the door when it was time to drive to the bus station, through the calls to come to supper when Mama and Vernon got back, through the rustling sounds as they got ready for bed in the room next door, through the quiet stillness that settled over the house. Some time long after midnight, I finished and closed the book.

I was grateful for this book as I had been for no other. The others had permitted me to escape from my loneliness and unhappiness to explore the larger world. This one had forced me to confront and, at least partially, accept myself. I knew then that, somehow, I would bear the mockery and torment

that certainly lay ahead for me in our little town, because I had no choice but to be myself.

I did not hate Richard anymore, and I wanted him to survive Korea and then escape from our little farm. But I also knew that I would never be able to forgive him fully, not so much for getting us caught in the smokehouse, but for his completely callous behavior afterward.

Sometime before sunrise, I finally drifted off to sleep in the middle of a waking dream in which I sat with my head against the knees of another Richard and softly strummed a lute in a far-off land.

FIVE
UNNATURAL DESIRES

How the single copy of *The City and the Pillar* wound up on the paperback book rack in Peavy's Drugs in Wilkinson, Georgia, I would never understand, but I had to believe it was put there especially for me. Now that I was working in the drugstore, I browsed through the books regularly during slack moments behind the soda fountain or in the stock room, quickly passing over the Max Brand and Luke Short westerns and Raymond Chandler mysteries, hoping for a rare find that would hold my interest.

When I pulled out the thin volume with the intriguing title, the author's strange name, Gore Vidal, and the cover drawing of two young men posed provocatively, my hands trembled. I flipped it over to read the back cover and saw "unnatural desires," and my heart almost stopped.

I had to have this book, but it was impossible for a timid, guilt-ridden sixteen-year-old like me to walk up to the counter and pay for it. The cashier, Mrs. Tennille, had been my Sunday School teacher when I was a child, and this book, and anyone who would want to read it, would be an abomination in her eyes.

With quivering hands and a drumming pulse, I crowded against the book rack, apprehensively glanced over my shoulder, and quickly stuffed the book under my belt beneath my apron and hid it in the stockroom until closing time. Then I nervously wished Mrs. Tennille a good night and walked out with my prize, the only thing I had ever stolen in my life, except for a pack of Luckies I took off the dash of Travis' car one night.

I had worked in the drugstore all summer, ever since Travis came out to the farm the Sunday night after school let out and enticed me into it. When he was home on weekends from the University in Athens, I had labored to avoid him since that day in the smokehouse. There was no way to avoid him when I answered the knock on the door and he stood there grinning.

"Hey, Jody. Where you been hiding? I've been looking for you downtown," he said.

"I've been pretty busy at school and all," I muttered. My face was flushed and I could not look him in the eye. I had never been so uncomfortable before.

For days after Richard left for Korea, I had girded myself for the taunts and insults I was sure would come when Travis finished spreading word around town about catching Richard and me. When nobody called me a queer or threatened to beat me up, I finally decided that Travis must have kept his mouth shut, probably concerned that he would be tarring Richard with the same brush if he talked about me. That knowledge made me no less uncomfortable around him, though, because he had seen, he knew.

We sat in the parlor with Mama and Vernon and sipped iced tea and munched on homemade cookies. I fidgeted and fretted and tried to come up with a believable reason to excuse myself.

"Does Richard have a new address?" Travis asked. "I keep writing him, but I never get an answer."

"No, it's the same one," Vernon said. "Richard never was much for writing."

"Jody just got a letter day before yesterday," Mama said, focusing attention on me. "Richard writes him more than he does us."

"He's doing okay," I said, clearing my throat so that I could talk. "He's not into any fighting yet, and he mostly complains about the food." I did not mention that he was still apologizing about that last day he was home.

After we socialized awhile, Travis thanked Mama for the tea and cookies and said he had to be going. "Come walk me to the car, Jody," he said.

"Here it comes," I thought. "He just wants to get me alone to torment me." That was the one thing I dreaded, but I had no choice but to walk across the front yard with him.

"What are you doing for the summer, now that Mr. McCluney has closed the farm down?" Travis asked.

"I don't know. I'm hoping to get a job," I said. After Richard was drafted, Vernon started doing maintenance at the Warner Robins air base, and all I had to do at the farm was tend a garden plot and look after a cow and some chickens. Mama and Vernon had strongly hinted that I could not just sit around all summer, and I knew I would have to shoulder the expense of

driving Richard's Studebaker when I got my license in July.

"You know I'm running the drugstore until Dad recovers from his heart attack," Travis said.

"Yeah, I was sorry to hear about your dad," I said.

"The reason I came out was I need some help behind the counter and in the stockroom and things. How'd you like to work for me?" he asked.

I took a deep breath and exhaled and leaned against the car for support. This was the last thing I had expected. "I don't know," I said. "I can't even make a banana split."

"I could teach you in five minutes," he laughed. "In fact, let's go down now. You can make us a split and I'll show you around. Then if you want the job, we'll talk about your pay."

Inside the empty store, he got me behind the counter and guided me through putting together a banana split and a sundae and we moved back around and sat on stools to eat them.

Just being close to him made my whole body tingle, as it always had done since I was ten. I caught myself nervously tapping my foot against the counter front and tried to will myself to calm down. Sitting there opened a floodgate of memories. When Travis had first started coming out to the farm, on the rare occasions when I had money enough to splurge on a soda, I liked to sit at this same counter on a Saturday and listen to Travis tease with the flock of girls around him and watch how his biceps flexed every time he dug the scoop into a tub of ice cream.

Without my even knowing it, he helped mold in me a lifetime standard of masculine attractiveness. By the time he was in his mid-teens, he was of medium height, with a slender, but definitely not fragile build. His chest and arms were particularly well developed, and I liked to watch the play of his muscles when he had his shirt off. He never put on the bulk that Richard began to acquire by the time he was sixteen.

Even when Travis was that age, I was not the only one who thought he looked like Tyrone Power, who had become my movie idol after I saw him in *The Mark of Zorro*. Travis had the same flawless classic features and the same intense quality in his eyes. Girls were always following him around and hanging all over him at school and falling in love with him. All this

time, I invented reasons to be around him and suffered from his teasing and his indifference.

As random memories of our six-year association flashed through my mind, I felt his eyes boring into me and turned to meet his gaze momentarily before I blushed and looked away.

"Why are you always so nervous around me?" he asked.

"I - I'm not nervous," I stammered.

"Like shit you're not," he scoffed. "You've been as fidgety as a piss ant around me as long as I've known you. Relax, I won't bite you."

After we finished our ice cream and washed up the dishes, he showed me a few things about the soda fountain and guided me around the store explaining about keeping the shelves stocked. We went in the stockroom and he talked about the importance of keeping careful inventory and told me what my job would involve if I took it.

As we talked, he sat on a hospital bed which I supposed they rented out for home care. He flopped on his back, one foot on the floor. "God, I'm tired," he said, rubbing his eyes. "Being here seven days a week has about whipped me. I don't have time for anything, anymore. I haven't even had a date in God knows how long." He idly fingered his crotch, and his movement drew my gaze like iron filings to a magnet.

"You need to take some time off," I said.

"That's not all I need," he said. He turned to look at me and caught me watching his slowly kneading fingers. He winked knowingly. "Come here," he almost whispered, gesturing me over with a toss of his head.

His piercing stare had me as transfixed as a bird charmed by a snake. Without breaking our gaze, I took a couple of tentative steps toward him, my chest tightening around my shallow breath, my hands quaking like sycamore leaves in a steady breeze. When I stopped beside him, he took one of my hands and dropped it on the swelling mound in his trousers. My mind instantly flashed to the etched-in image of him standing naked and erect in Ruby's doorway, an image that had fueled countless fantasies in the two years since my only full view of his body.

With my throat so tight and my mouth so cottony I could hardly swallow, I began gently massaging his bulging crotch,

wanting this as badly as I had ever wanted anything. Without either of us speaking, we kept our eyes locked on each other, and I no longer felt uncomfortable under his gaze.

"Turn out the light," he rasped out, his own throat so tight he could barely sound the words.

When I flicked the switch, plunging us into absolute darkness, and groped my way back to the bed, he had unbuckled his belt and opened his fly. I sat beside him and gingerly ran my hand up under his shirt across his firm abdomen and then back down to the waistband of his briefs. The head of his long cock protruded beyond his underwear, and I gently caressed it with thumb and forefinger. When I first touched it, he shrank back involuntarily and then thrust his pelvis forward, freeing even more of his cock.

I slid his pants and briefs down, and he raised his hips for me to clear them. I lifted his other leg onto the bed and worked his clothes on down to his ankles. He pried his shoes off with his toes and kicked them onto the floor, and I slid his pants over his feet. In the complete darkness, I had to rely solely upon touch, so I made a worshipful tactile exploration of his cock and balls. As I already knew from my one quick view two years before, he was much longer and substantially thicker than Richard.

When I first took him into my mouth, he drew in as much air as his lungs would hold and let it out with a long whooshing sound and spread his legs wider apart. A slight tremor ran through his entire body, and as my lips moved up and down his shaft, he almost imperceptibly flexed his buttocks and gently thrust into my mouth.

I used every technique to heighten his pleasure that Richard had ever taught me, so excited that my own cock throbbed and streams of precome soaked through my briefs. Travis did not make a sound through it all, and, except for the tremor running through his body and the slight sustained pelvic thrusts, he did not move until it was almost over. Then his thighs knotted and I heard him clawing and grasping at the mattress with both hands. He lifted his buttocks clear off the bed time after time in a rapidly accelerating rhythm, frantically jabbing his long cock deep into my mouth.

"God! Oh, God!" he moaned. He arched his back, and I

reached under to press the thick passageway behind his balls with the base of my palm, felt it pulse against my hand, and got the first musky taste of him as he came and came in my mouth, reaching to hold my head tight against him with one hand, until he finally sagged back onto the mattress.

I held my mouth on him and gently massaged his balls and caressed his abdomen until he finally twisted out from under me and sat up. "Thanks, Jody. That was nice," he said as he reached for his clothes.

We were awkward around each other when I turned the light back on, until he playfully punched me on the shoulder and asked, "Are you going to take the job?"

"Yeah," I said through a broad grin, "as long as it involves more nights in the stockroom."

I hardly slept that night. It was like a dream come true. I had wanted Travis for years, had hungered for that big cock and perfect body, and had despaired of ever doing more than casually observing him. Then, for a few minutes, he had lain desirous and vulnerable beneath my touch, his entire being crying out for the pleasure that I was able to give him. The experience had been so intense for me that I could recall every touch, every sound, every movement. As I relived those few short minutes throughout the night, my cock throbbed urgently and I stroked myself raw in excitement and anticipation of things to come.

And so began a summer of regular times on the hospital bed after we closed the store. We soon relaxed enough with each other that I could persuade him to leave the light on. Each time, I teasingly stripped all his clothes off and thrilled at seeing and touching his magnificent body. As much as I longed to be completely naked and lying beside him in a tight embrace, I never risked more than to take my shirt and shoes off. Except to run his hands through my hair and to grasp at my head frantically in his moments of approaching climax, he never touched me.

As he became more and more accustomed to our sessions in the stockroom, Travis gradually asserted himself verbally and physically, and I became a willing vessel for his experiments in pleasure. "Chew on my balls," he would say, and I would nibble away; "Lick my armpit," he would order, and I would

lap up every trace of sweat; "Suck my tit," he would beg, and I would ream it until he pulled my head away. He put us in all possible positions, with me kneeling in front of him, or him straddling my chest, or him on hands and knees with me awkwardly crouched beneath him.

For awhile, the excitement of having this body that I had coveted long before I understood why was enough to make me revel in the tremors and groans and frantic clutching at the mattress that I could evoke with my hands and mouth. After the newness wore off, however, I began to resent his selfish use of me without giving anything in return. I became unhappily aware that all I had done was substitute Travis for Richard.

"Did Richard ever - ?" he started to ask and then broke off one night after he had exhausted new possibilities of using my mouth.

"Did he ever what?" I said.

"Did he ever - you know - put it up in you?" he stammered.

"No," I lied. If he had asked weeks earlier, I would have consented, but I had decided that this was the ultimate intimacy, and in my growing disillusionment with our relationship, I did not want to be callously used in this way for his pleasure.

"Would you - would you let me do it?" he asked.

"Uh-uh," I said, shaking my head.

"Come on, let's try it. I really want to, Jody," he pleaded.

"No," I replied with finality. I took his cock in my mouth to end the conversation. He never asked again.

By the end of the summer, I respected Travis as an evenhanded employer and liked him as a friend. My feelings for him as a person had deepened, but so had my disenchantment with our physical relationship. Yet we had established a pattern I did not know how to break, and I was very conscious of the fact that, without our contact, I would have nothing.

Then I discovered *The City and the Pillar*. The night I stole it off the rack, I stayed up until daylight reading. I identified completely with Jim Willard's obsession over memories of an idyllic camping trip with a schoolmate, and I agonized for him when he raped and murdered his friend years later after the friend rejected his sexual advances.

I could not identify with the alien environment of New York bars and Hollywood parties and impersonal couplings with which the book was filled, but it did reveal to me a whole new world and fire me with the knowledge that somewhere, outside my little hometown, many men had the same desires and longings that I was experiencing.

I did not want the bars and the parties and the casual sex that Jim Willard was caught up in. I wanted to be plain Jody Garrett in my little Georgia farm town, but I also desperately wanted not to be alone, not to be the only person in town with what the world considered unnatural desires.

The only thing unnatural about it, to my thinking and in my limited experience, was the total lack of reciprocation, first by Richard, and then by Travis. My body and my spirit cried out for a companion who felt as I did. After contemplating the book and my situation, I decided that I had had enough "unnatural desire," and that I could wait until somewhere, someday, I met a person who would want me in the same way I wanted him.

After Travis had received his pleasure on the stockroom bed the next night, I announced, "This is the last time I'm doing this."

"Why?" he asked, obviously puzzled.

"Because I'm queer and you're not," I said flatly. It was the first time I had uttered the word out loud, and I discovered that it was not so terrible, after all. Then my feelings poured out. "I have needs, too, and you're not willing to satisfy them. I can't just keep being used."

"I didn't know you felt like that, Jody," he said. "I thought you liked what we were doing. I have been completely selfish, haven't I? Maybe we could figure out some ways to make it better for you. I can't do what you do for me, but maybe - "

"No, Travis," I cut him off. "You need to find a woman, and I need to wait for someone like me, someone who wants the same things I do."

I turned away from the beautiful body I was determined never to touch again and, without looking back, walked through the darkened store and out into the night.

SIX
NIGHT OF THE FIREFLIES

I sprawled on the blanket the man had spread in the tall grass, my hands locked behind my head, not able to bring myself to touch him. I watched the horde of fireflies we had kicked up in our trek across the pasture flashing overhead and tried not to think about anything. The man had removed both our shirts and now knelt close against my side. His moist, pudgy hands teased their way across my chest and squeezed my biceps, sending a slight quiver of excitement coursing all the way to my toes.

"You've got a great body, Jody, so hard and smooth," he whispered. His fingers tortured their way down my abdomen and probed gently under the waistband of my jeans. "Are you sure you don't play football?"

I did not answer. Thanks to hard work on the farm, I wasn't the ninety-eight-pound weakling who always got sand kicked in his face, but I wasn't exactly Charles Atlas, either. If he wanted to fantasize that I was some bulky football player, that was okay with me, as long as he didn't talk about it. I knew that, with too much talk, I would become repulsed by him and by what was happening. He bent over to chew and suck at one of my nipples, and his own hairy breasts, which sagged like the dugs of a nursing sow, brushed against my body. Trying to hurry things along, I unbuckled my belt and unsnapped the top of my jeans for good measure, making it easier for the man to get at what he so obviously craved.

I had kept thinking of him as "the man," although he had introduced himself as Burt, a salesman on the way to Macon, before I even settled into the seat beside him after accepting his offer of a ride. Richard's Studebaker was parked at home with a leaking water pump, which I could not afford to replace, so it was either hitchhike or walk the five miles home after work. Usually, I could count on somebody from a neighboring farm eventually giving me a ride almost all the way home. But it was rare to see an out-of-town car on the streets at night, and even rarer to see one as luxurious as the new 1952 Packard the man was driving.

I had accepted his offer partly out of a covetous desire to ride in his powder-blue convertible, the most beautiful car I had ever laid eyes on. But as I sank into the plush, cream-colored leather seat beside the obese, pink-faced stranger, I knew that I had gotten in partially to satisfy my curiosity, which he had aroused by circling the block twice before he pulled up beside me, reached over to open the door, and asked, "How far you going?" Then he had held my hand in his weak grasp an uncomfortably long time while he told me his name and asked me mine. I was almost sure of what he wanted before he drove away from the curb, not that I accepted the ride knowing with absolute certainty that I would go along with his intentions.

I had heard a couple of guys around town talk about letting queers pick them up for money, and I vaguely knew about the Trailways toilet stalls in Macon. One guy who had hitchhiked all the way to Florida and back even told a gang of us about letting an old man suck him off while he drove the man's car. We laughed along with him when he said he nearly swerved into a ditch as he shot off in the man's mouth.

Such talk among other guys intrigued me, but I never would have had the nerve to go looking for something like that. Even when Burt eased his hand on my thigh and suggested we "ride around" for a while before he dropped me off, I was still hesitant.

"Come on," he insisted. "The night's young. I'll even let you drive this baby some."

"Well, maybe for a little while," I agreed.

"You got a girlfriend?" he asked as I drove along the narrow, winding county road, wishing I could get on a main highway and really open it up.

"No," I said, shaking my head.

"Aw, you're pulling my leg," he said, as I concentrated on the hairpin curve ahead. "Good looking guy like you, I'll bet you're getting more than you can handle."

I laughed nervously. "I wish I was, but I'm not getting anything," I said.

"Honest?" he said. "Then I'll bet you're horny as a goat. You ever let another guy take care of you?"

"No," I muttered, feeling my face flush.

"How about giving it a try?" he said. This time, he dropped

his hand higher up on my thigh and inched toward my crotch.

"Uh-uh, I don't think so," I said, despite the tingling that had set up in my entire body.

"Come on," he wheedled. "I'll see you enjoy it. You won't have to do a thing. I'll even make it worth your while, so you can get your car fixed. What do you say?" His hand had reached my groin, and he squeezed my rapidly developing hard-on.

"Well, maybe," I said, "but I have to be home before too long."

In the pasture, by the time he slipped off my sneakers and socks and then worked my jeans over my hips, as excited as I was physically, I wished I had not let him talk me into it. As he slid my jeans and briefs down my legs and over my feet, leaving me completely naked, and began caressing and kissing his way back up my inner thighs toward my throbbing hard-on, I concentrated on the eerie phosphorescent pulsing of fireflies overhead to keep from watching his obscenely thick lips working on my body.

I remembered how, when Richard and Jo Ellen and Karen and I were kids, we would spend long summer nights chasing after lightning bugs. They put the ones they caught into a Mason jar with pinholes in the lid to make a glowing, greenish lantern, but I never would add mine to the collection. I would carefully hold one in my closed fist and peer in through thumb and forefinger to watch it glimmering in my palm and marvel at its production of light without heat, and then free it into the night air.

I forgot all about our childhood games when Burt grasped the base of my dick in his hand and took it into his mouth, his tongue lashing the head in great swirls, the fingers of his other hand flitting lightly across my abdomen and chest. I closed my eyes, and it was as if all the fireflies in the pasture had lighted on me and were pulsing and glowing over my entire body, only, instead of cold light, wherever his fingers and lips touched was intense, acutely pleasurable heat.

"You've got a nice big one," he said, "really nice for someone your size." As he talked, he barely took his mouth off my dick. His lips brushed against the head, and his warm, moist breath spread over the sensitive tip. I pushed upward,

lifting my hips off the ground. His mouth again took in my throbbing prick, and warm wetness embraced the shaft as he went lower and lower, tongue swirling maddeningly.

All at once, he shoved down, and I felt my dick slip into his throat, something I had never been able to do with Richard or Travis. When he had all of me in his mouth, he rhythmically constricted his throat muscles around my shaft, and the head of my prick rubbed against the soft slippery lining that held it in a tight embrace. Despite my earlier reluctance to touch him, I grabbed his head with both hands and pumped my dick into him, trying to drive it even deeper. He let it slide back and forth and continued to massage it with his throat muscles until he finally had to break my grip and come up for air. I sagged back onto the blanket and emitted a long sigh of sheer pleasure.

Holding my dick in one fist, he cradled my balls in his other palm and began licking and nipping them with his teeth, until I was writhing around and moaning with delight. Turning my dick and nuts loose, he raised my legs with his forearms and licked his way along the thick tube behind my balls. He worked his way back to them and sucked first one, then both of them into his mouth and pulled and tugged on my nutsac with his lips. Then he attacked my dick again, driving it deep into his throat time after time, pausing to lick and nibble at the head before every downstroke. Just when I was on the verge of exploding, he stopped and crawled from between my legs and knelt beside me.

Almost before I knew it, he had flipped me onto my stomach and tugged at my hips until I rested on knees and forearms, my ass thrust into the air. When he moved between my legs and spread them apart, I was afraid he planned to fuck me and prepared to resist his attempt. Then I realized that he had not even opened his fly. For several minutes, he just ran his hands over my lower back and buttocks, squeezing and parting my cheeks. What he was doing felt good, but I was in a hurry for him to get back to my dick. I was about to tell him so when his moist lips began exploring my cheeks. He spread them as wide as possible with both hands and buried his head between them. I felt his warm tongue exploring my crack. What he was doing was completely disgusting, but a curious pleasure began to override my distaste. When his tongue found its target and he

thrust it all the way up in me and rotated it, I backed into his face and gave him even better access. I had never considered this area of my body to be erotic, and Richard had never roused much pleasurable sensation in all the times he had used it. Burt's tongue action was setting me on fire, and I wiggled and squirmed under his touch and whimpered in newfound pleasure.

When he tired of tonguing my ass, Burt turned onto his back, scooted up under me, and took my dick in his mouth. I immediately thought of how Richard had enticed me to suck him with his "cow and calf" game that first winter I lived on the farm. I wondered if I had made him feel as good as Burt was making me. I sat back on my haunches, his hairy chest tickling my ass cheeks, grabbed his head with both hands and raised it off the ground. I began a slow, gyrating pumping into his mouth, working deeper and deeper until my cockhead was sliding into his throat with every thrust. He gurgled and grunted and tugged at my ass, pulling me even deeper into him. I threw back my head and emitted low guttural cries of pure pleasure. After a while, he flipped me onto my back and slowly, tantalizingly, excruciatingly brought me off. When I started coming, I lifted all the way off the blanket and clutched at his head and cried out loud in sheer ecstasy as I kept erupting time after time into his throat.

Burt hardly gave me time to sag back onto the blanket before he was all over me again, hands and lips flitting and toying, teasing me toward a second peak of excitement. Though I had just come so much I should have been completely satiated, my dick was still rock-hard and throbbing demandingly.

Burt took his time when he finally moved to my dick. He put a lot of effort into gently tonguing and licking all around the glans and up and down the shaft. I lay rigidly still, thighs trembling uncontrollably, eyes closed, and consciously luxuriated in every pleasurable move he made. Only when he had me on the verge of climax did I run my fingers through his hair and gyrate my pelvis, slowly rotating my dick in his mouth. It was as if we both were reluctant for it to end, but, inevitably, the stimulation of his warm mouth became too much to bear, and with a few savage lunges deep into his throat, I spewed out my second load, seemingly as copious as the first,

and equally enjoyable.

"Here's a little something for you," Burt said, thrusting some folded bills at me when he stopped to let me out at the dirt road leading to my house.

"I don't want any money," I said, opening the door. My ardor cooled, on the ride home I had felt more and more disgusted at what I had done. All I wanted now was to escape from him and be alone.

"Come on, buy yourself something nice," he said, again extending the bills to me. When I did not take them, he stuffed them in my shirt pocket. "Here," he said, "you were worth every penny, and I had a great time. Maybe I'll drop in at Peavy's Drugs to see you again sometime."

"I won't be there after school starts next week," I lied. I could think of few things worse than having him walk into Peavy's and greet me like an old friend. I never wanted to see him again. I got out of the car, closed the door, leaned back in to say, "Thanks for the ride," and walked away without looking back, but I knew that he sat watching me until I rounded a curve and moved out of his sight.

When I reached the house, I could not just go in and go to bed. I crawled through the strands of barbwire and walked across the pasture to the pond, kicking up fireflies on the way. I sat staring into the water for a long time, trying to sort through my feelings, questioning why physical sensation and emotional satisfaction were sometimes so widely separated. A pudgy, middle-aged stranger had just carried me to heights of physical excitement that I did not know existed, yet I felt nothing but disgust emotionally.

Most of my loathing was directed at myself. I had known from the beginning that I was not in the least attracted to Burt, and, now that it was over, I did not understand why I had consented to sex with him. I had walked away from Travis, who had long been my ideal, because I could not continue to be selfishly used by him. Yet I now realized that, in a different way, Burt had used me more completely than Richard or Travis ever did, had feasted voraciously on my body like a starving animal over a fresh kill, had aroused and manipulated my feelings and held me at a peak of desire until he was satiated.

When my thoughts became too complex, I reached out and

snagged a firefly and gazed at him through thumb and forefinger for a few seconds and then released him, cynically hoping that whatever female his sexual signal light attracted would bring him more genuine reward than I had just experienced.

Remembering the bills Burt had stuffed in my pocket, I pulled them out and peered at them in the faint light. My heart raced with excitement when I realized how much he had given me. It was more than twice as much as I made in a full week at fifty cents an hour behind the counter at Peavy's! I could get the Studebaker running and buy myself "something nice," and all for a few minutes of the purest sexual pleasure I had ever experienced.

Suddenly I realized where my greed was leading me. It was as if money had been my motive all along, as if I had sold myself to Burt like a cheap whore. Coming to my senses, I knew that I could not be a whore, even to my own feelings, and certainly not for money. I methodically tore the bills into tiny squares and, with one flourish, released them to hurtle through the air like a flushed covey of quail until they gently settled to earth.

Then I stripped and waded into the pond. Standing calf-deep in the tepid water, I ran my hands over my body, which so recently had been alive to Burt's touch. Now I recoiled from my flesh as if it were contaminated. Frantic with self-loathing, I scooped up handfuls of coarse sand from the pond floor and roughly scrubbed at my chest and abdomen and genitals - everywhere Burt had touched - until my skin was raw and oozing blood in places.

Then I began to swim. Driven by some inner fury, I battled the water back and forth, back and forth across the pond. When I was so near exhaustion that I could hardly lift my arms, I waded out onto the soft grass and stood quiet as an oak until the warm breeze dried me off.

As I trudged across the pasture toward home, the night air surrounding me now was empty of fireflies.

SEVEN
IN THE PRESENCE OF INNOCENCE

Maybe I missed all the early signs because I never believed something so awesome could occur. Without my even having dreamed about it, one of the most intelligent and most popular boys at school had singled me out for special attention. For weeks, I had been riding on a cloud, and by the time it started, I would have done anything to please him.

Brett Williams was Mr. Everything at Pelham County High. Tall and solidly-built, with an unruly shock of curly blond hair and a light bronze tan, he was a straight-"A" student, our star basketball player and team captain, president of the senior class, and editor of the school yearbook. His admirers ranged from the youngest elementary school kids to old men who came to cheer for him at every basketball game. Half the girls in the high school had a crush on him. I had worshipped him from a distance for years, and I was so nervous around him that I was practically tongue-tied.

That fall, my classmates chose me as the junior class representative on the yearbook staff, and every afternoon I met with Brett and several others to work on it. Brett hardly acknowledged my presence during the first few meetings, and I did not make any contributions to cause him to notice me.

All of that changed one afternoon when I called him over to look at the way I had cropped some photos and arranged them with some captions I had created on the dummy sheet. He studied the layout intently, then flashed me a pulse-quickening smile and said, "That's great, Jody! It's the most original idea I've seen so far." As I basked in his praise, he casually draped one arm across my shoulder and bent over until our heads were side by side and I could feel his breath on my cheek. He reached for a couple of photos in my layout and quickly rearranged them. "But remember, it's best to have people face the center instead of toward the margins." He straightened up and patted my shoulder. "You've got some real talent, Jody," he smiled down at me as I craned my neck to look up at him in awe. His hand trailed slowly across my back, as soft as a caress, and then he was gone, leaving me trembling and short of

breath.

"What are you doing after school?" he asked me as our work session ended, grabbing my elbow to hold me back as the others left the room.

"Nothing special," I said.

"How about meeting me at Peavy's for a soda?" he suggested.

I jumped at the invitation, but as we sat by ourselves in a back booth, surrounded by the noisy chatter of other students, I had to struggle to make conversation. Brett could easily have been anybody's ideal conception of the wholesome all-American boy, and just his presence made me all too aware of the feelings he aroused in me. I was convinced beyond doubt that Brett could never share those feelings, but this did not lessen my desire.

The next day, at the beginning of my library study period, he came over to my table. "You got stuff you really have to do this period?" he asked.

"Naw, I'm just reading a novel," I stammered.

"Good. Come on," he said, heading for the librarian's desk. I was no more than half a step behind him.

"I need Jody to work on the yearbook," he explained to Mrs. Resseau, who immediately wrote out a hall pass for me. Brett was so well respected that all the teachers invariably accepted whatever he said.

As soon as we got to the staff room, he showed me a mockup of the credits page. I was almost beside myself when I saw directly under his name as editor, "Jody Garrett, Assistant Editor and Junior Class Representative."

"What's this, some kind of joke?" I asked when I was able to speak.

"No joke, pal," he said, slapping me on the back. "I talked with Mr. Athorne this morning about how talented you are and told him I wanted you to be assistant editor. You deserve it, and, believe me, you'll earn it."

After I calmed down, we spent the rest of the period going over page after page of the slowly emerging yearbook. I was kept off balance by how often he made body contact, draping his arm across my shoulder, or laying his hand on my forearm, or lightly brushing against my thigh when he spread his legs

and stretched. Despite this distraction, my shyness at being around him soon disappeared and I began to talk freely, expressing my opinions and suggesting alternatives to the rather banal layouts before us. We wound up agreeing to scrap what we had entirely and take a new approach to the theme. When the period ended, I was so elated that my feet hardly touched the floor as we left the room.

In the hallway, he grabbed my arm and stopped me. "Oh, here," he said, handing me a sheet of paper. "This is an excuse from study hall any day we need to work. Just meet me in the staff room Monday afternoon, okay?" As I turned away from him, he called after me, "And come see my game tonight, y'hear?"

"I'll be there," I promised. I had forgotten that his team was playing, if I had ever known it.

I dumfounded my youngest stepsister, Karen, by offering to drive her and some of her girlfriends to the game. Usually, I paid very little attention to her. On the way to the gym, their thirteen-year old chatter and constant giggling got on my nerves, but it was better than showing up at the game alone.

Brett freed himself from the clutches of several cheerleaders and came over to speak to me. He was wearing the yellow and black Panther's warm-up jacket and tight nylon trunks, slightly split up the sides. As we talked, I had to concentrate to keep my eyes focused on his face, and not on the tight mound of his jockstrap or the nearly platinum sheen of fine hair on his firm legs.

"You brought your sister, huh? I was hoping we could go to the Dairy Queen afterward," he said.

"How about if I meet you there?" I suggested. "I'm going to dump them as soon as the game's over."

"I'll be waiting," he said with a smile that kept me in a state of excitement throughout the night.

Brett played a standout game, and on the way home, Karen and her friends gushed over him, oblivious to my presence.

"He's such a dreamboat!" Becky cooed.

"Oh, that hair! I could run my fingers through it all night," Karen added.

"If he ever hugged me against that scrumptious chest, I'd just die and go to Heaven. I know I would," Joanne said,

folding her arms across her breasts and shivering with exaggerated excitement.

I both envied and resented their ability to talk so openly among themselves, to put into words their adolescent dreams and maybe not so innocent desires for the whole world to hear. I was saddened by the knowledge that I would always have to cover up and disguise my feelings, which, in this case, were not so different from theirs.

"You girls are silly," I said. "Brett's a senior and doesn't even know you're alive. You should be concentrating on Allen and Steve and Cory. I saw how they were flirting with you around the concession stand."

"Ugh, those little drips make me want to puke," Karen said in a tone that questioned how I could possibly wish such a fate upon her.

I hurried to the Dairy Queen after I dropped the girls off. As soon as I pulled into the parking lot, Brett got out of a car where he sat with some of his teammates and sauntered over to the Studebaker with his burger and Coke. After I ordered, we sat munching on our burgers and talked about the game and plans for the yearbook. Again I was aware of how often he touched me, but he was such a straight-arrow and so popular among the girls that our contact gave me no hope that it was anything more than an unconscious expression of friendship.

Over the weekend, I fantasized more than ever, not daring to create overt sexual situations, but weaving dreams of the two of us becoming inseparable friends and putting together an award-winning yearbook. By Monday, my feelings for Brett had solidified into an overpowering infatuation.

In the days and weeks that followed, mostly at his urging, Brett and I began spending most of our free time together after school and on weekends. I started going to all home basketball games and meeting him somewhere afterwards. On Saturdays when I was working at Peavy's, he would come in and sit at the counter so long that I was afraid Mr. Peavy would chew me out about it. On Sundays, if I was not working, we would go for long drives or he would come out to the farm and we would tramp through the woods for hours, laughing and horsing around and just enjoying being together.

When I was not with him, I thought about him constantly. At

home I moped around avoiding my stepsisters and spent most of my time stretched out on my bed listening to Nat King Cole's honeyed version of "Too Young" or Gertrude Lawrence's "Hello, Young Lovers" on the tinny 45 rpm Silvertone record player I had ordered from Sears, Roebuck. Because of Brett, I assuredly had wings on my heels and was entranced in his presence. I was completely vulnerable emotionally, but completely insecure about his feelings for me.

One Sunday afternoon, we tramped through the woods on the farm, bundled up against the late autumn chill. Brett was in an especially playful mood. He poked and jabbed and tickled and laughed as we trudged along kicking at the thick mat of dried oak and beech leaves beneath our feet. From time to time, he would break away from me and run ahead through the trees, grabbing their trunks with one arm and whirling dizzily around them or jumping up to chin himself on a low-hanging branch.

As we stood at the top of a hill which sloped precipitously toward a meandering stream below, he scooped up a handful of leaves and crammed them down my collar and then danced away while I threw wads of them at him. When I chased him to the edge of the steep incline, he grappled me to the ground and we tumbled pell-mell down the hill, arms and legs flailing, both laughing hysterically. We came to rest in a soft bank of leaves with Brett on top of me, our chests crushed together, our arms wrapping each other in a tight embrace.

He raised up slightly, and our laughter stopped as if on a prearranged signal. The entire woods fell silent, and for a few seconds, I did not even hear the murmuring stream beside us. Brett was staring at me, and a vein was pulsing in his throat. For a fleeting moment, I saw something - uncertainty, fear, desire - something dominating his expression with such intensity that it frightened me. Just as quickly, his expression shifted and he laughed again and the sounds of the forest resumed. He sat up, threw a handful of leaves in my face and took off running, with me in hot pursuit.

Brett was waiting for me in the staff room Monday afternoon. He seemed tense and preoccupied, and as soon as I put my books down, he headed for the door. "Come on," he said. Wordlessly, I followed him outside the classroom building,

across the courtyard, and into the rear basement door of the gym.

"Where are we going?" I finally asked as we climbed the stairs to the main level.

"Come on," was all he said as he led me onto the darkened stage at the end of the gym. We stood quietly for a few seconds down against the front curtain. Gradually my eyes adjusted to the dark and I could distinguish Brett's features in the dim light bleeding in from the sides of the stage.

"What are we going to do here?" I asked.

"I've thought about you all night," he said, in a tight voice that hardly sounded like him. In the faint light, I detected a strange, almost pained expression on his face. "I like you, Jody. I like you a whole lot," he added.

Before I could respond to what he had said, he reached for my hand and jammed it into his groin. I was caught totally off guard. None of my fantasies of us had involved anything so specific. I was shocked that he would do this, that he would want to do this.

As I detected the heat of him through his jeans and studied the ever-changing expressions flitting across his face - a collage of boyish fear, raw desire, and disarming hesitation - I was certain that this was a major breakthrough for him, the culmination of an inner struggle which he finally had succumbed to. Part of me was terrified in the presence of what I considered his desperate innocence, and I wanted to run out into the light to evade its impending loss, but my legs were too weak to carry me even if I had tried it. The dominant part of me was captive to a thrill of possibility like nothing I had ever known before.

As he held my hand tight against him and kneaded it into the fabric of his jeans, which were rapidly tightening and swelling in my palm, I prayed for this to be what I had only dreamed of finding, a relationship equally strong on both sides. After a few seconds, I began squeezing and rubbing the bulge in his jeans without him having to move my hand.

"Take it out," he whispered, his voice a throaty croak.

My hands trembling almost beyond control, I unfastened his belt, unzipped his jeans, and ran my hands inside the front of his briefs, past a forest of rough hair, and freed his erection,

which snaked out along his thigh and then climbed straight up his abdomen. It gave off so much heat that I instinctively snatched my hand away from it.

"Go on and take it all the way out," he urged in the same husky voice.

I hooked my thumbs in the waistband of his briefs and tugged them and his jeans down his thighs. I stared in awe at what I had exposed to the dim light. His cock was fully as long as Travis' and nearly as thick. What intrigued me, though, was the full foreskin sheathing most of his bulbous cockhead. Both Richard and Travis were neatly clipped, as I was, so Brett's cock was strange and new. I stood looking so long that Brett became impatient.

"Play with it some," he whispered.

I wrapped my fingers around the strutted shaft of his beautiful dick and began moving my hand slowly, excited by the strange feel of his foreskin sliding back and forth over the glans.

Brett threw his head back and sighed. "Oh, yeah! That's good, Jody! Real good!" he said.

After a few seconds, he unfastened my jeans and slid them down. I had not been aware of my own erection until he freed it. He fingered my cock a little and then crouched down until our dicks were together, his beneath mine, dwarfing it, its flared head poking into my balls, which were drawn up so tight they hurt. He held both our dicks together and gently thrust into my balls a few times. Then he crouched lower and let his dick slide under, between my thighs. I squeezed my legs together, clutching his cock in a tight embrace. He grabbed both my ass cheeks and pulled me close against him. I risked wrapping my arms around his back in a bear hug. As he hunched between my legs, the fingers of one hand toyed and probed around the rim of my ass. I rested my head against his chest and sighed with happiness.

He stepped away from me and put both hands on my shoulders. "Take it in your mouth," he said, pressing my shoulders down.

"Uh-uh, I can't," I protested, suddenly afraid. Even though he had completely taken the lead, something in his ever-changing facial expressions, his voice, his trembling hands

told me that he was not at all confident in his leadership. I still had a sense of being in the presence of innocence, and I did not want to disenchant him and maybe drive him away by exposing him too quickly to my experience. I consciously wished for an equal innocence, knowing full well that it had been stolen from me years before by Richard, without my even knowing what I had lost.

"Yes you can, Jody. Come on, try, please," he insisted, pressing down on my shoulders even harder.

Caught up in an excitement greater than any I had ever experienced before, and desperately wanting to please him, I dropped to my knees in front of him and crouched there, unmoving, staring at his cock practically in my face. Brett put one hand behind my head and coaxed me toward him, while he guided his cock to my mouth with his other hand and rubbed it across my lips. Even with my mouth closed, I detected the musky taste of the fluid oozing from it.

"Come on, suck it," he urged, pushing against my lips forcefully. I opened up for him, and he eased into my mouth, the broad head of his dick stretching my jaws to capacity. When I had taken a couple of inches, he grabbed my head with both hands and slowly moved me back and forth on his dick.

He stopped his movements and gently toyed with my hair. "Keep going up and down on it," he told me, and I decided to do everything he wanted, but only if he instructed me. In that way, maybe I could feign an innocence I no longer had. My decision paid off, and as he got more and more excited, he expressed his desires openly. "Run your tongue around on it," he told me, and when I complied, he threw his head back and groaned.

I got caught up in pleasing him and began to toy with my own cock, which was aching for attention. As I stroked myself, he kept talking to me. "Oh, yeah! That's great, Jody! Tighten your lips a little, and play with my balls, too," he said. I reached for his nutsac and kneaded and squeezed while I flicked my tongue all around the head of his cock and licked up and down the shaft and pistoned my own rod through my hand.

After a few minutes, Brett began moaning and writhing around and again grabbed my head roughly with both hands.

He began a frenzied thrusting into my mouth, driving deeper and deeper. In the throes of impending orgasm, he was completely unmindful of me, except as the source of a moist, warm pleasure point for his pulsing cock.

I fought against his grip on my head and gagged on his thick cockhead battering my tonsils in an unrelenting assault. He gave out a loud series of staccato grunts. He pulled my head tight against him, and his body went rigid as his cock jerked and contracted and spurted jet after jet of come deep into my mouth.

I quit fighting against him and just held my mouth on him and tried not to swallow until he began to soften and then gingerly withdrew from me. I turned aside and spat several times onto the stage floor with exaggerated distaste, afraid that he might be repulsed at the idea of my swallowing his come.

I did not know what my emotions were at the moment. While it was happening, I was under the dominating spell of sensuality beyond thought, but, after his frenzied assault and unhesitating ejaculation in my mouth, I felt partly betrayed, partly angry for allowing myself to be used again in the same way Richard and Travis had used me. At the same time, an exhilarating excitement of a totally new magnitude still ruled me, and my whole body shivered from its effects.

Brett did not give me time to sort through my feelings. He tugged me to my feet and turned me around so that my back was to him. He pressed tight against me, and his moist, warm, nearly soft cock caressed my lower back. He wrapped one arm around my chest and leaned to whisper in my ear, "That was really great, Jody."

I heard him spit into his other hand. He reached for my rock-hard cock and began stroking me slowly. I pushed back against him and trembled from the pleasure of his moist hand gliding back and forth on me. His other hand slid down my body, across my abdomen, and toyed briefly with my thatch of pubic hair before he moved on down to my balls. He rolled them in his fingers and tickled beneath them as he stroked my dick faster and faster. In no time I was desperately hunching into his hand, establishing my own rhythm, and then, all too soon, I cried out loud and began shooting stream after stream onto the stage floor. Brett held me in his hand without moving

until I went completely soft.

Neither of us spoke as we pulled up our jeans and got ready to leave. Finally, Brett cleared his throat. "Are you okay about this?" he asked.

"Yeah, I guess," I muttered.

"I hope so," he said. "It was great for me. I can't believe I finally got up enough nerve to try it. You don't know how much I've thought about it and how much I wanted it to happen with you. So I hope it's okay with you. I don't want you to be mad at me or anything."

"I'm not," I said, not really sure what I was feeling.

"Good!" he said. He slapped me on the back playfully and then draped his arm over my shoulder casually as we left.

In the following hours, what we had done completely dominated my attention. I was fully aware that our sex had generated an overwhelming excitement in me, and I was just as aware that I had become deeply involved with him emotionally. At the same time, I was inundated by an intense sense that I had failed myself. Although Brett's jerking me off had been very pleasurable, and the fact that he had wanted to do it showed some feeling for me, his limited attempt to give me satisfaction represented a selfishness different only in degree from that of Richard and Travis. I had vowed that I would never again be a mere vessel for another's pleasure, but my ready submission to Brett, my urgent desire to please him, and my failure to insist that he reciprocate fully indicated that I had not kept my vow to myself.

I was still confused and unsure how I wanted to deal with Brett at school the next day. I consciously avoided him all morning, and that afternoon I reported to study hall instead of going to the publications office. I had hardly settled down to read when Brett slid quietly into the seat across the table. I looked up, my face flushed, and I quickly looked back down, unable to meet his eyes. The tension became almost palpable, and I could feel his stare boring into me. After what seemed forever, he whispered, "Jody." Still I averted my eyes. Again he whispered, "Jody, please," his voice desperate. I shyly met his gaze and he smiled weakly. "Please, let's go somewhere and talk," he said. I managed a smile as fragile as his.

We went to the publications office, but instead of talking, as

soon as he closed the door behind us, he wrapped his arms around me in a smothering embrace and just held me. I could feel the rapid beat of both our hearts and hear both our labored breathing. His hands strayed across my back and I wrapped my arms tightly around him and pushed myself snugly against him. We stayed that way for a long time, without either of us saying a word. I was acutely conscious of my throbbing erection, and of his bulging cock pulsing against my abdomen.

"Come on," he said finally.

Again we went through the lower door into the gym and up the stairs, but this time, instead of leading me to the stage, Brett went on into the gym, unlocked the door to a storage area beneath the seats, ushered me in, and locked the door behind us. It was almost completely dark inside, with only tiny pinpoints of light stealing in here and there from cracks in the seats above us. I could hardly make out his features with him standing tight against me.

"Is this safe?" I whispered, conscious as I had not been the first time of just how much we were risking.

"Sure. Don't worry," he answered. "Coach Sessions has the only other key, and he's in health class this period." His hand found my crotch, and instantly I was erect and trembling with anticipation.

The second time was almost a repeat of the first, except Brett took his pants all the way off and stretched out on some gym mats. He toyed idly with my hair and instructed me on techniques to increase his pleasure as I crouched between his legs and sucked his cock. He was much gentler than he had been the first time, just gyrating his pelvis and rolling his dick around in my mouth instead of jabbing down my throat and choking me. Even his climax was more restrained, with him trembling and sighing and rubbing his hands all over my back and through my hair as he came. When it was over, as he had the first time, he reached for me and brought me to a slow and agonizingly beautiful climax by hand. Then we lay close in a languid embrace and talked.

After that, I was almost comfortable around him in full light and was able to function around the other staff members with only a slight self-consciousness. It soon became apparent to everyone that he and I made a good team, and the yearbook

began to gel in a much more daringly creative form than anybody had anticipated.

I also became more relaxed with him during our moments of passion beneath the gym seats, and here, too, I became more daringly creative in my efforts to give him pleasure. No longer concerned that our relationship was not completely reciprocal, I learned to read and control every sensation that I evoked in him, and, day after day, I teased and tortured until he was writhing fitfully on the gym mats clutching at my hair before I allowed him to come. He was so caught up in the newness of it all that he readily experimented with positions I suggested and even created some himself. Sometimes he would be so excited that he would want to come a second time before we rushed back to class. As much as I relished the pleasure his hands brought me afterward, I derived an equal pleasure from knowing how fully I aroused and then satisfied him. I no longer felt that I was being used.

Outside the gym, we spent more and more time with each other and discussed books and music, our frustrations and aspirations in life, the unexpected intensity of our friendship - everything except the specifics of our sexual relationship. Brett was not nearly ready for open discussion, and, after making a few weak attempts to get him to talk, I backed off, afraid that I would scare him away by forcing him to confront things in himself which he was still trying to deny.

In the fourth week of our relationship, one day in the middle of our usual coupling, he caught me completely off guard. "I want to put it up in you," he whispered urgently.

Instinctively, I recoiled from the idea. I still considered this the ultimate intimacy and I was not ready to share it with him yet. Also, I felt a little prickle of fear. He was much larger than Richard, and it had now been two years since Richard had done it to me. Even when he was doing it regularly, I had endured but never enjoyed the experience. After such a long time, I was afraid that I could not handle Brett. I made a new assessment of the broad head and long, thick shaft with which my mouth had become so familiar.

"Uh-uh," I said flatly. "This big thing would split me open."

"Not if I went slow and easy," he persuaded, toying around

the ring of my ass with a finger.

"No way," I said, taking his cock back into my mouth.

"I really want to do it, Jody," he said in a quiet voice.

"Uh-uh," I muttered around his cockhead.

Alone and aroused in my bed that night, removed from the reality of his long, thick cock, I found his suggestion far less disturbing. I knew that I cared very deeply for him, and I could not come up with any rational reason to deny him this pleasure. Stroking myself, I circled the perimeter of my ass with a moistened finger and then slowly worked it up inside. With thoughts of Brett and the stimulation of my hand on my cock added to the titillation of my finger exploring around inside, by the time I experienced the first throes of orgasm, having Brett do it had become something almost to be desired.

The next time, as we sprawled naked on the gym mats with Brett's cock in my mouth, he sat up and bent over my back to knead my ass cheeks and probe at my opening. "I want to do it to you," he said, his voice filled with passion.

"I donno," I muttered, my hesitation again aroused by the reality of the huge cock in my hand.

"Let's try it," he pleaded.

"It'll hurt too much," I said.

"Look," he said, extricating himself from me. He fumbled beneath the corner of the gym mats. "I brought something to use." He showed me a small jar of Vaseline. "That'll make it go in easy."

"I donno," I repeated, a growing excitement now battling my fear.

"Come on, Jody, let me try," he begged. "I'll quit if you really want me to."

"Well, maybe," I said.

"Get on your hands and knees," he said, his voice trembling with excitement. He knelt behind me, scooped up a big gob of Vaseline onto two fingers and gradually worked it up inside me with first one and then both fingers. The stretch on my ass was uncomfortable, but not really painful. Brett took his time and slowly inserted his fingers deeper and deeper, rotating them back and forth. While he stretched and prepared me, he reached under with his other hand and slowly stroked my cock, restoring the erection I had lost.

Still fisting my cock, he reached for another gob of Vaseline and spread it all over his dick as I craned my neck to watch nervously. Holding my cock with one hand, he rubbed his dick between my cheeks with the other, sliding up and down across the surface of my opening. Then, without thrusting forward, he centered his cockhead over the opening and moved it around in tiny circles, causing me to squirm with pleasure.

"Reach back and spread yourself open," he said.

I threw my weight on one shoulder, with my head twisted awkwardly to one side against the mat, my ass thrust up and vulnerable. I reached back and spread my cheeks, again not at all sure I wanted this.

"Don't tighten up," he said. He turned my cock loose and circled that arm beneath me and clutched my opposite hip from below. In his eagerness, he shoved against me and his huge cock overcame my resistance and jabbed half way into me.

He had gone in before I was completely relaxed, and it was if I had been violated by a huge firebrand. The searing pain was much greater than it had ever been with Richard, even in his most drunken roughness. I tried to shrink away from him, but his encircling arm held me in position.

"Take it out; it hurts!" I cried out, struggling to twist away from him.

"Hold still," he said, grabbing both hips roughly. "It's in now. Hold still."

"I can't. It hurts, Brett," I complained. "Take it out, please."

"Just relax," he soothed. "Relax."

Wanting to please him, despite the pain, I quit struggling and willed myself to open up and accept him. He caressed my back with one hand, moving all the way down to stroke my cheek, and gradually the burning pain lessened.

All at once, he threw his weight against me and shoved another several inches into me. The pain returned, and again I tried to pull away from him. This time, he just kept lowering himself on me as I shrank away, until I lay flat against the mat with him stretched full length on top of me.

"Please quit! God, it hurts!" I cried, my eyes brimming with tears.

He did not answer. He just ran both hands through my hair

and craned his head down and kissed my neck and shoulders. Almost imperceptibly he pushed deeper into me until his rough pubic hair pressed against my buttocks. He rested for a moment, still kissing my neck, and then he began.

As his thrusts lengthened, the pain was excruciating. I tossed my head back and forth and clutched at the mat, tears streaming down my face. The tears were as much from anger at myself for letting it happen as they were from the pain.

Although Brett's assault was not brutal, it was relentless. Just about the time I decided I could not bear it, I passed a threshold and the pain was partially displaced by a new stimulation deep inside that arced through me like a pulsating electric charge. I started to gyrate my hips, lifting off the mat to meet Brett on his downstrokes.

"Oh, yeah!" he moaned. "This is so good!" He varied the pace and depth of his thrusts, sometimes withdrawing except for his broad cockhead, sometimes tunneling all the way in and rotating his pelvis, circling his cock against my inner walls.

I had forgotten the pain by the time he reached the peak of arousal. His movements became spasmodic, and he attacked me with a vengeance, trying to drive himself ever deeper into me, grunting with exertion on every stroke, his body dripping sweat. A time or two, in his compelling need, he withdrew until his cockhead popped all the way out and I closed up momentarily before he jabbed full length back into me, opening me back up with sharp stabbing pains each time. All of my pleasure and arousal destroyed, I lay beneath him and endured until, at last, he drove in with a few short, quick thrusts, one final deep one, and filled me with his hot fluid, his thick cock expanding and contracting rhythmically time after time.

When it was over, he collapsed on my back, his heart pounding, and gasped for breath. After he had rested for awhile, he raised up on elbows and kissed me on the neck. "Whew!" he exclaimed. "That was great! Fantastically great!"

He gingerly pulled back until his cockhead popped out and I was free. When he rolled off me, I immediately turned over and sat up. He reached to caress my cheek and encountered my tears.

"I hurt you," he said, that reality registering on him for the first time.

"I begged you to stop," I said. "You promised you would, and then you didn't."

"I'm sorry," he said, leaning in to kiss away my tears. "I didn't mean to hurt you. It was so fantastically new and great I just couldn't stop once I got started. God, I've wanted you that way so bad. I couldn't stop, Jody, but I didn't mean to hurt you. I'm so sorry."

He again kissed me on both cheeks and then moved down to kiss me on the mouth, the first time he had ever done that. As his tongue insinuated itself between my lips, I opened my mouth to receive it, and he grabbed me in a tight clench and I returned his kiss. I reached to caress his cheek and discovered that he was crying, too.

As our kiss lengthened, he reached between my legs and fondled my completely limp cock until it sprang back into life. Not breaking the kiss, he gently lowered me onto the mat, his hands darting all over my body. When I was completely reclining, he kissed his way down my neck onto my chest and sucked at one of my nipples, his hands still flitting and exploring my chest and abdomen and thighs. He worked his lips down my body, paused to tongue my navel, and buried his head in my pubic hair, my throbbing cock against his cheek. He turned slightly and kissed his way up my shaft, paused momentarily, and slipped the glans into his mouth.

I lay trembling from head to toe as Brett clamped his teeth down just below the glans and reamed my cockhead with his tongue, each circling swipe driving me wild. I clutched at his hair with both hands and held on as he sank deeper and deeper on my cock. I thrust into his mouth time after time, trying to be absorbed completely. Brett toyed and teased and dragged it out until I was practically exhausted. At last, he started to move up and down on my cock rapidly, taking most of me in each time, his tongue dancing all over on his downthrusts, his lips tightly suctioning on each upswing. In no time, I lifted all the way off the mat, cried out a primitive groan of ecstasy, and erupted into Brett's mouth. When the pulsations finally ceased, I sagged back onto the mat, totally drained.

Brett's head followed me down, my cock still deep in his mouth, and he lay holding me until I went completely soft. He sat up, swallowed, and then bent to take me into his mouth

again. He gently tongued my sensitive cockhead and played with my balls until my breathing became regular.

"You swallowed my cum!" I said when he sat up again.

"Yeah, how about that?" he said in amazement. He leaned in and kissed me and I tasted myself in his mouth. "I've never done any of this before," he said when he broke our kiss. He laughed happily. "I thought I was the only person in the world who wanted to do things like this. You're the only one I've had the courage to try it with, and from now on, I want to do everything with you."

My throat was too tight for me to answer, so I just hugged him to me and held on.

He pulled me even closer and wrapped both arms around me. "I'm sorry I hurt you," he said.

"You didn't kill me," I said, reaching for his cock. "But I do wish this thing wasn't so damn fuckin' big."

"Okay, then, I want you to do it to me next time. I want to feel you inside me."

"Well, okay..." I was dubious. I wouldn't mind doing him, but as his cock lengthened and stiffened in my hand, I knew that I was willing to endure the pain of him time and again.

"And if you ever let me do it again," he went on, "I promise I'll try not to hurt you."

I kissed the head of his magnificent cock. At last, I thought, I'd found someone who felt as I did, someone willing to give in a caring relationship. I was realist enough not to expect it to endure forever, but I was romantic enough to dream of at least a brief future with him. After all, it would be months before he finished school and left town for college. My feelings for him were so intense that even one day with him held the promise of a lifetime.

EIGHT
FROM THE CHILDLESS LAND

"Nothing I cared, in the lamb white days,
that time would take me
Up to the swallow thronged loft by the shadow of my hand,
In the moon that is always rising,
Nor that riding to sleep
I should hear him fly with the high fields
And wake to the farm forever fled from the childless land."
— Dylan Thomas, "Fern Hill"

My life in Wilkinson effectively ended one late spring Saturday just before I graduated from high school. The beginning of the end came with an authoritative knock on the front door, followed by Mama's tense call for me to come out of my room, where I had been holed up reading.

When I came into the parlor, Sheriff Stokes, hat in hand, dominated the middle of the room, his massive bulk squeezed into his too-tight uniform. Mama and Vernon huddled nervously to the side, their eyes burning into me imploringly as I walked in.

"I need to ask you a few questions, son," Sheriff Stokes growled before I even had a chance to speak to him. He was one of Vernon's hunting buddies, and I had grown up listening to him and Vernon swap tales around the fireplace on cold winter nights. His gruff manner had always frightened me a little bit, even in my own house, and I had heard rumors of him beating confessions out of Negroes and poor whites. Knowing that he had come to question me about something sent an involuntary shiver through me, although I had nothing to fear or feel guilty about.

"What is it?" I stammered. "I don't know of any way I can help you."

"You let me judge that," he said. He turned to Mama and Vernon. "I really need to talk to Jody private."

"I'd prefer to hear any discussion," Mama said.

Sheriff Stokes twirled his hat in his ham-like hands and cleared his throat. "What we need to talk about ain't fit for a

lady's ears, Miss Sarah," he said.

"Nevertheless, if my boy's involved, I insist on hearing it," Mama said.

Vernon patted her on the arm. "Why don't we menfolk go out in the yard to talk? I'll see Jody's alright," he assured Mama.

We silently walked to the sheriff's car, and he leaned heavily against the door. Vernon propped on a fender, and I stood facing them, looking down at my feet.

"Son, has that Dwight Akins been foolin' round with you?" Sheriff Stokes asked out of nowhere, catching me completely off guard.

"Wha - What do you mean, foolin' around?" I stammered, feeling my whole body heat up and the blood rush to my face.

"You know," the sheriff persisted. "Doin' things to you that's sinful, sinful for two males to do together."

"No - no sir!" I almost yelled.

Vernon straightened up and stepped toward me. "So that's it," he said. "That man always struck me as too sissified. If he's put a hand on you, I swear to God he ought to have his balls cut off. And I might just be the one to do it."

"But he hasn't done anything wrong," I stridently insisted. "He's just been interested in helping me in school and seeing that I go on to college."

"That ain't how some other boys tell it. We've got their statements, and they seem to think he's been messin' round with you, too," Sheriff Stokes said.

"Who said that? They're lying," I said, my knees suddenly so weak I could hardly stand.

"You tell it straight, Jody," Vernon said. "Man like that don't deserve you protecting him. I always did feel funny about your Mama letting you spend so much time with him, taking off for weekends in Atlanta and all."

"What I need is to take Jody down to the office for a statement, Vernon," the sheriff said. "I'm not arresting him, and there's no way he'll be charged with anything. You tell Miss Sarah I'll take good care of him and have him back in a couple of hours. Let's go, Jody."

. . .

Dwight Akins came into my life like the first flowers in spring or the songs of mockingbirds after a long, hard winter. Mr. Athorne finally had retired after teaching nearly forty years in Pelham County, but I had been so self-absorbed in my grief when Brett moved away during the summer that I had not even bothered to find out who his replacement was.

Then I walked into Senior English that first day of school and was confronted by a man - not a wizened old coot like Mr. Athorne - but a virile young man with a military bearing, a strikingly handsome man.

As we shuffled books and noisily settled down, Dwight Akins stood with one hand resting lightly on his desk top, and his eyes slowly moved from seat to seat, row to row, intense and piercing. When the room finally was still, he picked up his grade book and began calling roll, using only last names, pausing momentarily to glance in the direction of each, "Here," as if he were memorizing each face. When he called, "Garrett," I was so mesmerized that it took me a second to stammer, "Here."

"Oh, yes, Garrett," he said. "I will be faculty advisor for the yearbook, and I have been told I will need to talk to you." He smiled thinly, and a little knot of excitement jumped in the middle of my stomach.

And so began my association with the man who would influence my life more than anyone else ever would. Dwight Akins was everything I wasn't, but wanted to be. Obviously from a background of wealth and privilege, he embodied style and taste without the slightest pretension. In his early thirties, he held an advanced degree from a prestigious eastern university and had traveled extensively. He had been an Army officer during the war and had been decorated for bravery. He had a keen appreciation for art, music, theater, and literature. He was charmingly garrulous around other adults, but he made it obvious that he preferred the company of his students.

He practically ignored the Senior English textbook and, instead, talked about major modern writers I had never even heard of - Gide, Proust, Verlaine, Eliot, Auden and Yeats, Hemingway, Steinbeck, and Wolfe. Our little library had stopped with the nineteenth century, as had the knowledge of my previous teachers. Dwight Akins opened up a whole new

world of ideas for me, pulling books out of his personal library to feed my insatiable hunger.

From the beginning, he was a fireball of activity. In addition to advising the yearbook staff, he organized a literary club, a creative writing group, and a theater group. Taking on the yeoman's chore of rigging up makeshift lighting and constructing scenery, he cast and staged *Arsenic and Old Lace*, the first stage play in Pelham County, not counting annual "Womanless Wedding" performances for charity by the Elks Club.

Although he took up time with any of us who showed the slightest spark of creativity, he singled me out for attention from the beginning. He took an active interest in the yearbook and pitched in to help with the physical chores of layout and pasteup. This meant that he and I spent a great deal of time together, sometimes just the two of us working late into the night in the tiny publications room. Invariably, when we finished working, he would suggest that we go somewhere for a soda or a burger and coke.

I talked more with him than I ever had with an adult. He made me feel that he wanted to know absolutely everything about me, and he hung on every comment, no matter how banal. Catching me in a particularly morose mood once, he kept picking and encouraging me to talk about what was bothering me until I confessed some of my grief over parting with Brett, without revealing why Brett had been so important to me. Yet, I realized after a while that he seldom revealed any intimate information about himself. Except for dry biographical data, he remained pretty much a mystery.

One night as we worked alone in the publications office, poring over a layout that neither one of us was pleased with, he casually draped his arm over my shoulder. I felt a tightening in my stomach, and my whole body tingled. It was the first consciously sexual feeling I had had for him.

"You're trembling," he said, tightening his grip on my shoulder. "Do you feel all right?"

"Yeah, I'm fine," I choked out, having to clear my throat to speak.

With his other hand, he pulled my chin toward him and tilted my head back. "Let me look at you," he said.

"I'm all right, really," I assured him.

He stared deep into my eyes, and I returned his gaze, mesmerized. He bent down, and his lips brushed mine. He moved away and then leaned back in to kiss me harder on the lips.

"I - I'm sorry," he said, releasing me and turning his back hurriedly.

"It's all right," I said.

"No. No, it's not," he stammered. "I had no business -"

"But I didn't mind," I said. I swallowed hard and continued. "I've been kissed by a guy before."

"You have? Who? Brett?" he asked.

"Uh-huh," I muttered, staring at the floor, feeling my face flush.

"Well, I still had no right - I'm your teacher. You're just a boy. You can't really even know what it's all about," he said, all in one hurried breath.

"I might know more than you think," I said, looking up to meet his eyes.

He quickly turned away. "Let's lock up and go to the Dairy Queen before it closes," he said.

After that night, he seemed distant and impersonal toward me for a few days, and then he went back to being himself.

I began a more conscious effort to understand him. For one thing, I noticed that, except for school activities, he had no life in Wilkinson. He did not date. He did not hunt and fish or just stand around shooting the breeze with other men. Except for church every Sunday, he participated in no community functions unless they were school-related. Sometimes at night after I got off work at Peavey's, I would see him sitting in his car in front of Sammy's Billiards or Ray's Cafe, but I never saw him go inside. I decided that he was very lonely and starved for late-night company. When I pulled into the parking space beside him on the street a couple of times, though, it was almost as if my presence was disturbing, and so I quit stopping to talk to him.

Just before Christmas vacation, as we locked up the publications office one night, he said, "How about stopping by my place for some hot chocolate?"

"Sounds great!" I said. I followed him to the secluded

cottage that he rented behind Mr. and Mrs. Gilstrap's house, and we parked in the alley. He led me into the back door, through the kitchen, and into his tiny living room.

While he made chocolate, I browsed through his books, which filled the makeshift bookcases that stretched to the ceiling on every available wall space. Then I moved to his big, expensive stereo and flipped through row after row of albums. Most of them were names I had never heard or had only read about - Mahler, Stravinsky, Copeland, Brahms, Beethoven, Tchaikovsky. My musical knowledge was limited to the Grand Ole Opry and a few pop tunes. I had never heard a piece of classical music.

He came in with the chocolate as I read the jacket on a Mozart album. "Find something you like?" he asked, extending my cup to me.

"I've never heard it. I've never heard any of them," I admitted.

"Well, we can't neglect your musical education," he said, taking the album from me. "But Mozart is probably too formal to start with." He put the album down and thumbed through his collection and pulled out Tchaikovsky's, "Capriccio Italian." "This should be a good beginning for a young romantic like you," he said, putting the record on the turntable.

I sat on the couch, and he turned out the lights, except for a soft glow through the kitchen door. He started the record and sat beside me. "Close your eyes and just let it flow through you," he said. I noticed that he had turned so he could watch me. Then I closed my eyes and was swept away by the music.

When the stereo clicked off, I sat up and wiped at the tears that had flowed in rivulets down my cheeks. "Really got to you, huh?" he said.

"Uh-huh," I said. "It's so beautiful!"

He reached to wipe away a tear and left his palm against my cheek. "Maybe I underestimated you," he said. "Maybe you at least instinctively know a whole lot more than I've given you credit for. Maybe you picked up through his music that Tchaikovsky liked beautiful boys. Just as I do. And you are beautiful, Jody. God forgive my weakness, but you are beautiful!"

He took me in his arms and kissed me, and this time he did

not stop.

In the bedroom, he slowly undressed me and stretched me out on the bed. For a long time, he just explored my body worshipfully with his fingers and lips. By the time he finally took me in his mouth, my whole body was on fire and I was trembling uncontrollably. He explored my cock the way he had explored the rest of me until his slow ministrations caused me to cry out loud in pleasure and grasp at him frantically. When I knew I could not hold off much longer, I pulled away from him and flipped him on his back. He had taken off his shirt, and I kissed my way across his chest, alternately nibbling at each nipple. His breath came in great gasps. I traveled down his torso with my lips and unfastened his belt with trembling hands.

"You don't have to -" he said.

"I want to," I answered, tugging his pants and underwear over his hips to expose his thick cock. I pulled it away from his abdomen with two fingers and went down on it.

"Jody, I didn't expect - Oh, God, you're beautiful! Please don't stop! Oh, God, don't stop!" he sighed.

I tortured his cockhead with my tongue and slid my mouth down his thick shaft as far as I could. I fondled his balls with one hand and reached under with the other to run a finger around his ass ring. I had barely begun working on his cock when he suddenly grabbed at my head and tried to pull me away from him. "I'm going to come! I can't hold back any longer! I'm coming!" he cried out, just before he flooded my mouth. I swallowed it all down and held him until he was almost soft before I pulled away and turned onto my back. He immediately rolled over and once again launched a worshipful attack on my dick until I erupted seemingly unendingly in his mouth.

"Man, did I ever underestimate you," he said as he lay tight against my side and caressed my chest and stomach. "You're no novice at this sort of thing."

"I told you I knew more than you might think," I said. "Tonight is just the beginning of what I know."

· · ·

"Jody, the statements I've got are all from boys who don't go to school," Sheriff Stokes said, waving a stack of folders at me as I sat rigidly erect in front of his desk. "You know, the white trash boys that hang out all hours of the night down at the pool hall and raise hell every chance they get. Now, if we was to have a statement from a boy like you - a churchgoing boy from a good family, with good school grades, a jury would be more likely to view Mr. Dwight Akins in a harsher light. Y'know what I mean?"

"Yessir," I muttered. "But I can't tell you anything."

"These boys," he said, slapping the stack of folders against his desk. "These boys say they've seen your old Studebaker in the alley behind Akins' house. They say usually he couldn't wait to open the door and invite them in when they knocked, but on nights you was there, he'd crack the door and tell them he was busy and close the door in their face. They say they saw your car there lots of times."

"They might have," I said, surprised at how calm I was. "Mr. Akins sometimes invited a few of us over to discuss the yearbook. Sometimes the literary club would meet there to have a snack and discuss a book we'd all read."

"And sometimes you was there by yourself. Most of the time, in fact."

"A lot of times, yessir."

"And when you was there by yourself, the lights soon went off, according to old lady Gilstrap. Why was that?"

I silently cursed nosy old Mrs. Gilstrap. I wondered how much she had seen and heard. "Mr. Akins was exposing me to classical music. He said I could appreciate it more with the lights off," I said, squirming in my chair. With Dwight, it made perfect sense, but in front of Sheriff Stokes it sounded absurd.

"And after he exposed you to the music, did he expose himself to you?" the sheriff smirked.

"He never tried anything or tried to get me to do anything I wouldn't have approved of," I said.

"What about all them trips out of town, just the two of you?"

"Let's see, a group of us went to his parents' house in Atlanta and went to see a stage play," I said. "And I went back to his parents' with just him once and we went to hear a

symphony orchestra."

"And I understand just the two of you went all the way to Nashville during spring vacation. Was gone five days, just the two of you alone. What'd you do all that time, just the two of you together?" Sheriff Stokes made it all sound dirty by the way he asked his questions, smirking at me knowingly.

"Mr. Akins had Mama's permission for me to go with him. I went to Nashville to take some tests and talk with some professors at Vanderbilt who are friends of his. He was trying to help me get a scholarship for college. And he did, too. A full scholarship," I said, looking down at my lap.

"The hotel and motel rooms y'all stayed all them nights. They have one or two beds?"

"Two," I said, wondering how the sheriff knew all these things, and whether there was any way for him to check to see if I was lying.

. . .

Dwight and I drove from Nashville east through Knoxville and then down to Gatlinburg, where we spent the night. I had never been north of Atlanta, had never traveled outside of Georgia, and I was almost as thrilled at the wonderful newness of the mountainous countryside as I was at the near certainty of having a scholarship to Vanderbilt.

Outside Gatlinburg, the Great Smoky Mountains loomed in the near distance, and the landscape was covered with dogwood blossoms, snow trilium, and fiery red wild honeysuckle. The beautiful vista surrounding me made my eyes sting with tears.

After we ate at a quaint restaurant in the rustic village, we returned to the little cottage Dwight had rented for the night. There was still a chill in the air, and our little room was cold. Dwight had barely closed and locked the door before he was all over me, smothering me with kisses, grappling and struggling at the same time to get me undressed. I had never seen him so fired up, despite the fact that we had made love the night before and that morning as soon as we woke up.

We quickly jumped into bed and huddled together under the heavy blanket. My whole body was trembling, as much from

excitement as from the cold. Dwight pulled me tight against him and vigorously massaged my back, his hand eventually straying on down to my buttocks, where his touch changed into a caress. Our cocks throbbed in unison against our tightly pressed together abdomens.

Dwight turned me on my back and ducked his head beneath the covers. His warm mouth traveled slowly down my torso, lighting small fires wherever he nibbled and kissed. When he took my cock in his mouth, I arched up off the bed and threw the covers onto the floor. From that point on, we both were generating more than enough natural heat.

As he sucked my cock, his hands flitted maddeningly all over my body, and one settled between my legs, his fingers probing for my opening. He had been exploring my ass a lot lately, each time a little more demandingly, but he had never suggested anything other than mutual oral sex. But this trip, the success at Vanderbilt, the beautiful locale, made me want this night to be something special for us both.

"Why don't you fuck me?" I whispered.

He took his mouth off my cock. "I wouldn't want to hurt you," he said.

"You're big enough, but not that big," I said, reaching to stroke his thick shaft.

"You've done it before?" he asked.

"I'm not telling you all my secrets," I teased. "But I know you want to do it, and I want it, too."

"But if I hurt you –" he hesitated.

"Just do it. Quit talking and do it. Fuck me, Dwight," I said.

He kneeled between my legs and lubricated his cock. I swung my legs onto his shoulders, and, ever so gently, he entered me. After his broad cockhead parted my sphincter, he was so slow and gentle that I could barely detect his penetration. I was as fired up as I had ever been, and I became impatient.

"Shove it on in," I begged. "Don't worry about hurting me. I want you to hurt me. Fuck me, Dwight. Hard!"

"Okay, you're going to get fucked!" he said. With one lunge, he shoved all the way into me, almost taking my breath away. For the next fifteen minutes, he thrust and gyrated, varying the force and depth of his penetration, sighing and groaning with pleasure continuously.

As he got closer and closer to climax, he underwent a transformation, and I experienced a facet of him I had never seen before - an almost animalistic lust.

"Yeah, I've wanted your ass - your beautiful tight ass - from the very beginning. Now I'm going to fuck you all night! I'm going to cram my big dick so far in you it'll come out your mouth!" he growled.

I squeezed him tight against me and thrust upward each time to meet his assault, which became unrelenting. Finally, he was crying out loud and biting at my shoulders, and his thrusts became quick and spasmodic. My balls tightened painfully up against my body, my ass spasmed and contracted around his piledriving shaft, and I erupted all over my abdomen. Dwight kept thrusting, overcoming my muscular resistance, until I felt him bathe my insides with his hot fluid.

We lay still, both breathing heavily, until my cock softened between our bodies. I made a move to disengage myself, but Dwight held me in position. His cock was still rock hard.

"Not yet," he said. "I want some more of your hot ass. You were made to be fucked, and now that I've started, I plan to do it regularly."

He started all over, as aroused and needful as the first time, and before long my cock was erect and throbbing, and I got into the second round as much as the first. When he climaxed the second time, he immediately brought me off by mouth and then tenderly made love to me for a long time before he went back into me.

. . .

"Akins ever show you dirty magazines and pictures of naked boys when you visited?" Sheriff Stokes asked, opening the drawer of his desk.

"No sir," I answered truthfully.

"You never saw any of these?" he said, tossing a stack of magazines to the edge of the desk in front of me.

"No sir, I never did," I said, staring at cover photos of muscular young men in posing straps.

"Look through 'em," he urged. "I want you to make sure about things."

I flipped through a magazine that was filled with very good line drawings of naked men in all kinds of poses. Under other circumstances, they would have aroused me, but now they turned my stomach. "I never saw them," I said, tossing the magazine back onto the desk. "I don't look at such stuff."

"How about pictures?" he said, rifling through another folder. He handed me a stack of Polaroids of teenage boys in various stages of undress, most completely nude, some erect and fondling themselves.

"I never saw these," I said, handing them back. "I don't even know any of the people in them."

"I could show you some you would know. I got 'em. But who they are is confidential. Them," he said, gesturing to the stack on the table, "is of boys in Virginia, some of 'em rich kids from the fancy school where he taught last year, the school that just let him slip out of the state when he was caught at it, just let him come on down here to corrupt our kids. Oh, yeah, we know a lot about your Mr. Akins. And he ain't going to sneak out of our town unpunished."

He again reached into the folder and handed me a thinner stack of snapshots. "Recognize these?" he said.

They were of me! I suddenly was very nauseous and trembled all over. The revelations of a Dwight Akins I had never known and the implications of my involvement with him were overwhelming.

. . .

We were deep in the woods behind Dwight's parents' cabin on Lake Lanier. I had been a little puzzled the night before when we arrived in Atlanta and I discovered that Dwight's parents were out of town. He had told Mama that we were going to a concert with his parents. I didn't think much about it, though, as he rushed us out to eat in a fancy Atlanta restaurant and then rushed us back to his parents' house and into bed. Next morning, after making love, we drove out to Lake Lanier, stopping for breakfast on the way.

Dwight had just bought a new black and white Polaroid camera and took picture after picture of me. The camera had been on the market for several years, but I had never seen one.

I was intrigued at how the picture developed just moments after Dwight snapped it.

I willingly posed and hammed it up for him, first taking off my shirt and then my pants. He took a picture of me in my underwear and then tossed me the tight red bathing suit we had brought along. I modestly turned away from him, slipped off my underwear, and then tugged on the bathing suit. Just as I got it up to my thighs, I heard the whirr of the camera. He had gotten a picture of my naked butt.

He posed me in several provocative positions, leaning against and caressing a large pine.

"How about if I get some nude shots?" he asked.

"Uh-uh, I don't want to," I said.

"Aw, come on. Nobody'll see them except us," he persuaded.

"I don't want to, Dwight," I said firmly. "Somebody might see them. I don't even like the one you got with my bathing suit down."

"You're right, Jody. I don't need them. I have every detail of you memorized already," he said. He handed me the one of my exposed butt. "Here, tear this one up."

After I shredded the photo, he put the camera down and pushed me back against the pine. He kneeled in front of me, stripped my bathing suit off, and started sucking my cock. I locked my hands around his head and thrust in his mouth, throwing my head back against the tree and moaning.

He guided me down onto the thick mat of pine straw and switched to a sixty-nine position, and I took him in my mouth. As we both neared the peak of excitement, he took his mouth off my dick.

"I want you to fuck me, Jody," he said. "I never went in for it much, but you're special. I want to share that experience with you."

I lubricated myself, and he turned over on his stomach. I spread his legs and kneeled between them, probing with my spit-slickened finger before I guided my cockhead to the target. When I pushed in, violating his tight ass ring, he clenched his cheeks and stopped my progress.

"Go easy," he said. "You've got a big dick, and it's been a long time since I've been fucked. So let me get used to you."

I was so hot and wanted it so much that it was hard for me to be patient. With a whole lot of groaning and tensing up by him, I gradually worked about three-fourths of the way in and then lust overcame my concern for his comfort. I shoved the rest of the way in with one quick thrust.

"Oh, shit!" he cried out. "I don't think I can handle you!"

"I'm all the way in, and I'm not going to quit," I said. "Just relax and enjoy it. I'm going to fuck you the way you've been doing me."

I pounded away at his ass for all I was worth, caught up in an overpowering lust. I wanted him to feel it, wanted it to hurt, wanted to be dominant for a change, wanted him to know it and submit to it, as I had done with him for months. All too soon, a climax built somewhere deep inside me and then exploded in my cock, which twitched and jerked in his tight ass for what seemed like forever before I quit coming and collapsed against him.

Afterward, Dwight was more tender than he had ever been as he made love to every inch of my body, from head to toe. When he had me erect and demanding again, he crouched over me and sat down on my cock, a totally new experience for me. As he lifted and pushed back down and rocked back and forth on my dick, I reached for his cock and began to jerk it in rhythm with his movements on mine. In no time, he threw his head back, cried out, and sprayed his come up my body, some landing in my face. He kept moving on my cock with the same steady pace, and before long, I blasted another load up his ass.

We never did go swimming. We spent all afternoon there on the pine straw, and finally had to rush back to Atlanta for the concert.

. . .

"Why do I get the feeling you're lying to me, Jody," Sheriff Stokes asked, his piercing stare making me squirm uncomfortably.

"I don't know, sir. I just don't have anything to tell you," I said.

"You expect me to believe - after all we know about this man who's corrupted dozens of boys, in Virginia as well as here in

town - you expect me to believe everything was sweet and innocent between you two?" he asked, his tone uglier than before.

"I don't expect you to believe anything. I just don't have anything to say against him," I said.

"I know it's embarrassing to admit such things, Jody. But he's the one at fault, not you. Now, I want you to tell me truthfully everything he ever did to you. I want a statement from you that'll go a long way toward putting that bastard in prison. Now, you're going to give me that statement," he said, a menacing tone to his voice.

I don't know where I found the courage, but part of it came from my growing anger at his smug confidence that he could drag a statement out of me. I stood up. "I'm not making a statement, because I have nothing to say, Sheriff Stokes," I said.

"Maybe it's because you liked what was going on," he said. "Maybe you're one of them fairies like him."

"You can think whatever you want, sheriff," I said. "I'm leaving now. Don't bother to drive me home. I'll hitchhike." I turned and started for the door.

"Fuckin' sissy!" he hurled at me as I walked out of his office.

Monday at school, all everybody wanted to talk about was Mr. Akins being arrested. A grand jury was already in session, and by Tuesday had issued an indictment against him. It seemed that everything that went on in the jury room immediately was common knowledge. Kids at school talked openly about the boys who had testified against him and had all the details of what supposedly had gone on between them and Dwight.

When I got to school Wednesday, I was confronted by a group of redneck football players.

"Hey, Jody," Rick yelled. "I hear your buddy Mr. Akins is going to be sent away for about fifty years."

"Bet you're gonna miss your sweetie," Mike added.

I started past them without saying anything, but Joe grabbed my arm and spun me around. "Hey, we're talking to you," he said. "We hear you were his favorite. Did he pay you like he did the others?"

"Yeah, we hear he offered to pay double for kids to take it up the ass," Rick said. "He pay you double, or did you do it for free?"

I was overwhelmed by a blind fury. Without even thinking, I struck out and pummeled Rick with both fists until his friends wrestled me to the ground and started pounding on me. Even then I kicked and hit back until a couple of teachers pulled them off me and separated us. I had a bloody nose and a sore jaw, but I was pleased the next day to see that Rick had both eyes blackened and Joe had an angry contusion on his cheek.

As soon as I got to work, Mr. Peavy asked me to come back to his office. "Jody, I hate to do it, but I'm going to have to let you go," he said. He refused to look me in the eye.

"Why, Mr. Peavy?" I asked.

"Things have been sort of slow, and I'm having to cut back," he said.

"But you can't close the fountain, and you need help stocking," I argued.

"I just can't use you any more," he said.

"But, Mr. Peavy, I'm a good worker. I've never missed a day, and I'm always on time. I need the job through the summer, Mr. Peavy. I need to save as much as possible for college." I realized I was begging and quit talking.

"I have to let you go," he repeated.

"Then at least be honest and tell me the real reason why," I challenged.

"All that filth about that Akins fellow and all the talk going around, it's not good for business," he said. "You've been a good worker, Jody. I'm sorry." He handed me an envelope. "Here's your pay. I included a little extra as a bonus."

I opened the envelope and found twenty-five dollars more than I had earned. I flipped it on the desk in front of him. "I don't need your charity," I said.

Things were worse at home. Vernon had lit into me about being rude to Sheriff Stokes, and he and Mama kept pumping me about what had gone on between me and Dwight and lecturing me about how I should have told the sheriff anything I knew.

When I had heard all I could stand, I blurted out, "Maybe I didn't make a statement because I didn't mind what Dwight did with me." I immediately regretted my impetuousness, but there was no way to recall my words.

Mama was aghast, and Vernon was so angry I thought he was going to hit me for the first time. After that, communication between us was impossible. Mama went around with a hurt expression, looking as if she was carrying the weight of the world on her shoulders. I tried to imagine the battle waging between her love for me and her staunch Baptist concept of sin.

Conversation stopped when I walked into a room. Even my stepsisters quit talking to me, and we ate meals together in stony silence. I realized for the first time what it is like to be a pariah.

After I forced myself to attend graduation ceremonies, I made the first truly adult decision of my life. I packed my bags, left Mama a note, withdrew my savings from the bank, and hitchhiked to Macon, where I boarded a Trailways bus to Nashville. It was months before my scholarship started and a dorm room would be available, but I was confident that I could find some kind of job and survive until fall term began.

As the bus pulled out of the station in Macon, I knew that, in a way, I was leaving Wilkinson behind forever. I also knew that I already had left my childhood there on the farm.

Contributors
(Other Than the Editor, John Patrick)

"Fade to Black"
L. Amore

The author is 27 and has been in the book business for ten years. He has lived in upstate New York, Boston and New York City and now resides in Connecticut. He is currently working on his first novel, as yet untitled, and finishing a novella called, "The Night John Preston Flogged Me." The author's stories have also appeared in many other STARbooks anthologies.

"Novices"
Ken Anderson

The author lives in Georgia and is a frequent contributor to literary magazines. *The Intense Lover*, a book of Ken's poetry, was published by STARbooks earlier this year. The author is currently finishing a novel.

"Old Habits"
Mark Anderson

Retired from Ford Motor Co., the author is active with Toronto's Suicide Hot Line, and vacations often in Palm Springs, where he is occasionally inspired to write erotica for STARbooks.

"He Had No Idea"
Antler

The poet lives in Milwaukee when not traveling to perform his poems or wildernessing. His epic poem *Factory* was published by City Lights. His collection of poems *Last Words* was published by Ballantine. Winner of the Whitman Award from the Walt Whitman Society of Camden, New Jersey, and the Witter Bynner prize from the Academy and Institute of Arts & Letters in New York, his poetry has appeared in many periodicals (including *Utne Reader*, *Whole Earth Review* and *American Poetry Review*) and anthologies (including *Gay Roots*, *Erotic by Nature*, and *Gay and Lesbian Poetry of Our Time*).

"The New Page"
Edward Bangor

The author, an Englishman, was a frequent contributor to the anthologies of the late, lamented Acolyte Press. Under the name of Headbanger, he contributed a piece for the fourth issue of the American gay comic book *Cherubino*.

"Wherever You Want to Put It"
Kevin Bantan

The author lives in Ohio, where he is working on several new stories for STARbooks.

"When Bob Kissed Me..."
Greg Bowden

The author, who lives in California, has contributed many stories to gay magazines.

"Naked Skateboard Boy"
Frank Brooks

The author is a regular contributor to gay magazines. In addition to writing, his interests include figure drawing from the live model and mountain hiking.

"Strange Bedfellows"
Leo Cardini

Author of the best-selling *Mineshaft Nights*, Leo's short stories and theatre-related articles have appeared in numerous magazines. An enthusiastic nudist, he reports that, "A hundred and fifty thousand people have seen me naked, but I only had sex with half of them."

"In Angelo's Room"
William Cozad

The author is a regular contributor to gay magazines and his startling memoirs were published by STARbooks Press in *Lover Boys* and *Boys of the Night*. Another of his books, "The Preacher's Boy," appeared in *Secret Passions*.

"A Willing Learner,"
"A Good Spanking"
and "The Shooting Club"
Peter Gilbert

"Semi-retired" after a long career with the British Armed Forces, the author now lives in Germany but is contemplating a return to England. A frequent contributor to various periodicals, he also writes for television. He enjoys walking, photography and reading.

"Jonah's Island"
Jarred Goodall

When he is not accepting sabbatical appointments abroad, the author teaches English in a Midwestern university. Born in Wisconsin, he loves back-packing, mountain-climbing, chess and Victorian literature. His favorite color: blue-green; favorite pop-star: Leonard Bernstein; favorite car: WWII Jeep; favorite drink: water, preferably recycled; favorite actor: River Phoenix (alas); favorite hobby: "If you want to know that, read my stories."

"Hotter Than Hell"
Rick Hassett

This story was adapted especially for this collection from the author's first novel, *Sedona*. Rick has worked as a journalist in several western states, and edited the weekly newspaper in Sedona. He only recently started writing gay fiction and has completed a novel, *The All-American Boy*.

"Making Ends Meet"
James Hosier

The youthful author lives in a little town that is "definitely not sleepy." He says he is straight but admits that he lets guys do what they want: "I need the money and I happen to have a good body (thanks to the swimming club). Provided they're prepared to pay, I let them go ahead." Stay tuned.

"In the Presence of Innocence"
Thomas C. Humphrey

The author, who resides in Florida, is working on his first

novel, *All the Difference*, and has contributed stories to First Hand publications.

"Wild in the Woods"
Rick Jackson USMC

The oft-published author specializes in jarhead stories. When not travelling, he is based in Hawaii.

"After the Game"
William Joseph

This is the author's first story for STARbooks Press.

"Flexibility"
Cory James Legassie

The author wrote this memoir when he was in college in Maine. As a teenager, he had works published in a European journal. This story originally appeared in the now-defunct *Iris*.

"Burt's Trunks"
Terry McLearn

The author is a native of Connecticut. This is his first published story. His first gay novel is now being considered by publishers and he is at work on his second.

"Night School"
Edmund Miller

Edmund Miller, the author of the legendary poetry book *Fucking Animals* (reprinted by STARBooks) and frequent contributor of stories to gay magazines and anthologies, is the Chairman of the English Department at a large university in the New York area. He is currently working on a sonnet sequence about the go-go boys of New York.

"Hustling the Bone in Atlantic City"
Thom Nickels

The Cliffs of Aries, the author's first novel, was published in 1988 by Aegina Press. *Two Novellas: Walking Water & After All This*, was published in 1989 by Banned Books, and *The Boy on the Bicyle*, was published by STARbooks Press. Thom writes reviews and articles for *Lambda Book Report*, *Philadelphia Forum*

and *The City Paper.*

"Game for Anything"
Peter Z. Pan

A first-generation American of Cuban descent, this twentysomething author and producer of plays calls himself a "quintessential jack-of-all-trades: multimedia writer, theatrical director, and sometime actor-singer." Peter says he resides in Miami, "physically anyway." Spiritually, he says he will always live where Lost Boys forever frolic: "...second star to the right, and straight on till morning."

"Brady's Crotch"
Jack Ricardo

The author, who lives in Florida, is a novelist and frequent contributor to various gay magazines. His latest novel is *Last Dance at Studio 54.*

"Once, Upon An Island"
Rudy Roberts

The author lives in Canada and is a frequent contributor to STARbooks anthologies.

"The Birthday Present"
Ken Smith

The author, who lives in England, started life as a simple country lad. At the tender age of 15, he joined the Royal Navy, and says he has "ridden some big ones whilst at sea. Waves mostly." Ken has had several of his stories published in the London-based magazines *Vulcan, Mister,* and *Zipper.*

"Class Action" and "Junior Cum Laude"
Chad Stuart

The author, who now lives in Washington, was a regular contributor to gay magazines in the early '70s. He specializes in hustler stories.

"An Abuse of Authority"
Dan Veen

The author's first stories were based on his experiences as a

hustler in San Francisco and New Orleans. He has written erotic fiction for *Honcho, Mandate, Playguy, Torso, Inches, and First Hand* magazines. He writes regular film articles and erotic video reviews for *Honcho* under the name of V.C. Rand. He has a PhD. in English Literature and Germanic Languages.

The story herein originally appeared in a somewhat different form in *Honcho*.

NOW ON AUDIO TAPE

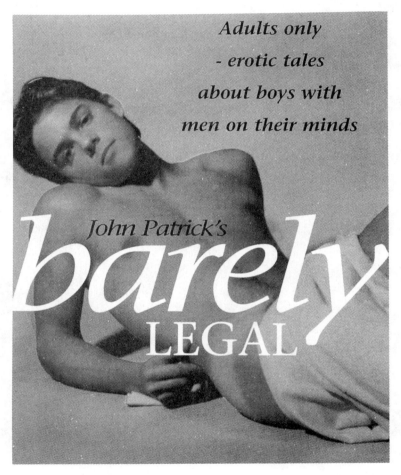

*Adults only
- erotic tales
about boys with
men on their minds*

John Patrick's
barely LEGAL

In cooperation with Prowler Press in London, STARbooks Press now makes available a special selection of stories from *Barely Legal*, our classic collection, on audio tape. Two cassettes. $16.95. Order from: STARbooks, P.O. Box 2737, Sarasota FL 34230-2737 U.S.A. Also available from Prowler Press, U.S.A. and London, via MaleXpress Ltd., 3 Broadbent Close, London N6 5GG, U.K.

ACKNOWLEDGEMENTS AND SOURCES

Main coverboy, Jim Darley, appears through the courtesy of the celebrated English photographer David Butt. Mr. Butt's photographs may be purchased through Suntown, Post Office Box 151, Danbury, Oxfordshire, OX16 8QN, United Kingdom. Ask for a full catalogue.

George Duroy's models appear through the courtesy of Bel-Ami Video. Write them at their U.S. offices: 484-B Washington Street #342, Monterey CA 93940-3030. Mr. Duroy's models also appear in the videos from International Collection distributed by Falcon Studios, which can be contacted at 1-800-227-3717; catalogue is $15, refundable with purchase.

SPECIAL OFFER

STARbooks Press now offers two very special international gay magazine packages: You can get the hottest American gay magazines, including *GAYME, All-Man, Torso, Advocate Men, Advocate Fresh Men, In Touch,* and *Playguy,* either singly for $6.99 each, or in a very special deluxe sampler package for only $25 for six big issues.

We also offer the sizzling British and European magazines, including *Euros, Euroboy, Prowl, Vulcan, HUNK,* and *Uniform* in a sampler package for only $39.95; six fabulous issues. Please add $2.75 post. Order from: STARbooks Press, P.O. Box 2737-B, Sarasota FL 34230-2737 USA.

Now available at bookstores or by mail: BEAUTIFUL BOYS, John Patrick's enormously entertaining look at boys who are really much more than just a pretty face. This unusual collection of hot erotic tales includes two big bonus books: "The Blessing," a sizzling novella by Leo Cardini, and another of John Patrick's revealing looks at the lives of porn stars, this one featuring the incredible bottom boy Kevin Kramer. This huge book is $14.95, plus $2.75 post from STARbooks Press, P.O. Box 2737-B, Sarasota FL 34230-2737 USA. *Or at your bookseller now.*

ABOUT THE EDITOR

John Patrick is a prolific, prize-winning author of fiction and non-fiction. One of his short stories, "The Well," was honored by PEN American Center as one of the best of 1987. His novels and anthologies, as well as his non-fiction works, including *Legends* and *The Best of the Superstars* series, continue to gain him new fans every day. One of his most famous short stories appears in the Badboy collection *Southern Comfort*.

A divorced father of two, the author is a longtime member of the American Booksellers Association, the Florida Publishers' Association, American Civil Liberties Union, and the Adult Video Association. He resides in Florida.